M000168111

THE ANNOTATED WUTHERING HEIGHTS

Emily Brontë

The Annotated Wuthering Heights

EDITED BY JANET GEZARI

THE BELKNAP PRESS OF HARVARD UNIVERSITY PRESS

Cambridge, Massachusetts, and London, England 2014

Printed in the United States of America

First printing

DESIGN BY ANNAMARIE MCMAHON WHY

Frontispiece: "On the Moor," one of twelve woodcuts by Clare Leighton (1898–1989), reproduced as full-page illustrations in the 1931 Random House edition of *Wuthering Heights.* Catherine dominates this scene, with Heathcliff crouching nearby and the hilly moorland, birds of prey, and windswept clouds behind.

Library of Congress Cataloging-in-Publication Data
Brontë, Emily, 1818–1848
[Wuthering Heights]
The annotated Wuthering Heights / Emily Brontë ; edited by Janet Gezari.
pages cm
Includes bibliographical references.
ISBN 978-0-674-72469-3 (alk. paper)
1. Triangles (Interpersonal relations)—Fiction. 2. Foundlings—Fiction. 3. Rural families—Fiction. 4. Rejection (Psychology)—Fiction. 5. Yorkshire (England)—Fiction. 6. Brontë, Emily, 1818–1848. Wuthering Heights. I. Gezari, Janet. II. Title.
PR4172.W7 2014b
823′.8—dc23 2014019429

CONTENTS

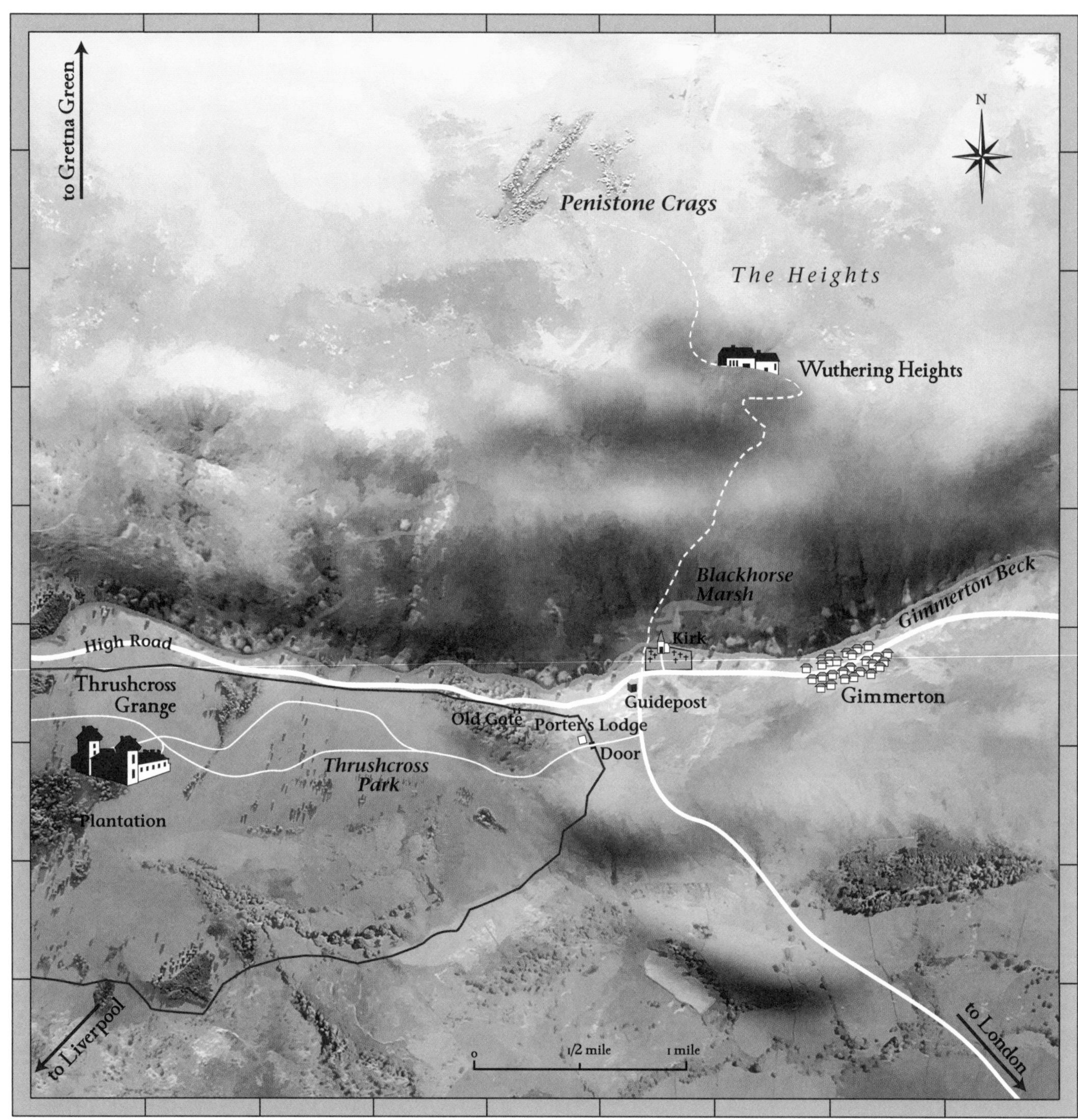

The world of *Wuthering Heights*.

THE ANNOTATED WUTHERING HEIGHTS

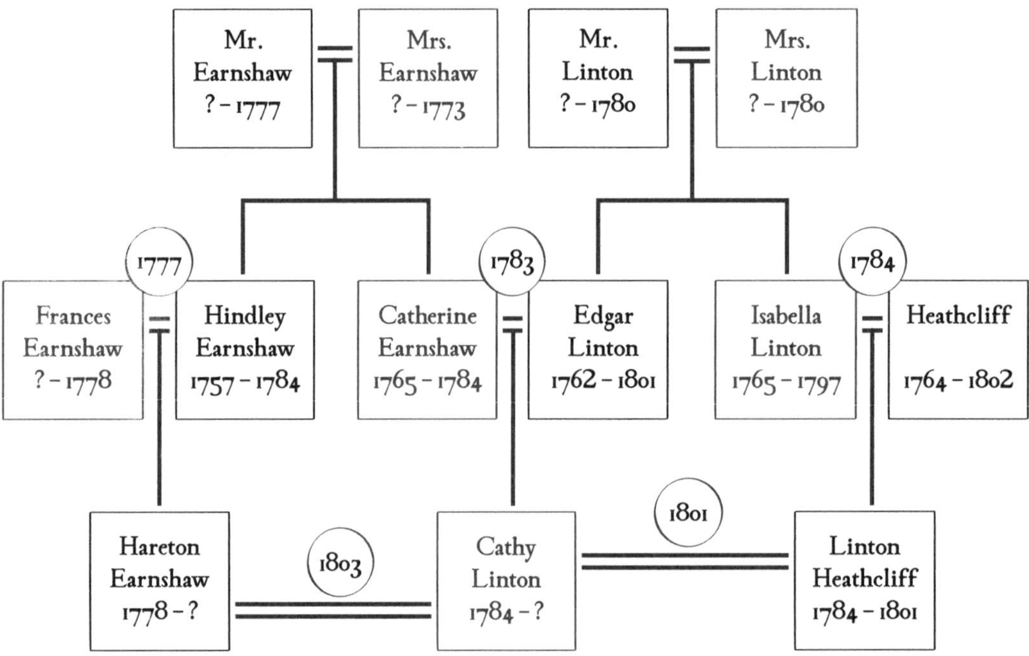

Genealogical chart.

INTRODUCTION

Emily Brontë clipped and saved five reviews of *Wuthering Heights.* This will surprise people who think of her as not just sphinx-like in her inscrutability and firm in her own convictions but so cut off from the world as to be entirely unconcerned about what other people thought of her novel. Emily's social isolation is a cornerstone of the Brontë myth that has had a long life in the popular imagination and still shapes the way many readers experience *Wuthering Heights.*[1] Writing as one of her first readers, Charlotte, her older sister, insists on it:

> If the auditor of her work when read in manuscript, shuddered under the grinding influence of natures so relentless and implacable, of spirits so lost and fallen; if it was complained that the mere hearing of certain vivid and fearful scenes banished sleep by night, and disturbed mental peace by day, [Emily] would wonder what was meant, and suspect the complaint of affectation.[2]

Even Charlotte was surprised to discover that the "vivid and fearful scenes" she encountered in *Wuthering Heights* were an ordinary part of her sister's imaginative life. There is also ample evidence, apart from her testimony here, that Emily did think that polite society required its members to affect ignorance of a great deal.[3] Knowing that she read the reviews of her novel and cared to keep some of them by her is, however, a useful corrective to the notion that she had no interest in what other people thought of her work and "no worldly wisdom."[4] *Wuthering Heights* is the expression of a supremely independent but not isolated mind. Brontë's determination to publish it is a warrant of her ambitious hope that it would find a fit audience.

As hugely talented sisters whose first novels came out within months of each other in 1847—*Jane Eyre* in October and *Wuthering Heights* in December—Emily and Charlotte have always been linked even more closely than Emily and Anne, the youngest Brontë sister, whose first novel, *Agnes Grey,* was published together with *Wuthering Heights* as the third part of a three-volume set. Yet *Jane Eyre* and *Wuthering Heights* are very different from each other. Despite its publisher's efforts to persuade readers that there was only one Brontë who had written both novels, *Wuthering Heights* did not achieve the same happy popularity as *Jane Eyre.* Some of their novels' themes have a family resemblance, but the difference between Emily's slant on them and Charlotte's is as great as the difference between Charlotte's Rochester and Emily's Heathcliff. In *Jane Eyre* and *Wuthering Heights,* women make large claims for themselves, fail to resent the free talk and shocking behavior of the men in their lives, and in general act far more independently than ladies should. Yet the rebellions mounted in *Jane Eyre* are different in their kind and course from those mounted in *Wuthering Heights.* In *Jane Eyre,* rebellion is the means to an agreeable and accommodating end. In *Wuthering Heights,* rebellion is an abiding state of mind and an end in itself.

The narrative programs of *Jane Eyre* and *Wuthering Heights* are also strikingly different. The heroine who gives her name to *Jane Eyre* provides the point of view from which every aspect of her life is seen. The novel repeatedly enforces the justice of Jane's point of view, and although she tells her story some ten years after her marriage to Mr. Rochester, there is hardly any perceptual gap between the young and the mature heroine. *Wuthering Heights,* in contrast, tells most of its story from the point of view of Nelly Dean, a self-educated upper servant who is both a reliable narrator and a thoroughly subjective one. She cleaves to her own idea of right and wrong, which is neither that of the characters whose story she relates nor her creator's. Nineteenth-century readers saw Nelly as "a specimen of true benevolence and homely fidelity," but at least since the middle of the twentieth century, she has also been seen as "one of the consummate villains in English literature."[5] Nelly's is not the only lens through which we see the characters and action of the novel. Her story includes the written accounts of other characters as well as their quoted speech, and all of these narrative components are framed by Lockwood's narration. Lockwood, the novel's master-narrator, has a name that may recall the Enlightenment philosopher Locke's but can't help suggesting confinement and hardened inaccessibility. As a London gentleman vacationing in a picturesque, rural part of England, he is very much a foreigner. The unfamiliarity of the customs and culture of the characters whose stories he hears makes him an unreli-

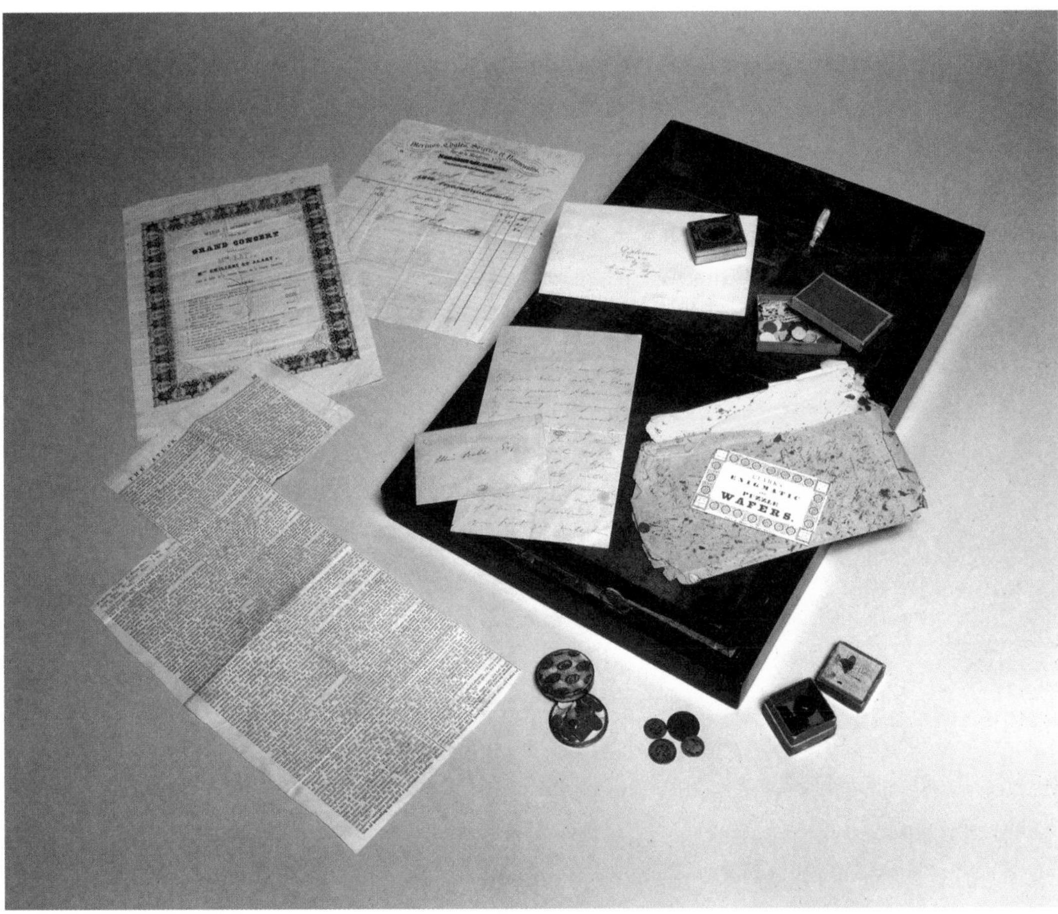

The writing slope or portable desk on which Emily wrote *Wuthering Heights*, and its contents at the time of her death, including five reviews of the novel and a letter from its publisher confirming his interest in securing her next novel.

able narrator, but so does his civilization, in the sense Freud fully develops in *Civilization and Its Discontents*. He is so distanced from his own instinctual life—the desire for sexual gratification and the aggressive and competitive impulses that civilization covers and curbs—that he can make only limited sense of the inhabitants of Wuthering Heights. Unlike Charlotte, Lockwood is a reader who shudders too little and sleeps (with one exception that every reader of *Wuthering Heights* will remember) too well.

The five reviews that Brontë preserved represent the contemporary response to *Wuthering Heights* and confirm the indelible impression it made at the time of its publication. Predictably, reviewers were disgusted or shocked by the novel's brutality, confounded by the absence of a reliable moral compass attributable to the author, and dismayed by the absence of characters to like or admire unreservedly. All but one of them complained that the story was "confused," or "unskilfully constructed," or "inartistic."[6] The origin of the one review that not only recognized the novel's consummate artistry but praised it unstintingly has not been traced, and we know about it only because Brontë preserved it. This reviewer is convinced that any reader will recognize in *Wuthering Heights* "the feelings of childhood, youth, manhood, and age, and all the emotions and passions which agitate the restless bosom of humanity."[7]

Wuthering Heights was eclipsed for the rest of the century by Charlotte's novels, and it was most often read in her "New Edition," published in 1850, two years after Emily's death. Restrained by Emily during her lifetime, bound by her requirements and always conciliatory, Charlotte was released by Emily's death to become her sister's editor and interpreter. Her "Biographical Notice of Ellis and Acton Bell" and her "Editor's Preface to the New Edition of 'Wuthering Heights'" (reprinted at the end of this edition) were meant to salvage Emily's reputation and largely succeeded. They represent her to her readers as a good woman and a gifted writer, but they also represent her novel as "a rude and strange production" and anticipate that readers will find its language, its manners, and the customs of its characters "repulsive."[8] If the "Editor's Preface" reveals Charlotte's concern for her sister's reputation, it also displays her anxiety about *Wuthering Heights.* Nevertheless, hers is the edition of *Wuthering Heights* that shaped Emily's reputation for the rest of the nineteenth century and for most of the twentieth.

A genuinely new work of art baffles its readers because it changes the rules of the game, and much of the difficulty Brontë's contemporaries had in recognizing the artistry of *Wuthering Heights* can be attributed to its originality. This has been the keynote of twentieth-century criticism of Brontë's novel. "No generalization that is true of Thackeray and Dickens, Trollope and Mrs. Gaskell, is true of her," David Cecil announced in 1935. "She writes about different subjects in a different manner and from a different point of view."[9] Writing in 1950, F. R. Leavis, one of the most influential critics of his time, famously called *Wuthering Heights* "a kind of 'sport,'" a spontaneous mutation owing little to the novels that preceded it and exerting little influence on novels to come: Emily Brontë "broke completely, and in the most challenging way, both with the Scott tradition that imposed on the novelist a romantic resolution of his themes, and with the tradition coming down from the eighteenth century that demanded a plane-mirror reflection of the surface of 'real' life."[10]

The assured status of *Wuthering Heights* as a classic has a lot to do with its having been read in such radically different ways by so many readers. In this it differs from other nineteenth-century British novels of comparable longevity. However much readers and critics of Jane Austen's *Pride and Prejudice* or George Eliot's *Middlemarch* differ in their approaches and emphases, they agree that Austen is writing a brilliant novel of manners and that *Middlemarch* is a great work in the genre of nineteenth-century realism. Yet there is no such agreement about the kind of thing *Wuthering Heights* is. The novel is at once a moral fable and a realistic account of particular lives; a timeless myth with affinities to fairy tales and ballads and a painstakingly accurate representation of changing relations of class and power in England during the first half of the nineteenth century; a metaphysical inquiry into eroticism and evil and a great romance; and so on. Like the perceptual groupings we identify as figure-ground problems, the novel is impossible to grasp as all of these things at once. It is for this reason that Dorothy Van Ghent calls it "the most treacherous [of all English novels] for the analytical understanding to approach."[11] It is not that the novel fails to provide, in Leavis's formulation, "a plane-mirror reflection of the surface of 'real' life," but that it provides so much more at the same time.

It is less striking that recent critics have approached *Wuthering Heights* armed with the tools of so wide a range of theoretical perspectives—Marxist, feminist, structuralist, semiotic, and so on—than it is that each of these different approaches has yielded so much. Over the course of a century and a half, Brontë's novel has demonstrated its capacity to generate an unusual "plurality" of readings, different for different times and readers, and yet not canceling each other out.[12] These readings are on display not only in the substantial critical literature attached to *Wuthering Heights* but also in the many film adaptations made since 1920; in still further adaptations for television, radio, theater, and opera; in illustrations for the novel; in the many poems and songs inspired by it, including Kate Bush's haunting debut single, "Wuthering Heights," which topped the UK charts in 1978; and in sequels. A simple way to take the measure of the imaginative range of adaptations the novel has inspired is to set Laurence Olivier, who plays Heathcliff in William Wyler's 1939 film of the novel, alongside James Howson, the unknown West Yorkshire black actor who plays Heathcliff in Andrea Arnold's 2011 film.

The drama of Emily Brontë's life and the lives of her talented sisters and their brother, Branwell, has always competed for attention with the drama of their works. Haworth, the village in the old West Riding of Yorkshire where they lived and wrote, is today the beating heart of a thriving Brontë industry. Among literary sites in England, only Stratford has more visitors. Every year, thousands of pilgrims climb Haworth's steep cobbled high street to visit the Parsonage (now housing a museum and a research library) and

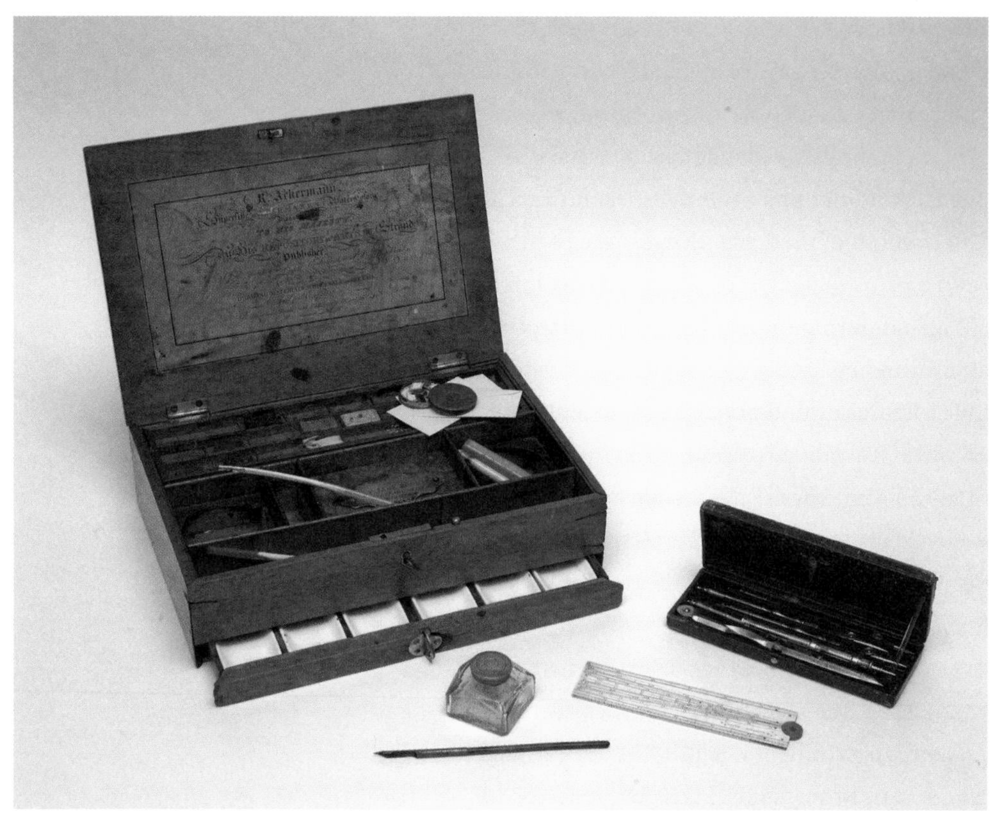

Regency period mahogany artist's box belonging to Emily. Bought at a Sotheby's auction in 2009, Emily's artist's box is a recent, important acquisition for the Brontë Parsonage Museum.

Emily's geometry set in its leather-covered box. Seven geometric diagrams drawn and labeled by Emily survive.

the church where the Brontës' father, Patrick, preached his sermons to a congregation of farmers, mill workers, household servants, substantial landowners, and others who worked in the cottage industries associated with wool manufacture. Since at least the last decades of the nineteenth century, the Brontës' admirers have been crossing the moors to Top Withens, where the blackened walls of a stone farmhouse still stand to mark an exposed, windy hilltop long associated with Wuthering Heights. When Ted Hughes and Sylvia Plath made their visit in 1956, the roofs' "Deadfall slabs were flaking, but mostly in place," as Plath's sketch of the building shows.[13] The rooms of the Parsonage, recently repainted after painstaking research into their appearance when the Brontës lived in them, contain relics in glass cases—not just drawings and letters but objects like Emily's writing slope and artist's box, the collar her dog Keeper wore, and her christening mug. The signs in the village streets and on the nearby moors are in Japanese as well as English, reminding visitors that although the three famous sisters lived mostly sequestered here, their works have traveled great distances and won admirers in places that would have been strange to them.

In the Brontë myth, Emily (1818–1848) is more mythic than the others. Even though he is composing a memorial to Charlotte, Matthew Arnold pays his highest tribute to Emily. His poem "Haworth Churchyard" (1855) recycles two of the most enduring ideas about her life and death: her "soul/ Knew no fellow for might,/ Passion, vehemence, grief,/ Daring," and she "sank/ Baffled, unknown, self-consumed." For Arnold and for countless others, Emily Brontë is a woman unlike all other women and, at the same time, all too much like them—not only frustrated and obscure but suicidal. In the end, she burns up in a flame she herself fuels. This particular myth about Brontë has been long-lived, like the story that the poet Keats was killed by a cruel review. In Brontë's case, as in Keats's, the actual villain was consumption. She caught cold at Branwell's funeral and never recovered her health. Less than two weeks before her death, Charlotte, painfully frustrated by Emily's rejection of any professional medical attention, wrote to a London specialist about her and asked him to prescribe a treatment. This letter has survived, but not intact. Portions of it describing the symptoms of Emily's illness have been torn off, probably in an effort to avoid indelicate revelations. (Jane Austen's sister, Cassandra, censored her sister's letters, often omitting references in them to physical ailments.[14]) What remains describes a cough accompanied by expectoration, emaciation, a rapid pulse, exhaustion, and drowsiness—all symptoms of miliary tuberculosis, a serious form of the disease in which the infection has spread throughout the body. Although Charlotte was distressed by Emily's insistence on self-medicating, the discovery of the bacterium that causes tuberculosis was three decades away, and it was only in the twentieth century that effective antibacterial drugs were developed. When Emily at last agreed to see a doctor a few hours before she died, she did so as one might ask for a priest or a minister, someone to preside over her death rather than forestall it.

The contrast with Anne (1820–1849), who sought and followed an exhausting prescribed course of treatment when she, in turn, was diagnosed with tuberculosis, is telling. The different ways in which these sisters met their illness and death correspond to the different faces they wore while they were still in good health. We know something about this from the diary papers they exchanged with each other at approximately four-year intervals. "I for my part cannot well be *flatter* or older in mind than I am now," Anne writes in 1845, but Emily is engaged with her life and sanguine about her prospects:

> I am quite contented for myself—not as idle as formerly, altogether as hearty and having learnt to make the most of the present and hope for the future with less fidgetiness that I cannot do all I wish—seldom or [n]ever troubled with nothing to do [illegible] and merely desiring that every body could be as comfortable as myself and as undesponding and then we should have a very tolerable world of it—[15]

Charlotte felt the contrast between her sisters: Anne "from her childhood, seemed preparing for an early death," but Emily "was torn conscious, panting, reluctant though resolute out of a happy life."[16] For Freud, the aim of an organism was to die in its own way. For Brontë, this aim, which the record of her last illness shows she shared with Freud, was connected to her determination to live in her own way. In life, she was remarkably unbaffled.

Here are a few facts about her life.[17] One of the family servants described her as "the prettiest of the children," a judgment corroborated by a reference to her as "the pet nursling" at the Clergy Daughters' School at Cowan Bridge, where she followed her two older sisters to school and was, at the age of six, the youngest child enrolled. Although there were other brief absences from Haworth—one as a pupil at Roe Head, where Charlotte (1816–1855) had a teaching post, and another as a teacher in a large school at Law Hill—Emily lived more at home than either of her sisters, and both home and the neighboring moors were more essential to her being than to theirs. She grew up tall and lanky, and by the time she accompanied Charlotte to Brussels for further

Patrick Branwell Brontë's portrait of Anne, Emily, and Charlotte. Painted c. 1834, when he was seventeen, it is known as the Pillar Portrait. The "pillar" between Emily (left) and Charlotte (right) covers Branwell's self-portrait, which was included in the painting at an earlier stage.

schooling at the age of twenty-three, she had lost her early prettiness. In Brussels, she worked "like a horse," teaching and studying music, learning French and German, sketching and painting.[18] The limp petticoats and leg-of-mutton sleeves she wore there made her look gawky and old-fashioned. She annoyed her pupils by insisting on giving them lessons during their play hours so as not to interfere with her own time for studying. Called back to England by her aunt's death, she remained at home for the rest of her life, except for a two-day holiday jaunt to York with Anne.

The Brontës' servant, Tabitha Ackroyd, presided over the kitchen, where Emily made the bread. Tabby spoke in the local dialect that figures so prominently in *Wuthering Heights,* and the traditional stories and ballads she told and sang were one of the kitchen's attractions. Another was the pleasure of repetitive physical work, like kneading bread, that quiets the body and leaves the mind free to range or to concentrate its force on a task like learning German. Emily was a great reader in a reading family and also a great walker in all weathers. Taller and physically hardier than either of her sisters, she was better suited for the physical burden of managing Branwell (1817–1848) when he was incapacitated by drink or opium. The myth that she was more sympathetic to him during his decline than her sisters still has its adherents, but there is no evidence to support it. The only idea that Brontë's writing will support is that pity probably played a larger role in her feelings about Branwell than disappointment or judgment.

Brontë's musical performance and her drawings are remarkable for their difference from the polite accomplishment expected of young ladies. In music, such accomplishment would have meant entertaining her family and company by playing the piano and singing, as Austen's Jane Fairfax does so much better than Emma. Brontë didn't sing at all, and the piano music she played was ambitious and demanding. She purchased *The Musical Library* in 1844, a multivolume publication designed to introduce "compositions of a superior order" to a wider audience, and we know that she studied a six-page excerpt from Beethoven's Pastoral Symphony, No. 6.[19] In addition to playing an instrument and singing, fashionable ladies and the governesses who hoped to educate them were encouraged to copy engravings of portraits, landscapes, fruit, and flowers. All of the Brontë sisters acquired this proficiency. None of them sketched or painted what Jane Eyre describes as visions seen with the "spiritual eye," unless we include Emily's doodlings on the manuscripts of her poems, which include a winged serpent, a frond or feather, and a Celtic cross. As the only boy in the family, Branwell felt authorized to sketch from nature, and Emily, although she also copied pictures, produced her best drawings and paintings in this way. During her nine months in Brussels, Emily would

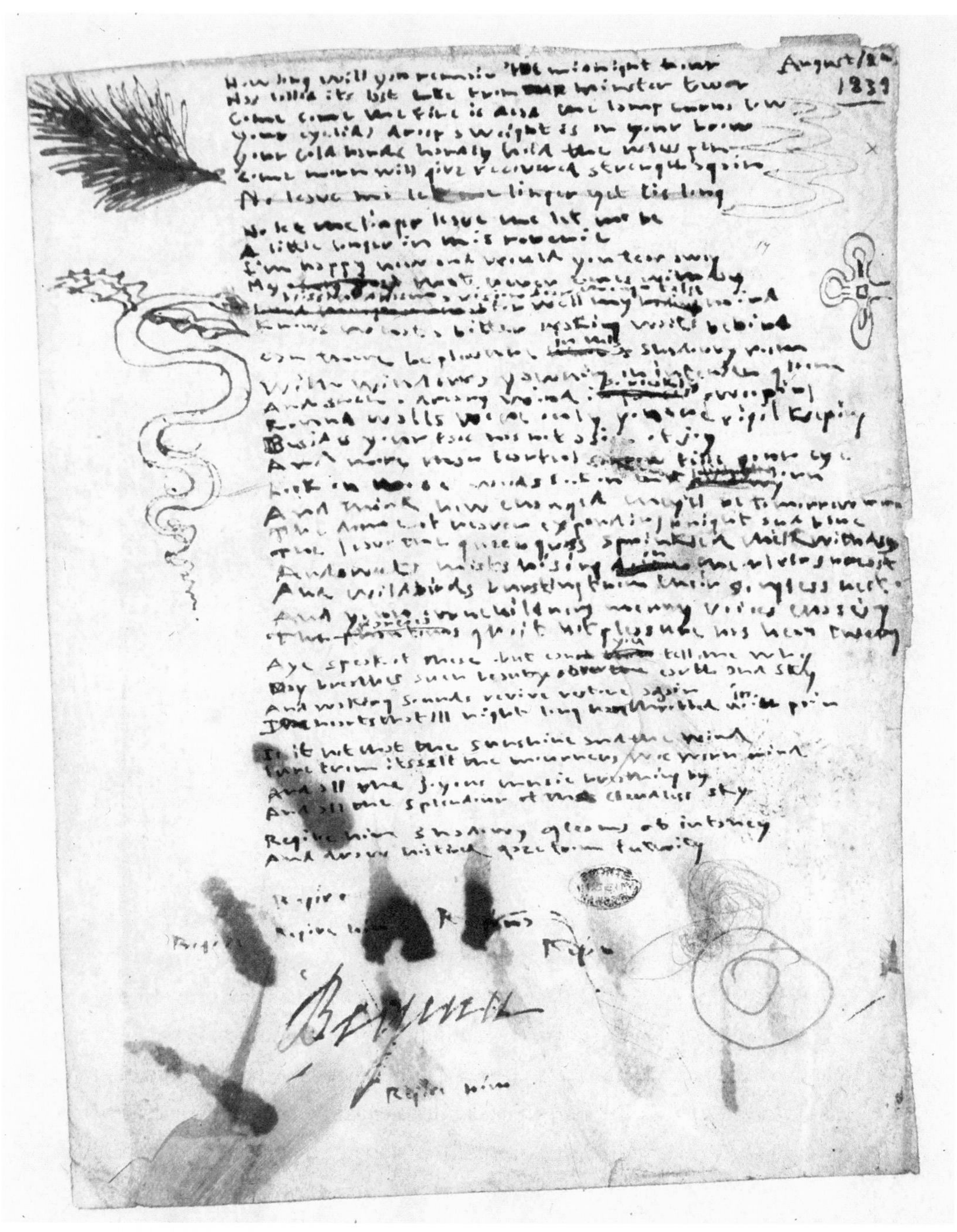

A single-leaf holograph manuscript dated 1839 and containing the only surviving copy of Brontë's poem "How long will you remain?" The page is decorated with sketches of a winged serpent, a frond or feather, a cross like a Celtic cross but lacking any circle, and a circle within a circle. Below the poem, Brontë has written and re-written the word *regive* and the phrase *regive him.*

have had the chance to attend several concerts; we don't know whether she did.[20] We do know that on her way to Brussels with Charlotte, Charlotte's friend Mary Taylor, and her father, she saw London for the first and only time (putting aside her return trip from Brussels, when she passed through the city) and visited some of its museums and galleries.

The event that famously stimulated the Brontë children's writing occurred in June 1826, when their father, the Reverend Patrick Brontë, returned from a trip to Leeds bringing wooden soldiers as a present for Branwell, who gave permission to each of his sisters to claim one as her own. Patrick Brontë's income was small, and although his children had books and toys, presents cannot have been frequent in the Parsonage. The children's lively enthusiasm for their father's gift contrasts sharply with the bitter disappointment of the children in Wuthering Heights when their father returns from his trip to Liverpool bearing "a dirty, ragged, black-haired child" who will be assigned the name "Heathcliff." Branwell and Charlotte named their toy soldiers after Napoleon and the Duke of Wellington, and they named Anne's soldier for her ("Waiting-Boy"). Probably they named Emily's soldier for her as well: Charlotte says that they called him "Gravey" because he was "a grave-looking fellow."[21] Emily later named her soldier "Parry" after the English admiral and explorer Sir William Edward Parry. This was probably in 1827, when his failed expedition to the North Pole brought him closer to earth's northernmost point than anyone had yet gone or would go for fifty years.

The story of the wooden soldiers suggests that Emily's combination of self-consciousness and self-assurance displayed itself very early. Her older siblings identify with military and political champions, but she names her soldier after a great navigator and explorer of unknown climes. Later, M. Heger, Charlotte's and Emily's French teacher in Brussels, told Elizabeth Gaskell, when she was doing research for her eloquent biography of Charlotte, that Emily "should have been a man—a great navigator." He found her "egotistical and exacting compared to Charlotte." Heger's teaching plan for his two English pupils bears a striking resemblance to the visual arts training women received by copying engravings. Heger would read masterpieces of French literature to them so that they could catch "the echo of a style" and practice "reproducing their own thoughts in a somewhat similar manner." According to Gaskell, Emily's response to this method was fierce and immediate: she "said that she saw no good to be derived from it; and that, by adopting it, they should lose all originality of thought and expression. She would have entered into an argument on the subject, but for this, M. Heger had no time."[22] Emily's readiness to argue with her teacher is as revealing as his refusal to argue with her. Without such willingness to engage in argument, there would have been fewer poems and no *Wuthering Heights.*

We know much less about Emily's life than about Charlotte's, and much of what we know relies on Charlotte's extensive correspondence. The difficulties are obvious. Charlotte is an acute but very partial observer. She was in awe of Emily, but she also condescended to her, believing that she was more mature and better grounded than her younger sister. We can read eight of Charlotte's letters to Emily, but none of the letters Emily wrote to her or Anne has survived. The three letters Emily wrote that have survived are addressed to Ellen Nussey, Charlotte's friend, and are just as brief as the arrangements they have to communicate will allow. Gaskell interviewed people who knew Emily, but she never met her, and the information given by those who spoke from firsthand knowledge of Emily is limited and not always reliable. When Emily was required to engage in social life, which wasn't often, she kept her thoughts to herself, but Mary Taylor says that she would break her usual silence, even in company, when something offended her. According to Mary, Emily was like Charlotte in her "habits of mind, but certainly never took her opinion, but always had one to offer."[23]

We know quite a lot about Charlotte's and Anne's religious convictions and much less about Emily's. History has it that she was the only one of the sisters who didn't teach in her father's Sunday school and didn't attend church regularly. She believed that her religion was nobody's business but hers and God's. "That's right," Mary Taylor, Charlotte's friend, recalls her saying in approval of Mary's having taken this position, and these words constituted her only contribution to the discussion of religion that Charlotte and her friends were having. In her poems, she represents the ecstatic release associated with mystical experience. They don't rebel against Christianity so much as press beyond it. In "No coward soul is mine," composed just two years before her death, she dismisses the "thousand creeds/ That move men's hearts" as "unutterably vain."[24] Nothing could be clearer than that by the time she went to Brussels, she was already familiar with these creeds and with the religious controversies that would be played out later in *Wuthering Heights.* Sue Lonoff finds "traces of Wesleyan and possibly Calvinist doctrine" in some references to the fall of man and to "an eternal empire of happiness and glory" in the short essays or "devoirs" she composed there in response to her teacher's prompts.[25] One devoir titled "Filial Love" bears the distinctive mark of Emily's ethical thinking. It begins with her own severe paraphrase of the fifth commandment: "Honor thy father and thy mother if thou wouldst live." For her, this commandment reveals God's view of "the baseness of our race": "To fulfill the gentlest, the holiest of all

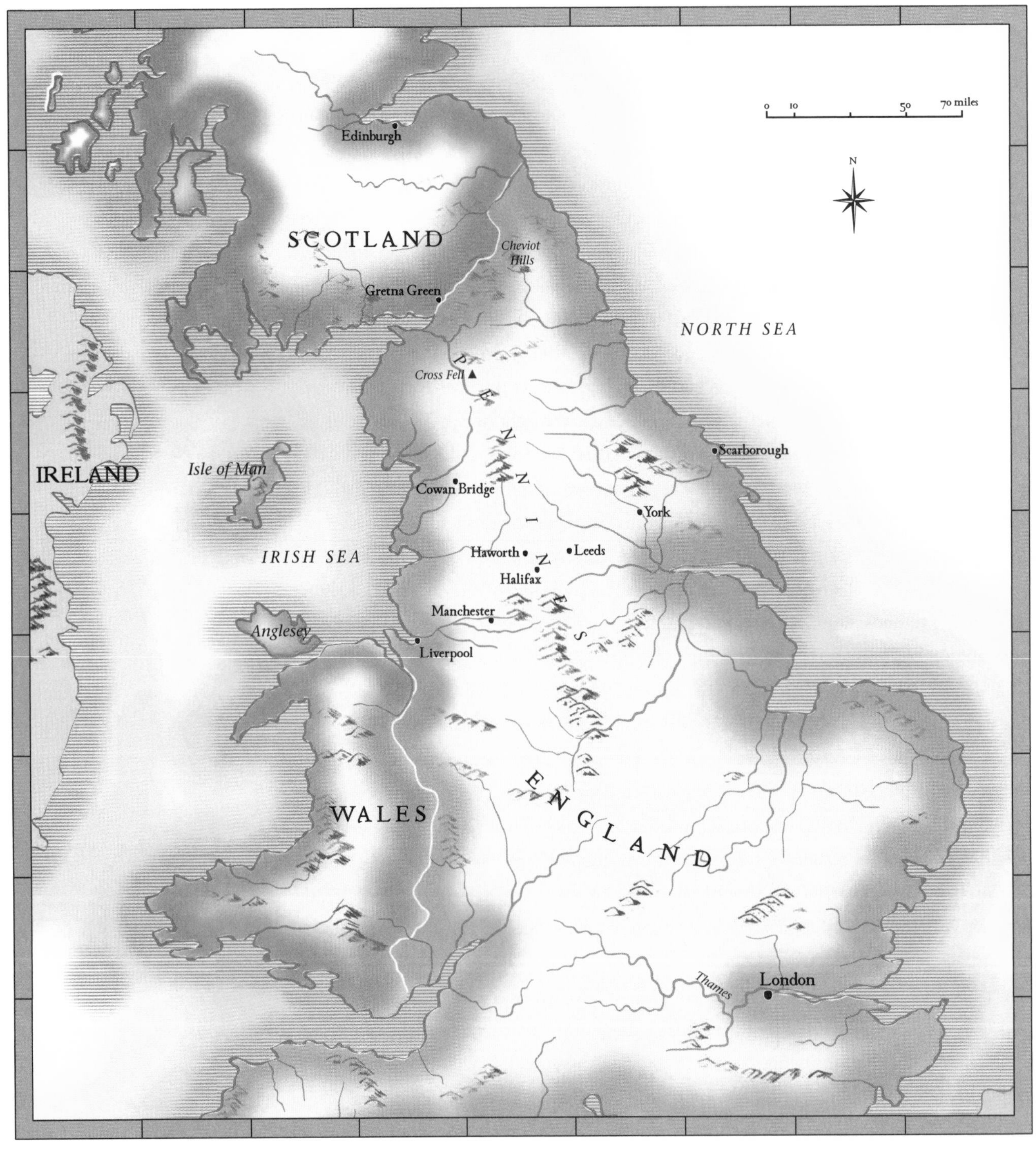

Emily Brontë's world.

duties man must be threatened."[26] No one who knew Emily doubted her moral rectitude, her "hypermorality." For Georges Bataille, the "intimate connection" between hypermorality and "transgression of the moral law" is "the ultimate meaning of Wuthering Heights."[27]

All four Brontë siblings had what Wordsworth called "the faculty of verse," but Emily's poetic gifts far exceeded the others'.[28] She is one of very few English writers—Thomas Hardy and D. H. Lawrence are others—who wrote memorable poems as well as memorable novels. One thing Brontë's poems call to our attention is that what Virginia Woolf called the "gigantic ambition" of *Wuthering Heights* had a history.[29] The earliest poem that survives, "Cold clear and blue the morning heaven," composed a few weeks before Brontë's eighteenth birthday, contains an unmistakable allusion to Sappho, the most famous woman poet in ancient Greece, and announces the dawning of a female planet. Brontë's poems have been much admired, in particular by other poets. Woolf thought that they might outlast her novel. Instead, they live alongside it as the record of her fine, musical ear; of the thinking, feeling, and reading that shaped her imaginative life; and of the distinctive self-idiom that informs and unifies the experiences she writes about. Readers of *Wuthering Heights* will easily recognize the novel's temper in Oscar Wilde's description of Brontë's poems as "instinct with tragic power and quite terrible in their bitter intensity of passion, the fierce fire of feeling seeming almost to consume the raiment of form."[30] Charlotte's novels, the poet Algernon Charles Swinburne wrote, are "rich in poetic spirit, poetic feeling, and poetic detail," but *Wuthering Heights* is "essentially and definitely a poem in the fullest and most positive sense of the term."[31]

In 1844, Brontë copied some of her poems into two fair-copy notebooks, one untitled, the other bearing the title "Gondal Poems." The Gondal poems are set in an imaginary kingdom Emily invented in collaboration with Anne and chronicled in prose narratives as well as poems. No Gondal prose has survived, so what we know about Gondal we know from Emily's and Anne's poems, from slight references to Gondal in their diary papers, and from the model provided by the chronicles of Angria, the imaginary kingdom invented by their older siblings, Charlotte and Branwell. The search for the sources of *Wuthering Heights* in the Gondal saga has not yielded much that is helpful. To say that the Gondal poems include doomed children, passionate and ambitious women with divided affections, and lovers who endure years of mourning will not explain the sea-change that transformed these materials into *Wuthering Heights.* Moreover, the quest for a key to the novel in the Gondal stories obscures the relevance of

Brontë's non-Gondal poems to her novel. We cannot characterize *her* Gondal fiction as juvenilia, as we can Charlotte's and Branwell's Angrian fiction, abandoned in favor of more mature endeavors. Months after the publication of *Wuthering Heights*, Emily was revising a Gondal poem about transgression and atonement, "Why ask to know the date—the clime." This poem's savage civil war, its remorseless mercenary soldier, and its damaged, surviving child belong to an imaginative cosmos continuous with her novel's, but so do the very different elements of "No coward soul is mine," a non-Gondal poem written just eight months earlier.

Charlotte's discovery of Emily's poems led to the publication of poems by all three sisters, and so to the publication of their novels. "One day, in the autumn of 1845," Charlotte writes, "I accidentally lighted on a MS. volume of verse in my sister Emily's handwriting. Of course, I was not surprised, knowing that she could and did write verse." Charlotte reports that "it took hours to reconcile [Emily] to the discovery I had made, and days to persuade her that such poems merited publication." The upshot was that Anne then showed Charlotte some of her poems, and the three of them succeeded in publishing a selection of their poems at their own expense. *Poems by Currer, Ellis, and Acton Bell* appeared in 1846. Sir Walter Scott had published his novels anonymously, and the title page of Jane Austen's *Sense and Sensibility* assigned authorship to "a lady." Three women living very quietly in a village where their father was the officiating clergyman would not be likely to publish their writing under their own names. It's more remarkable that the pseudonyms they chose were not unambiguously masculine (like "George Eliot"), though unlikely to be feminine. The Brontës had no reason to think that they would have a harder time finding a publisher for their poems and novels if they were presented as the work of women writers, but they had every reason to worry that their writing would be read differently—by reviewers as well as by publishers—if the authors were known to be women. Charlotte acerbically refers to their "vague impression that authoresses are liable to be looked on with prejudice" and to their having noticed that "critics sometimes use for their chastisement the weapon of personality, and for their reward, a flattery, which is not true praise."[32]

Although Charlotte says that the sisters began writing their first novels in the wake of the discouraging reception of *Poems* (the number of reviews it received—three—exceeded by one the number of copies actually sold in the first year), we know that she was already looking for a publisher for three "prose tales" a month before *Poems* was published. The manuscripts of all three novels—Charlotte's *The Professor*, Anne's *Agnes Grey*, and Emily's *Wuthering Heights*—duly made the rounds until Thomas Cautley

Newby agreed to publish Anne's and Emily's novels together in the three-decker format that was the norm at this time. Newby's printed text is the basis for this edition of the novel. In my Note on the Text I explain why and describe the first edition of *Wuthering Heights* in more detail as well as the ways in which this edition differs from it.

Emily Brontë died on December 19, 1848, almost exactly a year to the day after the publication of *Wuthering Heights.* She was thirty years old. There is convincing, if not conclusive, evidence that she was writing another work of fiction at the time of her death. If she wrote some pages of a new novel, Charlotte, who survived her, may have destroyed them. She was the keeper of her sister's flame, and her motives would have been the usual good Victorian ones. She may have found the writing inferior to *Wuthering Heights,* or she may have felt that what it expressed would damage her sister's reputation if it came to light. Charlotte's assessment of *Wuthering Heights* was complicated. She was awed by the novel's boldness and originality, yet she described her sister's creative power as "immature," particularly in comparison with her own. She predicted that had Emily lived, her work "would have attained a mellower ripeness and sunnier bloom," and she wrote a novel, *Shirley,* to prove it, modeling the heroine who bears the title's name—a man's name at the time—after Emily as she would have developed in happier circumstances.[33] This prediction alone, had it failed of fulfillment in a second novel by Emily, would have predisposed Charlotte to limit the world's knowledge of her sister's powers to *Wuthering Heights* and the handful of poems chosen for publication by Emily during her life and by Charlotte after her death.

POEMS

BY

CURRER, ELLIS, AND ACTON

BELL.

LONDON:

AYLOTT AND JONES, 8, PATERNOSTER-ROW.

1846.

The title page of *Poems* by Currer, Ellis, and Acton Bell (1846).

Any novel written more than 150 years ago wants annotating for a modern reader, and *Wuthering Heights* especially. The notes make the case that Brontë's practical knowledge of the world was greater than most readers have imagined, and that her confinement and isolation were less limiting. As a writer, she had all the advantages as well as all the disadvantages of being a woman in the middle of the nineteenth century. The disadvantages included limited, one-way access to the literary world, but the advantages included time to read, study, and write according to her own plan. In addition to providing new evidence of what Brontë was reading, the notes situate *Wuthering Heights* in its philosophical, historical, and religious contexts. They point to her knowledge of the laws regulating inheritance, wills, mortgages, divorce, separation, and domestic abuse and unpack her allusions to the Bible and to her other reading. Because language changes over time, the meanings of some words that were perfectly clear to Brontë's contemporaries are obscure to readers today. When Lockwood sees "a couple of horse-pistols" above the chimney in the family sitting room at Wuthering Heights, a reader will want to know that these are large pistols meant to be carried on horseback; when Nelly describes one of the characters as "half-silly," it is helpful to know that Nelly thinks her behavior almost feebleminded, not half-foolish. Familiar words like "doubt" had a larger range of meanings in Brontë's time. For example, when old Mr. Earnshaw tells his daughter, "I doubt thy mother and I must rue that we ever reared thee," he means that he begins to be afraid that they will regret having raised her. Language also varies from place to place, and much of the vocabulary of the novel and many of its idioms are specific to the part of England where the story is set. Lockwood glosses a few of these like "house" (referring to the sitting room in Wuthering Heights) and "wuthering" ("a significant provincial adjective, descriptive of . . . atmospheric tumult") that would have puzzled mid-nineteenth-century London readers as much as modern ones.

Dialect, the language and manner of speaking of a particular region and time, is a special case of the difficulties language presents for a reader of *Wuthering Heights*. Brontë was familiar with the use of dialect in Scottish literature, especially the novels, poems, and short stories of Scott and James Hogg, writers the Brontës read early and enthusiastically. The West Yorkshire dialect of Joseph, the surly, bigoted manservant at the Heights, has a great many words in common with the Lowland Scots spoken nearby, on the other side of the border with Scotland. Joseph always speaks in dialect, except when he is imitating Isabella Linton's standard English pronunciation of words like "bedroom": "'Bed-rume!' he repeated, in a tone of mockery." The novel's two houses—Wuthering Heights and Thrushcross Grange—and its two families—Earnshaws and Lintons—are divided by their speech as they are by almost everything else. Dialect words turn up in Mr. Earnshaw's speech, but not in Mr. Linton's.

The idea that dialect is political is by now a commonplace. Lockwood's standard English continually reminds us of the social distance between him and the characters whose story he is hearing. Joseph's heavy dialect speech separates him not just from Lockwood, the London tourist, but also from his employers at the Heights and from servants like Nelly who are steadily improving themselves. Language shifts repeatedly call our attention to the instability of social categories in this novel. Although Hareton's ancestors built Wuthering Heights and his family has lived continuously in it, his social standing is almost as unstable as Heathcliff's, and his dialect speech for most of the novel signifies his fall from the gentry class into which he was born. When Hareton sets about recovering his birthright, he has to learn not just to read but to speak differently, and his rise toward the end of the novel repeats a pattern already twice enacted by Heathcliff, who rises and falls and rises again. All these social transformations are marked by how the characters speak.

Brontë listened well to the speech of her neighbors, and those who knew their dialect, beginning with Charlotte, acknowledged her skill in representing it. Joseph's speech would have been almost as unintelligible to the London literary world in Brontë's time as it is to us today. "It seems to me advisable," Charlotte wrote in a letter to the publisher of the 1850 edition of *Wuthering Heights,* "to modify the orthography of the old servant Joseph's speeches—for though—as it stands—it exactly renders the Yorkshire accent to a Yorkshire ear—yet I am sure Southerns [Londoners] must find it unintelligible—and thus one of the most graphic characters in the book is lost on them."[34] The differences between the dialect Joseph speaks and Lockwood's standard English are primarily phonetic (differing pronunciations resulting in differing spellings) and lexical (different words). The notes in this edition sometimes supply translations of individual words, but more often translate whole sentences. All such translations are necessarily inexact insofar as they assimilate Joseph's speech to the speech of the other characters. Charlotte's effort to make Joseph's speech more comprehensible to London readers, even if it were more successful than it is, clashes with Emily's effort to represent the authentic texture of his thoughts and beliefs. For example, when Joseph fulminates against Cathy—"Bud yah're a nowt, and it's noa use talking—yah'll niver mend uh yer ill ways, bud goa raight tuh t'divil, like yer mother afore ye!"—she shows us Joseph's attitude toward women, his impatience, and the absolutism that may derive from his religion but goes far beyond it. Translating these sentences into standard English preserves the sense of Joseph's speech but loses the sounds, inflections, and rhythms that create him for us in all his unaccommodating strangeness. Dialect speech puts us on notice that we are, like Lockwood, foreigners in the world of *Wuthering Heights.*

Dialect speech emphasizes not just Lockwood's (and the implied London reader's) regional and class differences from the characters whose story the novel tells but the different ways in which the south and north of Britain developed over time. A simple way to put this is to say that Lockwood, because he belongs to the city, is modern, while the rest of the characters in the novel may be better imagined as continuous with people belonging to a much earlier period of time. Most of the dialect words we encounter in the novel came into the language from Old English or Old Norse and register the influence of Viking settlements in the ninth and tenth centuries in this part of England.[35] Dialect in *Wuthering Heights,* like archaisms (words that are old-fashioned or obsolete), persistently evokes this earlier time. So do the novel's references, which the notes explain, to fairy caves and elf-bolts and to the centuries-old Danish and Scottish or Border ballads that Nelly sings or hums. We know that times are changing because the young Cathy and Hareton, as we see them at the beginning and end of the novel, are much more familiar to Lockwood and to us than the characters who belong to the previous generation, Heathcliff and Catherine.

Wuthering Heights is a historical novel that represents actions that take place fifty to seventy-five years before the time of its publication, but it is a profound kind of historical novel because these actions hark back to an even older history. In Susan Stewart's elegant formulation of the novel's double plot, "Brontë juxtaposes the old ballad world of a love that destroys the reason to something emergent in the charity of Cathy's love for Hareton and Hareton's forgiveness of Cathy."[36] Brontë sets her story in a place where the passions of its central characters, Catherine and Heathcliff, are in tune with an earlier heroic ethos and a harsh, unaccommodating natural world. She puts these passions up against the forces of civilization dedicated to taming nature, enforcing orderly social relations and responsibilities, and securing the conventional comforts of home and family. The contest is complicated by Brontë's refusal to idealize either Catherine or Heathcliff (she can be selfish and spiteful, he vindictive and sadistic) and by her unmistakable appreciation of some of the characters whose way of being in the world opposes theirs.

The greatest challenge of preparing this edition has been to meet the demands of readers who are new to the novel while also meeting those of readers who know it well. Both kinds of readers may find the novel's chronology confusing, and the notes call attention to and sometimes provide a context for the dates on which events occur while also trying not to anticipate the plot. Here it may be helpful to have a general outline of that chronology. Lockwood, who has leased Thrushcross Grange from Heathcliff for a year and whose narrative frames the novel, first visits Wuthering Heights in late November 1801 (Chapter 1). By this time, Heathcliff's rages have subsided, and his tyran-

A contemporary pub sign in Haworth displaying Branwell's portrait of Emily, a famous quotation from the novel, and Fritz Eichenberg's cover illustration for the 1943 Random House edition of *Wuthering Heights.*

nical behavior has assumed a steady cast. The two young people in the household—Cathy Linton and Hareton Earnshaw—are cousins who have not yet formed a deeper bond. In Chapter 3, Lockwood happens on a Bible owned by Catherine Earnshaw some twenty-five years earlier and reads a kind of diary entry scribbled by her in its margins in 1777. In Chapter 4, Nelly, now the housekeeper at Thrushcross Grange, the manor house that Lockwood has rented as a holiday property, begins to tell him the story of the inhabitants of Wuthering Heights, and her story takes us back to the summer of 1771, when old Mr. Earnshaw set off for Liverpool and returned carrying a child who was about seven years old and will be given the name "Heathcliff." The story Nelly tells Lockwood spans the novel's two volumes and takes about two months for her to tell. In Chapter 17 of Volume II, Lockwood visits the Heights again, this time to tell Heathcliff that he is leaving Thrushcross Grange to return to London. The next chapter specifies the date—September 1802—of his return to Thrushcross Grange after an absence of eight months. Nelly then resumes her tale, bringing Lockwood up to date on events that have occurred during his eight-month absence. The narration of these events takes up most of Chapters 18 through 20. Lockwood himself narrates the novel's final paragraphs.

The small but crucial symmetry—three chapters at the beginning to edge readers into the body of the novel, and three chapters at the end to speed them on their way—is a signal feature of the structure of *Wuthering Heights*. The novel is overfull of symmetries. There are two characters named Catherine or Cathy, a mother and a daughter. In this introduction and in the notes, I consistently refer to the older Catherine as "Catherine" and to the younger Catherine as "Cathy," but the opposite practice would be equally defensible. The only characters in the novel who are consistent in naming mother and daughter are Heathcliff, who almost always refers to the older Catherine as "Cathy" and always refers to the younger as "Catherine," and Edgar, who always does the reverse. The genealogical tree included in this edition makes the symmetry of the pedigrees of the novel's two families clear at a glance.[37]

Characters belonging to each of these families resemble one another and differ from characters belonging to the other family. Earnshaws are hard and unrefined; the culture they acquire is always an overlay, a surface smoothness that does not alter the hard structure beneath. Heathcliff is an Earnshaw by nature, though not by blood, and his virtues are the Earnshaw virtues: steadfastness, determination, and an unswerving dedication to the objects of his devotion.[38] Earnshaws have fierce tempers and an appetite for violence. Turned outward, this appetite is expressed in Heathcliff's brutality toward Isabella and Cathy; turned inward, it results in Hindley's self-destruction. Lintons are soft and refined. Everything that belongs to them—the house they inhabit, the vast park that surrounds it, and the animals inside it—is cultivated. The great Linton virtues are gentleness and adaptability. While abstaining from violence, Lintons can be cowardly, quarrelsome, and petulant. Boundaries are breached as the characters belonging to one family are made (or led) to inhabit the house belonging to the other family. The characters crisscross the park and the moors, changing places with each other and longing to return to the homes they have left behind. Thus Catherine is transported from the Heights to the Grange, and Isabella from the Grange to the Heights; Linton Heathcliff and Cathy Linton are forced to come to the Heights, but—in one of the novel's gestures toward resolution—Hareton follows Cathy back to the Grange. Only Heathcliff always inhabits the Heights and enters the Grange only as a trespasser. When Earnshaws and Lintons intermarry, the names of wives and children mark combinations that are conflictual and unstable: Catherine Earnshaw Linton; Isabella Linton Heathcliff; Cathy Linton Heathcliff; Cathy Linton Earnshaw. Cathy's relationship with Hareton echoes her mother's relationship with Heathcliff but does not repeat it. Heathcliff and Catherine grow up together and sleep in the same bed as children, while Cathy and Hareton form their bond as young adults, waiting until nearly the last moment and coming together only after all the other members of their respective families have departed.

Wuthering Heights is a tale told by the fire, and most of the action in the novel takes place indoors. One way nature figures is by means of analogy.[39] Lockwood, the city dweller taking a rural holiday, is more familiar with beggars than he is with hawthorns. We find this out because when he makes his first visit to the Heights, he gauges "the power of the north wind, blowing over the edge" by "the excessive slant" of the "stunted firs at the end of the house; and by a range of gaunt thorns all stretching their limbs one way, as if craving alms of the sun." More memorably, the characters whose story Lockwood hears reverse this procedure, turning repeatedly to features of the landscape and to animal life for a language fit to convey the quality of their understanding and experience. Thus Catherine warns Isabella that Heathcliff is "an arid wilderness of furze and whinstone"; Heathcliff describes Edgar as a "sucking leveret"; and Nelly tells Lockwood that Heathcliff's history is a "cuckoo's" and that Hareton is "like an unfledged dunnock."

All the same, Nature is not a metaphor in *Wuthering Heights,* and the novel has always been praised for its capacity to convey the quality of the extrahuman life that surrounds the characters. Country-born and country-bred, Brontë names the flowers and trees that grow in the earth and the birds that fly in the sky, or nest, or fall prey to humans and other birds. Nature in the novel operates according to Darwinian principles. We learn how powerful it is at the novel's threshold when Lockwood is forced to make his way back to Thrushcross Grange from Wuthering Heights after a treacherous snowfall, a journey that leads to four weeks of illness. But regardless of whether nature is hostile, forbidding, glorious, or invigorating—its atmospheric and seasonal changes are felt in all these ways and more in the novel—its moods lack any intentionality that we can read as an expression of will, either human or divine. In this respect, Brontë differs from Thomas Hardy, a writer whose Dorchester landscape figures as largely in his novels as Brontë's Yorkshire landscape figures in hers.

Animals play an especially crucial role in the novel. There is nothing sentimental about Brontë's representation of them, and interactions between animals and humans carry some of the burden of revealing the natures of both. Dogs in particular are important to the contrast between the family at the Heights, where they are kept for hunting and guarding, and the family at the Grange, where they are also kept as pets. On his first visit to Wuthering Heights, Lockwood attempts to stroke a liver-colored bitch pointer who is guarding her litter. She snarls in response, and one of the first things he sees Heathcliff do is kick her. On his second visit, Lockwood amuses himself by teasing the guard dogs and is attacked by them. We get our first view of Thrushcross Grange and its inhabitants when, as children, Heathcliff and Catherine stand outside the drawing-room window watching Edgar and Isabella inside. Edgar is weeping and Isabella is screaming after disputing possession of a small, fluffy dog, perhaps the same springer spaniel that Heathcliff will later hang by a handkerchief from a bridle hook. There is also a bulldog at the Grange. We meet him when he clamps his teeth on Catherine's ankle as she and Heathcliff, discovered in their spying, try to get back to Wuthering Heights. On this occasion, Heathcliff observes that Catherine is calm and stoical despite her pain. She is kind and kin to animals, and she bears no grudge against the bulldog, whom she will later caress as if they had always been good friends.

Overshadowed by Charlotte's novels, *Wuthering Heights* lacked a popular audience for most of the nineteenth century. Mary Robinson, Brontë's first biographer, credited Swinburne with restoring Emily's claim to readers, but even Swinburne doubted that Emily's novel would ever be widely popular. Instead, he announced that those who like it "will like nothing very much better in the whole world of poetry or prose."[40] The novel's popular resurgence in adaptations, especially film and television adaptations, continues today. The first film of the novel was directed by A. V. Bramble in 1920. It has been eclipsed by William Wyler's 1939 film (starring Merle Oberon as Catherine and Laurence Olivier as Heathcliff), which won the New York Film Critics Award for best film and was nominated for eight Academy Awards. Wyler's film begins with Lockwood's arrival at the Heights, eliminates the second generation, and ends with a scene in which the ghosts of Heathcliff and Catherine climb Penistone Crag together. Almost all the films of *Wuthering Heights,* including the most recent one directed by Andrea

Arnold (2011), follow Wyler's lead, distorting the novel's plot and structure by eliminating most of the second volume.[41] (Arnold's film also eliminates Lockwood and reduces Nelly's role.)

All these films foreground a Heathcliff whose qualities have changed over time in relation to changing cultural imperatives, and especially to changing ideas of power, desire, and gender. In Wyler's film, Heathcliff is "a sad, half-mad sufferer" and looks more like his Byronic forebears and Jane Eyre's Rochester than Brontë's Heathcliff ever does.[42] In Robert Fuest's *Wuthering Heights* (1970), Heathcliff (as played by Timothy Dalton) is at first vulnerable, then dangerous; he has rough sex with Catherine and may be the father of her child. In Peter Kosminsky's *Emily Brontë's Wuthering Heights* (1992), which includes the younger generation and which many viewers will remember for its casting of Sinéad O'Connor as Emily Brontë, Heathcliff (as played by Ralph Fiennes) is crueler and more calculating than previous Heathcliffs. Andrea Arnold's *Wuthering Heights* (2011), which radically alters Brontë's plot by making Heathcliff nearly a teenager when he arrives at the Heights, will probably be remembered for being the first to cast two black actors, Solomon Glave and James Howson, as Heathcliff and for its inspired cinematography.

Novels that introduce vampire or zombie characters into already existing novels are called mashups, and *Wuthering Heights* has spawned one. Yet there's a notable difference between mashups like *Pride and Prejudice and Zombies* or *Little Vampire Women* and the novel titled *Heathcliff, Vampire of Wuthering Heights.* The transformation of Heathcliff into a supernatural being occurs over and over in Brontë's novel, at least in the imaginations of the other characters. In her letter to Nelly, written when she returns to Wuthering Heights after eloping with him, Isabella asks whether he is "a man," and "if not, is he a devil?" Warned earlier by Catherine that she likes Isabella too well to let him "absolutely seize and devour her up," Heathcliff responds that he likes her "too ill to attempt it . . . except in a very ghoulish fashion." Nelly describes him as "an evil beast" that is "waiting his time to spring and destroy," a vampire, and a goblin with the classic features of a vampire: "Those deep black eyes! That smile, and ghastly paleness." No wonder, then, that Bella Swan, the heroine of Stephanie Meyer's Twilight books, is a fan of *Wuthering Heights* and quotes from it. In 2010, sales of *Wuthering Heights* more than quadrupled after the release of *Eclipse,* the third volume in the series, and the one that reveals Bella's literary proclivities.[43]

Heathcliff is, of course, human, but then, so are vampires, in their way. Long before the vogue for vampire mashups, Leo Bersani observed that desire in *Wuthering Heights* is “essentially vampiristic.” The lack that constitutes desire for Heathcliff and Catherine has little to do with pleasure or sensation: “it is a hole in being, and it can be filled up only if other being is poured into it.”[44] Heathcliff rages against Catherine’s dying, digs up her corpse, and spends most of the novel’s second volume being teased by her ghost. Alive, Catherine warns that she will not stay buried until Heathcliff joins her. Dead, the two of them continue to ramble on the moors, or at least some of those above ground think so. Bersani’s persuasive account of how Heathcliff’s identity is shaped by psychological forces competes with compelling views of that identity as socially constructed. Terry Eagleton sees Catherine’s refusal to marry Heathcliff because he is socially inferior to Edgar as “the pivotal event of the novel” and the catalyst for Heathcliff’s transformation from rebellious outsider to champion of the values of capitalist social relations. For Eagleton, Heathcliff turns himself into a capitalist oppressor “in caricatured form.”[45]

In film and television adaptations of *Wuthering Heights,* as in Kate Bush’s hit song, Heathcliff dominates Catherine. In Brontë’s novel, however, Catherine is the dominant figure and the one whose wishes must be obeyed. She is the novel’s “principal ego” and the one who “expresses most clearly [its] psychological point of view.”[46] The geography of her dreams spans heaven and hell as well as the distance between Wuthering Heights and Thrushcross Grange. Before Brontë, no one had ever imagined a woman like Catherine Earnshaw, someone with many of the faults conventionally attributed to women—she is egotistical, demanding, and prone to tantrums and nervous attacks—but also someone with strengths of a kind not thought possible for a woman. A heroine’s decision to marry one man instead of another is a staple of the marriage plot in almost every nineteenth-century English novel, and there’s nothing unusual in Catherine’s belief that marriage is a social arrangement—the means by which a woman achieves her position in society as well as security, comfort, wealth, and independence from the men in her own family. Yet when I teach *Wuthering Heights,* I find that my students are much less sympathetic to Catherine than they are to other Victorian heroines who make convenient marriages like hers. The reason may be that Catherine expresses her sense of the wrong she is doing so originally. It’s not just that she wrongs Heathcliff, as he accusingly reminds her. She wrongs herself too, and perhaps she does this not by failing to marry Heathcliff but by marrying at all. The question Catherine asks and cannot then answer is how to live as a woman in the world while also being true to her deepest feelings.

Wuthering Heights has been called “the most beautiful, most profoundly violent love story of all time.”[47] Love is one of the names we give our deepest feelings, but in *Wuther-*

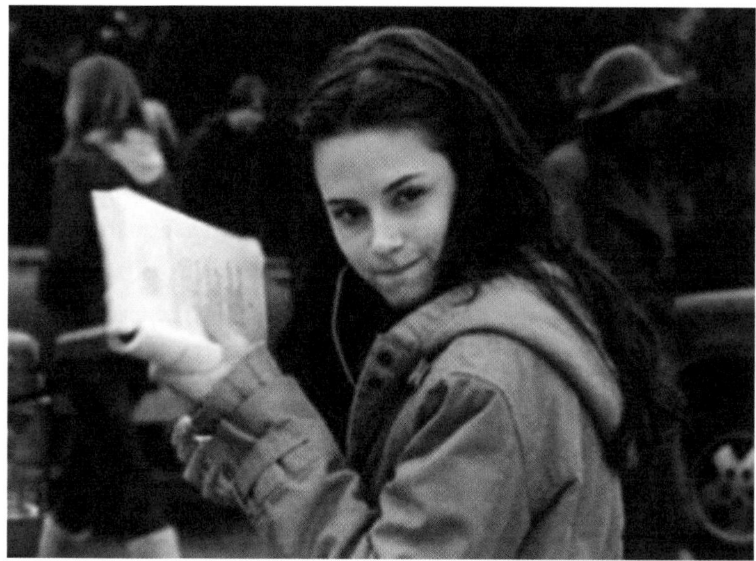

Bella Swan (played by Kristen Stewart), the heroine of the wildly popular Twilight saga, reading. Sales of *Wuthering Heights* more than quadrupled after Bella said *Wuthering Heights* was her favorite novel and compared her love for Edward to Catherine's love for Heathcliff.

ing Heights, it is too small a name to encompass everything the novel reaches out to include. To see this, we need only remember Catherine's claim: "I *am* Heathcliff." This is the simplest kind of sentence we can write in English. When we hear it, we know immediately that the formulation cannot be literally true. Yet Catherine doesn't mean that she is *like* Heathcliff, or that she has more in common with him than with Edgar, which may be true but trivializes her insight. In William Wyler's film version, Merle Oberon says, "I'm yours, Heathcliff. I've never been anyone else's." An assertion of consummate self-possession in the novel is thereby turned into a woman's longing to be possessed by a man. In the novel, Catherine's assertion emerges from questions that flicker like stars in the dark dreamscape of *Wuthering Heights.* How do we determine who and what we are? What do other people in and out of the family contribute to our sense of an identity? How is selfhood experienced differently by men and by women? Catherine's claim to *be* Heathcliff, and her intuition that she loses her connection to the universe when she loses him, is grounded in the novel's boldest collocation of coincidences: her separation from Heathcliff ("I was laid alone for the first time," she tells Nelly in Chapter 12 of the first volume) coincides with her father's death, her brother's inheritance of her father's property, the onset of her puberty, and the beginning of her transformation into the young lady who will become the mistress of Thrushcross Grange.

In preparing this edition, I have been inspired by Martin Gardner's epigraph to *The Annotated Alice:* "Wipe your glosses with what you know." I have been the fortunate beneficiary of the considerable intelligence and imagination of the many critics and scholars who have preceded me, and much of what I know I owe to them. I have not, however, used the notes to present the many interpretations *Wuthering Heights* has inspired in any detail. The reason is not, as Gardner put it in his introduction to *The Annotated Alice,* that the criticism is so "exceedingly easy to do" that "any clever reader" can do it for herself.[48] The main disadvantages of fully representing the critical commentary are that some of it is of interest to specialists only, and that too much of it may stand in the way of a reader's encounter with the novel and so constitute an interruption of thinking instead of an aid to it. Especially for a reader encountering the novel for the first time, critical interpretations that may prove both useful and engaging in the end can, along the way, either forestall a response or induce one. Charlotte's "Biographical Notice of Ellis and Acton Bell" and her "Editor's Preface to the New Edition of *Wuthering Heights*" have been included in this edition because they have played so large a role in the history of the novel's reception. We can easily read them today without subscribing to their view of the novel and its author. Particularly notable criticism of *Wuthering Heights* is recommended in the Further Reading section of this edition.

NOTES

1. "Since 1857," Lucasta Miller writes in *The Brontë Myth,* "hardly a year has gone by without some form of biographical material on the Brontës appearing—from articles in newspapers to full-length lives, from images on tea towels to plays, films, and novelizations" (New York: Knopf, 2004), p. xi.

2. "Editor's Preface to the New Edition of *Wuthering Heights,*" this edition, p. 443. Charlotte refers to herself as Emily's "auditor" and to her "hearing" of Emily's novel, not to her reading of it.

3. The evidence is supplied by Brontë's choice of Lockwood and Nelly to narrate her novel and by one of her Brussels school essays, "Letter," an invitation to a music recital, written by a pupil to her teacher, and the teacher's reply ("Letter," in Sue Lonoff, *The Belgian Essays: A Critical Edition* [New Haven: Yale Univ. Press, 1996], pp. 140–149).

4. "Editor's Preface," this edition, p. 440.

5. The first quotation is from the "Editor's Preface," this edition, p. 443. The second is from James Hafley, "The Villain in *Wuthering Heights,*" *Nineteenth-Century Fiction,* 13:3 (Dec. 1958), p. 199.

6. All these comments come from excerpts from the five reviews Brontë kept, which are collected in Miriam Allott, *The Brontës: The Critical Heritage* (London: Routledge & Kegan Paul, 1974), pp. 221, 224, 230, 224, 228, 231.

7. Allott, *The Brontës,* pp. 243–244.

8. "Editor's Preface," this edition, p. 441.

9. "Emily Brontë and *Wuthering Heights,*" from *Early Victorian Novelists: Essays in Revaluation,* reprinted in *The Brontë Sisters: Critical Assessments,* ed. Eleanor McNees, 4 vols. (Mountfield: Helm Information, 1996), 2, p. 103.

10. F. R. Leavis, *The Great Tradition: George Eliot, Henry James, Joseph Conrad* (New York: George W. Stewart, 1950): "The genius, of course, was Emily. I have said nothing about *Wuthering Heights* because that astonishing work seems to me a kind of sport" (p. 27).

11. "On *Wuthering Heights,*" from *The English Novel: Form and Function,* reprinted in McNees, ed., *The Brontë Sisters: Critical Assessments,* 2, p. 201.

12. Frank Kermode uses the word "plurality" in relation to *Wuthering Heights* in *The Classic: Literary Images of Permanence and Change* (Cambridge: Harvard Univ. Press, 1983), p. 133. The point is also made in J. Hillis Miller's deconstruction of *Wuthering Heights* in *Fiction and Repetition: Seven English Novels* (Cambridge: Harvard Univ. Press, 1985).

13. Ted Hughes, "Wuthering Heights," in *Collected Poems,* ed. Paul Keegan (New York: Farrar, Straus, and Giroux, 2003), p. 1080.

14. Terry Castle, *Boss Ladies, Watch Out!* (New York: Routledge, 2002), p. 126.

15. Quoted in Juliet Barker, *The Brontës* (London: Phoenix, 1994), pp. 455–456.

16. *The Letters of Charlotte Brontë,* 3 vols., ed. Margaret Smith (Oxford: Clarendon Press, 2000), 2, pp. 216 and 200.

17. There are several full-length biographies of Emily and of the Brontë family. Some of them are listed in the Further Reading section of this edition.

18. *Letters,* 1, p. 285.

19. Stevie Davies, *Emily Brontë* (Plymouth, UK: Northcote House Publishers Ltd., 1998), pp. 41–44.

20. Davies, *Emily Brontë,* p. 41.

21. "History of the Year" (1829), quoted in Winifred Gérin, *Emily Brontë: A Biography* (Oxford: Clarendon Press, 1971), p. 11.

22. Elizabeth Gaskell, *The Life of Charlotte Brontë,* ed. Angus Easson (Oxford: Oxford Univ. Press, 1996), p. 178.

23. Gérin, *Emily Brontë,* p. 121.

24. References to Emily Brontë's poems are to my edition of them, *Emily Jane Brontë: The Complete Poems,* ed. Janet Gezari (London: Penguin Books Ltd., 1992).

25. Lonoff, *The Belgian Essays,* p. lxii. The quotation at the end of the sentence in Lonoff's translation is from Brontë's essay "The Butterfly," in Lonoff's translation, p. 178.

26. Lonoff, *The Belgian Essays,* p. 156.

27. Georges Bataille, *Literature and Evil*, trans. Alastair Hamilton (London: Marion Boyars, 1957, rpt. 2001), p. 23.

28. Robert Southey quoted Wordsworth in his letter to Charlotte, who had written to him asking for his advice about her poetry in 1836 (*Letters*, 1, p. 166). For a fuller account of the poetry of the Brontës, see Janet Gezari, "The Poetry of the Brontës," in *The Brontës in Context*, ed. Marianne Thormählen (Cambridge: Cambridge Univ. Press, 2012), pp. 134–142.

29. "*Jane Eyre* and *Wuthering Heights*," in *Collected Essays*, 4 vols. (New York: Harcourt, Brace & World, Inc., 1967), 1, p. 187.

30. *Complete Writings of Oscar Wilde: Reviews* (New York: The Nottingham Society, 1909), p. 200.

31. Allott, *The Brontës*, pp. 439–440.

32. "Biographical Notice," this edition, p. 436.

33. "Biographical Notice," this edition, p. 437, and "Editor's Preface," this edition, p. 443.

34. *Letters*, 2, p. 479.

35. Irene Wiltshire, "Speech in Wuthering Heights: Joseph's Dialect and Charlotte's Emendations," *Brontë Studies*, 30 (March 2005), p. 26.

36. Susan Stewart, "The Ballad in Wuthering Heights," in *Representations* 86 (Spring 2004), p. 193.

37. "The Structure of *Wuthering Heights*," in McNees, ed., *The Brontë Sisters: Critical Assessments*, 2, p. 73.

38. I borrow this formulation from Anne Williams, "Natural Supernaturalism," *Studies in Philology*, 82:1 (Winter 1985), p. 114.

39. In a classic essay, Mark Schorer explores the way that Brontë "roots her analogies in the fierce life of animals and in the relentless life of the elements—fire, wind, water." "Fiction and the Matrix of Analogy," in McNees, ed., *The Brontë Sisters: Critical Assessments*, 2, p. 184.

40. Allott, *The Brontës*, p. 444.

41. Wikipedia lists two more recent adaptations of *Wuthering Heights;* a Hindi film, *Rockstar* (2011), in which the relationship of the rocker and his girl is loosely based on Heathcliff's and Catherine's; and a Philippine TV drama, *Walang Hanggan* [Infinity] (2012), loosely based on *Wuthering Heights* and a 1991 Philippine film.

42. Lin Haire-Sargeant, "Sympathy for the Devil: The Problem of Heathcliff in Film Versions of *Wuthering Heights*," in Emily Brontë, *Wuthering Heights*, ed. Richard Dunn (New York: W. W. Norton & Co., 2003), p. 418. Haire-Sargeant's account of four film adaptations of the novel has informed my account of the films.

43. These figures were widely reported. See, for example, "Wuthering Heights sales quadruple thanks to Twilight effect," in Book News, *The Telegraph*, April 10, 2010: http://www.telegraph.co.uk/culture/books/booknews/7570922/Wuthering-Heights-quadruple-double-thanks-to-Twilight-effect.html.

44. Leo Bersani, *A Future for Astyanax: Character and Desire in Literature* (New York: Columbia Univ. Press, 1979, rpt. 1984), p. 213.

45. Terry Eagleton, *Myths of Power: A Marxist Study of the Brontës* (London: Macmillan, 1975), pp. 111–113.

46. Bersani, *A Future for Astyanax,* p. 204.

47. Bataille, *Literature and Evil,* p. 16; quoted by Stewart, "The Ballad in Wuthering Heights," p. 181, in her own translation. My translation from the French differs slightly from Hamilton's and Stewart's.

48. Lewis Carroll, *The Annotated Alice: The Definitive Edition,* intro. and notes by Martin Gardner (New York: W. W. Norton & Co., 2000), p. xiv. The epigraph (quoting Joyce) has slipped out of this edition of *Alice* but can be found in earlier imprints (Cleveland and New York: Forum Books, 1960).

NOTE ON THE TEXT

This edition takes as its copy-text the first edition of the novel published by Thomas Cautley Newby in 1847. This is the only edition of the novel published during Brontë's lifetime. The posthumous second edition, edited by Charlotte Brontë and published in 1850, rejected Newby's division of the novel into two volumes, and most modern editions have followed suit. Although a strong case can be made that the division into two volumes was an accident of publication with no basis in Brontë's manuscript, this edition presents the text in the two-volume format approved by its author. This is also the format in which its first readers encountered it.

The problems an editor of *Wuthering Heights* faces are multiple. Brontë's manuscript, which would have provided information about her intentions, has not survived. Although she received proof-sheets, which she corrected and returned to Newby, he paid little attention to them. According to Charlotte, whose testimony on this matter is all we have, "almost all the errors that were corrected in the proof-sheets appear intact in what should have been the fair copies."[1] For this reason, the first edition cannot be said to represent Brontë's final intentions for her novel. Its reliability as a copy-text is further undermined by a large number of obvious errors: missing words and letters; type belonging to different fonts; and inconsistent or incorrect punctuation, capitalization, spelling, and paragraphing. In this edition, obvious typographical errors have been corrected silently.

The spelling of dialect words would have presented special problems for a London printer. According to K. M. Petyt, an expert on West Yorkshire dialect, "Newby's edition contains, besides obvious mistakes which are easily corrected, a number of impossible forms . . . and instances of standard and dialect spelling alongside each other."[2]

Petyt oversaw the spelling of dialect words for the Clarendon Press edition, and this edition reproduces the spellings approved by him for that publication.

In the several cases in which this edition emends the words of the text, the annotations explain my choices and thinking. One example is the substitution of "Fair Annie" for "Fairy Annie" as the title of a ballad Nelly sings. In cases where other editors have suggested emendations this edition rejects, the annotations also explain my thinking. One example is the choice to agree with 1847 in printing "sand-pillar" (not "hand-pillar") to identify the guidepost that points the way to Wuthering Heights, Thrushcross Grange, and Gimmerton.

Apart from such emendations, this edition does not try to reconstruct Brontë's manuscript, a task that is impossible with only the first and second editions of the novel to work from. In preparing her new edition of *Wuthering Heights,* Charlotte did not attempt to restore Emily's original text. Instead, her revisions try to make the novel more correct according to current standards and more easily accessible to a larger number of readers. Apart from presenting the novel in one volume, Charlotte made three important kinds of changes: she combined short paragraphs into longer ones; she altered punctuation, especially by eliminating unnecessary commas and replacing dashes with commas and periods; and she changed the spelling that represents Joseph's pronunciation and sometimes substituted standard English words for dialect words.

A text as close as possible to what Brontë wrote—a reconstruction of the manuscript—would not in any case constitute its author's final intentions for her book. It would not take into account her own corrections to the proof-sheets or the corrections she expected her publisher to make on her behalf. In this period, a responsible publisher would have improved his author's punctuation and normalized her spelling. Charlotte, whose novels were published by Smith, Elder & Co., a more reliable firm than the one headed by Newby, thanks her publisher for correcting the punctuation of *Jane Eyre.* Otherwise, it might have been as "mortifying" to her as she said the punctuation of the 1847 *Wuthering Heights* was to Emily.[3]

The most important evidence we have that Brontë understood and accepted the difference between a work in manuscript and a work in print is *Poems by Currer, Ellis, and Acton Bell* (1846), published during her lifetime. A comparison of the poems in manuscript with the poems in print shows important differences in punctuation and format. For example, while the poems in Brontë's manuscripts regularly lack punctuation at the ends of lines, *Poems* provides punctuation at the ends of all lines that are syntactically end-stopped, making Brontë's poems look more like other poems in print at the time.

Not just periods but colons and dashes terminate lines, suggesting that Brontë paid some attention to choosing her punctuation marks. There are also changes to the format of two poems: in the published versions of both "Faith and Despondency" and "The Philosopher," several four-line stanzas have been combined to create verse paragraphs or longer units.[4] We lack the evidence to determine how much of the punctuation and formatting of her poems should be attributed to the author's initiative and how much to the publisher's, but Emily accepted the poems as printed, and Charlotte expressed no dissatisfaction with their appearance.

My aim is to present *Wuthering Heights* in a form Brontë would have approved. No modern editor can do the work Newby left undone in 1847, or at least she cannot do it in collaboration with Brontë. What she can do is follow 1847 closely, while also providing a higher degree of consistency and correctness. In all cases, the features of 1847 that are distinctive have been preserved: frequent paragraphing; an abundance of exclamation points, often used where a reader would expect to see a comma; dashes instead of commas or periods; and italicized words. It is likely that all of these features belong to the manuscript, but there is an additional reason for preserving them: *Wuthering Heights* presents itself as a spoken text. There are important exceptions, including Catherine's diary entries in the margins of her Bible and Isabella's letter to Nelly, which is reproduced verbatim in the novel. The date at the beginning of the novel suggests that Lockwood himself is writing. For most of the novel, however, he is recounting a story that has been told to him by Nelly Dean, and Nelly's story includes stories told to her by other characters. Brontë's sentences are often long and crowded with qualifications. They convey the sense that she is taking the pulse of her characters' speech in a way that is unique to her novel. Dashes, exclamation points, and italicized words express the energies, emphases, urgencies, and hesitations of the speaking voices Brontë is hearing. They are as essential to her conception of her novel as the spellings she invents to represent West Riding dialect.

A distinguishing feature of *Wuthering Heights* is its embedded narratives. W. H. Stevenson usefully names the novel's form of narration "double-third-person": "Lockwood tells us what Nelly Dean told him." This form was "unique in 1847" and remains "unusual" still.[5] The edition of 1847 and subsequent editions avoid printing quotation marks within quotation marks when Nelly begins her narration, treating it as if it were not contained within Lockwood's narration. From a reader's point of view, this is a helpful simplification. Since Nelly's narrative contains the narratives of other characters, and since these narratives contain quite a lot of reported speech, omitting quotation marks around Nelly's narrative avoids banks of quotation marks within quotation marks. This edition differs from 1847 and from other editions in where the transitions from Lockwood's to Nelly's narration occur. Here, quotation marks around Nelly's narrative disappear when we no longer hear Lockwood talking or are being reminded that he is listening. Whenever the novel is presenting Nelly's narrative as direct discourse (flagged with interruptions like "she commenced, waiting no further invitation to her story"), quotation marks remain around that narrative.

I have not modernized punctuation and spelling or tried to normalize these features in accordance with usual mid-nineteenth-century practice. Instead, I have made the text more correct and more internally consistent. Readers who want to examine the 1847 edition of the novel can do so by consulting the original or the facsimile of it published by Orchises Press in 2007. In this edition, punctuation has been eliminated or altered when it departs from the norms established by the 1847 edition or confuses the sense of a sentence. The following more specific principles for changing punctuation and spelling have been applied:

Commas. Punctuation in the nineteenth century was a lot heavier than it is today, but one of the notable features of 1847 is an overabundance of commas. In her manuscript, Brontë may have left spaces between words and phrases that suggested or invited the addition of punctuation, but many unnecessary commas—some of them obscuring the sense—can probably be attributed to the typesetters. Commas are regularly used to set off adverbs and participial and prepositional phrases, and to divide compound predicates and subjects. They also usually precede subordinate clauses, including those beginning with "that." But even these punctuation protocols are not consistent throughout the text, and it is likely that several typesetters operated according to somewhat different principles.

This edition eliminates commas when they confuse a sentence's meaning, constitute an obvious eccentricity, or awkwardly interrupt or stall the flow of a sentence already replete with commas. For example, "This is certainly, a beautiful country!" becomes "This is certainly a beautiful country!" and "Catherine, we would fain have deluded, yet, but her own quick spirit refused to delude her" becomes "Catherine we would fain have deluded yet, but her own quick spirit refused to delude her." In the first example, the comma may have entered the text accidentally, but the typesetter's usual practice makes it more likely that he meant to put commas on both sides of the adverb "certainly." Adding rather than subtracting a comma would make Lockwood's compliment sound less glib than it is and disrupt the illusion of a spoken text. In the second example, the omission of the commas after "Catherine" and before "yet" makes the sentence's grammar, and with it the sentence's meaning, clearer. Although the commas have been removed in these instances, in some cases, though less frequently, commas have also been added.

Heavier marks of punctuation (semicolons, periods, and dashes) have in some instances replaced commas in order to make the logic of a sentence clearer, and, on a few occasions, commas have, for the same reason, replaced semicolons or dashes, but I have been wary both of hypercorrecting and of modernizing, since the semicolon was frequently used in the nineteenth century when today we would use a comma. Commas after "and" and "but" at the beginning of a clause have been retained when a good case can be made that they signal the rhythms of a character's speech, as in Catherine's enumeration of her reasons for marrying Edgar: "And, because he loves me."

Exclamation Points and Capitalization. Exclamation points are so frequent in 1847 that they are likely to belong to Brontë's manuscript. They signal that *Wuthering Heights* is an unusually excitable text. In Catherine's famous declaration to Nelly in Vol. I, Ch. 9, for example, the medial exclamation point compounds the emphasis already indicated by italics: "'*Here!* and *here!*' replied Catherine, striking one hand on her forehead, and the other on her breast." Lower-case letters following the exclamation point have been retained whenever the exclamation point follows an interjection ("Come! come to bed") or in other ways interrupts rather than ends a sentence. In such cases, the exclamation point often appears where a reader would expect to see a comma. One example of this use of the exclamation point is Hindley's speech to Heathcliff in Vol. I, Ch. 4:

> "Take my colt, gipsy, then!" said young Earnshaw, "and I pray that he may break your neck; take him, and be damned, you beggarly interloper! and wheedle my father out of all he has, only, afterwards, show him what you are, imp of Satan—And take that; I hope he'll kick out your brains!"

Quotation Marks. I have made Brontë's practice with respect to the use of quotation marks more consistent and correct than it is in 1847. Where quotation marks have been omitted around reported speech, I have reinstated them. Where indirect speech has been placed within quotation marks, I have omitted them.

Apostrophes. Apostrophes in 1847 are frequently omitted where they are required ("wont" for "won't"), and this edition silently adds them.

Spelling and Hyphenated Words. Corrections to the spelling of 1847 have been made when words are manifestly misspelled, but more than one spelling of some words was acceptable when the novel was published. Hyphenated words present a special case. According to the editors of the Clarendon edition of the novel, 1847 often prints words usually hyphenated as two words.[6] In several interesting cases, however, 1847 hyphenates words we don't expect to see hyphenated, and these forms have been preserved in this edition. Examples are "dis-relish" and "after-thought." The unusual word "preter-human" appears as a hyphenated compound in *Wuthering Heights* and, earlier, in Percy Shelley's *St. Irvyne,* although later instances of the word omit the hyphen.

In cases where different spellings of the same word were acceptable at the time and 1847 is inconsistent (for example, "to-day," "today," and "to day"), I have adopted the spelling that appears more often and applied it consistently. All three spellings of "to-day" appear in Brontë's poetical manuscripts, suggesting that her spelling of this word and others is likely to have been inconsistent in the manuscript of *Wuthering Heights.* We don't know whether she corrected herself in the proof-sheets she sent back to her publisher, but we can assume that she would have appreciated her publisher's making these corrections for her. I have also applied a principle of consistency to capitalization on the basis of frequency when words appear with both an upper- and a lower-case initial letter (for example, "bible"/"Bible").

NOTES

1. *The Letters of Charlotte Brontë,* 3 vols., ed. Margaret Smith (Oxford: Clarendon Press, 2000), 1, p. 580.
2. K. M. Petyt, "The Dialect Speech in Wuthering Heights," in *Wuthering Heights,* ed. Hilda Marsden and Ian Jack (Oxford: Clarendon Press, 1976), p. 501.
3. *Letters,* 1, p. 542.
4. References to Brontë's poems, here and throughout this edition, and the numbers given in parentheses are to my edition of the poems, *Emily Jane Brontë: The Complete Poems,* ed. Janet Gezari (London: Penguin Books, 1992).
5. "Wuthering Heights: The Facts," *Essays in Criticism,* 55:2 (1985), p. 153.
6. Marsden and Jack, eds., *Wuthering Heights,* p. xxx.

VOLUME I

CHAPTER 1

1801[1]—I have just returned from a visit to my landlord—the solitary neighbour that I shall be troubled with. This is certainly a beautiful country![2] In all England, I do not believe that I could have fixed on a situation so completely removed from the stir of society. A perfect misanthropist's Heaven—and Mr. Heathcliff[3] and I are such a suitable pair to divide the desolation between us. A capital fellow! He little imagined how my heart warmed towards him when I beheld his black eyes withdraw so suspiciously under their brows, as I rode up, and when his fingers sheltered themselves, with a jealous resolution, still further in his waistcoat, as I announced my name.

"Mr. Heathcliff?" I said.

A nod was the answer.

"Mr. Lockwood,[4] your new tenant, sir—I do myself the honour of calling as soon as possible after my arrival,[5] to express the hope that I have not inconvenienced you by my perseverance in soliciting the occupation of Thrushcross Grange:[6] I heard, yesterday, you had had some thoughts—"

"Thrushcross Grange is my own, sir," he interrupted wincing, "I should not allow any one to inconvenience me, if I could hinder it—walk in!"

The "walk in" was uttered with closed teeth and expressed the sentiment, "Go to the Deuce!"[7] Even the gate over which he leant

1 By beginning with a date, Brontë suggests that we are reading a diary or a journal and signals her careful attention to the internal chronology of her story. Lockwood, her primary narrator, has leased Thrushcross Grange from Heathcliff for a year; at the end of Chapter 16 of Volume II, we learn that the lease runs from October 1801 to October 1802. C. P. Sanger, whose timeline for *Wuthering Heights* (first published in 1926) remains largely uncontested, posits late November as the date of Lockwood's first visit to the Heights ("The Structure of Wuthering Heights," in *The Brontë Sisters: Critical Assessments,* ed. Eleanor McNees, 4 vols. [Mountfield: Helm Information, 1996], 2, pp. 71–82). Chapter 18 of Volume II, in which Lockwood returns to the Heights to settle his accounts with Heathcliff, also begins with a date: 1802. Inga-Stina Ewbank points out that "no less than twenty-two" of the novel's thirty-four chapters "begin with a sentence which, in one way or another, establishes a date" ("The Chronology of *Wuthering Heights,*" in Emily Brontë, *Wuthering Heights,* ed. Hilda Marsden and Ian Jack [Oxford: Clarendon Press, 1976], p. 488).

2 Region. "In English," Raymond Williams writes at the outset of *The Country and the City,* "'country' is both a nation and a part of a 'land'; 'the country' can be the whole society or its rural area" (New York: Oxford Univ. Press, 1973), p. 1. Yorkshire, the part of England where the action of *Wuthering Heights* takes place, presents a vast and various landscape that includes mountain vistas and flat marshes, hilly moorlands broken by craggy gritstone outcroppings, and verdant river valleys.

In Brontë's time, Lockwood would have been a familiar kind of cultural tourist. By 1801, well-to-do Englishmen like him were setting out from London in search of "picturesque countryside and sublime highland landscapes" (Gerald McLean, Donna Landry, and Joseph P. Ward, eds., *The Country and the City Revisited: England and the Politics of Culture, 1550–1850* [Cambridge: Cambridge Univ. Press, 1999], p. 14). The journey out was also a journey back into "a primitive past that lingered on the fringes of the modern nation" (Nancy Armstrong, "Emily's Ghost: The Cultural Politics of Victorian Fiction, Folklore, and Photography," *Novel: A Forum on Fiction,* 25:3 [Spring 1992], p. 247).

Generations of readers have taken the novel's fidelity to Yorkshire scenery for granted, but they haven't always agreed about where it can be found in the ordinary world. Traditionally, the novel's setting has been fixed in the country around Haworth, but at least one early reader recognized a more northern landscape: "Whoever has traversed the bleak heights of Hartside or Cross Fell, on his road from Westmoreland to the dales of Yorkshire, and has been welcomed there by the winds and rain on a 'gusty day,' will know how to estimate the comforts of Wuthering Heights in wintry weather" (From an unsigned review

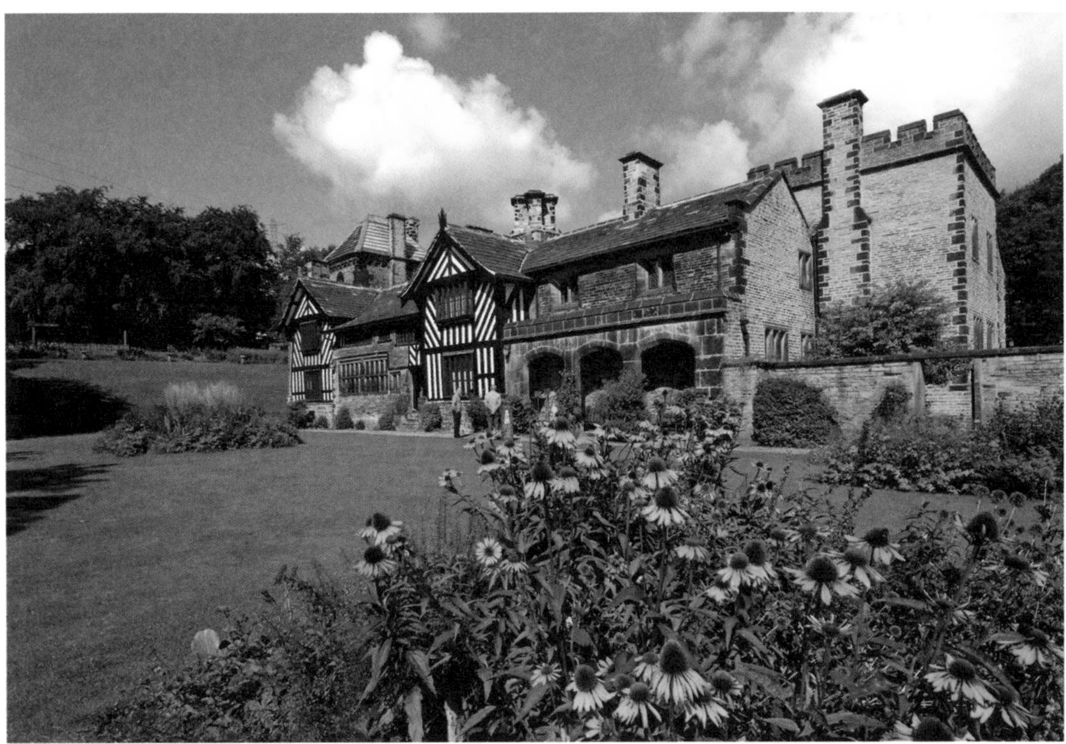

Shibden Hall, an important manor house a mile outside of Halifax and near Law Hill, the girls school where Brontë briefly taught. Its lush grounds and extensive park may have influenced the setting of Thrushcross Grange. When Brontë visited it, Shibden was occupied by Anne Lister, a formidable, independent woman who renovated the house, landscaped the property, traveled, and left a valuable diary record of her extensive activities and her lesbian relationships.

of *Wuthering Heights, Examiner* [January 1848], in Miriam Allott, *The Brontës: The Critical Heritage* [London: Routledge & Kegan Paul, 1974], p. 220). Christopher Heywood argues that the novel's two houses, Wuthering Heights and Thrushcross Grange, are situated in different landscapes. In the novel's first part, Heywood writes, Brontë represents a "limestone mountain landscape of the northern type," specifically the region around Ingleton, Thornton in Lonsdale, and Cowan Bridge. In its second part, she represents a landscape like the one surrounding Haworth, a "moorland of the southern Pennine type" (Christopher Heywood, ed., *Wuthering Heights* [Peterborough, ON: Broadview Press, 2002], pp. 18-22; see also Heywood, "Yorkshire Landscapes in 'Wuthering Heights,'" *Essays in Criticism,* 48:1 [Jan. 1998], pp. 13-34, and Heywood, "A Yorkshire Background for *Wuthering Heights,*" *Modern Language Review,* 88:4 [Oct. 1993], pp. 817-830).

3 The economy of names in *Wuthering Heights* has often been remarked on. Heathcliff has only one name, which does double duty as both his given name and his surname.

4 Lockwood has a given name, but the novel never tells us what it is.

5 Lockwood's claim that he is visiting "as soon as possible" after his arrival is likely true. His evident eagerness for company belies his representation of himself as a misanthrope and alerts readers to his unreliability at the outset of his narrative. Brontë was not the first novelist to exploit the resources of an unreliable narrator, but she is one of the subtlest. A thorough London gentleman, Lockwood will return to the life he knows months before his lease is up. His two brief sojourns as Heathcliff's tenant in Thrushcross Grange swell to contain a history of the novel's two houses and families—Earnshaws and Lintons—from the summer of 1771, when the child who will be named Heathcliff arrives at the Heights, to New Year's Day in 1803.

6 Thrushcross Grange is a gentleman's house set within an unusually large park. Located about four miles southwest of Wuthering Heights, it is the most important residence in the neighborhood. Brontë scholars and fans have devoted a lot of time to locating the historical original of the Grange, but no existing property closely fits the novel's description of either the building or its

manifested no sympathizing movement to the words; and I think that circumstance determined me to accept the invitation: I felt interested in a man who seemed more exaggeratedly reserved than myself.

When he saw my horse's breast fairly pushing the barrier, he did pull out his hand to unchain it, and then sullenly preceded me up the causeway,[8] calling, as we entered the court:

"Joseph, take Mr. Lockwood's horse; and bring up some wine."

"Here we have the whole establishment of domestics, I suppose," was the reflection, suggested by this compound order. "No wonder the grass grows up between the flags, and cattle are the only hedge-cutters."

Joseph was an elderly, nay, an old man, very old, perhaps, though hale and sinewy.[9]

"The Lord help us!" he soliloquised in an undertone of peevish displeasure, while relieving me of my horse: looking, meantime, in my face so sourly that I charitably conjectured he must have need of divine aid to digest his dinner, and his pious ejaculation had no reference to my unexpected advent.

Wuthering Heights is the name of Mr. Heathcliff's dwelling, "Wuthering" being a significant provincial adjective, descriptive of the atmospheric tumult to which its station is exposed, in stormy weather.[10] Pure, bracing ventilation they must have up there, at all times, indeed: one may guess the power of the north wind, blowing over the edge, by the excessive slant of a few, stunted firs at the end of the house; and by a range of gaunt thorns all stretching their limbs one way, as if craving alms of the sun.[11] Happily, the architect had foresight to build it strong: the narrow windows are deeply set in the wall; and the corners defended with large jutting stones.

Before passing the threshold, I paused to admire a quantity of grotesque carving lavished over the front, and especially about the principal door, above which, among a wilderness of crumbling griffins, and shameless little boys, I detected the date "1500," and the name "Hareton Earnshaw."[12] I would have made a few com-

grounds. Shibden Hall, an important manor house set within an extensive park, is a likely influence. It is located near Law Hill, the girls school on the outskirts of Halifax, where the twenty-year-old Emily worked as a teacher for about six months.

7 By the middle of the nineteenth century, "the Deuce" had come to mean "the Devil." This euphemism is better suited to Lockwood than to Heathcliff, who does not hesitate to refer to the devil directly just a few pages further on. Elizabeth Gaskell's biography of Charlotte remains the finest account of the character, customs, and behavior of the inhabitants of Haworth as seen by an outsider. Gaskell was born in London, raised in Cheshire, and settled in Manchester, where her husband was a Unitarian minister. She writes that "there is little display of any of the amenities of life among this wild rough population [of Haworth]. Their accost is curt; their accent and tone of speech blunt and harsh" (Elizabeth Gaskell, *The Life of Charlotte Brontë,* ed. Angus Easson [Oxford: Oxford Univ. Press, 1996], p. 15).

8 The flagstone path from the gate to the main door of the house. "Causeway" suggests that the ground around the path is wet and that the path itself may be raised.

9 As Lockwood observes, Joseph performs the work of both a farmhand and a domestic servant. Gaskell's praise of him is worth remembering. Although the feelings of Yorkshiremen "are not easily roused," she writes, "their duration is lasting. Hence there is much close friendship and faithful service; and for a correct exemplification of the form in which the latter frequently appears, I need only refer the reader of 'Wuthering Heights' to the character of 'Joseph'" (Gaskell, *The Life of Charlotte Brontë,* p. 16).

10 In Heathcliff's and Brontë's West Riding pronunciation, the vowel would have been lengthened to sound like the double "oo" in "wool." (The ancient West Riding of Yorkshire corresponds roughly to the modern English county of West Yorkshire.) The *OED* treats "wuthering" as a variant of "whithering," an adjective derived from the Scottish and dialect verb "whither": "to move with force or impetus, to rush; to make a rushing sound, to whizz; to bluster or rage, as the wind." Brontë's title announces her debt to Scottish literature, both the published fiction and poetry of her Border cousins, Sir Walter Scott and James Hogg, and the strange, magical folktales and ballads that nourished their writing as well as her own.

11 Hawthorns: shrubs or small flowering trees with thorny branches. A contemporary topographical and geological description of the region

ments, and requested a short history of the place from the surly owner, but his attitude at the door appeared to demand my speedy entrance, or complete departure, and I had no desire to aggravate his impatience, previous to inspecting the penetralium.[13]

One step brought us into the family sitting-room, without any introductory lobby, or passage: they call it here "the house" pre-eminently. It includes kitchen and parlor, generally, but I believe at Wuthering Heights, the kitchen is forced to retreat altogether into another quarter; at least I distinguished a chatter of tongues, and a clatter of culinary utensils, deep within;[14] and I observed no signs of roasting, boiling, or baking about the huge fire-place, nor any glitter of copper saucepans and tin cullenders[15] on the walls. One end, indeed, reflected splendidly both light and heat, from ranks of immense pewter dishes, interspersed with silver jugs and tankards, towering row after row in a vast oak dresser, to the very roof. The latter had never been under-drawn:[16] its entire anatomy lay bare to an inquiring eye, except where a frame of wood laden with oat-cakes and clusters of legs of beef, mutton, and ham concealed it. Above the chimney were sundry villainous[17] old guns, and a couple of horse-pistols,[18] and, by way of ornament, three gaudily painted canisters disposed along its ledge. The floor was of smooth, white stone: the chairs, high-backed, primitive structures, painted green; one or two heavy black ones lurking in the shade. In an arch, under the dresser, reposed a huge, liver-coloured bitch pointer surrounded by a swarm of squealing puppies, and other dogs haunted other recesses.

The apartment and furniture would have been nothing extraordinary as belonging to a homely, northern farmer with a stubborn countenance and stalwart limbs, set out to advantage in knee breeches and gaiters.[19] Such an individual, seated in his arm-chair, his mug of ale frothing on the round table before him, is to be seen in any circuit of five or six miles among these hills, if you go at the right time, after dinner. But Mr. Heathcliff forms a singular contrast to his abode and style of living. He is a dark skinned gipsy

around the village of Haworth notes that the country is "very hilly and bleak, as there are but few trees to arrest the wintry winds" (Babbage Report, Haworth, 1850, at http://freepages.genealogy.rootsweb.ancestry.com/~jeffreywright/Babbage%20Report).

12 The carvings commemorate the year in which the house was built and the man who owned it. Such inscriptions are typical of substantial houses in this part of England. Susan Stewart asks what Wuthering Heights could have been "in 1500 (a year of peace between Henry and James in anticipation of the wedding of James to Margaret in 1503)? The twelfth- and thirteenth-century Cistercians and Benedictines who founded the Yorkshire abbeys described 'a place uninhabited for all the centuries back, thick set with thorns, lying between the slopes of mountains and many rocks jutting out on both sides; fit rather to be the lair of wild beasts than the home of human beings'" ("The Ballad in *Wuthering Heights,*" *Representations,* 86 [Spring 2004], pp. 188–189).

Both the Grange and the Heights combine features of various houses and landscapes Brontë visited with those that belong entirely to her imagination. Top Withens, an Elizabethan farmhouse located at the summit of Haworth Moor about four miles from the village, has long been popularly associated with Wuthering Heights because of its lonely situation atop a windswept hill. Now roofless and in ruins, the house was already uninhabited in Brontë's time. Hilda Marsden and Ian Jack suggest that a better model for Wuthering Heights is High Sunderland Hall, a Gothic manor house just outside of Halifax: "While Halifax houses are remarkable for their ornate façades, Lockwood's description of the 'grotesque carving lavished over the front' [of Wuthering Heights] . . . corresponds closely to the singular and abundant carvings on the door and over the gateway of High Sunderland." These carvings included two griffins, mythological animals usually having an eagle's head and wings and a lion's body, two "mishapen nude men," "numerous Latin inscriptions," and various grotesque heads "with lewd faces" (Marsden and Jack, pp. 415–416). Paul Thompson points out that High Sunderland is, however, "too grand for a farmhouse" like Wuthering Heights. He suggests that Brontë's building looks more like Ponden Hall, located outside Stanbury, a village within easy walking distance of Haworth (www.wuthering-heights.co.uk). Ponden Hall has more often been cited as the model for Thrushcross Grange. It was rebuilt in 1801, and this date is inscribed on its front.

13 The *OED* cites this passage as an instance of the use of "penetralium" to mean "the interior of a building," but Lockwood may be using the word in its usual sense to mean a secret place that is difficult to penetrate. The first three chapters of the novel represent his efforts to

Top Withens, Pennine Way, on Haworth Moor. The location of Top Withens has long been associated with that of Wuthering Heights.

crack the hermeneutic codes that will unlock the mystery of Wuthering Heights and its occupants. His naive belief that the Heights is open to his inspection is repeatedly undermined, even as he enters more and more deeply into its innermost recesses and hidden places.

14 *Wuthering Heights* continues to persuade readers that the forces at play within it belong to an elemental natural world rather than to the domestic, social world represented in other English novels. Margaret Homans was the first critic to note that few of the novel's scenes actually take place outdoors ("Repression and Sublimation of Nature in *Wuthering Heights*," *PMLA*, 93:1 [Jan. 1978], pp. 9–19). John Bayley has remarked that the "real stuff [of the novel] is not so much among the moors and winds and harebells as in the kitchen and scullery" (*London Review of Books*, Dec. 20, 1990, p. 16). Emily differed as much from Charlotte in her enjoyment of housework as she did in her enthusiasm for ambitious outdoor rambles. At home in the Parsonage, Emily did the ironing, baked the family's bread, and "took the principal part of the cooking upon herself" (Gaskell, *The Life of Charlotte Brontë*, p. 110).

15 Colanders; this is the usual eighteenth- and nineteenth-century spelling.

16 The structure of the ceiling is exposed instead of being finished with plaster as it would have been in a more formal sitting room. The size of the dresser, the quantity of large pewter dishes and silver tankards, and the ample meat on display suggest prosperity and abundance.

17 Rustic.

18 Large pistols "carried at the pommel of the saddle when on horseback" *(OED)*.

19 Breeches are pants reaching to the knee or just below it. They were often worn with long gaiters, heavy cloth or leather coverings for the lower legs and ankles. Gentlemen shooting in the country would have worn a costume like Heathcliff's.

in aspect,[20] in dress and manners a gentleman; that is, as much a gentleman as many a country squire: rather slovenly, perhaps, yet not looking amiss with his negligence, because he has an erect and handsome figure—and rather morose—possibly, some people might suspect him of a degree of under-bred pride. I have a sympathetic chord within that tells me it is nothing of the sort; I know, by instinct, his reserve springs from an aversion to showy displays of feeling—to manifestations of mutual kindliness. He'll love and hate, equally under cover, and esteem it a species of impertinence to be loved or hated again—No, I'm running on too fast—I bestow my own attributes over liberally on him. Mr. Heathcliff may have entirely dissimilar reasons for keeping his hand out of the way, when he meets a would-be acquaintance,[21] to those which actuate me. Let me hope my constitution is almost peculiar: my dear mother used to say I should never have a comfortable home, and only last summer, I proved myself perfectly unworthy of one.

While enjoying a month of fine weather at the sea-coast, I was thrown into the company of a most fascinating creature, a real goddess, in my eyes, as long as she took no notice of me. I "never told my love"[22] vocally; still, if looks have language, the merest idiot might have guessed I was over head and ears[23]: she understood me, at last, and looked a return—the sweetest of all imaginable looks—and what did I do? I confess it with shame—shrunk icily into myself, like a snail, at every glance retired colder and farther; till, finally, the poor innocent was led to doubt her own senses, and, overwhelmed with confusion at her supposed mistake, persuaded her mamma to decamp.

By this curious turn of disposition I have gained the reputation of deliberate heartlessness, how undeserved I alone can appreciate.

I took a seat at the end of the hearthstone opposite that towards which my landlord advanced, and filled up an interval of silence by attempting to caress the canine mother, who had left her nursery and was sneaking wolfishly to the back of my legs, her lip curled

20 Lockwood is the first to remark on Heathcliff's dark-skinned complexion and to identify him as a "gipsy." Both spellings of the word ("gipsy" and "gypsy") are correct, but in all cases except this one, 1847 has "gipsy." I have changed the spelling here to make it consistent with the spelling of this word in the rest of the text.

21 Heathcliff does not offer to shake hands with Lockwood.

22 An allusion to Shakespeare's *Twelfth Night* (Act II, scene 4, line 110f). Lockwood appropriates Olivia's account of her imagined sister, who "never told her love" but concealed it, "pined in thought," and grew "melancholy." In the play, the story Viola tells the Duke about her fictive sister's silence glances at her own hidden love for him while also illustrating her point that women say less but feel more than men do. The Duke, who doesn't know that Viola is a woman when she makes this speech, is courting Olivia, who will herself fall in love with Viola.

The irony of Lockwood's association of himself with Viola is complex: like her, he hides his love, but unlike her, he is too timid or too cowardly to embrace love when he discovers that it is returned. This story is the only one we have about Lockwood's life prior to his appearance at Wuthering Heights. Seacoast destinations were widely sought in this period both for health and for pleasure. They provided opportunities for men and women to meet and encouraged gallantry as well as courtships that could lead to marriage.

Lockwood's story suggests how alert Brontë is to the conventions regulating female behavior and to the difficulties facing women who broke the rules by expressing their feelings too openly. She had an example close to home. Her brother, Branwell, seemed romantically attracted to Mary Taylor, Charlotte's friend, but then backed away, apparently because Mary's warm response disgusted him. "Mary is my study," Charlotte wrote, "for the contempt, the remorse—the misconstruction which follow the development of feelings in themselves noble, warm—generous—devoted and profound—but which being too freely revealed—too frankly bestowed—are not estimated at their real value." Charlotte is writing to Ellen Nussey, whose conventional wisdom she sometimes echoed with wry dismay: "no young lady should fall in love until the offer has been made, accepted . . . the marriage ceremony performed and the first half year of wedded life has passed away—a woman may then begin to love, but with great precaution—very coolly—very moderately—very rationally" (Smith, *The Letters*, 1, p. 234). See also Juliet Barker, *The Brontës* [London: Phoenix, 1994], pp. 338–339).

23 This expression, like "head over heels," means "wholly" or "desperately" (*Brewer's Dictionary of Phrase and Fable: Centenary Edition*, rev. Ivor H. Evans [New York: Harper & Row, 1970]).

"The Dog-Breaker," an etching by George Walker for *The Costume of Yorkshire* (1814). The picture shows the attire of a West Yorkshire gentleman hunter, including knee breeches and gaiters like the ones Heathcliff wears when Lockwood first meets him.

up, and her white teeth watering for a snatch. My caress provoked a long, guttural gnarl.[24]

"You'd better let the dog alone," growled Mr. Heathcliff, in unison, checking fiercer demonstrations with a punch of his foot. "She's not accustomed to be spoiled—not kept for a pet."

Then, striding to a side-door, he shouted again.

"Joseph!"

Joseph mumbled indistinctly in the depths of the cellar, but, gave no intimation of ascending; so his master dived down to him, leaving me *vis-à-vis*[25] the ruffianly bitch and a pair of grim, shaggy sheep dogs, who shared with her a jealous guardianship over all my movements.

24 "Gnarl" combines "snarl" and "growl" (Johnson, *A Dictionary of the English Language* [London: 1755], Digital Edition). According to the *OED*, which cites this passage, the use of "gnarl" as a noun rather than a verb is rare.

25 "Vis-à-vis," meaning facing or opposite to, entered English from French in the middle of the eighteenth century. Here, and in the next chapter when Lockwood uses the Latin abbreviation "N.B." *(nota bene),* Brontë calls attention to the difference between his vocabulary and that of the country people he is observing. Lockwood's use of foreign tags like "vis-à-vis" and "N.B." indicates that he wants to be seen as a man of the world, but cannot prove that he has more than a passing knowledge of French and Latin.

Brontë herself worked hard at learning languages. She knew less French than Charlotte when the two of them went to study and teach in Brussels, and her French improved considerably while she was there. She also studied German in Brussels and continued to teach herself

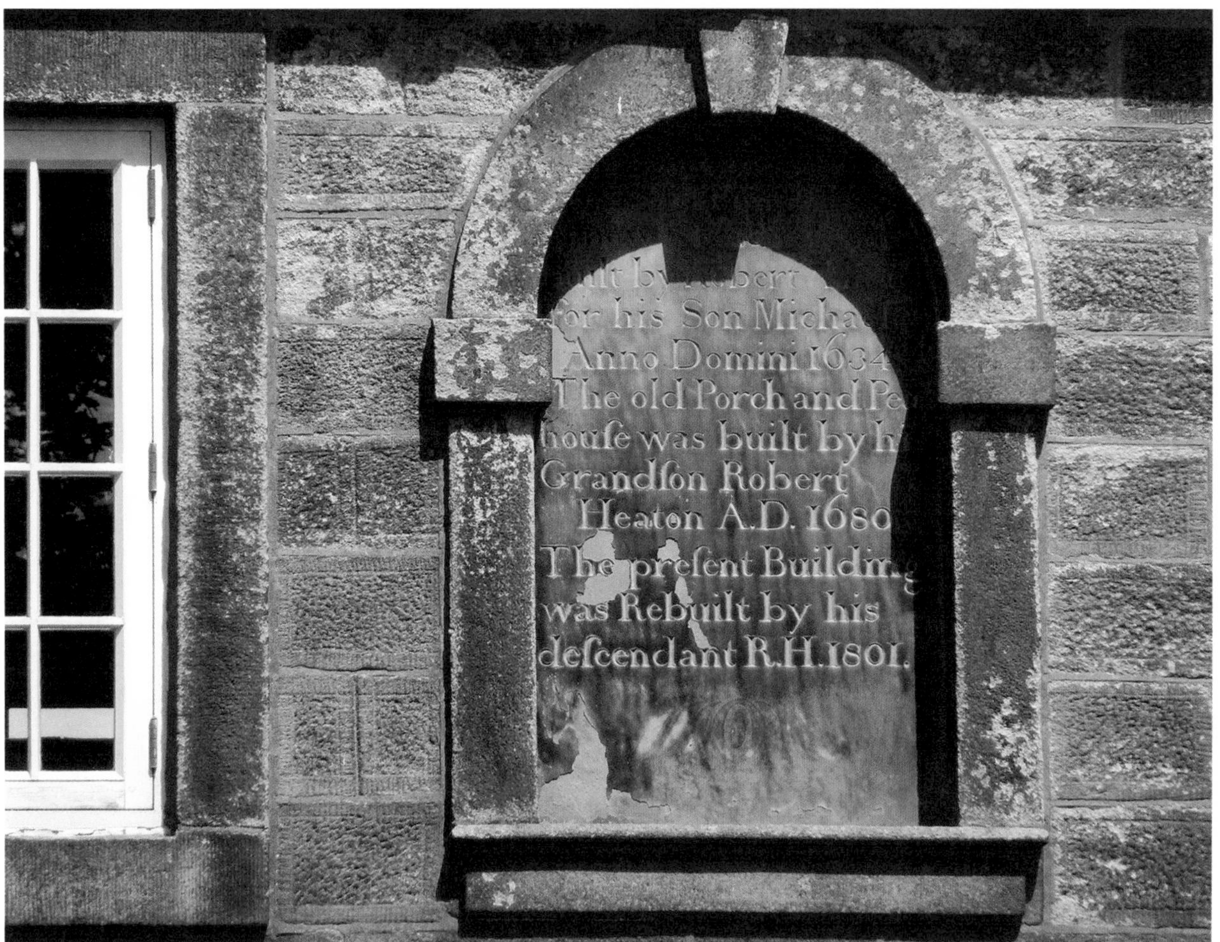

The carved stone plaque over the door of Ponden Hall, a few miles' walk from the Parsonage, provides the names of the men who built the house and the date of its most recent renovation (1801). The Heaton family at Ponden and the Brontës were on friendly terms, and the Brontë children made use of the Ponden library.

Not anxious to come in contact with their fangs, I sat still—but imagining they would scarcely understand tacit insults, I unfortunately indulged in winking and making faces at the trio, and some turn of my physiognomy[26] so irritated madam, that she suddenly broke into a fury, and leapt on my knees. I flung her back, and hastened to interpose the table between us. This proceeding roused the whole hive. Half-a-dozen four-footed fiends, of various sizes and ages, issued from hidden dens to the common centre. I felt my heels and coat-laps[27] peculiar subjects of assault; and, parrying off the larger combatants as effectually as I could with the poker, I was constrained to demand, aloud, assistance from some of the household in re-establishing peace.

Mr. Heathcliff and his man climbed the cellar steps with vexatious phlegm.[28] I don't think they moved one second faster than usual, though the hearth was an absolute tempest of worrying and yelping.

Happily, an inhabitant of the kitchen made more dispatch; a lusty dame, with tucked up gown, bare arms, and fire-flushed cheeks, rushed into the midst of us flourishing a frying-pan; and used that weapon and her tongue to such purpose, that the storm subsided magically, and she only remained, heaving like a sea after a high wind, when her master entered on the scene.

"What the devil is the matter?" he asked, eyeing me in a manner that I could ill endure after this inhospitable treatment.

"What the devil, indeed!" I muttered. "The herd of possessed swine[29] could have had no worse spirits in them than those animals of yours, sir. You might as well leave a stranger with a brood of tigers!"

"They won't meddle with persons who touch nothing," he remarked, putting the bottle before me, and restoring the displaced table. "The dogs do right to be vigilant. Take a glass of wine?"

"No, thank you."

"Not bitten, are you?"

"If I had been, I would have set my signet on the biter."

Heathcliff's countenance relaxed into a grin.[30]

German when she returned to Haworth. As the boy in the family, Branwell studied classical literature with his father, and his sisters may have shared some of his lessons. Emily, at least, learned enough Latin to translate portions of Virgil's *Aeneid.*

26 Lockwood intends to deceive the dogs, but they easily comprehend his insults and hold him accountable. The term "physiognomy" refers to his facial features and expression. Along with phrenology, physiognomy gained popularity at the end of the eighteenth century in response to increasing interest in decoding physical form. According to Johann Kaspar Lavater, who popularized it and whose work appeared in translation in England in the 1780s and 1790s, physiognomy was "'the science or knowledge of the correspondence between the external and internal man, the visible superficies and the invisible contents.' The premises of physiognomy were religious: God had inscribed a language on the face of nature for all to read. It necessarily followed, therefore, that an absolute correspondence existed between outer human form and inner moral quality, since otherwise, 'eternal order is degraded to a juggler, whose purpose it is to deceive'" (Sally Shuttleworth, *Charlotte Brontë and Victorian Psychology* [Cambridge: Cambridge Univ. Press, 1996], p. 59).

27 Coat lapels. The dogs are not only biting at Lockwood's heels but leaping up on him.

28 One of the four humors, here indicating an apathetic response to Lockwood's predicament.

29 The story of Jesus casting the demons into a herd of swine, which then rush into a lake and drown, can be found in Matthew 8:30–37, Mark 5:1–20, and Luke 8:27–38.

30 Since the "signet" is located on Lockwood's ring, setting it on the biter is a fancy way for him to threaten to strike the dog. Heathcliff grins at Lockwood's boast, retracting his lips and displaying his teeth. Unlike a smile, a grin can be threatening or malicious. Later in the novel, Catherine shows her feelings about the child her father brings home from Liverpool by spitting and grinning at him. Charles Darwin recorded his observation that grinning was common among dogs and monkeys as well as humans in *The Expression of the Emotions in Man and Animals,* rev. and abridged by C. M. Beadnell (London: Watts and Co., 1948).

Gaskell reports that "someone," speaking of Emily to her, said that "she never showed regard to any human creature; all her love was reserved for animals." Emily's English mastiff mix, "Keeper," walked with Patrick Brontë at the head of her funeral procession, "followed Emily's coffin to the vault where she was buried, lay in the family pew . . . while the burial service was being read and then took up his forlorn station outside the door of Emily's room, where he howled pitifully for many days" (Barker, *The Brontës,* p. 578). Keeper was said to be as fierce as he was faithful: "he who struck him with a stick or whip, roused the relentless nature of the brute, who flew at his throat forthwith, and held him there till one or the other was at the point of death" (Gaskell, *The Life of Charlotte Brontë,* p. 214).

Gaskell tells the story of Brontë's punishing Keeper for lying on the "delicate white counterpane" that covered one of the beds in the Parsonage. She struck him with her fists "till his eyes were swelled up" and he was "half-blind" and "stupefied." Afterward, she tended his wounds (Gaskell, *The Life of Charlotte Brontë,* pp. 214–215). This story is probably apocryphal. It conforms to the myth of Emily, who combines masculine force with feminine tenderness. It also contradicts Ellen Nussey's more plausible account of Emily's and Keeper's relationship. Ellen writes that Emily could make him "spring and roar like a lion" and

"Come, come," he said, "you are flurried, Mr. Lockwood. Here, take a little wine. Guests are so exceedingly rare in this house that I and my dogs, I am willing to own, hardly know how to receive them. Your health, sir!"

I bowed and returned the pledge; beginning to perceive that it would be foolish to sit sulking for the misbehaviour of a pack of curs: besides, I felt loath to yield the fellow further amusement, at my expense, since his humour took that turn.

He—probably swayed by prudential considerations of the folly of offending a good tenant—relaxed a little, in the laconic style of chipping of his pronouns and auxiliary verbs;[31] and introduced what he supposed would be a subject of interest to me, a discourse

A watercolor titled *Keeper—from life,* signed by Emily Brontë and dated April 24, 1838, soon after her return to Haworth from her teaching post at Law Hill. Keeper was a cross-bred dog with the look of a bullmastiff. He and Emily were deeply attached to each other. He died three years after her and was buried in the Parsonage garden.

on the advantages and disadvantages of my present place of retirement.

I found him very intelligent on the topics we touched; and before I went home, I was encouraged so far as to volunteer another visit to-morrow.

He evidently wished no repetition of my intrusion. I shall go, notwithstanding. It is astonishing how sociable I feel myself compared with him.

"taught him this kind of occasional play without any coercion" (Ellen Nussey, "Reminiscences of Charlotte Brontë," in McNees, ed., *The Brontë Sisters: Critical Assessments,* 2, p. 111).

31 Lockwood's reference to a "laconic style" suggests that Heathcliff chops or shortens his pronouns and auxiliary verbs (the verb "chip" has this sense in the south of Scotland [*OED*]). Joseph's speech provides many examples of the contraction of standard English words.

CHAPTER 2

Yesterday afternoon set in misty and cold. I had half a mind to spend it by my study fire, instead of wading through heath and mud[1] to Wuthering Heights.

On coming up from dinner, however (N. B. I dine between twelve and one o'clock; the housekeeper, a matronly lady taken as a fixture along with the house, could not, or would not, comprehend my request that I might be served at five[2])—on mounting the stairs with this lazy intention, and stepping into the room, I saw a servant-girl on her knees, surrounded by brushes and coal-scuttles; and raising an infernal dust as she extinguished the flames with heaps of cinders. This spectacle drove me back immediately; I took my hat, and, after a four miles walk, arrived at Heathcliff's garden gate just in time to escape the first feathery flakes of a snow shower.

On that bleak hill top the earth was hard with a black frost,[3] and the air made me shiver through every limb. Being unable to remove the chain, I jumped over, and, running up the flagged causeway bordered with straggling gooseberry bushes,[4] knocked vainly for admittance, till my knuckles tingled, and the dogs howled.

"Wretched inmates!" I ejaculated, mentally, "you deserve perpetual isolation from your species for your churlish inhospitality. At least, I would not keep my doors barred in the day time—I don't care—I will get in!"

1 Gaskell reports on the forbidding terrain and the difficulties of travel in the country around Haworth: "Men hardly past middle life talk of the days of their youth, spent in this part of the country, when, during the winter months, they rode up to the saddle-girths in mud; when absolute business was the only reason for stirring beyond the precincts of home" (Elizabeth Gaskell, *The Life of Charlotte Brontë,* ed. Angus Easson [Oxford: Oxford Univ. Press, 1996], p. 20). The heath Lockwood wades through is "open uncultivated ground" or "wilderness . . . naturally clothed with low herbage and dwarf shrubs" like heath and heather *(OED).*

2 "Dinner," the main meal of the day, is eaten in the middle of the day at Thrushcross Grange. Lockwood's preference for a later dinner reminds us of his city habits. By the end of the eighteenth century, fashionable people living in cities would have stayed up much later than their working neighbors or people living in rural settings like this one. Evening parties, new public entertainments, and artificial lighting had changed the shape of the day and the night. Lockwood's supper, the light meal taken before bedtime, would also have been served later, and he would have left his bed later in the morning.

3 A dry freeze severe enough to blacken the shrubby vegetation.

4 The gooseberry bushes that border the flagstone path bear edible fruit as well as thorns. Like the animals at the Heights, working animals rather than pets, and in contrast to the plants cultivated at Thrushcross Grange, the gooseberries are more useful than ornamental.

Sir Walter Scott, engraving by Charles Turner (1810), after a painting by Sir Henry Raeburn (1756–1823).

5 Joseph speaks entirely in the West Riding dialect that signals his locality, class, and lack of formal schooling. "What do you want?" he asks Lockwood. Heathcliff is "down in the [sheep] fold," and Lockwood will have to go around the end of the barn if he wants to speak to him.

Educated speakers were expected to speak standard English at least from the fifteenth century, but dialect speech held its own throughout England well into the twentieth. The Elementary Education Act of 1880, which made education for children between the ages of five and ten free and compulsory, significantly increased the spread of standard English. The Brontës spoke standard English with an Irish accent in the Parsonage, but most of their neighbors as well as their servants were dialect speakers. According to F. W. Moorman, who compiled an anthology of Yorkshire dialect verse (published in 1916 and 1917), "there is no such thing as a standard Yorkshire dialect. The speech of the North and East Ridings is far removed from that of the industrial south-west. The difference consists, not so much in idiom or vocabulary, as in pronunciation—especially in the pronunciation of the long vowels and diphthongs" (*Yorkshire Dialect Poems,* Project Gutenberg Ebook [release date Jan. 10, 2009, updated Feb. 6, 2013], p. 10). Brontë listened well to the speech of her neighbors, and her skill in phonetically representing her local dialect has often been remarked. In the early 1970s, K. M. Petyt observed that "the speech of the country people in the area around still presents many of the features that Emily records" (Hilda Marsden and Ian Jack, eds., *Wuthering Heights* [Oxford: Clarendon Press, 1976], p. 593).

Maria Edgeworth, Walter Scott, and James Hogg had already represented Irish and Scottish dialect speech in their novels and stories. In her preface to *Castle Rackrent,* Edgeworth writes that she considered translating her narrator's language into "plain English" but found his idiom untranslatable and inextricable from the "authenticity of his story" (*Castle Rackrent and Ennui,* ed. Marilyn Butler [London: Penguin Books Ltd., 1992], p. 63). Brontë would have agreed with her, but when Charlotte edited *Wuthering Heights* in 1850, she altered Emily's representation of Joseph's speech, often by substituting standard English spellings. These standardized spellings have an odd look alongside the dialect spellings Charlotte retains or alters only slightly. For example, "I" replaces "Aw," and "uh" ["of"] becomes "o.'" In explaining her practice to her publisher, Charlotte writes that although Emily's spelling "as it stands . . . exactly renders Yorkshire dialect to a Yorkshire ear—yet, I am sure Southerns must find it unintelligible" (Margaret Smith, ed., *The Letters of Charlotte Brontë,* 3 vols. [Oxford: Clarendon Press, 2000], 2, p. 479). In 1850, this passage reads: "'What are ye for?' he shouted. 'T'maister's down i' t' fowld. Go round by th'end ot' laith, if ye went to spake tull him.'"

So resolved, I grasped the latch, and shook it vehemently. Vinegar-faced Joseph projected his head from a round window of the barn.

"Whet are ye for?" he shouted. "T' maister's dahn t'fowld. Goa rahnd by th' end ut' laith, if yah went tuh spake tull him."[5]

"Is there nobody inside to open the door?" I hallooed, responsively.

"They's nobbut t' missis; and shoo'll nut oppen't an ye mak yer flaysome dins till neeght."[6]

"Why? Cannot you tell her who I am, eh, Joseph?"

"Nor-ne me! Aw'll hae noa hend wi't,"[7] muttered the head vanishing.

The snow began to drive thickly. I seized the handle to essay another trial; when a young man, without coat, and shouldering a pitchfork, appeared in the yard behind. He hailed me to follow him, and, after marching through a washhouse and a paved area containing a coal-shed, pump, and pigeon cote, we at length arrived in the large, warm, cheerful apartment where I was formerly received.

It glowed delightfully in the radiance of an immense fire compounded of coal, peat, and wood: and near the table, laid for a plentiful evening meal, I was pleased to observe the "missis," an individual whose existence I had never previously suspected.

I bowed and waited, thinking she would bid me take a seat. She looked at me, leaning back in her chair, and remained motionless and mute.

"Rough weather!" I remarked. "I'm afraid, Mrs. Heathcliff, the floor must bear the consequence of your servants' leisure attendance: I had hard work to make them hear me!"

She never opened her mouth. I stared—she stared also. At any rate, she kept her eyes on me, in a cool, regardless manner, exceedingly embarrassing and disagreeable.

"Sit down," said the young man, gruffly. "He'll be in soon."

I obeyed; and hemmed,[8] and called the villain Juno, who deigned, at this second interview, to move the extreme tip of her tail, in token of owning my acquaintance.

"A beautiful animal!" I commenced again. "Do you intend parting with the little ones, madam?"

"They are not mine," said the amiable hostess more repellingly than Heathcliff himself could have replied.

"Ah, your favourites are among these!" I continued, turning to an obscure cushion full of something like cats.

"A strange choice of favourites," she observed scornfully.

Unluckily, it was a heap of dead rabbits—I hemmed once more, and drew closer to the hearth, repeating my comment on the wildness of the evening.

"You should not have come out," she said, rising and reaching from the chimney piece two of the painted canisters.

Her position before was sheltered from the light: now, I had a distinct view of her whole figure and countenance. She was slender, and apparently scarcely past girlhood: an admirable form, and the most exquisite little face that I have ever had the pleasure of beholding: small features, very fair; flaxen ringlets, or rather golden, hanging loose on her delicate neck; and eyes—had they been agreeable in expression, they would have been irresistible—fortunately for my susceptible heart, the only sentiment they evinced hovered between scorn and a kind of desperation, singularly unnatural to be detected there.

The canisters were almost out of her reach; I made a motion to aid her; she turned upon me as a miser might turn, if any one attempted to assist him in counting his gold.

"I don't want your help," she snapped, "I can get them for myself."

"I beg your pardon," I hastened to reply.

"Were you asked to tea?" she demanded, tying an apron over her neat black frock,[9] and standing with a spoonful of the leaf poised over the pot.

6 "There's no one but the missis; and she'll not open it if you make your dreadful noises till night." This is the first of many occasions when characters are locked out of Wuthering Heights. They are also locked into it. The main entry is through a door leading directly into the sitting room and not, as here, through rooms that remind Lockwood and us that the Heights is a working farmhouse, a place where laundry is washed, coal stored, water pumped, and pigeons cultivated.

7 "Nor-ne me!" emphatically refuses Lockwood's request: "I'll have no hand in it."

8 Either Lockwood clears his throat, or he stammers in his speech *(OED)*. Both expressions might register how unsettled he is by Mrs. Heathcliff's "cool" stare.

9 Lockwood does not comment on his hostess's dress, except to note its color; she is dressed in black because she is in mourning.

"I shall be glad to have a cup," I answered.

"Were you asked?" she repeated.

"No," I said, half smiling. "You are the proper person to ask me."

She flung the tea back, spoon and all; and resumed her chair in a pet, her forehead corrugated, and her red under-lip pushed out, like a child's, ready to cry.

Meanwhile, the young man had slung onto his person a decidedly shabby upper garment, and, erecting himself before the blaze, looked down on me, from the corner of his eyes, for all the world as if there were some mortal feud unavenged between us. I began to doubt[10] whether he were a servant or not; his dress and speech were both rude, entirely devoid of the superiority observable in Mr. and Mrs. Heathcliff; his thick, brown curls were rough and uncultivated, his whiskers encroached bearishly over his cheeks, and his hands were embrowned like those of a common labourer; still his bearing was free, almost haughty; and he showed none of a domestic's assiduity in attending on the lady of the house.

In the absence of clear proofs of his condition, I deemed it best to abstain from noticing his curious conduct, and, five minutes afterwards, the entrance of Heathcliff relieved me, in some measure, from my uncomfortable state.

"You see, sir, I am come according to promise!" I exclaimed, assuming the cheerful, "and I fear I shall be weather-bound for half an hour, if you can afford me shelter during that space."

"Half an hour?" he said, shaking the white flakes from his clothes; "I wonder you should select the thick of a snow-storm to ramble about in. Do you know that you run a risk of being lost in the marshes?[11] People familiar with these moors often miss their road on such evenings, and, I can tell you, there is no chance of a change at present."

"Perhaps I can get a guide among your lads, and he might stay at the Grange till morning—could you spare me one?"

"No, I could not."

10 Be uncertain about.

11 The marshes consist of land that is waterlogged for some part of the year. The moors Hareton refers to in the next sentence contain spongy marshland as well as stretches of rocky soil carpeted by low-growing vegetation.

"Oh, indeed! Well then, I must trust to my own sagacity."

"Umph."

"Are you going to mak th' tea?" demanded he of the shabby coat, shifting his ferocious gaze from me to the young lady.

"Is *he* to have any?" she asked, appealing to Heathcliff.

"Get it ready, will you?" was the answer, uttered so savagely that I started. The tone in which the words were said revealed a genuine bad nature. I no longer felt inclined to call Heathcliff a capital fellow.

When the preparations were finished, he invited me with—

"Now, sir, bring forward your chair." And we all, including the rustic youth, drew round the table, an austere silence prevailing while we discussed[12] our meal.

I thought if I had caused the cloud, it was my duty to make an effort to dispel it. They could not every day sit so grim and taciturn, and it was impossible, however ill-tempered they might be, that the universal scowl they wore was their every day countenance.

"It is strange," I began in the interval of swallowing one cup of tea and receiving another, "it is strange how custom can mould our tastes and ideas; many could not imagine the existence of happiness in a life of such complete exile from the world as you spend, Mr. Heathcliff; yet, I'll venture to say, that, surrounded by your family, and with your amiable lady as the presiding genius[13] over your home and heart—"

"My amiable lady!" he interrupted, with an almost diabolical sneer on his face. "Where is she—my amiable lady?"

"Mrs. Heathcliff, your wife, I mean."

"Well, yes—Oh! You would intimate that her spirit has taken the post of ministering angel, and guards the fortunes of Wuthering Heights, even when her body is gone.[14] Is that it?"

Perceiving myself in a blunder, I attempted to correct it. I might have seen there was too great a disparity between the ages of the parties to make it likely that they were man and wife. One was

12 "Discussed" means "consumed," and Lockwood calls attention here to the humorous contrast between the silence around the table and the earnest eating. The *OED* cites Scott's *Guy Mannering* (1815) as the first use of "discuss" in this sense.

13 Lockwood's amiability, an attempt on his part to lighten the mood at the Heights, is patently disingenuous. Heathcliff's "amiable lady" has so far been downright unfriendly. Lockwood's gallant reference to her as the "presiding genius" of the Heights associates her with the ideal wife soon to be celebrated in Coventry Patmore's *The Angel in the House* (1854).

14 Heathcliff's reference to his deceased wife as a "ministering angel" and guardian of "the fortunes of the Heights" is profoundly sardonic. The Heights has no "presiding genius." As Lockwood will have to go to sleep to learn, it has instead a presiding ghost.

15 Mrs. Heathcliff (Cathy Heathcliff née Cathy Linton) is about 17.5 years old; Heathcliff is not older than 38.

16 This is Hareton Earnshaw, who gives his name just below. Lockwood disparages him as a rustic and a lout.

about forty; a period of mental vigour at which men seldom cherish the delusion of being married for love by girls: that dream is reserved for the solace of our declining years. The other did not look seventeen.[15]

Then it flashed upon me: the clown[16] at my elbow, who is drinking his tea out of a basin, and eating his bread with unwashed hands, may be her husband, Heathcliff junior, of course. Here is the consequence of being buried alive: she has thrown herself away upon that boor, from sheer ignorance that better individuals existed! A sad pity—I must beware how I cause her to regret her choice.

The last reflection may seem conceited; it was not. My neighbour struck me as bordering on repulsive. I knew, through experience, that I was tolerably attractive.

"Mrs. Heathcliff is my daughter-in-law," said Heathcliff, corroborating my surmise. He turned, as he spoke, a peculiar look in her direction, a look of hatred unless he has a most perverse set of facial muscles that will not, like those of other people, interpret the language of his soul.

"Ah, certainly—I see now; you are the favoured possessor of the beneficent fairy," I remarked, turning to my neighbour.

This was worse than before: the youth grew crimson, and clenched his fist with every appearance of a meditated assault. But he seemed to recollect himself presently; and smothered the storm in a brutal curse, muttered on my behalf, which, however, I took care not to notice.

"Unhappy in your conjectures, sir!" observed my host; "we neither of us have the privilege of owning your good fairy; her mate is dead. I said she was my daughter-in-law; therefore, she must have married my son."

"And this young man is—"

"Not my son, assuredly!"

Heathcliff smiled again, as if it were rather too bold a jest to attribute the paternity of that bear to him.

"My name is Hareton Earnshaw,"[17] growled the other, "and I'd counsel you to respect it!"

"I've shown no disrespect," was my reply, laughing internally at the dignity with which he announced himself.

He fixed his eye on me longer than I cared to return the stare, for fear I might be tempted either to box his ears, or render my hilarity audible. I began to feel unmistakably out of place in that pleasant family circle. The dismal spiritual atmosphere overcame, and more than neutralized the glowing physical comforts round me; and I resolved to be cautious how I ventured under those rafters a third time.

The business of eating being concluded, and no one uttering a word of sociable conversation, I approached a window to examine the weather.

A sorrowful sight I saw: dark night coming down prematurely, and sky and hills mingled in one bitter whirl of wind and suffocating snow.

"I don't think it possible for me to get home now, without a guide," I could not help exclaiming. "The roads will be buried already; and, if they were bare, I could scarcely distinguish a foot in advance."

"Hareton, drive those dozen sheep into the barn porch. They'll be covered if left in the fold all night; and put a plank before them," said Heathcliff.

"How must I do?" I continued, with rising irritation.

There was no reply to my question; and, on looking round, I saw only Joseph bringing in a pail of porridge[18] for the dogs; and Mrs. Heathcliff, leaning over the fire, diverting herself with burning a bundle of matches[19] which had fallen from the chimney-piece as she restored the tea-canister to its place.

The former, when he had deposited his burden, took a critical survey of the room; and, in cracked tones, grated out[20]:

"Aw woonder hagh yah can faishion tuh stand thear i' idleness un' war, when all on 'em's goan aght! Bud yah're a nowt, and it's noa

17 Lockwood saw the name carved over the entrance to Wuthering Heights, along with the date of the house's construction, 1500, but he fails to connect Hareton's pride in announcing it with his identity as the descendant of the Hareton Earnshaw who caused the house to be built.

18 Any kind of watery mash; here oat flakes or meal boiled in water.

19 The ancestor of the modern match, the safety match, was invented in 1844. Cathy is using the fire to ignite the kind of matches used in an earlier time. These were pieces of cord, cloth, or wood dipped in melted sulphur so that they could be easily lit with a flint.

20 Spoke out harshly. This unusual and expressive phrasal verb, together with Lockwood's reference to Joseph's "cracked tones," captures the impression his unfamiliar Yorkshire dialect makes on Lockwood as well as Joseph's attitude toward Cathy.

use talking—yah'll niver mend uh yer ill ways, bud goa raight tuh t' divil, like yer mother afore ye!"[21]

I imagined, for a moment, that this piece of eloquence was addressed to me; and, sufficiently enraged, stepped towards the aged rascal with an intention of kicking him out of the door.

Mrs. Heathcliff, however, checked me by her answer.

"You scandalous old hypocrite!" she replied. "Are you not afraid of being carried away bodily, whenever you mention the devil's name? I warn you to refrain from provoking me, or I'll ask your abduction as a special favour. Stop, look here, Joseph," she continued, taking a long, dark book from a shelf. "I'll show you how far I've progressed in the Black Art—I shall soon be competent to make a clear house of it. The red cow didn't die by chance; and your rheumatism can hardly be reckoned among providential visitations!"[22]

"Oh, wicked, wicked!" gasped the elder, "may the Lord deliver us from evil!"

"No, reprobate! you are a castaway—be off, or I'll hurt you seriously! I'll have you all modelled in wax and clay;[23] and the first who passes the limits I fix shall—I'll not say what he shall be done to—but, you'll see![24] Go, I'm looking at you!"

The little witch put a mock malignity into her beautiful eyes, and Joseph, trembling with sincere horror, hurried out praying and ejaculating "wicked" as he went.

I thought her conduct must be prompted by a species of dreary fun; and, now that we were alone, I endeavoured to interest her in my distress.

"Mrs. Heathcliff," I said, earnestly, "you must excuse me for troubling you—I presume, because, with that face, I'm sure you cannot help being good-hearted. Do point out some landmarks by which I may know my way home—I have no more idea how to get there than you would have how to get to London!"

21 "I wonder how you can have the face to stand there in idleness and worse, when everyone else has gone out [to work]! But you're a nothing, and it's no use talking—you'll never mend your bad ways, but go right to the devil, like your mother before you!" This is the first unmistakable sign of Joseph's fierce Calvinism. In Chapter 5, Nelly will describe him as "the wearisomest, self-righteous pharisee that ever ransacked a Bible to rake the promises to himself, and fling the curses on his neighbours." Patrick Brontë condemned extreme Calvinist beliefs, including the belief in eternal damnation. Charlotte satirizes them in her portrait of the Evangelical Calvinist Mr. Brocklehurst in *Jane Eyre.*

22 Unlike Lockwood, who imagines kicking the old man out of the house, Cathy fights back by fanning the fires of Joseph's paranoia. Magic and a belief in ghosts, demons, fairies, and goblins still have considerable sway with him. The book Cathy takes from the shelf isn't a witch's manual, but since Joseph can't read, he won't know this.

23 Cathy threatens Joseph with both his theology and her (pretended) black magic. A "reprobate" or a "castaway" is a sinner consigned to eternal punishment. Witches were thought to burn wax or clay figures representing those they were cursing.

24 An echo of the passage from Shakespeare's *King Lear* in which Lear fulminates against his daughters and stammers his own helplessness: "I will have such revenges on you both/That all the world shall—I will do such things—/What they are, yet I know not, but they shall be/The terrors of the earth" (Act II, Scene iv, ll. 282–285).

"Take the road you came," she answered, ensconcing herself in a chair, with a candle and the long book open before her. "It is brief advice, but as sound as I can give."

"Then, if you hear of me being discovered dead in a bog, or a pit full of snow, your conscience won't whisper that it is partly your fault?"

"How so? I cannot escort you. They wouldn't let me go to the end of the garden-wall."

"*You!* I should be sorry to ask you to cross the threshold, for my convenience, on such a night," I cried. "I want you to *tell* me my way, not to *show* it; or else to persuade Mr. Heathcliff to give me a guide."

"Who? There is himself, Earnshaw, Zillah, Joseph, and I. Which would you have?"

"Are there no boys at the farm?"

"No, those are all."

"Then, it follows that I am compelled to stay."

"That you may settle with your host. I have nothing to do with it."

"I hope it will be a lesson to you, to make no more rash journeys on these hills," cried Heathcliff's stern voice from the kitchen entrance. "As to staying here, I don't keep accommodations for visiters; you must share a bed with Hareton or Joseph, if you do."

"I can sleep on a chair in this room," I replied.

"No, no! A stranger is a stranger, be he rich or poor—it will not suit me to permit anyone the range of the place while I am off guard!" said the unmannerly wretch.

With this insult my patience was at an end. I uttered an expression of disgust, and pushed past him into the yard, running against Earnshaw in my haste. It was so dark that I could not see the means of exit, and, as I wandered round, I heard another specimen of their civil behaviour amongst each other.

At first, the young man appeared about to befriend me.

"I'll go with him as far as the park," he said.

"You'll go with him to hell!" exclaimed his master, or whatever relation he bore. "And who is to look after the horses, eh?"

"A man's life is of more consequence than one evening's neglect of the horses; somebody must go," murmured Mrs. Heathcliff, more kindly than I expected.

"Not at your command!" retorted Hareton. "If you set store on him,[25] you'd better be quiet."

"Then I hope his ghost will haunt you; and I hope Mr. Heathcliff will never get another tenant, till the Grange is a ruin!" she answered sharply.

"Hearken, hearken, shoo's cursing on em!"[26] muttered Joseph, towards whom I had been steering.

He sat within earshot, milking the cows, by the aid of a lantern, which I seized unceremoniously, and calling out that I would send it back on the morrow, rushed to the nearest postern.[27]

"Maister, maister, he's staling t' lantern!" shouted the ancient, pursuing my retreat. "Hey, Gnasher! Hey, dog! Hey, Wolf,[28] holld him, holld him!"[29]

On opening the little door, two hairy monsters flew at my throat, bearing me down, and extinguishing the light, while a mingled guffaw, from Heathcliff and Hareton, put the copestone[30] on my rage and humiliation.

Fortunately, the beasts seemed more bent on stretching their paws, and yawning, and flourishing their tails, than devouring me alive; but they would suffer no resurrection, and I was forced to lie till their malignant masters pleased to deliver me: then hatless, and trembling with wrath, I ordered the miscreants to let me out—on their peril to keep me one minute longer—with several incoherent threats of retaliation that, in their indefinite depth of virulency, smacked of King Lear.[31]

The vehemence of my agitation brought on a copious bleeding at the nose, and still Heathcliff laughed, and still I scolded. I don't know what would have concluded the scene had there not been

25 Esteem or value him highly; this sense is now obsolete except in dialect speech *(OED)*.

26 "She's putting a curse on him!"

27 Lockwood is in the yard and chooses the nearest postern (or door) to make his exit. By mistake, he opens the door to the kennel and releases the dogs. This is another instance in which egress from the Heights is blocked, and violence is the result of an attempted escape.

28 One of the dogs is named "Gnasher"; the other is probably named "Wolf." The lower-case "w" in the 1847 edition has been emended to an upper-case "W" in this edition. This follows Charlotte's emendation in 1850.

29 Joseph accuses Lockwood of stealing the lantern and commands the dogs to keep him from leaving the property.

30 The highest stone of a structure; figuratively, the attack of the dogs crowns or completes Lockwood's "rage and humiliation."

31 This is Brontë's second allusion to the passage in which Lear expresses his helplessness in his contest with his two powerful daughters. (See *King Lear,* Act II, Scene iv, ll. 282–285.)

one person at hand rather more rational than myself, and more benevolent than my entertainer. This was Zillah, the stout housewife,[32] who at length issued forth to inquire into the nature of the uproar. She thought that some of them had been laying violent hands on me; and, not daring to attack her master, she turned her vocal artillery against the younger scoundrel.

"Well, Mr. Earnshaw," she cried, "I wonder what you'll have agait next! Are we going to murder folk on our very door-stones? I see this house will never do for me—look at t' poor lad, he's fair choking! Wisht, wisht! you munn't go on so—come in, and I'll cure that. There now, hold ye still."[33]

With these words she suddenly splashed a pint of icy water down my neck, and pulled me into the kitchen. Mr. Heathcliff followed, his accidental merriment expiring quickly in his habitual moroseness.

I was sick exceedingly, and dizzy and faint, and thus compelled, perforce, to accept lodgings under his roof. He told Zillah to give me a glass of brandy, and then passed on to the inner room, while she condoled with me on my sorry predicament, and having obeyed his orders, whereby I was somewhat revived, ushered me to bed.

32 Female domestic servant.

33 "Agait" is dialect for "a-foot" or "a-going," and "wisht" is dialect for "hush": "Hush, hush! you mustn't go on like that—come in, and I'll take care of that." The "door-stone" is the flagstone in front of the door to the house.

1 The "clothes-press" is a tall, free-standing armoire for holding linens or clothes, and the "large oak case" is a box-bed. Box-beds were cupboard-like structures built against the wall of a room and enclosing a sleeping compartment. In addition to creating a private place for sleeping in a room also serving other purposes, box-beds protected sleepers against cold drafts. They were more common in the north of England and Scotland than in the south and certainly old-fashioned enough to be entirely unfamiliar to Lockwood in 1801. The squares cut out near the top of this box-bed are an unusual feature. The suggestion that they look like coach windows calls attention to the idea that dreams transport dreamers to faraway places. Brontë describes the magic of nighttime travel in "Stars":

> Thought followed thought, star followed star,
> Through boundless regions, on;
> While one sweet influence, near and far,
> Thrilled through, and proved us one!
>
> Why did the morning dawn to break
> So great, so pure, a spell;
> And scorch with fire, the tranquil cheek,
> Where your cool radiance fell?

2 The names scratched into the paint tell the stories of both Catherines, the mother—born Catherine Earnshaw, who has left this record of her existence for Lockwood to find—and the daughter, born Catherine Linton, the Mrs. Heathcliff Lockwood has already introduced us to. It is Lockwood who puts the names into an order—"Catherine Earnshaw—Heathcliff—Linton"—that forecasts the plot of Catherine Earnshaw's story. Frank Kermode observes that the daughter's story is the mother's story in reverse: Catherine Linton—Heathcliff—Earnshaw. The "movement of the book" is "away from Earnshaw and back, like the movement of the house itself. And all the movement must be *through* Heathcliff" (*The Classic: Literary Images of Permanence and Change* [Cambridge: Harvard Univ. Press, 1983], p. 122).

CHAPTER 3

While leading the way up-stairs, she recommended that I should hide the candle, and not make a noise, for her master had an odd notion about the chamber she would put me in, and never let anybody lodge there willingly.

I asked the reason.

She did not know, she answered; she had only lived there a year or two; and they had so many queer goings on, she could not begin to be curious.

Too stupified to be curious myself, I fastened my door and glanced round for the bed. The whole furniture consisted of a chair, a clothes-press, and a large oak case, with squares cut out near the top, resembling coach windows.[1]

Having approached this structure, I looked inside, and perceived it to be a singular sort of old-fashioned couch, very conveniently designed to obviate the necessity for every member of the family having a room to himself. In fact, it formed a little closet, and the ledge of a window, which it enclosed, served as a table.

I slid back the panelled sides, got in with my light, pulled them together again, and felt secure against the vigilance of Heathcliff, and every one else.

The ledge, where I placed my candle, had a few mildewed books piled up in one corner; and it was covered with writing scratched

A modern reconstruction of a box-bed, from Peter Kosminsky's film adaptation of *Wuthering Heights* (1992).

on the paint. This writing, however, was nothing but a name repeated in all kinds of characters, large and small—*Catherine Earnshaw;* here and there varied to *Catherine Heathcliff,* and then again to *Catherine Linton.*[2]

In vapid listlessness I leant my head against the window, and continued spelling over Catherine Earnshaw—Heathcliff—Linton, till my eyes closed; but they had not rested five minutes when a glare of white letters started from the dark, as vivid as spectres—the air swarmed with Catherines; and rousing myself to dispel the obtrusive name, I discovered my candle wick reclining on one of the antique volumes, and perfuming the place with an odour of roasted calf-skin.

I snuffed it off, and, very ill at ease under the influence of cold and lingering nausea, sat up and spread open the injured tome on my knee. It was a Testament in lean type,[3] and smelling dreadfully musty: a fly-leaf bore the inscription—"Catherine Earnshaw, her book," and a date some quarter of a century back.

I shut it and took up another, and another, till I had examined all. Catherine's library was select; and its state of dilapidation proved it to have been well used, though not altogether for a legitimate purpose; scarcely one chapter had escaped a pen-and-ink commentary—at least, the appearance of one—covering every morsel of blank that the printer had left.

Some were detached sentences; other parts took the form of a regular diary, scrawled in an unformed, childish hand. At the top of an extra page, quite a treasure probably when first lighted on, I was greatly amused to behold an excellent caricature of my friend Joseph, rudely yet powerfully sketched.[4]

An immediate interest kindled within me for the unknown Catherine, and I began, forthwith, to decypher her faded hieroglyphics.

"An awful Sunday!"[5] commenced the paragraph beneath. "I wish my father were back again. Hindley is a detestable substitute—his conduct to Heathcliff is atrocious—H. and I are going to rebel—we took our initiatory step this evening.

"All day had been flooding with rain; we could not go to church, so Joseph must needs get up a congregation in the garret; and, while Hindley and his wife basked down stairs before a comfortable fire, doing anything but reading their Bibles, I'll answer for it; Heathcliff, myself, and the unhappy plough-boy were commanded to take our Prayer-books and mount—we were ranged in a row, on a sack of corn,[6] groaning and shivering, and hoping that Joseph would shiver too, so that he might give us a short homily[7] for his own sake. A vain idea! The service lasted precisely three hours; and yet my brother had the face to exclaim, when he saw us descending,

3 A New Testament in a font whose letters fall inside the "normal" length of a line composed of all the letters of the alphabet. This is "lean type" as opposed to "fat type" (Robert Luce, "Fat and Lean Type," in *Writing for the Press: A Manual* [Boston: Clipping Bureau Press, 1907]).

4 Caricatures—unlike copies of engravings of flowers, figures, and landscapes—were not among the accomplishments expected of fashionable ladies. Like Catherine, the Brontë children left numerous sketches in their school books and in the books belonging to their father's library, a habit he "surprisingly tolerated" (Christine Alexander and Jane Sellars, *The Art of the Brontës* [Cambridge: Cambridge Univ. Press, 1995], p. 4). They also produced very competent pencil sketches and watercolor paintings. Branwell was for a time destined and prepared for a career as a portrait painter.

The twenty-nine paintings and drawings by Emily that survive include images of the family's dogs and a pet hawk named Nero that she rescued from an abandoned nest on the moors; an extraordinary pencil sketch, "Study of a fir tree," taken outdoors while she and Charlotte were studying in Brussels; and various doodles, sketches, and caricatures preserved in the diary papers she exchanged with Anne and in her poem manuscripts.

5 A day in November 1777, five weeks before Christmas and soon after the death of old Mr. Earnshaw. Catherine is twelve years old. Since it is now November 1801, Lockwood's observation that the fly-leaf of the Testament "bears a date some quarter of a century back" is accurate. Margaret Homans points out that "the diary fragment is the most authentic, as well as the most distant, of the narrative layers" of the novel. It is also the "only unmediated record of the veritable voice and attitudes of one of the central characters" (Homans, "Repression and Sublimation of Nature in *Wuthering Heights*," *PMLA*, 93:1 [Jan. 1978], p. 10).

6 Corn can be any species of cereal grain; here it is likely oats.

7 Sermon.

8 Unnecessary or idle talk. English sailors learned the word from Portuguese traders on the west coast of Africa, who used it to denote their conversations with the natives. It passed "from nautical slang into colloquial use" in the eighteenth century *(OED)*.

9 This is the same oak server that Lockwood observed on his first visit to the Heights. Under its arch, where Catherine and Heathcliff are crouching, Lockwood saw a "liver-coloured bitch pointer" and her puppies.

"'What, done already?'"

"On Sunday evenings we used to be permitted to play, if we did not make much noise; now a mere titter is sufficient to send us into corners!

"'You forget you have a master here,' says the tyrant. 'I'll demolish the first who puts me out of temper! I insist on perfect sobriety and silence. Oh, boy! was that you? Frances, darling, pull his hair as you go by; I heard him snap his fingers.'

"Frances pulled his hair heartily; and then went and seated herself on her husband's knee, and there they were, like two babies, kissing and talking nonsense by the hour—foolish palaver[8] that we should be ashamed of.

"We made ourselves as snug as our means allowed in the arch of the dresser.[9] I had just fastened our pinafores[10] together, and hung them up for a curtain, when in comes Joseph, on an errand from the stables. He tears down my handywork, boxes my ears, and croaks:

"'T' maister nobbut just buried, and Sabbath nut oe'red, and t' sahnd uh t'gospel still i' yer lugs, and yah darr be laiking! shame on ye! sit ye dahn, ill childer! they's good books eneugh if ye'll read 'em; sit ye dahn, and think uh yer sowls!'[11]

"Saying this, he compelled us so to square our positions that we might receive, from the far-off fire, a dull ray to show us the text of the lumber he thrust upon us.

"I could not bear the employment. I took my dingy volume by the scroop,[12] and hurled it into the dog-kennel, vowing I hated a good book.

"Heathcliff kicked his to the same place. Then there was a hubbub!

"'Maister Hindley!' shouted our chaplain. 'Maister, coom hither! Miss Cathy's riven th' back off "Th' Helmet uh Salvation," un' Heathcliff's pawsed his fit intuh t' first part uh "T' Brooad Way to Destruction"! It's fair flaysome ut yah let 'em goa on this gait. Ech! th' owd man ud uh laced 'em properly—bud he's goan!'[13]

Nero, signed E. J. B. and dated October 27, 1841. Brontë's watercolor depicts the merlin hawk she kept briefly as a pet. Nero lived in a cage, but Brontë paints him as a free creature.

10 Pinafores or aprons were worn by both boys and girls to protect their clothes from dirt.

11 "The master's only just buried, and the Sabbath's not over, and the sound of the gospel's still in your ears, and you dare to be playing! shame on you! sit down, bad children! there are good books enough if you'll read them; sit down, and think of your souls!"

As a strict Calvinist, Joseph disapproves of the children's play under any circumstances. Playing on the Sabbath and while the house is in mourning heightens their offense. Many Evangelical Christians also disapproved of worldly activities and entertainment, especially on the Sabbath. Patrick Brontë seems not to have enforced solemnity in the Parsonage and to have left his children free to amuse themselves as they liked.

George Whitefield (1714–1770), one of the founders of the Evangelical movement within the Anglican Church and of Methodism, preaching in Moorfields in London. Lithograph illustration after Eyre Crowe for H. D. M. Spence-Jones's *The Church of England: A History for the People* (c. 1910).

"Hindley hurried up from his paradise on the hearth, and seizing one of us by the collar and the other by the arm, hurled both into the back-kitchen,[14] where, Joseph asseverated, 'owd Nick'[15] would fetch us as sure as we were living; and, so comforted, we each sought a separate nook to await his advent.

"I reached this book and a pot of ink from a shelf, and pushed the house-door ajar to give me light, and I have got the time on with writing for twenty minutes; but my companion is impatient and proposes that we should appropriate the dairy woman's cloak, and have a scamper on the moors under its shelter. A pleasant suggestion—and then, if the surly old man come in, he may believe his prophesy verified—we cannot be damper, or colder, in the rain than we are here."[16]

****

I suppose Catherine fulfilled her project, for the next sentence took up another subject; she waxed lachrymose.

12 *OED* treats "scroop" as a mistake for "scruff," which refers to the back of the cover of a book. The word "scroop" does not appear in Joseph Wright's authoritative *English Dialect Dictionary* (London, Oxford, New York: G. P. Putnam's Sons, 1898).

13 Catherine has torn the back off *The Helmet of Salvation,* and Heathcliff has kicked *The Broad Way to Destruction.* "It's frightful that you let them go on this way. Ech! The old man [Mr. Earnshaw] would've beaten them properly—but he's gone."

I have not been able to find these titles, and Brontë probably invented them. They are perfectly suited to Joseph's brand of theology as well as likely to be in a God-fearing Mr. Earnshaw's library. One title, "The Helmet of Salvation," owes something to *Christian in Compleat Armour* by William Gurnall (1617–1679), which contains sermons and lectures on Ephesians 6: 10–20 that Gurnall delivered during his ministry. The biblical passage begins with the instruction "Put on the whole armour of God" and includes the phrase "the helmet of salvation." The second title refers to a passage from the Sermon on the Mount, well known and often cited in nineteenth-century sermons: "Enter ye in at the strait gate: for wide is the gate, and broad is the way, that leadeth to destruction, and many there be which go in thereat" (Matthew 7: 13).

"How little did I dream that Hindley would ever make me cry so!" she wrote. "My head aches, till I cannot keep it on the pillow; and still I can't give over. Poor Heathcliff! Hindley calls him a vagabond,[17] and won't let him sit with us, nor eat with us any more; and, he says, he and I must not play together, and threatens to turn him out of the house if we break his orders.

"He has been blaming our father (how dared he?) for treating H. too liberally; and swears he will reduce him to his right place—"

****

I began to nod drowsily over the dim page; my eye wandered from manuscript to print. I saw a red ornamented title—"Seventy Times Seven, and the First of the Seventy First. A Pious Discourse delivered by the Reverend Jabes Branderham, in the Chapel of Gimmerden Sough."[18] And while I was, half consciously, worrying my brain to guess what Jabes Branderham would make of his subject, I sank back in bed, and fell asleep.

Alas, for the effects of bad tea and bad temper! What else could it be that made me pass such a terrible night? I don't remember another that I can at all compare with it since I was capable of suffering.

I began to dream, almost before I ceased to be sensible of my locality. I thought it was morning; and I had set out on my way home, with Joseph for a guide. The snow lay yards deep in our road; and, as we floundered on, my companion wearied me with constant reproaches that I had not brought a pilgrim's staff: telling me I could never get into the house without one, and boastfully flourishing a heavy-headed cudgel, which I understood to be so denominated.

For a moment I considered it absurd that I should need such a weapon to gain admittance into my own residence. Then, a new idea flashed across me. I was not going there; we were journeying to hear the famous Jabes Branderham preach from the text—"Seventy Times Seven"—and either Joseph, the preacher, or I had

14 Apparently, Brontë has a clear image of the layout of the farmhouse in which the action of the first three chapters largely takes place. The kitchen to which Catherine and Heathcliff are banished is the back-kitchen and located behind the house or family sitting room. A ladder from the back-kitchen leads to the garret rooms, in one of which Joseph sleeps. The house has a large fireplace where water is boiled for tea, but the serious cooking and the washing up are done in the much smaller back-kitchen.

15 The Devil.

16 A gap in the text of the first edition and a row of asterisks mark the interruption of Catherine's narrative and the absence of her account of this romp on the moors with Heathcliff.

17 By deriding Heathcliff as a "vagabond" (someone who lacks a regular occupation or obvious means of support), Hindley justifies the separation of Heathcliff from Catherine that initiates the novel's tragic action. Thus Hindley's first act as master of the Heights is to punish his old enemy and his sister. Catherine is being instructed to accept her place in the civilized social world, where affinities are determined by paternity and property, not by instinct and feeling. The Grange represents this civilized, social world better than the Heights, as Hindley may always have known but has certainly confirmed during his sojourn in the south.

18 Marianne Thormählen disputes the usual identification of Jabes Branderham with Jabez Bunting (1779–1858), a popular preacher and one of the founders of Methodism. She suggests that a likelier source is Jabez Burns (1805–1876), a Baptist preacher who was named after Jabez Bunting by his Methodist mother. Burns was a vigorous advocate for temperance and the author of many popular religious books, including (in Brontë's lifetime) *The Golden Pot of Manna; or Christian's Portion, containing Daily Exercises on the Person, Offices, Work, and Glory of the Redeemer* and *The Pulpit Cyclopaedia; and Christian Minister's Companion,* containing hundreds of "skeletal sermons" (*The Brontës and Religion* [Cambridge: Cambridge Univ. Press, 1999], pp. 17–18). If Burns is Brontë's model, her comedy is prescient: he went on to publish books with Branderhamish titles like *One Hundred and Fifty Original Sketches and Plans of Sermons* (1866) and *Two Hundred Sketches and Outlines of Sermons* (1875). How do we choose between Burns and Bunting? In Brontë studies, the quest for historical originals regularly assumes that the author has a single source in mind. Charlotte usually does, but Emily's art is more often combinatory.

19 Branderham's text is Matthew 18:21–22, where Jesus instructs his disciples on the importance of forgiveness: "Then came Peter to him, and said, Lord, how oft shall my brother sin against me, and I forgive him? till seven times? Jesus saith unto him, I say not unto thee, Until seven times: but, Until seventy times seven." Brontë's satire is acerbic. Branderham's literal-mindedness—as if the command to forgive the first 490 sins frees us not to forgive the 491st sin—is part of her joke. Instead of using his chosen text to enable his listeners to become better Christians, this preacher encourages them to fulfill the desire for revenge that the Scriptural text countermands. Meanwhile, Lockwood refuses to forgive Branderham for committing "the sin that no Christian need pardon": he bores his listeners with his interminable, and interminably divided, sermon.

20 In the dream, and in the title of the sermon in the book that Lockwood is reading, the chapel is called Gimmerden Sough. Gimmerton (not Gimmerden) is the nearest village to the Heights and the Grange, and Lockwood has passed Gimmerton Chapel in his walks. Gimmerton Kirk, the established church where the Lintons and Earnshaws worshipped on Sundays, has lost its minister by 1801.

"Gimmer" (pronounced with a hard "g") is a dialect word for a young sheep, and Gimmerden means "young sheep valley." A sough (rhymes with "tough") is "a boggy or swampy place" *(OED)*. Lockwood casually mentions the embalming properties of the peaty soil in the Gimmerton churchyard where the dead are buried. The wet, acidic conditions of peat bogs were known to preserve cadavers from decay; records of bog bodies, usually discovered while peat was being harvested for fuel, go back to at least the mid-seventeenth century.

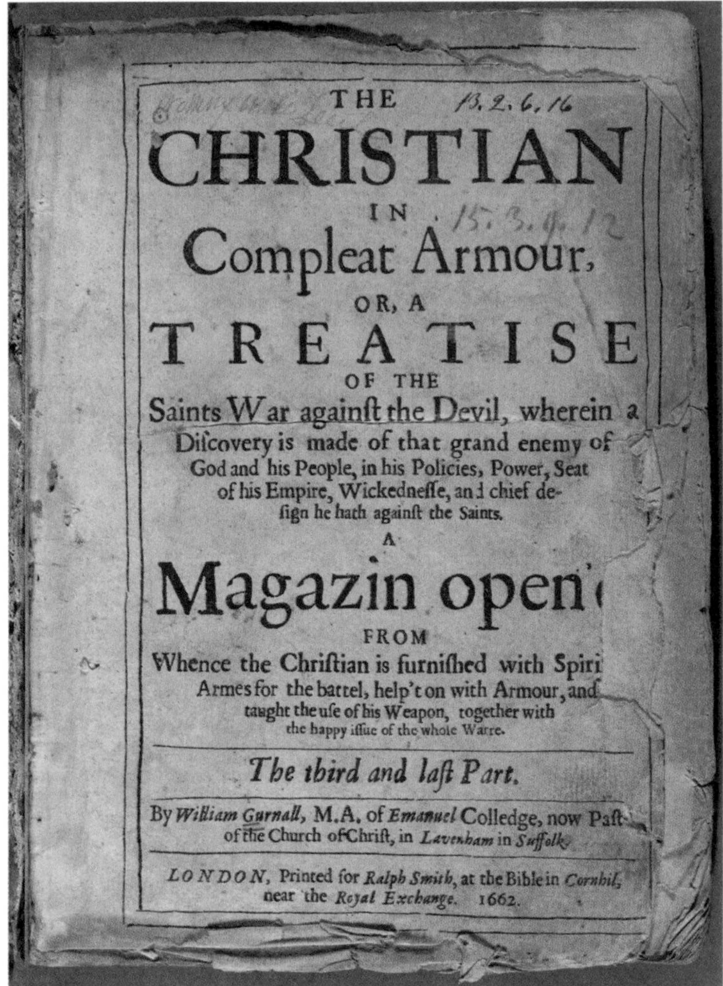
THE
CHRISTIAN
IN
Compleat Armour,
OR, A
TREATISE
OF THE
Saints War againſt the Devil, wherein a Diſcovery is made of that grand enemy of God and his People, in his Policies, Power, Seat of his Empire, Wickedneſſe, and chief deſign he hath againſt the Saints.
A
Magazin open
FROM
Whence the Chriſtian is furniſhed with Spiri Armes for the battel, help't on with Armour, and taught the uſe of his Weapon, together with the happy iſſue of the whole Warre.

The third and laſt Part.

By *William Gurnall*, M.A. of *Emanuel* Colledge, now Paſt of the Church of Chriſt, in *Lavenham* in *Suffolk*.

LONDON, Printed for *Ralph Smith*, at the Bible in *Cornhil*, near the *Royal Exchange*. 1662.

Title page of William Gurnall's *The Christian in Compleat Armour,* published in three volumes (1655, 1658, and 1662). It comprises Gurnall's sermons and was popular among Christians engaged in spritual warfare.

committed the "First of the Seventy First," and were to be publicly exposed and excommunicated.[19]

We came to the chapel—I have passed it really in my walks, twice or thrice: it lies in a hollow, between two hills—an elevated hollow—near a swamp, whose peaty moisture is said to answer all the purposes of embalming on the few corpses deposited there.[20] The roof has been kept whole hitherto, but, as the clergyman's stipend is only twenty pounds per annum, and a house with two rooms threatening speedily to determine[21] into one, no clergyman will undertake the duties of pastor, especially, as it is currently reported that his flock would rather let him starve than increase the living by one penny from their own pockets.[22] However, in my dream, Jabes had a full and attentive congregation: and he preached—good God—what a sermon! Divided into *four hundred and ninety* parts—each fully equal to an ordinary address from the pulpit—and each discussing a separate sin! Where he searched for them, I cannot tell; he had his private manner of interpreting the phrase, and it seemed necessary the brother should sin different sins on every occasion.

They were of the most curious character—odd trangressions that I never imagined previously.

Oh, how weary I grew. How I writhed, and yawned, and nodded, and revived! How I pinched and pricked myself, and rubbed my eyes, and stood up, and sat down again, and nudged Joseph to inform me if he would *ever* have done!

I was condemned to hear all out—finally, he reached the *"First of the Seventy-First."* At that crisis, a sudden inspiration descended on me; I was moved to rise and denounce Jabes Branderham as the sinner of the sin that no Christian need pardon.

"Sir," I exclaimed, "sitting here, within these four walls, at one stretch I have endured and forgiven the four hundred and ninety heads of your discourse. Seventy times seven times have I plucked up my hat and been about to depart—Seventy times seven times have you preposterously forced me to resume my seat. The four hundred and ninety-first is too much. Fellow martyrs, have at him! Drag him down, and crush him to atoms, that the place which knows him may know him no more!"[23]

"Thou art the Man!"[24] cried Jabes, after a solemn pause, leaning over his cushion. "Seventy times seven times didst thou gapingly contort thy visage—seventy times seven did I take counsel with my soul—Lo, this is human weakness; this also may be absolved!

21 "To end consequentially" (Johnson, *Dictionary*); to become.

22 The clergyman's remuneration—20 pounds annually and the tenancy of a two-room house—is meager. Patrick Brontë was paid a yearly salary of 200 pounds and given Haworth Parsonage, a modest but comfortable house, for his residence. Charlotte earned an annual salary of 20 pounds in her first position as a governess. Anne earned 40 pounds annually as governess at Thorp Green, while Branwell, employed as tutor to the family's only son, earned twice that amount. "Accounts of conditions in and around parish churches in the late eighteenth and early nineteenth centuries are full of horrors," Marianne Thormählen writes: "crumbling houses of worship; fonts filled with coffin ropes and candle ends; frayed and dirty cloths on altars used to serving as meal-tables or even chairs; and clergymen who nonchalantly asked whether a member of the congregation happened to have a corkscrew handy on one of the rare occasions when Holy Communion was administered" (Thormählen, *The Brontës and Religion,* pp. 175–176).

23 Lockwood alludes to Job 7: 9–10, where an anguished Job remonstrates with God: "As the cloud is consumed and vanished away: so he that goeth down to the grave shall come up no more. He shall return no more to his house, neither shall his place know him any more."

24 Jabes quotes 2 Samuel 12:7, where the prophet Nathan tells David a story that leads him to condemn himself to death for murdering Uriah and marrying his wife Bathsheba. With "Thou art the Man," Nathan reveals that David himself is guilty of murder and adultery. Anne also alludes to 2 Samuel 12 in *Agnes Grey* (Chap. 15), and "Thou Art the Man" is the title of an Edgar Allan Poe short story published in 1844. Poe was popular in England as well as in the United States, and the Brontës read him. Charlotte quotes the refrain of "The Raven," published in 1845, in a letter she wrote after Emily's death (Margaret Smith, ed., *The Letters of Charlotte Brontë,* 3 vols. [Oxford: Clarendon Press, 2000], 2, p. 186).

Jabez Burns (1805–1876), a Baptist writer and preacher widely known for his sermons on temperance.

Jabez Bunting (1779–1858), a popular Methodist preacher. Calotype by David Octavius Hill and Robert Adamson, c. 1843–1848.

The First of the Seventy-First is come. Brethren, execute upon him the judgment written! Such honour have all His saints!"

With that concluding word, the whole assembly, exalting their pilgrim's staves, rushed round me in a body, and I, having no weapon to raise in self-defence, commenced grappling with Joseph, my nearest and most ferocious assailant, for his. In the confluence of the multitude, several clubs crossed; blows, aimed at me, fell on other sconses. Presently the whole chapel resounded with rappings and counter-rappings. Every man's hand was against his neighbour;[25] and Branderham, unwilling to remain idle, poured forth his zeal in a shower of loud taps on the boards of the pulpit, which responded so smartly, that, at last, to my unspeakable relief, they woke me.[26]

And what was it that had suggested the tremendous tumult, what had played Jabes' part in the row? Merely, the branch of a fir-tree that touched my lattice[27] as the blast wailed by, and rattled its dry cones against the panes!

25 Variants of this proverbial phrase appear a few times in the Bible, including in Isaiah 19: 2. A scene of civil strife (here rendered comically) is also the subject of Brontë's last surviving poem, "Why ask to know what date what clime," the only poem she is known to have written after the publication of *Wuthering Heights*. Stevie Davies observes that although the "poem has been called 'paranoid,'" Brontë "would have called it truthful" (*Emily Brontë* [Plymouth: Northcote House Publishers, 1998], p. 29). Both Lockwood's nightmare and the poem invite apocalyptic readings.

26 Lockwood's first dream has received little critical attention, unlike the still more wonderful dream that follows it. This scene in Branderham's chapel is Brontë's only direct representation of organized religion. Her religious satire is very different from Charlotte's, which concentrates on the hypocrisy of the clergy, and from Anne's careful attempts to address doctrinal matters in her fiction and poetry. It is irreverent and rambunctious.

Emily was reticent about her own religious beliefs. When Mary Taylor took the position that her religion was nobody's business but God's, Emily made one of her few recorded assertions: "That's right." Although Emily didn't attend church regularly, she would have heard and read hundreds of sermons. They were an important part of services

Pencil sketch of a mullioned window. Brontë made this drawing, the earliest example of her art that survives, at the age of ten. It shows a casement window with stone mullions and small diamond-shaped panes. A shape like a hand breaks through the glass at the right of the central section.

in churches like her father's, and printed sermons were well represented in the Parsonage library. Ellen Nussey describes a church service she attended in Haworth in 1833 during which the sexton with his long staff "continually walked round in the aisles 'knobbing' sleepers when he dare" until the sermon began, and the congregation began to pay attention to the preacher (Juliet Barker, *The Brontës* [London: Phoenix, 1994], pp. 97–98). For a fuller discussion of the influence of sermons on the Brontës' writing, see Jennifer M. Stolpa, "Preaching to the Clergy: *Agnes Grey* as a Treatise on Sermon Style and Delivery," in *Victorian Literature and Culture*, 31.1 (2003), pp. 225–240.

27 A window made of small panes of glass, rectangular or diamond-shaped and separated by wooden laths. Lockwood's analysis of the role the fir tree branch brushing against his window plays in his dream is consistent with Scott's in *Letters on Demonology and Witchcraft* (1830), a book Brontë certainly read with interest. Scott points out that any "external impression upon our organs in sleep" will be

> instantly adopted . . . and accommodated to the tenor of the current train of thought, whatever that may happen to be; and nothing is more remarkable than the rapidity with which imagination supplies a complete explanation of the interruption, according to the previous train of ideas expressed in the dream, even when scarce a moment of time is allowed for that purpose. In dreaming, for example, of a duel, the external sound becomes, in the twinkling of an eye, the discharge of the combatants' pistols;—is an orator haranguing in his sleep, the sound becomes the applause of his supposed audience;—is the dreamer wandering among supposed ruins, the noise is that of the fall of some part of the mass. (Walter Scott, *Letters on Demonology and Witchcraft* [New York: Harper & Brothers, 1843], p. 33)

I listened doubtingly an instant; detected the disturber, then turned and dozed, and dreamt again; if possible, still more disagreebly than before.

This time, I remembered I was lying in the oak closet, and I heard distinctly the gusty wind and the driving of the snow; I heard also the fir-bough repeat its teasing sound, and ascribed it to the right cause: but it annoyed me so much, that I resolved to silence it, if possible; and I thought I rose and endeavoured to unhasp the casement. The hook was soldered into the staple, a circumstance observed by me, when awake, but forgotten.

"I must stop it, nevertheless!" I muttered, knocking my knuckles through the glass, and stretching an arm out to seize the importunate branch: instead of which, my fingers closed on the fingers of a little, ice-cold hand!

The intense horror of nightmare came over me; I tried to draw back my arm, but the hand clung to it, and a most melancholy voice sobbed,

"Let me in—let me in!"[28]

"Who are you?" I asked, struggling, meanwhile, to disengage myself.

"Catherine Linton," it replied, shiveringly (why did I think of *Linton?* I had read *Earnshaw* twenty times for Linton). "I'm come home. I'd lost my way on the moor!"

As it spoke, I discerned, obscurely, a child's face looking through the window—Terror made me cruel; and, finding it useless to attempt shaking the creature off, I pulled its wrist on to the broken pane, and rubbed it to and fro till the blood ran down and soaked the bed-clothes[29]: still it wailed—"Let me in!" and maintained its tenacious gripe, almost maddening me with fear.

"How can I?" I said at length. "Let *me* go, if you want me to let you in!"

The fingers relaxed; I snatched mine through the hole, hurriedly piled the books up in a pyramid against it, and stopped my ears to exclude the lamentable prayer.

I seemed to keep them closed above a quarter of an hour, yet, the instant I listened again, there was the doleful cry moaning on!

"Begone!" I shouted, "I'll never let you in, not if you beg for twenty years!"

"It's twenty years," mourned the voice, "twenty years—I've been a waif[30] for twenty years!"

Thereat began a feeble scratching outside, and the pile of books moved as if thrust forward.

28 Compare Scott's account of a nightmare confided to him by "a late nobleman":

> He had fallen asleep, with some uneasy feelings arising from indigestion. They operated in their usual course of visionary terrors. At length they were all summed up in the apprehension, that the phantom of a dead man held the sleeper by the wrist, and endeavored to drag him out of bed. He awaked in horror, and still felt the cold dead grasp of a corpse's hand on his right wrist. It was a minute before he discovered that his own left hand was in a state of numbness, and with it he had accidentally encircled his right arm. (Scott, *Letters on Demonology and Witchcraft*, p. 49)

Unlike the phantom in the nobleman's nightmare, Lockwood's phantom wants to pull herself into the bed, not pull him out of it.

29 In another contemporary account of dreaming, John Addington Symonds notes "that curious suspension of the moral sense, which is sometimes experienced" in dreams (*Sleep and Dreams* [London: John Murray, 1851], p. 61). The question Dorothy Van Ghent asks in her classic essay on *Wuthering Heights* is still pertinent: "Why should Lockwood, the well-mannered urbanite, dream *this?*" Her answer to it takes into account not just the dream but the dreamer, the city dweller sleeping in a strange bed: "Lockwood, more successfully than anyone else in the book, has shut out the powers of darkness (the pun in his name is obvious in this context); and his lack of any dramatically thorough motivation for dreaming the cruel dream suggests those powers as existing autonomously, not only in the 'outsideness' of external nature, beyond the physical windowpane, but also within, even in the soul least prone to passionate excursion" (*The English Novel: Form and Function* [New York: Holt, Rinehart and Winston, 1953], pp. 160–161).

Van Ghent's interpretation of the meaning of Lockwood's second dream relies on an insight we owe to modern psychoanalysis: dreams give access to the dreamer's subconscious. There was a revival of interest in dreams in the late eighteenth and early nineteenth centuries, but there was little agreement about their meaning and source. Coleridge believed dreams were prophetic and caused by spirits that could "enter the dreamer's mind and shape a dream at will" (p. 142). He considered himself an authority on nightmares, being himself "plagued by a 'dreadful labyrinth of strangling, hell-pretending Dreams'" (Jennifer Ford, *Coleridge on Dreaming: Romanticism, Dreams and the Medical Imagination* [Cambridge: Cambridge Univ. Press, 1998], pp. 142 and 108–129).

30 A remarkable choice of a word to describe the child outside the window. A "waif" can be a homeless person, an "unowned or neglected child," or something "borne or driven by the wind." The *OED* cites 1854 as the first instance of this last meaning of the word.

I tried to jump up, but could not stir a limb; and so yelled aloud, in a frenzy of fright.

To my confusion, I discovered the yell was not ideal.[31] Hasty footsteps approached my chamber door: somebody pushed it open, with a vigorous hand, and a light glimmered through the squares at the top of the bed. I sat shuddering, yet, and wiping the perspiration from my forehead: the intruder appeared to hesitate and muttered to himself.

At last, he said in a half-whisper, plainly not expecting an answer,

"Is any one here?"

I considered it best to confess my presence, for I knew Heathcliff's accents, and feared he might search further, if I kept quiet.

With this intention, I turned and opened the panels—I shall not soon forget the effect my action produced.

Heathcliff stood near the entrance, in his shirt and trousers; with a candle dripping over his fingers, and his face as white as the wall behind him. The first creak of the oak startled him like an electric shock: the light leaped from his hold to a distance of some feet, and his agitation was so extreme, that he could hardly pick it up.[32]

"It is only your guest, sir," I called out, desirous to spare him the humiliation of exposing his cowardice further. "I had the misfortune to scream in my sleep, owing to a frightful nightmare. I'm sorry I disturbed you."

"Oh, God confound you, Mr. Lockwood! I wish you were at the—" commenced my host setting the candle on a chair, because he found it impossible to hold it steady.

"And who showed you up to this room?" he continued, crushing his nails into his palms, and grinding his teeth to subdue the maxillary[33] convulsions. "Who was it? I've a good mind to turn them out of the house this moment!"

"It was your servant, Zillah," I replied, flinging myself on to the floor, and rapidly resuming my garments. "I should not care if

31 The conversation with the ghost of Catherine has taken place silently, within Lockwood's dream, or so he imagines, but his yell is real enough to be heard by the other sleepers in the Heights. Brontë's poems frequently juxtapose a dream (or ideal) world and waking (or ordinary) experience. Several of her poems, notably "To Imagination," "How Clear She Shines," and "Stars," celebrate the night's dreams and lament the daylight that ends them.

32 The first half of the nineteenth century saw the invention of the electric battery, the electric motor, and the electric telegraph, but it wasn't until 1879, fully three decades after Brontë's death, that Thomas Edison created the first practical incandescent light bulb. Her image of Heathcliff's being startled by the sound of the panels of the box-bed opening as by an electric shock, followed by the light of Heathcliff's candle leaping from his hand when he sees Lockwood within the box-bed, connects lightning and lighting as well as repeating the motif of inside and outside so prominent in this scene. Victor Frankenstein decides to abandon alchemy in favor of science after seeing a tree destroyed by lightning. We know that Brontë read Percy Bysshe Shelley's poetry. It's hard to imagine that she didn't also read Mary Shelley's *Frankenstein; or, The Modern Prometheus,* but we lack evidence that she (or either of her sisters) did read it.

33 Relating to the jaw.

34 A child left to replace one stolen by the fairies; changelings were thought to be ugly, stupid, or wicked.

you did, Mr. Heathcliff; she richly deserves it. I suppose that she wanted to get another proof that the place was haunted, at my expense—Well, it is—swarming with ghosts and goblins! You have reason in shutting it up, I assure you. No one will thank you for a doze in such a den!"

"What do you mean?" asked Heathcliff, "and what are you doing? Lie down and finish out the night, since you *are* here; but for Heaven's sake! don't repeat that horrid noise—Nothing could excuse it, unless you were having your throat cut!"

"If the little fiend had got in at the window, she probably would have strangled me!" I returned. "I'm not going to endure the persecutions of your hospitable ancestors again—Was not the Reverend Jabes Branderham akin to you on the mother's side? And that minx, Catherine Linton, or Earnshaw, or however she was called—she must have been a changeling[34]—wicked little soul! She told me she had been walking the earth these twenty years: a just punishment for her mortal transgressions, I've no doubt!"

Scarcely were these words uttered, when I recollected the association of Heathcliff's with Catherine's name in the book, which had completely slipped from my memory till thus awakened. I blushed at my inconsideration; but without showing further consciousness of the offence, I hastened to add, "The truth is, sir, I passed the first part of the night in"—here, I stopped afresh—I was about to say "perusing those old volumes," then it would have revealed my knowledge of their written, as well as their printed contents; so correcting myself, I went on—"in spelling over the name scratched on that window-ledge. A monotonous occupation, calculated to set me asleep, like counting, or—"

"What *can* you mean, by talking in this way to *me!*" thundered Heathcliff with savage vehemence. "How—how *dare* you, under my roof—God! he's mad to speak so!" And he struck his forehead with rage.

I did not know whether to resent this language, or pursue my explanation; but he seemed so powerfully affected that I took pity and proceeded with my dreams, affirming I had never heard the appellation of "Catherine Linton" before, but reading it often over produced an impression which personified itself when I had no longer my imagination under control.

Heathcliff gradually fell back into the shelter of the bed as I spoke, finally sitting down almost concealed behind it. I guessed, however, by his irregular and intercepted breathing, that he struggled to vanquish an access of violent emotion.

Not liking to show him that I heard the conflict, I continued my toilette rather noisily, looked at my watch, and soliloquised on the length of the night: "Not three o'clock yet! I could have taken oath it had been six—time stagnates here—we must surely have retired to rest at eight!"

"Always at nine in winter, and always rise at four," said my host, suppressing a groan; and, as I fancied, by the motion of his shadow's arm, dashing a tear from his eyes.

"Mr. Lockwood," he added, "you may go into my room; you'll only be in the way, coming down stairs so early: and your childish outcry has sent sleep to the devil for me."

"And for me too," I replied. "I'll walk in the yard till daylight, and then I'll be off; and you need not dread a repetition of my intrusion. I am now quite cured of seeking pleasure in society, be it country or town. A sensible man ought to find sufficient company in himself."

"Delightful company!" muttered Heathcliff. "Take the candle, and go where you please. I shall join you directly. Keep out of the yard, though—the dogs are unchained—and the house—Juno mounts sentinel there—and—nay, you can only ramble about the steps and passages—but away with you! I'll come in two minutes."

I obeyed, so far as to quit the chamber; when, ignorant where the narrow lobbies led, I stood still, and was witness, involuntarily, to a piece of superstition on the part of my landlord, which belied, oddly, his apparent sense.

He got on to the bed, and wrenched open the lattice, bursting, as he pulled at it, into an uncontrollable passion of tears.

"Come in! come in!" he sobbed. "Cathy, do come. Oh do—*once* more! Oh! my heart's darling, hear me *this* time—Catherine, at last!"[35]

The spectre showed a spectre's ordinary caprice; it gave no sign of being; but the snow and wind whirled wildly through, even reaching my station, and blowing out the light.

There was such anguish in the gush of grief that accompanied this raving, that my compassion made me overlook its folly, and I drew off, half angry to have listened at all, and vexed at having related my ridiculous nightmare, since it produced that agony; though *why* was beyond my comprehension.

I descended cautiously to the lower regions and landed in the back-kitchen, where a gleam of fire, raked compactly together, enabled me to rekindle my candle.

Nothing was stirring except a brindled, grey cat, which crept from the ashes, and saluted me with a querulous mew.

Two benches, shaped in sections of a circle, nearly enclosed the hearth; on one of these I stretched myself, and Grimalkin[36] mounted the other. We were both of us nodding, ere any one invaded our retreat; and then it was Joseph, shuffling down a wooden ladder that vanished in the roof through a trap, the ascent to his garret, I suppose.

He cast a sinister look at the little flame which I had enticed to play between the ribs,[37] swept the cat from its elevation, and bestowing himself in the vacancy, commenced the operation of stuffing a three-inch pipe with tobacco; my presence in his sanctum was evidently esteemed a piece of impudence too shameful for remark. He silently applied the tube to his lips, folded his arms, and puffed away.

I let him enjoy the luxury, unannoyed; and after sucking out the last wreath, and heaving a profound sigh, he got up, and departed as solemnly as he came.

35 Italics are used precisely and judiciously here to express Heathcliff's unresolved longing. His words echo those of Byron's Manfred beseeching the phantom of Astarte:

> Speak to me! though it be in wrath;—but say—
> I reck not what—but let me hear thee once—
> This once—once more! (*Manfred,* II, iv, ll. 515–517)

It would be hard to overestimate the influence of Byron (1788–1824), both his life and his works, on Brontë, and this allusion to *Manfred* is richly suggestive. Manfred and Astarte are brother and sister, and their love is both inevitable and forbidden. Like *Manfred, Wuthering Heights* explores a forbidden passion and the fascination of a self that is "both same and different" (Loren Glass, "Blood and Affection: The Poetics of Incest in *Manfred* and *Parisina,*" *Romanticism,* 34:2 [Summer 1995], pp. 211–219). The crimes for which Manfred is finally punished remain unspecified, but they are connected to Astarte's death and to his incestuous love for her. Brontë read Thomas Moore's *Letters and Journals of Lord Byron with Notices of his Life* (1833) and knew about Byron's love for his half-sister Augusta Leigh. The first name of one of the principal heroines of her Gondal poems is Augusta.

The Byronic hero was born in *Childe Harold's Pilgrimage* (1812–1818). He is wounded, proud, and defiant, but also capable of a devotion so intense that it dwarfs the feelings of everyone around him. His avatars appear regularly in nineteenth-century fiction, and contemporary reviewers of *Wuthering Heights* easily identified Heathcliff as one of them. One of the five reviews that Brontë clipped and saved compared Heathcliff to Conrad, the hero of Byron's best-selling verse tale, *The Corsair* (1814), who is "linked to one virtue and a thousand crimes" (Miriam Allott, *The Brontës: The Critical Heritage* [London: Routledge & Kegan Paul, 1974], p. 220).

In this scene, Brontë contrasts Heathcliff's tormented and frustrated longing for union with something outside the self to Lockwood's horror at the invasion of something outside the self. As Eugenia C. DeLamotte observes, "Even barricading the window will not keep it out; even wrenching open the lattice will not bring it in" (*Perils of the Night: A Feminist Study of Nineteenth-Century Gothic* [Oxford: Oxford Univ. Press, 1990], p. 132).

36 A name given to an old female cat *(OED).* In the opening scene of *Macbeth* (a play Brontë knew well and alludes to in her poems), one of the three witches calls her familiar "Graymalkin."

37 The ribs belong to the fireplace grate, the metal frame that holds the fuel.

A more elastic footstep entered next, and now I opened my mouth for a "good morning," but closed it again, the salutation unachieved; for Hareton Earnshaw was performing his orisons,[38] *sotto voce,*[39] in a series of curses directed against every object he touched, while he rummaged a corner for a spade or shovel to dig through the drifts. He glanced over the back of the bench dilating his nostrils, and thought as little of exchanging civilities with me as with my companion, the cat.

I guessed by his preparations that egress was allowed, and leaving my hard couch, made a movement to follow him. He noticed this, and thrust at an inner door with the end of his spade, intimating by an inarticulate sound, that there was the place where I must go, if I changed my locality.

It opened into the house,[40] where the females were already astir; Zillah urging flakes of flame up the chimney with a colossal bellows; and Mrs. Heathcliff, kneeling on the hearth, reading a book by the aid of the blaze.

She held her hand interposed between the furnace-heat and her eyes, and seemed absorbed in her occupation: desisting from it only to chide the servant for covering her with sparks, or to push away a dog, now and then, that snoozled[41] its nose over forwardly into her face.

I was surprised to see Heathcliff there also. He stood by the fire, his back towards me, just finishing a stormy scene to poor Zillah, who ever and anon interrupted her labour to pluck up the corner of her apron, and heave an indignant groan.

"And you, you worthless—" he broke out as I entered, turning to his daughter-in-law, and employing an epithet as harmless as duck or sheep, but generally represented by a dash.[42]

"There you are at your idle tricks again! The rest of them do earn their bread—you live on my charity! Put your trash away, and find something to do. You shall pay me for the plague of having you eternally in my sight—do you hear, damnable jade?"

38 Prayers, here used ironically.

39 In music, *sotto voce* directs the player or vocalist to soften his tones. Compare Charlotte's use of the term in *Jane Eyre*: "'I will indeed send her to school soon,' murmured Mrs. Reed, *sotto voce*."

40 As above, the sitting room.

41 Nuzzled. The dogs that reacted so fiercely to Lockwood nose Mrs. Heathcliff affectionately.

42 Here and elsewhere in his narrative, Lockwood omits words that would be offensive in polite society. In the following paragraph, Heathcliff addresses his daughter-in-law as a "damnable jade" or worthless horse. Presumably, he uses the name of an animal on this earlier occasion, but one that Lockwood will not name (bitch?). In her "Editor's Preface to the New Edition of *Wuthering Heights*," Charlotte imagines how her sister's novel looks to "other people" who have been "trained from their cradle to observe the utmost evenness of manner and guardedness of language." They will

> hardly know what to make of the rough, strong utterance, the harshly manifested passions, the unbridled aversions, and headlong partialities of unlettered moorland hinds and rugged moorland squires, who have grown up untaught and unchecked, except by mentors as harsh as themselves. A large class of readers, likewise, will suffer greatly from the introduction into the pages of this work of words printed with all their letters, which it has become the custom to represent by the initial and final letter only—a blank line filling the interval. I may as well say at once that, for this circumstance, it is out of my power to apologize; deeming it, myself, a rational plan to write words at full length. The practice of hinting by single letters those expletives with which profane and violent persons are wont to garnish their discourse, strikes me as a proceeding which, however well meant, is weak and futile. I cannot tell what good it does—what feeling it spares—what horror it conceals. (this edition, pp. 441–442)

“I’ll put my trash away because you can make me, if I refuse,” answered the young lady, closing her book, and throwing it on a chair. “But I’ll not do anything, though you should swear your tongue out, except what I please!”

Heathcliff lifted his hand, and the speaker sprang to a safer distance, obviously acquainted with its weight.

Having no desire to be entertained by a cat and dog combat, I stepped forward briskly, as if eager to partake the warmth of the hearth, and innocent of any knowledge of the interrupted dispute. Each had enough decorum to suspend further hostilities; Heathcliff placed his fists out of temptation, in his pockets: Mrs. Heathcliff curled her lip, and walked to a seat far off, where she kept her word by playing the part of a statue during the remainder of my stay.

That was not long. I declined joining their breakfast, and, at the first gleam of dawn, took an opportunity of escaping into the free air, now clear, and still, and cold as impalpable ice.

My landlord hallooed for me to stop ere I reached the bottom of the garden, and offered to accompany me across the moor. It was well he did, for the whole hill-back was one billowy,[43] white ocean; the swells and falls not indicating corresponding rises and depressions in the ground—many pits, at least, were filled to a level; and entire ranges of mounds, the refuse of the quarries, blotted from the chart which my yesterday’s walk left pictured in my mind.[44]

I had remarked on one side of the road, at intervals of six or seven yards, a line of upright stones, continued through the whole length of the barren:[45] these were erected, and daubed with lime, on purpose to serve as guides in the dark, and also, when a fall,[46] like the present, confounded the deep swamps on either hand with the firmer path: but, excepting a dirty dot pointing up here and there, all traces of their existence had vanished; and my companion found it necessary to warn me frequently to steer to the right or left, when I imagined I was following, correctly, the windings of the road.

43 Brontë describes the moors as “billowy” in one of her poems, “I paused on the threshold I turned to the sky,” probably written while she was a teacher at Law Hill in Halifax. In another poem we know was written there in December 1838, “A little while, a little while,” she also uses the word “billowy” to describe a landscape that combines features of Gondal, the imaginary kingdom she and Anne created, with others belonging to the Yorkshire world in which they lived. The poem’s setting is a wide common ringed by mountains and populated by both “Wild moor-sheep” and deer:

> That was the scene—I knew it well
> I knew the pathways far and near
> That winding o’er each billowy swell
> Marked out the tracks of wandering deer

For more about the combinatory landscape of *Wuthering Heights,* see Chapter 1, note 2, above.

44 As Lockwood now fully understands, the landscape is treacherous, and he cannot find his way back to the Grange without Heathcliff’s help. Brontë’s poem “It was night and on the mountains” describes snow so deep that even the shepherd who knows his pastures well stands “a wildered stranger/ On his own unbounded moor.” Stone quarries were an important part of the economy of the West Riding in the nineteenth century, and abandoned quarries were a hazard.

45 A tract of land producing little or no vegetation. The upright stones, coated with lime to mark the path, can’t be seen after the heavy snowfall. Even in daylight, Lockwood has to depend on Heathcliff or Hareton, who know the way from the Heights to the Grange.

46 Snowfall.

We exchanged little conversation, and he halted at the entrance of Thrushcross park, saying, I could make no error there. Our adieux were limited to a hasty bow, and then I pushed forward, trusting to my own resources, for the porter's lodge is untenanted as yet.

The distance from the gate to the Grange is two miles: I believe I managed to make it four; what with losing myself among the trees, and sinking up to the neck in snow, a predicament which only those who have experienced it can appreciate. At any rate, whatever were my wanderings, the clock chimed twelve as I entered the house; and that gave exactly an hour for every mile of the usual way from Wuthering Heights.

My human fixture and her satellites rushed to welcome me; exclaiming, tumultuously, they had completely given me up; everybody conjectured that I perished last night; and they were wondering how they must set about the search for my remains.

I bid them be quiet, now that they saw me returned, and, benumbed to my very heart, I dragged up-stairs, whence, after putting on dry clothes and pacing to and fro, thirty or forty minutes, to restore the animal heat, I am adjourned to my study, feeble as a kitten, almost too much so to enjoy the cheerful fire and smoking coffee which the servant has prepared for my refreshment.

CHAPTER 4

What vain weather-cocks we are![1] I, who had determined to hold myself independent of all social intercourse, and thanked my stars that, at length, I had lighted on a spot where it was next to impracticable—I, weak wretch, after maintaining till dusk a struggle with low spirits and solitude, was finally compelled to strike my colours;[2] and, under pretence of gaining information concerning the necessities of my establishment, I desired Mrs. Dean, when she brought in supper, to sit down while I ate it, hoping sincerely she would prove a regular gossip, and either rouse me to animation or lull me to sleep by her talk.

"You have lived here a considerable time," I commenced; "did you not say sixteen years?"

"Eighteen, sir; I came, when the mistress[3] was married, to wait on her; after she died, the master retained me for his housekeeper."

"Indeed."

There ensued a pause. She was not a gossip, I feared, unless about her own affairs, and those could hardly interest me.

However, having studied[4] for an interval, with a fist on either knee, and a cloud of meditation over her ruddy countenance, she ejaculated—

"Ah, times are greatly changed since then!"

"Yes," I remarked, "you've seen a good many alterations, I suppose?"

1 "Vain" and "vaine" (or "vane") go back to different roots. Lockwood's pun acknowledges both his changeability and the futility of his determination to avoid company. Brontë is probably recalling *Love's Labour's Lost* IV.i.94: "What plume of fethers is he that indited this letter? What vaine? What Wethercock?"

2 A nautical and military phrase that refers to lowering the flag or the topsail as a sign of surrender.

3 Catherine Earnshaw Linton. The date of her marriage and of Nelly's moving with her to the Grange is March 1783.

4 Thought intently.

"I have: and troubles too," she said.

"Oh, I'll turn the talk on my landlord's family!" I thought to myself. "A good subject to start—and that pretty girl—widow, I should like to know her history; whether she be a native of the country, or, as is more probable, an exotic that the surly indigenae[5] will not recognise for kin."

With this intention I asked Mrs. Dean why Heathcliff let Thrushcross Grange, and preferred living in a situation and residence so much inferior.

"Is he not rich enough to keep the estate in good order?" I enquired.

"Rich, sir!" she returned. "He has, nobody knows what money, and every year it increases. Yes, yes, he's rich enough to live in a finer house than this; but he's very near—close-handed; and, if he had meant to flit to Thrushcross Grange, as soon as he heard of a good tenant, he could not have borne to miss the chance of getting a few hundreds more. It is strange people should be so greedy, when they are alone in the world!"

"He had a son, it seems?"

"Yes, he had one—he is dead."

"And that young lady, Mrs. Heathcliff, is his widow?"

"Yes."

"Where did she come from originally?"

"Why, sir, she is my late master's daughter; Catherine Linton was her maiden name.[6] I nursed her, poor thing! I did wish Mr. Heathcliff would remove here, and then we might have been together again."

"What, Catherine Linton!" I exclaimed, astonished. But a minute's reflection convinced me it was not my ghostly Catherine. "Then," I continued, "my predecessor's name was Linton?"

"It was."

"And who is that Earnshaw, Hareton Earnshaw, who lives with Mr. Heathcliff? Are they relations?"

"No; he is the late Mrs. Linton's nephew."[7]

5 Natives of the country; aboriginals. Mrs. Heathcliff does not seem to Lockwood to belong to the world of Wuthering Heights, any more than he himself does. His word for the inhabitants of the Heights parades its Latin origin, once again calling attention to his London breeding.

6 Although Heathcliff always calls Catherine Linton (Mrs. Heathcliff) "Catherine," partly to distinguish her from her mother, whom he almost always calls "Cathy," Nelly and Edgar usually call the second Catherine "Cathy." I refer to the younger Catherine consistently as "Cathy" in the notes to distinguish her from her mother, whom I refer to as "Catherine."

7 Nelly places Hareton in relation to Catherine Earnshaw Linton, not to her brother, Hindley Earnshaw, who is Hareton's father. She also places Cathy Linton in relation to Edgar Linton, her father, rather than in relation to Catherine Earnshaw Linton, her mother. Nelly goes on to describe Hareton as "the last" of the Earnshaws and Cathy as the last of the Lintons. For more about the two families and the genealogy of the characters, see the Introduction and the Genealogical Chart in this edition.

"The young lady's[8] cousin, then?"

"Yes; and her husband was her cousin also—one, on the mother's—the other, on the father's side—Heathcliff married Mr. Linton's sister."

"I see the house at Wuthering Heights has 'Earnshaw' carved over the front door. Are they an old family?"

"Very old, sir; and Hareton is the last of them, as our Miss Cathy is of us—I mean, of the Lintons. Have you been to Wuthering Heights? I beg pardon for asking; but I should like to hear how she is!"

"Mrs. Heathcliff? She looked very well, and very handsome; yet, I think, not very happy."

"Oh dear, I don't wonder! And how did you like the master?"

"A rough fellow, rather, Mrs. Dean. Is not that his character?"

"Rough as a saw-edge, and hard as whinstone![9] The less you meddle with him the better."

"He must have had some ups and downs in life to make him such a churl.[10] Do you know anything of his history?"

"It's a cuckoo's, sir.[11] I know all about it, except where he was born, and who were his parents, and how he got his money, at first —And Hareton has been cast out like an unfledged dunnock[12]—The unfortunate lad is the only one, in all this parish, that does not guess how he has been cheated!"

"Well, Mrs. Dean, it will be a charitable deed to tell me something of my neighbours—I feel I shall not rest, if I go to bed; so, be good enough to sit, and chat an hour."

"Oh, certainly, sir! I'll just fetch a little sewing, and then sit as long as you please, but you've caught cold; I saw you shivering, and you must have some gruel[13] to drive it out."

The worthy woman bustled off; and I crouched nearer the fire: my head felt hot, and the rest of me chill: moreover I was excited, almost to a pitch of foolishness through my nerves and brain. This caused me to feel, not uncomfortable, but rather fearful, as I am still, of serious effects from the incidents of to-day and yesterday.

8 Cathy's. Cathy and Hareton are first cousins.

9 A generic name for various hard, dark rocks, including those in the neighborhood of Wuthering Heights.

10 A rude, low-born character.

11 Cuckoos are brood parasites that lay their eggs in other birds' nests, including those of the "dunnock" or hedge-sparrow. Hareton has been flung out of the nest unfeathered; in other words, he has been deprived too early of a parent's protection and cheated of his inheritance. *A History of British Birds,* a book the Brontës owned and perused with admiration, contains a detailed account of how the young cuckoo gets rid of the hedge-sparrow's offspring and "becomes the sole object of the care of its foster parents" (Thomas Bewick, *A History of British Birds* [Newcastle: J. Blackwell and Co., 1847], vol. 1, p. 269).

More than one cuckoo usurper has been cited as a historical model for Heathcliff. The most famous is "Welsh Brunty," a child said to have been found in the hold of a merchant vessel traveling from Liverpool to Ireland and adopted by Patrick Brontë's great-grandfather. Although this story continues to be treated as a source for the novel, Juliet Barker points out that it is a fanciful fabrication. It didn't inspire the novel but was inspired by it and first recorded almost fifty years after *Wuthering Heights* was written ("The Brontës in Ireland," *New York Times,* Dec. 3, 1995). Jack Sharp, whose history resembles Heathcliff's less closely than Welsh's, is a more likely influence. An orphan adopted and brought up by his uncle, Jack Sharp took over his uncle's business, displacing the legitimate heir and then ruining him, perhaps by leading him to drink and gamble. Sharp built Law Hill, the building that housed the boarding school where Brontë briefly taught, and his story was well known there. Sharp was also reputed to have had a manservant named Joseph (Christine Alexander and Margaret Smith, eds., *The Oxford Companion to the Brontës* [Oxford: Oxford Univ. Press, 2003], p. 292; and Winifred Gérin, *Emily Brontë: A Biography* [Oxford: Oxford Univ. Press, 1971], pp. 75–80).

12 Hedge-sparrow (see the previous note).

13 A very thin porridge made by boiling a small quantity of oats in water or milk and often prescribed for invalids and those recovering from an illness.

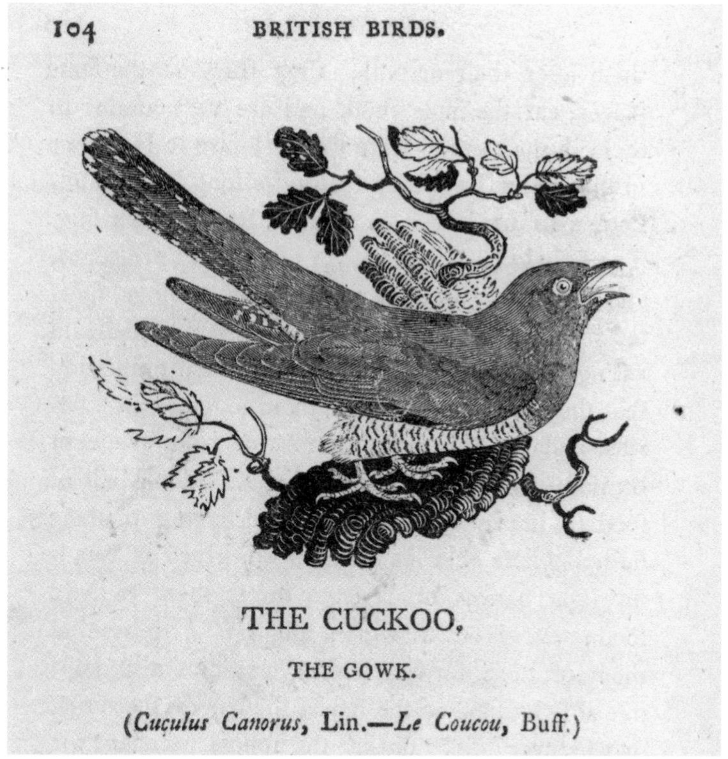

Wood engraving of a cuckoo from Thomas Bewick's *A History of British Birds* (Volume 1, "Land Birds," 1797, and Volume 2, "Water Birds," 1804). Patrick Brontë owned a copy, and Bewick's illustrations made an indelible impression on the Brontë children. At the start of *Jane Eyre,* Jane is admiring Bewick's pictures when her mean-spirited cousin John Reed finds her. He tells her she is a "dependent" with no right to "our books" and hurls the Bewick back at her with such force that she falls, striking her head.

She returned presently, bringing a smoking basin and a basket of work; and, having placed the former on the hob,[14] drew in her seat, evidently pleased to find me so companionable.

"Before I came to live here," she commenced,[15] waiting no further invitation to her story, "I was almost always at Wuthering Heights because my mother had nursed Mr. Hindley Earnshaw, that was Hareton's father, and I got used to playing with the children—I ran errands too, and helped to make hay, and hung about the farm ready for anything that anybody would set me to."[16]

14 A place where pots can be set to warm in a fireplace.

15 So begins Nelly's story in earnest; "she commenced" reminds us that her narrative is embedded in Lockwood's. W. H. Stevenson calls the novel's form of narration "double-third-person": "Lockwood tells us what Nelly Dean told him." This form was "unique in 1847" and remains "unusual" still ("*Wuthering Heights:* The Facts," *Essays in Criticism,* 55:2 [1985], p. 153). Other narratives are also embedded in Nelly's narrative, just as Catherine's narrative, written in the margins of her Testament, has already been embedded in Lockwood's. A succession of narratives framing other narratives is often compared to a set of Chinese boxes of graduated sizes, each one nested inside another. Marie-Laure Ryan suggests that we visualize embedded narratives instead as "a 'stack,' like the spring-loaded stack of plates at a cafeteria. Each successive narrative pushes the one framing it out of view the way the plates do as they are stacked one [on] top of the other. Take a plate off, and the one supporting it comes back into view in the same way a framing narrative reappears when we leave the narrative embedded in it" (H. Porter Abbott, *The Cambridge Introduction to Narrative* [Cambridge: Cambridge Univ. Press, 2008], p. 29).

16 Beginning with the next paragraph, I omit quotation marks around the story Nelly tells Lockwood until Chapter 7, when she interrupts her narrative of past events and returns to present time and her conversation with Lockwood. This follows the practice of both 1847 and modern editions of the novel, which seek to avoid the confusion of printing banks of quotation marks. In this edition, I have also inserted a vertical space into the text to mark the transitions from Lockwood's narration to Nelly's and from Nelly's narration back to Lockwood's.

****

One fine summer morning—it was the beginning of harvest, I remember—Mr. Earnshaw, the old master, came down stairs, dressed for a journey; and, after he had told Joseph what was to be done during the day, he turned to Hindley, and Cathy, and me—for I sat eating my porridge with them, and he said, speaking to his son, "Now my bonny man, I'm going to Liverpool to-day . . . What shall I bring you? You may choose what you like; only let it be little, for I shall walk there and back; sixty miles each way,[17] that is a long spell!"

Hindley named a fiddle, and then he asked Miss Cathy; she was hardly six years old, but she could ride any horse in the stable, and she chose a whip.

He did not forget me, for he had a kind heart, though he was rather severe sometimes. He promised to bring me a pocketful of apples and pears, and then he kissed his children good bye, and set off.

It seemed a long while to us all—the three days of his absence—and often did little Cathy ask when he would be home: Mrs. Earnshaw expected him by supper-time on the third evening; and she put the meal off hour after hour; there were no signs of his coming, however, and at last the children got tired of running down to the gate to look—Then it grew dark, she would have had them to bed, but they begged sadly to be allowed to stay up; and, just about eleven o'clock, the door-latch was raised quietly and in stept the master. He threw himself into a chair, laughing and groaning, and bid them all stand off, for he was nearly killed—he would not have such another walk for the three kingdoms.[18]

"And at the end of it, to be flighted[19] to death!" he said opening his great coat, which he held bundled up in his arms. "See here, wife; I was never so beaten[20] with anything in my life; but you must e'en take it as a gift of God; though it's as dark almost as if it came from the devil."

We crowded round, and, over Miss Cathy's head, I had a peep at a dirty, ragged, black-haired child, big enough both to walk and

17 Approximately the distance from Haworth to Liverpool. This small fact—that Mr. Earnshaw walks the sixty miles to Liverpool and back in 1771—would have reminded Brontë's contemporary readers of how importantly travel had changed by 1847. The opening of the Liverpool and Manchester Railway in 1830 inaugurated the Railway Age. It was the first rail link between two major cities in England as well as the first passenger railway that ran on a timetable and was powered mainly by steam engines. The Manchester and Leeds Railway opened in 1839 and was soon linked to the Liverpool and Manchester line.

In a letter to Ellen Nussey, Charlotte reported Branwell's success in securing employment as a railway clerk: "A distant relation of mine, one Patrick Boanerges, has set off to seek his fortune, in the wild, wandering, adventurous, romantic, knight-errant-like capacity of clerk on the Leeds and Manchester Railroad. Leeds and Manchester, where are they? Cities in a wilderness–like Tadmor, alias Palmyra–are they not?" (Margaret Smith, ed., *The Letters of Charlotte Brontë,* 3 vols. [Oxford: Clarendon Press, 2000], 1, p. 228). Barker, who quotes this letter, hears "derision" in it, but we can also hear Charlotte's romantic enthusiasm for the strange, vast, and exciting metropolitan world the railroad brought nearer to people living in rural villages like Haworth. Such enthusiasm helps to account for the three sisters' investment of a portion of their small capital in railroad shares. Emily managed this investment and, according to Charlotte, "made herself mistress of the necessary degree of knowledge for conducting the matter, by dint of carefully reading every paragraph & every advertisement in the news-papers that related to rail-roads" (Barker, "The Brontës in Ireland," p. 346; Smith, *Letters,* 2, p. 390).

18 England, Ireland, and Scotland. The Acts of Union joined the Kingdoms of England and Scotland to create Great Britain in 1706 and 1707. The Acts of Union united the Kingdoms of Great Britain and Ireland in 1800.

19 Frightened.

20 Bruised with walking or hard work (Joseph Wright, *English Dialect Dictionary* [London, Oxford, New York: G. P. Putnam's Sons, 1898]).

A Train of the First Class of Carriages, with the Mail.
A Train of the Second Class, for outside Passengers.

A Train of Waggons, with Goods, etc., etc.
A Train of Carriages with Cattle.

PLATE XX
TRAVELLING ON THE LIVERPOOL AND MANCHESTER RAILWAY

"Travelling on the Liverpool to Manchester Railway," 1831, from "Ackermann's Long Prints." Plates show trains of first-class carriages with the mail; second-class carriages for outside passengers; wagons with freight; and carriages with cattle.

21 "Unintelligible speech, belonging to no known language" *(OED)*. Heathcliff's speech combines with his dark skin and black hair to mark an origin that has remained mysterious. We don't know what language this child speaks any more than we know how dark he is. What we do know is that, importantly, he is racially different from the Earnshaws. His having been found in Liverpool, a port city, is a key fact. A stray child in Liverpool's streets might trace his ancestry back to Indian sailors, Irish immigrants, African slaves, gypsies, Americans, and others.

Most of the novel's characters—Nelly, Mrs. Earnshaw, Hindley, Mrs. Linton, Isabella, and Lockwood—identify Heathcliff as a gypsy, and this account of his origins continues to be not just probable but richly germane to Brontë's representation of social inequality. People who were called gypsies belong to a widely dispersed ethnic group nomadic throughout Europe. They called themselves Romani. The name "gypsy," a corruption of "Egyptian," belongs to a time when distinctions among non-European people were unclear to most Europeans, but it was known as early as 1782 that the Romani spoke an Indo-Aryan language with affinities to Hindi. For most of the characters, gypsies are foreign, lazy, disreputable, and predatory, but Brontë would also have been familiar with representations of gypsies as emblems of rural poverty and hardship and as noble savages or exotics who led a free, simple life in close contact with nature.

Terry Eagleton's argument that Heathcliff is Irish depends on metaphorical flourish rather than historical evidence, as Eagleton himself acknowledges. If Heathcliff has some Irish in him, Eagleton writes, it's because he is a "little Caliban" with "a nature on which nurture will never stick; and that is simply an English way of saying that he is quite possibly Irish" (*Heathcliff and the Great Hunger: Studies in Irish Culture* [London: Verso, 1995], pp. 3–11). Branwell visited Liverpool in August 1845, when Emily may have been thinking about her novel, but Irish immigrants only flooded the city two years later, in 1847 and 1848, at the height of the Irish famine. In 1861, Henry Mayhew would describe them as "mere paupers, half-naked and starving." They "landed, for the most part, during the winter, and became, immediately on landing, applicants for parochial relief" (Henry Mayhew, *London Labour and the London Poor*, vol. 1, p. 112 [Digital edition: http://hdl.handle.net/10427/53837. From the Edwin C. Bolles papers (MS004), Digital Collections and Archives, Tufts University, Medford, MA]). The Brontës could have seen pictures of them in the *Illustrated London News*—"scarecrows with a few rags on them and an animal growth of black hair almost obscuring their features" (Gérin, *Emily Brontë*, p. 226)—but not in time to influence Emily's conception of Heathcliff.

The case for Heathcliff's African ancestry directs our attention to the date of his arrival at the Heights, which is 1771. Until 1807, when the Slave Trade Act was passed, Liverpool was the most important slaving port in Britain. The New Exchange/Town Hall was ornamented with "busts of blackamoors and elephants, emblematical of the African

talk—indeed, its face looked older than Catherine's—yet, when it was set on its feet, it only stared round, and repeated over and over again, some gibberish[21] that nobody could understand. I was frightened, and Mrs. Earnshaw was ready to fling it out of doors: she did fly up[22]—asking how he could fashion to bring that gipsy brat into the house, when they had their own bairns to feed and fend for? What he meant to do with it, and whether he were mad?

The master tried to explain the matter; but, he was really half dead with fatigue, and all that I could make out, amongst her scolding, was a tale of his seeing it starving, and houseless, and as good as dumb in the streets of Liverpool, where he picked it up and inquired for its owner—Not a soul knew to whom it belonged, he said, and his money and time being both limited, he thought it better to take it home with him at once, than run into vain expences there, because he was determined he would not leave as he found it.

Well, the conclusion was that my mistress grumbled herself calm; and Mr. Earnshaw told me to wash it, and give it clean things, and let it sleep with the children.

Hindley and Cathy contented themselves with looking and listening till peace was restored: then, both began searching their father's pockets for the presents he had promised them. The former was a boy of fourteen, but when he drew out, what had been a fiddle crushed to morsels in the great coat, he blubbered aloud, and Cathy, when she learnt the master had lost her whip in attending on the stranger, showed her humour[23] by grinning and spitting at the stupid little thing, earning for her pains a sound blow from her father to teach her cleaner[24] manners.

They entirely refused to have it in bed with them, or even in their room, and I had no more sense, so I put it on the landing of the stairs, hoping it might be gone on the morrow. By chance, or else attracted by hearing his voice, it crept to Mr. Earnshaw's door and there he found it on quitting his chamber. Inquiries were made as to how it got there; I was obliged to confess, and in recompense for my cowardice and inhumanity was sent out of the house.

Four-Masted Clipper Ship in Liverpool Harbour, c. 1810, oil on panel painted by Robert Salmon (1775–1848). American clipper ships like this one were a frequent sight in the Liverpool harbor.

trade" responsible for the city's prosperity. The date of Earnshaw's walk to Liverpool (1771) is close to the date of a famous trial in which an English court ruled that an African American slave, James Sommersett, who had been brought by his owner to London, could not be compelled to return to the colonies and to slavery (Maja-Lisa Von Sneidern, "*Wuthering Heights* and the Liverpool Slave Trade," ELH, 62, 1 [1995], pp. 171–172). In her 2011 film adaptation of the novel, Andrea Arnold cast two black actors in the role of the young and older Heathcliff, although she had begun her search for an actor to play Heathcliff by "tramping the Dales and the odd gypsy site" (Richard Brooks, *The Sunday Times* [London], April 11, 2010, p. 12).

In her "Editor's Preface to the New Edition of Wuthering Heights," Charlotte elaborates on Earnshaw's description of the child he brings to the Heights. She quotes from memory, and quotes inaccurately. "Heathcliff, indeed, stands unredeemed," she writes; "never once swerving in his arrow-straight course to perdition, from the time when 'the little black-haired, swarthy thing, as dark as if it came from the Devil,' was first unrolled out of the bundle and set on its feet in the farm-house kitchen" (this edition, p. 443). Charlotte's description of Heathcliff as a "swarthy thing" is consistent with her reference to him, in the next paragraph, as neither "Lascar nor gipsy, but a man's shape animated by demon life—a Ghoul—an Afreet" (this edition, p. 444). A Lascar is an Indian sailor. Charlotte's reference to Ghouls and Afreets recalls a line from Byron's Oriental romance *The Giaour* (1813): "Then stalking to thy sullen grave—Go—and with Ghouls and Afrits rave." Ghouls (the word comes into English from Arabic) prey on human corpses, and Afreets are powerful demons in Muslim mythology. Charlotte does not mention a less exotic supernatural creature, the Brownie or Brown Man of the Moors, a Scottish folk figure who may also have influenced the creation of Heathcliff. Douglas Gifford makes the case for the influence of the Brownie on Heathcliff in "Hogg, Scottish Literature and *Wuthering Heights* or Was Heathcliff a Brownie," *Studies in Hogg and His World* (The James Hogg Society, no. 23, 2013), pp. 5–22.

22 Become (very) excited. Wright cites a related North Yorkshire dialect use of the phrase "to fly out of the head," meaning "to become excited or insane" (Wright, *English Dialect Dictionary).*

23 Her mood and temper.

24 More proper.

This was Heathcliff's first introduction to the family: on coming back a few days afterwards, for I did not consider my banishment perpetual, I found they had christened him "Heathcliff": it was the name of a son who died in childhood, and it has served him ever since, both for Christian and surname.

Miss Cathy and he were now very thick; but Hindley hated him, and to say the truth I did the same; and we plagued and went on with him shamefully, for I wasn't reasonable enough to feel my injustice, and the mistress never put in a word on his behalf, when she saw him wronged.

He seemed a sullen, patient child; hardened, perhaps, to ill-treatment: he would stand Hindley's blows without winking or shedding a tear, and my pinches moved him only to draw in a breath, and open his eyes as if he had hurt himself by accident, and nobody was to blame.

This endurance made old Earnshaw furious when he discovered his son persecuting the poor, fatherless child, as he called him. He took to Heathcliff strangely,[25] believing all he said (for that matter, he said precious little, and generally the truth), and petting him up far above Cathy, who was too mischievous and wayward for a favourite.

So, from the very beginning, he bred bad feeling in the house; and at Mrs. Earnshaw's death, which happened in less than two years after,[26] the young master had learnt to regard his father as an oppressor rather than a friend, and Heathcliff as a usurper of his parent's affections, and his privileges, and he grew bitter with brooding over these injuries.

I sympathised awhile, but when the children fell ill of the measles and I had to tend them, and take on me the cares of a woman at once,[27] I changed my ideas. Heathcliff was dangerously sick, and while he lay at the worst, he would have me constantly by his pillow; I suppose he felt I did a good deal for him, and he hadn't wit to guess that I was compelled to do it. However, I will say this, he was the quietest child that ever nurse watched over. The dif-

25 Some have suggested that Heathcliff is Mr. Earnshaw's illegitimate son. But on the principle of Occam's razor, the conjecture is weak: neither Mr. Earnshaw's preference for Heathcliff nor Mrs. Earnshaw's immediate dislike of him requires that he be Earnshaw's son.

26 In 1773.

27 After Mrs. Earnshaw's death, Nelly assumes full care of the children. She would have been sixteen years old, about Hindley's age. Catherine and Heathcliff are eight and nine years old, respectively.

ference between him and the others forced me to be less partial: Cathy and her brother harassed me terribly: *he* was as uncomplaining as a lamb; though hardness, not gentleness, made him give little trouble.

He got through, and the doctor affirmed it was in a great measure owing to me, and praised me for my care. I was vain of his commendations, and softened towards the being by whose means I earned them, and thus Hindley lost his last ally; still I couldn't dote on Heathcliff, and I wondered often what my master saw to admire so much in the sullen boy who never, to my recollection, repaid his indulgence by any sign of gratitude. He was not insolent to his benefactor; he was simply insensible, though knowing perfectly the hold he had on his heart, and conscious he had only to speak and all the house would be obliged to bend to his wishes.

As an instance, I remember Mr. Earnshaw once bought a couple of colts at the parish fair, and gave the lads each one. Heathcliff took the handsomest, but it soon fell lame, and when he discovered it, he said to Hindley,

"You must exchange horses with me; I don't like mine, and if you won't, I shall tell your father of the three thrashings you've given me this week, and show him my arm, which is black to the shoulder."

Hindley put out his tongue, and cuffed[28] him over the ears.

"You'd better do it, at once," he persisted, escaping to the porch (they were in the stable), "you will have to, and, if I speak of these blows, you'll get them again with interest."

"Off dog!" cried Hindley, threatening him with an iron weight, used for weighing potatoes and hay.

"Throw it," he replied, standing still, "and then I'll tell how you boasted that you would turn me out of doors as soon as he died, and see whether he will not turn you out directly."

Hindley threw it, hitting him on the breast, and down he fell, but staggered up immediately, breathless and white, and had not I prevented it, he would have gone just so to the master, and got full

28 Struck.

revenge by letting his condition plead for him, intimating who had caused it.

"Take my colt, gipsy, then!" said young Earnshaw, "and I pray that he may break your neck; take him, and be damned, you beggarly interloper! and wheedle my father out of all he has, only, afterwards, show him what you are, imp of Satan—And take that; I hope he'll kick out your brains!"

Heathcliff had gone to loose the beast, and shift it to his own stall—He was passing behind it, when Hindley finished his speech by knocking him under its feet, and without stopping to examine whether his hopes were fulfilled, ran away as fast as he could.

I was surprised to witness how coolly the child gathered himself up, and went on with his intention, exchanging saddles and all; and then sitting down on a bundle of hay to overcome the qualm which the violent blow occasioned, before he entered the house.

I persuaded him easily to let me lay the blame of his bruises on the horse; he minded little what tale was told since he had what he wanted. He complained so seldom, indeed, of such stirs as these, that I really thought him not vindictive—I was deceived, completely, as you will hear.

CHAPTER 5

In the course of time, Mr. Earnshaw began to fail. He had been active and healthy, yet his strength left him suddenly; and when he was confined to the chimney-corner he grew grievously irritable. A nothing vexed him, and suspected slights of his authority nearly threw him into fits.

This was especially to be remarked if any one attempted to impose upon, or domineer over his favourite: he was painfully jealous lest a word should be spoken amiss to him, seeming to have got into his head the notion that, because he liked Heathcliff, all hated, and longed to do him an ill-turn.

It was a disadvantage to the lad, for the kinder among us did not wish to fret the master, so we humoured his partiality; and that humouring was rich nourishment to the child's pride and black tempers. Still it became in a manner necessary; twice or thrice, Hindley's manifestations of scorn, while his father was near, roused the old man to a fury. He seized his stick to strike him, and shook with rage that he could not do it.

At last, our curate (we had a curate then who made the living[1] answer by teaching the little Lintons and Earnshaws, and farming his bit of land himself), he advised that the young man should be sent to college,[2] and Mr. Earnshaw agreed, though with a heavy spirit, for he said—

1 A curate in the Church of England is the clergyman who officiates in a parish or assists the incumbent in a parish. His "living" can refer to his benefice in the church, the duties he is required to perform, or the revenues he receives for performing them. Curates were low on the ecclesiastical ladder, but most were university graduates. Their advancement depended less on their own efforts than on patrons willing to use influence on their behalf. The Gimmerton curate's remuneration for performing his ecclesiastical duties is so meager that he has to supplement it by farming and by tutoring the children of the chief families in his parish.

2 Hindley, born in 1757, is now about seventeen years old, too old to continue being tutored by the curate. His father therefore decides to send him away to college, either a university or a preparatory secondary school.

"Hindley was naught, and would never thrive as where[3] he wandered."

I hoped heartily we should have peace now. It hurt me to think the master should be made uncomfortable by his own good deed. I fancied the discontent of age and disease arose from his family disagreements, as he would have it that it did—really, you know, sir, it was in his sinking frame.

We might have got on tolerably, notwithstanding, but for two people, Miss Cathy and Joseph, the servant; you saw him, I dare say, up yonder. He was, and is yet, most likely, the wearisomest, self-righteous pharisee[4] that ever ransacked a Bible to rake the promises to himself, and fling the curses on his neighbours. By his knack of sermonizing and pious discoursing, he contrived to make a great impression on Mr. Earnshaw, and, the more feeble the master became, the more influence he gained.

He was relentless in worrying him about his soul's concerns, and about ruling his children rigidly. He encouraged him to regard Hindley as a reprobate; and, night after night, he regularly grumbled out a long string of tales against Heathcliff and Catherine, always minding to flatter Earnshaw's weakness by heaping the heaviest blame on the last.

Certainly, she had ways with her such as I never saw a child take up before; and she put all of us past our patience fifty times and oftener in a day: from the hour she came down stairs, till the hour she went to bed, we had not a minute's security that she wouldn't be in mischief. Her spirits were always at high-water mark, her tongue always going—singing, laughing, and plaguing everybody who would not do the same. A wild, wick[5] slip she was—but, she had the bonniest eye, and sweetest smile, and lightest foot in the parish; and, after all, I believe she meant no harm; for when once she made you cry in good earnest, it seldom happened that she would not keep you company, and oblige you to be quiet that you might comfort her.

3 The sense is that Hindley will come to nothing no matter where he goes.

4 The Pharisees were noted for their rigorous observance of religious law, and Jesus criticized their hypocrisy.

5 A northern variant of "quick": full of life, lively *(OED)*.

The young Catherine (Shannon Beer) and the young Heathcliff (Solomon Glave) sharing a view of the moor in Andrea Arnold's film adaptation of *Wuthering Heights* (2011).

She was much too fond of Heathcliff. The greatest punishment we could invent for her was to keep her separate from him: yet she got chided more than any of us on his account.

In play, she liked exceedingly to act the little mistress; using her hands freely,[6] and commanding her companions: she did so to me, but I would not bear slapping and ordering; and so I let her know.

Now, Mr. Earnshaw did not understand jokes from his children: he had always been strict and grave with them; and Catherine, on her part, had no idea why her father should be crosser and less patient in his ailing condition than he was in his prime.

His peevish reproofs wakened in her a naughty delight to provoke him; she was never so happy as when we were all scolding her at once, and she defying us with her bold, saucy look, and her ready words; turning Joseph's religious curses into ridicule, baiting me, and doing just what her father hated most, showing how her pretended insolence, which he thought real, had more power over

6 Slapping.

Heathcliff than his kindness. How the boy would do *her* bidding in anything, and *his* only when it suited his own inclination.

After behaving as badly as possible all day, she sometimes came fondling to make it up at night.

"Nay, Cathy," the old man would say, "I cannot love thee; thou'rt worse than thy brother.[7] Go, say thy prayers, child, and ask God's pardon. I doubt[8] thy mother and I must rue that we ever reared thee!"

That made her cry, at first; and then, being repulsed continually hardened her, and she laughed if I told her to say she was sorry for her faults, and beg to be forgiven.

But the hour came, at last, that ended Mr. Earnshaw's troubles on earth. He died quietly in his chair one October evening, seated by the fire-side.[9]

A high wind blustered round the house, and roared in the chimney: it sounded wild and stormy, yet it was not cold, and we were all together—I, a little removed from the hearth, busy at my knitting, and Joseph reading his Bible near the table, (for the servants generally sat in the house then,[10] after their work was done). Miss Cathy had been sick, and that made her still; she leant against her father's knee, and Heathcliff was lying on the floor with his head in her lap.

I remember the master, before he fell into a doze, stroking her bonny hair—it pleased him rarely to see her gentle—and saying—

"Why canst thou not always be a good lass, Cathy?"

And she turned her face up to his, and laughed, and answered, "Why cannot you always be a good man, father?"

But as soon as she saw him vexed again, she kissed his hand, and said she would sing him to sleep. She began singing very low, till his fingers dropped from hers, and his head sank on his breast. Then I told her to hush, and not stir, for fear she should wake him. We all kept as mute as mice a full half-hour, and should have done longer, only Joseph, having finished his chapter, got up and said that he must rouse the master for prayers and bed. He stepped for-

7 "Thee," "thou," and "thy" are the familiar pronouns, used here by a parent addressing a child. It would be inappropriate for Catherine to use these pronouns when she addresses her father, so she uses the polite form "you" when she responds to him. Later, both Hindley and Joseph use the familiar pronouns when they address Hareton. Hareton uses them when he speaks condescendingly to Linton Heathcliff and when he wants to assert himself after Cathy orders him to bring her horse as if he were her servant (Irene Wiltshire, "Speech in Wuthering Heights: Joseph's Dialect and Charlotte's Emendations," *Brontë Studies,* 30 [March 2005], pp. 21–22).

8 Begin to be afraid that. Further on in the sentence, "rue" means "be sorry."

9 The year is 1777, and Catherine is now about twelve years old.

10 Nelly parenthetically notes the changes brought about by time and Hindley's efforts to gentrify the Heights. By 1801, when she is telling the story to Lockwood, it would no longer have been customary for servants to occupy the sitting room along with their masters.

ward, and called him by name, and touched his shoulder, but he would not move—so he took the candle and looked at him.

I thought there was something wrong as he set down the light; and seizing the children each by an arm, whispered them to "frame up-stairs, and make little din[11]—they might pray alone that evening—he had summut to do."

"I shall bid father good-night first," said Catherine, putting her arms round his neck, before we could hinder her.

The poor thing discovered her loss directly—she screamed out—

"Oh, he's dead, Heathcliff, he's dead!"

And they both set up a heart-breaking cry.

I joined my wail to theirs, loud and bitter; but Joseph asked what we could be thinking of to roar in that way over a saint in Heaven.

He told me to put on my cloak and run to Gimmerton for the doctor and the parson. I could not guess the use that either would be of, then. However, I went, through wind and rain, and brought one, the doctor, back with me; the other said he would come in the morning.

Leaving Joseph to explain matters, I ran to the children's room; their door was ajar. I saw they had never laid down, though it was past midnight; but they were calmer, and did not need me to console them. The little souls were comforting each other with better thoughts than I could have hit on; no parson in the world ever pictured Heaven so beautifully as they did, in their innocent talk; and while I sobbed and listened, I could not help wishing we were all there safe together.[12]

11 "Go upstairs, quietly."

12 Nelly's family name is "Dean," a word that can refer to a wide or deep vale or, in an ecclesiastical context, to a cleric holding a position of authority. Here she voices a belief that was widely shared in Victorian England: life in Heaven is better than life on earth, and families will be reunited there. Apparently Catherine and Heathcliff share her view of Heaven at this early stage of their lives.

CHAPTER 6

Mr. Hindley came home to the funeral; and—a thing that amazed us, and set the neighbours gossipping right and left—he brought a wife with him.[1]

What she was, and where she was born, he never informed us; probably, she had neither money nor name to recommend her, or he would scarcely have kept the union from his father.

She was not one that would have disturbed the house much on her own account. Every object she saw, the moment she crossed the threshold, appeared to delight her; and every circumstance that took place about her, except the preparing for the burial, and the presence of the mourners.

I thought she was half silly[2] from her behaviour while that went on; she ran into her chamber, and made me come with her, though I should have been dressing the children; and there she sat, shivering and clasping her hands, and asking repeatedly—

"Are they gone yet?"

Then she began describing with hysterical emotion the effect it produced on her to see black; and started, and trembled, and, at last, fell a weeping—and when I asked what was the matter, answered, she didn't know; but she felt so afraid of dying!

I imagined her as little likely to die as myself. She was rather thin, but young, and fresh complexioned, and her eyes sparkled as

1 Hindley, who is twenty-one years old, has secretly married Frances during his time away at college. We don't know her age.

2 Feeble-minded.

3 Apart from her sensitivity to sudden noises, Frances displays the classic symptoms of consumption, or tuberculosis, the disease that ended Emily Brontë's life as well as the lives of her brother and sister, Branwell and Anne.

4 Brontë does not tell us where Hindley's college is located, but Frances's designation as a "foreigner" may mean they met in the south, probably in the vicinity of London. Gaskell remarks on the sourness with which Yorkshire natives met non-natives: "a stranger can hardly ask a question without receiving some crusty reply, if, indeed, he receive any at all. Yet, if the 'foreigner' takes all this churlishness good-humouredly, or as a matter of course, and makes good any claim upon their latent kindliness and hospitality, they are faithful and generous, and thoroughly to be relied upon" (Elizabeth Gaskell, *The Life of Charlotte Brontë,* ed. Angus Easson [Oxford: Oxford Univ. Press, 1996], p. 19).

5 Another reference to the separation of servants and masters that makes the labor of the servants "less visible and creates a sharper distinction in everyday life between kin and other members of the household" (Beth Newman, "Wuthering Heights in its Context(s)," in *Social Issues in Literature: Class Conflict in Emily Brontë's Wuthering Heights,* ed. Dedria Bryfonski [Detroit: Greenhaven Press, 2011], p. 47). Hindley's altered dress and speech signal his new ambitions for his family.

6 The case containing dishes, probably the same oak dresser Lockwood remarked on earlier., Delf or delft was tin-glazed earthenware pottery, either plain white or decorated. Originating in the Netherlands in the sixteenth century (and named for the Dutch city of Delft), delftware was later produced in England as well. The main centers of production were London, Bristol, and Liverpool. The pottery at the Heights probably comes from Liverpool.

7 Nelly's strong word emphasizes the importance of both work and education in determining social position.

8 So long as.

bright as diamonds. I did remark, to be sure, that mounting the stairs made her breathe very quick, that the least sudden noise set her all in a quiver, and that she coughed troublesomely sometimes: but I knew nothing of what these symptoms portended,[3] and had no impulse to sympathize with her. We don't in general take to foreigners[4] here, Mr. Lockwood, unless they take to us first.

Young Earnshaw was altered considerably in the three years of his absence. He had grown sparer, and lost his colour, and spoke and dressed quite differently: and, on the very day of his return, he told Joseph and me we must thenceforth quarter ourselves in the back-kitchen, and leave the house[5] for him. Indeed he would have carpeted and papered a small spare room for a parlour; but his wife expressed such pleasure at the white floor and huge glowing fire-place, at the pewter dishes, and delf-case,[6] and dog-kennel, and the wide space there was to move about in, where they usually sat, that he thought it unnecessary to her comfort, and so dropped the intention.

She expressed pleasure, too, at finding a sister among her new acquaintance, and she prattled to Catherine, and kissed her, and ran about with her, and gave her quantities of presents, at the beginning. Her affection tired very soon, however, and when she grew peevish, Hindley became tyrannical. A few words from her, evincing a dislike to Heathcliff, were enough to rouse in him all his old hatred of the boy. He drove him from their company to the servants, deprived him of the instructions of the curate, and insisted that he should labour out of doors instead, compelling him to do so, as hard as any other lad on the farm.

He bore his degradation[7] pretty well at first, because Cathy taught him what she learnt, and worked or played with him in the fields. They both promised fair to grow up as rude as savages, the young master being entirely negligent how they behaved, and what they did, so[8] they kept clear of him. He would not even have seen after their going to church on Sundays, only Joseph and the curate

A delftware bowl possibly painted by William Jackson, Liverpool, England, ca. 1765–1770.

Drawing in India ink by Balthasar Klossowski de Rola, known as Balthus (1908–2001), illustrating "Parce que Cathy lui enseignait ce qu'elle apprenait." Balthus illustrated the first volume of *Wuthering Heights* in the early 1930s. This image shows Catherine and Heathcliff after Hindley has assumed control of the Heights and banished Heathcliff from the family: "He bore his degradation pretty well at first, because Cathy taught him what she learnt, and worked or played with him in the fields." Balthus's drawing depicts the intensity and harmony of teenage intimacy. Heathcliff appears dominant, yet only Catherine has access to the book and pen that are the properties of dominance in the novel.

reprimanded his carelessness when they absented themselves, and that reminded him to order Heathcliff a flogging, and Catherine a fast from dinner or supper.

But it was one of their chief amusements to run away to the moors in the morning and remain there all day, and the after-punishment grew a mere thing to laugh at. The curate might set as many chapters as he pleased for Catherine to get by heart,[9] and Joseph might thrash Heathcliff till his arm ached; they forgot everything the minute they were together again, at least the minute they had contrived some naughty plan of revenge, and many a time I've cried to myself to watch them growing more reckless daily, and I not daring to speak a syllable for fear of losing the small power I still retained over the unfriended[10] creatures.

One Sunday evening, it chanced that they were banished from the sitting-room, for making a noise, or a light offence of the kind, and when I went to call them to supper, I could discover them nowhere.

We searched the house, above and below, and the yard and stables; they were invisible; and, at last, Hindley in a passion told us to bolt the doors, and swore nobody should let them in that night.

The household went to bed; and I, too anxious to lie down, opened my lattice and put my head out to hearken, though it rained, determined to admit them in spite of the prohibition, should they return.

In a while, I distinguished steps coming up the road, and the light of a lantern glimmered through the gate.

I threw a shawl over my head and ran to prevent them from waking Mr. Earnshaw by knocking. There was Heathcliff, by himself; it gave me a start to see him alone.

"Where is Miss Catherine?" I cried hurriedly. "No accident, I hope?"

"At Thrushcross Grange," he answered, "and I would have been there too, but they had not the manners to ask me to stay."

9 Rote learning was a subject much debated in the nineteenth century. Maria and Richard Lovell Edgeworth eloquently opposed it in *Essays on Practical Education* (1798), but its proponents argued that filling "the storehouse of the memory is the rational business of education at a season of life when the powers of reason have not acquired a useful degree of action" (David Blair, *The Universal Preceptor* [1811], quoted in

"Well, you will catch it!"[11] I said, "you'll never be content till you're sent about your business. What in the world led you wandering to Thrushcross Grange?"

"Let me get off my wet clothes, and I'll tell you all about it, Nelly," he replied.

I bid him beware of rousing the master, and while he undressed, and I waited to put out the candle, he continued—

"Cathy and I escaped from the wash-house[12] to have a ramble at liberty, and getting a glimpse of the Grange lights, we thought we would just go and see whether the Lintons passed their Sunday evenings standing shivering in corners, while their father and mother sat eating and drinking, and singing and laughing, and burning their eyes out before the fire. Do you think they do? Or reading sermons, and being catechised[13] by their man-servant, and set to learn a column of Scripture names, if they don't answer properly?"

"Probably not," I responded. "They are good children, no doubt, and don't deserve the treatment you receive for your bad conduct."

"Don't you cant,[14] Nelly," he said, "nonsense! We ran from the top of the Heights to the park without stopping—Catherine completely beaten in the race, because she was barefoot. You'll have to seek for her shoes in the bog to-morrow. We crept through a broken hedge, groped our way up the path, and planted ourselves on a flower-plot under the drawing-room window. The light came from thence; they had not put up the shutters, and the curtains were only half closed. Both of us were able to look in by standing on the basement,[15] and clinging to the ledge, and we saw—Ah! it was beautiful—a splendid place carpeted with crimson, and crimson-covered chairs and tables, and a pure white ceiling bordered by gold, a shower of glass-drops hanging in silver chains from the centre, and shimmering with little soft tapers.[16] Old Mr. and Mrs. Linton were not there. Edgar and his sister had it entirely to themselves; shouldn't they have been happy? We should have

Marianne Thormählen, *The Brontës and Education* [Cambridge: Cambridge Univ. Press, 2007], p. 188). Rote learning had important practical advantages: little time and limited competence were required of teachers whose only task was to see that the child got it right. *Wuthering Heights* suggests that Emily adamantly opposed it. We know she opposed the milder constraints on originality imposed on her and Charlotte by Monsieur Heger, their French teacher in Brussels.

10 "[W]anting friends" and "unsupported." Johnson cites Shakespeare's use of the word in *Twelfth Night (Dictionary)*. Shakespeare also uses the word in *King Lear*.

11 You will "get a thrashing or a scolding. *colloq*." *(OED)*.

12 The place where the washing is done.

13 Given religious instruction by being made to repeat the instruction until it has been learned by heart. Joseph's teaching method arouses Heathcliff's resentment, but so does his sense that Joseph is a servant who has been put into an inappropriate position of authority over him and Catherine. This is an early instance of Heathcliff's class pride.

14 "Affect religious or pietistic phraseology" *(OED)*. So begins Heathcliff's longest speech in the first volume. He speaks standard, not dialect, English, and speaks in Catherine's idiolect rather than Nelly's. His extensive vocabulary, formal diction, and elaborate syntax provide solid evidence of his education up to this point in his life and of the achieved social standing he is about to lose.

15 Heathcliff and Catherine are standing on "a ledge or surbase above the basement-window level" and holding on to the sill of the window (Hilda Marsden and Ian Jack, eds., *Wuthering Heights* [Oxford: Clarendon Press, 1976], p. 420).

16 The carpet, the upholstered furniture, the gilded ceiling, and the elaborate chandelier with molded (not dipped) candles emphasize Thrushcross Grange's difference from Wuthering Heights. Raymond Williams observes that this scene directly renders the contrast between "two kinds of life": "an exposed unaccommodated wrenching of living from the heath and a sheltered refined civilised and *rentier* settlement in the valley" (*The English Novel from Dickens to Lawrence* [Oxford: Oxford Univ. Press, 1970], p. 65).

The crimson drawing room at Windsor Castle in an 1838 chromolithograph after James Baker Pyne (1800–1870). This famous drawing room was created for King George IV. It's much grander than the crimson drawing room at Thrushcross Grange so admired by Heathcliff, but it may have inspired Brontë's description of it.

thought ourselves in heaven! And now, guess what your good children were doing? Isabella, I believe she is eleven, a year younger than Cathy, lay screaming at the farther end of the room, shrieking as if witches were running red hot needles into her. Edgar stood on the hearth, weeping silently, and in the middle of the table sat a little dog, shaking its paw and yelping, which, from their mutual accusations, we understood they had nearly pulled in two between them. The idiots! That was their pleasure! to quarrel who should hold a heap of warm hair, and each begin to cry because both, after struggling to get it, refused to take it. We laughed outright at the petted things, we did despise them! When would you catch me wishing to have what Catherine wanted? or find us by ourselves, seeking entertainment in yelling, and sobbing, and rolling on the ground, divided by the whole room? I'd not exchange, for a thousand lives, my condition here for Edgar Linton's at Thrushcross Grange—not if I might have the privilege of flinging Joseph off the highest gable, and painting the house-front with Hindley's blood!"

"Hush, hush!" I interrupted. "Still you have not told me, Heathcliff, how Catherine is left behind?"

"I told you we laughed," he answered. "The Lintons heard us, and with one accord, they shot like arrows to the door; there was silence, and then a cry, 'Oh, mamma, mamma! Oh, papa! Oh, mamma, come here. Oh papa, oh!' They really did howl out, something in that way. We made frightful noises to terrify them still more, and then we dropped off the ledge, because somebody was drawing the bars, and we felt we had better flee. I had Cathy by the hand, and was urging her on, when all at once she fell down.

"'Run, Heathcliff, run!' she whispered. 'They have let the bull-dog loose, and he holds me!'

"The devil had seized her ankle, Nelly; I heard his abominable snorting. She did not yell out—no! She would have scorned to do it, if she had been spitted on the horns of a mad cow.[17] I did, though; I vociferated curses enough to annihilate any fiend in Christendom, and I got a stone and thrust it between his jaws, and tried with all my might to cram it down his throat. A beast of a servant came up with a lantern at last, shouting—

"'Keep fast, Skulker, keep fast!'

"He changed his note, however, when he saw Skulker's game.[18] The dog was throttled off, his huge, purple tongue hanging half a foot out of his mouth, and his pendant lips streaming with bloody slaver.

17 Charlotte based an episode in *Shirley* on Emily's stoical response to being bitten by an apparently rabid dog. Telling no one about the incident "till the danger was well-nigh over, for fear of the terrors that might beset their weaker minds," Emily cauterized the wound with a red-hot iron and continued about her ordinary business (Gaskell, *The Life of Charlotte Brontë*, p. 214).

18 Prey.

"The man took Cathy up; she was sick, not from fear, I'm certain, but from pain. He carried her in; I followed grumbling execrations and vengeance.

"'What prey, Robert?' hallooed Linton from the entrance.

"'Skulker has caught a little girl, sir,' he replied, 'and there's a lad here,' he added, making a clutch at me, 'who looks an out-and-outer![19] Very like, the robbers were for putting them through the window to open the doors to the gang, after all were asleep, that they might murder us at their ease. Hold your tongue, you foul-mouthed thief, you! You shall go to the gallows for this. Mr. Linton, sir, don't lay by your gun!'

"'No, no, Robert!' said the old fool. 'The rascals knew that yesterday was my rent day;[20] they thought to have me cleverly. Come in; I'll furnish them a reception. There, John, fasten the chain. Give Skulker some water, Jenny. To beard a magistrate in his stronghold,[21] and on the Sabbath, too! where will their insolence stop? Oh, my dear Mary, look here! Don't be afraid, it is but a boy—yet, the villain scowls so plainly in his face, would it not be a kindness to the country to hang him at once, before he shows his nature in acts, as well as features?'[22]

"He pulled me under the chandelier, and Mrs. Linton placed her spectacles on her nose and raised her hands in horror. The cowardly children crept nearer also, Isabella lisping—

"'Frightful thing! Put him in the cellar, papa. He's exactly like the son of the fortune-teller that stole my tame pheasant.[23] Isn't he, Edgar?'

"While they examined me, Cathy came round; she heard the last speech, and laughed.

"Edgar Linton, after an inquisitive stare, collected sufficient wit to recognise her. They see us at church, you know, though we seldom meet them elsewhere.

"'That's Miss Earnshaw!' he whispered to his mother, 'and look how Skulker has bitten her—how her foot bleeds!'

19 Someone who is beyond the norm; here, an interloper or a foreigner.

20 The day when Mr. Linton collects rent from his tenants. This rent is payment for the use of land to grow crops as well as for a dwelling rather than a payment for lodging in our modern sense. Wuthering Heights also has tenants; later (Vol. II, Chap. 4) the villagers will report that Heathcliff is "a cruel hard landlord."

21 As in "to beard the lion in his den": "To defy personally or have it out FACE TO FACE" (*Brewer's Dictionary of Phrase and Fable,* 89). As a magistrate or justice of the peace, Mr. Linton is empowered to judge and sentence Heathcliff. Sentences were harsh at this time. Data collected for 1785 show that the majority of the ninety-seven offenses for which the penalty imposed was hanging were offenses against property, including burglary and housebreaking (Leon Radzinowicz, *A History of English Criminal Law,* 1, 148, cited in Marsden and Jack, *Wuthering Heights,* p. 421).

22 Another allusion to physiognomy, here used by Mr. Linton to predict Heathcliff's character from his appearance. Although physiognomy was seen as a progressive science in its own time, it promoted racial stereotyping and other prejudices.

23 Another reference to Heathcliff's looking like a gypsy (because gypsies were associated with fortune-telling).

24 In its secular sense, someone stranded or thrown overboard; in its religious sense, someone damned.

25 Mrs. Linton's given name is Mary, but Mr. Linton, Edgar's and Isabella's father, is always called "Linton" or "Mr. Linton."

26 A warm drink made with sweetened red wine, sherry, or port.

"'Miss Earnshaw? Nonsense!' cried the dame, 'Miss Earnshaw scouring the country with a gipsy! And yet, my dear, the child is in mourning—surely it is—and she may be lamed for life!'

"'What culpable carelessness in her brother!' exclaimed Mr. Linton, turning from me to Catherine. 'I've understood from Shielders (that was the curate, sir) that he lets her grow up in absolute heathenism. But who is this? Where did she pick up this companion? Oho! I declare he is that strange acquisition my late neighbour made in his journey to Liverpool—a little Lascar, or an American or Spanish castaway.'[24]

"'A wicked boy, at all events,' remarked the old lady, 'and quite unfit for a decent house! Did you notice his language, Linton?[25] I'm shocked that my children should have heard it.'

"I recommenced cursing—don't be angry, Nelly—and so Robert was ordered to take me off—I refused to go without Cathy—he dragged me into the garden, pushed the lantern into my hand, assured me that Mr. Earnshaw should be informed of my behaviour, and bidding me march directly, secured the door again.

"The curtains were still looped up at one corner; and I resumed my station as spy, because if Catherine had wished to return, I intended shattering their great glass panes to a million fragments, unless they let her out.

"She sat on the sofa quietly; Mrs. Linton took off the grey cloak of the dairy maid which we had borrowed for our excursion, shaking her head, and expostulating with her, I suppose; she was a young lady, and they made a distinction between her treatment and mine. Then the woman servant brought a basin of warm water, and washed her feet; and Mr. Linton mixed a tumbler of negus,[26] and Isabella emptied a plateful of cakes into her lap, and Edgar stood gaping at a distance. Afterwards, they dried and combed her beautiful hair, and gave her a pair of enormous slippers, and wheeled her to the fire, and I left her, as merry as she could be, dividing her food between the little dog and Skulker,

Drawing in India ink by Balthasar Klossowski de Rola, known as Balthus (1908–2001), illustrating "Nous avons couru depuis le sommet des Hauts." "We ran from the top of the Heights to the park without stopping—Catherine completely beaten in the race, because she was barefoot." Here again Balthus has chosen to illustrate a turning point in the novel, a moment when Catherine embodies the pure freedom she is about to give up by exchanging the Heights for the Grange.

whose nose she pinched as he ate; and kindling a spark of spirit in the vacant blue eyes of the Lintons—a dim reflection from her own enchanting face—I saw they were full of stupid admiration; she is so immeasurably superior to them—to everybody on earth—is she not, Nelly?"

"There will more come of this business than you reckon on," I answered covering him up and extinguishing the light, "you are incurable, Heathcliff, and Mr. Hindley will have to proceed to extremities, see if he won't."

My words came truer than I desired. The luckless adventure made Earnshaw furious—And then, Mr. Linton, to mend matters, paid us a visit himself, on the morrow; and read the young master such a lecture on the road he guided his family that he was stirred to look about him in earnest.

Heathcliff received no flogging, but he was told that the first word he spoke to Miss Catherine should ensure a dismissal; and Mrs. Earnshaw undertook to keep her sister-in-law in due restraint when she returned home, employing art, not force—with force she would have found it impossible.

CHAPTER 7

Cathy stayed at Thrushcross Grange five weeks, till Christmas. By that time her ankle was thoroughly cured, and her manners much improved. The mistress visited her often, in the interval, and commenced her plan of reform by trying to raise her self-respect with fine clothes, and flattery, which she took readily: so that, instead of a wild, hatless little savage jumping into the house, and rushing to squeeze us all breathless, there lighted from a handsome black pony a very dignified person with brown ringlets falling from the cover of a feathered beaver, and a long cloth habit[1] which she was obliged to hold up with both hands that she might sail in.

Hindley lifted her from her horse, exclaiming delightedly, "Why Cathy, you are quite a beauty! I should scarcely have known you—you look like a lady now—Isabella Linton is not to be compared with her, is she, Frances?"

"Isabella has not her natural advantages,"[2] replied his wife, "but she must mind and not grow wild again here. Ellen,[3] help Miss Catherine off with her things—Stay, dear, you will disarrange your curls—let me untie your hat."

I removed the habit, and there shone forth beneath a grand plaid silk frock, white trousers,[4] and burnished shoes; and, while her eyes sparkled joyfully when the dogs came bounding up to welcome her, she dare hardly touch them lest they should fawn upon her splendid garments.

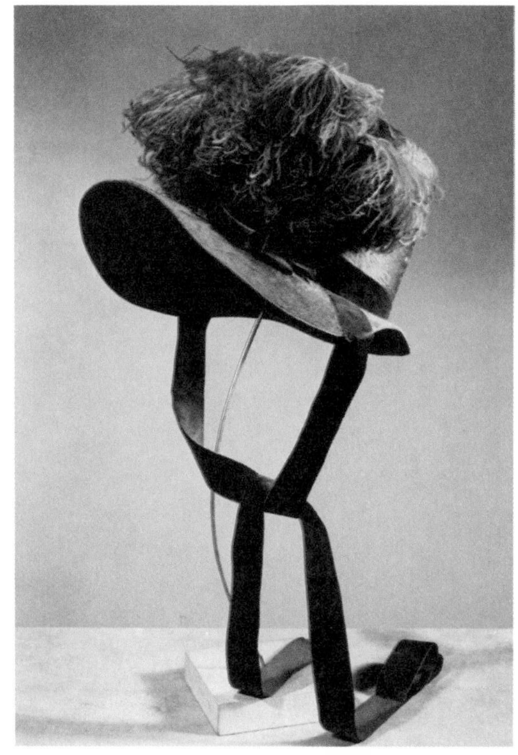

Made in 1816, this beaver felt poke bonnet is decorated with ribbon and ostrich feathers. The feathered beaver Catherine wears on her return to the Heights from Thrushcross Grange may have looked like this one.

1 Catherine's hat, riding habit, and fashionably curled hair mark her new alignment with the Lintons and her increased social distance from Heathcliff. Her hat is made of beaver felt decorated with feathers, and she wears a long riding coat probably made of fine wool.

2 A polite way of saying that Catherine is handsomer than Isabella.

3 Nelly's given name is Ellen, but Frances is the first character to use it in addressing her, signaling again the imposition of a new distance between servants and their masters and mistresses at the Heights.

4 Frilled or trimmed drawers reaching to the ankles, similar to "what is worn when bathing," were popular in riding costumes in the second quarter of the nineteenth century (C. Willett and Phillis Cunnington, *Handbook of English Costume in the Nineteenth Century* [London: Faber and Faber, 1959], p. 391).

5 A long wooden bench with a high back and arms.

6 A reference to Catherine's previously uncurled and tousled hair.

She kissed me gently; I was all flour making the Christmas cake, and it would not have done to give me a hug; and, then, she looked round for Heathcliff. Mr. and Mrs. Earnshaw watched anxiously their meeting, thinking it would enable them to judge, in some measure, what grounds they had for hoping to succeed in separating the two friends.

Heathcliff was hard to discover, at first—If he were careless, and uncared for, before Catherine's absence, he had been ten times more so since.

Nobody but I even did him the kindness to call him a dirty boy, and bid him wash himself, once a week; and children of his age, seldom have a natural pleasure in soap and water. Therefore, not to mention his clothes, which had seen three month's service in mire and dust, and his thick uncombed hair, the surface of his face and hands was dismally beclouded.

He might well skulk behind the settle,[5] on beholding such a bright, graceful damsel enter the house, instead of a rough-headed[6] counterpart to himself, as he expected.

"Is Heathcliff not here?" she demanded, pulling off her gloves, and displaying fingers wonderfully whitened with doing nothing, and staying in doors.

"Heathcliff you may come forward," cried Mr. Hindley enjoying his discomfiture and gratified to see what a forbidding young blackguard he would be compelled to present himself. "You may come and wish Miss Catherine welcome, like the other servants."

Cathy, catching a glimpse of her friend in his concealment, flew to embrace him, she bestowed seven or eight kisses on his cheek within the second, and then stopped, and drawing back, burst into a laugh, exclaiming,

"Why, how very black and cross you look! and how—how funny and grim! But that's because I'm used to Edgar and Isabella Linton. Well, Heathcliff, have you forgotten me?"

She had some reason to put the question, for shame and pride threw double gloom over his countenance, and kept him immoveable.

THAT'S OUR HEATHCLIFF
NOW THAT I AM BACK FROM MY STAY AT THE LINTONS, I AM QUITE THE LADY
!
HEATHCLIFF! HA HA OH YES I'VE FORGOTTEN HOW GROSS AND DIRTY YOU ARE NOW
I WILL NOT BE LAUGHED AT!

GOD, AND YOU JUST KNOW HE'LL LOCK THAT IN HIS HEART FOREVER UNTIL REVENGE COMES

Frames from *Hark! A Vagrant,* Kate Beaton's smart and engaging webcomic about historical and literary characters transported into the twenty-first century. Beaton was born in Cape Breton, Nova Scotia, in 1983.

"Shake hands, Heathcliff," said Mr. Earnshaw, condescendingly; "once in a way, that is permitted."

"I shall not!" replied the boy finding his tongue at last, "I shall not stand to be laughed at, I shall not bear it!"

And he would have broken from the circle, but Miss Cathy seized him again.

"I did not mean to laugh at you," she said. "I could not hinder myself, Heathcliff, shake hands, at least! What are you sulky for? It was only that you looked odd—If you wash your face, and brush your hair, it will be all right. But you are so dirty!"

She gazed concernedly at the dusky fingers she held in her own, and also at her dress, which she feared had gained no embellishment from its contact with his.

"You needn't have touched me!" he answered, following her eye and snatching away his hand. "I shall be as dirty as I please, and I like to be dirty, and I will be dirty."

With that he dashed head foremost out of the room, amid the merriment of the master and mistress, and to the serious disturbance of Catherine, who could not comprehend how her remarks should have produced such an exhibition of bad temper.

After playing lady's maid[7] to the newcomer, and putting my cakes in the oven, and making the house and kitchen cheerful with great fires befitting Christmas eve, I prepared to sit down and amuse myself by singing carols, all alone; regardless of Joseph's af-

7 Ladies had personal maids. Nelly's suggestion that she is only "playing" this role takes in Catherine's new pretensions as well as the difference between the servant economies of the Heights and the Grange. Nelly performs the functions of nurse, housekeeper, and cook at the Heights; several different servants perform these functions at the Grange.

firmations that he considered the merry tunes I chose as next door to songs.[8]

He had retired to private prayer in his chamber, and Mr. and Mrs. Earnshaw were engaging Missy's attention by sundry gay trifles bought for her to present to the little Lintons, as an acknowledgment of their kindness.

They had invited them to spend the morrow at Wuthering Heights, and the invitation had been accepted, on one condition; Mrs. Linton begged that her darlings might be kept carefully apart from that "naughty, swearing boy."

Under these circumstances I remained solitary. I smelt the rich scent of the heating spices; and admired the shining kitchen utensils, the polished clock, decked in holly, the silver mugs ranged on a tray ready to be filled with mulled ale for supper; and, above all, the speckless purity of my particular care—the scoured and well-swept floor.

I gave due inward applause to every object, and, then, I remembered how old Earnshaw used to come in when all was tidied, and call me a cant[9] lass, and slip a shilling into my hand, as a Christmas box:[10] and, from that, I went on to think of his fondness for Heathcliff, and his dread lest he should suffer neglect after death had removed him; and that naturally led me to consider the poor lad's situation now, and from singing, I changed my mind to crying. It struck me soon, however, there would be more sense in endeavouring to repair some of his wrongs than shedding tears over them —I got up and walked into the court to seek him.

He was not far; I found him smoothing the glossy coat of the new pony in the stable, and feeding the other beasts, according to custom.

"Make haste, Heathcliff!" I said "the kitchen is so comfortable—and Joseph is up-stairs; make haste, and let me dress you smart before Miss Cathy comes out—and then you can sit together, with the whole hearth to yourselves, and have a long chatter till bedtime."

8 Secular songs. Nelly's carols are too much like these for Joseph's taste. Like Calvin, Joseph values religious songs only as "spurs to incite us to pray to and praise God, and to meditate upon his works in order to love, fear, honor and glorify him" (Calvin, quoted by John Barber, "Luther and Calvin on Music and Worship," *Reformed Perspective Magazine,* 8:26, June 25–July 1, 2006). Calvin limited even church singing to songs including the words of God as found in the Psalms. Haworth was known for its musicians, and Patrick Brontë oversaw the building of a fine new organ in the parish church in 1834. Several of Emily's poems show the influence of hymn forms, Anne composed hymns that are still being sung in churches today, and Branwell sometimes played the church organ at services.

9 Lively, adroit.

10 A tip, given to a servant at Christmas in acknowledgment of services rendered during the year.

"Christmas-Eve in Yorkshire," drawn by Dodgson, depicts festivities similar to those at the Heights, where the sitting room is less grand but still very handsome before Hindley's decline. Wuthering Heights also has pewter dishes on display in the oak dresser, joints hanging from the ceiling, and dancing (*The Illustrated London News,* Christmas Supplement, 1849, p. 420).

He proceeded with his task and never turned his head towards me.

"Come—are you coming?" I continued. "There's a little cake for each of you, nearly enough; and you'll need half an hour's donning."[11]

I waited five minutes, but getting no answer left him . . . Catherine supped with her brother and sister-in-law; Joseph and I joined at an unsociable meal seasoned with reproofs on one side, and sauciness on the other. His cake and cheese remained on the table all night, for the fairies. He managed to continue work till nine o'clock, and then marched dumb and dour to his chamber.

Cathy sat up late, having a world of things to order for the reception of her new friends: she came into the kitchen, once, to

11 Dressing (chiefly Northern dialect).

speak to her old one, but he was gone, and she only stayed to ask what was the matter with him, and then went back.

In the morning, he rose early; and, as it was a holiday, carried his ill-humour onto the moors, not re-appearing till the family were departed for church. Fasting and reflection seemed to have brought him to a better spirit. He hung about me for a while, and having screwed up his courage, exclaimed abruptly, "Nelly, make me decent; I'm going to be good."

"High time, Heathcliff," I said, "you *have* grieved Catherine; she's sorry she ever came home, I dare say! It looks as if you envied her, because she is more thought of than you."

The notion of *envying* Catherine was incomprehensible to him, but the notion of grieving her, he understood clearly enough.

"Did she say she was grieved?" he inquired, looking very serious.

"She cried when I told her you were off again this morning."

"Well, I cried last night," he returned, "and I had more reason to cry than she."

"Yes, you had the reason of going to bed, with a proud heart and an empty stomach," said I. "Proud people breed sad sorrows for themselves—but if you be ashamed of your touchiness, you must ask pardon, mind, when she comes in. You must go up, and offer to kiss her, and say—you know best what to say—only, do it heartily, and not as if you thought her converted into a stranger by her grand dress. And now, though I have dinner to get ready, I'll steal time to arrange you so that Edgar Linton shall look quite a doll beside you: and that he does—you are younger, and yet, I'll be bound, you are taller and twice as broad across the shoulders—you could knock him down in a twinkling; don't you feel that you could?"

Heathcliff's face brightened a moment; then, it was overcast afresh, and he sighed.

"But, Nelly, if I knocked him down twenty times, that wouldn't make him less handsome, or me more so. I wish I had light hair and a fair skin, and was dressed and behaved as well, and had a chance of being as rich as he will be!"

"And cried for mamma at every turn," I added, "and trembled if a country lad heaved his fist against you, and sat at home all day for a shower of rain—O, Heathcliff, you are showing a poor spirit! Come to the glass, and I'll let you see what you should wish. Do you mark those two lines between your eyes, and those thick brows, that instead of rising arched, sink in the middle, and that couple of black fiends, so deeply buried, who never open their windows boldly, but lurk glinting under them, like devil's spies? Wish and learn to smooth away the surly wrinkles, to raise your lids frankly, and change the fiends to confident, innocent angels, suspecting and doubting nothing, and always seeing friends where they are not sure of foes—Don't get the expression of a vicious cur that appears to know the kicks it gets are its desert, and yet, hates all the world as well as the kicker for what it suffers."

"In other words, I must wish for Edgar Linton's great blue eyes and even forehead," he replied. "I do—and that won't help me to them."

"A good heart will help you to a bonny face my lad," I continued, "if you were a regular black;[12] and a bad one will turn the bonniest into something worse than ugly. And now that we've done washing, and combing, and sulking—tell me whether you don't think yourself rather handsome? I'll tell you, I do. You're fit for a prince in disguise. Who knows, but your father was Emperor of China, and your mother an Indian queen, each of them able to buy up, with one week's income, Wuthering Heights and Thrushcross Grange together? And you were kidnapped by wicked sailors, and brought to England. Were I in your place, I would frame high notions of my birth; and the thoughts of what I was should give me courage and dignity to support the oppressions of a little farmer!"[13]

So I chattered on; and Heathcliff gradually lost his frown, and began to look quite pleasant; when, all at once, our conversation was interrupted by a rumbling sound moving up the road and en-

12 References to any dark-skinned person as "black" or "a black" go back to at least the early sixteenth century.

13 Nelly's encouraging speech evokes the familiar comedy plot in which an apparently low-born protagonist is ultimately revealed to have noble ancestry, a reversal of fortune that enables him to marry the woman of his choice. At the same time, it reminds us that Nelly's world is large enough to make an English landowner look like "a little farmer." She also has the political vocabulary to see English landowners as oppressors, and she puts more stress on the wealth of Heathcliff's putative ancestors than on their nobility, driving home the lesson that in her world, money trumps birth.

John Barrell points to the presentation of gypsies under a double aspect in many Romantic poems and to the way the figure of the gypsy unites the exotic and the familiar ("Afterword: Moving Stories, Still Lives," in Gerald MacLean, Donna Landry, and Joseph P. Ward, eds., *The Country and the City Revisited: England and the Politics of Culture, 1550–1850* [Cambridge: Cambridge Univ. Press, 1999], pp. 216–222). Wordworth's "Beggars," for example, brings together two gypsy boys, who offend the poem's narrator by lying to him without compunction, and a beautiful gypsy woman, whom he takes to be their mother and enthusiastically admires:

> Her skin was of Egyptian brown:
> Haughty, as if her eye had seen
> Its own light to a distance thrown,
> She towered, fit person for a Queen
> To lead those ancient Amazonian files;
> Or ruling Bandit's wife among the Grecian isles.

14 Someone whose appearance is showy.

15 Grip.

tering the court. He ran to the window, and I to the door, just in time to behold the two Lintons descend from the family carriage, smothered in cloaks and furs, and the Earnshaws dismount from their horses—they often rode to church in winter. Catherine took a hand of each of the children, and brought them into the house, and set them before the fire, which quickly put colour into their white faces.

I urged my companion to hasten now, and show his amiable humour, and he willingly obeyed: but ill luck would have it that, as he opened the door leading from the kitchen on one side, Hindley opened it on the other; they met, and the master, irritated at seeing him clean and cheerful, or, perhaps, eager to keep his promise to Mrs. Linton, shoved him back with a sudden thrust, and angrily bade Joseph "keep the fellow out of the room—send him into the garret till dinner is over. He'll be cramming his fingers in the tarts, and stealing the fruit, if left alone with them a minute."

"Nay, sir," I could not avoid answering, "he'll touch nothing, not he—and, I suppose, he must have his share of the dainties as well as we."

"He shall have his share of my hand, if I catch him down stairs again till dark," cried Hindley. "Begone, you vagabond! What, you are attempting the coxcomb,[14] are you? Wait till I get hold of those elegant locks—see if I won't pull them a bit longer!"

"They are long enough already," observed Master Linton, peeping from the door-way. "I wonder they don't make his head ache. It's like a colt's mane over his eyes!"

He ventured this remark without any intention to insult; but Heathcliff's violent nature was not prepared to endure the appearance of impertinence from one whom he seemed to hate, even then, as a rival. He seized a tureen of hot apple-sauce, the first thing that came under his gripe[15]; and dashed it full against the speaker's face and neck—who instantly commenced a lament that brought Isabella and Catherine hurrying to the place.

Mr. Earnshaw snatched up the culprit directly and conveyed him to his chamber, where, doubtless, he administered a rough remedy to cool the fit of passion, for he reappeared red and breathless. I got the dish-cloth, and, rather spitefully, scrubbed Edgar's nose and mouth, affirming it served him right for meddling. His sister began weeping to go home, and Cathy stood by confounded, blushing for all.

"You should not have spoken to him!" she expostulated with Master Linton. "He was in a bad temper, and now you've spoilt your visit, and he'll be flogged—I hate him to be flogged! I can't eat my dinner. Why did you speak to him, Edgar?"

"I didn't," sobbed the youth, escaping from my hands, and finishing the remainder of the purification with his cambric[16] pocket-handkerchief. "I promised mamma that I wouldn't say one word to him, and I didn't!"

"Well, don't cry!" replied Catherine, contemptuously. "You're not killed—don't make more mischief—my brother is coming—be quiet! Give over, Isabella! Has anybody hurt *you?*"

"There, there, children—to your seats!" cried Hindley, bustling in. "That brute of a lad has warmed me nicely. Next time, Master Edgar, take the law into your own fists—it will give you an appetite!"

The little party recovered its equanimity at sight of the fragrant feast. They were hungry after their ride, and easily consoled, since no real harm had befallen them.

Mr. Earnshaw carved bountiful platefuls; and the mistress made them merry with lively talk. I waited[17] behind her chair, and was pained to behold Catherine, with dry eyes and an indifferent air, commence cutting up the wing of a goose before her.

"An unfeeling child," I thought to myself, "how lightly she dismisses her old playmate's troubles. I could not have imagined her to be so selfish."

She lifted a mouthful to her lips; then, she set it down again: her cheeks flushed, and the tears gushed over them. She slipped her

Head study of a rakish gypsy by the French painter Henri Alexandre Georges Regnault (1843–1871).

16 A delicate linen fabric.

17 As this is a special occasion, Nelly stands behind Frances and serves the guests at the table.

fork to the floor, and hastily dived under the cloth to conceal her emotion. I did not call her unfeeling long, for I perceived she was in purgatory throughout the day, and wearying to find an opportunity of getting by herself, or paying a visit to Heathcliff, who had been locked up by the master, as I discovered on endeavouring to introduce to him a private mess of victuals.[18]

In the evening we had a dance. Cathy begged that he might be liberated then, as Isabella Linton had no partner; her entreaties were vain, and I was appointed to supply the deficiency.

We got rid of all gloom in the excitement of the exercise, and our pleasure was increased by the arrival of the Gimmerton band, mustering fifteen strong: a trumpet, a trombone, clarionets,[19] bassoons, French horns, and a bass viol, besides singers. They go the rounds of all the respectable houses, and receive contributions every Christmas, and we esteemed it a first-rate treat to hear them.[20]

After the usual carols had been sung, we set them to songs and glees.[21] Mrs. Earnshaw loved the music, and so they gave us plenty.

Catherine loved it too; but she said it sounded sweetest at the top of the steps, and she went up in the dark: I followed. They shut the house door below, never noting our absence, it was so full of people. She made no stay at the stairs' head, but mounted farther, to the garret where Heathcliff was confined; and called him. He stubbornly declined answering for a while—she persevered, and finally persuaded him to hold communion with her through the boards.

I let the poor things converse unmolested, till I supposed the songs were going to cease, and the singers to get some refreshment: then, I clambered up the ladder to warn her.

Instead of finding her outside, I heard her voice within. The little monkey had crept by the skylight of one garret, along the roof, into the skylight of the other, and it was with the utmost difficulty I could coax her out again.

When she did come, Heathcliff came with her; and she insisted that I should take him into the kitchen, as my fellow-servant had

18 Portion of food.

19 Clarinets.

20 Such bands "were a feature of social life in the West Riding. They played at Christmas and on other festive occasions" (Hilda Marsden and Ian Jack, eds., *Wuthering Heights* [Oxford: Clarendon Press, 1976], p. 421). Haworth had its own traveling band.

21 Musical compositions "for three or more voices (one voice to each part) . . . and (in strict use) without accompaniment" *(OED).*

gone to a neighbour's to be removed from the sound of our "devil's psalmody," as it pleased him to call it.[22]

I told them I intended, by no means, to encourage their tricks; but as the prisoner had never broken his fast since yesterday's dinner, I would wink at his cheating Mr. Hindley that once.

He went down; I set him a stool by the fire, and offered him a quantity of good things; but he was sick and could eat little, and my attempts to entertain him were thrown away. He leant his two elbows on his knees, and his chin on his hands, and remained wrapt in dumb meditation. On my inquiring the subject of his thoughts, he answered gravely—

"I'm trying to settle how I shall pay Hindley back. I don't care how long I wait, if I can only do it, at last. I hope he will not die before I do!"

"For shame, Heathcliff!" said I. "It is for God to punish wicked people; we should learn to forgive."

"No, God won't have the satisfaction that I shall," he returned. "I only wish I knew the best way! Let me alone, and I'll plan it out: while I'm thinking of that, I don't feel pain."

"But, Mr. Lockwood, I forget these tales cannot divert you. I'm annoyed how I should dream of chattering on at such a rate; and your gruel cold, and you nodding for bed! I could have told Heathcliff's history, all that you need hear, in half-a-dozen words."

Thus interrupting herself, the housekeeper rose and proceeded to lay aside her sewing; but I felt incapable of moving from the hearth, and I was very far from nodding.

"Sit still, Mrs. Dean," I cried, "do sit still, another half hour! You've done just right to tell the story leisurely. That is the method I like; and you must finish in the same style. I am interested in every character you have mentioned, more or less."

"The clock is on the stroke of eleven, sir."

"No matter—I'm not accustomed to go to bed in the long hours.[23] One or two is early enough for a person who lies till ten."

22 Joseph disapproves of Christmas carols. A "devil's psalmody" is the antithesis of God's psalmody, literally words from the Book of Psalms set to music.

23 Those denoted by the large numbers, eleven and twelve. Brontë again reminds us that Lockwood's city habits clash with Nelly's country habits.

24 Lockwood cuts Nelly off, just as she is about to summarize the period between Christmas 1777, when Edgar and Isabella Linton return from church for dinner and music at Wuthering Heights, and summer 1780, when Edgar proposes to Catherine.

"You shouldn't lie till ten. There's the very prime of the morning gone long before that time. A person who has not done one half his day's work by ten o'clock runs a chance of leaving the other half undone."

"Nevertheless, Mrs. Dean, resume your chair; because to-morrow I intend lengthening the night till afternoon. I prognosticate for myself an obstinate cold, at least."

"I hope not, sir. Well, you must allow me to leap over some three years; during that space, Mrs. Earnshaw—"[24]

"No, no, I'll allow nothing of the sort! Are you acquainted with the mood of mind in which, if you were seated alone, and the cat licking its kitten on the rug before you, you would watch the operation so intently that puss's neglect of one ear would put you seriously out of temper?"

"A terribly lazy mood, I should say."

"On the contrary, a tiresomely active one. It is mine at present, and, therefore, continue minutely. I perceive that people in these regions acquire over people in towns the value that a spider in a dungeon does over a spider in a cottage to their various occupants; and yet, the deepened attraction is not entirely owing to the situation of the looker-on. They *do* live more in earnest, more in themselves, and less in surface change and frivolous external things. I could fancy a love for life here almost possible; and I was a fixed unbeliever in any love of a year's standing—one state resembles setting a hungry man down to a single dish on which he may concentrate his entire appetite, and do it justice—the other, introducing him to a table laid out by French cooks; he can perhaps extract as much enjoyment from the whole; but each part is a mere atom in his regard and remembrance."

"Oh! here we are the same as anywhere else, when you get to know us," observed Mrs. Dean, somewhat puzzled at my speech.

"Excuse me," I responded; "you, my good friend, are a striking evidence against that assertion. Excepting a few provincialisms of slight consequence, you have no marks of the manners that I am habituated to consider as peculiar to your class. I am sure you have thought a great deal more than the generality of servants think. You have been compelled to cultivate your reflective faculties, for want of occasions for frittering your life away in silly trifles."

Mrs. Dean laughed.

"I certainly esteem myself a steady, reasonable kind of body," she said, "not exactly from living among the hills, and seeing one set of faces, and one series of actions, from year's end to year's end: but I have undergone sharp discipline which has taught me wisdom; and then, I have read more than you would fancy, Mr. Lockwood. You could not open a book in this library that I have not looked into, and got something out of also; unless it be that range of Greek and Latin, and that of French—and those I know one from another; it is as much as you can expect of a poor man's daughter.

"However, if I am to follow my story in true gossip's fashion, I had better go on; and instead of leaping three years, I will be content to pass to the next summer—the summer of 1778, that is, nearly twenty-three years ago."[25]

25 The first edition omits quotation marks around this paragraph, but since Nelly is talking to Lockwood, who narrates the conversation, I have restored them. Quotation marks are eliminated in the following paragraph, when Nelly resumes her uninterrupted narrative of past events.

CHAPTER 8

On the morning of a fine June day, my first bonny little nursling, and the last of the ancient Earnshaw stock was born.

We were busy with the hay in a far away field, when the girl that usually brought our breakfasts came running, an hour too soon, across the meadow and up the lane, calling me as she ran.

"Oh, such a grand bairn!" she panted out. "The finest lad that ever breathed! but the doctor says missis must go; he says she's been in a consumption these many months. I heard him tell Mr. Hindley—and now she has nothing to keep her, and she'll be dead before winter. You must come home directly. You're to nurse it, Nelly—to feed it with sugar and milk, and take care of it, day and night[1]—I wish I were you, because it will be all yours when there is no missis!"

"But is she very ill?" I asked, flinging down my rake, and tying my bonnet.

"I guess she is; yet she looks bravely," replied the girl, "and she talks as if she thought of living to see it grow a man. She's out of her head for joy, it's such a beauty! If I were her I'm certain I should not die. I should get better at the bare sight of it, in spite of Kenneth.[2] I was fairly mad at him. Dame Archer[3] brought the cherub down to master in the house, and his face just began to light up; then the old croaker steps forward, and says he: 'Earnshaw, it's a blessing your wife has been spared to leave you this

1 Nelly is summoned to act as Hareton's dry nurse, a woman who cares for a child but does not suckle it.

2 The doctor, named here for the first time. Dr. Kenneth has already made two appearances in the novel, the first when Heathcliff fell ill soon after arriving at the Heights and the second when old Mr. Earnshaw died.

3 Dame Archer is the midwife.

son. When she came, I felt convinced we shouldn't keep her long; and now, I must tell you, the winter will probably finish her. Don't take on, and fret about it too much, it can't be helped. And besides, you should have known better than to choose such a rush of a lass!"[4]

"And what did the master answer?" I enquired.

"I think he swore—but I didn't mind him; I was straining to see the bairn," and she began again to describe it rapturously. I, as zealous as herself, hurried eagerly home to admire, on my part, though I was very sad for Hindley's sake; he had room in his heart only for two idols—his wife and himself—he doted on both, and adored one, and I couldn't conceive how he would bear the loss.

When we got to Wuthering Heights, there he stood at the front door; and, as I passed in, I asked, how was the baby?

"Nearly ready to run about, Nell!" he replied, putting on a cheerful smile.

"And the mistress?" I ventured to inquire, "the doctor says she's—"

"Damn the doctor!" he interrupted, reddening. "Frances is quite right—she'll be perfectly well by this time next week. Are you going up-stairs? Will you tell her that I'll come, if she'll promise not to talk. I left her because she would not hold her tongue; and she must—tell her Mr. Kenneth says she must be quiet."

I delivered this message to Mrs. Earnshaw; she seemed in flighty spirits, and replied merrily—"I hardly spoke a word, Ellen, and there he has gone out twice, crying. Well, say I promise I won't speak; but that does not bind me not to laugh at him!"

Poor soul! Till within a week of her death that gay heart never failed her; and her husband persisted doggedly, nay, furiously, in affirming her health improved every day. When Kenneth warned him that his medicines were useless at that stage of the malady, and he needn't put him to further expense by attending her, he retorted—"I know you need not—she's well—she does not want any more attendance from you! She never was in a consumption. It

4 According to Kenneth, Frances is too fragile to survive childbirth or a challenging environment like that of Wuthering Heights, and Hindley should have known better than to marry her and bring her there. The use of a rush as the type of something slight or insignificant goes back to the fourteenth century.

Death is a frequent and ordinary happening in the novel, yet it is no less profound and intolerable for that. Brontë was more familiar with death than most people, even in the nineteenth century. The 1850 *Report to the General Board of Health on the Hamlet of Haworth* found that the mortality rate—63.3 deaths per 1,000 annually—was 44.3 percent above the rate in neighboring hamlets and "only to be met with in very unhealthy places." The average age at death was 25.8 years, about the same as in three of the most unhealthy districts in London. The Board of Health Report attributed Haworth's high death rate to poor sanitation: not enough privies, no sewers, and a dearth of safe water for drinking and cooking. Patrick Brontë had campaigned for this inspection.

was a fever; and it is gone—her pulse is as slow as mine now, and her cheek as cool."

He told his wife the same story, and she seemed to believe him; but one night, while leaning on his shoulder, in the act of saying she thought she should be able to get up to-morrow, a fit of coughing took her—a very slight one—he raised her in his arms; she put her two hands about his neck, her face changed, and she was dead.

As the girl had anticipated, the child Hareton fell wholly into my hands. Mr. Earnshaw, provided he saw him healthy, and never heard him cry, was contented, as far as regarded him. For himself, he grew desperate; his sorrow was of that kind that will not lament, he neither wept nor prayed—he cursed and defied—execrated God and man, and gave himself up to reckless dissipation.

The servants could not bear his tyrannical and evil conduct long: Joseph and I were the only two that would stay. I had not the heart to leave my charge; and besides, you know, I had been his foster sister,[5] and excused his behaviour more readily than a stranger would.

Joseph remained to hector over tenants[6] and labourers; and because it was his vocation to be where he had plenty of wickedness to reprove.

The master's bad ways and bad companions formed a pretty example for Catherine and Heathcliff. His treatment of the latter was enough to make a fiend of a saint. And, truly, it appeared as if the lad *were* possessed of something diabolical at that period. He delighted to witness Hindley degrading himself past redemption; and became daily more notable for savage sullenness and ferocity.

I could not half tell what an infernal house we had. The curate dropped calling, and nobody decent came near us at last; unless Edgar Linton's visits to Miss Cathy might be an exception. At fifteen she was the queen of the country-side; she had no peer: and she did turn out a haughty, headstrong creature! I own I did not like her, after her infancy was past; and I vexed her frequently by trying to bring down her arrogance; she never took an aversion to

5 Nelly calls herself Hindley's "foster sister" because her mother nursed them both. She and Hindley are roughly the same age, and they played together like brother and sister before they took up the different social roles assigned to them, Hindley's as a landowner and Nelly's as a servant. Unlike Hindley, Heathcliff, and Catherine, Nelly would not have had lessons from the curate. She calls attention to her social position and her social aspirations at several points in her narrative. The narrative itself calls attention to Nelly's aspirations by not being delivered in the dialect spoken by the other servants.

6 Like the Lintons, the Earnshaws have tenants who pay rent on the land they farm.

me, though. She had a wondrous constancy to old attachments; even Heathcliff kept his hold on her affections unalterably, and young Linton, with all his superiority, found it difficult to make an equally deep impression.

"He was my late master; that is his portrait over the fireplace. It used to hang on one side, and his wife's on the other; but hers has been removed, or else you might see something of what she was. Can you make that out?"

Mrs. Dean raised the candle, and I discerned a soft-featured face, exceedingly resembling the young lady at the Heights, but more pensive and amiable in expression. It formed a sweet picture. The long light hair curled slightly on the temples; the eyes were large and serious; the figure almost too graceful. I did not marvel how Catherine Earnshaw could forget her first friend for such an individual. I marvelled much how he, with a mind to correspond with his person, could fancy my idea of Catherine Earnshaw.

"A very agreeable portrait," I observed to the housekeeper. "Is it like?"

"Yes," she answered, "but he looked better when he was animated; that is his every day countenance; he wanted spirit in general."

Catherine had kept up her acquaintance with the Lintons since her five weeks' residence among them; and as she had no temptation to show her rough side in their company, and had the sense to be ashamed of being rude where she experienced such invariable courtesy, she imposed unwittingly on the old lady and gentleman, by her ingenious cordiality; gained the admiration of Isabella, and the heart and soul of her brother—acquisitions that flattered her from the first, for she was full of ambition—and led her to adopt a double character without exactly intending to deceive anyone.

In the place where she heard Heathcliff termed a "vulgar young ruffian," and "worse than a brute," she took care not to act like him;

India ink and pencil drawing by Balthasar Klossowski de Rola, known as Balthus (1908–2001), "Alors, pourquoi as-tu cette robe de soie?" This image is keyed to Heathcliff's question to Catherine, who is dressing for Edgar Linton's visit: "Why have you that silk frock on, then?" In Balthus's erotic oil painting *La Toilette de Cathy* [*Cathy Dressing*], which is based on this drawing, Cathy's dressing gown is wide open, revealing her naked body, and Balthus has given his own features to Heathcliff, making his identification with him clear. In the drawing, Cathy is fully clothed, but her enlarged head and the dress that clings to her body call attention to her erotic power.

but at home she had small inclination to practise politeness that would only be laughed at, and restrain an unruly nature when it would bring her neither credit nor praise.

Mr. Edgar seldom mustered courage to visit Wuthering Heights openly. He had a terror of Earnshaw's reputation, and shrunk from encountering him, and yet, he was always received with our best attempts at civility: the master himself avoided offending him—knowing why he came—and if he could not be gracious, kept out of the way. I rather think his appearance there was distasteful to Catherine; she was not artful, never played the coquette, and had evidently an objection to her two friends meeting at all: for when Heathcliff expressed contempt of Linton in his presence, she could not half coincide, as she did in his absence; and when Linton evinced disgust and antipathy to Heathcliff, she dare not treat his sentiments with indifference, as if depreciation of her playmate were of scarcely any consequence to her.

I've had many a laugh at her perplexities and untold troubles, which she vainly strove to hide from my mockery. That sounds ill-natured—but she was so proud, it became really impossible to pity her distresses, till she should be chastened into more humility.

She did bring herself, finally, to confess and confide in me. There was not a soul else that she might fashion into an adviser.

Mr. Hindley had gone from home one afternoon; and Heathcliff presumed to give himself a holiday, on the strength of it. He had reached the age of sixteen then, I think, and without having bad features or being deficient in intellect, he contrived to convey an impression of inward and outward repulsiveness that his present aspect retains no traces of.

In the first place, he had, by that time, lost the benefit of his early education: continual hard work, begun soon and concluded late, had extinguished any curiosity he once possessed in pursuit of knowledge, and any love for books or learning. His childhood's sense of superiority, instilled into him by the favours of old Mr. Earnshaw, was faded away. He struggled long to keep up an equality with Catherine in her studies, and yielded with poignant though silent regret: but he yielded completely; and there was no prevailing on him to take a step in the way of moving upward, when he found he must, necessarily, sink beneath his former level. Then, personal appearance sympathised with mental deterioration; he acquired a slouching gait and ignoble look; his naturally reserved disposition was exaggerated into an almost idiotic excess of unsociable moroseness; and he took a grim pleasure, apparently, in exciting the aversion rather than the esteem of his few acquaintance.

Catherine and he were constant companions still, at his seasons of respite from labour; but he had ceased to express his fondness for her in words, and recoiled with angry suspicion from her girlish caresses, as if conscious there could be no gratification in lavishing such marks of affection on him. On the before-named occasion, he came into the house[7] to announce his intention of doing nothing, while I was assisting Miss Cathy to arrange her dress—she had not reckoned on his taking it into his head to be idle, and imagining she would have the whole place to herself, she managed, by some means, to inform Mr. Edgar of her brother's absence, and was then preparing to receive him.

"Cathy, are you busy, this afternoon?" asked Heathcliff. "Are you going anywhere?"

"No, it is raining," she answered.

"Why have you that silk frock on, then?" he said. "Nobody coming here, I hope?"

"Not that I know of," stammered Miss, "but you should be in the field now, Heathcliff. It is an hour past dinner time; I thought you were gone."

"Hindley does not often free us from his accursed presence," observed the boy. "I'll not work any more to-day; I'll stay with you."

"O, but Joseph will tell," she suggested; "you'd better go!"

"Joseph is loading lime on the farther side of Pennistow Crag;[8] it will take him till dark, and he'll never know."

7 This scene is set in the sitting room.

8 Variant spellings in the first edition include Pennistow, Peniston, and Penistone, and this edition retains them. Etymologically, all derive from the Welsh, Cumbric, and Cornish root word "pen," meaning a headland or hill. A crag (a word of Celtic origin) is a "steep or precipitous rugged rock" *(OED)*. Visitors today can still climb Penistone Hill and walk across the expanse of moorland near Haworth where the Brontës walked. There are sandstone outcroppings as well as waste rock left behind during quarrying. In Brontë's time, many villagers were employed in the Penistone quarries. The lime Joseph is loading on "the farther side of Pennistow Crag" would be used for construction or for agricultural purposes.

9 Still a common spelling in the nineteenth century and earlier; here a calendar of months and days together with other useful information.

So saying he lounged to the fire, and sat down, Catherine reflected an instant, with knitted brows—she found it needful to smooth the way for an intrusion.

"Isabella, and Edgar Linton talked of calling this afternoon," she said at the conclusion of a minute's silence. "As it rains, I hardly expect them; but they may come, and if they do, you run the risk of being scolded for no good."

"Order Ellen to say you are engaged, Cathy," he persisted. "Don't turn me out for those pitiful, silly friends of yours! I'm on the point sometimes of complaining that they—but I'll not—"

"That they what?" cried Catherine, gazing at him with a troubled countenance. "Oh Nelly!" she added petulantly, jerking her head away from my hands, "you've combed my hair quite out of curl! That's enough, let me alone. What are you on the point of complaining about, Heathcliff?"

"Nothing—only look at the almanack[9] on that wall." He pointed to a framed sheet hanging near the window, and continued,

"The crosses are for the evenings you have spent with the Lintons, the dots for those spent with me—Do you see, I've marked every day?"

"Yes—very foolish; as if I took notice!" replied Catherine in a peevish tone. "And where is the sense of that?"

"To show that I *do* take notice," said Heathcliff.

"And should I always be sitting with you," she demanded, growing more irritated. "What good do I get—What do you talk about? You might be dumb or a baby for anything you say to amuse me, or for anything you do, either!"

"You never told me before that I talked too little, or that you disliked my company, Cathy!" exclaimed Heathcliff in much agitation.

"It is no company at all, when people know nothing and say nothing," she muttered.

Her companion rose up, but he hadn't time to express his feelings further, for a horse's feet were heard on the flags, and, having knocked gently, young Linton entered, his face brilliant with delight at the unexpected summons he had received.

Doubtless Catherine marked the difference between her friends as one came in, and the other went out. The contrast resembled what you see in exchanging a bleak, hilly, coal country, for a beautiful fertile valley; and his voice and greeting were as opposite as his aspect—he had a sweet, low manner of speaking, and pronounced his words as you do, that's less gruff than we talk here and softer.[10]

"I'm not come too soon, am I?" he said, casting a look at me. I had begun to wipe the plate, and tidy some drawers at the far end in the dresser.

"No," answered Catherine. "What are you doing there, Nelly?"

"My work, Miss," I replied. (Mr. Hindley had given me directions to make a third party in any private visits Linton chose to pay.)

She stepped behind me and whispered crossly, "Take yourself and your dusters off! When company are in the house, servants don't commence scouring and cleaning in the room where they are!"

"It's a good opportunity, now that master is away," I answered aloud. "He hates me be fidgeting over these things in his presence—I'm sure Mr. Edgar will excuse me."

"I hate you to be fidgeting in *my* presence," exclaimed the young lady imperiously, not allowing her guest time to speak—she had failed to recover her equanimity since the little dispute with Heathcliff.

"I'm sorry for it, Miss Catherine!" was my response; and I proceeded assiduously with my occupation.

She, supposing Edgar could not see her, snatched the cloth from my hand, and pinched me with a prolonged wrench, very spitefully on the arm.

I've said I did not love her, and rather relished mortifying her vanity, now and then; besides, she hurt me extremely, so I started up from my knees, and screamed out.

10 As befits someone who inhabits Thrushcross Grange, Edgar's pronunciation is more like Lockwood's than like that of the inhabitants of the Heights. But the contrast between his nature and Heathcliff's exceeds all differences of habit, manners, nurture, and education. It is so fundamental and inalienable that it can only be conveyed by means of analogies to natural elements, weathers, landscapes, and animal species: for example, "a bleak, hilly, coal country" vs. "a beautiful fertile valley." As various readers have observed approvingly or disapprovingly ever since *Wuthering Heights* was published, such analogies undermine the rational preferences and moral judgments that are the usual business of Victorian novels. Behind them is Brontë's abiding belief that the same life force courses through human beings, nonhuman animals, and elemental nature.

"O, Miss, that's a nasty trick! You have no right to nip me, and I'm not going to bear it!"

"I didn't touch you, you lying creature!" cried she, her fingers tingling to repeat the act, and her ears red with rage. She never had power to conceal her passion; it always set her whole complexion in a blaze.

"What's that then?" I retorted showing a decided purple witness to refute her.

She stamped her foot, wavered a moment, and then, irresistibly impelled by the naughty spirit within her, slapped me on the cheek a stinging blow that filled both eyes with water.

"Catherine, love! Catherine!" interposed Linton, greatly shocked at the double fault of falsehood and violence which his idol had committed.

"Leave the room, Ellen!" she repeated, trembling all over.

Little Hareton, who followed me everywhere, and was sitting near me on the floor, at seeing my tears commenced crying himself, and sobbed out complaints against "wicked aunt Cathy," which drew her fury on to his unlucky head: she seized his shoulders, and shook him till the poor child waxed livid, and Edgar thoughtlessly laid hold of her hands to deliver him. In an instant one was wrung free, and the astonished young man felt it applied over his own ear in a way that could not be mistaken for jest.

He drew back in consternation—I lifted Hareton in my arms, and walked off to the kitchen with him, leaving the door of communication open, for I was curious to watch how they would settle their disagreement.

The insulted visiter moved to the spot where he had laid his hat, pale and with a quivering lip.

"That's right!" I said to myself. "Take warning and begone! It's a kindness to let you have a glimpse of her genuine disposition."

"Where are you going?" demanded Catherine, advancing to the door.

He swerved aside and attempted to pass. "You must not go!" she exclaimed energetically.

"I must and shall!" he replied in a subdued voice.

"No," she persisted, grasping the handle; "not yet, Edgar Linton—sit down, you shall not leave me in that temper. I should be miserable all night, and I won't be miserable for you!"

"Can I stay after you have struck me?" asked Linton.

Catherine was mute.

"You've made me afraid, and ashamed of you," he continued; "I'll not come here again!"

Her eyes began to glisten and her lids to twinkle.

"And you told a deliberate untruth!" he said.

"I didn't!" she cried, recovering her speech. "I did nothing deliberately—Well, go, if you please—get away! And now I'll cry—I'll cry myself sick!"

She dropped down on her knees by a chair and set to weeping in serious earnest.

Edgar persevered in his resolution as far as the court; there, he lingered. I resolved to encourage him.

"Miss is dreadfully wayward, sir!" I called out. "As bad as any marred[11] child—you'd better be riding home, or else she will be sick, only to grieve us."[12]

The soft thing looked askance through the window—he possessed the power to depart, as much as a cat possesses the power to leave a mouse half killed, or a bird half eaten—

Ah, I thought, there will be no saving him—He's doomed, and flies to his fate!

And so it was; he turned abruptly, hastened into the house again, shut the door behind him; and, when I went in a while after to inform them that Earnshaw had come home rabid drunk, ready to pull the old place about our ears (his ordinary frame of mind in that condition), I saw the quarrel had merely effected a closer intimacy—had broken the outworks of youthful timidity, and enabled

11 Spoiled.

12 Here Nelly goes out of her way to urge Edgar to give Catherine up, and this is one passage that calls attention to her role as a character in the story she tells. Nelly's reputation with readers has undergone dramatic shifts during the life of *Wuthering Heights.* In her "Editor's Preface," Charlotte praises her as "a specimen of true benevolence and homely fidelity." Her contemporaries would have agreed, as does Q. D. Leavis more than a century later in her classic essay on the novel. According to Leavis, Nelly is "most carefully, consistently and convincingly created for us as the normal woman, whose truly feminine nature satisfies itself in nurturing all the children in the book in turn" (*Collected Essays: The Englishness of the English Novel,* vol. 1, ed. G. Singh [Cambridge: Cambridge Univ. Press, 1983], p. 234). James Hafley was the first of many critics to demur. According to Hafley, Nelly is "one of the consummate villains in English literature" ("The Villain in *Wuthering Heights,*" *Nineteenth-Century Fiction,* 13:3 [Dec. 1958], p. 199).

Readers will probably continue to disagree about whether Nelly is a villain or an admirable woman. Is she harsher than she should be in judging Catherine? Does she keep information from her that might change her behavior? How thoroughly should we trust her view of Catherine's feelings for Edgar or Heathcliff? Certainly the novel provides ample evidence that Nelly resents Catherine and wants to humble her, even though she continues to receive Catherine's confidences and offer her advice.

them to forsake the disguise of friendship, and confess themselves lovers.

Intelligence of Mr. Hindley's arrival drove Linton speedily to his horse, and Catherine to her chamber. I went to hide little Hareton, and to take the shot out of the master's fowling piece, which he was fond of playing with in his insane excitement, to the hazard of the lives of any who provoked, or even attracted, his notice too much; and I had hit upon the plan of removing it, that he might do less mischief, if he did go the length of firing the gun.

CHAPTER 9

He entered, vociferating oaths dreadful to hear; and caught me in the act of stowing his son away in the kitchen cupboard. Hareton was impressed with a wholesome terror of encountering either his wild beast's fondness, or his madman's rage—for in one he ran a chance of being squeezed and kissed to death, and in the other of being flung into the fire, or dashed against the wall—and the poor thing remained perfectly quiet wherever I chose to put him.

"There I've found it out at last!" cried Hindley, pulling me back by the skin of the neck, like a dog. "By Heaven and Hell, you've sworn between you to murder that child! I know how it is, now that he is always out of my way. But, with the help of Satan, I shall make you swallow the carving knife, Nelly! you needn't laugh, for I've just crammed Kenneth head-downmost in the Blackhorse marsh; and two is the same as one—and I want to kill some of you, I shall have no rest till I do!"

"But I don't like the carving knife, Mr. Hindley," I answered; "it has been cutting red herrings—I'd rather be shot if you please."

"You'd rather be damned!" he said, "and so you shall—No law in England can hinder a man from keeping his house decent, and mine's abominable! Open your mouth."

He held the knife in his hand, and pushed its point between my teeth: but, for my part, I was never much afraid of his vagaries. I spat out, and affirmed it tasted detestably—I would not take it on any account.

"Oh!" said he, releasing me, "I see that hideous little villain is not Hareton—I beg your pardon, Nell—if it be, he deserves flaying alive for not running to welcome me, and for screaming as if I were a goblin. Unnatural cub, come hither! I'll teach thee to impose on a good-hearted, deluded father—Now, don't you think the lad would be handsomer cropped?[1] It makes a dog fiercer, and I love something fierce—Get me a scissors—something fierce and trim! Besides, it's infernal affectation—devilish conceit, it is, to cherish our ears—we're asses enough without them.[2] Hush, child, hush! well then, it is my darling! Wisht,[3] dry thy eyes—there's a joy; kiss me; what, it won't? Kiss me, Hareton! Damn thee, kiss me! By God, as if I would rear such a monster! As sure as I'm living, I'll break the brat's neck."

Poor Hareton was squalling and kicking in his father's arms with all his might, and redoubled his yells when he carried him up-stairs and lifted him over the bannister. I cried out that he would frighten the child into fits, and ran to rescue him.

As I reached them, Hindley leant forward on the rails to listen to a noise below, almost forgetting what he had in his hands.

"Who is that?" he asked, hearing some one approaching the stair's-foot.

I leant forward also for the purpose of signing to Heathcliff, whose step I recognized, not to come further; and, at the instant when my eye quitted Hareton, he gave a sudden spring, delivered himself from the careless grasp that held him, and fell.

There was scarcely time to experience a thrill of horror before we saw that the little wretch was safe. Heathcliff arrived underneath just at the critical moment; by a natural impulse, he arrested his descent, and setting him on his feet, looked up to discover the author of the accident.

A miser who has parted with a lucky lottery ticket for five shillings and finds next day he has lost in the bargain five thousand

1 A reference to the practice of cropping a dog's ears. There's no evidence that cropping a dog's ears makes the dog fiercer, although it may make him look that way.

2 An allusion to Bottom, a comic character in Shakespeare's *A Midsummer Night's Dream*. In the play Puck, a mischievous jester with magical powers, replaces Bottom's human head with the head of a jackass, then gives Bottom back his human head. Bottom remains himself, always a jackass, regardless of which head he wears.

3 Hush.

pounds could not show a blanker countenance than he did on beholding the figure of Mr. Earnshaw above—It expressed, plainer than words could do, the intensest anguish at having made himself the instrument of thwarting his own revenge. Had it been dark, I dare say, he would have tried to remedy the mistake by smashing Hareton's skull on the steps; but we witnessed his salvation; and I was presently below with my precious charge pressed to my heart.

Hindley descended more leisurely, sobered and abashed.

"It is your fault, Ellen," he said, "you should have kept him out of sight; you should have taken him from me! Is he injured anywhere?"

"Injured!" I cried angrily. "If he's not killed, he'll be an idiot! Oh! I wonder his mother does not rise from her grave to see how you use him. You're worse than a heathen—treating your own flesh and blood in that manner!"

He attempted to touch the child, who, on finding himself with me, sobbed off his terror directly. At the first finger his father laid on him, however, he shrieked again louder than before, and struggled as if he would go into convulsions.

"You shall not meddle with him!" I continued. "He hates you—they all hate you—that's the truth! A happy family you have; and a pretty state you're come to!"

"I shall come to a prettier yet, Nelly!" laughed the misguided man, recovering his hardness. "At present, convey yourself and him away—And, hark you, Heathcliff! clear you too, quite from my reach and hearing . . . I wouldn't murder you to-night, unless, perhaps, I set the house on fire; but that's as my fancy goes—"

While saying this he took a pint bottle of brandy from the dresser, and poured some into a tumbler.

"Nay, don't!" I entreated. "Mr. Hindley, do take warning. Have mercy on this unfortunate boy, if you care nothing for yourself!"

"Any one will do better for him than I shall," he answered.

"Have mercy on your own soul!" I said, endeavouring to snatch the glass from his hand.

"Not I! On the contrary, I shall have great pleasure in sending it to perdition to punish its maker," exclaimed the blasphemer. "Here's to its hearty damnation!"

He drank the spirits, and impatiently bade us go, terminating his command with a sequel of horrid imprecations, too bad to repeat or remember.

"It's a pity he cannot kill himself with drink," observed Heathcliff, muttering an echo of curses back when the door was shut. "He's doing his very utmost; but his constitution defies him—Mr. Kenneth says he would wager his mare that he'll outlive any man on this side Gimmerton, and go to the grave a hoary sinner; unless some happy chance out of the common course befall him."

I went into the kitchen and sat down to lull my little lamb to sleep. Heathcliff, as I thought, walked through to the barn. It turned out, afterwards, that he only got as far as the other side the settle, when he flung himself on a bench by the wall, removed from the fire, and remained silent.

I was rocking Hareton on my knee, and humming a song that began,

> "It was far in the night, and the bairnies grat,
> The mither beneath the mools heard that,"[4]

when Miss Cathy, who had listened to the hubbub from her room, put her head in and whispered,

"Are you alone, Nelly?"

"Yes, Miss," I replied.

She entered and approached the hearth. I, supposing she was going to say something, looked up. The expression of her face seemed disturbed and anxious. Her lips were half asunder as if she meant to speak; and she drew a breath, but it escaped in a sigh, instead of a sentence.

I resumed my song, not having forgotten her recent behaviour.

"Where's Heathcliff?" she said, interrupting me.

4 Nelly is humming a Danish ballad, "Svend Dyring," whose theme is appropriate to Hindley's decline and his harsh treatment of Hareton after Frances's death. Brontë would have heard ballads sung by Tabitha Ackroyd, the family's beloved servant. She would also have encountered the words to this particular ballad, translated as "The Ghaist's Warning," in one of Scott's footnotes to Canto 4, part 12, of *The Lady of the Lake:* "'Twas lang i' the night, and the bairnies grat [cried]:/ Their mither [mother] she under the mools [grave] heard that. . . ." "The Ghaist's Warning" tells the story of seven children whose unkind treatment by their stepmother brings their dead mother back to tend to them and warn their father that she will return if he does not see to their welfare. Earlier in this chapter, after Hareton escaped from his father's grasp and was saved from falling onto the stone floor below by Heathcliff, Nelly wondered that "his mother does not rise from her grave" at the sight of Hindley's treatment of their son.

"About his work in the stable," was my answer.

He did not contradict me; perhaps he had fallen into a doze.[5]

There followed another long pause, during which I perceived a drop or two trickle from Catherine's cheek to the flags.

Is she sorry for her shameful conduct? I asked myself. That will be a novelty; but she may come to the point as she will—I shan't help her!

No, she felt small trouble regarding any subject, save her own concerns.

"Oh, dear!" she cried at last, "I'm very unhappy!"

"A pity," observed I, "you're hard to please—so many friends and so few cares, and can't make yourself content!"

"Nelly, will you keep a secret for me?" she pursued, kneeling down by me, and lifting her winsome eyes to my face with that sort of look which turns off bad temper, even when one has all the right in the world to indulge it.

"Is it worth keeping?" I inquired less sulkily.

"Yes, and it worries me, and I must let it out! I want to know what I should do—To-day, Edgar Linton has asked me to marry him, and I've given him an answer—Now, before I tell you whether it was a consent or denial—you tell me which it ought to have been."

"Really, Miss Catherine, how can I know?" I replied. "To be sure, considering the exhibition you performed in his presence this afternoon, I might say it would be wise to refuse him—since he asked you after that, he must either be hopelessly stupid or a venturesome fool."

"If you talk so, I won't tell you any more," she returned peevishly, rising to her feet. "I accepted him, Nelly; be quick, and say whether I was wrong!"

"You accepted him? Then what good is it discussing the matter? You have pledged your word, and cannot retract."

"But say whether I should have done so—do!" she exclaimed in an irritated tone; chafing her hands together and frowning.

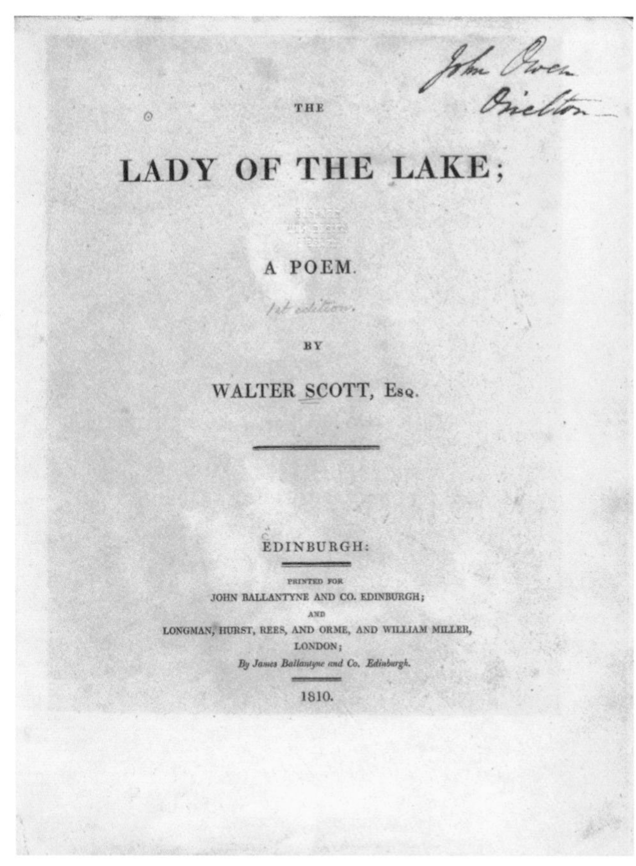

THE

LADY OF THE LAKE;

A POEM.

BY

WALTER SCOTT, Esq.

EDINBURGH:

PRINTED FOR

JOHN BALLANTYNE AND CO. EDINBURGH;

AND

LONGMAN, HURST, REES, AND ORME, AND WILLIAM MILLER,

LONDON;

By James Ballantyne and Co. Edinburgh.

1810.

Title page of *Lady of the Lake,* the long narrative poem Sir Walter Scott published in 1810.

5 As Nelly tells the story to Lockwood, she takes account of Heathcliff's presence, but she claims that she did not know that Heathcliff was on the other side of the settle until he got up to leave.

"There are many things to be considered before that question can be answered properly," I said sententiously. "First and foremost, do you love Mr. Edgar?"

"Who can help it? Of course I do," she answered.

Then I put her through the following catechism—for a girl of twenty-two it was not injudicious.

"Why do you love him, Miss Cathy?"

"Nonsense, I do—that's sufficient."

"By no means; you must say why."

"Well, because he is handsome and pleasant to be with."

"Bad," was my commentary.

"And because he is young and cheerful."

"Bad, still."

"And because he loves me."

"Indifferent, coming there."

"And he will be rich, and I shall like to be the greatest woman of the neighbourhood, and I shall be proud of having such a husband."

"Worst of all! And now, say how you love him?"

"As every body loves—You're silly, Nelly."

"Not at all—Answer."

"I love the ground under his feet, and the air over his head, and everything he touches, and every word he says—I love all his looks, and all his actions, and him entirely and altogether. There now!"

"And why?"

"Nay—you are making a jest of it; it is exceedingly ill-natured! It's no jest to me!" said the young lady scowling, and turning her face to the fire.

"I'm very far from jesting, Miss Catherine," I replied, "you love Mr. Edgar because he is handsome, and young, and cheerful, and rich, and loves you. The last, however, goes for nothing—You would love him without that, probably, and with it, you wouldn't unless he possessed the four former attractions."

"No, to be sure not—I should only pity him—hate him, perhaps, if he were ugly and a clown."

"But there are several other handsome, rich young men in the world; handsomer, possibly, and richer than he is—What should hinder you from loving them?"

"If there be any, they are out of my way—I've seen none like Edgar."

"You may see some; and he won't always be handsome and young, and may not always be rich."

"He is now; and I have only to do with the present—I wish you would speak rationally."

"Well, that settles it—if you have only to do with the present, marry Mr. Linton."

"I don't want your permission for that—I *shall* marry him; and yet, you have not told me whether I'm right."

"Perfectly right; if people be right to marry only for the present. And now, let us hear what you are unhappy about. Your brother will be pleased . . . The old lady and gentleman will not object, I think—you will escape from a disorderly, comfortless home into a wealthy respectable one; and you love Edgar, and Edgar loves you. All seems smooth and easy—where is the obstacle?"

"*Here!* and *here!*" replied Catherine, striking one hand on her forehead, and the other on her breast. "In whichever place the soul lives—in my soul, and in my heart,[6] I'm convinced I'm wrong!"

"That's very strange! I cannot make it out."

"It's my secret; but if you will not mock at me, I'll explain it; I can't do it distinctly—but I'll give you a feeling of how I feel."

She seated herself by me again: her countenance grew sadder and graver, and her clasped hands trembled.

"Nelly, do you never dream queer dreams?" she said, suddenly, after some minutes' reflection.

"Yes, now and then," I answered.

"And so do I. I've dreamt in my life dreams that have stayed with me ever after, and changed my ideas; they've gone through and

6 In her late, great poem "No coward soul is mine," composed in January 1846, when she may also have been writing *Wuthering Heights*, Brontë locates the soul in the breast rather than in the head, addressing it as the "God within my breast," the "Life, that in me has rest," and "Being and Breath." The poem holds eternity firmly in view and celebrates its speaker's indomitable creative spirit.

"No coward soul is mine" on a page of the Honresfeld fair-copy notebook, into which Brontë transcribed poems that didn't belong to her Gondal saga. Charlotte published it in her 1850 edition of *Wuthering Heights,* where she identified it as her sister's last poem. She was wrong about this (Emily's last poem was the Gondal poem "Why ask to know what date what clime"), but "No coward soul is mine" is a fiercely final assertion of the immortality of being and breath.

through me, like wine through water, and altered the colour of my mind. And this is one—I'm going to tell it—but take care not to smile at any part of it."

"Oh don't, Miss Catherine!" I cried. "We're dismal enough without conjuring up ghosts and visions to perplex us. Come, come, be merry, and like yourself! Look at little Hareton—he's dreaming nothing dreary. How sweetly he smiles in his sleep!"

"Yes; and how sweetly his father curses in his solitude! You remember him, I dare say, when he was just such another as that

7 The doctrine Nelly expresses is that the wicked would lack the capacity to enjoy the bliss of heaven: "They would be in the same position as a blind man before a beautiful view, or a deaf man at a concert" (Geoffrey Rowell, *Hell and the Victorians* [Oxford: Clarendon Press, 1974], p. 44).

8 Catherine's rejoinder—"But it is not for that [reason]"—does not dispute Nelly's doctrinal point but insists instead on the psychological and emotional truth conveyed by her dream. In the dream, heaven stands in for the splendid, worldly abode of the Lintons. Heathcliff has already described Thrushcross Grange in this way. Spying on Edgar and Isabella through the drawing-room window of the Grange, he tells

chubby thing—nearly as young and innocent. However, Nelly, I shall oblige you to listen—it's not long; and I've no power to be merry to-night."

"I won't hear it, I won't hear it!" I repeated, hastily.

I was superstitious about dreams then, and am still; and Catherine had an unusual gloom in her aspect that made me dread something from which I might shape a prophecy, and foresee a fearful catastrophe.

She was vexed, but she did not proceed. Apparently taking up another subject, she re-commenced in a short time.

"If I were in heaven, Nelly, I should be extremely miserable."

"Because you are not fit to go there," I answered. "All sinners would be miserable in heaven."[7]

"But it is not for that. I dreamt, once, that I was there."

"I tell you I won't harken to your dreams, Miss Catherine! I'll go to bed," I interrupted again.

She laughed, and held me down, for I made a motion to leave my chair.

"This is nothing," cried she. "I was only going to say that heaven did not seem to be my home; and I broke my heart with weeping to come back to earth; and the angels were so angry that they flung me out, into the middle of the heath on the top of Wuthering Heights, where I woke sobbing for joy. That will do to explain my secret, as well as the other.[8] I've no more business to marry Edgar Linton than I have to be in heaven; and if the wicked man in there had not brought Heathcliff so low, I shouldn't have thought of it. It would degrade me to marry Heathcliff now; so he shall never know how I love him; and that, not because he's handsome, Nelly, but because he's more myself than I am. Whatever our souls are made of, his and mine are the same, and Linton's is as different as a moonbeam from lightning, or frost from fire."[9]

Ere this speech ended I became sensible of Heathcliff's presence. Having noticed a slight movement, I turned my head, and saw him rise from the bench, and steal out, noiselessly. He had lis-

Nelly that he and Catherine, in their place, would have thought themselves "in heaven" (Chapter 6).

Yet it would be a mistake to limit the meaning of Catherine's dream to her own interpretation of it as a warning against marrying Edgar. The dream also tells us how much she prefers her life at the Heights (not inside the Heights but on the heath, the moors, and the windy hilltop) to any afterlife she can imagine. Brontë's poems give us speakers who celebrate life as often as speakers who long for death. In "I see around me tombstones grey," a walk through a graveyard elicits a speech promising Earth that humans don't forget her easily:

Indeed no dazzling land above
Can cheat thee of thy children's love—
We all in life's departing shine
Our last dear longings blend with thine;
And struggle still, and strive to trace
With clouded gaze thy darling face
We would not leave our native home
For *any* world beyond the Tomb
No—rather on thy kindly breast
Let us be laid in lasting rest
Or waken but to share with thee
A mutual immortality—

The speaker of "I see around me tombstones grey" longs for life, as Emily herself did, according to Charlotte's report: "she was torn conscious, panting, reluctant though resolute out of a happy life" (*The Letters of Charlotte Brontë*, 3 vols., ed. Margaret Smith [Oxford: Clarendon Press, 2000], 2, p. 200). In "The Philosopher," even the longing for oblivion is attributed to our illimitable human needs and aspirations:

No promised heaven, these wild desires,
Could all, or half fulfill;
No threatened hell, with quenchless fires,
Subdue this quenchless will!

9 Catherine's analysis of the mistake she is about to make by marrying Edgar has no precedent in the English novel. She shares the social ambition that is a staple feature of these novels and their marriage plots—she wants to be rich and "the greatest woman of the neighborhood"—but she also reaches out toward a truth that belongs to an entirely different domain. Thus she expresses the alternatives Heathcliff and Edgar offer her by means of analogies to elemental natural forces. Here and throughout the novel, these natural forces are oppositional and incompatible rather than good or bad, lovable or unlovable in themselves.

tened till he heard Catherine say it would degrade her to marry him, and then he stayed to hear no farther.[10]

My companion, sitting on the ground, was prevented by the back of the settle from remarking his presence or departure; but I started, and bade her hush!

"Why?" she asked, gazing nervously round.

"Joseph is here," I answered, catching, opportunely, the roll of his cartwheels up the road, "and Heathcliff will come in with him. I'm not sure whether he were not at the door this moment."

"Oh, he couldn't overhear me at the door!" said she. "Give me Hareton, while you get the supper, and when it is ready, ask me to sup with you. I want to cheat my uncomfortable conscience, and be convinced that Heathcliff has no notion of these things—he has not, has he? He does not know what being in love is?"

"I see no reason that he should not know, as well as you," I returned, "and, if *you* are his choice, he'll be the most unfortunate creature that ever was born! As soon as you become Mrs. Linton, he loses friend, and love, and all! Have you considered how you'll bear the separation, and how he'll bear to be quite deserted in the world? Because, Miss Catherine—"

"He quite deserted! We separated!" she exclaimed, with an accent of indignation. "Who is to separate us, pray? They'll meet the fate of Milo![11] Not as long as I live, Ellen—for no mortal creature. Every Linton on the face of the earth might melt into nothing, before I could consent to forsake Heathcliff. Oh, that's not what I intend—that's not what I mean! I shouldn't be Mrs. Linton were such a price demanded! He'll be as much to me as he has been all his lifetime. Edgar must shake off his antipathy and tolerate him, at least. He will when he learns my true feeling towards him. Nelly, I see now you think me a selfish wretch, but did it never strike you that, if Heathcliff and I married, we should be beggars? whereas if I marry Linton, I can aid Heathcliff to rise, and place him out of my brother's power."[12]

10 Gérin cites an incident recorded in Thomas Moore's *Life of Byron* that may have influenced this scene. When Byron was fifteen and in love with Mary Chaworth, he "either was told of, or overheard, Miss Chaworth saying to her maid, 'Do you think I could care anything for that lame boy?' This speech, as he himself described it, was like a shot through the heart" (Moore, quoted in Winifred Gérin, *Emily Brontë: A Biography* [Oxford: Oxford Univ. Press, 1971], p. 45). Brontë's watercolor "The North Wind" was copied from William Finden's engraving of Richard Westall's "Ianthe," published as the frontispiece to volume 2 of Moore's *Life* as well as elsewhere.

11 According to legend, Milo, a great Greek athlete and warrior, tried to tear apart a tree that had been split with a wedge. The wedge fell out, and the tree closed on his hand. Held captive by the tree, he was devoured by wolves.

12 As a woman, Catherine's rank and support depend on the novel's land-owning males, Hindley and Edgar. Terry Eagleton sees her choosing Edgar rather than Heathcliff as "the pivotal event of the novel" and the "decisive catalyst of the tragedy; and if this is so, then the crux of *Wuthering Heights* must be conceded by even the most remorselessly mythological and mystical of critics to be a social one. In a crucial act of self-betrayal and bad faith, Catherine rejects Heathcliff as a suitor because he is socially inferior to Linton; and it is from this that the train of destruction follows" (Eagleton, *Myths of Power: A Marxist Study of the Brontës* [London: Macmillan, 1975], p. 101).

Oil portrait of a pensive George Gordon, Lord Byron (1813), by Richard Westall (1765–1836).

"With your husband's money, Miss Catherine?" I asked. "You'll find him not so pliable as you calculate upon: and, though I'm hardly a judge, I think that's the worst motive you've given yet for being the wife of young Linton."

"It is not," retorted she, "it is the best! The others were the satisfaction of my whims; and for Edgar's sake too, to satisfy him. This is for the sake of one who comprehends in his person my feelings to Edgar and myself. I cannot express it, but surely you and every body have a notion that there is, or should be, an existence of yours beyond you. What were the use of my creation if I were entirely contained here? My great miseries in this world have been Heathcliff's miseries, and I watched and felt each from the beginning; my great thought in living is himself. If all else perished, and *he* remained, I should still continue to be; and, if all else remained, and he were annihilated, the Universe would turn to a mighty stranger. I should not seem a part of it. My love for Linton is like the foliage in the woods. Time will change it, I'm well aware, as winter changes the trees—my love for Heathcliff resembles the eternal rocks beneath—a source of little visible delight, but necessary. Nelly, I *am* Heathcliff[13]—he's always, always in my mind—not as a pleasure, any more than I am always a pleasure to myself—but as my own being—so don't talk of our separation again—it is impracticable; and—"

She paused, and hid her face in the folds of my gown; but I jerked it forcibly away. I was out of patience with her folly!

"If I can make any sense of your nonsense, Miss," I said, "it only goes to convince me that you are ignorant of the duties you undertake in marrying; or else, that you are a wicked, unprincipled girl. But trouble me with no more secrets. I'll not promise to keep them."

"You'll keep that?" she asked, eagerly.

"No, I'll not promise," I repeated.

She was about to insist when the entrance of Joseph finished our conversation; and Catherine removed her seat to a corner, and nursed Hareton, while I made the supper.

After it was cooked, my fellow servant and I began to quarrel who should carry some to Mr. Hindley; and we didn't settle it till all was nearly cold. Then we came to the agreement that we would let him ask, if he wanted any, for we feared particularly to go into his presence when he had been sometime alone.

13 This declaration—the climax of Catherine's most famous speech—is the simplest kind of sentence one can speak in English, yet it has puzzled generations of readers. Leo Bersani points out that Catherine does not mean that she is *like* Heathcliff: "She is sociable, high-spirited, indeed often manic; he is quiet, closed, and he hoards his feelings in a way dramatically opposed to Catherine's wild display of feelings" (*A Future for Astyanax* [New York: Columbia Univ. Press, 1984], p. 204). William Wyler's 1939 film adaptation of the novel has Catherine express her love for Heathcliff in terms not of identification but of possession: "I'm yours. I've never been anyone else's." Percy Shelley's *Epipsychidion* (1821) has been cited as an influence. Addressed to Emilia or Emily, the speaker's soulmate, the poem is a meditation on ideal love, ideal union, and ideal liberty. In particular, a line from the poem, "I am not thine: I am a part of *thee*" (l. 52), has been adduced as an important source of Catherine's claim to *be* Heathcliff.

How close to Shelley's formulation is Brontë's? Catherine's identification with Heathcliff is premised on ideas she formulates earlier in the paragraph: everybody has "a notion that there is, or should be, an existence of yours beyond you," and "If all else perished, and *he* remained, I should still continue to be; and, if all else remained, and he were annihilated, the Universe would turn to a mighty stranger." Like Coleridge, Brontë intuited "the one life within us and abroad" ("The Eolian Harp"). And like Wordsworth, she represents, in her poems and her novel, our desperate human longing to re-establish a connection to the world that is felt most fully in childhood. With Brontë's affinities to these defining Romantic ideas in mind, we can better understand why Catherine's words here echo words Brontë had already set down in "No coward soul is mine":

> Though Earth and moon were gone
> And suns and universes ceased to be
> And thou wert left alone
> Every Existence would exist in thee

In the poem, Brontë's most triumphant assertion of her faith in an infinite, enduring life pervading the universe, the speaker locates this "Life" in her own soul or breast, not outside her either on earth or in heaven. But Catherine locates the pervasive vital principle that keeps her from being isolated and self-contained, adrift in an alien universe, in Heathcliff. She would not cease to exist in a world lacking him, but she would be cut off from that world, an existence without an existence beyond her own.

From Catherine's point of view, marrying Edgar—the topic on which she has just asked for Nelly's advice—is entirely compatible with her relationship to Heathcliff. Marriage, Catherine thinks, is not an expression of one person's view of another as an extension of her own be-

Oil portrait of Percy Bysshe Shelley (1819) by Amelia Curran (1775–1847).

"Und hah isn't that nowt comed in frough th' field, be this time? What is he abaht? girt eedle seeght!"[14] demanded the old man, looking round for Heathcliff.

"I'll call him," I replied. "He's in the barn, I've no doubt."

I went and called, but got no answer. On returning, I whispered to Catherine that he had heard a good part of what she said, I was sure; and told how I saw him quit the kitchen just as she complained of her brother's conduct regarding him.

ing. Instead, it is a means of social advancement and economic consolidation as well as a provision of worldly powers and pleasures. Unlike Heathcliff, Edgar is well qualified for this more conventional kind of human relation. Patsy Stoneman translates Catherine's "argument" into simpler language: "If I love Edgar and I *am* Heathcliff, then Heathcliff must love Edgar" ("Catherine Earnshaw's Journey to Her Home among the Dead: Fresh Thoughts on *Wuthering Heights* and 'Epipsychidion,'" *Review of English Studies,* 47:188 [Nov. 1966], p. 530). Generations of readers, along with Nelly, Heathcliff, and Edgar, have balked at so radical an idea.

14 "And how is it that nobody has come in from the field by this time? What is he doing? great idle spectacle!"

15 "Badly behaved enough for any foul manners."

16 Sheepfold.

She jumped up in a fine fright—flung Hareton onto the settle, and ran to seek for her friend herself, not taking leisure to consider why she was so flurried, or how her talk would have affected him.

She was absent such a while that Joseph proposed we should wait no longer. He cunningly conjectured they were staying away in order to avoid hearing his protracted blessing. They were "ill eneugh for ony fahl manners,"[15] he affirmed. And, on their behalf, he added that night a special prayer to the usual quarter of an hour's supplication before meat, and would have tacked another to the end of the grace, had not his young mistress broken in upon him with a hurried command that he must run down the road, and, wherever Heathcliff had rambled, find and make him re-enter directly!

"I want to speak to him, and I *must,* before I go up-stairs," she said. "And the gate is open; he is somewhere out of hearing, for he would not reply, though I shouted at the top of the fold[16] as loud as I could."

Joseph objected at first; she was too much in earnest, however, to suffer contradiction; and, at last, he placed his hat on his head and walked grumbling forth.

Meantime, Catherine paced up and down the floor, exclaiming—

"I wonder where he is—I wonder where he *can* be!—What did I say, Nelly? I've forgotten. Was he vexed at my bad humour this afternoon? Dear! tell me what I've said to grieve him? I do wish he'd come. I do wish he would!"

"What a noise for nothing!" I cried, though rather uneasy myself. "What a trifle scares you! It's surely no great cause of alarm that Heathcliff should take a moonlight saunter on the moors, or even lie, too sulky to speak to us, in the hay-loft. I'll engage he's lurking there. See if I don't ferret him out!"

I departed to renew my search; its result was disappointment, and Joseph's quest ended in the same.

"Yon lad gets war un war!" observed he on re-entering. "He's left th' yate ut t' full swing, and miss's pony has trodden dahn two rigs uh corn, un'plottered through, raight o'er intuh t' meadow! Hahsomdiver, t' maister 'ull play t' divil to-morn, and he'll do weel. He's patience itsseln wi' sich careless, offald craters—patience itsseln he is! Bud he'll nut be soa allus—yah's see, all on ye! Yah munn't drive him aht uf his heead fur nowt!"[17]

"Have you found Heathcliff, you ass?" interrupted Catherine. "Have you been looking for him, as I ordered?"

"Aw sud more likker look for th' horse," he replied. "It 'ud be tuh more sense. Bud aw can look for norther horse nur man uf a neeght loike this—as black as t' chimbley! und Hathecliff's noan t' chap tuh coom ut *maw* whistle—happen he'll be less hard uh hearing wi' *ye!*"[18]

It *was* a very dark evening for summer: the clouds appeared inclined to thunder, and I said we had better all sit down; the approaching rain would be certain to bring him home without further trouble.

However, Catherine would not be persuaded into tranquillity. She kept wandering to and fro, from the gate to the door, in a state of agitation which permitted no repose: and, at length, took up a permanent situation on one side of the wall, near the road, where, heedless of my expostulations and the growling thunder, and the great drops that began to plash around her, she remained calling, at intervals, and then listening, and then crying outright. She beat Hareton, or any child, at a good, passionate fit of crying.

About midnight, while we still sat up, the storm came rattling over the Heights in full fury. There was a violent wind, as well as thunder, and either one or the other split a tree off at the corner of the building; a huge bough fell across the roof, and knocked down a portion of the east chimney-stack, sending a clatter of stones and soot into the kitchen fire.

We thought a bolt[19] had fallen in the middle of us, and Joseph swung onto his knees, beseeching the Lord to remember the Patri-

17 "That lad gets worse and worse. . . . He's left the gate wide open, and miss's pony has trodden down two rows of grain, and floundered through, right over into the meadow! In any case, the master will be furious tomorrow, and he'll do well [to be furious]. He's patience itself with such careless, worthless creatures—patience itself he is! But he'll not be so always—you'll see, all of you! You mustn't drive him out of his head for no reason!"

18 "I should more likely look for the horse. That would make more sense. But I can look for neither horse nor man on a night like this—as black as the chimney! and Heathcliff's not the chap to come at *my* whistle—perhaps he'll be less hard of hearing with *you!*"

19 A flash of lightning imagined as a hot solid body and often interpreted as a sign of divine vengeance.

archs Noah and Lot;[20] and, as in former times, spare the righteous, though he smote the ungodly. I felt some sentiment that it must be a judgment on us also. The Jonah,[21] in my mind, was Mr. Earnshaw, and I shook the handle of his den that I might ascertain if he were yet living. He replied audibly enough, in a fashion which made my companion vociferate more clamorously than before that a wide distinction might be drawn between saints like himself, and sinners like his master. But the uproar passed away in twenty minutes, leaving us all unharmed, excepting Cathy, who got thoroughly drenched for her obstinacy in refusing to take shelter and standing bonnetless and shawlless to catch as much water as she could with her hair and clothes.

She came in, and lay down on the settle, all soaked as she was, turning her face to the back, and putting her hands before it.

"Well, Miss!" I exclaimed, touching her shoulder. "You are not bent on getting your death, are you? Do you know what o'clock it is? Half-past twelve. Come! come to bed—there's no use waiting longer on that foolish boy—he'll be gone to Gimmerton, and he'll stay there now. He guesses we shouldn't wake[22] for him till this late hour; at least, he guesses that only Mr. Hindley would be up; and he'd rather avoid having the door opened by the master."

"Nay, nay, he's noan at Gimmerton!" said Joseph. "Aw's niver wonder, bud he's at t' bothom of a bog-hoile. This visitation worn't for nowt, and aw wod hev ye tuh look aht, Miss—yah muh be t' next. Thank Hivin for all! All warks togither for gooid tuh them as is chozzen, and piked aht froo' th' rubbidge! Yah knaw whet t' Scripture ses—"[23]

And he began quoting several texts, referring us to the chapters and verses where we might find them.

I, having vainly begged the wilful girl to rise and remove her wet things, left him preaching and her shivering, and betook myself to bed with little Hareton, who slept as fast as if every one had been sleeping round him.

20 God spared the righteous patriarchs Noah (from the flood) and Lot (by sending him out of Sodom before he destroyed the city).

21 Nelly thinks that Hindley is the object of God's wrath, as Jonah was when he refused to go to Nineveh. When a violent storm threatens the ship that Jonah has boarded to sail away from Nineveh, he orders the sailors to throw him overboard.

22 Wait up for.

23 "Nay, nay, he's not at Gimmerton. . . . I wouldn't wonder if he were at the bottom of a bog-hole. This visitation wasn't for nothing, and I'd have you look out, Miss—you may be the next. Thank Heaven for all! All works together for the good to them that are chosen, and picked out from the rubbish! You know what the Scripture says—" Joseph refers to Romans 8:28: "And we know that all things work together for good to them that love God, to them who are the called according to his purpose."

I heard Joseph read on a while afterwards; then, I distinguished his slow step on the ladder, and then I dropt asleep.

Coming down somewhat later than usual, I saw, by the sunbeams piercing the chinks of the shutters, Miss Catherine still seated near the fire-place. The house door was ajar too: light entered from its unclosed windows. Hindley had come out, and stood on the kitchen hearth, haggard and drowsy.

"What ails you, Cathy?" he was saying when I entered. "You look as dismal as a drowned whelp—Why are you so damp and pale, child?"

"I've been wet," she answered reluctantly, "and I'm cold, that's all."

"Oh, she is naughty!" I cried, perceiving the master to be tolerably sober. "She got steeped in the shower of yesterday evening, and there she has sat, the night through, and I couldn't prevail on her to stir."

Mr. Earnshaw stared at us in surprise. "The night through," he repeated. "What kept her up? Not fear of the thunder, surely? That was over, hours since."

Neither of us wished to mention Heathcliff's absence, as long as we could conceal it; so I replied, I didn't know how she took it into her head to sit up; and she said nothing.

The morning was fresh and cool; I threw back the lattice, and presently the room filled with sweet scents from the garden: but Catherine called peevishly to me.

"Ellen, shut the window. I'm starving!"[24] And her teeth chattered as she shrunk closer to the almost extinguished embers.

"She's ill—" said Hindley, taking her wrist. "I suppose that's the reason she would not go to bed—Damn it! I don't want to be troubled with more sickness here—What took you into the rain?"

"Running after t'lads, as usuald!" croaked Joseph, catching an opportunity, from our hesitation, to thrust in his evil tongue. "If Aw wur yah, maister, Aw'd just slam t'boards i' their faces, all on

24 Freezing.

'em, gentle and simple! Never a day ut yah're off, but yon cat uh Linton comes sneaking hither—and Miss Nelly, shoo's a fine lass! shoo sits watching for ye i' t'kitchen; and as yah're in at one door, he's aht at t'other—Und, then, wer grand lady goes a coorting uf hor side! It's bonny behaviour, lurking among t'fields after twelve ut' night, wi that fahl, flaysome divil of a gipsy, Heathcliff! They think *Aw'm* blind; but Aw'm noan, now't ut t'soart! Aw seed young Linton, boath coming and going, and Aw seed *yah* (directing his discourse to me)—yah gooid fur nowt, slattenly witch! nip up und bolt intuh th' hahs t' minute yah heard t'maister's horse fit clatter up t' road."[25]

"Silence, eavesdropper!" cried Catherine. "None of your insolence before me! Edgar Linton came yesterday, by chance, Hindley: and it was *I* who told him to be off because I knew you would not like to have met him as you were."

"You lie, Cathy, no doubt," answered her brother, "and you are a confounded simpleton! But never mind Linton, at present—Tell me, were you not with Heathcliff last night? Speak the truth, now. You need not be afraid of harming him—Though I hate him as much as ever, he did me a good turn a short time since that will make my conscience tender of breaking his neck. To prevent it, I shall send him about his business this very morning; and after he's gone, I'd advise you all to look sharp; I shall only have the more humour for you!"

"I never saw Heathcliff last night," answered Catherine, beginning to sob bitterly, "and if you do turn him out of doors, I'll go with him. But perhaps you'll never have an opportunity—perhaps he's gone." Here she burst into uncontrollable grief, and the remainder of her words were inarticulate.

Hindley lavished on her a torrent of scornful abuse, and bid her get to her room immediately, or she shouldn't cry for nothing! I obliged her to obey; and I shall never forget what a scene she acted when we reached her chamber. It terrified me—I thought she was going mad, and I begged Joseph to run for the doctor.

25 Joseph's idea of Catherine is drenched in gall. "If I were you, master, I'd just slam the doors in their faces, all of them, masters and servants! Never a day that you're off, but that cat of a Linton comes sneaking here—and Miss Nelly, she's a fine lass! She sits watching for you in the kitchen; and as you're in at one door, he's out at the other—And, then, our grand lady goes courting for her part! It's fine behavior, lurking in the fields after midnight, with that wicked, dreadful devil of a gypsy, Heathcliff! They think *I'm* blind; but I'm not, nothing of the kind! I've seen young Linton both coming and going, and I've seen *you* . . . you good for nothing, slatternly witch!—jump up and bolt into the house the minute you heard the master's horse's feet clatter up the road."

It proved the commencement of delirium; Mr. Kenneth, as soon as he saw her, pronounced her dangerously ill; she had a fever.

He bled her,[26] and he told me to let her live on whey and water gruel; and take care she did not throw herself down stairs, or out of the window; and then he left, for he had enough to do in the parish where two or three miles was the ordinary distance between cottage and cottage.

Though I cannot say I made a gentle nurse, and Joseph and the master were no better, and, though our patient was as wearisome and headstrong as a patient could be, she weathered it through.

Old Mrs. Linton paid us several visits, to be sure; and set things to rights, and scolded and ordered us all; and when Catherine was convalescent, she insisted on conveying her to Thrushcross Grange, for which deliverance we were very grateful. But the poor dame had reason to repent of her kindness; she and her husband both took the fever, and died within a few days of each other.

Our young lady returned to us saucier, and more passionate, and haughtier than ever. Heathcliff had never been heard of since the evening of the thunder-storm, and one day, I had the misfortune, when she had provoked me exceedingly, to lay the blame of his disappearance on her (where indeed it belonged, as she well knew). From that period for several months, she ceased to hold any communication with me save in the relation of a mere servant. Joseph fell under a ban also; he *would* speak his mind, and lecture her all the same as if she were a little girl; and she esteemed herself a woman, and our mistress, and thought that her recent illness gave her a claim to be treated with consideration. Then the doctor had said that she would not bear crossing much, she ought to have her own way; and it was nothing less than murder, in her eyes, for any one to presume to stand up and contradict her.

From Mr. Earnshaw and his companions she kept aloof; and tutored by Kenneth and serious threats of a fit that often attended her rages, her brother allowed her whatever she pleased to demand, and generally avoided aggravating her fiery temper. He was

26 Bleeding by means of venisection, cupping, or leeches (the method used to treat Lockwood in the next chapter) was still the first medical treatment for a serious fever in the nineteenth century.

27 Emended from "ought" (1847).

rather *too* indulgent in humouring her caprices—not from affection, but from pride; he wished earnestly to see her bring honour to the family by an alliance with the Lintons, and, as long as she let him alone, she might trample us like slaves for aught[27] he cared!

Edgar Linton, as multitudes have been before and will be after him, was infatuated, and believed himself the happiest man alive on the day he led her to Gimmerton Chapel, three years subsequent to his father's death.

Much against my inclination, I was persuaded to leave Wuthering Heights and accompany her here. Little Hareton was nearly five years old, and I had just begun to teach him his letters. We made a sad parting, but Catherine's tears were more powerful than ours—When I refused to go, and when she found her entreaties did not move me, she went lamenting to her husband and brother. The former offered me munificent wages; the latter ordered me to pack up—he wanted no women in the house, he said, now that there was no mistress; and as to Hareton, the curate should take him in hand, by and by. And so, I had but one choice left: to do as I was ordered—I told the master he got rid of all decent people only to run to ruin a little faster; I kissed Hareton good bye; and, since then, he has been a stranger, and it's very queer to think it, but I've no doubt he has completely forgotten all about Ellen Dean and that he was ever more than all the world to her, and she to him!

At this point of the housekeeper's story she chanced to glance towards the time-piece over the chimney; and was in amazement on seeing the minute-hand measure half past one. She would not hear of staying a second longer—In truth, I felt rather disposed to defer the sequel of her narrative myself: and now that she is vanished to her rest, and I have meditated for another hour or two, I shall summon courage to go also, in spite of aching laziness of head and limbs.

CHAPTER 10

A charming introduction to a hermit's life! Four weeks' torture, tossing and sickness! Oh, these bleak winds and bitter, northern skies, and impassable roads, and dilatory country surgeons![1] And, oh, this dearth of the human physiognomy, and, worse than all, the terrible intimation of Kenneth that I need not expect to be out of doors till spring!

Mr. Heathcliff has just honoured me with a call. About seven days ago he sent me a brace of grouse—the last of the season.[2]

Scoundrel! He is not altogether guiltless in this illness of mine; and that I had a great mind to tell him. But alas! how could I offend a man who was charitable enough to sit at my bedside a good hour, and talk on some other subject than pills and draughts, blisters and leeches?[3]

This is quite an easy interval. I am too weak to read, yet I feel as if I could enjoy something interesting. Why not have up Mrs. Dean to finish her tale? I can recollect its chief incidents, as far as she had gone. Yes, I remember her hero had run off, and never been heard of for three years: and the heroine was married. I'll ring; she'll be delighted to find me capable of talking cheerfully.

Mrs. Dean came.

"It wants twenty minutes, sir, to taking the medicine," she commenced.

"Away, away with it!" I replied; "I desire to have—"

1 Surgical practice included the nonsurgical treatment of diseases, fevers, and broken bones. The surgeon who visits Lockwood is probably Kenneth, the only medical practitioner named in the novel. Most people, in cities as well as in the country, relied on apothecaries, surgeons, or surgeon-apothecaries for their medical needs. Physicians, who were certified by the College of Physicians, had to be graduates of Oxford or Cambridge. There were fewer of them, and their services were more costly. The respectability of apothecaries and surgeons increased steadily during the nineteenth century.

2 In 1801, when Lockwood received Heathcliff's gift, there was no close season for hunting game birds, and the novel's reference to one is therefore anachronistic. Lockwood's speaking of the grouse he receives as "the last of the season" makes sense only if Brontë has in mind the Game Act of 1831, which stipulated an open season for hunting grouse that stretched from August 12 to December 10. The latter date has been crucial in establishing the date on which the novel begins. Since Lockwood has already been ill for three weeks, he must have made his first visit to Wuthering Heights in the middle of November (C. P. Sanger, "The Structure of Wuthering Heights," in Eleanor McNees, ed., *The Brontë Sisters: Critical Assessments,* 4 vols. [Mountfield: Helm Information, 1996], 2, p. 103). The novel also refers to the beginning of "the shooting season" in Volume II, Chapter 9.

The Game Act of 1831 also required hunters to purchase licenses. Like enclosures, about which so much more has been written, game licensing contributed to the increasing restriction of the rights of common people.

3 Bleeding, here by means of leeches, blistering (placing hot plasters on the skin), pills, and liquid medicines, including purges, were all standard treatments for fever in this period.

A nineteenth-century ceramic leech jar, English School.

"The doctor says you must drop the powders."

"With all my heart! Don't interrupt me. Come and take your seat here. Keep your fingers from that bitter phalanx of vials. Draw your knitting out of your pocket—that will do—now continue the history of Mr. Heathcliff, from where you left off to the present day. Did he finish his education on the Continent, and come back a gentleman? Or did he get a sizar's place at college? Or escape to America, and earn honours by drawing blood from his foster country? Or make a fortune more promptly on the English highways?"[4]

"He may have done a little in all these vocations, Mr. Lockwood; but I couldn't give my word for any. I stated before that I didn't know how he gained his money; neither am I aware of the means he took to raise his mind from the savage ignorance into which it was sunk; but, with your leave, I'll proceed in my own fashion, if you think it will amuse and not weary you. Are you feeling better this morning?"

"Much."

"That's good news."

I got Miss Catherine and myself to Thrushcross Grange: and to my agreeable disappointment, she behaved infinitely better than I dared to expect. She seemed almost over fond of Mr. Linton; and even to his sister, she showed plenty of affection. They were both very attentive to her comfort, certainly. It was not the thorn bending to the honeysuckles, but the honeysuckles embracing the thorn. There were no mutual concessions: one stood erect, and the others yielded; and who *can* be ill-natured, and bad-tempered, when they encounter neither opposition nor indifference?

I observed that Mr. Edgar had a deep-rooted fear of ruffling her humour. He concealed it from her; but if ever he heard me answer sharply, or saw any other servant grow cloudy at some imperious order of hers, he would show his trouble by a frown of displeasure

4 Brontë neither confirms nor rejects any of Lockwood's conjectures about how Heathcliff has spent his three years away from the Heights. That he has obtained a university education is unlikely. In England, he would have had to enter a university as a sizar, an undergraduate who received financial aid for performing duties later performed by college servants. (In 1802, Patrick Brontë entered St. John's College, Cambridge, as a sizar.) It's possible that Heathcliff makes his fortune in the Atlantic slave economy (Christopher Heywood makes this case in his edition of *Wuthering Heights* [Peterborough, ON: Broadview Press, 2002], p. 61), but the period of Heathcliff's absence from the scene of the novel makes a brief career as a soldier in the American Revolutionary War especially plausible. The signing of the Treaty of Paris that officially ended the war in September 1783 coincides neatly with the date of Heathcliff's return.

It's tempting to imagine Heathcliff as a mercenary fighting on "foreign sod." The phrase comes from the last poem in Brontë's *Gondal Poems* notebook, "Why ask to know what date what clime," the only poem she is known to have written after the publication of *Wuthering Heights*. This poem is an incomplete reworking of a much longer poem that precedes it in the same notebook, "Why ask to know the date—the clime," dated September 14, 1846. The protagonist of the longer poem is a mercenary soldier, and mercenaries were a notable feature of the American war. German mercenaries (called "Hessians") supplemented British troops; French soldiers fought alongside American troops; Native Americans and African Americans fought on both sides. The education of the hero of George Sand's *Mauprat* (1837) includes a six-year absence in America, where he fights for American independence. Patricia Thomson argues that Brontë read Sand's novel in French, and that it influenced *Wuthering Heights* ("*Wuthering Heights* and *Mauprat*," R.E.S., 24:93, 1973, pp. 26–37).

Oil portrait (1832) of George Sand (1804–1876), the much revered and criticized French novelist, by Auguste Charpentier (1813–1880).

that never darkened on his own account. He, many a time, spoke sternly to me about my pertness;[5] and averred that the stab of a knife could not inflict a worse pang than he suffered at seeing his lady vexed.

Not to grieve a kind master, I learnt to be less touchy; and, for the space of half a year, the gunpowder lay as harmless as sand, because no fire came near to explode it. Catherine had seasons of gloom and silence, now and then; they were respected with sympathizing silence by her husband, who ascribed them to an altera-

5 "Smartness bordering upon impudence" *(OED).*

6 A reference to Heathcliff's acquired accent.

tion in her constitution produced by her perilous illness, as she was never subject to depression of spirits before. The return of sunshine was welcomed by answering sunshine from him. I believe I may assert that they were really in possession of deep and growing happiness.

It ended. Well, we *must* be for ourselves in the long run; the mild and generous are only more justly selfish than the domineering—and it ended when circumstances caused each to feel that the one's interest was not the chief consideration in the other's thoughts.

On a mellow evening in September, I was coming from the garden with a heavy basket of apples which I had been gathering. It had got dusk, and the moon looked over the high wall of the court, causing undefined shadows to lurk in the corners of the numerous projecting portions of the building. I set my burden on the house steps by the kitchen door, and lingered to rest and draw in a few more breaths of the soft, sweet air; my eyes were on the moon, and my back to the entrance, when I heard a voice behind me say—

"Nelly, is that you?"

It was a deep voice, and foreign in tone;[6] yet there was something in the manner of pronouncing my name which made it sound familiar. I turned about to discover who spoke, fearfully, for the doors were shut, and I had seen nobody on approaching the steps.

Something stirred in the porch; and moving nearer, I distinguished a tall man dressed in dark clothes, with dark face and hair. He leant against the side, and held his fingers on the latch, as if intending to open for himself.

"Who can it be?" I thought. "Mr. Earnshaw? Oh, no! The voice has no resemblance to his."

"I have waited here an hour," he resumed, while I continued staring, "and the whole of that time all round has been as still as death: I dared not enter. You do not know me? Look, I'm not a stranger!"

A ray fell on his features; the cheeks were sallow and half covered with black whiskers; the brows lowering, the eyes deep set and singular. I remembered the eyes.

"What!" I cried, uncertain whether to regard him as a worldly[7] visitor, and I raised my hands in amazement. "What! you come back? Is it really you? Is it?"

"Yes, Heathcliff," he replied, glancing from me up to the windows which reflected a score of glittering moons, but showed no lights from within. "Are they at home—where is she? Nelly, you are not glad—you needn't be so disturbed. Is she here? Speak! I want to have one word with her—your mistress. Go, and say some person from Gimmerton desires to see her."

"How will she take it?" I exclaimed. "What will she do? The surprise bewilders me—it will put her out of her head! And you *are* Heathcliff? But altered! Nay, there's no comprehending it. Have you been for a soldier?"

"Go, and carry my message," he interrupted impatiently; "I'm in hell till you do!"

He lifted the latch, and I entered; but when I got to the parlour where Mr. and Mrs. Linton were, I could not persuade myself to proceed.

At length, I resolved on making an excuse to ask if they would have the candles lighted, and I opened the door.

They sat together in a window whose lattice lay back against the wall, and displayed beyond the garden trees, and the wild green park, the valley of Gimmerton, with a long line of mist winding nearly to its top (for very soon after you pass the chapel, as you may have noticed, the sough[8] that runs from the marshes joins a beck[9] which follows the bend of the glen). Wuthering Heights[10] rose above this silvery vapour; but our old house was invisible—it rather dips down on the other side.

Both the room, and its occupants, and the scene they gazed on, looked wondrously peaceful. I shrank reluctantly from performing my errand, and was actually going away, leaving it unsaid, af-

7 Earthly, mortal.

8 A channel for draining off water, as here from the marshes.

9 Stream.

10 The hill, not the house itself, as the rest of Nelly's sentence indicates.

11 An occasion of celebration; figuratively, and commonly in biblical contexts, a time of restitution or release.

ter having put my question about the candles, when a sense of my folly compelled me to return, and mutter:

"A person from Gimmerton wishes to see you, ma'am."

"What does he want?" asked Mrs. Linton.

"I did not question him," I answered.

"Well, close the curtains, Nelly," she said, "and bring up tea. I'll be back again directly."

She quitted the apartment. Mr. Edgar inquired carelessly, who it was?

"Some one the mistress does not expect," I replied. "That Heathcliff, you recollect him, sir, who used to live at Mr. Earnshaw's."

"What, the gipsy—the plough-boy?" he cried. "Why did you not say so to Catherine?"

"Hush! you must not call him by those names, master," I said. "She'd be sadly grieved to hear you. She was nearly heartbroken when he ran off; I guess his return will make a jubilee[11] to her."

Mr. Linton walked to a window on the other side of the room that overlooked the court. He unfastened it and leant out. I suppose they were below, for he exclaimed, quickly—

"Don't stand there, love! Bring the person in, if it be any one particular."

Ere long, I heard the click of the latch, and Catherine flew upstairs, breathless and wild, too excited to show gladness; indeed, by her face, you would rather have surmised an awful calamity.

"Oh, Edgar, Edgar!" she panted, flinging her arms round his neck. "Oh, Edgar, darling! Heathcliff's come back—he is!" And she tightened her embrace to a squeeze.

"Well, well," cried her husband, crossly, "don't strangle me for that! He never struck me as such a marvellous treasure. There is no need to be frantic!"

"I know you didn't like him," she answered, repressing a little the intensity of her delight. "Yet for my sake, you must be friends now. Shall I tell him to come up?"

"Here," he said, "into the parlour?"

Catherine (Juliette Binoche) insisting that Heathcliff (Ralph Fiennes) and Edgar (Simon Shepherd) become friends in Peter Kosminsky's film adaptation of *Wuthering Heights* (1992).

"Where else?" she asked.

He looked vexed, and suggested the kitchen as a more suitable place for him.

Mrs. Linton eyed him with a droll expression—half angry, half laughing at his fastidiousness.

"No," she added, after a while; "I cannot sit in the kitchen. Set two tables here, Ellen; one for your master and Miss Isabella, being gentry; the other for Heathcliff and myself, being of the lower orders. Will that please you, dear? Or must I have a fire lighted elsewhere? If so, give directions. I'll run down and secure my guest. I'm afraid the joy is too great to be real!"[12]

She was about to dart off again, but Edgar arrested her.

"*You* bid him step up," he said, addressing me, "and, Catherine, try to be glad without being absurd! The whole household need not witness the sight of your welcoming a runaway servant as a brother."[13]

I descended and found Heathcliff waiting under the porch, evidently anticipating an invitation to enter. He followed my guidance without waste of words, and I ushered him into the presence of the master and mistress, whose flushed cheeks betrayed signs of

12 Catherine's joy at Heathcliff's return makes her doubt her senses, and the familiarity of her feeling ("this is too good to be true") may obscure the attention Brontë gives such feelings in her poems as well as her novel. In "To Imagination," published in 1846, her speaker contrasts the ordinary world in which we live most of the time to the one her imagination shows her in "cherished dreams." But imagination not only offers an escape from a "hopeless" ordinary world into dreams or fancies. It also intimates the existence of "real" worlds just as "bright" as the "world within." Heathcliff's return reawakens Catherine's hope that there is such a real world for her, a world in which she can love both Heathcliff and Edgar.

13 Edgar's allusion to the abolitionist conjunction of slave and brother would not have escaped Brontë's notice. His words recall the famous legend on the 1787 medallion designed by Josiah Wedgwood for the British antislavery campaign: "Am I not a man and a brother?" Brontë would have read abolitionist literature depicting the brutal treatment of runaway slaves, and her novel is alert to the analogy between Hindley's treatment of Heathcliff and the treatment of slaves by their masters. On this occasion, Edgar's unwitting allusion to slavery suggests his isolation from the powerful storms shaking the world outside Thrushcross Grange and its correspondence to his unwillingness to acknowledge the powerful storms shaking the foundations of his marriage.

A famous Slave Emancipation Society medallion (c. 1787–1790) in jasperware, designed by William Hackwood (c. 1757–1829) and produced by Josiah Wedgwood and Sons.

warm talking. But the lady's glowed with another feeling when her friend appeared at the door; she sprang forward, took both his hands, and led him to Linton; and then she seized Linton's reluctant fingers and crushed them into his.

Now fully revealed by the fire and candlelight, I was amazed, more than ever, to behold the transformation of Heathcliff. He had grown a tall, athletic, well-formed man beside whom my master seemed quite slender and youth-like. His upright carriage suggested the idea of his having been in the army. His countenance was much older in expression and decision of feature than Mr. Linton's; it looked intelligent, and retained no marks of former degradation. A half-civilized ferocity lurked yet in the depressed brows and eyes full of black fire, but it was subdued; and his manner was even dignified, quite divested of roughness, though too stern for grace.

My master's surprise equalled or exceeded mine: he remained for a minute at a loss how to address the plough-boy, as he had called him; Heathcliff dropped his slight hand, and stood looking at him coolly till he chose to speak.

"Sit down, sir," he said, at length. "Mrs. Linton, recalling old times, would have me give you a cordial reception, and, of course, I am gratified when anything occurs to please her."

"And I also," answered Heathcliff, "especially if it be anything in which I have a part. I shall stay an hour or two willingly."

He took a seat opposite Catherine, who kept her gaze fixed on him as if she feared he would vanish were she to remove it. He did not raise his to her often; a quick glance now and then sufficed; but it flashed back, each time, more confidently, the undisguised delight he drank from hers.

They were too much absorbed in their mutual joy to suffer embarrassment; not so Mr. Edgar: he grew pale with pure annoyance, a feeling that reached its climax when his lady rose—and stepping across the rug, seized Heathcliff's hands again, and laughed like one beside herself.

"I shall think it a dream to-morrow!" she cried. "I shall not be able to believe that I have seen, and touched, and spoken to you once more—and yet, cruel Heathcliff! you don't deserve this welcome. To be absent and silent for three years, and never to think of me!"

"A little more than you have thought of me!" he murmured. "I heard of your marriage, Cathy, not long since; and, while waiting in the yard below, I meditated this plan—just to have one glimpse of your face—a stare of surprise, perhaps, and pretended pleasure; afterwards settle my score with Hindley; and then prevent the law by doing execution on myself. Your welcome has put these ideas out of my mind; but beware of meeting me with another aspect next time! Nay, you'll not drive me off again—you were really sorry for me, were you? Well, there was cause. I've fought through a bitter life since I last heard your voice, and you must forgive me, for I struggled only for you!"

"Catherine, unless we are to have cold tea, please to come to the table," interrupted Linton, striving to preserve his ordinary tone, and a due measure of politeness. "Mr. Heathcliff will have a long walk, wherever he may lodge to-night; and I'm thirsty."

She took her post before the urn; and Miss Isabella came, summoned by the bell; then, having handed their chairs forward, I left the room.

The meal hardly endured ten minutes—Catherine's cup was never filled, she could neither eat nor drink. Edgar had made a slop in his saucer,[14] and scarcely swallowed a mouthful.

Their guest did not protract his stay, that evening, above an hour longer. I asked, as he departed, if he went to Gimmerton?

"No, to Wuthering Heights," he answered. "Mr. Earnshaw invited me when I called this morning."

Mr. Earnshaw invited *him!* and *he* called on Mr. Earnshaw! I pondered this sentence painfully, after he was gone. Is he turning out a bit of a hypocrite, and coming into the country to work mischief under a cloak? I mused—I had a presentiment, in the bottom of my heart, that he had better have remained away.

14 The "slop" is the tea that has left the cup for the saucer. In his distress over Heathcliff's re-appearance and Catherine's welcome, Edgar has spilled more tea than he has drunk.

15 Vexation or thwarting.

About the middle of the night, I was wakened from my first nap by Mrs. Linton gliding into my chamber, taking a seat on my bedside, and pulling me by the hair to rouse me.

"I cannot rest, Ellen," she said by way of apology. "And I want some living creature to keep me company in my happiness! Edgar is sulky, because I'm glad of a thing that does not interest him—He refuses to open his mouth, except to utter pettish, silly speeches; and he affirmed I was cruel and selfish for wishing to talk when he was so sick and sleepy. He always contrives to be sick at the least cross![15] I gave a few sentences of commendation to Heathcliff, and he, either for a headache or a pang of envy, began to cry: so I got up and left him."

"What use is it praising Heathcliff to him?" I answered. "As lads they had an aversion to each other, and Heathcliff would hate just as much to hear him praised—it's human nature. Let Mr. Linton alone about him, unless you would like an open quarrel between them."

"But does it not show great weakness?" pursued she. "I'm not envious—I never feel hurt at the brightness of Isabella's yellow hair, and the whiteness of her skin; at her dainty elegance, and the fondness all the family exhibit for her. Even you, Nelly, if we have a dispute sometimes, you back Isabella at once; and I yield like a foolish mother—I call her a darling, and flatter her into a good temper. It pleases her brother to see us cordial, and that pleases me. But they are very much alike: they are spoiled children, and fancy the world was made for their accommodation; and, though I humour both, I think a smart chastisement might improve them all the same."

"You're mistaken, Mrs. Linton," said I. "They humour you—I know what there would be to do if they did not! You can well afford to indulge their passing whims, as long as their business is to anticipate all your desires—You may, however, fall out, at last, over something of equal consequence to both sides; and then those you term weak are very capable of being as obstinate as you!"

"And then we shall fight to the death, shan't we, Nelly?" she returned laughing. "No! I tell you, I have such faith in Linton's love that I believe I might kill him, and he wouldn't wish to retaliate."

I advised her to value him the more for his affection.

"I do," she answered, "but he needn't resort to whining for trifles. It is childish; and, instead of melting into tears because I said that Heathcliff was now worthy of any one's regard, and it would honour the first gentleman in the country to be his friend, he ought to have said it for me, and been delighted from sympathy—He must get accustomed to him, and he may as well like him—considering how Heathcliff has reason to object to him, I'm sure he behaved excellently!"

"What do you think of his going to Wuthering Heights?" I inquired. "He is reformed in every respect, apparently—quite a Christian—offering the right hand of fellowship to his enemies all round!"

"He explained it," she replied. "I wondered as much as you—He said he called to gather information concerning me from you, supposing you resided there still; and Joseph told Hindley, who came out and fell to questioning him of what he had been doing, and how he had been living: and finally, desired him to walk in. There were some persons sitting at cards—Heathcliff joined them; my brother lost some money to him; and, finding him plentifully supplied, he requested that he would come again in the evening, to which he consented. Hindley is too reckless to select his acquaintance prudently; he doesn't trouble himself to reflect on the causes he might have for mistrusting one whom he has basely injured—But Heathcliff affirms his principal reason for resuming a connection with his ancient persecutor is a wish to install himself in quarters at walking distance from the Grange, and an attachment to the house where we lived together, and, likewise, a hope that I shall have more opportunities of seeing him there than I could have if he settled in Gimmerton. He means to offer liberal payment for permission to lodge at the Heights; and doubtless my brother's covetousness will prompt him to accept the terms; he was always greedy, though what he grasps with one hand, he flings away with the other."

"It's a nice place for a young man to fix his dwelling in!" said I. "Have you no fear of the consequences, Mrs. Linton?"

"None for my friend," she replied; "his strong head will keep him from danger—a little for Hindley, but he can't be made morally worse than he is; and I stand between him and bodily harm—The event of this evening has reconciled me to God and humanity! I had risen in angry rebellion against providence—Oh, I've endured very, very bitter misery, Nelly! If that creature knew how bitter, he'd be ashamed to cloud its removal with idle petulance—It was kindness for him which induced me to bear it alone: had I expressed the agony I frequently felt, he would have been taught to long for its alleviation as ardently as I—However, it's over, and I'll take no revenge on his folly—I can afford to suffer anything hereafter! Should the meanest thing alive slap me on the cheek, I'd not only turn the other, but I'd ask pardon for provoking it—and, as a proof, I'll go make my peace with Edgar instantly—Good night—I'm an angel!"

In this self-complacent conviction she departed; and the success of her fulfilled resolution was obvious on the morrow—Mr. Linton had not only abjured his peevishness (though his spirits seemed still subdued by Catherine's exuberance of vivacity) but he ventured no objection to her taking Isabella with her to Wuthering Heights in the afternoon; and she rewarded him with such a summer of sweetness and affection in return as made the house a paradise for several days, both master and servants profiting from the perpetual sunshine.

Heathcliff—Mr. Heathcliff, I should say in future, used the liberty of visiting at Thrushcross Grange cautiously at first: he seemed estimating how far its owner would bear his intrusion. Catherine also deemed it judicious to moderate her expressions of pleasure in receiving him; and he gradually established his right to be expected.

He retained a great deal of the reserve for which his boyhood was remarkable, and that served to repress all startling demonstrations of feeling. My master's uneasiness experienced a lull, and further circumstances diverted it into another channel for a space.

His new source of trouble sprang from the not anticipated misfortune of Isabella Linton evincing a sudden and irresistible attraction towards the tolerated guest—She was at that time a charming young lady of eighteen;[16] infantile in manners, though possessed of keen wit, keen feelings, and a keen temper too, if irritated. Her brother, who loved her tenderly, was appalled at this fantastic preference. Leaving aside the degradation of an alliance with a nameless man, and the possible fact that his property, in default of heirs male, might pass into such a one's power,[17] he had sense to comprehend Heathcliff's disposition—to know that, though his exterior was altered, his mind was unchangeable, and unchanged. And he dreaded that mind; it revolted him; he shrank forebodingly from the idea of committing Isabella to its keeping.

He would have recoiled still more had he been aware that her attachment rose unsolicited, and was bestowed where it awakened no reciprocation of sentiment; for the minute he discovered its existence, he laid the blame on Heathcliff's deliberate designing.

We had all remarked, during some time, that Miss Linton fretted and pined over something. She grew cross and wearisome, snapping at and teasing Catherine continually, at the imminent risk of exhausting her limited patience. We excused her to a certain extent, on the plea of ill health—she was dwindling and fading before our eyes—but one day, when she had been peculiarly wayward, rejecting her breakfast, complaining that the servants did not do what she told them; that the mistress would allow her to be nothing in the house, and Edgar neglected her; that she had caught a cold with the doors being left open, and we let the parlour fire go

16 Isabella, born in 1765, is less than a year younger than Catherine, although Nelly describes her manners as "infantile" and Catherine addresses her as "child."

17 Edgar's estate is entailed. An estate tail prefers males to females: a son of Edgar's takes precedence over Isabella, or any of Isabella's offspring, but a son of Isabella's takes precedence over a daughter of Edgar's. Additionally, Edgar appears to have only a life interest in the estate. If he dies without having children, or produces a daughter only, that daughter will be passed over in favor of Isabella, who also has a life interest in the estate. Marriage would give Heathcliff possession of Isabella's personal property as well as a husband's power over her, and that power was considerable at this time. As C. P. Sanger observes, Brontë clearly studied inheritance law, and her "ten or twelve legal references," including this one, enable her readers to understand Heathcliff's plot to gain legal possession of both the Heights and the Grange (Sanger, "The Structure of Wuthering Heights," in McNees, ed., *The Brontë Sisters: Critical Assessments,* 2, pp. 76–79).

out on purpose to vex her; with a hundred yet more frivolous accusations—Mrs. Linton peremptorily insisted that she should get to bed, and, having scolded her heartily, threatened to send for the doctor.

Mention of Kenneth caused her to exclaim, instantly, that her health was perfect, and it was only Catherine's harshness which made her unhappy.

"How can you say I am harsh, you naughty fondling?"[18] cried the mistress, amazed at the unreasonable assertion. "You are surely losing your reason. When have I been harsh, tell me?"

"Yesterday," sobbed Isabella, "and now!"

"Yesterday!" said her sister-in-law. "On what occasion?"

"In our walk along the moor; you told me to ramble where I pleased, while you sauntered on with Mr. Heathcliff!"

"And that's your notion of harshness?" said Catherine, laughing. "It was no hint that your company was superfluous; we didn't care whether you kept with us or not; I merely thought Heathcliff's talk would have nothing entertaining for your ears."

"Oh, no," wept the young lady, "you wished me away, because you knew I liked to be there!"

"Is she sane?" asked Mrs. Linton, appealing to me. "I'll repeat our conversation, word for word, Isabella; and you point out any charm it could have had for you."

"I don't mind the conversation," she answered: "I wanted to be with—"

"Well!" said Catherine, perceiving her hesitate to complete the sentence.

"With him; and I won't be always sent off!" she continued, kindling up. "You are a dog in the manger,[19] Cathy, and desire no one to be loved but yourself!"

"You are an impertinent little monkey!" exclaimed Mrs. Linton, in surprise. "But I'll not believe this idiocy! It is impossible that you can covet the admiration of Heathcliff—that you can consider

18 Someone much indulged; a pet.

19 A phrase derived from an ancient fable and used to describe someone who selfishly prevents someone else from having something, even though she herself has no use for it.

him an agreeable person! I hope I have misunderstood you, Isabella?"

"No, you have not," said the infatuated girl. "I love him more than ever you loved Edgar; and he might love me if you would let him!"

"I wouldn't be you for a kingdom, then!" Catherine declared, emphatically—and she seemed to speak sincerely. "Nelly, help me to convince her of her madness. Tell her what Heathcliff is—an unreclaimed creature, without refinement—without cultivation; an arid wilderness of furze and whinstone.[20] I'd as soon put that little canary into the park on a winter's day as recommend you to bestow your heart on him! It is deplorable ignorance of his character, child, and nothing else, which makes that dream enter your head. Pray don't imagine that he conceals depths of benevolence and affection beneath a stern exterior! He's not a rough diamond—a pearl-containing oyster of a rustic; he's a fierce, pitiless, wolfish man. I never say to him let this or that enemy alone, because it would be ungenerous or cruel to harm them—I say, let them alone because I should hate them to be wronged: and he'd crush you like a sparrow's egg, Isabella, if he found you a troublesome charge. I know he couldn't love a Linton; and yet, he'd be quite capable of marrying your fortune and expectations. Avarice is growing with him a besetting sin. There's my picture; and I'm his friend—so much so, that had he thought seriously to catch you, I should, perhaps, have held my tongue, and let you fall into his trap."

Miss Linton regarded her sister-in-law with indignation.

"For shame! for shame!" she repeated, angrily. "You are worse than twenty foes, you poisonous friend!"[21]

"Ah! you won't believe me then?" said Catherine. "You think I speak from wicked selfishness?"

"I'm certain you do," retorted Isabella, "and I shudder at you!"

"Good!" cried the other. "Try for yourself, if that be your spirit; I have done, and yield the argument to your saucy insolence."

20 Brontë's geological and botanical knowledge is extensive, and the information she conveys, as here in the metaphors Catherine uses to describe Heathcliff to Isabella, is always specific and precise. "Furze" are spiny evergreen shrubs that grow in barren soils, and "whinstone" refers to any of "various very hard dark-coloured rocks or stones" *(OED)*. Appealing to Isabella's good sense, she characterizes her as a pet canary living in a cage and a sparrow's egg (both the fragile casing and the unfledged bird it contains). The bird references, together with Catherine's explanation of how she exercises her authority over Heathcliff—she always appeals to his desire to please her, not to his conscience—anticipates her memory of the fledgling lapwings that Heathcliff killed by setting a trap above their nest so that the parents could not feed them. (See Chapter 12 below.)

21 An echo of "The Conference," a poem by Charles Churchill (1732–1764), an English poet and satirist: "Her spirit seems her interest to oppose,/ And where she make one friend, makes twenty foes" (ll. 13–14). Brontë turns Churchill's juxtaposition of "one friend" and "twenty foes" into a new aphorism.

22 "'Nelly,' he said, 'we're going to have a coroner's inquest soon enough, at our house. One of them almost got his finger cut off with keeping the other one from sticking himself like a calf. That's the master, you know, who's so set on going to the grand assizes. He's not afraid of the Bench of judges, neither Paul, nor Peter, nor John, nor Matthew, nor any of them, not he! He'd like—he longs—to set his brazen face against them! And that bonny lad, Heathcliff, you mind me, he's a rare one! He can bare his teeth in a laugh as well as anybody at a right devil's jest. Does he never say anything about his fine living with us when he goes to the Grange? This is the way of it—up at sun-down, dice, brandy, closed shutters and candle-light till the next day at noon—then, the fool goes cursing and raving to his chamber, making decent folks dig their fingers in their ears for very shame; and the knave, why he can count his money, and eat, and sleep, and off to his neighbor's to gossip with the wife. While this is going on, he tells Dame Catherine how her father's gold runs into his pockets, and her father's son gallops down the Broad road, while he flies ahead to open the gates.'"

"Sticking" refers to slaughtering an animal, usually a pig or a calf, by thrusting a knife into its throat. A coroner's inquest would be held to inquire into the causes of a violent death.

"And I must suffer for her egotism!" she sobbed, as Mrs. Linton left the room. "All, all is against me; she has blighted my single consolation. But she uttered falsehoods, didn't she? Mr. Heathcliff is not a fiend; he has an honourable soul, and a true one, or how could he remember her?"

"Banish him from your thoughts, miss," I said. "He's a bird of bad omen; no mate for you. Mrs. Linton spoke strongly, and yet, I can't contradict her. She is better acquainted with his heart than I, or any one besides; and she never would represent him as worse than he is. Honest people don't hide their deeds. How has he been living? How has he got rich? Why is he staying at Wuthering Heights, the house of a man whom he abhors? They say Mr. Earnshaw is worse and worse since he came. They sit up all night together continually: and Hindley has been borrowing money on his land; and does nothing but play and drink, I heard only a week ago; it was Joseph who told me—I met him at Gimmerton."

"'Nelly,' he said, 'we's hae a Crahnr's 'quest enah, at ahr folks. One on 'em's a'most getten his finger cut off wi' hauding t'other froo' sticking hisseln loike a cawlf. That's maister, yah knaw, ut's soa up uh going tuh t'grand 'sizes. He's noan feard uh t' Bench uh judges, norther Paul, nur Peter, nur John, nor Mathew, nor noan on 'em, nut he! He fair likes—he langs—tuh set his brazened face agean 'em! And yon bonny lad Heathcliff, yah mind, he's a rare un! He can girn a laugh as weel's onybody at a raight divil's jest. Does he niver say nowt of his fine living amang us when he goas tuh t' Grange? This is t' way on't—up at sun-dahn, dice, brandy, cloised shutters and can'le leeght till next day at nooin—then, t' fooil gangs banning un raving tuh his cham'er, makking dacent fowks dig thur fingers i' thur lugs fur varry shaume; un' the' knave, wah, he can cahnt his brass, un ate, un' sleep, un' off tuh his neighbour's tuh gossip wi' t' wife. I' course, he tells Dame Catherine hah hor father's goold runs intuh his pocket, and her fathur's son gallops dahn t' Broad road, while he flees afore tuh oppen t' pikes?'[22] Now, Miss Linton, Joseph is an old rascal, but no liar; and, if his account of Heathcliff's conduct be true, you would never think of desiring such a husband, would you?"

"You are leagued with the rest, Ellen!" she replied. "I'll not listen to your slanders. What malevolence you must have to wish to convince me that there is no happiness in the world!"

Whether she would have got over this fancy if left to herself, or persevered in nursing it perpetually, I cannot say; she had little time to reflect. The day after, there was a justice-meeting at the next town;[23] my master was obliged to attend; and Mr. Heathcliff, aware of his absence, called rather earlier than usual.

Catherine and Isabella were sitting in the library, on hostile terms but silent—the latter alarmed at her recent indiscretion, and the disclosure she had made of her secret feelings in a transient fit of passion; the former, on mature consideration, really offended with her companion; and, if she laughed again at her pertness, inclined to make it no laughing matter to *her.*

She did laugh as she saw Heathcliff pass the window. I was sweeping the hearth, and I noticed a mischievous smile on her lips. Isabella, absorbed in her meditations, or a book, remained till the door opened, and it was too late to attempt an escape, which she would gladly have done had it been practicable.

"Come in, that's right!" exclaimed the mistress gaily, pulling a chair to the fire. "Here are two people sadly in need of a third to thaw the ice between them, and you are the very one we should both of us choose. Heathcliff, I'm proud to show you, at last, somebody that dotes on you more than myself. I expect you to feel flattered—nay, it's not Nelly; don't look at her! My poor little sister-in-law is breaking her heart by mere contemplation of your physical and moral beauty. It lies in your own power to be Edgar's brother! No, no, Isabella, you sha'n't run off," she continued, arresting, with feigned playfulness, the confounded girl, who had risen indignantly. "We were quarrelling like cats about you, Heathcliff; and I was fairly beaten in protestations of devotion, and admiration; and, moreover, I was informed that if I would but have the man-

23 A court session for dealing with criminal and civil cases, held quarterly before justices of the peace. As a justice of the peace, Edgar is obliged to attend.

"Mercenaries embarking from Hesse to America. 1776," a copperplate engraving contemporary with the event it records. About 30,000 German soldiers called Hessians fought for the British in the American Revolutionary War.

ners to stand aside, my rival, as she will have herself to be, would shoot a shaft into your soul that would fix you for ever, and send my image into eternal oblivion!"

"Catherine," said Isabella, calling up her dignity, and disdaining to struggle from the tight grasp that held her. "I'd thank you to adhere to the truth and not slander me, even in joke! Mr. Heathcliff, be kind enough to bid this friend of yours release me—she forgets that you and I are not intimate acquaintances, and what amuses her is painful to me beyond expression."

As the guest answered nothing, but took his seat, and looked thoroughly indifferent what sentiments she cherished concerning him, she turned and whispered an earnest appeal for liberty to her tormenter.

"By no means!" cried Mrs. Linton in answer. "I won't be named a dog in the manger again. You *shall* stay, now then! Heathcliff, why don't you evince satisfaction at my pleasant news? Isabella swears that the love Edgar has for me, is nothing to that she entertains for you. I'm sure she made some speech of the kind, did she not, Ellen? And she has fasted ever since the day before yesterday's walk, from sorrow and rage that I despatched her out of your society, under the idea of its being unacceptable."

"I think you belie her," said Heathcliff, twisting his chair to face them. "She wishes to be out of my society now at any rate!"

And he stared hard at the object of discourse, as one might do at a strange repulsive animal, a centipede from the Indies, for instance, which curiosity leads one to examine in spite of the aversion it raises.

The poor thing couldn't bear that; she grew white and red in rapid succession, and, while tears beaded her lashes, bent the strength of her small fingers to loosen the firm clutch of Catherine, and perceiving that, as fast as she raised one finger off her arm, another closed down, and she could not remove the whole together, she began to make use of her nails, and their sharpness presently ornamented the detainer's with crescents of red.

"There's a tigress!" exclaimed Mrs. Linton, setting her free, and shaking her hand with pain. "Begone, for God's sake, and hide your vixen face! How foolish to reveal those talons to *him*. Can't you fancy the conclusions he'll draw? Look, Heathcliff! they are instruments that will do execution—you must beware of your eyes."

"I'd wrench them off her fingers, if they ever menaced me," he answered, brutally, when the door had closed after her. "But what did you mean by teasing the creature in that manner, Cathy? You were not speaking the truth, were you?"

"I assure you I was," she returned. "She has been pining for your sake several weeks, and raving about you this morning, and pouring forth a deluge of abuse because I represented your failings in a plain light for the purpose of mitigating her adoration. But don't notice it further. I wished to punish her sauciness, that's all—I like her too well, my dear Heathcliff, to let you absolutely seize and devour her up."

"And I like her too ill to attempt it," said he, "except in a very ghoulish fashion. You'd hear of odd things, if I lived alone with that mawkish,[24] waxen face; the most ordinary would be painting on its white the colours of the rainbow, and turning the blue eyes black, every day or two; they detestably resemble Linton's."

"Delectably," observed Catherine. "They are dove's eyes—angel's!"

24 Insipid, nauseating.

25 Catherine's sons will be Isabella's nephews. Her confidence that she will live to give birth to several sons, thereby securing Edgar's lineage and their eldest son's claim to his estate, is often overlooked by readers, who doubt her commitment to her marriage and her life with Edgar at this point in the novel.

26 Hindley.

"She's her brother's heir, is she not?" he asked, after a brief silence.

"I should be sorry to think so," returned his companion. "Half-a-dozen nephews shall erase her title, please Heaven![25] Abstract your mind from the subject at present—you are too prone to covet your neighbour's goods: remember *this* neighbour's goods are mine."

"If they were *mine,* they would be none the less that," said Heathcliff, "but though Isabella Linton may be silly, she is scarcely mad; and—in short we'll dismiss the matter as you advise."

From their tongues, they did dismiss it; and Catherine, probably, from her thoughts. The other, I felt certain, recalled it often in the course of the evening; I saw him smile to himself—grin rather—and lapse into ominous musing whenever Mrs. Linton had occasion to be absent from the apartment.

I determined to watch his movements. My heart invariably cleaved to the master's, in preference to Catherine's side; with reason, I imagined, for he was kind, and trustful, and honourable: and she—she could not be called the *opposite,* yet she seemed to allow herself such wide latitude that I had little faith in her principles, and still less sympathy for her feelings. I wanted something to happen which might have the effect of freeing both Wuthering Heights and the Grange of Mr. Heathcliff quietly, leaving us as we had been prior to his advent. His visits were a continual nightmare to me; and, I suspected, to my master also. His abode at the Heights was an oppression past explaining. I felt that God had forsaken the stray sheep[26] there to its own wicked wanderings, and an evil beast prowled between it and the fold, waiting his time to spring and destroy.

CHAPTER 11

Sometimes, while meditating on these things in solitude, I've got up in a sudden terror, and put on my bonnet to go see how all was at the farm; I've persuaded my conscience that it was a duty to warn him how people talked regarding his ways; and then I've recollected his confirmed bad habits, and, hopeless of benefiting him, have flinched from re-entering the dismal house, doubting if I could bear to be taken at my word.

One time, I passed the old gate, going out of my way, on a journey to Gimmerton. It was about the period that my narrative has reached—a bright, frosty afternoon; the ground bare, and the road hard and dry.

I came to a stone where the highway branches off on to the moor at your left hand, a rough sand-pillar,[1] with the letters W. H. cut on its north side, on the east G., and on the south-west T. G. It serves as guide-post to the Grange, and Heights, and village.

The sun shone yellow on its grey head, reminding me of summer; and I cannot say why, but all at once, a gush of child's sensations flowed into my heart. Hindley and I held it a favourite spot twenty years before.

I gazed long at the weather-worn block; and, stooping down, perceived a hole near the bottom still full of snail-shells and pebbles, which we were fond of storing there with more perishable things—and, as fresh as reality, it appeared that I beheld my early

1 The term "sand-pillar" to denote a guidepost is apparently unique. In his edition of *Wuthering Heights,* Christopher Heywood emends the text to read "hand-pillar" on the model of "finger-post," a name for a guidepost with one or more arms that sometimes terminate in the shape of a finger. He conjectures that Brontë's "formation of the letters *h* and *s*" in her *Gondal Poems* notebook explains "a printer's misreading of '*hand-pillar*'" (Heywood, ed., *Wuthering Heights* [Peterborough, ON: Broadview Press, 2002], p. 202). Brontë transcribed the poems in her *Gondal Poems* notebook in block, not cursive, letters. She used a clear cursive hand in her fair-copy Ashley Library poems manuscript and in her school essays for M. Heger, and it is likely that she would also have written a manuscript as long as *Wuthering Heights* in cursive. Nelly describes the head of the pillar as "grey" in the paragraph below, where the sun shines "yellow" on it, and then she calls the pillar itself a "weather-worn block." Perhaps the guidepost, which Nelly later refers to as a "guide-stone," is made of sandstone, which varies in color. Both sandstone and gritstone (a hard, coarse-grained form of sandstone) were quarried in the West Riding.

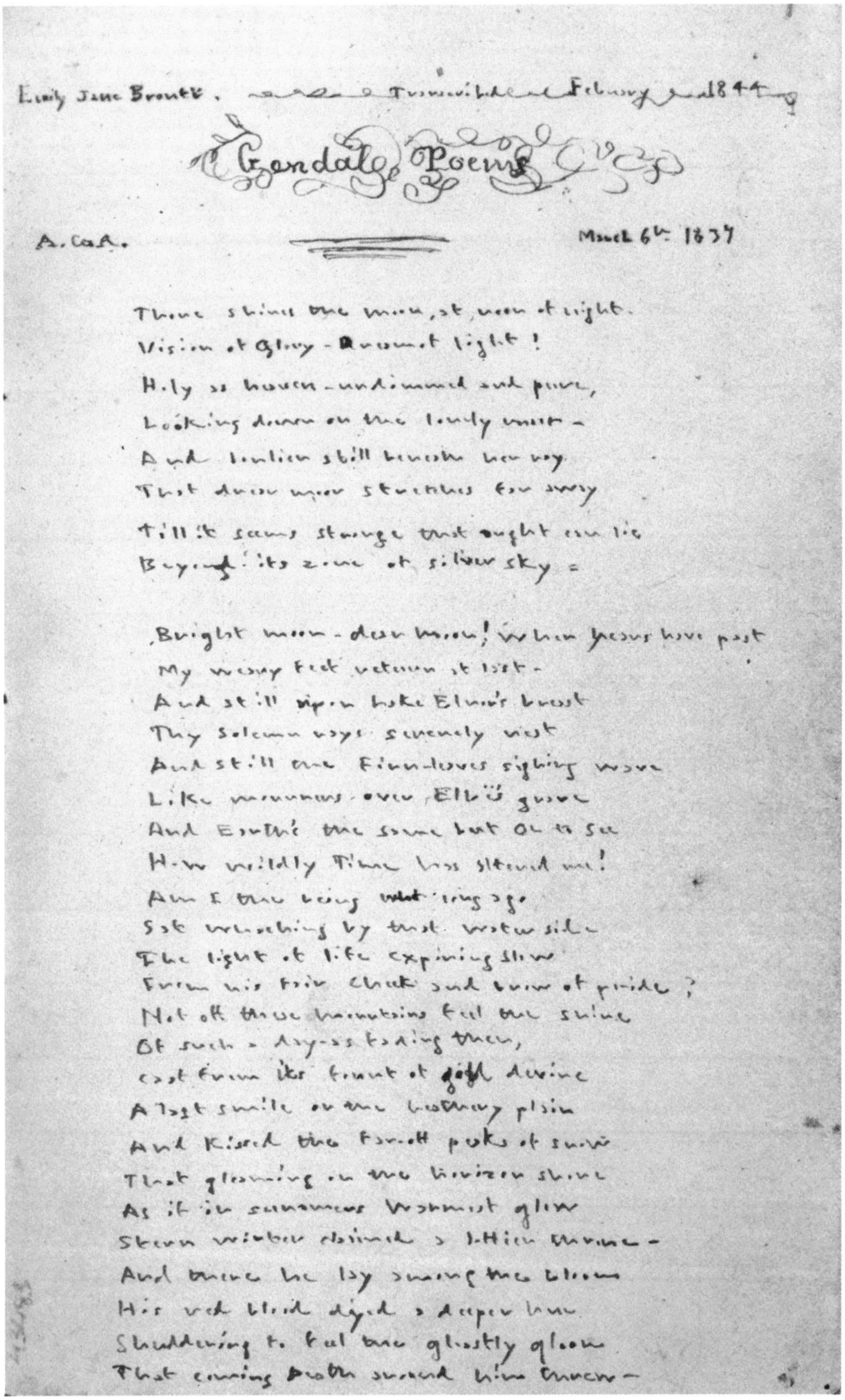

Emily Jane Brontë. Transcribed February 1844

Gondal Poems

A.G.A. March 6th 1837

There shines the moon, at noon of night.
Vision of Glory - Dream of light!
Holy as heaven - undimmed and pure,
Looking down on the lonely moor -
And lonelier still beneath her ray
That drear moor stretches far away
Till it seems strange that aught can lie
Beyond its zone of silver sky =

Bright moon - dear moon! when years have past
My weary feet return at last -
And still upon Lake Elnor's breast
Thy solemn rays serenely rest
And still the Fern-leaves sighing wave
Like mourners over Elbë's grave
And Earth's the same but Oh to see
How wildly Time has altered me!
Am I the being who long ago
Sat watching by that water side
The light of life expiring slow
From his fair cheek and brow of pride?
Not oft these mountains feel the shine
Of such a day - as fading then,
Cast from its fount of gold divine
A last smile on the heathery plain
And kissed the far-off peaks of snow
That gleaming on the horizon shone
As if in summer's warmest glow
Stern winter claimed a loftier throne -
And there he lay among the bloom
His red blood dyed a deeper hue
Shuddering to feel the ghostly gloom
That coming Death around him threw -

The first page of Emily's *Gondal Poems* notebook with the name she preferred written with a flourish: Emily Jane Brontë. This notebook has sixty-eight pages and contains fair-copy versions of forty-four poems. Since no Gondal fiction has survived, these poems tell us most of what we know about the imaginary country whose history and current affairs Anne and Emily chronicled in fiction and poetry. The poem that begins the notebook, "There shines the moon, at noon of night—," was composed in 1837 and first published in 1936 in Virginia Moore's *The Life and Eager Death of Emily Brontë.* The initials A. G. A. (to the left of the date) identify the speaker as Augusta G. Almeda, one of Gondal's tragic heroines.

playmate seated on the withered turf, his dark, square head bent forward, and his little hand scooping out the earth with a piece of slate.

"Poor Hindley!" I exclaimed, involuntarily.

I started—my bodily eye was cheated into a momentary belief that the child lifted its face and stared straight into mine! It vanished in a twinkling; but immediately, I felt an irresistible yearning to be at the Heights. Superstition urged me to comply with this impulse—Supposing he should be dead! I thought—or should die soon!—supposing it were a sign of death!

The nearer I got to the house the more agitated I grew: and, on catching sight of it, I trembled every limb. The apparition had outstripped me; it stood looking through the gate. That was my first idea on observing an elf-locked,[2] brown-eyed boy setting his ruddy countenance against the bars. Further reflection suggested this must be Hareton, my Hareton, not altered greatly since I left him, ten months since.

"God bless thee, darling!" I cried, forgetting instantaneously my foolish fears. "Hareton, it's Nelly—Nelly, thy nurse."

He retreated out of arm's length, and picked up a large flint.

"I am come to see thy father, Hareton," I added, guessing from the action that Nelly, if she lived in his memory at all, was not recognised as one with me.

He raised his missile to hurl it; I commenced a soothing speech, but could not stay his hand. The stone struck my bonnet, and then ensued, from the stammering lips of the little fellow, a string of curses which, whether he comprehended them or not, were delivered with practised emphasis, and distorted his baby features into a shocking expression of malignity.[3]

You may be certain this grieved more than angered me. Fit to cry, I took an orange from my pocket, and offered it to propitiate him.

He hesitated, and then snatched it from my hold, as if he fancied I only intended to tempt and disappoint him.

2 Tangled hair was sometimes superstitiously attributed to the agency of elves.

3 Charlotte told Elizabeth Gaskell about an incident that occurred in 1839 when she was a governess for the Sidgwick family at Stonegappe. Her pupil John, whom she described as "pampered spoilt & turbulent," threw stones at her when she tried to make him leave the stable yard, where he was not allowed. One of them struck her hard enough to leave a noticeable mark on her forehead (Juliet Barker, *The Brontës* [London: Phoenix, 1994], pp. 311–312).

4 Child.

5 Give.

6 Way.

7 Abide, or put up with.

8 I don't know.

9 Dashes replace Hareton's curses, an expurgation we can attribute to either Nelly or Lockwood.

I showed another, keeping it out of his reach. "Who has taught you those fine words, my barn,"[4] I inquired. "The curate?"

"Damn the curate, and thee! Gie[5] me that," he replied.

"Tell us where you got your lessons, and you shall have it," said I. "Who's your master?"

"Devil daddy," was his answer.

"And what do you learn from Daddy?" I continued.

He jumped at the fruit; I raised it higher. "What does he teach you?" I asked.

"Naught," said he, "but to keep out of his gait[6]—Daddy cannot bide[7] me because I swear at him."

"Ah! and the devil teaches you to swear at Daddy?" I observed.

"Aye—nay," he drawled.

"Who then?"

"Heathcliff."

I asked if he liked Mr. Heathcliff?

"Aye!" he answered again.

Desiring to have his reasons for liking him, I could only gather the sentences. "I known't[8]—he pays Dad back what he gies to me—he curses Daddy for cursing me—He says I mun do as I will."

"And the curate does not teach you to read and write, then?" I pursued.

"No, I was told the curate should have his—teeth dashed down his—[9] throat, if he stepped over the threshold—Heathcliff had promised that!"

I put the orange in his hand; and bade him tell his father that a woman called Nelly Dean was waiting to speak with him, by the garden gate.

He went up the walk, and entered the house; but instead of Hindley, Heathcliff appeared on the door stones, and I turned directly and ran down the road as hard as ever I could race, making no halt till I gained the guide post, and feeling as scared as if I had raised a goblin.

This is not much connected with Miss Isabella's affair; except that it urged me to resolve further on mounting vigilant guard, and doing my utmost to check the spread of such bad influence at the Grange, even though I should wake a domestic storm by thwarting Mrs. Linton's pleasure.

The next time Heathcliff came, my young lady chanced to be feeding some pigeons in the court. She had never spoken a word to her sister-in-law for three days; but she had likewise dropped her fretful complaining, and we found it a great comfort.

Heathcliff had not the habit of bestowing a single unnecessary civility on Miss Linton, I knew. Now, as soon as he beheld her, his first precaution was to take a sweeping survey of the house-front. I was standing by the kitchen window, but I drew out of sight. He then stept across the pavement to her, and said something: she seemed embarrassed, and desirous of getting away; to prevent it, he laid his hand on her arm—she averted her face; he apparently put some question which she had no mind to answer. There was another rapid glance at the house, and supposing himself unseen, the scoundrel had the impudence to embrace her.

"Judas! Traitor!" I ejaculated; "you are a hypocrite too, are you? A deliberate deceiver."

"Who is, Nelly?" said Catherine's voice at my elbow—I had been over-intent on watching the pair outside to mark her entrance.

"Your worthless friend!" I answered warmly, "the sneaking rascal yonder—Ah, he has caught a glimpse of us—he is coming in! I wonder will he have the art to find a plausible excuse for making love to Miss, when he told you he hated her?"

Mrs. Linton saw Isabella tear herself free, and run into the garden; and a minute after, Heathcliff opened the door.

I couldn't withhold giving some loose to my indignation; but Catherine angrily insisted on silence, and threatened to order me out of the kitchen, if I dared be so presumptuous as to put in my insolent tongue.

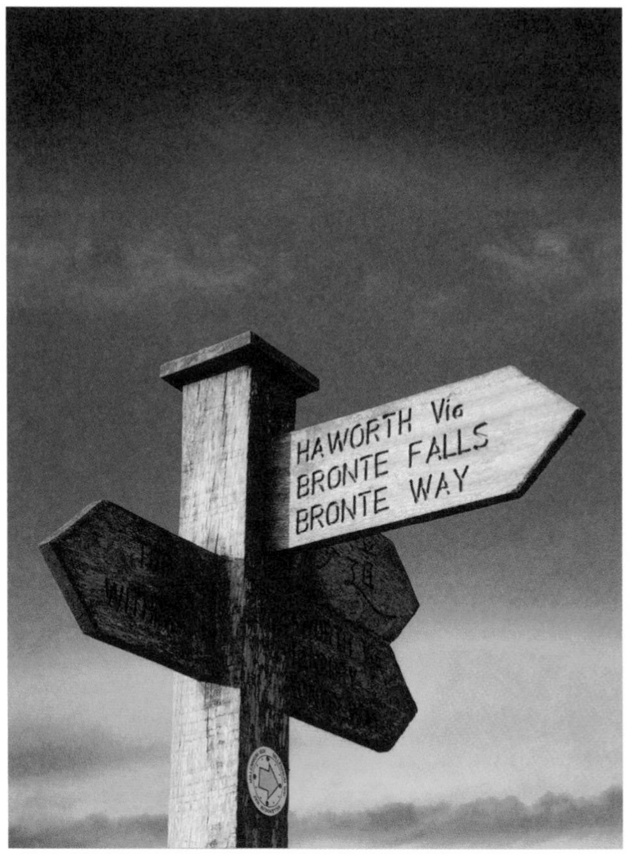

A modern guidepost in Brontë country points the way to some of the most popular tourist destinations.

"To hear you, people might think *you* were the mistress!" she cried. "You want setting down in your right place! Heathcliff, what are you about, raising this stir? I said you must let Isabella alone!—I beg you will unless you are tired of being received here, and wish Linton to draw the bolts against you!"

"God forbid that he should try!" answered the black villain—I detested him just then. "God keep him meek and patient! Every day I grow madder[10] after sending him to heaven!"

"Hush!" said Catherine shutting the inner door! "Don't vex me. Why have you disregarded my request? Did she come across you on purpose?"

"What is it to you?" he growled, "I have a right to kiss her, if she chooses, and you have no right to object—I'm not *your* husband; *you* needn't be jealous of me!"

"I'm not jealous of you," replied the mistress, "I'm jealous for you.[11] Clear your face, you shan't scowl at me! If you like Isabella, you shall marry her. But, do you like her, tell the truth, Heathcliff? There, you wont answer. I'm certain you don't!"

"And would Mr. Linton approve of his sister marrying that man?" I inquired.

"Mr. Linton should approve," returned my lady decisively.

"He might spare himself the trouble," said Heathcliff, "I could do as well without his approbation—And, as to you, Catherine, I have a mind to speak a few words, now, while we are at it—I want you to be aware that I *know* you have treated me infernally—infernally! Do you hear? And if you flatter yourself that I don't perceive it, you are a fool—and if you think I can be consoled by sweet words, you are an idiot—and if you fancy I'll suffer unrevenged, I'll convince you of the contrary in a very little while! Meantime, thank you for telling me your sister-in-law's secret—I swear I'll make the most of it, and stand you aside!"

"What new phase of his character is this?" exclaimed Mrs. Linton, in amazement. "I've treated you infernally—and you'll take revenge! How will you take it, ungrateful brute? How have I treated you infernally?"

10 "Chiefly Brit. With infinitive: wildly desirous (to do something)" *(OED).*

11 "Jealous" is a word that appears frequently in the novel. Here Catherine distinguishes between Heathcliff's idea that she is jealous *of* him and her own conviction that she is jealous *for* him. In her 1850 edition, Charlotte italicizes the words *"of"* and *"for"* to call attention to the distinction Catherine is making. When she says she is jealous "for" Heathcliff, she means she is jealous on his behalf because she identifies his wishes with hers. Most readers of the novel continue to find Heathcliff's point of view, which is also Isabella's, easier to understand than Catherine's. They dismiss her belief that she can love both Heathcliff and Edgar as merely self-deluding. William Wyler's 1939 film adaptation of the novel firmly rejects Catherine's view of her situation by making her look guilty about Heathcliff in front of Edgar, and so suggesting that she's contemplating adultery. In Luis Bunuel's film adaptation of the novel, *Abismos de Pasion* (1954), the love between Alejandro (Heathcliff) and Catalina (Catherine) is unarguably adulterous.

(left) A poster for William Wyler's film adaptation of *Wuthering Heights* (1939), with Laurence Olivier as Heathcliff, Merle Oberon as Catherine, and David Niven as Edgar.

(above) Heathcliff (Jorge Mistral as Alejandro) embracing Isabella (Lilia Prado as Isabel) in Luis Buñuel's 1954 film adaptation of *Wuthering Heights, Abismos de pasión.* In the film, Alejandro never kisses Isabel on the lips but always fastens his mouth on her neck, like a vampire.

"I seek no revenge on you," replied Heathcliff less vehemently. "That's not the plan—The tyrant grinds down his slaves, and they don't turn against him, they crush those beneath them[12]—You are welcome to torture me to death for your amusement, only allow me to amuse myself a little in the same style—And refrain from insult, as much as you are able. Having levelled my palace, don't erect a hovel and complacently admire your own charity in

12 In the public discourse during Brontë's lifetime, slavery was widely said to corrupt slaveholders. Here Heathcliff asserts that slavery corrupts slaves. Brontë would have been familiar with the arguments of the abolitionists from her reading of periodicals like *Blackwood's* and *Fraser's*, both received at the Parsonage. William Wilberforce, a prominent leader of the abolitionist movement, was briefly one of Patrick Brontë's patrons. Heathcliff's idea of love as tyranny and of the one who loves as a slave who torments those who are weaker than he is provides one explanation of his brutal treatment of Isabella.

giving me that for a home. If I imagined you really wished me to marry Isabella, I'd cut my throat!"

"Oh the evil is that I am *not* jealous, is it?" cried Catherine. "Well, I won't repeat my offer of a wife—It is as bad as offering Satan a lost soul—Your bliss lies, like his, in inflicting misery—You prove it—Edgar is restored from the ill-temper he gave way to at your coming; I begin to be secure and tranquil; and you, restless to know us at peace, appear resolved on exciting a quarrel—quarrel with Edgar if you please, Heathcliff, and deceive his sister; you'll hit on exactly the most efficient method of revenging yourself on me."

The conversation ceased—Mrs. Linton sat down by the fire, flushed and gloomy. The spirit which served her was growing intractable: she could neither lay[13] nor control it. He stood on the hearth with folded arms, brooding on his evil thoughts; and in this position I left them to seek the master, who was wondering what kept Catherine below so long.

"Ellen," said he, when I entered, "have you seen your mistress?"

"Yes, she's in the kitchen, sir," I answered. "She's sadly put out by Mr. Heathcliff's behaviour: and indeed, I do think it's time to arrange his visits on another footing. There's harm in being too soft, and now it's come to this—." And I related the scene in the court, and, as near as I dared, the whole subsequent dispute. I fancied it could not be very prejudicial to Mrs. Linton, unless she made it so, afterwards, by assuming the defensive for her guest.

Edgar Linton had difficulty in hearing me to the close—His first words revealed that he did not clear his wife of blame.

"This is insufferable!" he exclaimed. "It is disgraceful that she should own him for a friend, and force his company on me! Call me two men out of the hall, Ellen—Catherine shall linger no longer to argue with the low ruffian—I have humoured her enough."

He descended, and, bidding the servants wait in the passage, went, followed by me, to the kitchen. Its occupants had recommenced their angry discussion; Mrs. Linton, at least, was scold-

13 Prevent a spirit or ghost from walking. The *OED* cites Shakespeare's *Romeo and Juliet:* "To raise a spirit in his Mistres circle . . . making it . . . stand till she had laid it, and coniurde it downe" (ii.s.26).

ing with renewed vigour; Heathcliff had moved to the window, and hung his head somewhat cowed by her violent rating[14] apparently.

14 Scolding.

He saw the master first, and made a hasty motion that she should be silent, which she obeyed abruptly on discovering the reason of his intimation.

"How is this?" said Linton, addressing her; "what notion of propriety must you have to remain here, after the language which has been held to you by that blackguard? I suppose because it is his ordinary talk, you think nothing of it—you are habituated to his baseness, and perhaps imagine I can get used to it too!"

"Have you been listening at the door, Edgar?" asked the mistress, in a tone particularly calculated to provoke her husband, implying both carelessness and contempt of his irritation.

Heathcliff, who had raised his eyes at the former speech, gave a sneering laugh at the latter, on purpose, it seemed, to draw Mr. Linton's attention to him.

He succeeded; but Edgar did not mean to entertain him with any high flights of passion.

"I have been so far forbearing with you, sir," he said, quietly; "not that I was ignorant of your miserable, degraded character, but I felt you were only partly responsible for that; and Catherine wishing to keep up your acquaintance, I acquiesced—foolishly. Your presence is a moral poison that would contaminate the most virtuous—for that cause, and to prevent worse consequences, I shall deny you, hereafter, admission into this house, and give notice now that I require your instant departure. Three minutes' delay will render it involuntary and ignominious."

Heathcliff measured the height and breadth of the speaker with an eye full of derision.

"Cathy, this lamb of yours threatens like a bull!" he said. "It is in danger of splitting its skull against my knuckles. By God, Mr. Linton, I'm mortally sorry that you are not worth knocking down!"

My master glanced towards the passage, and signed me to fetch the men—he had no intention of hazarding a personal encounter.

I obeyed the hint; but Mrs. Linton, suspecting something, followed, and when I attempted to call them, she pulled me back, slammed the door to, and locked it.

"Fair means!" she said, in answer to her husband's look of angry surprise. "If you have not the courage to attack him, make an apology, or allow yourself to be beaten. It will correct you of feigning more valour than you possess. No, I'll swallow the key before you shall get it! I'm delightfully rewarded for my kindness to each! After constant indulgence of one's weak nature and the other's bad one, I earn, for thanks, two samples of blind ingratitude, stupid to absurdity! Edgar, I was defending you and yours; and I wish Heathcliff may flog you sick for daring to think an evil thought of me!"

It did not need the medium of a flogging to produce that effect on the master. He tried to wrest the key from Catherine's grasp; and for safety she flung it into the hottest part of the fire; whereupon Mr. Edgar was taken with a nervous trembling, and his countenance grew deadly pale. For his life he could not avert that access of emotion—mingled anguish and humiliation overcame him completely. He leant on the back of a chair, and covered his face.

"Oh! Heavens! In old days this would win you knighthood!" exclaimed Mrs. Linton. "We are vanquished. We are vanquished! Heathcliff would as soon lift a finger at you as the king would march his army against a colony of mice. Cheer up, you sha'n't be hurt! Your type is not a lamb, it's a sucking leveret."[15]

"I wish you joy of the milk-blooded coward, Cathy!" said her friend. "I compliment you on your taste: and that is the slavering, shivering thing you preferred to me! I would not strike him with my fist, but I'd kick him with my foot and experience considerable satisfaction. Is he weeping, or is he going to faint for fear?"

The fellow approached and gave the chair on which Linton rested a push. He'd better have kept his distance: my master quickly

15 Literally, a young hare that is not yet weaned; figuratively, someone of little spirit. Since Catherine called Heathcliff a "wolfish man" in Chapter 10, he and Edgar, like the wolf and the hare, are natural enemies. Does Edgar's anguish and humiliation proceed from his terror of Heathcliff, as Catherine seems to think, or from his discovery of her deep sympathy with Heathcliff and her increasing alienation from him? If from the latter, then Edgar's understanding of the scene is fuller than Nelly's or Catherine's, although the novel provides no reliable access to his point of view.

That the strong triumph over the weak is clear here and elsewhere in the novel. In a school essay Brontë wrote while she was in Brussels, "The Butterfly," the speaker, "in one of those black humors," concludes that Nature "exists on a principle of destruction. Every being must be the tireless instrument of death to others, or itself must cease to live." In the essay, Brontë produces a magical outcome that restores her speaker's faith in God's "eternal empire of happiness and glory" ("Le Papillon," in Sue Lonoff, ed. and trans., *The Belgian Essays: A Critical Edition* [New Haven: Yale Univ. Press, 1997], pp. 176–179). But in a poem, "Stanzas to—," composed in 1839 and published in 1846, she offers a different kind of moral calculation and one that is especially pertinent to *Wuthering Heights*. The occasion for this poem, which Brontë transcribed into her non-Gondal fair-copy notebook, the so-called Honresfeld manuscript, is the death of someone whose ambitions were disappointed and whose fame was "blighted." As in "The Butterfly," a too easy judgment is rebuked and opposed to a wider view of the order of the universe. This wider view appeals not to God's hidden plan, as in "The Butterfly," but instead to a Blakean order in which each creature performs its unique nature:

> Do I despise the timid deer,
> Because his limbs are fleet with fear?
> Or, would I mock the wolf's death-howl,
> Because his form is gaunt and foul?
> Or hear with joy the leveret's cry,
> Because it cannot bravely die?

The poem suggests that Brontë may be more sympathetic to Edgar than Catherine is.

sprang erect, and struck him full on the throat a blow that would have levelled a slighter man.

It took his breath for a minute; and, while he choked, Mr. Linton walked out by the back door into the yard, and from thence, to the front entrance.

"There! you've done with coming here," cried Catherine. "Get away, now—he'll return with a brace of pistols, and half-a-dozen assistants. If he did overhear us, of course, he'd never forgive you. You've played me an ill turn, Heathcliff! But go—make haste! I'd rather see Edgar at bay than you."

"Do you suppose I'm going with that blow burning in my gullet?" he thundered. "By Hell, no! I'll crush his ribs in like a rotten hazel-nut before I cross the threshold! If I don't floor him now, I shall murder him sometime, so as you value his existence, let me get at him!"

"He is not coming," I interposed, framing a bit of a lie. "There's the coachman, and the two gardeners; you'll surely not wait to be thrust into the road by them! Each has a bludgeon, and master will very likely be watching from the parlour windows to see that they fulfil his orders."

The gardeners and coachman *were* there; but Linton was with them. They had already entered the court—Heathcliff, on second thoughts, resolved to avoid a struggle against three underlings; he seized the poker, smashed the lock from the inner door, and made his escape as they tramped in.

Mrs. Linton, who was very much excited, bid me accompany her up-stairs. She did not know my share in contributing to the disturbance, and I was anxious to keep her in ignorance.

"I'm nearly distracted, Nelly!" she exclaimed, throwing herself on the sofa. "A thousand smiths'[16] hammers are beating in my head! Tell Isabella to shun me—this uproar is owing to her; and should she or any one else aggravate my anger at present, I shall get wild. And, Nelly, say to Edgar, if you see him again to-night, that I'm in danger of being seriously ill—I wish it may prove true. He

16 Blacksmiths or farriers.

17 Gained knowledge of (as opposed to hearing).

18 Declared his thoughts and feelings about me.

19 Brain fever.

has startled and distressed me shockingly! I want to frighten him. Besides, he might come and begin a string of abuse or complainings; I'm certain I should recriminate, and God knows where we should end! Will you do so, my good Nelly? You are aware that I am no way blameable in this matter. What possessed him to turn listener? Heathcliff's talk was outrageous after you left us; but I could soon have diverted him from Isabella, and the rest meant nothing. Now, all is dashed wrong by the fool's-craving to hear evil of self that haunts some people like a demon! Had Edgar never gathered[17] our conversation, he would never have been the worse for it. Really, when he opened on me[18] in that unreasonable tone of displeasure, after I had scolded Heathcliff till I was hoarse for *him,* I did not care hardly what they did to each other, especially as I felt that, however the scene closed, we should all be driven asunder for nobody knows how long! Well, if I cannot keep Heathcliff for my friend—if Edgar will be mean and jealous, I'll try to break their hearts by breaking my own. That will be a prompt way of finishing all, when I am pushed to extremity! But it's a deed to be reserved for a forlorn hope—I'd not take Linton by surprise with it. To this point he has been discreet in dreading to provoke me; you must represent the peril of quitting that policy; and remind him of my passionate temper, verging, when kindled, on frenzy[19]—I wish you could dismiss that apathy out of your countenance, and look rather more anxious about me!"

The stolidity with which I received these instructions was, no doubt, rather exasperating; for they were delivered in perfect sincerity, but I believed a person who could plan the turning of her fits of passion to account beforehand might, by exerting her will, manage to control herself tolerably even while under their influence; and I did not wish to "frighten" her husband, as she said, and multiply his annoyances for the purpose of serving her selfishness.

Therefore I said nothing when I met the master coming towards the parlour; but I took the liberty of turning back to listen whether they would resume their quarrel together.

He began to speak first.

"Remain where you are, Catherine," he said, without any anger in his voice, but with much sorrowful despondency. "I shall not stay. I am neither come to wrangle, nor be reconciled: but I wish just to learn whether, after this evening's events, you intend to continue your intimacy with—"

"Oh, for mercy's sake," interrupted the mistress, stamping her foot, "for mercy's sake, let us hear no more of it now! Your cold blood cannot be worked into a fever—your veins are full of ice-water—but mine are boiling, and the sight of such chillness makes them dance."

"To get rid of me—answer my question," persevered Mr. Linton. "You *must* answer it; and that violence does not alarm me. I have found that you can be as stoical as any one when you please. Will you give up Heathcliff hereafter, or will you give up me? It is impossible for you to be *my* friend, and *his* at the same time; and I absolutely *require* to know which you choose."

"I require to be let alone!" exclaimed Catherine furiously. "I demand it! Don't you see I can scarcely stand? Edgar, you—you leave me!"

She rung the bell till it broke with a twang: I entered leisurely. It was enough to try the temper of a saint, such senseless, wicked rages! There she lay dashing her head against the arm of the sofa and grinding her teeth, so that you might fancy she would crash them to splinters!

Mr. Linton stood looking at her in sudden compunction and fear. He told me to fetch some water. She had no breath for speaking.

I brought a glass full; and, as she would not drink, I sprinkled it on her face. In a few seconds she stretched herself out stiff, and turned up her eyes, while her cheeks, at once blanched and livid, assumed the aspect of death.

Linton looked terrified.

"There is nothing in the world the matter," I whispered. I did not want him to yield, though I could not help being afraid in my heart.

"She has blood on her lips!" he said, shuddering.

"Never mind!" I answered tartly. And I told him how she had resolved, previous to his coming, on exhibiting a fit of frenzy.

I incautiously gave the account aloud, and she heard me, for she started up—her hair flying over her shoulders, her eyes flashing, the muscles of her neck and arms standing out preternaturally. I made up my mind for broken bones at least; but she only glared about her for an instant, and then rushed from the room.

The master directed me to follow; I did, to her chamber door; she hindered me from going farther by securing it against me.

As she never offered to descend to breakfast next morning, I went to ask whether she would have some carried up.

"No!" she replied peremptorily.

The same question was repeated at dinner, and tea; and again on the morrow after, and received the same answer.

Mr. Linton, on his part, spent his time in the library, and did not inquire concerning his wife's occupations. Isabella and he had had an hour's interview, during which he tried to elicit from her some sentiment of proper horror for Heathcliff's advances; but he could make nothing of her evasive replies, and was obliged to close the examination unsatisfactorily, adding, however, a solemn warning, that if she were so insane as to encourage that worthless suitor, it would dissolve all bonds of relationship between herself and him.

CHAPTER 12

While Miss Linton moped about the park and garden, always silent, and almost always in tears; and her brother shut himself up among books that he never opened—wearying, I guessed, with a continual vague expectation that Catherine, repenting her conduct, would come of her own accord to ask pardon, and seek a reconciliation; and *she* fasted pertinaciously, under the idea, probably, that at every meal Edgar was ready to choke for her absence, and pride alone held him from running to cast himself at her feet; I went about my household duties, convinced that the Grange had but one sensible soul in its walls, and that lodged in my body.

I wasted no condolences on miss, nor any expostulations on my mistress, nor did I pay attention to the sighs of my master, who yearned to hear his lady's name, since he might not hear her voice.

I determined they should come about as they pleased for me; and though it was a tiresomely slow process, I began to rejoice at length in a faint dawn of its progress, as I thought at first.

Mrs. Linton, on the third day, unbarred her door; and having finished the water in her pitcher and decanter, desired a renewed supply, and a basin of gruel, for she believed she was dying. That I set down as a speech meant for Edgar's ears; I believed no such thing, so I kept it to myself, and brought her some tea and dry toast.

1 Not a mistake but a form of the past tense of the verb still in use at this time. Charlotte substitutes "ate" in 1850.

2 An unnatural sleep or apathy, but also, in medical parlance, a kind of apoplexy.

3 Nelly's retort is wonderfully barbed. Her sympathies are entirely with Edgar, who is being made to spend more time with his books than he should or would spend, if Catherine were behaving like a good wife. But Nelly's report that Edgar's studies "occupy him" is misleading: at the beginning of the chapter, Nelly reports that Edgar "never opened" his books while Catherine remained in her bedroom.

She eat[1] and drank eagerly; and sank back on her pillow again clenching her hands and groaning.

"Oh, I will die," she exclaimed, "since no one cares anything about me. I wish I had not taken that."

Then a good while after, I heard her murmur,

"No, I'll not die—he'd be glad—he does not love me at all—he would never miss me!"

"Did you want anything, ma'am?" I enquired, still preserving my external composure, in spite of her ghastly countenance, and strange exaggerated manner.

"What is that apathetic being doing?" she demanded, pushing the thick entangled locks from her wasted face. "Has he fallen into a lethargy,[2] or is he dead?"

"Neither," replied I, "if you mean Mr. Linton. He's tolerably well, I think, though his studies occupy him rather more than they ought; he is continually among his books, since he has no other society."[3]

I should not have spoken so, if I had known her true condition, but I could not get rid of the notion that she acted a part of her disorder.

"Among his books!" she cried, confounded. "And I dying! I on the brink of the grave! My God! does he know how I'm altered?" continued she, staring at her reflection in a mirror, hanging against the opposite wall. "Is that Catherine Linton? He imagines me in a pet—in play, perhaps. Cannot you inform him that it is frightful earnest? Nelly, if it be not too late, as soon as I learn how he feels, I'll choose between these two—either to starve, at once, that would be no punishment unless he had a heart—or to recover and leave the country. Are you speaking the truth about him now? Take care. Is he actually so utterly indifferent for my life?"

"Why, ma'am," I answered, "the master has no idea of your being deranged; and, of course, he does not fear that you will let yourself die of hunger."

"You think not? Cannot you tell him I will?" she returned; "persuade him—speak of your own mind—say you are certain I will!"

"No, you forget, Mrs. Linton," I suggested, "that you have eaten some food with a relish this evening, and to-morrow you will perceive its good effects."

"If I were only sure it would kill him," she interrupted, "I'd kill myself directly! These three awful nights, I've never closed my lids—and oh, I've been tormented! I've been haunted, Nelly! But I begin to fancy you don't like me. How strange! I thought, though everybody hated and despised each other, they could not avoid loving me—and they have all turned to enemies in a few hours. *They* have, I'm positive; the people *here.* How dreary to meet death, surrounded by their cold faces! Isabella, terrified and repelled, afraid to enter the room, it would be so dreadful to watch Catherine go. And Edgar standing solemnly by to see it over; then offering prayers of thanks to God for restoring peace to his house, and going back to his *books!*[4] What in the name of all that feels, has he to do with *books,* when I am dying?"

She could not bear the notion which I had put into her head of Mr. Linton's philosophical resignation. Tossing about, she increased her feverish bewilderment to madness, and tore the pillow with her teeth, then raising herself up all burning, desired that I would open the window. We were in the middle of winter, the wind blew strong from the northeast,[5] and I objected.

Both the expressions flitting over her face, and the changes of her moods, began to alarm me terribly; and brought to my recollection her former illness, and the doctor's injunction that she should not be crossed.

A minute previously she was violent; now, supported on one arm, and not noticing my refusal to obey her, she seemed to find childish diversion in pulling the feathers from the rents she had just made, and ranging them on the sheet according to their different species: her mind had strayed to other associations.

4 Catherine's resentment of books is two-pronged. They substitute for her in Edgar's life and will, she anticipates, console him after her death. They epitomize how cultivated and mediated life at the Grange is in contrast to the unrefined and unmediated life Catherine has known at the Heights.

Books have earlier been connected to social mobility. When Lockwood complimented Nelly on her having "no marks of the manners . . . peculiar to [her] class," she explained that she has "looked into" all the books in the library at Thrushcross Grange, "unless it be that range of Greek and Latin, and that of French" (Vol. I, Chap. 8). Heathcliff rebelled against his education by kicking a book, but apart from separating him from Catherine, the worst punishment Hindley can inflict on him is to stop his book-learning. Hareton is also deprived of the curate's teaching and later will have to be taught to read by his cousin in order to become worthy of her.

5 From the direction of Wuthering Heights.

"That's a turkey's," she murmured to herself; "and this is a wild-duck's; and this is a pigeon's. Ah, they put pigeons' feathers in the pillows—no wonder I couldn't die! Let me take care to throw it on the floor when I lie down. And here is a moor-cock's; and this—I should know it among a thousand—it's a lapwing's.[6] Bonny bird, wheeling over our heads in the middle of the moor. It wanted to get to its nest, for the clouds touched the swells, and it felt rain coming. This feather was picked up from the heath, the bird was not shot—we saw its nest in the winter, full of little skeletons. Heathcliff set a trap over it, and the old ones dare not come. I made him promise he'd never shoot a lapwing after that, and he didn't. Yes, here are more! Did he shoot my lapwings, Nelly? Are they red, any of them? Let me look."[7]

"Give over with that baby-work!" I interrupted, dragging the pillow away, and turning the holes towards the mattress, for she was removing its contents by handfuls. "Lie down and shut your eyes; you're wandering. There's a mess! The down is flying about like snow!"

I went here and there collecting it.

"I see in you, Nelly," she continued, dreamily, "an aged woman—you have grey hair, and bent shoulders. This bed is the fairy cave under Peniston Crag, and you are gathering elf-bolts[8] to hurt our heifers; pretending, while I am near, that they are only locks of wool. That's what you'll come to fifty years hence; I know you are not so now. I'm not wandering, you're mistaken, or else I should believe you really *were* that withered hag, and I should think I *was* under Penistone Crag, and I'm conscious it's night, and there are two candles on the table making the black press[9] shine like jet.

"The black press? Where is that?" I asked. "You are talking in your sleep!"[10]

"It's against the wall, as it always is," she replied. "It *does* appear odd—I see a face in it!"

"There is no press in the room, and never was," said I, resuming my seat, and looping up the curtain that I might watch her.

6 Richard Blakeborough records Yorkshire accounts of the use of pigeon feathers to delay death and of their removal from the bedding when a person seemed unable to die (*Wit, Character, Folklore & Customs of the North Riding of Yorkshire* [London: Henry Frowde, 1898], p. 116). A moor-cock is a male black or red grouse, probably the kind of grouse that Heathcliff brought Lockwood near the end of the shooting season. Lapwings are crested plovers, common on the moors and known for vigorously defending their nests against intruders.

Catherine's monologue recalls the distracted speech in which Ophelia sets out the meanings assigned to particular plants: "There's rosemary, that's for remembrance—pray you, love, remember. And there is pansies, that's for thoughts." As the gentleman in *Hamlet* says, "Her speech is nothing,/ Yet the unshaped use of it doth move/ The hearers to collection" (*Hamlet*, IV. v. 177f.; 7–9). Catherine's rambling identification of the different species of birds whose feathers fill her pillow is saner than Ophelia's speech and culminates in one of her most important memories of her childhood with Heathcliff.

7 Catherine's memory of Heathcliff's cruelty—he sentences the fledgling lapwings to death for the pleasure of it, and this is before he has been deprived of social and educational advantages by Hindley—is oddly consoling, since it demonstrates the power she once had over him. The surfacing of this memory also reveals how thoroughly Heathcliff's pursuit of an alliance with Isabella has shaken Catherine's confidence in her own authority. Her search for bloodied lapwing feathers that would provide evidence of an earlier, previously unimaginable deception is one of Brontë's clearest representations of Catherine's tortured unconscious, revealed to us in ravings that Nelly is unable to interpret.

8 Neolithic arrowheads, once commonly found in Scotland's offshore islands, were called "elf-bolts." The fairies were supposed to have shot them at cattle (Samuel Johnson, *A Journey to the Western Islands of Scotland* [1775], p. 63).

9 A large cupboard, especially one placed in a recess in a wall, used for holding clothes, dishes, or other household items. Now chiefly Scottish and Irish English *(OED)*.

10 Anxious to prove to Nelly that she is lucid, Catherine insists that she can distinguish what she imagines from what she actually sees. Writing of Johnson's hypochondria, Boswell similarly distinguishes between a disorder that affects the imagination and one that impairs judgment:

> This distinction was made to me by the late Professor Gaubius of Leyden, physician to the Prince of Orange, in a conversation

Male and female lapwings, a color engraving by Edouard Travies (1809–c. 1865). These are Northern lapwings, large-winged birds in the plover family. The *OED* derives the name from the Old English words *hleápan* (to leap) and *winc* (to totter), both referring to the way lapwings fly. Lapwing eggs were highly prized in the Victorian period.

"Don't *you* see that face?" she enquired, gazing earnestly at the mirror.

And say what I could, I was incapable of making her comprehend it to be her own; so I rose and covered it with a shawl.[11]

"It's behind there still!" she pursued, anxiously. "And it stirred. Who is it? I hope it will not come out when you are gone! Oh! Nelly, the room is haunted! I'm afraid of being alone!"

I took her hand in mine, and bid her be composed, for a succession of shudders convulsed her frame, and she *would* keep straining her gaze towards the glass.

"There's nobody here!" I insisted. "It was *yourself,* Mrs. Linton; you knew it a while since."

"Myself," she gasped, "and the clock is striking twelve! It's true then; that's dreadful!"[12]

Her fingers clutched the clothes,[13] and gathered them over her eyes. I attempted to steal to the door with an intention of calling

> which I had with him several years ago, and he expanded it thus: "If (said he) a man tells me that he is grievously disturbed, for that he *imagines* he sees a ruffian coming against him with a drawn sword, though at the same time he is *conscious* it is a delusion, I pronounce him to have a disordered imagination; but if a man tells me that he *sees* this, and in consternation calls me to look at it, I pronounce him to be *mad.* (*Boswell's Life of Johnson,* ed. George Birkbeck Hill [Oxford: Clarendon, 1934; rpt. 1971], vol. 1, pp. 65–66)

There is no press in Catherine's room in Thrushcross Grange, but there is one in her bedroom in Wuthering Heights.

11 In Yorkshire folklore, doors and windows are opened at the moment of death, and mirrors are covered. Susan Stewart suggests that Nelly's draping the mirror here and then opening the window predict Catherine's death (Stewart, "The Ballad in *Wuthering Heights,*" *Representations,* 86:1 [Spring 2004], p. 185). Leo Bersani points to "the danger of being haunted by alien versions of the self" that the mirror threatens (Bersani, *A Future for Astyanax: Character and Desire in Literature* [New York: Columbia Univ. Press, 1976, rpt. 1984], p. 208). More specifically, it is the image of "Mrs. Linton"—so Nelly addresses her—that Catherine fails to recognize as her own image in this mirror.

her husband; but I was summoned back by a piercing shriek. The shawl had dropped from the frame.

"Why what *is* the matter?" cried I. "Who is coward now? Wake up! That is the glass—the mirror, Mrs. Linton; and you see yourself in it, and there am I too by your side."

Trembling and bewildered, she held me fast, but the horror gradually passed from her countenance; its paleness gave place to a glow of shame.

"Oh, dear! I thought I was at home," she sighed. "I thought I was lying in my chamber at Wuthering Heights. Because I'm weak, my brain got confused, and I screamed unconsciously. Don't say anything; but stay with me. I dread sleeping, my dreams appal me."

"A sound sleep would do you good, ma'am," I answered, "and I hope this suffering will prevent your trying starving again."

"Oh, if I were but in my own bed in the old house!" she went on bitterly, wringing her hands. "And that wind sounding in the firs by the lattice. Do let me feel it—it comes straight down the moor—do let me have one breath!"

To pacify her, I held the casement ajar a few seconds. A cold blast rushed through; I closed it, and returned to my post.

She lay still now: her face bathed in tears—Exhaustion of body had entirely subdued her spirit; our fiery Catherine was no better than a wailing child!

"How long is it since I shut myself in here?" she asked suddenly reviving.

"It was Monday evening," I replied, "and this is Thursday night, or rather Friday morning, at present."

"What! of the same week?" she exclaimed. "Only that brief time?"

"Long enough to live on nothing but cold water and ill-temper," observed I.

"Well, it seems a weary number of hours," she muttered doubtfully; "it must be more—I remember being in the parlour, after they had quarrelled; and Edgar being cruelly provoking, and me

12 Cinderella is one of many folk and literary figures who undergo a transformation at midnight. When her disguise disappears, she becomes again who she really is (or was) before her metamorphosis into the rich and beautiful princess who captures her prince's heart. The story of Cinderella exists in many versions, but Charles Perrault's *Tales and Stories of the Past with Morals* (better known by its subtitle, *Tales of Mother Goose*) includes the version that would have been most widely known in nineteenth-century England. First published in French in 1697, it was translated into English in 1729.

13 Bedclothes, that is, the sheets and blankets.

running into this room desperate—As soon as ever I had barred the door, utter blackness overwhelmed me, and I fell on the floor—I couldn't explain to Edgar how certain I felt of having a fit, or going raging mad, if he persisted in teasing me! I had no command of tongue, or brain, and he did not guess my agony perhaps; it barely left me sense to try to escape from him and his voice—Before I recovered sufficiently to see, and hear, it began to be dawn; and Nelly, I'll tell you what I thought, and what has kept recurring and recurring till I feared for my reason—I thought as I lay there with my head against that table leg, and my eyes dimly discerning the grey square of the window, that I was enclosed in the oak-panelled bed at home; and my heart ached with some great grief which, just waking, I could not recollect—I pondered, and worried myself to discover what it could be; and most strangely, the whole last seven years of my life grew a blank! I did not recall that they had been at all. I was a child; my father was just buried, and my misery arose from the separation that Hindley had ordered between me and Heathcliff—I was laid alone, for the first time,[14] and rousing from a dismal doze after a night of weeping—I lifted my hand to push the panels aside, it struck the table-top! I swept it along the carpet, and then, memory burst in—my late anguish was swallowed in a paroxysm of despair—I cannot say why I felt so wildly wretched—it must have been temporary derangement for there is scarcely cause—But, supposing at twelve years old, I had been wrenched from the Heights, and every early association, and my all in all, as Heathcliff was at that time, and been converted, at a stroke into Mrs. Linton, the lady of Thrushcross Grange, and the wife of a stranger, an exile and outcast, thenceforth, from what had been my world—You may fancy a glimpse of the abyss where I grovelled! Shake your head as you will, Nelly, *you* have helped to unsettle me! You should have spoken to Edgar, indeed you should, and compelled him to leave me quiet! Oh, I'm burning! I wish I were out of doors—I wish I were a girl again, half savage and hardy, and free . . . and laughing at injuries, not maddening under them!

14 Before her father's death, Catherine and Heathcliff slept together in the oak box-bed. Hindley's separation of them therefore coincides with old Mr. Earnshaw's death and with Catherine's puberty (she is twelve at the time). The separation of Catherine and Heathcliff when they are discovered looking through the window at Thrushcross Grange—he is sent back to Wuthering Heights, she is brought into the house for an extended stay—completes her transformation from a wild girl into a fine lady.

Why am I so changed? Why does my blood rush into a hell of tumult at a few words? I'm sure I should be myself were I once among the heather on those hills . . . Open the window again wide, fasten it open! Quick, why don't you move?"

"Because, I won't give you your death of cold," I answered.

"You won't give me a chance of life, you mean," she said sullenly. "However, I'm not helpless yet, I'll open it myself."

And sliding from the bed before I could hinder her, she crossed the room, walking very uncertainly, threw it back, and bent out, careless of the frosty air that cut about her shoulders as keen as a knife.

I entreated, and finally attempted to force her to retire. But I soon found her delirious strength much surpassed mine; (she *was* delirious, I became convinced by her subsequent actions and ravings).

There was no moon, and every thing beneath lay in misty darkness; not a light gleamed from any house, far or near; all had been extinguished long ago; and those at Wuthering Heights were never visible . . . still she asserted she caught their shining.

"Look!" she cried eagerly, "that's my room, with the candle in it, and the trees swaying before it . . . and the other candle is in Joseph's garret . . . Joseph sits up late, doesn't he? He's waiting till I come home that he may lock the gate . . . Well, he'll wait a while yet. It's a rough journey, and a sad heart to travel it; and we must pass by Gimmerton Kirk to go that journey! We've braved its ghosts often together, and dared each other to stand among the graves and ask them to come . . . But Heathcliff, if I dare you now, will you venture? If you do, I'll keep you. I'll not lie there by myself; they may bury me twelve feet deep, and throw the church down over me; but I won't rest till you are with me . . . I never will!"

She paused, and resumed with a strange smile, "He's considering . . . he'd rather I'd come to him! Find a way, then! not through that Kirkyard . . . You are slow! Be content, you always followed me!"

Perceiving it vain to argue against her insanity, I was planning how I could reach something to wrap about her, without quitting my hold of herself, for I could not trust her alone by the gaping lattice; when, to my consternation, I heard the rattle of the door-handle, and Mr. Linton entered. He had only then come from the library; and, in passing through the lobby, had noticed our talking and been attracted by curiosity or fear to examine what it signified at that late hour.

"Oh, sir!" I cried, checking the exclamation risen to his lips at the sight which met him, and the bleak atmosphere of the chamber.

"My poor Mistress is ill, and she quite masters me; I cannot manage her at all; pray, come and persuade her to go to bed. Forget your anger, for she's hard to guide any way but her own."

"Catherine ill?" he said hastening to us. "Shut the window, Ellen! Catherine! why . . ."

He was silent; the haggardness of Mrs. Linton's appearance smote him speechless, and he could only glance from her to me in horrified astonishment.

"She's been fretting here," I continued, "and eating scarcely anything, and never complaining; she would admit none of us till this evening, and so we couldn't inform you of her state, as we were not aware of it ourselves, but it is nothing."

I felt I uttered my explanations awkwardly; the master frowned. "It is nothing, is it, Ellen Dean?" he said sternly. "You shall account more clearly for keeping me ignorant of this!" And he took his wife in his arms, and looked at her with anguish.

At first she gave him no glance of recognition . . . he was invisible to her abstracted gaze. The delirium was not fixed, however; having weaned her eyes from contemplating the outer darkness, by degrees she centred her attention on him, and discovered who it was that held her.

"Ah! you are come, are you, Edgar Linton?" she said with angry animation . . . "You are one of those things that are ever found when least wanted, and when you are wanted, never! I suppose we shall have plenty of lamentations, now . . . I see we shall . . . but they can't keep me from my narrow home out yonder—my resting place, where I'm bound before Spring is over! There it is, not among the Lintons, mind, under the chapel-roof; but in the open air with a head-stone, and you may please yourself, whether you go to them, or come to me!"[15]

"Catherine, what have you done?" commenced the master. "Am I nothing to you, any more? Do you love that wretch, Heath—"

"Hush!" cried Mrs. Linton. "Hush, this moment! You mention that name and I end the matter, instantly, by a spring from the window! What you touch at present, you may have; but my soul will be on that hilltop before you lay hands on me again. I don't want you, Edgar; I'm past wanting you . . . Return to your books . . . I'm glad you possess a consolation, for all you had in me is gone."

"Her mind wanders, sir," I interposed. "She has been talking nonsense the whole evening; but let her have quiet and proper attendance, and she'll rally . . . Hereafter, we must be cautious how we vex her."

"I desire no further advice from you," answered Mr. Linton. "You knew your mistress's nature, and you encouraged me to harass her. And not to give me one hint of how she has been these three days! It was heartless! Months of sickness could not cause such a change!"

I began to defend myself, thinking it too bad to be blamed for another's wicked waywardness!

"I knew Mrs. Linton's nature to be headstrong and domineering," cried I; "but I didn't know that you wished to foster her fierce temper! I didn't know that, to humour her, I should wink at Mr. Heathcliff. I performed the duty of a faithful servant in telling you, and I have got a faithful servant's wages! Well, it will teach me to be careful next time. Next time you may gather intelligence for yourself!"

Engraved portrait of Matthew Arnold (1822–1888), English School. Arnold's memorable praise of Emily appears in "Haworth Churchyard," the elegy he wrote on the occasion of Charlotte's death.

15 Catherine insists on being buried in the open air rather than inside the church and offers Edgar the option of being buried alongside her there, instead of inside the church with his own family. With the exception of Anne, who is buried in a graveyard in Scarborough, the Brontës are all buried in a family vault inside Haworth church. In his elegy on the occasion of Charlotte's death, "Haworth Churchyard," Matthew Arnold mistakenly locates the Brontës' graves in the Haworth churchyard. Although Arnold visited Haworth in 1852, he seems not to have visited the church itself. He was dismayed when Gaskell told him of his mistake: "I am almost sorry you told me about the place of their burial," he wrote her. "It really seems to me to put the finishing touch to the strange cross-grained character of the fortunes of that ill-fated family that they would even be placed after death in the wrong, uncongenial spot" (Quoted in Miriam Allott, ed., *The Brontës: The Critical Heritage* [London: Routledge & Kegan Paul, 1974], p. 306).

"The next time you bring a tale to me, you shall quit my service, Ellen Dean," he replied.

"You'd rather hear nothing about it, I suppose, then, Mr. Linton?" said I. "Heathcliff has your permission to come a-courting to Miss and to drop in at every opportunity your absence offers, on purpose to poison the mistress against you?"

Confused as Catherine was, her wits were alert at applying our conversation.

"Ah! Nelly has played traitor," she exclaimed passionately. "Nelly is my hidden enemy—you witch! So you do seek elf-bolts to hurt us! Let me go, and I'll make her rue! I'll make her howl a recantation!"

A maniac's fury kindled under her brows; she struggled desperately to disengage herself from Linton's arms. I felt no inclination to tarry the event;[16] and resolving to seek medical aid on my own responsibility, I quitted the chamber.

In passing the garden to reach the road, at a place where a bridle hook is driven into the wall, I saw something white moved irregularly, evidently by another agent than the wind. Notwithstanding my hurry, I stayed to examine it, lest ever after I should have the conviction impressed on my imagination that it was a creature of the other world.

My surprise and perplexity were great to discover, by touch more than vision, Miss Isabella's springer[17] Fanny, suspended to a handkerchief, and nearly at its last gasp.

I quickly released the animal and lifted it into the garden. I had seen it follow its mistress up-stairs when she went to bed, and wondered much how it could have got out there, and what mischievous person had treated it so.

While untying the knot round the hook, it seemed to me that I repeatedly caught the beat of horses' feet galloping at some distance; but there were such a number of things to occupy my reflections that I hardly gave the circumstance a thought, though it was a strange sound, in that place, at two o'clock in the morning.

16 Wait for the outcome.

17 Springer spaniel.

A watercolor painting of Flossy (c. 1843), Anne's dog, a black and white spaniel. The painting was long attributed to Charlotte but is now thought to be Emily's work. The spaniel looks like a springer, a breed appropriate as both a pet and a field dog. The abundant life of the dog, which Emily paints in energetic motion, suggests a context for Heathcliff's parting gesture on leaving Thrushcross Grange: he hangs Isabella's springer spaniel from a bridle hook.

Mr. Kenneth was fortunately just issuing from his house to see a patient in the village as I came up the street; and my account of Catherine Linton's malady induced him to accompany me back immediately.

He was a plain, rough man; and he made no scruple to speak his doubts of her surviving this second attack; unless she were more submissive to his directions than she had shown herself before.

"Nelly Dean," said he, "I can't help fancying there's an extra cause for this. What has there been to do at the Grange? We've odd reports up here. A stout, hearty lass like Catherine does not fall ill for a trifle; and that sort of people should not either. It's hard work bringing them through fevers, and such things. How did it begin?"

"The master will inform you," I answered; "but you are acquainted with the Earnshaws' violent dispositions, and Mrs. Linton caps them all. I may say this: it commenced in a quarrel. She was struck during a tempest of passion with a kind of fit. That's her account, at least; for she flew off in the height of it, and locked herself up. Afterwards, she refused to eat, and now she alternately raves, and remains in a half dream, knowing those about her, but having her mind filled with all sorts of strange ideas and illusions."

"Mr. Linton will be sorry?" observed Kenneth, interrogatively.

"Sorry? he'll break his heart should anything happen!" I replied. "Don't alarm him more than necessary."

"Well, I told him to beware," said my companion, "and he must bide the consequences of neglecting my warning! Hasn't he been thick with Mr. Heathcliff lately?"

"Heathcliff frequently visits at the Grange," answered I, "though more on the strength of the mistress having known him when a boy, than because the master likes his company. At present, he's discharged from the trouble of calling, owing to some presumptuous aspirations after Miss Linton which he manifested. I hardly think he'll he taken in again."

"And does Miss Linton turn a cold shoulder on him?" was the doctor's next question.

"I'm not in her confidence," returned I, reluctant to continue the subject.

"No, she's a sly one," he remarked, shaking his head. "She keeps her own counsel! But she's a real little fool. I have it from good authority, that, last night—and a pretty night it was!—she and Heathcliff were walking in the plantation at the back of your house above two hours; and he pressed her not to go in again, but just mount his horse and away with him! My informant said she could only put him off by pledging her word of honour to be prepared on their first meeting after that; when it was to be, he didn't hear, but you urge Mr. Linton to look sharp!"

This news filled me with fresh fears; I outstripped Kenneth, and ran most of the way back. The little dog was yelping in the garden yet. I spared a minute to open the gate for it, but instead of going to the house door, it coursed up and down snuffing the grass, and would have escaped to the road, had I not seized and conveyed it in with me.

On ascending to Isabella's room, my suspicions were confirmed: it was empty. Had I been a few hours sooner, Mrs. Linton's illness might have arrested her rash step. But what could be done now? There was a bare possibility of overtaking them if pursued instantly. *I* could not pursue them, however; and I dare not rouse the family, and fill the place with confusion, still less unfold the business to my master, absorbed as he was in his present calamity, and having no heart to spare for a second grief!

I saw nothing for it, but to hold my tongue, and suffer matters to take their course: and Kenneth being arrived, I went with a badly composed countenance to announce him.

Catherine lay in a troubled sleep; her husband had succeeded in soothing the access of frenzy; he now hung over her pillow, watching every shade, and every change of her painfully expressive features.

The doctor, on examining the case for himself, spoke hopefully to him of its having a favourable termination, if we could only preserve around her perfect and constant tranquillity. To me, he signified the threatening danger was not so much death as permanent alienation of intellect.[18]

I did not close my eyes that night, nor did Mr. Linton; indeed, we never went to bed: and the servants were all up long before the usual hour, moving through the house with stealthy tread, and exchanging whispers as they encountered each other in their vocations. Every one was active but Miss Isabella; and they began to remark how sound she slept—her brother too asked if she had risen, and seemed impatient for her presence, and hurt that she showed so little anxiety for her sister-in-law. I trembled lest he should send me to call her; but I was spared the pain of being the first proclaimant of her flight. One of the maids, a thoughtless girl, who had been on an early errand to Gimmerton, came panting upstairs, open-mouthed, and dashed into the chamber, crying, "Oh, dear, dear! What mun we have next? Master, master, our young lady—"

"Gretna-Green," an illustration in *The Illustrated London News* accompanying an article titled "Gretna-Green Marriages" (Sept. 9, 1848, p. 157). The article points out that marriages in Scotland are almost always celebrated by a clergyman, except at sites like Gretna Green, where English couples went to avoid English marriage laws. The article quoted one authority who, "in 1771, described couples as married [in Gretna-Green] by a fisherman, a joiner, or a blacksmith, at from two guineas a job to a dram of whisky." In 1848, a bill to stop these "stolen," "runaway," or "border" marriages was introduced into Parliament.

18 Insanity. Kenneth will diagnose Catherine's illness as "a brain fever."

"Hold your noise!" cried I hastily, enraged at her clamorous manner.

"Speak lower, Mary—What is the matter?" said Mr. Linton. "What ails your young lady?"

"She's gone, she's gone! Yon' Heathcliff's run off wi' her!" gasped the girl.

"That is not true!" exclaimed Linton, rising in agitation. "It cannot be—how has the idea entered your head? Ellen Dean, go and seek her—it is incredible—it cannot be."

As he spoke he took the servant to the door, and then repeated his demand to know her reasons for such an assertion.

"Why, I met on the road a lad that fetches milk here," she stammered, "and he asked whether we wern't[19] in trouble at the Grange—I thought he meant for Missis's sickness, so I answered, yes. 'Then,' says he, 'they's somebody gone after 'em, I guess?' I stared. He saw I knew naught about it, and he told how a gentleman and lady had stopped to have a horse's shoe fastened at a blacksmith's shop, two miles out of Gimmerton, not very long after midnight! and how the blacksmith's lass had got up to spy who they were: she knew them both directly—And she noticed the man, Heathcliff it was, she felt certain, nob'dy could mistake him, besides—put a sovereign in her father's hand for payment. The lady had a cloak about her face; but having desired a sup of water, while she drank it fell back, and she saw her very plain—Heathcliff held both bridles as they rode on, and they set their faces from the village, and went as fast as the rough roads would let them. The lass said nothing to her father, but she told it all over Gimmerton this morning."[20]

I ran and peeped, for form's sake into Isabella's room, confirming when I returned the servant's statement—Mr. Linton had resumed his seat by the bed; on my re-entrance, he raised his eyes, read the meaning of my blank aspect, and dropped them without giving an order, or uttering a word.

"Are we to try any measures for overtaking and bringing her back?" I inquired. "How should we do?"

19 I have let the word stand as printed in 1847; its spelling registers Mary's pronunciation.

20 Heathcliff and Isabella are headed for the Scottish border because the Marriage Act of 1753 did not apply in Scotland. In order for a marriage to be valid in England, it had to be preceded by the publication of banns or the obtaining of a license, and Gretna Green, just across the Scottish border, was famous as a site of runaway marriages. In the geography of the novel, Gimmerton is north and east of Thrushcross Grange, and the main road would have taken Heathcliff and Isabella through the village on their way to Scotland. See the map on p. vi of this edition, and Chapter 11 above, where Nelly comes to the "sand-pillar, with the letters W.H. cut on its north side, on the east G., and on the south-west T.G."

"She went of her own accord," answered the master; "she had a right to go if she pleased—Trouble me no more about her—Hereafter, she is only my sister in name; not because I disown her, but because she has disowned me."

And that was all he said on the subject; he did not make a single inquiry further, or mention her in any way, except directing me to send what property she had in the house to her fresh home, wherever it was, when I knew it.

CHAPTER 13

For two months the fugitives remained absent; in those two months, Mrs. Linton encountered and conquered the worst shock of what was denominated a brain fever.[1] No mother could have nursed an only child more devotedly than Edgar tended her. Day and night, he was watching, and patiently enduring, all the annoyances that irritable nerves and a shaken reason could inflict; and, though Kenneth remarked that what he saved from the grave would only recompense his care by forming the source of constant future anxiety—in fact, that his health and strength were being sacrificed to preserve a mere ruin of humanity—he knew no limits in gratitude and joy, when Catherine's life was declared out of danger; and hour after hour, he would sit beside her, tracing the gradual return to bodily health, and flattering his too sanguine hopes with the illusion that her mind would settle back to its right balance also, and she would soon be entirely her former self.

The first time she left her chamber was at the commencement of the following March. Mr. Linton had put on her pillow, in the morning, a handful of golden crocuses; her eye, long stranger to any gleam of pleasure, caught them in waking, and shone delighted as she gathered them eagerly together.

"These are the earliest flowers at the Heights!" she exclaimed. "They remind me of soft thaw winds,[2] and warm sunshine, and

1 By the end of the eighteenth century, "brain fever" had replaced an earlier diagnosis of "phrenzy." Medical practitioners believed that brain fevers could be caused by shocks to the nervous system or mental fatigue as well as by contagion. Women were thought to be more susceptible to this kind of shock or fatigue than men, although both men and women suffer from brain fever in nineteenth-century fiction. In 1858, James Copland's *A Dictionary of Practical Medicine* listed the symptoms of brain fever as "acute pain in the head, with intolerance of light and sound; watchfulness, delirium; flushed countenance, and redness of the conjunctiva, or a heavy suffused state of the eyes; quick pulse; frequently spasmodic twitchings or convulsions, passing into somnolency, coma, and complete relaxation of the limbs" (quoted in Audrey C. Peterson, "Brain Fever in Nineteenth-Century Literature: Fact and Fiction," *Victorian Studies,* vol. 19, no. 4, June 1976, pp. 445–464).

2 Melting winds. In Brontë's poem "My Comforter," the Comforter is compared to "A thaw-wind, melting quietly/ The snow-drift, on some wintry lea." The Comforter plays a role like that of Hope and Imagination in other poems: it calms the speaker's "resentful mood" and tames her "savage heart."

3 Catherine and Edgar have been married almost exactly a year.

nearly melted snow—Edgar, is there not a south wind, and is not the snow almost gone?"

"The snow is quite gone down here, darling!" replied her husband, "and I only see two white spots on the whole range of moors—The sky is blue, and the larks are singing, and the becks and brooks are all brim full. Catherine, last spring at this time, I was longing to have you under this roof[3]—now, I wish you were a mile or two up those hills; the air blows so sweetly, I feel that it would cure you."

"I shall never be there, but once more!" said the invalid; "and then you'll leave me, and I shall remain for ever. Next spring you'll long again to have me under this roof, and you'll look back and think you were happy to-day."

Linton lavished on her the kindest caresses, and tried to cheer her by the fondest words; but vaguely regarding the flowers, she let the tears collect on her lashes, and stream down her cheeks unheeding.

We knew she was really better, and therefore decided that long confinement to a single place produced much of this despondency, and it might be partially removed by a change of scene.

The master told me to light a fire in the many-weeks deserted parlour, and to set an easy-chair in the sunshine by the window; and then he brought her down, and she sat a long while enjoying the genial heat, and, as we expected, revived by the objects round her, which, though familiar, were free from the dreary associations investing her hated sick-chamber. By evening, she seemed greatly exhausted; yet no arguments could persuade her to return to that apartment, and I had to arrange the parlour sofa for her bed, till another room could be prepared.

To obviate the fatigue of mounting and descending the stairs, we fitted up this, where you lie at present, on the same floor with the parlour: and she was soon strong enough to move from one to the other, leaning on Edgar's arm.

Ah, I thought to myself, she might recover, so waited on as she was. And there was double cause to desire it, for on her existence depended that of another; we cherished the hope that in a little while, Mr. Linton's heart would be gladdened, and his lands secured from a stranger's gripe, by the birth of an heir.[4]

I should mention that Isabella sent to her brother, some six weeks from her departure, a short note announcing her marriage with Heathcliff. It appeared dry and cold; but at the bottom was dotted in with pencil an obscure apology, and an entreaty for kind remembrance and reconciliation, if her proceeding had offended him, asserting that she could not help it then, and being done, she had now no power to repeal it.

Linton did not reply to this, I believe; and, in a fortnight more, I got a long letter which I considered odd coming from the pen of a bride just out of the honeymoon. I'll read it, for I keep it yet. Any relic of the dead is precious, if they were valued living.

"DEAR ELLEN," it begins.[5]

"I came, last night, to Wuthering Heights, and heard, for the first time, that Catherine has been, and is yet, very ill. I must not write to her, I suppose, and my brother is either too angry, or too distressed to answer what I send him. Still, I must write to somebody, and the only choice left me is you.

"Inform Edgar that I'd give the world to see his face again—that my heart returned to Thrushcross Grange in twenty-four hours after I left it, and is there at this moment, full of warm feelings for him and Catherine! *I can't follow it, though* (those words are underlined)—they need not expect me, and they may draw what conclusions they please, taking care, however, to lay nothing at the door of my weak will or deficient affection.

"The remainder of the letter is for yourself alone. I want to ask you two questions: the first is,

"'How did you contrive to preserve the common sympathies of human nature when you resided here?' I cannot recognise any sentiment which those around, share with me.

"The second question I have great interest in; it is this—

4 Catherine is pregnant.

5 Isabella's letter to Nelly takes up almost the entire chapter. Like the young Catherine's diary fragment, which was embedded in Lockwood's narration, it is embedded in Nelly's narration and supplies a part of the story that Nelly has not herself witnessed. Isabella's letter describes domestic abuse from the point of view of an abused wife. Judith E. Pike points out that "Brontë's introduction of a young bride from the gentry class into the domestic mayhem of the Heights is highly unorthodox for the mid-Victorian period" ("'My Name was Isabella Linton': Coverture, Domestic Violence and Mrs. Heathcliff's Narrative in *Wuthering Heights*," *Nineteenth-Century Literature* [Dec. 2009], 64:3, pp. 354–357). Anne also takes up the topic of domestic violence and a married woman's escape from it in her second novel, *The Tenant of Wildfell Hall* (1848).

"'Is Mr. Heathcliff a man? If so, is he mad? And if not, is he a devil?' I shan't tell my reasons for making this inquiry; but, I beseech you to explain, if you can, what I have married—that is, when you call to see me; and you must call, Ellen, very soon. Don't write but come, and bring me something from Edgar.

"Now, you shall hear how I have been received in my new home, as I am led to imagine the Heights will be. It is to amuse myself that I dwell on such subjects as the lack of external comforts; they never occupy my thoughts, except at the moment when I miss them—I should laugh and dance for joy, if I found their absence was the total of my miseries, and the rest was an unnatural dream!

"The sun set behind the Grange as we turned on to the moors; by that, I judged it to be six o'clock; and my companion halted half-an-hour, to inspect the park, and the gardens, and, probably, the place itself as well as he could; so it was dark when we dismounted in the paved yard of the farm-house, and your old fellow-servant, Joseph, issued out to receive us by the light of a dip candle.[6] He did it with a courtesy that redounded to his credit. His first act was to elevate his torch to a level with my face, squint malignantly, project his under-lip, and turn away.

"Then he took the two horses, and led them into the stables, reappearing for the purpose of locking the outer gate, as if we lived in an ancient castle.

"Heathcliff stayed to speak to him, and I entered the kitchen—a dingy, untidy hole[7]; I dare say you would not know it, it is so changed since it was in your charge.

"By the fire stood a ruffianly child, strong in limb, and dirty in garb, with a look of Catherine in his eyes, and about his mouth.

"This is Edgar's legal nephew, I reflected—mine in a manner; I must shake hands, and—yes—I must kiss him. It is right to establish a good understanding at the beginning.

"I approached, and, attempting to take his chubby fist, said—'How do you do, my dear?'

"He replied in a jargon I did not comprehend. 'Shall you and I be friends, Hareton?' was my next essay at conversation.

6 A candle made by repeatedly dipping the wick in melted tallow; more refined candles, like the ones seen earlier in Thrushcross Grange, were made by pouring wax into a mold.

7 "Hole" in dialect usage can mean "room," and Isabella, though she is not herself a dialect speaker, may be using it in this way here and below, when she refers to the "lumber-hole." See Malcolm Petyt, "The Dialect Speech in *Wuthering Heights*," in Hilda Marsden and Ian Jack, *Wuthering Heights* (Oxford: Clarendon Press, 1976), p. 511.

"An oath and a threat to set Throttler on me if I did not 'frame off' rewarded my perseverance.

"'Hey, Throttler, lad!' whispered the little wretch, rousing a half-bred bull-dog from its lair in a corner. 'Now, wilt tuh be ganging?' he asked authoritatively.

"Love for my life urged a compliance; I stepped over the threshold to wait till the others should enter. Mr. Heathcliff was nowhere visible; and Joseph, whom I followed to the stables, and requested to accompany me in, after staring and muttering to himself, screwed up his nose and replied—

'Mim! mim! mim![8] Did iver Christian body hear owt like it? Minching un' munching! Hah can Aw tell whet ye say?'[9]

"'I say, I wish you to come with me into the house!' I cried, thinking him deaf, yet highly disgusted at his rudeness.

"'Nor nuh me! Aw getten summut else to do,'[10] he answered, and continued his work, moving his lantern jaws[11] meanwhile, and surveying my dress and countenance (the former a great deal too fine, but the latter, I'm sure, as sad as he could desire) with sovereign contempt.

"I walked round the yard and through a wicket to another door, at which I took the liberty of knocking, in hopes some more civil servant might shew himself.

"After a short suspense it was opened by a tall, gaunt man, without neckerchief, and otherwise extremely slovenly; his features were lost in masses of shaggy hair that hung on his shoulders; and *his* eyes, too, were like a ghostly Catherine's, with all their beauty annihilated.

"'What's your business here?' he demanded, 'Who are you?'

"'My name *was* Isabella Linton,' I replied. 'You've seen me before, sir. I'm lately married to Mr. Heathcliff; and he has brought me here—I suppose by your permission.'

"'Is he come back, then?' asked the hermit, glaring like a hungry wolf.

"'Yes—we came just now,' I said; 'but he left me by the kitchen door; and when I would have gone in, your little boy played sen-

8 Priggish or affected, especially with reference to speech. Marsden and Jack cite Charlotte Brontë's novel *Shirley*, Ch. VII: "Some o't' bonniest and mimmest-looking too" (p. 426), but Charlotte's character uses the word more approvingly than Joseph does, perhaps to mean "demure" or "proper" without the usual connotation of affectation.

9 "Did ever a Christian body hear anything like it? Minching and muching! How can I tell what you're saying?"

Joseph mocks Isabella for working her jaws to little effect. He sees her speaking, but her locution is so different from his that he claims not to understand her.

10 "Not I! I've got other things to do."

11 "Long thin jaws, giving a hollow appearance to the cheek" *(OED)*.

tinel over the place, and frightened me off by the help of a bull-dog.'

"'It's well the hellish villain has kept his word!' growled my future host, searching the darkness beyond me in expectation of discovering Heathcliff, and then he indulged in a soliloquy of execrations, and threats of what he would have done had the 'fiend' deceived him.

"I repented having tried this second entrance; and was almost inclined to slip way before he finished cursing, but ere I could execute that intention, he ordered me in, and shut and re-fastened the door.

"There was a great fire, and that was all the light in the huge apartment, whose floor had grown a uniform grey; and the once brilliant pewter dishes which used to attract my gaze when I was a girl partook of a similar obscurity created by tarnish and dust.

"I inquired whether I might call the maid, and be conducted to a bed-room? Mr. Earnshaw vouchsafed no answer. He walked up and down, with his hands in his pockets, apparently quite forgetting my presence; and his abstraction was evidently so deep, and his whole aspect so misanthropical, that I shrank from disturbing him again.

"You'll not be surprised, Ellen, at my feeling particularly cheerless, seated in worse than solitude, on that inhospitable hearth, and remembering that four miles distant lay my delightful home, containing the only people I loved on earth: and there might as well be the Atlantic to part us, instead of those four miles—I could not overpass them!

"I questioned with myself—where must I turn for comfort? And —mind you don't tell Edgar, or Catherine—above every sorrow beside, this rose pre-eminent—despair at finding nobody who could or would be my ally against Heathcliff!

"I had sought shelter at Wuthering Heights, almost gladly because I was secured by that arrangement from living alone with him; but he knew the people we were coming amongst, and he did not fear their intermeddling.

"I sat and thought a doleful time; the clock struck eight, and nine, and still my companion paced to and fro, his head bent on his breast, and perfectly silent, unless a groan, or a bitter ejaculation forced itself out at intervals.

"I listened to detect a woman's voice in the house, and filled the interim with wild regrets, and dismal anticipations, which, at last, spoke audibly in irrepressible sighing and weeping.

"I was not aware how openly I grieved, till Earnshaw halted opposite, in his measured walk, and gave me a stare of newly awakened surprise. Taking advantage of his recovered attention, I exclaimed—

"'I'm tired with my journey, and I want to go to bed! Where is the maid-servant? Direct me to her, as she won't come to me!'

"'We have none,' he answered; 'you must wait on yourself!'

"'Where must I sleep, then?' I sobbed—I was beyond regarding self-respect, weighed down by fatigue and wretchedness.

"'Joseph will show you Heathcliff's chamber,' said he; 'open that door—he's in there.'

"I was going to obey, but he suddenly arrested me, and added in the strangest tone—'Be so good as to turn your lock, and draw your bolt—don't omit it!'

"'Well!' I said. 'But why, Mr. Earnshaw?' I did not relish the notion of deliberately fastening myself in with Heathcliff.

"'Look here!' he replied, pulling from his waistcoat a curiously constructed pistol, having a double-edged spring knife attached to the barrel.[12] 'That's a great tempter to a desperate man, is it not? I cannot resist going up with this, every night, and trying his door. If once I find it open, he's done for! I do it invariably, even though the minute before I have been recalling a hundred reasons that should make me refrain—it is some devil that urges me to thwart my own schemes by killing him—you fight against that devil, for love, as long as you may; when the time comes, not all the angels in heaven shall save him!'

"I surveyed the weapon inquisitively; a hideous notion struck me. How powerful I should be possessing such an instrument! I

12 Pocket pistol knives were well known in England in 1784, even though Isabella has never seen one. See Vol. 2, Chap. 3, note 21 for a fuller description of Hindley's pistol knife.

took it from his hand, and touched the blade. He looked astonished at the expression my face assumed during a brief second. It was not horror, it was covetousness. He snatched the pistol back jealously; shut the knife, and returned it to its concealment.

"'I don't care if you tell him,' said he. 'Put him on his guard, and watch for him. You know the terms we are on, I see; his danger does not shock you.'

"'What has Heathcliff done to you?' I asked. 'In what has he wronged you to warrant this appalling hatred? Wouldn't it be wiser to bid him quit the house?'

"'No,' thundered Earnshaw, 'should he offer to leave me, he's a dead man; persuade him to attempt it, and you are a murderess! Am I to lose *all,* without a chance of retrieval? Is Hareton to be a beggar? Oh, damnation! I *will* have it back; and I'll have *his* gold too; and then his blood; and hell shall have his soul! It will be ten times blacker with that guest than ever it was before!'

"You've acquainted me, Ellen, with your old master's habits. He is clearly on the verge of madness—he was so, last night at least. I shuddered to be near him, and thought on the servant's ill-bred moroseness as comparatively agreeable.

"He now recommenced his moody walk, and I raised the latch, and escaped into the kitchen.

"Joseph was bending over the fire, peering into a large pan that swung above it; and a wooden bowl of oatmeal stood on the settle close by. The contents of the pan began to boil, and he turned to plunge his hand into the bowl; I conjectured that this preparation was probably for our supper, and, being hungry, I resolved it should be eatable—so crying out sharply—'*I'll* make the porridge!' —I removed the vessel out of his reach, and proceeded to take off my hat and riding habit. 'Mr. Earnshaw,' I continued, 'directs me to wait on myself—I will—I'm not going to act the lady among you, for fear I should starve.'

"'Gooid Lord!' he muttered, sitting down, and stroking his ribbed stockings from the knee to the ankle. 'If they's tuh be fresh ortherings—just when Aw getten used tuh two maisters, if Aw mun hev a *mistress* set o'er my heead, it's loike time tuh be flitting. Aw niver *did* think tuh say t' day ut Aw mud lave th' owld place—but Aw daht it's nigh at hend!'[13]

"This lamentation drew no notice from me; I went briskly to work; sighing to remember a period when it would have been all merry fun; but compelled speedily to drive off the remembrance. It racked me to recall past happiness, and the greater peril there was of conjuring up its apparition, the quicker the thible[14] ran round, and the faster the handfuls of meal fell into the water.

"Joseph beheld my style of cookery with growing indignation.

"'Thear!' he ejaculated. 'Hareton, thah willn't sup thy porridge tuh neeght; they'll be nowt bud lumps as big as maw nave. Thear, agean! Aw'd fling in bowl un all, if Aw wer yah! Thear, pale t' guilp off, un' then yah'll hae done wi't. Bang, bang. It's a marcy t' bothom isn't deaved aht!'[15]

"It *was* rather a rough mess, I own, when poured into the basins; four had been provided, and a gallon pitcher of new milk was brought from the dairy, which Hareton seized and commenced drinking and spilling from the expansive lip.

"I expostulated, and desired that he should have his in a mug, affirming that I could not taste the liquid treated so dirtily. The old cynic chose to be vastly offended at this nicety; assuring me, repeatedly, that 'the barn was every bit as gooid' as I, 'and every bit as wollsome,'[16] and wondering how I could fashion to be so conceited; meanwhile, the infant ruffian continued sucking; and glowered up at me defyingly, as he slavered into the jug.

"'I shall have my supper in another room,' I said. 'Have you no place you call a parlour?'

"'*Parlour!*' he echoed, sneeringly, '*parlour!* Nay, we've noa *parlours*. If yah dunnut loike wer company, they's maister's; un' if yah dunnut loike maister, they's us.'[17]

"'Then I shall go up-stairs,' I answered; 'shew me a chamber!'

13 "If there are to be new ways of doing things—just when I've gotten used to two masters, if I'm to have a *mistress* set over me, it's high time to be going. I never *did* think I'd see the day that I'd have to leave the old place—but I suspect it's near at hand."

14 A wooden spoon for stirring porridge.

15 "There! . . . Hareton, thou will not eat thy porridge to-night; there'll be nothing but lumps as big as my fist. There, again! I'd throw in bowl and all, if I were you! There, peal the scum off, and then you'll have done with it. Bang, bang. It's a mercy the bottom isn't knocked out."

The meaning of the dialect word "guilp" has been much disputed, and there is no agreement about it. I take Joseph's meaning to be that Isabella has not stirred the porridge properly so that it's lumpy and the bottom of the pan is scorched. He therefore advises Hareton to take his portion from the top.

16 Hareton is Isabella's social equal, and every bit as healthy.

17 "*Parlour . . . parlour!* Nay, we've no *parlours*. If you don't like our company, there's master's; and if you don't like master, there's us."

Joseph mocks Isabella's pronunciation of the word *parlour*. What she has in mind is a separate room, nicely furnished, where someone can have privacy or where guests can be entertained. Catherine and Edgar are sitting in the parlor at Thrushcross Grange when Heathcliff returns after his three-year absence. Hindley thought of creating a parlour out of a spare room at Wuthering Heights to please Frances, but she discouraged him from doing so.

"I put my basin on a tray, and went myself to fetch some more milk.

"With great grumblings, the fellow rose, and preceded me in my ascent: we mounted to the garrets; he opening a door, now and then, to look into the apartments we passed.

"'Here's a rahm,' he said at last, flinging back a cranky board on hinges. 'It's weel eneugh tuh ate a few porridge in. They's a pack uh corn i' t' corner thear, meeterly clane; if yah're feared uh muckying yer grand silk cloes, spread yer hankerchir ut t' top on't.'[18]

"The 'rahm' was a kind of lumber-hole smelling strong of malt and grain, various sacks of which articles were piled around, leaving a wide, bare space in the middle.

"'Why, man!' I exclaimed, facing him angrily, 'this is not a place to sleep in. I wish to see my bed-room.'

"'*Bed-rume!*'" he repeated, in a tone of mockery. 'Yah's see all t' *bed-rumes* thear is—yon's mine.'[19]

"He pointed into the second garret, only differing from the first in being more naked about the walls, and having a large, low, curtainless bed, with an indigo-coloured quilt at one end.

"'What do I want with yours?' I retorted. 'I suppose Mr. Heathcliff does not lodge at the top of the house, does he?'

"'Oh! it's Maister *Hathecliff's* yah're wenting?' cried he, as if making a new discovery. 'Couldn't ye uh said soa, at onst? un then, Aw mud uh telled ye, baht all this wark, ut that's just one yah cannut sea—he allas keeps it locked, un' nob'dy iver mells on't but hisseln.'[20]

"'You've a nice house, Joseph,' I could not refrain from observing, 'and pleasant inmates; and I think the concentrated essence of all the madness in the world took up its abode in my brain the day I linked my fate with theirs! However, that is not to the present purpose—there are other rooms. For heaven's sake, be quick, and let me settle somewhere!'

"He made no reply to this adjuration, only plodding doggedly down the wooden steps, and halting before an apartment which,

18 "Here's a room. . . . It's good enough to eat some porridge in. There's a sack of grain in the corner there, pretty clean; if you're afraid of soiling your grand silk clothes, spread your handkerchief on top of it."

19 As before, Joseph mocks Isabella's pronunciation (of the word bedroom) as well as her assumption that there are rooms set aside for sleeping and not used for multiple purposes in a house like Wuthering Heights.

20 "Oh! It's Master *Heathcliff's* you're wanting? . . . Couldn't you have said so at first? And then, I might have told you, without all this work, that that's just one you cannot see—he always keeps it locked, and nobody ever meddles with it but himself."

This is, we know, the room that Catherine and Heathcliff slept in together before old Mr. Earnshaw died and Hindley separated them. It is also the room that Lockwood slept in when he had his nightmares, and the room that Catherine longed to occupy again at the onset of her brain fever.

from that halt, and the superior quality of its furniture, I conjectured to be the best one.

"There was a carpet, a good one, but the pattern was obliterated by dust; a fire-place hung with cut paper[21] dropping to pieces; a handsome oak-bedstead with ample crimson curtains of rather expensive material and modern make. But they had evidently experienced rough usage: the valances hung in festoons, wrenched from their rings; and the iron rod supporting them was bent in an arc on one side, causing the drapery to trail upon the floor. The chairs were also damaged, many of them severely; and deep indentations deformed the panels of the walls.

"I was endeavouring to gather resolution for entering, and taking possession, when my fool of a guide announced—

"'This here is t' maister's.'[22]

"My supper by this time was cold, my appetite gone, and my patience exhausted. I insisted on being provided instantly with a place of refuge, and means of repose.

"'Whear the divil,' began the religious elder. 'The Lord bless us! The Lord forgie us! Whear the *hell* wold ye gang? ye marred, wearisome nowt? Yah seen all bud Hareton's bit of a cham'er. They's nut another hoile tuh lig dahn in i' th' hahse!'[23]

"I was so vexed, I flung my tray and its contents on the ground; and then seated myself at the stairs-head, hid my face in my hands, and cried.

"'Ech! ech!' exclaimed Joseph. 'Weel done, Miss Cathy! weel done, Miss Cathy![24] Hahsiver, t' maister sall just tum'le o'er them brocken pots; un' then we's hear summut; we's hear hah it's tuh be. Gooid-fur-nowt madling! yah desarve pining froo this tuh Churstmas, flinging t' precious gifts uh God under fooit i' yer flaysome rages! Bud Aw'm mista'en if yah shew yer sperrit lang. Will Hathecliff bide sich bonny ways, think ye? Aw nobbut wish he muh cotch ye i' that plisky. Aw nobbut wish he may.'[25]

"And so he went scolding to his den beneath, taking the candle with him, and I remained in the dark.

21 "[P]ictures or floral designs cut from coloured paper and usually pasted on—here probably pasted to a chimney-board placed in the fireplace during the summer, but perhaps festooned above the mantlepiece" (Marsden and Jack, p. 427).

22 This is Hindley's room, and the best sleeping room in Wuthering Heights. Its condition, described by Isabella in the previous paragraph, calls attention to Hindley's violence and the servants' neglect.

23 "The Lord bless us! The Lord forgive us! Where the *hell* would you go, you spoiled, wearisome nothing? You've seen all but Hareton's bit of a room. There's not another room to lie down in in the house!"

24 Possibly Joseph blames Catherine for the current state of affairs: Isabella has left the Grange, where she belongs; she has married Heathcliff; and she is disturbing Joseph's peace by crying her eyes out in frustration and wounded pride. More likely, Joseph conflates Isabella and Catherine, two characters who are connected for him by their gender and the explosive behavior that is its natural consequence. Joseph's mistake invites a larger interpretation. As Patricia Parker points out, Catherine and Isabella exchange places as a result of their marriages. Catherine moves from the Heights to the Grange when she marries Edgar, and Isabella moves in the opposite direction ("The (Self-) Identity of the Literary Text: Property, Propriety, Proper Place, and Proper Name in *Wuthering Heights*," in Mario J. Valdes and Owen Miller, eds., *Identity of the Literary Text* [Toronto: Univ. of Toronto Press, 1985], p. 100).

25 "Nevertheless, the master shall just tumble over those broken pots; and then we'll hear something; we'll hear how it's to be. Good-for-nothing crazy! You deserve to pine from now until Christmas, flinging God's precious goods under foot in your frightful rages! But I'm mistaken if you will show your spirit long. Will Heathcliff stand such affected behavior, do you think? I only wish he might catch you in that tantrum. I only wish he may."

26 "There's room for both you and your pride, I should think, in the sitting-room. It's empty; you may have it all to yourself, with Him [the Devil] who always makes a third in such bad company!"

"The period of reflection succeeding this silly action compelled me to admit the necessity of smothering my pride, and choking my wrath, and bestirring myself to remove its effects.

"An unexpected aid presently appeared in the shape of Throttler, whom I now recognised as a son of our old Skulker; it had spent its whelphood at the Grange, and was given by my father to Mr. Hindley. I fancy it knew me—it pushed its nose against mine by way of salute, and then hastened to devour the porridge, while I groped from step to step, collecting the shattered earthenware, and drying the spatters of milk from the bannister with my pocket-handherchief.

"Our labours were scarcely over when I heard Earnshaw's tread in the passage; my assistant tucked in his tail, and pressed to the wall; I stole into the nearest doorway. The dog's endeavour to avoid him was unsuccessful, as I guessed by a scutter down stairs and a prolonged, piteous yelping. I had better luck. He passed on, entered his chamber, and shut the door.

"Directly after, Joseph came up with Hareton, to put him to bed. I had found shelter in Hareton's room, and the old man, on seeing me, said—

"'They's rahm fur boath yah un yer pride, nah, Aw sud think, i' th hahse. It's empty; yah muh hev it all tuh yerseln, un Him as allas maks a third, i' sich ill company!'[26]

"Gladly did I take advantage of this intimation; and the minute I flung myself into a chair by the fire, I nodded and slept.

"My slumber was deep and sweet, though over far too soon. Mr. Heathcliff awoke me; he had just come in, and demanded, in his loving manner, what I was doing there?

"I told him the cause of my staying up so late—that he had the key of our room in his pocket.

"The adjective *our* gave mortal offence. He swore it was not, nor ever should be, mine; and he'd—but I'll not repeat his language, nor describe his habitual conduct; he is ingenious and unresting in seeking to gain my abhorrence! I sometimes wonder at him with an intensity that deadens my fear: yet, I assure you, a tiger, or a venomous serpent could not rouse terror in me equal to that which he wakens. He told me of Catherine's illness, and accused my brother of causing it; promising that I should be Edgar's proxy in suffering, till he could get a hold of him.

"I do hate him—I am wretched—I have been a fool! Beware of uttering one breath of this to any one at the Grange. I shall expect you every day—don't disappoint me!

"ISABELLA."

CHAPTER 14

As soon as I had perused this epistle, I went to the master, and informed him that his sister had arrived at the Heights, and sent me a letter expressing her sorrow for Mrs. Linton's situation, and her ardent desire to see him; with a wish that he would transmit to her, as early as possible, some token of forgiveness by me.

"Forgiveness?" said Linton. "I have nothing to forgive her, Ellen—you may call at Wuthering Heights this afternoon, if you like, and say that I am not *angry,* but I'm *sorry* to have lost her: especially as I can never think she'll be happy. It is out of the question my going to see her, however; we are eternally divided; and should she really wish to oblige me, let her persuade the villain she has married to leave the country."

"And you won't write her a little note, sir?" I asked, imploringly.

"No," he answered. "It is needless. My communication with Heathcliff's family shall be as sparing as his with mine. It shall not exist!"

Mr. Edgar's coldness depressed me exceedingly; and all the way from the Grange, I puzzled my brains how to put more heart into what he said when I repeated it; and how to soften his refusal of even a few lines to console Isabella.

I dare say she had been on the watch for me since morning: I saw her looking through the lattice, as I came up the garden causeway, and I nodded to her; but she drew back, as if afraid of being observed.

I entered without knocking. There never was such a dreary, dismal scene as the formerly cheerful house presented! I must confess that, if I had been in the young lady's place, I would, at least, have swept the hearth, and wiped the tables with a duster. But she already partook of the pervading spirit of neglect which encompassed her. Her pretty face was wan and listless; her hair uncurled, some locks hanging lankly down, and some carelessly twisted round her head. Probably she had not touched her dress since yester evening.

Hindley was not there. Mr. Heathcliff sat at a table, turning over some papers in his pocket-book;[1] but he rose when I appeared, asked me how I did, quite friendly, and offered me a chair.

He was the only thing there that seemed decent, and I thought he never looked better. So much had circumstances altered their positions, that he would certainly have struck a stranger as a born and bred gentleman, and his wife as a thorough little slattern!

She came forward eagerly to greet me; and held out one hand to take the expected letter.

I shook my head. She wouldn't understand the hint, but followed me to a sideboard, where I went to lay my bonnet, and importuned me in a whisper to give her directly what I had brought.

Heathcliff guessed the meaning of her manoeuvres, and said—

"If you have got anything for Isabella, as no doubt you have, Nelly, give it to her. You needn't make a secret of it; we have no secrets between us."

"Oh, I have nothing," I replied, thinking it best to speak the truth at once. My master bid me tell his sister that she must not expect either a letter or a visit from him at present. He sends his love, ma'am, and his wishes for your happiness, and his pardon for the grief you have occasioned; but he thinks that after this time, his household, and the household here, should drop intercommunication, as nothing good could come of keeping it up."

1 A small notebook, intended to be carried in the pocket.

2 Neighborhood.

Mrs. Heathcliff's lip quivered slightly, and she returned to her seat in the window. Her husband took his stand on the hearthstone near me, and began to put questions concerning Catherine.

I told him as much as I thought proper of her illness, and he extorted from me, by cross-examination, most of the facts connected with its origin.

I blamed her, as she deserved, for bringing it all on herself; and ended by hoping that he would follow Mr. Linton's example, and avoid future interference with his family, for good or evil.

"Mrs Linton is now just recovering," I said, "she'll never be like she was, but her life is spared, and if you really have a regard for her, you'll shun crossing her way again. Nay, you'll move out of this country[2] entirely; and that you may not regret it, I'll inform you Catherine Linton is as different now from your old friend Catherine Earnshaw as that young lady is different from me! Her appearance is changed greatly, her character much more so; and the person who is compelled, of necessity, to be her companion, will only sustain his affection hereafter, by the remembrance of what she once was, by common humanity, and a sense of duty!"

"That is quite possible," remarked Heathcliff, forcing himself to seem calm, "quite possible that your master should have nothing but common humanity and a sense of duty to fall back upon. But do you imagine that I shall leave Catherine to his *duty* and *humanity?* and can you compare my feelings respecting Catherine to his? Before you leave this house, I must exact a promise from you that you'll get me an interview with her—consent or refuse, I *will* see her! What do you say?"

"I say, Mr. Heathcliff," I replied, "you must not—you never shall through my means. Another encounter between you and the master would kill her altogether!"

"With your aid that may be avoided," he continued, "and should there be danger of such an event—should he be the cause of adding a single trouble more to her existence—Why, I think I shall be justified in going to extremes! I wish you had sincerity enough to tell me whether Catherine would suffer greatly from his loss. The fear that she would restrains me: and there you see the distinction between our feelings—Had he been in my place and I in his, though I hated him with a hatred that turned my life to gall, I never would have raised a hand against him. You may look incredulous, if you please! I never would have banished him from her society, as long as she desired his. The moment her regard ceased, I would have torn his heart out, and drank his blood! But till then—if you don't believe me, you don't know me—till then, I would have died by inches before I touched a single hair of his head!"

"And yet," I interrupted, "you have no scruples in completely ruining all hopes of her perfect restoration by thrusting yourself into her remembrance, now, when she has nearly forgotten you, and involving her in a new tumult of discord and distress."

"You suppose she has nearly forgotten me?" he said. "Oh Nelly! you know she has not! You know as well as I do that for every thought she spends on Linton, she spends a thousand on me! At a most miserable period of my life, I had a notion of the kind; it haunted me on my return to the neighbourhood last summer, but only her own assurance could make me admit the horrible idea again. And then, Linton would be nothing, nor Hindley, nor all the dreams that ever I dreamt. Two words would comprehend my future, *death* and *hell*—existence after losing her would be hell.[3]

"Yet I was a fool to fancy for a moment that she valued Edgar Linton's attachment more than mine—If he loved with all the powers of his puny being, he couldn't love as much in eighty years, as I could in a day. And Catherine has a heart as deep as I have; the sea could be as readily contained in that horse-trough, as her whole affection be monopolized by him—Tush! He is scarcely a degree dearer to her than her dog, or her horse[4]—It is not in him to be loved like me, how can she love in him what he has not?

"Catherine and Edgar are as fond of each other as any two people can be!" cried Isabella with sudden vivacity. "No one has a right

3 Heathcliff's definition of hell as his "existence" if Catherine were to abandon him is his counterpart to her idea that if Heathcliff "were annihilated, the Universe would turn to a mighty stranger" and she "should not seem a part of it." (See Vol. I, Chap. 9, for Catherine's account of their separation.) Both of them adapt formulations familiar in religious discourse to describe their relationship, but her formulation is heterodox while his is blasphemous, since Catherine occupies the place reserved for God in it.

4 An allusion to Tennyson's "Locksley Hall," published in *Poems* (1842): "He will hold thee, when his passion shall have spent its novel force,/ Something better than his dog, a little dearer than his horse" (ll. 49–50). The similarity between Tennyson's disappointed lover and Brontë's Heathcliff is well worth noting. Both are angry at childhood sweethearts who have chosen to marry wealthy gentlemen. The differences are as important. Tennyson's lover believes that women have "shallower" brains than men and that their passions are weaker, but Heathcliff's faith in the power of Catherine's intelligence and the depth of her feelings never wavers.

to talk in that manner, and I won't hear my brother depreciated in silence!"

"Your brother is wondrous fond of you too, isn't he?" observed Heathcliff scornfully. "He turns you adrift on the world with surprising alacrity."

"He is not aware of what I suffer," she replied. "I didn't tell him that."

"You have been telling him something, then—you have written, have you?"

"To say that I was married, I did write—you saw the note."

"And nothing since?"

"No."

"My young lady is looking sadly the worse for her change of condition," I remarked. "Somebody's love comes short in her case, obviously—whose I may guess; but perhaps I shouldn't say."

"I should guess it was her own," said Heathcliff. "She degenerates into a mere slut![5] She is tired of trying to please me uncommonly early—You'd hardly credit it, but the very morrow of our wedding, she was weeping to go home. However, she'll suit this house so much the better for not being over nice,[6] and I'll take care she does not disgrace me by rambling abroad."[7]

"Well, sir," returned I, "I hope you'll consider that Mrs. Heathcliff is accustomed to be looked after, and waited on; and that she has been brought up like an only daughter whom every one was ready to serve—You must let her have a maid to keep things tidy about her, and you must treat her kindly—Whatever be your notion of Mr. Edgar, you cannot doubt that she has a capacity for strong attachments, or she wouldn't have abandoned the elegancies, and comforts, and friends of her former home to fix contentedly in such a wilderness as this, with you."

"She abandoned them under a delusion," he answered, "picturing in me a hero of romance,[8] and expecting unlimited indulgences from my chivalrous devotion. I can hardly regard her in the light of a rational creature, so obstinately has she persisted in forming a

5 Nelly has already observed that Isabella looks like a slattern.

6 Overly fastidious.

7 Heathcliff is hardly likely to be concerned about the impression Isabella makes in the village and its effect on his reputation. He counts on Nelly's sharing his and his period's view of female propriety and his understanding of a husband's legal rights. These include the right to confine his wife. From a conventional point of view, Isabella's disheveled appearance constitutes evidence that she ought to be confined.

8 Isabella's view of Heathcliff and of marriage was, we know, determinedly sentimental and likely to have been supported by her reading of romantic fiction.

Oil portrait of Alfred Lord Tennyson (1809–1892) c. 1840 by Samuel Laurence (1812–1884).

fabulous notion of my character, and acting on the false impressions she cherished. But at last, I think she begins to know me—I don't perceive the silly smiles and grimaces that provoked me at first; and the senseless incapability of discerning that I was in earnest when I gave her my opinion of her infatuation, and herself—It

9 Bitch-hound.

10 In order to protect himself against giving Isabella grounds for a separation, Heathcliff has apparently limited his brutality toward her. It was not until 1857 that the Matrimonial Causes Act transferred jurisdiction over divorce from the ecclesiastical to the civil courts. In 1784, when Heathcliff returns to Wuthering Heights with Isabella, ecclesiastical courts still issued divorces *a mensa et thoro* (from bed and board) in cases of adultery, desertion, or extreme cruelty. Divorces were both expensive and difficult to achieve. After a divorce neither party could remarry, and a woman separated from her husband was almost certain to lose not just custody of her children but contact with them ("Divorce," in *Victorian Britain: An Encyclopedia*, ed. Sally Mitchell [New York: Garland Publishing, Inc., 1988], p. 223).

was a marvellous effort of perspicacity to discover that I did not love her. I believed, at one time, no lessons could teach her that, and yet it is poorly learnt; for this morning she announced, as a piece of appalling intelligence, that I had actually succeeded in making her hate me! A positive labour of Hercules, I assure you! If it be achieved, I have cause to return thanks—Can I trust your assertion, Isabella, are you sure you hate me? If I let you alone for half-a-day, won't you come sighing and wheedling to me again? I dare say she would rather I had seemed all tenderness before you; it wounds her vanity to have the truth exposed. But I don't care who knows that the passion was wholly on one side, and I never told her a lie about it. She cannot accuse me of showing a bit of deceitful softness. The first thing she saw me do, on coming out of the Grange, was to hang up her little dog , and when she pleaded for it the first words I uttered were a wish that I had the hanging of every being belonging to her, except one: possibly, she took that exception for herself—But no brutality disgusted her—I suppose, she has an innate admiration of it, if only her precious person were secure from injury! Now, was it not the depth of absurdity—of genuine idiocy, for that pitiful, slavish, mean-minded brach[9] to dream that I could love her? Tell your master, Nelly, that I never, in all my life, met with such an abject thing as she is—She even disgraces the name of Linton; and I've sometimes relented, from pure lack of invention, in my experiments on what she could endure, and still creep shamefully cringing back! But tell him also, to set his fraternal and magisterial heart at ease, that I keep strictly within the limits of the law—I have avoided, up to this period, giving her the slightest right to claim a separation; and what's more, she'd thank nobody for dividing us—if she desired to go she might—the nuisance of her presence outweighs the gratification to be derived from tormenting her!"[10]

"Mr. Heathcliff," said I, "this is the talk of a madman, and your wife, most likely, is convinced you are mad; and, for that reason, she has borne with you hitherto: but now that you say she may go, she'll doubtless avail herself of the permission—You are not so bewitched ma'am, are you, as to remain with him, of your own accord?"

"Take care, Ellen!" answered Isabella, her eyes sparkling irefully—there was no misdoubting by their expression the full success of her partner's endeavours to make himself detested. "Don't put faith in a single word he speaks. He's a lying fiend, a monster, and not a human being! I've been told I might leave him before; and I've made the attempt, but I dare not repeat it! Only Ellen, promise you'll not mention a syllable of his infamous conversation to my brother or Catherine—whatever he may pretend, he wishes to provoke Edgar to desperation—he says he has married me on purpose to obtain power over him; and he shan't obtain it—I'll die first! I just hope, I pray, that he may forget his diabolical prudence and kill me! The single pleasure I can imagine is to die, or to see him dead!"

"There—that will do for the present!" said Heathcliff. "If you are called upon in a court of law, you'll remember her language, Nelly![11] And take a good look at that countenance—she's near the point which would suit me. No, you're not fit to be your own guardian, Isabella, now; and I, being your legal protector, must retain you in my custody, however distasteful the obligation may be—Go up-stairs; I have something to say to Ellen Dean, in private. That's not the way—up-stairs, I tell you! Why this is the road up-stairs, child!"

He seized, and thrust her from the room; and returned muttering, "I have no pity! I have no pity! The more the worms writhe, the more I yearn to crush out their entrails![12] It is a moral teething,[13] and I grind with greater energy in proportion to the increase of pain."

"Do you understand what the word *pity* means?" I said hastening to resume my bonnet. "Did you ever feel a touch of it in your life?"

"Put that down!" he interrupted, perceiving my intention to depart. "You are not going yet—Come here now, Nelly—I must either persuade or compel you to aid me in fulfilling my determi-

11 Heathcliff has clearly imagined a future confrontation with Isabella in a court of law. Her words, which he orders Nelly to remember so that she can testify to them, would support his case that Isabella is violent, unwomanly, and arguably mad. His threat is that a court of law will award him legal custody of her. In *Jane Eyre,* Charlotte represents just such a situation in the marriage of Rochester to Bertha Mason, whom he might have sent to an asylum for the insane but instead imprisons in the attic of Thornfield Hall.

12 An emendation of 1847, where the sentence reads as follows: "The worms writhe, the more I yearn to crush out their entrails!" Compare Chapter 5 above: " . . . the more feeble the master became, the more influence he gained."

13 A kind of metaphysical conceit, famously defined by Johnson as the violent yoking together of heterogeneous ideas. Teething is not a moral (or an immoral) activity, and the pain that stimulates an animal's teething is its own. The pain that stimulates Heathcliff's teething is ambiguously his and Isabella's. Compare his formulation in Chapter 11: "The tyrant grinds down his slaves, and they don't turn against him, they crush those beneath them."

14 How well Heathcliff knows Nelly! Here he appeals to her need to avoid violence and blame.

nation to see Catherine, and that without delay—I swear that I meditate no harm; I don't desire to cause any disturbance, or to exasperate or insult Mr. Linton; I only wish to hear from herself how she is, and why she has been ill; and to ask if anything that I could do would be of use to her. Last night, I was in the Grange garden six hours, and I'll return there to-night; and every night I'll haunt the place, and every day, till I find an opportunity of entering. If Edgar Linton meets me, I shall not hesitate to knock him down, and give him enough to ensure his quiescence while I stay —If his servants oppose me, I shall threaten them off with these pistols—But wouldn't it be better to prevent my coming in contact with them, or their master. And you could do it so easily! I'd warn you when I came, and then you might let me in unobserved, as soon as she was alone, and watch till I departed—your conscience quite calm, you would be hindering mischief."[14]

I protested against playing that treacherous part in my employer's house; and besides, I urged the cruelty and selfishness of his destroying Mrs. Linton's tranquillity for his satisfaction.

"The commonest occurrence startles her painfully," I said. "She's all nerves, and she couldn't bear the surprise, I'm positive—Don't persist, sir! or else, I shall be obliged to inform my master of your designs, and he'll take measures to secure his house and its inmates from any such unwarrantable intrusions!"

"In that case, I'll take measures to secure you, woman!" exclaimed Heathcliff; "you shall not leave Wuthering Heights till to-morrow morning. It is a foolish story to assert that Catherine could not bear to see me; and as to surprising her, I don't desire it; you must prepare her—ask her if I may come. You say she never mentions my name, and that I am never mentioned to her. To whom should she mention me if I am a forbidden topic in the house? She thinks you are all spies for her husband—Oh, I've no doubt she's in hell among you! I guess, by her silence as much as any thing, what she feels. You say she is often restless and anxious looking—is that a proof of tranquillity? You talk of her mind being unsettled—How the devil could it be otherwise, in her frightful isolation? And that insipid, paltry creature attending her from *duty* and *humanity!* From *pity* and *charity!*[15] He might as well plant an oak in a flowerpot and expect it to thrive as imagine he can restore her to vigour in the soil of his shallow cares! Let us settle it at once; will you stay here, and am I to fight my way to Catherine over Linton and his footmen? Or will you be my friend, as you have been hitherto, and do what I request? Decide! because there is no reason for my lingering another minute, if you persist in your stubborn ill-nature!"

Well, Mr. Lockwood, I argued, and complained, and flatly refused him fifty times; but in the long run he forced me to an agreement—I engaged to carry a letter from him to my mistress; and should she consent, I promised to let him have intelligence of Linton's next absence from home, when he might come, and get in as he was able—I wouldn't be there, and my fellow servants should be equally out of the way.

Was it right or wrong? I fear it was wrong, though expedient. I thought I prevented another explosion by my compliance; and I thought, too, it might create a favourable crisis in Catherine's mental illness: and then, I remembered Mr. Edgar's stern rebuke of my carrying tales; and I tried to smooth away all disquietude on the subject, by affirming, with frequent iteration, that that betrayal of trust, if it merited so harsh an appellation, should be the last.

Notwithstanding, my journey homeward was sadder than my journey thither; and many misgivings I had, ere I could prevail on myself to put the missive into Mrs. Linton's hand.

But here is Kenneth—I'll go down, and tell him how much better you are. My history is *dree,*[16] as we say, and will serve to wile away another morning.

Dree and dreary! I reflected, as the good woman descended to receive the doctor; and not exactly of the kind which I should have chosen to amuse me; but never mind! I'll extract wholesome med-

15 Duty and humanity—the social virtues—join forces here with pity and charity—the Christian virtues. Heathcliff scorns them all.

16 Dreary or doleful. Both "dreary" and "drear" appear in Brontë's poems. "Dree," which is a dialect word, does not, although she would have heard it often as well as read it in the poems of Burns and Scott.

17 Situation or plight. Obsolete in this sense, except to this day in Scotland. *(OED)*

icines from Mrs. Dean's bitter herbs; and firstly, let me beware of the fascination that lurks in Catherine Heathcliff's brilliant eyes. I should be in a curious taking[17] if I surrendered my heart to that young person, and the daughter turned out a second edition of the mother!

THE END OF VOL. I

VOLUME II

CHAPTER 1

Another week over—and I am so many days nearer health and spring! I have now heard all my neighbour's history, at different sittings, as the housekeeper could spare time from more important occupations. I'll continue it in her own words, only a little condensed. She is, on the whole, a very fair narrator, and I don't think I could improve her style.

"In the evening," she said, "the evening of my visit to the Heights, I knew as well as if I saw him, that Mr. Heathcliff was about the place; and I shunned going out, because I still carried his letter in my pocket, and didn't want to be threatened or teased any more."[1]

I had made up my mind not to give it till my master went somewhere, as I could not guess how its receipt would affect Catherine. The consequence was that it did not reach her before the lapse of three days. The fourth was Sunday, and I brought it into her room, after the family were gone to church.

There was a man servant left to keep the house with me, and we generally made a practice of locking the doors during the hours of service; but on that occasion, the weather was so warm and pleasant that I set them wide open; and to fulfil my engagement, as I knew who would be coming, I told my companion that the mistress wished very much for some oranges, and he must run over to

Charlotte Brontë's 1850 edition of *Wuthering Heights* numbered the thirty-four chapters of the novel consecutively, and most modern editions have followed this practice. This edition follows 1847: Volume I contains fourteen chapters, and Volume II contains twenty. The first volume therefore ends with Heathcliff's return to the Heights and with Nelly's promise to carry a letter from him to Catherine. "Was it right, or wrong? I fear it was wrong, though expedient," Nelly says to Lockwood. Nelly's decision to act as Heathcliff's agent is a crucial turning point in the story. The tension between what she believes to be right and what she feels is convenient is the keynote of her character.

The decision to end Volume I after Chapter 14 can probably be attributed to the publisher. Christopher Heywood conjectures that Brontë's manuscript "presented its 34 chapters in two parts, each numbered 1–17," and that Newby obscured Brontë's symmetry in order to create his own: a three-decker "novel" with a substantial second volume—Volume II of *Wuthering Heights*—flanked by two slimmer volumes, Volume I of *Wuthering Heights* and the whole of *Agnes Grey* (*Wuthering Heights* [Peterborough, ON: Broadview Press, 2002], pp. 34–36; 80–81). Heywood's conjecture cannot be proved or disproved, but the symmetry that his hypothesis foregrounds belongs to the novel and is important to observe, even if Brontë did not present her novel to Newby in two parts. At the end of Chapter 3 (Chapter 17 if chapters are numbered consecutively), Hindley dies, leaving Heathcliff in possession of the Heights and in control of Hareton. In the following chapter, Nelly compresses the next twelve years into a few paragraphs and resumes her story when Cathy is thirteen years old.

1 The 1847 edition omits quotation marks at the end of this paragraph and at the beginning of subsequent paragraphs, reserving them for Nelly's speech within her narrative and for the speech of the other characters. I have closed the first paragraph with quotation marks and added a space break to mark the beginning of Nelly's uninterrupted narrative.

the village and get a few, to be paid for on the morrow. He departed, and I went up-stairs.

Mrs. Linton sat in a loose, white dress, with a light shawl over her shoulders, in the recess of the open window, as usual. Her thick, long hair had been partly removed at the beginning of her illness; and now, she wore it simply combed in its natural tresses over her temples and neck. Her appearance was altered, as I had told Heathcliff, but when she was calm, there seemed unearthly beauty in the change.

The flash of her eyes had been succeeded by a dreamy and melancholy softness: they no longer gave the impression of looking at the objects around her; they appeared always to gaze beyond, and far beyond—you would have said out of this world[2]—Then, the paleness of her face, its haggard aspect having vanished as she recovered flesh, and the peculiar expression arising from her mental state, though painfully suggestive of their causes, added to the touching interest which she wakened, and invariably to me, I know, and to any person who saw her, I should think, refuted more tangible proofs of convalescence and stamped her as one doomed to decay.

A book lay spread on the sill before her, and the scarcely perceptible wind fluttered its leaves at intervals. I believe Linton had laid it there, for she never endeavoured to divert herself with reading, or occupation of any kind; and he would spend many an hour in trying to entice her attention to some subject which had formerly been her amusement.

She was conscious of his aim, and in her better moods, endured his efforts placidly; only showing their uselessness by now and then suppressing a wearied sigh, and checking him at last, with the saddest of smiles and kisses. At other times, she would turn petulantly away, and hide her face in her hands, or even push him off angrily; and then he took care to let her alone, for he was certain of doing no good.

2 Catherine's "unearthly beauty," so visible here to Nelly, connects her to the heroine of one of Brontë's best-known poems, "The Prisoner (A Fragment)," published in 1846:

> The captive raised her face, it was as soft and mild
> As sculptured marble saint, or slumbering unwean'd child;
> It was so soft and mild, it was so sweet and fair,
> Pain could not trace a line, nor grief a shadow there!

The woman in the longer poem from which the published one has been excerpted is named A. G. Rochelle. Like Catherine, she has turned her face away from life and welcomes death as "eternal liberty." This is probably the poem Charlotte read in the autumn of 1845 when she made the famous discovery of Emily's poems that led to the publication of *Poems by Currer, Ellis, and Acton Bell* in 1846. The prison poems of the summer and fall of 1845, and the Gondal story to which they belonged, gave Brontë practice in imagining Catherine's desperation when she feels betrayed by Edgar, abandoned by Heathcliff, and locked inside both Thrushcross Grange and her own body.

Gimmerton Chapel bells were still ringing; and the full, mellow flow of the beck in the valley came soothingly on the ear. It was a sweet substitute for the yet absent murmur of the summer foliage which drowned that music about the Grange, when the trees were in leaf. At Wuthering Heights it always sounded on quiet days, following a great thaw, or a season of steady rain—and, of Wuthering Heights, Catherine was thinking as she listened; that is, if she thought, or listened, at all; but she had the vague, distant look I mentioned before, which expressed no recognition of material things either by ear or eye.

"There's a letter for you, Mrs. Linton," I said, gently inserting it in one hand that rested on her knee. "You must read it immediately, because it wants an answer. Shall I break the seal?"

"Yes," she answered, without altering the direction of her eyes.

I opened it—it was very short.

"Now," I continued, "read it."

She drew away her hand, and let it fall. I replaced it in her lap, and stood waiting till it should please her to glance down; but that movement was so long delayed that at last I resumed—

"Must I read it, ma'am? It is from Mr. Heathcliff."

There was a start, and a troubled gleam of recollection, and a struggle to arrange her ideas. She lifted the letter, and seemed to peruse it; and when she came to the signature, she sighed; yet still I found she had not gathered its import; for upon my desiring to hear her reply, she merely pointed to the name, and gazed at me with mournful and questioning eagerness.

"Well, he wishes to see you," said I, guessing her need of an interpreter. "He's in the garden by this time, and impatient to know what answer I shall bring."

As I spoke, I observed a large dog lying on the sunny grass beneath raise its ears, as if about to bark; and then smoothing them back, announce by a wag of the tail that some one approached whom it did not consider a stranger.

Mrs. Linton bent forward, and listened breathlessly. The minute after, a step traversed the hall; the open house was too tempting for Heathcliff to resist walking in: most likely he supposed that I was inclined to shirk my promise, and so resolved to trust to his own audacity.

With straining eagerness Catherine gazed towards the entrance of her chamber. He did not hit the right room directly; she motioned me to admit him; but he found it out, ere I could reach the door, and in a stride or two was at her side, and had her grasped in his arms.

He neither spoke, nor loosed his hold, for some five minutes, during which period he bestowed more kisses than ever he gave in his life before, I dare say; but then my mistress had kissed him first, and I plainly saw that he could hardly bear, for downright agony, to look into her face! The same conviction had stricken him as me, from the instant he beheld her, that there was no prospect of ultimate recovery there—she was fated, sure to die.

"Oh, Cathy! Oh, my life! how can I bear it?" was the first sentence he uttered, in a tone that did not seek to disguise his despair.

And now he stared at her so earnestly that I thought the very intensity of his gaze would bring tears into his eyes; but they burned with anguish, they did not melt.[3]

"What now?" said Catherine, leaning back, and returning his look with a suddenly clouded brow—her humour was a mere vane for constantly varying caprices.[4] "You and Edgar have broken my heart, Heathcliff! And you both come to bewail the deed to me, as if you were the people to be pitied! I shall not pity you, not I. You have killed me—and thriven on it, I think. How strong you are! How many years do you mean to live after I am gone?"

Heathcliff had knelt on one knee to embrace her; he attempted to rise, but she seized his hair, and kept him down.

"I wish I could hold you," she continued, bitterly, "till we were both dead! I shouldn't care what you suffered. I care nothing for

3 "Anguish" is an important word for Brontë and appears often in her poems and in *Wuthering Heights*, especially in the second volume. The poem that most urgently expresses an anguish like Heathcliff's, as he acknowledges the inevitability of Catherine's death, is titled "Death." A summary of its plot will suggest its relation to Catherine's story so far. The poem's speaker begins her life happily but then experiences the ravages of sorrow and guilt. The poem does not tell us what she has done to provoke suffering, her own or anyone else's. Instead, it emphasizes her recuperative powers. So long as "Life's restoring tide" flows through her—it seems "for ever"—Hope "[laughs her] out of sadness," and she blossoms into a glorious "second May." The word "anguish" appears in the poem's penultimate stanza:

> Cruel Death! The young leaves droop and languish;
> Evening's gentle air may still restore—
> No! the morning sunshine mocks my anguish—
> Time, for me, must never blossom more!

The ordinary but intolerable truth is that life goes on but the individual does not. For a fuller discussion of "Death," see Janet Gezari, *Last Things* (Oxford: Oxford Univ. Press, 2007).

4 Catherine's mood is unpredictable and shifts like a weathervane in the wind.

your sufferings. Why shouldn't you suffer? I do! Will you forget me—will you be happy when I am in the earth? Will you say twenty years hence, 'That's the grave of Catherine Earnshaw. I loved her long ago, and was wretched to lose her; but it is past. I've loved many others since—my children are dearer to me than she was, and, at death, I shall not rejoice that I am going to her, I shall be sorry that I must leave them!' Will you say so, Heathcliff?"

"Don't torture me till I'm as mad as yourself," cried he, wrenching his head free, and grinding his teeth.

The two, to a cool spectator, made a strange and fearful picture. Well might Catherine deem that Heaven would be a land of exile to her,[5] unless, with her mortal body, she cast away her mortal character also. Her present countenance had a wild vindictiveness in its white cheek, and a bloodless lip, and scintillating[6] eye; and she retained, in her closed fingers, a portion of the locks she had been grasping. As to her companion, while raising himself with one hand, he had taken her arm with the other; and so inadequate was his stock of gentleness to the requirements of her condition, that on his letting go, I saw four distinct impressions left blue in the colourless skin.[7]

"Are you possessed with a devil," he pursued, savagely, "to talk in that manner to me, when you are dying? Do you reflect that all those words will be branded in my memory, and eating deeper eternally, after you have left me? You know you lie to say I have killed you; and, Catherine, you know that I could as soon forget you as my existence! Is it not sufficient for your infernal selfishness that while you are at peace I shall writhe in the torments of hell?"[8]

"I shall not be at peace," moaned Catherine, recalled to a sense of physical weakness by the violent, unequal throbbing of her heart, which beat visibly and audibly under this excess of agitation.

She said nothing further till the paroxysm was over; then she continued, more kindly—

5 Nelly recalls Catherine's dream in Chapter 9 (Vol. I) and interprets it literally. In the dream, Catherine was miserable when she found herself in heaven and exultant when she was cast out on the heath at the top of Wuthering Heights.

6 Sparkling. The phrase "scintillating eye" also appears in an early prose work of Percy Shelley's, *Zastrozzi: A Romance,* a Gothic thriller published in 1810. In combination with a "commanding countenance" and a "bold expressive gaze," it describes Shelley's antiheroine, Matilda.

7 Catherine and Heathcliff come closest to a sexual embrace as adults with the intimate and extreme violence of this reunion. The drama of their assault on and resistance to each other is heightened by the physical damage they do: Catherine pulls Heathcliff's hair out at the roots, and he bruises her arm. "The basis of sexual effusion is the negation of the isolation of the ego which only experiences ecstasy by exceeding itself, by surpassing itself in the embrace in which the being loses its solitude," Georges Bataille writes in *Literature and Evil,* which puts Brontë into the company of Baudelaire, Blake, Sade, and Genet. "And the anguish of pure love is all the more symbolic of the ultimate truth of love as the death of those whom it unites approaches them and strikes them. To no mortal love does this apply as much as to the union between the heroes of *Wuthering Heights,* Catherine Earnshaw and Heathcliff. Nobody revealed this truth more forcefully than Emily Brontë" (Georges Bataille, *Literature and Evil,* trans. Alistair Hamilton [London: Marion Boyars, 2001], pp. 16–17).

8 When he says that he could as soon forget her as "[his] existence," Heathcliff comes close to Catherine's "I-*am*-Heathcliff" formulation of their relation to each other. Heathcliff's concept of hell as life without Catherine owes something to Byron's idea of the hell he and his half-sister Augusta inhabited when they were separated from each other. Byron's famous poem about his exile from her, "Stanzas to Augusta," was first published in Moore's *Life of Byron.*

9 Brontë's poems frequently represent death as an enlargement of a spirit that is confined by the body during life. In "The Prisoner [A Fragment]," the flesh is a "chain" that keeps the spirit from soaring; so long as the senses function, the "inward essence" cannot "feel." "Aye, there it is! It wakes tonight," composed in 1841, also expresses the longing to escape into "that glorious world" its speaker sees only "dimly through tears":

> Thus truly when that breast is cold
> Thy prisoned soul shall rise
> The dungeon mingle with the mould—
> The captive with the skies—

"I'm not wishing you greater torment than I have, Heathcliff! I only wish us never to be parted—and should a word of mine distress you hereafter, think I feel the same distress underground, and for my own sake, forgive me! Come here and kneel down again! You *never* harmed me in your life. Nay, if you nurse anger, that will be worse to remember than my harsh words! Won't you come here again? Do!"

Heathcliff went to the back of her chair, and leant over, but not so far as to let her see his face, which was livid with emotion. She bent round to look at him; he would not permit it; turning abruptly, he walked to the fire-place, where he stood, silent, with his back towards us.

Mrs. Linton's glance followed him suspiciously: every movement woke a new sentiment in her. After a pause, and a prolonged gaze, she resumed, addressing me in accents of indignant disappointment.

"Oh, you see, Nelly! he would not relent a moment, to keep me out of the grave! *That* is how I'm loved! Well, never mind! That is not *my* Heathcliff. I shall love mine yet; and take him with me—he's in my soul. And," added she, musingly, "the thing that irks me most is this shattered prison, after all. I'm tired, tired of being enclosed here. I'm wearying to escape into that glorious world, and to be always there; not seeing it dimly through tears, and yearning for it through the walls of an aching heart; but really with it, and in it.[9] Nelly, you think you are better and more fortunate than I; in full health and strength—you are sorry for me—very soon that will be altered. I shall be sorry for *you*. I shall be incomparably beyond and above you all. I *wonder* he won't be near me!" She went on to herself, "I thought he wished it. Heathcliff, dear! you should not be sullen now. Do come to me, Heathcliff."

In her eagerness she rose, and supported herself on the arm of the chair. At that earnest appeal, he turned to her, looking absolutely desperate. His eyes wide, and wet at last, flashed fiercely on her; his breast heaved convulsively. An instant they held asunder; and then how they met I hardly saw, but Catherine made a spring, and he caught her, and they were locked in an embrace from which I thought my mistress would never be released alive. In fact, to my eyes, she seemed directly insensible. He flung himself into the nearest seat, and on my approaching hurriedly to ascertain if she had fainted, he gnashed at me, and foamed like a mad dog, and gathered her to him with greedy jealousy. I did not feel as if I were in the company of a creature of my own species; it appeared that he would not understand, though I spoke to him; so I stood off, and held my tongue, in great perplexity.

A movement of Catherine's relieved me a little presently: she put up her hand to clasp his neck, and bring her cheek to his, as he held her: while he, in return, covering her with frantic caresses, said wildly—

"You teach me now how cruel you've been—cruel and false. *Why* did you despise me? *Why* did you betray your own heart, Cathy? I have not one word of comfort—you deserve this. You have killed yourself. Yes, you may kiss me, and cry; and wring out my kisses and tears. They'll blight you—they'll damn you. You loved me—then what *right* had you to leave me? What right—answer me—for the poor fancy you felt for Linton? Because misery, and degradation, and death, and nothing that God or Satan could inflict would have parted us, *you,* of your own will, did it. I have not broken your heart—you have broken it—and in breaking it, you have broken mine.[10] So much the worse for me that I am strong. Do I want to live? What kind of living will it be when you—Oh, God! would *you* like to live with your soul in the grave?"

"Let me alone. Let me alone," sobbed Catherine. "If I've done wrong, I'm dying for it. It is enough! You left me too; but I won't upbraid you! I forgive you. Forgive me!"

"It is hard to forgive, and to look at those eyes, and feel those wasted hands," he answered. "Kiss me again; and don't let me see

10 Brontë may be remembering two lines from a song by Byron, "I speak not, I trace not, I breathe not thy name," printed for the first time in Moore's *Life of Byron:* "But the heart which is thine shall expire undebased,/ And *man* shall not break it—whatever *thou* mayst" (*Letters and Journals of Lord Byron with Notices of His Life,* 3 vols. [London: John Murray, 1833], 2, p. 70). Brontë's formulation is more complicated than Byron's. Catherine hasn't just broken Heathcliff's heart (as only she could): she's broken her own heart, and his breaks because of it.

your eyes! I forgive what you have done to me. I love my murderer—but *yours!* How can I?"

They were silent—their faces hid against each other, and washed by each other's tears. At least, I suppose the weeping was on both sides; as it seemed Heathcliff *could* weep on a great occasion like this.

I grew very uncomfortable, meanwhile, for the afternoon wore fast away; the man whom I had sent off returned from his errand; and I could distinguish, by the shine of the westering sun up the valley, a concourse thickening outside Gimmerton Chapel porch.

"Service is over," I announced. "My master will be here in half-an-hour."

Heathcliff groaned a curse, and strained Catherine closer—she never moved.

Ere long I perceived a group of the servants passing up the road towards the kitchen wing. Mr. Linton was not far behind; he opened the gate himself, and sauntered slowly up, probably enjoying the lovely afternoon that breathed as soft as summer.

"Now he is here," I exclaimed. "For Heaven's sake, hurry down! You'll not meet any one on the front stairs. Do be quick; and stay among the trees till he is fairly in."

"I must go, Cathy," said Heathcliff, seeking to extricate himself from his companion's arms. "But if I live, I'll see you again before you are asleep. I won't stray five yards from your window."

"You must not go!" she answered, holding him as firmly as her strength allowed. "You shall not, I tell you."

"For one hour," he pleaded, earnestly.

"Not for one minute," she replied.

"I *must*—Linton will be up immediately," persisted the alarmed intruder.

He would have risen, and unfixed her fingers by the act—she clung fast gasping; there was mad resolution in her face.

"No!" she shrieked. "Oh, don't, don't go. It is the last time! Edgar will not hurt us. Heathcliff, I shall die! I shall die!"

"Damn the fool. There he is," cried Heathcliff, sinking back into his seat. "Hush, my darling! Hush, hush, Catherine! I'll stay. If he shot me so, I'd expire with a blessing on my lips."

And there they were fast again. I heard my master mounting the stairs—the cold sweat ran from my forehead; I was horrified.

"Are you going to listen to her ravings?" I said, passionately. "She does not know what she says. Will you ruin[11] her, because she has not wit to help herself? Get up! you could be free instantly. That is the most diabolical deed that ever you did. We are all done for—master, mistress, and servant."

I wrung my hands, and cried out; and Mr. Linton hastened his step at the noise. In the midst of my agitation, I was sincerely glad to observe that Catherine's arms had fallen relaxed, and her head hung down.

"She's fainted or dead," I thought, "so much the better. Far better that she should be dead, than lingering a burden and a misery-maker to all about her."

Edgar sprang to his unbidden guest, blanched with astonishment and rage. What he meant to do, I cannot tell; however, the other stopped all demonstrations, at once, by placing the lifeless-looking form in his arms.

"Look there," he said, "unless you be a fiend, help her first—then you shall speak to me!"

He walked into the parlour, and sat down. Mr. Linton summoned me, and, with great difficulty, and after resorting to many means, we managed to restore her to sensation; but she was all bewildered; she sighed, and moaned, and knew nobody. Edgar, in his anxiety for her, forgot her hated friend. I did not. I went, at the earliest opportunity, and besought him to depart, affirming that Catherine was better, and he should hear from me in the morning how she passed the night.

11 Damage her irreparably. If Edgar finds Heathcliff and Catherine locked in an embrace, her reputation will be destroyed, Edgar will be made miserable, and Nelly's trustworthiness will be called into question.

12 Ominous.

"I shall not refuse to go out of doors," he answered, "but I shall stay in the garden; and, Nelly, mind you keep your word to-morrow. I shall be under those larch trees, mind! or I pay another visit, whether Linton be in or not."

He sent a rapid glance through the half-open door of the chamber, and ascertaining that what I stated was apparently true, delivered the house of his luckless[12] presence.

CHAPTER 2

About twelve o'clock, that night,[1] was born the Catherine you saw at Wuthering Heights, a puny, seven months' child;[2] and two hours after, the mother died, having never recovered sufficient consciousness to miss Heathcliff, or know Edgar.

The latter's distraction at his bereavement is a subject too painful to be dwelt on; its after effects showed how deep the sorrow sunk.

A great addition, in my eyes, was his being left without an heir. I bemoaned that, as I gazed on the feeble orphan; and I mentally abused old Linton for what was only natural partiality, the securing his estate to his own daughter, instead of his son's.[3]

An unwelcomed infant it was, poor thing! It might have wailed out of life, and nobody cared a morsel, during those first hours of existence. We redeemed the neglect afterwards; but its beginning was as friendless as its end is likely to be.

Next morning—bright and cheerful out of doors—stole softened, in through the blinds of the silent room, and suffused the couch and its occupant with a mellow, tender glow.

Edgar Linton had his head laid on the pillow, and his eyes shut. His young and fair features were almost as death-like as those of the form beside him, and almost as fixed; but *his* was the hush of exhausted anguish, and *hers* of perfect peace. Her brow smooth, her lids closed, her lips wearing the expression of a smile. No angel

1 The date is Sunday, March 19, 1784, almost exactly a year after Catherine's marriage to Edgar. She is eighteen years old; Heathcliff is about nineteen; Edgar is twenty-two. Inga-Stina Ewbank cites the date of Catherine's death (March 20, about 2 A.M.) as evidence that Brontë did not use a calendar. March 20 was a Saturday in 1784, not a Monday, as in the novel (Hilda Marsden and Ian Jack, *Wuthering Heights* [Oxford: Clarendon Press, 1976], p. 489).

2 Victorian novels were reticent about pregnancy and childbirth. Although Nelly referred obliquely to Catherine's pregnancy in Volume I, Chapter 13, there has been no notice of its progress apart from the loose dress Nelly tells us Catherine wears. In 1859, a reviewer of George Eliot's *Adam Bede* objected strenuously to any discussion of the stages of pregnancy: "Let us copy the old masters of the art, who, if they gave us a baby, gave it us all at once. A decent author and a decent public may take the premonitory symptoms for granted" (Quoted in Jill L. Matus, *Unstable Bodies: Victorian Representations of Sexuality and Maternity* [Manchester: Manchester Univ. Press, 1995], p. 1).

3 Here Nelly reminds us that Edgar's daughter will not inherit his estate when he dies. It passes to his sister, Isabella, who has a life interest in it; when she dies, her son is preferred to Edgar's daughter.

in heaven could be more beautiful than she appeared; and I partook of the infinite calm in which she lay. My mind was never in a holier frame, than while I gazed on that untroubled image of Divine rest. I instinctively echoed the words she had uttered, a few hours before. "Incomparably beyond, and above us all! Whether still on earth or now in Heaven, her spirit is at home with God!"

I don't know if it be a peculiarity in me, but I am seldom otherwise than happy while watching in the chamber of death, should no frenzied or despairing mourner share the duty with me. I see a repose that neither earth nor hell can break; and I feel an assurance of the endless and shadowless hereafter—the Eternity they have entered—where life is boundless in its duration, and love in its sympathy, and joy in its fulness. I noticed on that occasion how much selfishness there is even in a love like Mr. Linton's, when he so regretted Catherine's blessed release![4]

To be sure one might have doubted, after the wayward and impatient existence she had led, whether she merited a haven of peace at last. One might doubt in seasons of cold reflection, but not then, in the presence of her corpse. It asserted its own tranquillity, which seemed a pledge of equal quiet to its former inhabitant.

"Do you believe such people *are* happy in the other world, sir? I'd give a great deal to know."

I declined answering Mrs. Dean's question, which struck me as something heterodox.[5] She proceeded:

"Retracing the course of Catherine Linton I fear we have no right to think she is: but we'll leave her with her Maker."

The master looked asleep, and I ventured soon after sunrise to quit the room and steal out to the pure, refreshing air. The servants thought me gone to shake off the drowsiness of my protracted watch; in reality my chief motive was seeing Mr. Heathcliff. If he had remained among the larches all night he would have heard

4 Nelly expresses the most widely held Victorian belief about death. It ends the suffering of mortal beings and transports them to a better place. In *The Excursion* (1814), Wordsworth's description of death's "twofold aspect" glosses Nelly's and Edgar's immediate responses to Catherine's death. On the one hand, death has a "wintry" aspect: "Cold, sullen, blank, from hope and joy shut out." On the other, death is "Replete with vivid promise, bright as spring."

5 Not in keeping with orthodox beliefs.

Heathcliff awaiting news of Catherine's death in the garden at Thrushcross Grange. This wood engraving by Fritz Eichenberg (1901–1990) appears on the cover of the 1943 Random House edition of the novel.

6 Blackbirds.

7 Subdued.

nothing of the stir at the Grange, unless, perhaps, he might catch the gallop of the messenger going to Gimmerton. If he had come nearer he would probably be aware, from the lights flitting to and fro, and the opening and shutting of the outer doors, that all was not right within.

I wished yet feared to find him. I felt the terrible news must be told, and I longed to get it over, but *how* to do it I did not know.

He was there—at least a few yards further in the park; leant against an old ash tree, his hat off, and his hair soaked with the dew that had gathered on the budded branches, and fell pattering round him. He had been standing a long time in that position, for I saw a pair of ousels[6] passing and repassing, scarcely three feet from him, busy in building their nest, and regarding his proximity no more than that of a piece of timber. They flew off at my approach, and he raised his eyes and spoke:

"She's dead!" he said; "I've not waited for you to learn that. Put your handkerchief away—don't snivel before me. Damn you all! she wants none of *your* tears!"

I was weeping as much for him as her: we do sometimes pity creatures that have none of the feeling either for themselves or others; and when I first looked into his face I perceived that he had got intelligence of the catastrophe; and a foolish notion struck me that his heart was quelled,[7] and he prayed, because his lips moved, and his gaze was bent on the ground.

"Yes, she's dead!" I answered, checking my sobs, and drying my cheeks. "Gone to heaven, I hope, where we may, everyone, join her, if we take due warning, and leave our evil ways to follow good!"

"Did *she* take due warning, then?" asked Heathcliff, attempting a sneer. "Did she die like a saint? Come, give me a true history of the event. How did—"

He endeavoured to pronounce the name, but could not manage it; and compressing his mouth, he held a silent combat with his inward agony, defying, meanwhile, my sympathy with an unflinching, ferocious stare.

“Heathcliff’s Grief,” woodcut by Clare Leighton (1898–1989).

8 The fate of body and soul after death was controversial throughout the Victorian period. If humans are immortal, where does a future existence take place? In heaven or hell, or in some intermediate place where the dead await a Last Judgment? Heathcliff's uncertainty about where Catherine continues to exist after her death is more heterodox than this, and it contributed to the view that Heathcliff is damned. His love for Catherine, Charlotte writes, "is a sentiment fierce and inhuman: a passion such as might boil and glow in the bad essence of some evil genius; a fire that might form the tormented centre—the ever-suffering soul of a magnate of the infernal world: and by its quenchless and ceaseless ravage effect the execution of the degree which dooms him to carry Hell with him wherever he wanders" ("Editor's Preface," this edition, pp. 443–444).

"How did she die?" he resumed, at last—fain, notwithstanding his hardihood, to have a support behind him, for, after the struggle, he trembled, in spite of himself, to his very finger-ends.

"Poor wretch!" I thought; "you have a heart and nerves the same as your brother men! Why should you be so anxious to conceal them? Your pride cannot blind God! You tempt him to wring them, till he forces a cry of humiliation!"

"Quietly as a lamb!" I answered, aloud. "She drew a sigh, and stretched herself, like a child reviving, and sinking again to sleep; and five minutes after, I felt one little pulse at her heart, and nothing more!"

"And—and did she ever mention me?" he asked, hesitating, as if he dreaded the answer to his question would introduce details that he could not bear to hear.

"Her senses never returned—she recognised nobody from the time you left her," I said. "She lies with a sweet smile on her face; and her latest ideas wandered back to pleasant early days. Her life closed in a gentle dream—may she wake as kindly in the other world!"

"May she wake in torment!" he cried, with frightful vehemence, stamping his foot, and groaning in a sudden paroxysm of ungovernable passion. "Why, she's a liar to the end! Where is she? Not *there*—not in heaven—not perished—where?[8] Oh!—you said you cared nothing for my sufferings! And I pray one prayer—I repeat it till my tongue stiffens—Catherine Earnshaw, may you not rest, as long as I am living! You said I killed you—haunt me then! The murdered *do* haunt their murderers. I believe—I know that ghosts *have* wandered on earth. Be with me always—take any form—drive me mad! Only *do* not leave me in this abyss, where I cannot find you! Oh, God! it is unutterable! I *cannot* live without my life! I *cannot* live without my soul!"

He dashed his head against the knotted trunk; and, lifting up his eyes, howled, not like a man but like a savage beast getting goaded to death with knives and spears.

I observed several splashes of blood about the bark of the tree, and his hand and forehead were both stained; probably the scene I witnessed was a repetition of others acted during the night. It hardly moved my compassion—it appalled me; still I felt reluctant to quit him so. But the moment he recollected himself enough to notice me watching, he thundered a command for me to go, and I obeyed. He was beyond my skill to quiet or console!

Mrs. Linton's funeral was appointed to take place on the Friday following her decease; and till then her coffin remained uncovered, and strewn with flowers and scented leaves, in the great drawing-room. Linton spent his days and nights there, a sleepless guardian; and—a circumstance concealed from all but me—Heathcliff spent his nights, at least, outside, equally a stranger to repose.

I held no communication with him; still I was conscious of his design to enter, if he could; and on the Tuesday, a little after dark, when my master from sheer fatigue, had been compelled to retire a couple of hours, I went and opened one of the windows, moved by his perseverance to give him a chance of bestowing on the fading image of his idol one final adieu.

He did not omit to avail himself of the opportunity, cautiously and briefly; too cautiously to betray his presence by the slightest noise; indeed, I shouldn't have discovered that he had been there, except for the disarrangement of the drapery about the corpse's face, and for observing on the floor a curl of light hair, fastened with a silver thread, which, on examination, I ascertained to have been taken from a locket hung round Catherine's neck. Heathcliff had opened the trinket, and cast out its contents, replacing them by a black lock of his own. I twisted the two, and enclosed them together.[9]

Mr. Earnshaw was, of course, invited to attend the remains of his sister to the grave; and he sent no excuse, but he never came; so that besides her husband, the mourners were wholly composed of tenants and servants. Isabella was not asked.

Oil portrait of the young Queen Victoria, painted by Franz Xaver Winterhalter (1805–1873) in 1843. The queen commissioned the portrait as a birthday present for Prince Albert and wears a locket containing a lock of his hair.

9 Victorian couples frequently exchanged locks of hair, and it is Linton's hair that Heathcliff has removed from Catherine's locket. It was also common practice for a lock of hair to be taken from a dead person and worn as a remembrance by the living. Here Heathcliff reverses that practice, not taking a lock of Catherine's hair but arranging for her to be buried with a lock of his. Nelly's decision to combine Heathcliff's and Edgar's hair in Catherine's locket is another example of her readiness to prefer her own judgment to everyone else's.

The opposition between light and dark hair is a recurrent motif in the novel. Two children who are temperamentally opposite but bound to each other also figure in a Gondal poem, "A. E. and R. C.," dated May 28, 1845, and first published in Charlotte Brontë's 1850 edition of *Wuthering Heights* under her title, "The Two Children." The girl has "sunbright hair/And seablue seadeep eyes," and the boy is described as a "mournful boy" whose "grim Fate" has never "Smiled since he was born."

The place of Catherine's interment, to the surprise of the villagers, was neither in the chapel, under the carved monument of the Lintons, nor yet by the tombs of her own relations, outside. It was dug on a green slope, in a corner of the kirkyard, where the walk is so low that heath and bilberry plants have climbed over it from the moor; and peat mould almost buries it.[10] Her husband lies in the same spot, now; and they have each a simple headstone above, and a plain grey block at their feet, to mark the graves.

10 Heath carpets the Heights and also evokes Heathcliff's name. Bilberry is a small, hardy shrub adorned with a blue-black berry. According to Wordsworth, it is "never so beautiful as in early spring" (William Wordsworth, *A Description of the Scenery of the Lakes in Northern England* [London: Longman, Hurst, Rees, Orme, and Brown, 1810, rpt. 1822], p. 34).

CHAPTER 3

That Friday made the last of our fine days, for a month. In the evening, the weather broke; the wind shifted from south to north-east, and brought rain first, and then sleet and snow.

On the morrow one could hardly imagine that there had been three weeks of summer:[1] the primroses and crocuses were hidden under wintry drifts: the larks were silent, the young leaves of the early trees smitten and blackened—And dreary, and chill, and dismal that morrow did creep over! My master kept his room—I took possession of the lonely parlour, converting it into a nursery; and there I was sitting, with the moaning doll of a child laid on my knee, rocking it to and fro, and watching, meanwhile, the still driving flakes build up[2] the uncurtained window, when the door opened, and some person entered out of breath and laughing!

My anger was greater than my astonishment for a minute; I supposed it one of the maids, and I cried, "Have done! How dare you show your giddiness, here? What would Mr. Linton say if he heard you?"

"Excuse me!" answered a familiar voice, "but I know Edgar is in bed, and I cannot stop myself."

With that, the speaker came forward to the fire, panting and holding her hand to her side.

"I have run the whole way from Wuthering Heights!" she continued, after a pause. "Except where I've flown—I couldn't count

1 Catherine's funeral is held on March 24. The sleet, snow, and blossoming primroses and crocuses confirm that the season is early spring. Nelly's reference to the following day as "three weeks" into the summer harks back to an earlier sense of the English year as divided into two rather than four seasons. This stark opposition of summer and winter can be found in Boethius's *Consolation of Philosophy,* written around 524, and in many Middle English songs and poems.

2 Obstruct.

3 A reference to the low neckline of Isabella's dress. Short-sleeved and made of light silk, it reminds us that the change in the weather on the night of Catherine's burial is sudden.

4 Some of Isabella's scratches and bruises have been acquired on the way to the Grange; others, including the deep cut under her ear, are evidence of Heathcliff's physical abuse. Isabella's battered appearance may but need not imply sexual trauma. Heathcliff has certainly exercised his conjugal rights long enough to ensure that she is pregnant, but perhaps not longer. His violence toward Isabella has increased, as it was likely to do along with his own torment, in the few days since Catherine's death. Isabella's distracted appearance and disorderly dress threaten to mark her as a woman no longer entitled to respect, perhaps even as a lunatic, like Bertha Rochester in *Jane Eyre*. This provides an additional motive for Nelly to insist that she change her clothes before she goes on to Gimmerton.

the number of falls I've had—Oh, I'm aching all over! Don't be alarmed—There shall be an explanation as soon as I can give it—only just have the goodness to step out, and order the carriage to take me on to Gimmerton, and tell a servant to seek up a few clothes in my wardrobe."

The intruder was Mrs. Heathcliff—she certainly seemed in no laughing predicament; her hair streamed on her shoulders, dripping with snow and water; she was dressed in the girlish dress she commonly wore, befitting her age more than her position; a low frock,[3] with short sleeves, and nothing on either head or neck. The frock was of light silk, and clung to her with wet; and her feet were protected merely by thin slippers; add to this a deep cut under one ear, which only the cold prevented from bleeding profusely, a white face scratched and bruised,[4] and a frame hardly able to support itself through fatigue, and you may fancy my first fright was not much allayed when I had leisure to examine her.

"My dear young lady," I exclaimed "I'll stir nowhere, and hear nothing, till you have removed every article of your clothes, and put on dry things; and certainly, you shall not go to Gimmerton to-night; so it is needless to order the carriage."

"Certainly, I shall," she said, "walking or riding—yet I've no objection to dress myself decently; and—ah, see how it flows down my neck now! The fire does make it smart."

She insisted on my fulfilling her directions, before she would let me touch her; and not till after the coachman had been instructed to get ready, and a maid set to pack up some necessary attire, did I obtain her consent for binding the wound, and helping to change her garments.

"Now Ellen," she said when my task was finished, and she was seated in an easy chair on the hearth, with a cup of tea before her, "You sit down opposite me, and put poor Catherine's baby away—I don't like to see it! You mustn't think I care little for Catherine, because I behaved so foolishly on entering—I've cried too, bitterly—yes, more than any one else has reason to cry—we parted unreconciled, you remember, and I shan't forgive myself. But for all that, I was not going to sympathise with him—the brute beast! O, give me the poker! This is the last thing of his I have about me," she slipped the gold ring from her third finger, and threw it on the floor. "I'll smash it!" she continued, striking with childish spite, "and then I'll burn it!" And she took and dropped the misused article among the coals. "There! he shall buy another, if he gets me back again. He'd be capable of coming to seek me, to tease[5] Edgar—I dare not stay, lest that notion should possess his wicked head! And besides, Edgar has not been kind, has he? And I won't come suing for his assistance; nor will I bring him into more trouble—Necessity compelled me to seek shelter here; though if I had not learnt he was out of the way, I'd have halted at the kitchen, washed my face, warmed myself, got you to bring what I wanted, and departed again to anywhere out of the reach of my accursed—of that incarnate goblin! Ah, he was in such a fury—if he had caught me! It's a pity, Earnshaw is not his match in strength—I wouldn't have run till I'd seen him all but demolished, had Hindley been able to do it!"

"Well, don't talk so fast, Miss!" I interrupted, "you'll disorder the handkerchief I have tied round your face, and make the cut bleed again—Drink your tea, and take breath and give over laughing—Laughter is sadly out of place under this roof, and in your condition!"

"An undeniable truth," she replied, "Listen to that child! It maintains a constant wail—send it out of my hearing for an hour; I shan't stay any longer."

I rang the bell, and committed it to a servant's care; and then I inquired what had urged her to escape from Wuthering Heights in such an unlikely plight—and where she meant to go, as she refused remaining with us.

"I ought, and I wish, to remain," answered she, "to cheer Edgar, and take care of the baby, for two things, and because the Grange is my right home—but I tell you, he wouldn't let me! Do you think he

5 Isabella uses the word to mean "vex" or "torment," not in the lighter sense more usual today.

could bear to see me grow fat and merry; and could bear to think that we were tranquil, and not resolve on poisoning our comfort? Now, I have the satisfaction of being sure that he detests me to the point of its annoying him seriously to have me within ear-shot, or eye-sight—I notice, when I enter his presence, the muscles of his countenance are involuntarily distorted into an expression of hatred; partly arising from his knowledge of the good causes I have to feel that sentiment for him, and partly from original aversion—It is strong enough to make me feel pretty certain that he would not chase me over England, supposing I contrived a clear escape; and therefore I must get quite away. I've recovered from my first desire to be killed by him. I'd rather he'd kill himself! He has extinguished my love effectually, and so I'm at my ease. I can recollect yet how I loved him; and can dimly imagine that I could still be loving him, if—No, no! Even if he had doted on me, the devilish nature would have revealed its existence, somehow. Catherine had an awfully perverted taste to esteem him so dearly, knowing him so well—Monster! would that he could be blotted out of creation,[6] and out of my memory!"

"Hush, hush! He's a human being," I said. "Be more charitable; there are worse men than he is yet!"

"He's not a human being," she retorted; "and he has no claim on my charity—I gave him my heart, and he took and pinched it to death; and flung it back to me—people feel with their hearts, Ellen, and since he has destroyed mine, I have not power to feel for him, and I would not, though he groaned from this to his dying day; and wept tears of blood for Catherine! No, indeed, indeed, I wouldn't!" And here Isabella began to cry; but, immediately dashing the water from her lashes, she recommenced.

"You asked, what has driven me to flight at last? I was compelled to attempt it because I had succeeded in rousing his rage a pitch above his malignity. Pulling out the nerves with red-hot pincers requires more coolness than knocking on the head.[7] He was worked up to forget the fiendish prudence he boasted of, and pro-

6 An allusion to Genesis 6: 7 ("And the Lord said, I will destroy man whom I have created from the face of the earth") and more particularly to John Wesley's note on this passage: "I will wipe off man from off the earth; as dirt is wiped off from a place which should be clean, and thrown to the dunghill. Or, I will blot out man from the earth, as those lines are blotted out of a book which displease the author, or as the name of a citizen is blotted out of the rolls of the freemen when he is disenfranchised" (*The Wesley Center Online, John Wesley's Notes on the Bible,* Wesleyan Heritage Publishing, July 5, 2013, *Genesis* 6: 7, http://wesley.nnu.edu/john-wesley/john-wesleys-notes-on-the-bible/). Wesley was an Anglican clergyman and one of the founders of Methodism.

7 Red-hot pincers were an infamous instrument of torture, but Isabella's idea of using them to extract the nerves is startling. Her point is that Heathcliff's refined methods of torture require more coolness than rough violence does.

ceeding to murderous violence. I experienced pleasure in being able to exasperate him: the sense of pleasure woke my instinct of self-preservation; so, I fairly broke free, and if ever I come into his hands again, he is welcome to a signal[8] revenge.

"Yesterday, you know, Mr. Earnshaw should have been at the funeral. He kept himself sober, for the purpose—tolerably sober; not going to bed mad[9] at six o'clock and getting up drunk at twelve. Consequently, he rose in suicidal low spirits, as fit for the church as for a dance; and instead, he sat down by the fire, and swallowed gin or brandy by tumblerfuls.

"Heathcliff—I shudder to name him!—has been a stranger in the house from last Sunday till to-day—Whether the angels have fed him, or his kin beneath, I cannot tell; but he has not eaten a meal with us for nearly a week—He has just come home at dawn, and gone upstairs to his chamber, locking himself in—as if anybody dreamt of coveting his company! There he has continued, praying like a methodist;[10] only the deity he implored is senseless dust and ashes; and God, when addressed, was curiously confounded with his own black father![11] After concluding these precious orisons[12]—and they lasted generally till he grew hoarse and his voice was strangled in his throat—he would be off again; always straight down to the Grange! I wonder Edgar did not send for a constable, and give him into custody![13] For me, grieved as I was about Catherine, it was impossible to avoid regarding this season of deliverance from degrading oppression as a holiday.

"I recovered spirits sufficient to hear Joseph's eternal lectures without weeping; and to move up and down the house, less with the foot of a frightened thief than formerly. You wouldn't think that I should cry at anything Joseph could say, but he and Hareton are detestable companions. I'd rather sit with Hindley, and hear his awful talk, than with 't' little maister,' and his staunch supporter, that odious old man!

"When Heathcliff is in, I'm often obliged to seek the kitchen,[14] and their society, or starve among the damp, uninhabited cham-

8 Remarkable or exceptional.

9 Deranged or dazed.

10 Heathcliff's noisy expressions of grief in the days between Catherine's death and her funeral make him sound like a Methodist at a prayer meeting, shouting and groaning in an unseemly way. Although Brontë's mother and aunt had been brought up as Wesleyan Methodists (both became members of the Church of England), Methodists are regularly treated contemptuously or comically in Charlotte's and Branwell's early writings and in Charlotte's *Shirley.* In this novel, the name of the preacher in Lockwood's first dream, Jabes Branderham, connects him to Jabez Bunting, one of the founders of Methodism, and to Jabez Burns, a Baptist preacher named after him by his Methodist mother.

11 The devil.

12 Prayers.

13 An officer of the peace. As a magistrate, Edgar could easily have had Heathcliff arrested.

14 Isabella means the back-kitchen, not the sitting room, where Heathcliff would sit if he were at home.

15 A quotation from I Corinthians 3: 15: "If any man's work shall be burned, he shall suffer loss: but he himself shall be saved; yet so as by fire."

bers; when he is not, as was the case this week, I establish a table and chair at one corner of the house fire, and never mind how Mr. Earnshaw may occupy himself; and he does not interfere with my arrangements: he is quieter now than he used to be, if no one provokes him; more sullen and depressed, and less furious. Joseph affirms he's sure he's an altered man; that the Lord has touched his heart, and he is saved "so as by fire."[15] I'm puzzled to detect signs of the favourable change, but it is not my business.

"Yester-evening, I sat in my nook reading some old books, till late on towards twelve. It seemed so dismal to go up-stairs, with the wild snow blowing outside, and my thoughts continually reverting to the kirkyard, and the new-made grave! I dared hardly lift my eyes from the page before me, that melancholy scene so instantly usurped its place.

"Hindley sat opposite; his head leant on his hand, perhaps meditating on the same subject. He had ceased drinking at a point below irrationality, and had neither stirred nor spoken during two or three hours. There was no sound through the house, but the moaning wind which shook the windows every now and then: the faint crackling of the coals; and the click of my snuffers as I removed at intervals the long wick of the candle. Hareton and Joseph were probably fast asleep in bed. It was very, very sad, and while I read, I sighed, for it seemed as if all joy had vanished from the world, never to be restored.

"The doleful silence was broken, at length, by the sound of the kitchen latch—Heathcliff had returned from his watch earlier than usual, owing, I suppose, to the sudden storm.

"That entrance was fastened; and we heard him coming round to get in by the other. I rose with an irrepressible expression of what I felt on my lips, which induced my companion, who had been staring towards the door, to turn and look at me.

"'I'll keep him out five minutes,' he exclaimed. 'You won't object?'

"'No, you may keep him out the whole night, for me,' I answered. 'Do! put the key in the lock, and draw the bolts.'

"Earnshaw accomplished this, ere his guest reached the front; he then came, and brought his chair to the other side of my table, leaning over it, and searching in my eyes a sympathy with the burning hate that gleamed from his: as he both looked and felt like an assassin, he couldn't exactly find that; but he discovered enough to encourage him to speak.

"'You and I,' he said, 'have each a great debt to settle with the man out yonder! If we were neither of us cowards, we might combine to discharge it. Are you as soft as your brother? Are you willing to endure to the last, and not once attempt a repayment?'

"'I'm weary of enduring now,' I replied, 'and I'd be glad of a retaliation that wouldn't recoil on myself; but treachery, and violence, are spears pointed at both ends—they wound those who resort to them, worse than their enemies.'

"'Treachery and violence are a just return for treachery and violence!' cried Hindley. 'Mrs. Heathcliff, I'll ask you to do nothing but sit still, and be dumb—Tell me now, can you? I'm sure you would have as much pleasure as I in witnessing the conclusion of the fiend's existence; he'll be *your* death unless you overreach[16] him—and he'll be *my* ruin—Damn the hellish villain! He knocks at the door as if he were master here already! Promise to hold your tongue, and before that clock strikes—it wants three minutes of one—you're a free woman!'

"He took the implements[17] which I described to you in my letter from his breast, and would have turned down the candle[18]—I snatched it away, however, and seized his arm.

"'I'll not hold my tongue!' I said. 'You mustn't touch him . . . Let the door remain shut and be quiet!'

"'No! I've formed my resolution, and by God, I'll execute it!' cried the desperate being. 'I'll do you a kindness, in spite of yourself, and Hareton justice! And you needn't trouble your head to

16 Outwit or get the better of him.

17 The pistol with a double-edged spring knife attached to its barrel.

18 Brontë seems to be thinking of an oil lamp with a flame that can be turned down, not of a candle.

19 Upright bars dividing the panes of the casement window.

20 Snarled, showing his teeth.

screen me, Catherine is gone—Nobody alive would regret me, or be ashamed, though I cut my throat this minute—and it's time to make an end!'

"I might as well have struggled with a bear; or reasoned with a lunatic. The only resource left me was to run to a lattice, and warn his intended victim of the fate which awaited him.

"'You'd better seek shelter somewhere else to-night!' I exclaimed in a rather triumphant tone. 'Mr. Earnshaw has a mind to shoot you, if you persist in endeavouring to enter.'

"'You'd better open the door, you—' he answered, addressing, me by some elegant term that I don't care to repeat.

"'I shall not meddle in the matter,' I retorted again. 'Come in, and get shot, if you please! I've done my duty.'

"With that I shut the window, and returned to my place by the fire, having too small a stock of hypocrisy at my command to pretend any anxiety for the danger that menaced him.

"Earnshaw swore passionately at me, affirming that I loved the villain yet; and calling me all sorts of names for the base spirit I evinced. And I, in my secret heart (and conscience never reproached me), thought what a blessing it would be for *him*, should Heathcliff put him out of misery: and what a blessing for *me*, should he send Heathcliff to his right abode! As I sat nursing these reflections, the casement behind me was banged on to the floor by a blow from the latter individual; and his black countenance looked blightingly through. The stanchions[19] stood too close to suffer his shoulders to follow; and I smiled, exulting in my fancied security. His hair and clothes were whitened with snow, and his sharp cannibal teeth, revealed by cold and wrath, gleamed through the dark.

"'Isabella let me in, or I'll make you repent!' he 'girned,'[20] as Joseph calls it.

"'I cannot commit murder,' I replied. 'Mr. Hindley stands sentinel with a knife and loaded pistol.'

"'Let me in by the kitchen door!' he said.

"'Hindley will be there before me,' I answered. 'And that's a poor love of yours, that cannot bear a shower of snow! We were left at peace in our beds, as long as the summer moon shone, but the moment a blast of winter returns, you must run for shelter! Heathcliff, if I were you, I'd go stretch myself over her grave, and die like a faithful dog . . . The world is surely not worth living in now, is it? You had distinctly impressed on me the idea that Catherine was the whole joy of your life—I can't imagine how you think of surviving her loss.'

"'He's there . . . is he?' exclaimed my companion, rushing to the gap. 'If I can get my arm out I can hit him!'

"I'm afraid, Ellen, you'll set me down as really wicked—but you don't know all, so don't judge! I wouldn't have aided or abetted an attempt on even *his* life, for anything—Wish that he were dead, I must; and therefore I was fearfully disappointed, and unnerved by terror for the consequences of my taunting speech when he flung himself on Earnshaw's weapon and wrenched it from his grasp.

"The charge exploded, and the knife, in springing back, closed into its owner's wrist.[21] Heathcliff pulled it away by main force, slitting up the flesh as it passed on, and thrust it dripping into his pocket. He then took a stone, struck down the division between two windows and sprung in. His adversary had fallen senseless with excessive pain, and the flow of blood that gushed from an artery, or a large vein.

"The ruffian kicked and trampled on him, and dashed his head repeatedly against the flags, holding me with one hand, meantime, to prevent me summoning Joseph.

"He exerted preter-human[22] self-denial in abstaining from finishing him completely; but getting out of breath, he finally desisted, and dragged the apparently inanimate body onto the settle.

"There he tore off the sleeve of Earnshaw's coat, and bound up the wound with brutal roughness, spitting and cursing during the operation, as energetically as he had kicked before.

21 Hindley's pistol fires as Heathcliff grasps it, but the bullet misses him and the knife blade springs back, striking Hindley's wrist. Heathcliff then takes the pistol from Hindley, slicing his wrist in the process and recalling Lockwood's rubbing the ghost child's wrist against the broken window glass in Volume I, Chapter 3.

Christopher Heywood identifies Hindley's weapon as "the Lacroix muzzle-loading version (around 1835) of a widely manufactured weapon, the Saloon Pistol Knife" (*Wuthering Heights* [Peterborough, ON: Broadview Press, 2002], p. 46), but it is more likely that Brontë has in mind a flintlock pistol with a spring-loaded blade, a weapon well known in England in the 1780s. According to Donald J. La Rocca, Curator, Arms and Armor, Metropolitan Museum of Art, the "blade was mounted either on the top, side, or underside of the barrel and, when released by a simple catch, would flip or snap into position. It is easy to imagine how the blade could fold back and impale someone's wrist during a tussle."

22 Super-human. Brontë may be remembering Percy Shelley's use of the word to describe the outcast Wolfstein's meeting with "the superior Ginotti" in his Gothic horror novel, *St. Irvyne; or, The Rosicrucian, A Romance.* Shelley's novel was published in 1811 and reprinted in 1840 in William Hazlitt's *The Romancist and the Novelist's Library: The Best Works of the Best Authors,* vol. 3 (London: John Clements, Little Pulteney, 1841).

"Being at liberty, I lost no time in seeking the old servant; who, having gathered by degrees the purport of my hasty tale, hurried below, gasping as he descended the steps two at once.

"'Whet is thur tuh do, nah?[23] whet is thur tuh do, nah?'

"'There's this to do,' thundered Heathcliff, 'that your master's mad; and should he last another month, I'll have him to an asylum. And how the devil did you come to fasten me out, you toothless hound? Don't stand muttering and mumbling there. Come, I'm not going to nurse him. Wash that stuff away; and mind the sparks of your candle—it[24] is more than half brandy!'

"'Und soa, yah been murthering on him?' exclaimed Joseph, lifting his hands and eyes in horror. 'If iver Aw seed a seeght loike this! May the Lord—'

"Heathcliff gave him a push onto his knees, in the middle of the blood, and flung a towel to him; but instead of proceeding to dry it up, he joined his hands, and began a prayer which excited my laughter from its odd phraseology. I was in the condition of mind to be shocked at nothing; in fact, I was as reckless as some malefactors show themselves at the foot of the gallows.

"'Oh, I forgot you,' said the tyrant, 'you shall do that. Down with you. And you conspire with him against me, do you, viper?[25] There, that is work fit for you!'

"He shook me till my teeth rattled, and pitched me beside Joseph, who steadily concluded his supplications, and then rose, vowing he would set off for the Grange directly. Mr. Linton was a magistrate, and though he had fifty wives dead he should inquire into this.[26]

"He was so obstinate in his resolution that Heathcliff deemed it expedient to compel, from my lips, a recapitulation of what had taken place; standing over me, heaving with malevolence, as I reluctantly delivered the account in answer to his questions.

"It required a great deal of labour to satisfy the old man that he was not the aggressor, especially with my hardly wrung replies. However, Mr. Earnshaw soon convinced him that he was alive still;

23 The dialect word "nah" is an intensifier or an expression of surprise.

24 Hindley's blood, which Heathcliff has just ordered Joseph to wash away.

25 A venomous snake native to England. Heathcliff alludes to the popular fable of the viper that turns on the person who has fed it.

26 Even though Edgar is mourning Catherine's death, Joseph thinks he should do his job as a magistrate and punish Heathcliff for attacking Hindley.

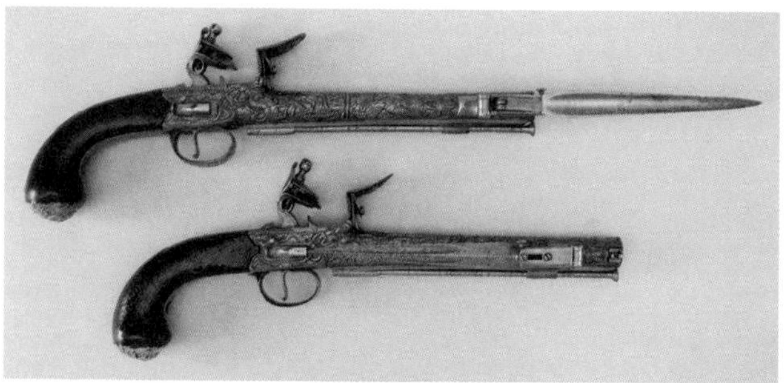

Pair of flintlock pistols with spring blades. With blades folded the pistols, made of steel, brass, silver, and wood, measure 8 7/8 inches. (The Metropolitan Museum of Art, Gift of Charles M. Schott, Jr., 1917 [19.53.17, .18].)

he hastened to administer a dose of spirits, and by their succour his master presently regained motion and consciousness.

"Heathcliff, aware that he was ignorant of the treatment received while insensible, called him deliriously intoxicated; and said he should not notice his atrocious conduct further, but advised him to get to bed. To my joy, he left us after giving this judicious counsel, and Hindley stretched himself on the hearth-stone. I departed to my own room, marvelling that I had escaped so easily.

"This morning, when I came down, about half-an-hour before noon, Mr. Earnshaw was sitting by the fire, deadly sick; his evil genius almost as gaunt and ghastly, leant against the chimney. Neither appeared inclined to dine, and having waited till all was cold on the table, I commenced alone.

"Nothing hindered me from eating heartily; and I experienced a certain sense of satisfaction and superiority, as, at intervals, I cast a look towards my silent companions, and felt the comfort of a quiet conscience within me.

"After I had done, I ventured on the unusual liberty of drawing near the fire; going round Earnshaw's seat, and kneeling in the corner beside him.

"Heathcliff did not glance my way, and I gazed up, and contemplated his features, almost as confidently as if they had been turned to stone. His forehead, that I once thought so manly, and that I now think so diabolical, was shaded with a heavy cloud; his basilisk eyes[27] were nearly quenched[28] by sleeplessness—and weeping, perhaps, for the lashes were wet then: his lips devoid of their ferocious sneer, and sealed in an expression of unspeakable sadness. Had it been another, I would have covered my face, in the presence of such grief. In *his* case, I was gratified: and ignoble as it seems to insult a fallen enemy, I couldn't miss this chance of sticking in a dart; his weakness was the only time when I could taste the delight of paying wrong for wrong."[29]

"Fie, fie, Miss!" I interrupted. "One might suppose you had never opened a Bible in your life. If God afflict your enemies,

27 The basilisk is a fabulous serpent said to kill with its look and breath. The eyes of the dark-haired, fair-cheeked Byronic stranger in Brontë's poem beginning "And now the house dog stretched once more" have a "basilisk charm."

28 Blinded. Compare the invocation to Book 3 of *Paradise Lost,* where Milton refers to his own blind eyes "that roll in vain/ To find thy piercing ray, and find no dawn;/ So thick a drop serene hath quencht thir Orbs" (*Paradise Lost,* Book 3, ll. 23–25). Brontë may well have been thinking of Milton's Satan as she wrote this chapter. Like Satan, Heathcliff is enraged and bent "On desperate revenge, that shall redound/ Upon his own rebellious head" (*Paradise Lost,* Book 3, ll. 85–86). Later in this paragraph, Isabella refers to Heathcliff as "a fallen enemy."

29 Moore's account of Byron's mutability and of the violently contradictory emotions that possessed him provides a model for Isabella's portrait of Heathcliff:

> The various crosses he had met with, in themselves sufficiently irritating and wounding,—were rendered still more so by the high, impatient temper with which he encountered them. What others would have bowed to, as misfortunes, his proud spirit rose against, as wrongs; and the vehemence of this reaction produced, at once, a revolution throughout his whole character, in which, as in revolutions of the political world, all that was bad and irregular in his nature burst forth with all that was most energetic and grand. The very virtues and excellencies of his disposition ministered to the violence of this change. The same ardour that had burned through his friendships and loves now fed the fierce explosions of his indignation and scorn. His natural vivacity and humour but lent a fresher flow to his bitterness, till he, at last, revelled in it as an indulgence; and that hatred of hypocrisy, which had hitherto only shown itself in a too shadowy colouring of his own youthful frailties, now hurried him, from his horror of all false pretensions to virtue, into the still more dangerous boast and ostentation of vice. (Thomas Moore, *Letters and Journals of Lord Byron with Notices of His Life,* 3 vols. [London: John Murray, 1833], 1, p. 237)

30 Exodus 21: 23–25: ". . . thou shalt give life for life, / Eye for eye, tooth for tooth, hand for hand, foot for foot, / Burning for burning, wound for wound, stripe for stripe." Isabella's Old Testament rule responds to Nelly's not quite New Testament one: "If God afflict your enemies, surely that ought to suffice you." So much for Jesus's direction to turn the other cheek. *Wuthering Heights* is a revenge story, and even placid Nelly takes the view that humans want to see their enemies punished.

A basilisk. According to ancient souces, the basilisk was a snake hatched from a cock's egg. Its hissing drove other serpents away, and its gaze was believed to be as deadly as its venom.

surely that ought to suffice you. It is both mean and presumptuous to add your torture to his!"

"In general, I'll allow that it would be, Ellen," she continued. "But what misery laid on Heathcliff could content me, unless I have a hand in it? I'd rather he suffered *less,* if I might cause his sufferings, and he might *know* that I was the cause. Oh, I owe him so much. On only one condition can I hope to forgive him. It is, if I may take an eye for an eye, a tooth for a tooth,[30] for every wrench of agony, return a wrench, reduce him to my level. As he was the first to injure, make him the first to implore pardon; and then—why then, Ellen, I might show you some generosity. But it is utterly impossible I can ever be revenged, and therefore I cannot forgive him. Hindley wanted some water, and I handed him a glass, and asked him how he was."

"'Not as ill as I wish,' he replied. 'But leaving out my arm, every inch of me is as sore as if I had been fighting with a legion of imps!'

"'Yes, no wonder,' was my next remark. 'Catherine used to boast that she stood between you and bodily harm—she meant that certain persons would not hurt you, for fear of offending her. It's well people don't *really* rise from their grave, or, last night, she might have witnessed a repulsive scene! Are not you bruised, and cut over your chest and shoulders?'

"'I can't say,' he answered; 'but what do you mean? Did he dare to strike me when I was down?'

"'He trampled on, and kicked you, and dashed you on the ground,' I whispered. 'And his mouth watered to tear you with his teeth; because he's only half a man—not so much.'

"Mr. Earnshaw looked up, like me, to the countenance of our mutual foe; who, absorbed in his anguish, seemed insensible to anything around him; the longer he stood, the plainer his reflections revealed their blackness through his features.

"'Oh, if God would but give me strength to strangle him in my last agony, I'd go to hell with joy,' groaned the impatient man writhing to rise, and sinking back in despair, convinced of his inadequacy for the struggle.

"'Nay, it's enough that he has murdered one of you,' I observed aloud. 'At the Grange, every one knows your sister would have been living now, had it not been for Mr. Heathcliff. After all, it is preferable to be hated than loved by him. When I recollect how happy we were—how happy Catherine was before he came—I'm fit to curse the day.'

"Most likely, Heathcliff noticed more the truth of what was said, than the spirit of the person who said it. His attention was roused, I saw, for his eyes rained down tears among the ashes, and he drew his breath in suffocating sighs.

"I stared full at him, and laughed scornfully. The clouded windows of hell[31] flashed a moment towards me; the fiend which usu-

31 His eyes.

32 Hareton's hanging the puppies is either a task he's been assigned or a sadistic amusement. Isabella does not connect the puppy hanging that marks her flight from Wuthering Heights to the hanging of her spaniel that marked her flight from Thrushcross Grange in Chapter 12 of Volume I.

ally looked out, however, was so dimmed and drowned that I did not fear to hazard another sound of derision.

"'Get up, and begone out of my sight,' said the mourner.

"I guessed he uttered those words, at least, though his voice was hardly intelligible.

"'I beg your pardon,' I replied. 'But I loved Catherine too; and her brother requires attendance which, for her sake, I shall supply. Now that she's dead, I see her in Hindley; Hindley has exactly her eyes, if you had not tried to gouge them out, and made them black and red, and her—'

"'Get up, wretched idiot, before I stamp you to death!' he cried, making a movement that caused me to make one also.

"'But then,' I continued, holding myself ready to flee, 'if poor Catherine had trusted you, and assumed the ridiculous, contemptible, degrading title of Mrs. Heathcliff, she would soon have presented a similar picture! *She* wouldn't have borne your abominable behaviour quietly; her detestation and disgust must have found voice.'

"The back of the settle, and Earnshaw's person interposed between me and him; so instead of endeavouring to reach me, he snatched a dinner knife from the table, and flung it at my head. It struck beneath my ear, and stopped the sentence I was uttering; but pulling it out, I sprang to the door, and delivered another, which I hope went a little deeper than his missile.

"The last glimpse I caught of him was a furious rush, on his part, checked by the embrace of his host; and both fell locked together on the hearth.

"In my flight through the kitchen I bid Joseph speed to his master; I knocked over Hareton, who was hanging a litter of puppies from a chair back in the doorway;[32] and, blest as a soul escaped from purgatory, I bounded, leaped, and flew down the steep road: then, quitting its windings, shot direct across the moor, rolling over banks, and wading through marshes; precipitating myself, in fact, towards the beacon light of the Grange. And far rather would I be condemned to a perpetual dwelling in the infernal regions, than even for one night abide beneath the roof of Wuthering Heights again."

Isabella ceased speaking, and took a drink of tea; then she rose, and bidding me put on her bonnet, and a great shawl I had brought, and turning a deaf ear to my entreaties for her to remain another hour, she stepped onto a chair, kissed Edgar's and Catherine's portraits, bestowed a similar salute on me, and descended to the carriage accompanied by Fanny, who yelped wild with joy at recovering her mistress. She was driven away, never to revisit this neighbourhood; but a regular correspondence was established between her and my master when things were more settled.

I believe her new abode was in the south, near London; there she had a son born, a few months subsequent to her escape. He was christened Linton, and, from the first, she reported him to be an ailing, peevish creature.

Mr. Heathcliff, meeting me one day in the village, inquired where she lived. I refused to tell. He remarked that it was not of any moment, only she must beware of coming to her brother; she should not be with him, if he had to keep her himself.

Though I would give no information, he discovered, through some of the other servants, both her place of residence, and the existence of the child. Still he didn't molest her; for which forbearance she might thank his aversion, I suppose.

He often asked about the infant, when he saw me; and on hearing its name, smiled grimly, and observed: "They wish me to hate it too, do they?"

"I don't think they wish you to know any thing about it," I answered.

"But I'll have it," he said, "when I want it. They may reckon on that!"

Fortunately, its mother died before the time arrived, some thirteen years after the decease of Catherine, when Linton was twelve, or a little more.[33]

33 Isabella (1765–1797) is thirty-two years old at the time of her death.

On the day succeeding Isabella's unexpected visit, I had no opportunity of speaking to my master: he shunned conversation, and was fit for discussing nothing. When I could get him to listen, I saw it pleased him that his sister had left her husband, whom he abhorred with an intensity which the mildness of his nature would scarcely seem to allow. So deep and sensitive was his aversion that he refrained from going anywhere where he was likely to see or hear of Heathcliff. Grief, and that together, transformed him into a complete hermit: he threw up his office of magistrate, ceased even to attend church, avoided the village on all occasions, and spent a life of entire seclusion within the limits of his park and grounds: only varied by solitary rambles on the moors, and visits to the grave of his wife, mostly at evening, or early morning, before other wanderers were abroad.

But he was too good to be thoroughly unhappy long. *He* didn't pray for Catherine's soul to haunt him: time brought resignation, and a melancholy sweeter than common joy. He recalled her memory with ardent, tender love, and hopeful aspiring to the better world, where, he doubted not, she was gone.

And he had earthly consolation and affections also. For a few days, I said, he seemed regardless of the puny successor to the departed: that coldness melted as fast as snow in April, and ere the tiny thing could stammer a word or totter a step, it wielded a despot's sceptre in his heart.

It was named Catherine, but he never called it the name in full, as he had never called the first Catherine short, probably because Heathcliff had a habit of doing so. The little one was always Cathy; it formed to him a distinction from the mother, and yet, a connection with her; and his attachment sprang from its relation to her, far more than from its being his own.

I used to draw a comparison between him and Hindley Earnshaw, and perplex myself to explain satisfactorily why their conduct was so opposite in similar circumstances. They had both been fond husbands, and were both attached to their children; and I could not see how they shouldn't both have taken the same road, for good or evil. But, I thought in my mind, Hindley with apparently the stronger head, has shown himself sadly the worse and the weaker man. When his ship struck, the captain abandoned his post; and the crew, instead of trying to save her, rushed into riot and confusion, leaving no hope for their luckless vessel. Linton, on the contrary, displayed the true courage of a loyal and faithful soul: he trusted God; and God comforted him. One hoped, and the other despaired: they chose their own lots, and were righteously doomed to endure them.

"But you'll not want to hear my moralizing, Mr. Lockwood: you'll judge as well as I can, all these things; at least, you'll think you will and that's the same."

The end of Earnshaw was what might have been expected: it followed fast on his sister's; there was scarcely six months between them.[34] We, at the Grange, never got a very succinct account of his state preceding it; all that I did learn was on occasion of going to aid in the preparations for the funeral. Mr. Kenneth came to announce the event to my master.

"Well, Nelly," said he, riding into the yard one morning, too early not to alarm me with an instant presentiment of bad news. "It's yours and my turn to go into mourning at present. Who's given us the slip now, do you think?"

"Who?" I asked in a flurry.

"Why, guess!" he returned, dismounting, and slinging his bridle on a hook by the door. "And nip up the corner of your apron; I'm certain you'll need it."[35]

"Not Mr. Heathcliff, surely?" I exclaimed.

"What! would you have tears for him?" said the doctor. No, Heathcliff's a tough young fellow; he looks blooming to-day—I've just seen him. He's rapidly regaining flesh since he lost his better half.[36]

34 Hindley (1757–1784) dies in September, about six months after Catherine.

35 For drying her tears.

36 His wife, Isabella.

37 Nelly has begun to cry.

38 Nelly anticipates Joseph's concerns. See note 41 below.

39 Nelly's mother nursed both her and Hindley.

"Who is it then, Mr. Kenneth?" I repeated impatiently.

"Hindley Earnshaw! Your old friend Hindley—" he replied. "And my wicked gossip, though he's been too wild for me this long while. There! I said we should draw water[37]—But cheer up! He died true to his character, drunk as a lord—Poor lad; I'm sorry too. One can't help missing an old companion, though he had the worst tricks with him that ever man imagined; and has done me many a rascally turn—He's barely twenty-seven, it seems; that's your own age; who would have thought you were born in one year!"

I confess this blow was greater to me than the shock of Mrs. Linton's death: ancient associations lingered round my heart; I sat down in the porch, and wept as for a blood relation, desiring Kenneth to get another servant to introduce him to the master.

I could not hinder myself from pondering on the question—"Had he had fair play?"[38] Whatever I did, that idea would bother me: it was so tiresomely pertinacious that I resolved on requesting leave to go to Wuthering Heights, and assist in the last duties to the dead. Mr. Linton was extremely reluctant to consent, but I pleaded eloquently for the friendless condition in which he lay; and I said my old master, and foster brother,[39] had a claim on my services as strong as his own. Besides, I reminded him that the child, Hareton, was his wife's nephew; and, in the absence of nearer kin, he ought to act as its guardian; and he ought to and must inquire how the property was left, and look over the concerns of his brother-in-law.

He was unfit for attending to such matters then, but he bid me speak to his lawyer; and at length permitted me to go. His lawyer had been Earnshaw's also: I called at the village, and asked him to accompany me. He shook his head, and advised that Heathcliff should be let alone; affirming, if the truth were known, Hareton would be found little else than a beggar.

"His father died in debt," he said; "the whole property is mortgaged, and the sole chance for the natural heir is to allow him an opportunity of creating some interest in the creditor's heart, that he may be inclined to deal leniently towards him."

When I reached the Heights, I explained that I had come to see everything carried on decently, and Joseph, who appeared in sufficient distress, expressed satisfaction at my presence. Mr. Heathcliff said he did not perceive that I was wanted, but I might stay and order the arrangements for the funeral, if I chose.

"Correctly," he remarked, "that fool's body should be buried at the cross-roads, without ceremony of any kind[40]—I happened to leave him ten minutes, yesterday afternoon; and, in that interval, he fastened the two doors of the house against me, and he has spent the night in drinking himself to death deliberately! We broke in this morning, for we heard him snorting like a horse; and there he was, laid over the settle—flaying and scalping would not have wakened him—I sent for Kenneth, and he came; but not till the beast had changed into carrion—he was both dead and cold, and stark; and so you'll allow, it was useless making more stir about him!"

The old servant confirmed this statement, but muttered, "Aw'd raythег he'd goan hisseln fur t'doctor! Aw sud uh taen tent uh t'maister better nur him—un' he warn't deead when Aw left, nowt uh t'soart!"[41]

I insisted on the funeral being respectable—Mr. Heathcliff said I might have my own way there too; only, he desired me to remember that the money for the whole affair came out of his pocket.

He maintained a hard, careless deportment, indicative of neither joy nor sorrow; if anything, it expressed a flinty gratification at a piece of difficult work successfully executed. I observed once, indeed, something like exultation in his aspect. It was just when the people were bearing the coffin from the house; he had the hypocrisy to represent a mourner; and previous to following with Hareton, he lifted the unfortunate child on to the table, and muttered with peculiar gusto,

"Now, my bonny lad, you are *mine!* And we'll see if one tree won't grow as crooked as another, with the same wind to twist it!"[42]

40 Suicides were buried at a cross-road, not in consecrated ground.

41 "I'd rather he'd gone himself for the doctor! I would have taken care of the master better than him—and he wasn't dead when I left, nothing of the sort!"

Joseph implies that Heathcliff has hastened Hindley's death or even murdered him, and many readers, including John Sutherland, have followed Joseph's lead (*Is Heathcliff a Murderer?: Great Puzzles in Nineteenth-Century Fiction* [Oxford: Oxford Univ. Press, 1998]). Does Heathcliff smother Hindley while Hindley is in a drunken stupor? He's certainly capable of it, though the novel doesn't show him doing it.

42 Heathcliff's comparison of his own rearing to the plans he has for Hareton supports readings of the novel that attribute Heathcliff's character as an adult to nurture rather than nature. "The novel says quite explicitly," Terry Eagleton writes, "that Hindley's systematic degradation of Heathcliff 'was enough to make a fiend of a saint'; and we should not be surprised that what it does, more precisely, is to produce a pitiless capitalist landlord out of an oppressed child" (Terry Eagleton, *Myths of Power: A Marxist Study of the Brontës* [London: Macmillan, 1975], p. 111). It's Nelly who says this, not "the novel," and she complicates her sociological analysis with the superstitious speculation that immediately follows: "it appeared as if the lad *were* possessed of something diabolical at that period [just after Frances's death]. He delighted to witness Hindley degrading himself past redemption; and became daily more notable for savage sullenness and ferocity" (Vol. I, Chap. 8).

The unsuspecting thing was pleased at this speech; he played with Heathcliff's whiskers, and stroked his cheek, but I divined its meaning and observed tartly,

"That boy must go back with me to Thrushcross Grange, Sir—There is nothing in the world less yours than he is!"

"Does Linton say so?" he demanded.

"Of course—he has ordered me to take him," I replied.

"Well," said the scoundrel, "We'll not argue the subject now; but I have a fancy to try my hand at rearing a young one, so intimate to your master that I must supply the place of this with my own, if he attempt to remove it; I don't engage to let Hareton go undisputed; but I'll be pretty sure to make the other come! Remember to tell him."

This hint was enough to bind our hands. I repeated its substance, on my return, and Edgar Linton, little interested at the commencement, spoke no more of interfering. I'm not aware that he could have done it to any purpose, had he been ever so willing.

The guest was now the master of Wuthering Heights: he held firm possession, and proved to the attorney, who, in his turn, proved it to Mr. Linton, that Earnshaw had mortgaged every yard of land he owned for cash to supply his mania for gaming: and he, Heathcliff, was the mortgagee.

In that manner, Hareton, who should now be the first gentleman in the neighbourhood, was reduced to a state of complete dependence on his father's inveterate enemy; and lives in his own house as a servant deprived of the advantage of wages, and quite unable to right himself because of his friendlessness, and his ignorance that he has been wronged.

CHAPTER 4

The twelve years," continued Mrs. Dean, "following that dismal period, were the happiest of my life: my greatest troubles, in their passage, rose from our little lady's trifling illnesses which she had to experience in common with all children, rich and poor."[1]

For the rest, after the first six months, she grew like a larch; and could walk and talk too, in her own way, before the heath blossomed a second time over Mrs. Linton's dust.

She was the most winning thing that ever brought sunshine into a desolate house—a real beauty in face—with the Earnshaws' handsome dark eyes, but the Lintons' fair skin, and small features, and yellow curling hair. Her spirit was high, though not rough, and qualified by a heart sensitive and lively to excess in its affections. That capacity for intense attachments reminded me of her mother; still she did not resemble her; for she could be soft and mild as a dove,[2] and she had a gentle voice, and pensive expression: her anger was never furious; her love never fierce; it was deep and tender.

However, it must be acknowledged, she had faults to foil[3] her gifts. A propensity to be saucy was one; and a perverse will that indulged children invariably acquire, whether they be good tempered or cross. If a servant chanced to vex her, it was always: "I shall tell papa!" And if he reproved her, even by a look, you would

1 This edition follows 1847 by putting Nelly's narrative in this first paragraph back into quotation marks; "continued Mrs. Dean" reminds us that Lockwood is narrating.

2 Compare the description of the heroine's face in "The Prisoner [A Fragment]": "it was as soft and mild / As sculptured marble saint, or slumbering unwean'd child."

3 Set off by contrast.

have thought it a heart-breaking business: I don't believe he ever did speak a harsh word to her.

He took her education entirely on himself, and made it an amusement: fortunately, curiosity and a quick intellect urged her into an apt scholar; she learnt rapidly and eagerly, and did honour to his teaching.

Till she reached the age of thirteen, she had not once been beyond the range of the park by herself. Mr. Linton would take her with him, a mile or so outside, on rare occasions; but he trusted her to no one else. Gimmerton was an unsubstantial name in her ears; the chapel, the only building she had approached, or entered, except her own home; Wuthering Heights and Mr. Heathcliff did not exist for her; she was a perfect recluse; and, apparently, perfectly contented. Sometimes, indeed, while surveying the country from her nursery window, she would observe—

"Ellen, how long will it be before I can walk to the top of those hills? I wonder what lies on the other side—is it the sea?"

"No, Miss Cathy," I would answer, "it is hills again just like these."

"And what are those golden rocks like, when you stand under them?" she once asked.

The abrupt descent of Penistone Craggs[4] particularly attracted her notice, especially when the setting sun shone on it and the topmost Heights, and the whole extent of landscape besides lay in shadow.

I explained that they were bare masses of stone, with hardly enough earth in their clefts to nourish a stunted tree.

"And why are they bright so long after it is evening here?" she pursued.

"Because they are a great deal higher up than we are," replied I; "you could not climb them, they are too high and steep. In winter the frost is always there before it comes to us; and, deep into summer, I have found snow under that black hollow on the north-east side!"

4 Both spellings of "Crag" (or "Cragg") have been retained in this edition, as have variant spellings of Penistone.

"Oh, you have been on them!" she cried, gleefully. "Then I can go, too, when I am a woman. Has papa been, Ellen?"

"Papa would tell you, Miss," I answered, hastily, "that they are not worth the trouble of visiting. The moors, where you ramble with him, are much nicer; and Thrushcross park is the finest place in the world."

"But I know the park, and I don't know those," she murmured to herself. "And I should delight to look round me, from the brow of that tallest point—my little pony, Minny, shall take me sometime."

One of the maids, mentioning the Fairy cave,[5] quite turned her head with a desire to fulfil this project; she teased Mr. Linton about it; and he promised she should have the journey when she got older: but Miss Catherine measured her age by months, and—

"Now, am I old enough to go to Penistone Craggs?" was the constant question in her mouth.

The road thither wound close by Wuthering Heights. Edgar had not the heart to pass it; so she received as constantly the answer,

"Not yet, love, not yet."

I said Mrs. Heathcliff lived above a dozen years after quitting her husband. Her family were of a delicate constitution: she and Edgar both lacked the ruddy health that you will generally meet in these parts. What her last illness was, I am not certain; I conjecture they died of the same thing, a kind of fever, slow at its commencement, but incurable, and rapidly consuming life towards the close.

She wrote to inform her brother of the probable conclusion of a four months' indisposition, under which she had suffered; and entreated him to come to her, if possible, for she had much to settle, and she wished to bid him adieu, and deliver Linton safely into his hands. Her hope was that Linton might be left with him, as he had been with her; his father, she would fain convince herself, had no desire to assume the burden of his maintenance or education.

My master hesitated not a moment in complying with her request; reluctant as he was to leave home at ordinary calls, he flew to answer this; commending Catherine to my peculiar vigilance in

5 In Vol. I, Chap. 12, Catherine imagined her bed in the Grange as "the fairy cave under Peniston Crag" and accused Nelly of "gathering elf-bolts to hurt our heifers" (see note 8 in that chapter). Later in this chapter, Hareton will show Cathy "the mysteries of the Fairy cave, and twenty other queer places."

his absence, with reiterated orders that she must not wander out of the park, even under my escort; he did not calculate on her going unaccompanied.

He was away three weeks: the first day or two, my charge sat in a corner of the library, too sad for either reading or playing: in that quiet state she caused me little trouble; but it was succeeded by an interval of impatient, fretful weariness; and being too busy, and too old then, to run up and down amusing her, I hit on a method by which she might entertain herself.

I used to send her on her travels round the grounds—now on foot, and now on a pony, indulging her with a patient audience of all her real and imaginary adventures when she returned.

The summer shone in full prime; and she took such a taste for this solitary rambling that she often contrived to remain out from breakfast till tea; and then the evenings were spent in recounting her fanciful tales. I did not fear her breaking bounds, because the gates were generally locked, and I thought she would scarcely venture forth alone, if they had stood wide open.

Unluckily, my confidence proved misplaced. Catherine came to me, one morning at eight o'clock, and said she was that day an Arabian merchant, going to cross the Desert with his caravan; and I must give her plenty of provision for herself and beasts, a horse and three camels, personated by a large hound and a couple of pointers.

I got together good store of dainties,[6] and slung them in a basket on one side of the saddle; and she sprang up as gay as a fairy, sheltered by her wide-brimmed hat and gauze veil from the July sun, and trotted off with a merry laugh, mocking my cautious counsel to avoid gallopping and come back early.

The naughty thing never made her appearance at tea. One traveller, the hound, being an old dog and fond of its ease, returned; but neither Cathy, nor the pony, nor the two pointers were visible in any direction; and I despatched emissaries down this path, and that path, and, at last, went wandering in search of her myself.

6 "Something nice or delicate; a delicacy; something of exquisite taste" (Johnson, *Dictionary*).

Hand-colored etching of "A Scotch Poney, commonly call'd a Galloway," by James Gillray (1757–1815).

There was a labourer working at a fence round a plantation, on the borders of the grounds. I enquired of him if he had seen our young lady?

"I saw her at morn," he replied; "she would have me to cut her a hazel switch; and then she leapt her galloway[7] over the hedge yonder, where it is lowest, and gallopped out of sight."

You may guess how I felt at hearing this news. It struck me directly she must have started for Penistone Craggs.

"What will become of her?" I ejaculated, pushing through a gap which the man was repairing; and making straight to the high road.

7 Cathy wants the hazel switch to urge her mare on. Any small horse, standing between thirteen and fourteen hands, could be called "a Galloway, from a beautiful breed of little horses once found in the south of Scotland. . . . The pure galloway was said to be nearly fourteen hands high, and sometimes more; of a bright bay, or brown, with black legs, small head and neck, and peculiarly deep and clean legs" (W. Youatt, *Horse* [1831], quoted in *OED*). Galloways were prized for their sure-footedness.

A scene from Andrea Arnold's film adaptation of *Wuthering Heights* (2011) showing the pastoral landscape associated with Thrushcross Grange in the novel.

I walked as if for a wager, mile after mile, till a turn brought me in view of the Heights, but no Catherine could I detect, far or near.

The Craggs lie about a mile and a half beyond Mr. Heathcliff's place, and that is four from the Grange, so I began to fear night would fall ere I could reach them.

"And what if she should have slipped in clambering among them," I reflected, "and been killed, or broken some of her bones?"

My suspense was truly painful; and, at first, it gave me delightful relief to observe, in hurrying by the farm-house, Charlie, the fiercest of the pointers, lying under a window, with swelled head, and bleeding ear.

I opened the wicket, and ran to the door, knocking vehemently for admittance. A woman whom I knew, and who formerly lived at Gimmerton, answered—she had been servant there since the death of Mr. Earnshaw.

"Ah," said she, "you are come a'seeking your little mistress! Don't be frightened. She's here safe—but I'm glad it isn't the master."

"He is not at home then, is he?" I panted, quite breathless with quick walking and alarm.

"No, no," she replied, "both he and Joseph are off, and I think they won't return this hour or more. Step in and rest you a bit."

I entered, and beheld my stray lamb, seated on the hearth, rocking herself in a little chair that had been her mother's, when a child. Her hat was hung against the wall, and she seemed perfectly at home, laughing and chattering, in the best spirits imaginable, to Hareton, now a great, strong lad of eighteen, who stared at her with considerable curiosity and astonishment; comprehending precious little of the fluent succession of remarks and questions which her tongue never ceased pouring forth.

"Very well, Miss," I exclaimed, concealing my joy under an angry countenance. "This is your last ride, till papa comes back. I'll not trust you over the threshold again, you naughty, naughty girl."

"Aha, Ellen!" she cried, gaily, jumping up, and running to my side. "I shall have a pretty story to tell to-night—and so you've found me out. Have you ever been here in your life before?"

"Put that hat on, and home at once," said I. "I'm dreadfully grieved at you, Miss Cathy, you've done extremely wrong! It's no use pouting and crying; that won't repay the trouble I've had, scouring the country after you. To think how Mr. Linton charged me to keep you in; and you stealing off so; it shows you are a cunning little fox, and nobody will put faith in you any more."

"What have I done?" sobbed she, instantly checked. "Papa charged me nothing—he'll not scold me, Ellen—he's never cross, like you!"

"Come, come!" I repeated. "I'll tie the riband.[8] Now, let us have no petulance. Oh, for shame. You thirteen years old, and such a baby!"

This exclamation was caused by her pushing the hat from her head, and retreating to the chimney out of my reach.

"Nay," said the servant, "don't be hard on the bonny lass, Mrs. Dean. We made her stop—she'd fain have ridden forwards, afeard

8 The ribbon on Cathy's bonnet.

you should be uneasy. But Hareton offered to go with her, and I thought he should. It's a wild road over the hills."

Hareton, during the discussion, stood with his hands in his pockets, too awkward to speak, though he looked as if he did not relish my intrusion.

"How long am I to wait?" I continued, disregarding the woman's interference. "It will be dark in ten minutes. Where is the pony, Miss Cathy? And where is Phenix? I shall leave you, unless you be quick, so please yourself."

"The pony is in the yard," she replied, "and Phenix is shut in there. He's bitten—and so is Charlie. I was going to tell you all about it; but you are in a bad temper, and don't deserve to hear."

I picked up her hat, and approached to reinstate it; but perceiving that the people of the house took her part, she commenced capering round the room; and, on my giving chase, ran like a mouse, over and under, and behind the furniture, rendering it ridiculous for me to pursue.

Hareton and the woman laughed; and she joined them, and waxed more impertinent still; till I cried, in great irritation,

"Well, Miss Cathy, if you were aware whose house this is, you'd be glad enough to get out."

"It's *your* father's, isn't it?" said she, turning to Hareton.

"Nay," he replied, looking down, and blushing bashfully.

He could not stand a steady gaze from her eyes, though they were just his own.

"Whose then—your master's?" she asked. He coloured deeper, with a different feeling, muttered an oath, and turned away.

"Who is his master?" continued the tiresome girl, appealing to me. "He talked about 'our house,' and 'our folk.' I thought he had been the owner's son. And he never said 'Miss'; he should have done, shouldn't he, if he's a servant?"

Hareton grew black as a thunder-cloud at this childish speech. I silently shook my questioner, and, at last, succeeded in equipping her for departure.

"Now, get my horse," she said, addressing her unknown kinsman as she would one of the stable-boys at the Grange. "And you may come with me. I want to see where the goblin hunter rises in the marsh, and to hear about the *fairishes,*[9] as you call them—but make haste! What's the matter? Get my horse, I say."

"I'll see thee damned, before I be *thy*[10] servant!" growled the lad.

"You'll see me *what?*" asked Catherine in surprise.

"Damned—thou saucy witch!" he replied.

"There, Miss Cathy! you see you have got into pretty company," I interposed. "Nice words to be used to a young lady! Pray don't begin to dispute with him—Come, let us seek for Minny ourselves, and be gone."

"But Ellen," cried she, staring, fixed in astonishment. "How dare he speak so to me? Mustn't he be made to do as I ask him? You wicked creature, I shall tell papa what you said—Now then!"

Hareton did not appear to feel this threat; so the tears sprung into her eyes with indignation. "You bring the pony," she exclaimed, turning to the woman, "and let my dog free this moment!"

"Softly, Miss," answered the addressed. "You'll lose nothing, by being civil. Though Mr. Hareton, there, be not the master's son, he's your cousin; and I was never hired to serve you."

"*He* my cousin!" cried Cathy with a scornful laugh.

"Yes, indeed," responded her reprover.

"Oh, Ellen! don't let them say such things," she pursued in great trouble. "Papa is gone to fetch my cousin from London—my cousin is a gentleman's son—That my—" she stopped, and wept outright; upset at the bare notion of relationship with such a clown.[11]

"Hush, hush!" I whispered, "people can have many cousins and of all sorts, Miss Cathy, without being any the worse for it; only they needn't keep their company, if they be disagreeable and bad."

9 Fairies. Cathy mocks Hareton by using his dialect word.

10 Hareton speaks to Cathy as if she were a child, using the familiar forms of the second-person pronouns—"thee" and "thou"—to express his condescension in response to her assumption of social superiority. She is thirteen, and he is nineteen. No nineteenth-century English novel uses language to register social status, aspiration, and mobility more pointedly than this one or more poignantly than here in this exchange between the two cousins, separated from birth and reared under such different circumstances.

11 Someone of low breeding. Cathy's assertion that her cousin Linton (Heathcliff's son) is "a gentleman's son," unlike her cousin Hareton (Hindley's son), is richly ironic. Lockwood also disparaged Hareton as a "clown" when he met him in the opening chapters of the novel.

"He's not, he's not my cousin, Ellen!" she went on, gathering fresh grief from reflection, and flinging herself into my arms for refuge from the idea.

I was much vexed at her and the servant for their mutual revelations; having no doubt of Linton's approaching arrival, communicated by the former, being reported to Mr. Heathcliff; and feeling as confident that Catherine's first thought on her father's return would be to seek an explanation of the latter's assertion concerning her rude-bred kindred.

Hareton, recovering from his disgust at being taken for a servant, seemed moved by her distress; and, having fetched the pony round to the door, he took, to propitiate her, a fine crooked-legged terrier whelp[12] from the kennel; and putting it into her hand, bid her wisht[13] for he meant naught.

Pausing in her lamentations, she surveyed him with a glance of awe and horror, then burst forth anew.

I could scarcely refrain from smiling at this antipathy to the poor fellow, who was a well-made, athletic youth, good looking in features, and stout and healthy, but attired in garments befitting his daily occupations of working on the farm, and lounging among the moors after rabbits and game. Still, I thought I could detect in his physiognomy[14] a mind owning better qualities than his father ever possessed. Good things lost amid a wilderness of weeds, to be sure, whose rankness far over-topped their neglected growth; yet, notwithstanding, evidence of a wealthy soil that might yield luxuriant crops, under other and favourable circumstances. Mr. Heathcliff, I believe, had not treated him physically ill; thanks to his fearless nature, which offered no temptation to that course of oppression; it had none of the timid susceptibility that would have given zest to ill-treatment, in Heathcliff's judgment. He appeared to have bent his malevolence on making him a brute: he was never taught to read or write; never rebuked for any bad habit which did not annoy his keeper; never led a single step towards virtue, or guarded by a single precept against vice. And from what I heard,

12 Terriers were originally bred to pursue vermin and to flush out or kill rabbits, foxes, and badgers, but they have long been popular as house dogs. Some terriers have crooked forelegs like those of dachshunds and basset hounds. As Nelly's description of the dog as "fine" suggests, this has not usually been considered a fault. Since the dogs at the Heights are working animals rather than pets, the puppy Hareton gives Cathy is likely to be small enough to go underground. Perhaps it is a Yorkshire terrier, a small breed with a reputation as an excellent house dog and companion. (Rawdon Briggs, *A History and Description of the Modern Dogs of Great Britain and Ireland: The Terriers,* Elibron Classics facsimile reprint of the 1894 edition, online.) Hareton's peace offering to Cathy, here so distressed by her discovery of "her rude-bred kindred," is a puppy bred like Hareton at the Heights yet also suitable for the Grange.

13 Hush.

14 Facial features. Nelly's use of the word suggests that she knows something about current scientific theories. For more about physiognomy, see Vol. I, Chap. 1, note 26 above.

15 Worthless or wicked. This edition corrects the spelling in 1847 ("offalld") to make it consistent with the spelling of this word in its earlier appearance in Volume I.

16 Denunciations, and especially threats of divine punishment.

17 Stingy.

Joseph contributed much to his deterioration by a narrow-minded partiality which prompted him to flatter and pet him as a boy, because he was the head of the old family. And as he had been in the habit of accusing Catherine Earnshaw and Heathcliff, when children, of putting the master past his patience, and compelling him to seek solace in drink, by what he termed their "offald ways,"[15] so at present, he laid the whole burden of Hareton's faults on the shoulders of the usurper of his property.

If the lad swore, he wouldn't correct him; nor however culpably he behaved. It gave Joseph satisfaction, apparently, to watch him go the worst lengths. He allowed that he was ruined; that his soul was abandoned to perdition; but then, he reflected that Heathcliff must answer for it. Hareton's blood would be required at his hands; and there lay immense consolation in that thought.

Joseph had instilled into him a pride of name, and of his lineage; he would, had he dared, have fostered hate between him and the present owner of the Heights, but his dread of that owner amounted to superstition; and he confined his feelings regarding him to muttered inuendos and private comminations.[16]

I don't pretend to be intimately acquainted with the mode of living customary in those days, at Wuthering Heights. I only speak from hearsay, for I saw little. The villagers affirmed Mr. Heathcliff was *near,*[17] and a cruel hard landlord to his tenants; but the house, inside, had regained its ancient aspect of comfort under female management; and the scenes of riot common in Hindley's time were not now enacted within its walls. The master was too gloomy to seek companionship with any people, good or bad, and he is yet—

This, however, is not making progress with my story. Miss Cathy rejected the peace-offering of the terrier, and demanded her own dogs, Charlie and Phenix. They came limping, and hanging their heads; and we set out for home, sadly out of sorts, every one of us.

I could not wring from my little lady how she had spent the day; except that, as I supposed, the goal of her pilgrimage was Penis-

A lecturer demonstrating the science of physiognomy in an etching published in *The Universal Museum and Complete Magazine* (London, 1765). The heads provide examples of different outward appearances that the lecturer is connecting to inward capacities and characteristics.

tone Crags; and she arrived without adventure to the gate of the farm-house, when Hareton happened to issue forth, attended by some canine followers, who attacked her train.

They had a smart battle, before their owners could separate them: that formed an introduction. Catherine told Hareton who she was, and where she was going, and asked him to show her the way; finally, beguiling him to accompany her.

He opened the mysteries of the Fairy cave, and twenty other queer places; but being in disgrace, I was not favoured with a description of the interesting objects she saw.

I could gather, however, that her guide had been a favourite till she hurt his feelings by addressing him as a servant, and Heathcliff's housekeeper hurt hers by calling him her cousin.

Then the language he had held to her rankled in her heart; she who was always "love," and "darling," and "queen," and "angel," with everybody at the Grange; to be insulted so shockingly by a stranger! She did not comprehend it; and hard work I had, to obtain a promise that she would not lay the grievance before her father.

I explained how he objected to the whole household at the Heights, and how sorry he would be to find she had been there; but I insisted most on the fact that if she revealed my negligence of his orders, he would perhaps be so angry that I should have to leave; and Cathy couldn't bear that prospect: she pledged her word, and kept it, for my sake—after all, she was a sweet little girl.

CHAPTER 5

A letter, edged with black,[1] announced the day of my master's return. Isabella was dead; and he wrote to bid me get mourning[2] for his daughter, and arrange a room, and other accommodations, for his youthful nephew.

Catherine ran wild with joy at the idea of welcoming her father back: and indulged most sanguine anticipations of the innumerable excellencies of her "real" cousin.

The evening of their expected arrival came. Since early morning, she had been busy, ordering her own small affairs; and now, attired in her new black frock—poor thing! her aunt's death impressed her with no definite sorrow—she obliged me, by constant worrying, to walk with her down through the grounds to meet them.

"Linton is just six months younger than I am," she chattered as we strolled leisurely over the swells and hollows of mossy turf, under shadow of the trees. "How delightful it will be to have him for a playfellow! Aunt Isabella sent papa a beautiful lock of his hair; it was lighter than mine—more flaxen, and quite as fine. I have it carefully preserved in a little glass box; and I've often thought what pleasure it would be to see its owner—Oh! I am happy—and papa, dear, dear papa! Come, Ellen, let us run—come run!"

She ran, and returned and ran again, many times before my sober footsteps reached the gate, and then she seated herself on the

1 Black-bordered cards and stationery indicated that a household was in mourning.

2 Mourning clothing, worn as an outward sign of inward sorrow and as a show of respect for the dead. Rules about exactly what could or could not be worn during the mourning period, as well as rules about how long the mourning period lasted, were very specific. A child would be expected to wear mourning for a parent for a year; Cathy's period of mourning for her aunt would be shorter. By at least the beginning of the nineteenth century, mourning dress had achieved an important place in the realm of women's fashion.

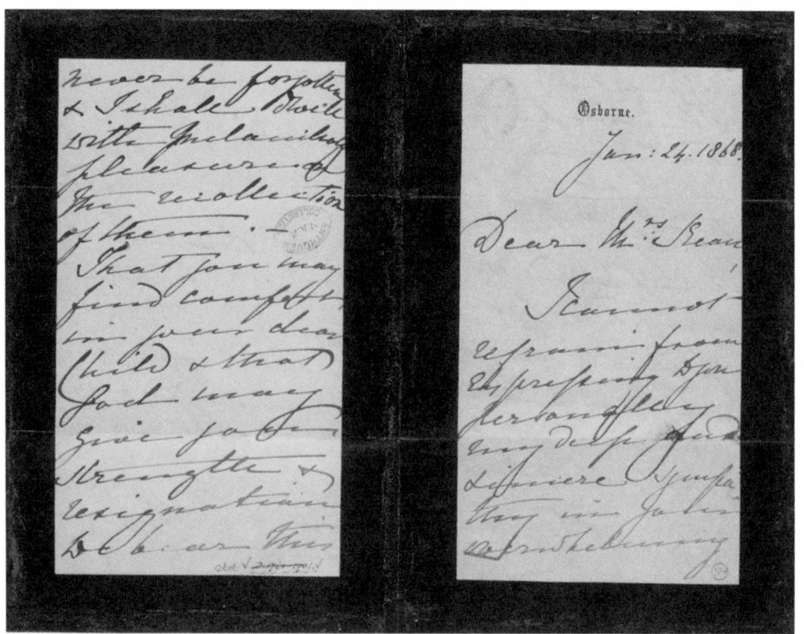

Osborne.

Jan: 24. 1868.

Dear Mrs Kea[illegible]

I cannot refrain from expressing to you personally my deep & sincere sympathy in your overwhelming

never be forgotten & I shall think with melancholy pleasure of the recollection of them. — That you may find comfort in your dear child & that God may give you strength & resignation to bear this

Facsimile of an autograph letter from Queen Victoria written on mourning paper. The letter is dated January 24, 1868, and expresses sympathy on the death of the recipient's husband. Prince Albert had died almost exactly six years earlier, and the queen's long mourning was a keynote of her reign.

grassy bank beside the path, and tried to wait patiently; but that was impossible; she couldn't be still a minute.

"How long they are!" she exclaimed. "Ah, I see some dust on the road—they are coming! No! When will they be here? May we not go a little way—half a mile, Ellen, only just half a mile—do say yes—to that clump of birches at the turn!"

I refused staunchily: and, at length, her suspense was ended: the travelling carriage[3] rolled in sight.

Miss Cathy shrieked, and stretched out her arms, as soon as she caught her father's face, looking from the window. He descended, nearly as eager as herself; and a considerable interval elapsed, ere they had a thought to spare for any but themselves.

While they exchanged caresses, I took a peep in to see after Linton. He was asleep, in a corner, wrapped in a warm, fur-lined cloak, as if it had been winter. A pale, delicate, effeminate boy, who might have been taken for my master's younger brother, so strong was the resemblance, but there was a sickly peevishness in his aspect that Edgar Linton never had.

3 Although the Lintons own a carriage, this is probably a vehicle better suited to long journeys and hired by Edgar to transport his nephew comfortably from London to Thrushcross Grange.

The latter saw me looking; and, having shaken hands, advised me to close the door, and leave him undisturbed; for the journey had fatigued him.

Cathy would fain have taken one glance; but her father told her to come on, and they walked together up the park, while I hastened before, to prepare the servants.

"Now, darling," said Mr. Linton, addressing his daughter, as they halted at the bottom of the front steps. "Your cousin is not so strong or so merry as you are, and he has lost his mother, remember, a very short time since; therefore, don't expect him to play, and run about with you directly. And don't harass him much by talking—let him be quiet this evening, at least, will you?"

"Yes, yes, papa," answered Catherine; "but I do want to see him; and he hasn't once looked out."

The carriage stopped; and the sleeper, being roused, was lifted to the ground by his uncle.

"This is your cousin Cathy, Linton," he said, putting their little hands together. "She's fond of you already; and mind you don't grieve her by crying to-night. Try to be cheerful now; the travelling is at an end, and you have nothing to do but rest and amuse yourself as you please."

"Let me go to bed then," answered the boy, shrinking from Catherine's salute;[4] and he put his fingers to his eyes to remove incipient tears.

"Come, come, there's a good child," I whispered, leading him in. "You'll make her weep too—see how sorry she is for you!"

I do not know whether it were sorrow for him, but his cousin put on as sad a countenance as himself, and returned to her father. All three entered, and mounted to the library, where tea was laid[5] ready.

I proceeded to remove Linton's cap and mantle,[6] and placed him on a chair by the table; but be was no sooner seated than he began to cry afresh. My master inquired what was the matter.

"I can't sit on a chair," sobbed the boy.

4 Kiss.

5 Set out.

6 A loose sleeveless coat.

"Go to the sofa then; and Ellen shall bring you some tea," answered his uncle, patiently.

He had been greatly tried during the journey, I felt convinced, by his fretful, ailing charge.

Linton slowly trailed himself off,[7] and lay down. Cathy carried a foot-stool and her cup to his side.

At first she sat silent; but that could not last; she had resolved to make a pet of her little cousin, as she would have him to be; and she commenced stroking his curls, and kissing his cheek, and offering him tea in her saucer, like a baby. This pleased him, for he was not much better; he dried his eyes, and lightened into a faint smile.

"Oh, he'll do very well," said the master to me, after watching them a minute. "Very well, if we can keep him, Ellen. The company of a child of his own age will instil new spirit into him soon: and by wishing for strength he'll gain it."

Aye, if we can keep him! I mused to myself; and sore misgivings came over me that there was slight hope of that. And then, I thought, however will that weakling live at Wuthering Heights, between his father and Hareton? What playmates and instructors they'll be.

Our doubts were presently decided; even earlier than I expected. I had just taken the children up-stairs, after tea was finished; and seen Linton asleep—he would not suffer me to leave him, till that was the case—I had come down, and was standing by the table in the hall, lighting a bed-room candle for Mr. Edgar, when a maid stepped out of the kitchen, and informed me that Mr. Heathcliff's servant, Joseph, was at the door, and wished to speak with the master.

"I shall ask him what he wants first," I said, in considerable trepidation. "A very unlikely hour to be troubling people, and the instant they have returned from a long journey. I don't think the master can see him."

7 Linton moves from his chair to the sofa without energy or will. The *OED* cites Dickens, *Cricket on Hearth* iii (1845), as the first instance of this use of "trail off."

Joseph had advanced through the kitchen as I uttered these words, and now presented himself in the hall. He was donned[8] in his Sunday garments, with his most sanctimonious and sourest face; and holding his hat in one hand, and his stick in the other, he proceeded to clean his shoes on the mat.

"Good evening, Joseph," I said, coldly. "What business brings you here to-night?"

"It's Maister Linton Aw mun spake tull,"[9] he answered, waving me disdainfully aside.

"Mr. Linton is going to bed; unless you have something particular to say, I'm sure he won't hear it now," I continued. "You had better sit down in there, and entrust your message to me."

"Which is his rahm?" pursued the fellow, surveying the range of closed doors.

I perceived he was bent on refusing my mediation; so, very reluctantly, I went up to the library, and announced the unseasonable visiter; advising that he should be dismissed till next day.

Mr. Linton had no time to empower me to do so, for he mounted close at my heels, and pushing into the apartment, planted himself at the far side of the table, with his two fists clapped on the head of his stick, and began in an elevated tone, as if anticipating opposition.

"Hathecliff has send me for his lad, un' Aw munn't goa back baht him."[10]

Edgar Linton was silent a minute; an expression of exceeding sorrow overcast his features; he would have pitied the child on his own account; but, recalling Isabella's hopes and fears, and anxious wishes for her son, and her commendations of him to his care, he grieved bitterly at the prospect of yielding him up, and searched in his heart how it might be avoided. No plan offered itself: the very exhibition of any desire to keep him would have rendered the claimant more peremptory: there was nothing left but to resign him. However, he was not going to rouse him from his sleep.

BRITISH BIRDS. 231
THE WHINCHAT.
(Motacilla rubetra, Lin.—Le grand Traquet, ou le tarier, Buff.)

Wood engraving of a whinchat from Thomas Bewick's *A History of British Birds* (1797). Emily faithfully copied this engraving in 1829. Bewick describes whinchats as "solitary" birds that sing "a simple unvaried note."

8 Dressed. In Chapter 7, Vol. I, Nelly tells Heathcliff he'll "need half an hour's donning."

9 "It's Master Linton I must speak to."

10 "Heathcliff has sent me for his boy, and I mustn't go back without him."

"Tell Mr. Heathcliff," he answered, calmly, "that his son shall come to Wuthering Heights to-morrow. He is in bed, and too tired to go the distance now. You may also tell him that the mother of Linton desired him to remain under my guardianship; and, at present, his health is very precarious."

"Noa!" said Joseph, giving a thud with his prop on the floor, and assuming an authoritative air. "Noa! that manes nowt—Hathecliff maks noa 'cahnt uh t' mother, nur yah norther—bud he'll hev his lad; and Aw mun tak him—soa nah yah knaw!"[11]

"You shall not to-night!" answered Linton, decisively. "Walk down stairs at once, and repeat to your master what I have said. Ellen, show him down. Go—"

And, aiding the indignant elder with a lift by the arm, he rid the room of him, and closed the door.

"Varrah weel!" shouted Joseph, as he slowly drew off. "Tuh morn, he's come hisseln, un' thrust *him* aht, if yah darr!"[12]

11 "No! That means nothing—Heathcliff takes no account of the mother, nor of you either—but he'll have his boy; and I must take him —so now you know!"

12 "In the morning, he'll come himself, and thrust *him* out, if you dare!"

CHAPTER 6

To obviate the danger of this threat being fulfilled, Mr. Linton commissioned me to take the boy home early, on Catherine's pony, and, said he—

"As we shall now have no influence over his destiny, good or bad, you must say nothing of where he is gone to my daughter; she cannot associate with him hereafter; and it is better for her to remain in ignorance of his proximity, lest she should be restless, and anxious to visit the Heights—merely tell her, his father sent for him suddenly, and he has been obliged to leave us."

Linton was very reluctant to be roused from his bed at five o'clock, and astonished to be informed that he must prepare for further travelling: but I softened off the matter by stating that he was going to spend some time with his father, Mr. Heathcliff, who wished to see him so much, he did not like to defer the pleasure till he should recover from his late journey.

"My father?" he cried, in strange perplexity. "Mamma never told me I had a father. Where does he live? I'd rather stay with uncle."

"He lives a little distance from the Grange," I replied, "just beyond those hills—not so far, but you may walk over here, when you get hearty. And you should be glad to go home, and to see him. You must try to love him, as you did your mother, and then he will love you."

1 "A state of mental abstraction or musing: 'gloomy meditations' (Johnson)" *(OED)*.

"But why have I not heard of him before?" asked Linton; "why didn't mamma and he live together as other people do?"

"He had business to keep him in the north," I answered, "and your mother's health required her to reside in the south."

"And why didn't mamma speak to me about him?" persevered the child. "She often talked of uncle, and I learnt to love him long ago. How am I to love papa? I don't know him."

"Oh, all children love their parents," I said. "Your mother, perhaps, thought you would want to be with him, if she mentioned him often to you. Let us make haste. An early ride on such a beautiful morning is much preferable to an hour's more sleep."

"Is *she* to go with us," he demanded. "The little girl I saw yesterday?"

"Not now," replied I.

"Is uncle?" he continued.

"No, I shall be your companion there," I said.

Linton sank back on his pillow, and fell into a brown study.[1]

"I won't go without uncle," he cried at length; "I can't tell where you mean to take me."

I attempted to persuade him of the naughtiness of showing reluctance to meet his father: still he obstinately resisted any progress towards dressing; and I had to call for my master's assistance, in coaxing him out of bed.

The poor thing was finally got off with several delusive assurances that his absence should be short; that Mr. Edgar and Cathy would visit him; and other promises, equally ill-founded, which I invented and reiterated, at intervals, throughout the way.

The pure heather-scented air, and the bright sunshine, and the gentle canter of Minny relieved his despondency, after a while. He began to put questions concerning his new home, and its inhabitants, with greater interest, and liveliness.

"Is Wuthering Heights as pleasant a place as Thrushcross Grange?" he inquired, turning to take a last glance into the valley, whence a light mist mounted, and formed fleecy cloud, on the skirts of the blue.

"It is not so buried in trees," I replied, "and it is not quite so large, but you can see the country beautifully, all round; and the air is healthier for you—fresher, and dryer. You will, perhaps, think the building old and dark, at first—though it is a respectable house, the next best in the neighbourhood. And you will have such nice rambles on the moors! Hareton Earnshaw—that is Miss Cathy's other cousin; and so yours in a manner—will show you all the sweetest spots; and you can bring a book in fine weather, and make a green hollow your study; and, now and then, your uncle may join you in a walk; he does, frequently, walk out on the hills."

"And what is my father like?" he asked. "Is he as young and handsome as uncle?"

"He's as young," said I "but he has black hair, and eyes; and looks sterner, and he is taller and bigger altogether. He'll not seem to you so gentle and kind at first, perhaps, because it is not his way—still, mind you be frank and cordial with him; and naturally, he'll be fonder of you than any uncle, for you are his own."

"Black hair and eyes!" mused Linton. "I can't fancy[2] him. Then I am not like him, am I?"

"Not much," I answered . . . Not a morsel, I thought: surveying with regret the white complexion, and slim frame of my companion, and his large languid eyes . . . his mother's eyes save that, unless a morbid touchiness kindled them a moment, they had not a vestige of her sparkling spirit.

"How strange that he should never come to see mama and me," he murmured. "Has he ever seen me? If he have, I must have been a baby—I remember not a single thing about him!"

"Why, Master Linton," said I, "three hundred miles[3] is a great distance: and ten years seem very different in length to a grown-up person, compared with what they do to you. It is probable Mr. Heathcliff proposed going, from summer to summer, but never

2 Picture or imagine.

3 A distance of three hundred miles from London would put Gimmerton very close to the Scottish border and facilitate the hasty marriages in the novel. But the other information the novel provides about the location of Gimmerton—that Wuthering Heights, a few miles north of the village, is about sixty miles from Liverpool (see Volume I, Chapter 4)—is incompatible with this distance from London. For purposes of comparison, Haworth is about sixty miles from Liverpool and about two hundred miles from London.

4 Linton is shaking, as if in a fever.

5 The ancient Greeks used sour milk and snails for medicinal purposes. Doctors were still prescribing snail preparations for internal and external use in the nineteenth century. Linton looks like an invalid. When Heathcliff says he wasn't "sanguine" about his son, he means he wasn't hopeful, but the word reminds us of the contrast between Heathcliff's own blood-red color and Linton's pallor.

found a convenient opportunity: and now it is too late—Don't trouble him with questions on the subject: it will disturb him for no good."

The boy was fully occupied with his own cogitations for the remainder of the ride, till we halted before the farm-house garden gate. I watched to catch his impressions in his countenance. He surveyed the carved front and low-browed lattices, the straggling gooseberry bushes and crooked firs, with solemn intentness, and then shook his head: his private feelings entirely disapproved of the exterior of his new abode; but he had sense to postpone complaining—there might be compensation within.

Before he dismounted, I went and opened the door. It was half-past six; the family had just finished breakfast; the servant was clearing and wiping down the table: Joseph stood by his master's chair telling some tale concerning a lame horse; and Hareton was preparing for the hay-field.

"Hallo, Nelly!" cried Mr. Heathcliff, when he saw me. "I feared I should have to come down and fetch my property myself—You've brought it, have you? Let us see what we can make of it."

He got up and strode to the door: Hareton and Joseph followed in gaping curiosity. Poor Linton ran a frightened eye over the faces of the three.

"Sure-ly," said Joseph after a grave inspection, "he's swopped wi' ye, maister, an' yon's his lass!"

Heathcliff, having stared his son into an ague of confusion,[4] uttered a scornful laugh.

"God! what a beauty! what a lovely, charming thing!" he exclaimed. "Haven't they reared it on snails and sour milk,[5] Nelly? Oh, damn my soul!—but that's worse than I expected—and the devil knows I was not sanguine!"

I bid the trembling and bewildered child get down, and enter. He did not thoroughly comprehend the meaning of his father's speech, or whether it were intended for him: indeed, he was not yet certain that the grim, sneering stranger was his father; but he clung to me with growing trepidation; and on Mr. Heathcliff's taking a seat, and bidding him "come hither," he hid his face on my shoulder, and wept.

"Tut, tut!" said Heathcliff, stretching out a hand and dragging him roughly between his knees, and then holding up his head by the chin. "None of that nonsense! we're not going to hurt thee, Linton—isn't that thy name? Thou art thy mother's child, entirely! Where is my share in thee, puling[6] chicken?"

He took off the boy's cap and pushed back his thick flaxen curls, felt his slender arms, and his small fingers; during which examination, Linton ceased crying, and lifted his great blue eyes to inspect the inspector.

"Do you know me?" asked Heathcliff, having satisfied himself that the limbs were all equally frail and feeble.

"No!" said Linton, with a gaze of vacant fear.

"You've heard of me, I dare say?"

"No," he replied again.

"No? What a shame of your mother, never to waken your filial regard for me! You are my son, then, I'll tell you; and your mother was a wicked slut to leave you in ignorance of the sort of father you possessed—Now, don't wince, and colour up! Though it *is* something to see you have not white blood—Be a good lad; and I'll do for you—Nelly, if you be tired you may sit down, if not get home again—I guess you'll report what you hear, and see, to the cipher at the Grange; and this thing won't be settled while you linger about it."

"Well," replied I, "I hope you'll be kind to the boy, Mr. Heathcliff, or you'll not keep him long, and he's all you have a-kin, in the wide world that you will ever know—remember."

"I'll be *very* kind to him you needn't fear!" he said laughing. "Only nobody else must be kind to him—I'm jealous of monopolizing his affection—And, to begin my kindness, Joseph!—bring the lad some breakfast—Hareton, you infernal calf, begone to your work. Yes, Nell," he added when they were departed, "my son is

6 Whining or crying weakly.

prospective owner of your place, and I should not wish him to die till I was certain of being his successor. Besides, he's *mine,* and I want the triumph of seeing *my* descendent fairly lord of their estates; my child hiring their children, to till their fathers' lands for wages—That is the sole consideration which can make me endure the whelp—I despise him for himself, and hate him for the memories he revives! But that consideration is sufficient; he's as safe with me, and shall be tended as carefully, as your master tends his own—I have a room up-stairs, furnished for him, in handsome style—I've engaged a tutor, also, to come three times a week, from twenty miles distance, to teach him what he pleases to learn. I've ordered Hareton to obey him: and in fact, I've arranged every thing with a view to preserve the superior and the gentleman in him, above his associates—I do regret, however, that he so little deserves the trouble—if I wished any blessing in the world, it was to find him a worthy object of pride, and I'm bitterly disappointed with the whey-faced[7] whining wretch!"

While he was speaking, Joseph returned, bearing a basin of milk-porridge, and placed it before Linton. He stirred round the homely mess with a look of aversion, and affirmed he could not eat it.

I saw the old man servant shared largely in his master's scorn of the child, though he was compelled to retain the sentiment in his heart, because Heathcliff plainly meant his underlings to hold him in honour.

"Cannot ate it?" repeated he, peering in Linton's face, and subduing his voice to a whisper, for fear of being overheard. "But Maister Hareton nivir ate nowt else, when he wer a little un: und what wer gooid eneugh fur him's gooid eneugh fur yah, Aw's rayther think!"[8]

"I *shan't* eat it!" answered Linton, snappishly. "Take it away."

Joseph snatched up the food indignantly, and brought it to us.

"Is there owt ails th' victuals?"[9] he asked, thrusting the tray under Heathcliff's nose.

7 Linton's complexion is pale, like whey, the watery part of the milk that remains after the curd has been removed. Johnson notes that "whey" can imply cowardice *(Dictionary).* Brontë, like Johnson, was familiar with Macbeth's use of the word to address his servant:

> Go prick thy face, and over-red thy fear,
> Thou lily-liver'd boy. What soldiers, patch?
> Death of thy soul! those linen cheeks of thine
> Are counsellors to fear. What soldiers, whey-face? (*Macbeth,* v.iii.17–18)

8 "But Master Hareton never ate anything else, when he was a little one: and what was good enough for him's good enough for you, I rather think!"

9 "Is there anything wrong with the food?"

"What should ail them?" he said.

"Wah!" answered Joseph, "yon dainty chap says he cannut ate 'em. Bud Aw guess it's raight! His mother wer just soa—we wer a'most too mucky tuh sow t' corn fur makking her breead."[10]

"Don't mention his mother to me," said the master, angrily. "Get him something that he can eat, that's all. What is his usual food, Nelly?"

I suggested boiled milk or tea; and the housekeeper received instructions to prepare some.

Come, I reflected, his father's selfishness may contribute to his comfort. He perceives his delicate constitution, and the necessity of treating him tolerably. I'll console Mr. Edgar by acquainting him with the turn Heathcliff's humour has taken.

Having no excuse for lingering longer, I slipped out, while Linton was engaged in timidly rebuffing the advances of a friendly sheep-dog. But he was too much on the alert to be cheated—as I closed the door, I heard a cry, and a frantic repetition of the words—

"Don't leave me! I'll not stay here! I'll not stay here!"

Then the latch was raised and fell—they did not suffer him to come forth. I mounted Minny, and urged her to a trot; and so my brief guardianship ended.

10 "What! . . . that dainty chap says he cannot eat them. But I guess that's right! His mother was just so—we were almost too low to sow the oats for making her bread."

1 Become (without the sense of growth or increase).

2 Earlier, Joseph mocked Isabella's request to be taken to the parlor: "Nay, we've no *parlours*" (Vol. I, Chap. 13). That Wuthering Heights now contains a room that can be called a parlor and is well furnished shows Heathcliff's effort to bring Linton up as a gentleman and also to separate him from the other inhabitants of the Heights.

CHAPTER 7

We had sad work with little Cathy that day: she rose in high glee, eager to join her cousin; and such passionate tears and lamentations followed the news of his departure that Edgar himself was obliged to sooth her, by affirming he should come back soon; he added, however, "if I can get him"; and there were no hopes of that.

This promise poorly pacified her; but time was more potent; and though still, at intervals, she inquired of her father when Linton would return; before she did see him again, his features had waxed[1] so dim in her memory that she did not recognise him.

When I chanced to encounter the housekeeper of Wuthering Heights, in paying business-visits to Gimmerton, I used to ask how the young master got on; for he lived almost as secluded as Catherine herself, and was never to be seen. I could gather from her that he continued in weak health, and was a tiresome inmate. She said Mr. Heathcliff seemed to dislike him ever longer and worse, though he took some trouble to conceal it. He had an antipathy to the sound of his voice, and could not do at all with his sitting in the same room with him many minutes together.

There seldom passed much talk between them; Linton learnt his lessons, and spent his evenings in a small apartment they called the parlour;[2] or else lay in bed all day; for he was constantly getting coughs, and colds, and aches, and pains of some sort.

"And I never knew such a faint-hearted creature," added the woman; "nor one so careful of hisseln. He *will* go on, if I leave the window open, a bit late in the evening. Oh!—it's killing, a breath of night air! And he must have a fire in the middle of summer; and Joseph's 'bacca pipe is poison; and he must always have sweets and dainties, and always milk, milk for ever—heeding naught how the rest of us are pinched in winter—and there he'll sit, wrapped in his furred cloak in his chair by the fire, and some toast and water, or other slop on the hob to sip at; and if Hareton, for pity, comes to amuse him—Hareton is not bad-natured, though he's rough—they're sure to part, one swearing, and the other crying. I believe the master would relish Earnshaw's thrashing him to a mummy, if he were not his son: and, I'm certain, he would be fit to turn him out of doors, if he knew half the nursing he gives hisseln. But then, he won't go into danger of temptation; he never enters the parlour, and should Linton show those ways in the house where he is, he sends him up-stairs directly."

I divined, from this account, that utter lack of sympathy had rendered young Heathcliff selfish and disagreeable, if he were not so originally; and my interest in him, consequently, decayed; though still I was moved with a sense of grief at his lot, and a wish that he had been left with us.

Mr. Edgar encouraged me to gain information; he thought a great deal about him, I fancy, and would have run some risk to see him; and he told me once to ask the housekeeper whether he ever came into the village.

She said he had only been twice, on horseback, accompanying his father: and both times he pretended to be quite knocked up for three or four days afterwards.

That housekeeper left, if I recollect rightly, two years after he came; and another, whom I did not know, was her successor: she lives there still.

Time wore on at the Grange in its former pleasant way, till Miss Cathy reached sixteen.[3] On the anniversary of her birth we never

3 The year is 1800. Almost three years have passed since Linton's arrival at Thrushcross Grange.

4 Any game birds found on the moors, but primarily grouse.

manifested any signs of rejoicing, because it was also the anniversary of my late mistress's death. Her father invariably spent that day alone in the library; and walked, at dusk, as far as Gimmerton kirkyard, where he would frequently prolong his stay beyond midnight. Therefore Catherine was thrown on her own resources for amusement.

This twentieth of March was a beautiful spring day, and when her father had retired, my young lady came down dressed for going out, and said she had asked to have a ramble on the edge of the moors with me; and Mr. Linton had given her leave, if we went only a short distance, and were back within the hour.

"So make haste, Ellen!" she cried. "I know where I wish to go; where a colony of moor-game[4] are settled; I want to see whether they have made their nests yet."

"That must be a good distance up," I answered; "they don't breed on the edge of the moor."

"No, it's not," she said. "I've gone very near with papa."

I put on my bonnet and sallied out; thinking nothing more of the matter. She bounded before me, and returned to my side, and was off again like a young greyhound; and, at first, I found plenty of entertainment in listening to the larks singing far and near; and enjoying the sweet, warm sunshine; and watching her, my pet and my delight, with her golden ringlets flying loose behind, and her bright cheek, as soft and pure in its bloom as a wild rose, and her eyes radiant with cloudless pleasure. She was a happy creature, and an angel, in those days. It's a pity she could not be content.

"Well," said I, "where are your moor-game, Miss Cathy? We should be at them—the Grange park-fence is a great way off now."

"Oh, a little further—only a little further, Ellen," was her answer, continually. "Climb to that hillock, pass that bank, and by the time you reach the other side, I shall have raised the birds."

But there were so many hillocks and banks to climb and pass, that, at length, I began to be weary, and told her we must halt, and retrace our steps.

I shouted to her, as she had outstripped me, a long way; she either did not hear, or did not regard, for she still sprang on, and I was compelled to follow. Finally, she dived into a hollow; and before I came in sight of her again, she was two miles nearer Wuthering Heights than her own home; and I beheld a couple of persons arrest[5] her, one of whom I felt convinced was Mr. Heathcliff himself.

Cathy had been caught in the fact of plundering,[6] or, at least, hunting out the nests of the grouse.

The Heights were Heathcliff's land, and he was reproving the poacher.

"I've neither taken any nor found any," she said, as I toiled to them, expanding her hands in corroboration of the statement. "I didn't mean to take them; but papa told me there were quantities up here, and I wished to see the eggs."

Heathcliff glanced at me with an ill-meaning smile, expressing his acquaintance with the party, and, consequently, his malevolence towards it, and demanded who "papa" was?

"Mr. Linton of Thrushcross Grange," she replied. "I thought you did not know me, or you wouldn't have spoken in that way."

"You suppose papa is highly esteemed and respected then?" he said, sarcastically.

"And what are you?" inquired Catherine, gazing curiously on the speaker. "That man I've seen before. Is he your son?"

She pointed to Hareton, the other individual; who had gained nothing but increased bulk and strength by the addition of two years[7] to his age: he seemed as awkward and rough as ever.

"Miss Cathy," I interrupted, "it will be three hours instead of one that we are out, presently. We really must go back."

"No, that man is not my son," answered Heathcliff, pushing me aside. "But I have one, and you have seen him before too; and, though your nurse is in a hurry, I think both you and she would be the better for a little rest. Will you just turn this nab[8] of heath, and walk into my house? You'll get home earlier for the ease; and you shall receive a kind welcome."

5 Detain.

6 Did Brontë write "fact of plundering" or "act of plundering"? This may be a printer's error that she would have corrected in the lost proof-sheets.

7 Hareton is now twenty-one, almost six years older than Cathy.

8 The "jutting part of a hill or rock" *(OED)*.

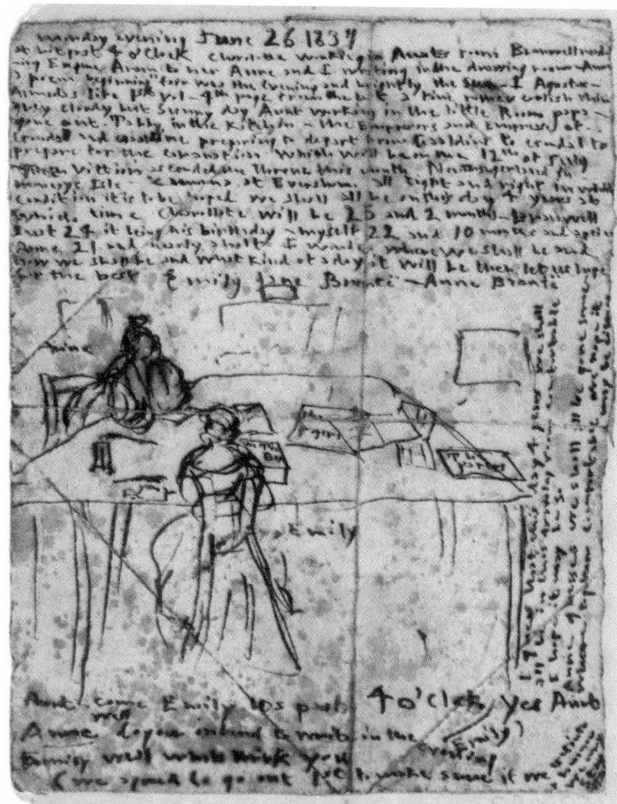

Emily's diary paper, bearing the date of Branwell's twentieth birthday, June 26, 1837. Anne and Emily each wrote and shared diary papers at intervals of approximately four years.The ink sketch shows Emily and Anne writing a diary paper, with Emily in the foreground surrounded by books and papers. The tin box in which the diary papers were kept can also be seen on the table. This diary paper records information about the daily life of the family and Anne's and Emily's writing plans. To the right of her sketch, Emily records her hopes and Anne's for the future:

> I guess that this day 4 years we shall all be in this drawing room comfortable I hope it may be so
> Anne guesses we shall all be gone somewhere together comfortable
> we hope it may be either

At the bottom of the page, she records a conversation that took place:

> AUNT. come Emily it's past 4 o'clock
> EMILY. Yes Aunt
> ANNE. well do you intend to write in the evening
> EMILY. well what think you
> (we agreed to go out 1st to make sure if we get into a humour we may stay [out?]

I whispered Catherine that she mustn't, on any account, accede to the proposal; it was entirely out of the question.

"Why?" she asked, aloud. "I'm tired of running, and the ground is dewy—I can't sit here. Let us go, Ellen! Besides, he says I have seen his son. He's mistaken, I think; but I guess where he lives, at the farm-house I visited in coming from Penistone Craggs. Don't you?"

"I do. Come, Nelly, hold your tongue—it will be a treat for her to look in on us. Hareton get forwards with the lass. You shall walk with me, Nelly."

"No, she's not going to any such place," I cried, struggling to release my arm which he had seized; but she was almost at the door-stones already, scampering round the brow[9] at full speed. Her appointed companion did not pretend to escort her; he shyed off by the road side, and vanished.

"Mr. Heathcliff, it's very wrong," I continued, "you know you mean no good; and there she'll see Linton, and all will be told, as soon as ever we return; and I shall have the blame."

"I want her to see Linton," he answered: "he's looking better these few days; it's not often he's fit to be seen. And we'll soon persuade her to keep the visit secret—where is the harm of it?"

"The harm of it is, that her father would hate me, if he found I suffered her to enter your house; and I am convinced you have a bad design in encouraging her to do so," I replied.

"My design is as honest as possible. I'll inform you of its whole scope," he said. "That the two cousins may fall in love, and get married. I'm acting generously to your master; his young chit[10] has no expectations, and should she second my wishes, she'll be provided for, at once, as joint successor with Linton."[11]

"If Linton died," I answered, "and his life is quite uncertain, Catherine would be the heir."

"No, she would not," he said. "There is no clause in the will to secure it so; his property would go to me; but, to prevent disputes, I desire their union, and am resolved to bring it about."[12]

"And I'm resolved she shall never approach your house with me again," I returned, as we reached the gate, where Miss Cathy waited our coming.

Heathcliff bid me be quiet; and preceding us up the path, hastened to open the door. My young lady gave him several looks, as if she could not exactly make up her mind what to think of him; but now he smiled when he met her eye, and softened his voice in addressing her, and I was foolish enough to imagine the memory of her mother might disarm him from desiring her injury.

Linton stood on the hearth. He had been out, walking in the fields; for his cap was on, and he was calling to Joseph to bring him dry shoes.

He had grown tall of his age, still wanting some months of sixteen. His features were pretty yet, and his eye and complexion brighter than I remembered them, though with merely temporary lustre borrowed from the salubrious air and genial sun.

"Now, who is that?" asked Mr. Heathcliff, turning to Cathy. "Can you tell?"

"Your son?" she said, having doubtfully surveyed, first one, and then the other.

"Yes, yes," answered he; "but is this the only time you have beheld him? Think! Ah! you have a short memory. Linton, don't you recall your cousin, that you used to tease us so, with wishing to see?"

"What, Linton!" cried Cathy, kindling into joyful surprise at the name. "Is that little Linton? He's taller than I am! Are you Linton?"

The youth stepped forward, and acknowledged himself: she kissed him fervently, and they gazed with wonder at the change time had wrought in the appearance of each.

Catherine had reached her full height; her figure was both plump and slender,[13] elastic as steel, and her whole aspect sparkling with health and spirits. Linton's looks and movements were very languid, and his form extremely slight; but there was a grace in his manner that mitigated these defects, and rendered him not unpleasing.

9 Slope or hilly ascent.

10 An animal's young offspring and a contemptuous term for a young child.

11 Heathcliff's claim that when Cathy marries Linton she will be "provided for" as "joint successor with Linton" does not hold water, as Heathcliff knows. The immediate consequence of Cathy's marrying Linton is that her moveable property, including any of it that she inherits from her father at the time of his death, becomes Linton's and can be willed to his father by him.

12 As Sanger points out, the inheritance of real (as opposed to moveable) property was no simple matter in the nineteenth century. Heathcliff may simply be putting his own construction on things when he tells Nelly that he will inherit Linton's property. His claim would not have been valid in 1800 when he makes it, but it would have been valid after the passage of the Inheritance Act of 1833. Before the Act, it was "considered unnatural that an inheritance should ascend directly" (C. P. Sanger, "The Structure of Wuthering Heights," in Eleanor McNees, ed., *The Brontë Sisters: Critical Assessments* [Mountfield: Helm Information, 1996], 2, pp. 77–78). If Brontë is relying on the Inheritance Act of 1833, this would be the second instance of an anachronism in the novel. The first is her reference to the Game Act of 1831, which is assumed to be in effect in two places in the novel. For the Game Act of 1831, see Vol. I, Chap. 10, note 2.

13 Cathy is slim but shapely. She is sixteen years old and about a half-year older than Linton.

After exchanging numerous marks of fondness with him, his cousin went to Mr. Heathcliff, who lingered by the door, dividing his attention between the objects inside and those that lay without, pretending, that is, to observe the latter, and really noting the former alone.

"And you are my uncle, then!" she cried, reaching up to salute him. "I thought I liked you, though you were cross, at first. Why don't you visit at the Grange with Linton? To live all these years such close neighbours, and never see us, is odd; what have you done so for?"

"I visited it once or twice too often before you were born," he answered. "There—damn it! If you have any kisses to spare, give them to Linton—they are thrown away on me."

"Naughty Ellen!" exclaimed Catherine, flying to attack me next with her lavish caresses. "Wicked Ellen!—to try to hinder me from entering. But I'll take this walk every morning in future—may I, uncle—and sometimes bring papa? Won't you be glad to see us?"

"Of course!" replied the uncle, with a hardly surpressed grimace, resulting from his deep aversion to both the proposed visiters. "But stay," he continued, turning towards the young lady. "Now I think of it, I'd better tell you. Mr. Linton has a prejudice against me; we quarrelled at one time of our lives, with unchristian ferocity; and, if you mention coming here to him, he'll put a veto on your visits altogether. Therefore, you must not mention it, unless you be careless of seeing your cousin hereafter—you may come, if you will, but you must not mention it."

"Why did you quarrel?" asked Catherine, considerably crestfallen.

"He thought me too poor to wed his sister," answered Heathcliff, "and was grieved that I got her—his pride was hurt, and he'll never forgive it."

"That's wrong!" said the young lady: "sometime, I'll tell him so; but Linton and I have no share in your quarrel. I'll not come here, then; he shall come to the Grange."

FACSIMILE OF TWO PAGES OF EMILY BRONTË'S DIARY.

Emily's diary paper, bearing the date of her twenty-seventh birthday, Thursday, July 30, 1845. Her sketch at the bottom shows her writing in her tiny bedroom, previously the room the Brontë children called their "study." Her dog Keeper lies at her feet, while Anne's dog Flossy and a cat occupy the bed.

"It will be too far for me," murmured her cousin, "to walk four miles would kill me. No, come here, Miss Catherine, now and then, not every morning, but once or twice a week."

The father launched towards his son a glance of bitter contempt.

"I am afraid, Nelly, I shall lose my labour," he muttered to me. "Miss Catherine, as the ninny calls her, will discover his value, and send him to the devil. Now, if it had been Hareton—do you know that, twenty times a day, I covet Hareton, with all his degradation? I'd have loved the lad had he been some one else. But I think he's safe from *her* love. I'll pit him against that paltry creature, unless it bestir itself briskly. We calculate it will scarcely last till it is eighteen. Oh, confound the vapid thing. He's absorbed in drying his feet, and never looks at her—Linton!"

"Yes, father," answered the boy.

"Have you nothing to show your cousin, any where about; not even a rabbit, or a weasel's nest? Take her into the garden, before you change your shoes; and into the stable to see your horse."

"Wouldn't you rather sit here?" asked Linton, addressing Cathy in a tone which expressed reluctance to move again.

"I don't know," she replied, casting a longing look to the door, and evidently eager to be active.

He kept his seat, and shrank closer to the fire.

Heathcliff rose, and went into the kitchen, and from thence to the yard, calling out for Hareton.

Hareton responded, and presently the two re-entered. The young man had been washing himself, as was visible by the glow on his cheeks, and his wetted hair.

"Oh, I'll ask *you,* uncle;" cried Miss Cathy, recollecting the housekeeper's assertion. "That's not my cousin, is he?"

"Yes," he replied, "your mother's nephew. Don't you like him?"

Catherine looked queer.

"Is he not a handsome lad?" he continued.

The uncivil little thing stood on tiptoe, and whispered a sentence in Heathcliff's ear.

He laughed; Hareton darkened; I perceived he was very sensitive to suspected slights, and had obviously a dim notion of his inferiority. But his master or guardian chased the frown by exclaiming—

"You'll be the favourite among us, Hareton! She says you are a—What was it? Well, something very flattering—Here!—you go with her round the farm. And behave like a gentleman, mind! Don't use any bad words; and don't stare, when the young lady is not looking at you, and be ready to hide your face when she is; and, when you speak, say your words slowly, and keep your hands out of your pockets. Be off, and entertain her as nicely as you can."

He watched the couple walking past the window. Earnshaw had his countenance completely averted from his companion. He seemed studying the familiar landscape with a stranger's and an artist's interest.

Catherine took a sly look at him, expressing small admiration. She then turned her attention to seeking out objects of amusement for herself, and tripped merrily on, lilting[14] a tune to supply the lack of conversation.

"I've tied his tongue," observed Heathcliff. "He'll not venture a single syllable, all the time! Nelly, you recollect me at his age—nay, some years younger—Did I ever look so stupid, so 'gaumless,'[15] as Joseph calls it."

"Worse," I replied, "because more sullen with it."

"I've a pleasure in him!" he continued reflecting aloud. "He has satisfied my expectations—If he were a born fool I should not enjoy it half so much—But he's no fool; and I can sympathise with all his feelings, having felt them myself—I know what he suffers now, for instance, exactly—it is merely a beginning of what he shall suffer, though. And he'll never be able to emerge from his bathos[16] of coarseness, and ignorance. I've got him faster than his scoundrel of a father secured me, and lower; for he takes a pride in his brutishness. I've taught him to scorn everything extra-animal[17] as silly and weak—Don't you think Hindley would be proud of his son, if he could see him? almost as proud as I am of mine—But there's this difference, one is gold put to the use of paving stones; and the other is tin polished to ape a service of silver—*Mine* has nothing valuable about it; yet I shall have the merit of making it go as far as such poor stuff can go. *His* had first-rate qualities, and they are lost—rendered worse than unavailing—I have nothing to regret; he would have more than any, but I, are aware of—And the best of

14 Cheerfully singing.

15 Gormless; without sense or discernment *(OED)*.

16 Depth.

17 Heathcliff has taught Hareton to despise feelings and behaviors (such as pity and manners) that humans don't share with animals.

it is, Hareton is damnably fond of me! You'll own that I've outmatched Hindley there—If the dead villain could rise from his grave to abuse me for his offspring's wrongs, I should have the fun of seeing the said offspring fight him back again, indignant that he should dare to rail at the one friend he has in the world!"

Heathcliff chuckled a fiendish laugh at the idea; I made no reply, because I saw that he expected none.

Meantime, our young companion, who sat too removed from us to hear what was said, began to evince symptoms of uneasiness: probably repenting that he had denied himself the treat of Catherine's society, for fear of a little fatigue.

His father remarked the restless glances wandering to the window, and the hand irresolutely extended towards his cap.

"Get up, you idle boy!" he exclaimed with assumed heartiness. "Away after them—they are just at the corner, by the stand of hives."[18]

Linton gathered his energies, and left the hearth. The lattice was open and, as he stepped out, I heard Cathy inquiring of her unsociable attendant, what was that inscription over the door?

Hareton stared up, and scratched his head like a true clown.[19]

"It's some damnable writing," he answered. "I cannot read it."

"Can't read it?" cried Catherine, "I can read it . . . It's English . . . but I want to know why it is there."

Linton giggled—the first appearance of mirth he had exhibited.

"He does not know his letters," he said to his cousin. "Could you believe in the existence of such a colossal dunce?"

"Is he all as he should be?" asked Miss Cathy seriously, "or is he simple[20] . . . not right? I've questioned him twice now, and each time he looked so stupid, I think he does not understand me; I can hardly understand *him,* I'm sure!"

Linton repeated his laugh, and glanced at Hareton tauntingly, who certainly, did not seem quite clear of comprehension at that moment.

18 Beehives.

19 Ironically, Hareton's inability to read even his own name inscribed over the entry means that he lacks this confirmation of his own position as the direct descendant of the man who built the house.

20 Lacking learning or intelligence, perhaps even mentally deficient.

"There's nothing the matter but laziness, is there, Earnshaw?" he said. "My cousin fancies you are an idiot . . . There you experience the consequence of scorning 'book-larning,' as you would say . . . Have you noticed, Catherine, his frightful Yorkshire pronunciation?"

"Why, where the devil is the use on't?" growled Hareton, more ready in answering his daily companion. He was about to enlarge further, but the two youngsters broke into a noisy fit of merriment, my giddy Miss being delighted to discover that she might turn his strange talk to matter of amusement.

"Where is the use of the devil in that sentence?" tittered Linton. "Papa told you not to say any bad words, and you can't open your mouth without one . . . Do try to behave like a gentleman, now do!"

"If thou wern't more a lass than a lad, I'd fell thee this minute, I would; pitiful lath of a crater!"[21] retorted the angry boor retreating, while his face burnt with mingled rage, and mortification; for he was conscious of being insulted, and embarrassed how to resent it.

Mr. Heathcliff having overheard the conversation, as well as I, smiled when he saw him go, but immediately afterwards, cast a look of singular aversion on the flippant pair, who remained chattering in the door-way. The boy finding animation enough while discussing Hareton's faults, and deficiencies, and relating anecdotes of his goings on; and the girl relishing his pert and spiteful sayings, without considering the ill-nature they evinced: but I began to dislike, more than to compassionate, Linton, and to excuse his father, in some measure, for holding him cheap.

We staid till afternoon: I could not tear Miss Cathy away before: but happily, my master had not quitted his apartment, and remained ignorant of our prolonged absence.

As we walked home, I would fain have enlightened my charge on the characters of the people we had quitted; but she got it into her head that I was prejudiced against them.

21 "Pitiful, fragile creature."

"Aha!" she cried, "you take papa's side, Ellen—you are partial . . . I know, or else you wouldn't have cheated me so many years, into the notion that Linton lived a long way from here. I'm really extremely angry, only I'm so pleased, I can't show it! But you must hold your tongue about my uncle . . . he's my uncle, remember, and I'll scold papa for quarrelling with him."

And so she ran on, till I dropped endeavouring to convince her of her mistake.

She did not mention the visit that night, because she did not see Mr. Linton. Next day it all came out, sadly to my chagrin; and still I was not altogether sorry: I thought the burden of directing and warning would be more efficiently borne by him than me, but he was too timid in giving satisfactory reasons for his wish that she would shun connection with the household of the Heights, and Catherine liked good reasons for every restraint that harassed her petted will.

"Papa!" she exclaimed after the morning's salutations, "guess whom I saw yesterday, in my walk on the moors . . . Ah, papa, you started! you've not done right, have you, now? I saw—But listen, and you shall hear how I found you out, and Ellen, who is in league with you, and yet pretended to pity me so, when I kept hoping, and was always disappointed about Linton's coming back!"

She gave a faithful account of her excursion and its consequences; and my master, though he cast more than one reproachful look at me, said nothing, till she had concluded. Then he drew her to him, and asked if she knew why he had concealed Linton's near neighbourhood from her? Could she think it was to deny her a pleasure that she might harmlessly enjoy?

"It was because you disliked Mr. Heathcliff," she answered.

"Then you believe I care more for my own feelings than yours, Cathy?" he said. "No, it was not because I disliked Mr. Heathcliff; but because Mr. Heathcliff dislikes me; and is a most diabolical man, delighting to wrong and ruin those he hates, if they give him the slightest opportunity. I knew that you could not keep up an acquaintance with your cousin, without being brought into contact with him; and I knew he would detest you, on my account; so, for your own good, and nothing else, I took precautions that you should not see Linton again—I meant to explain this, some time, as you grew older, and I'm sorry I delayed it!"

"But Mr. Heathcliff was quite cordial, papa," observed Catherine, not at all convinced; "and *he* didn't object to our seeing each other: he said I might come to his house, when I pleased, only I must not tell you, because you had quarrelled with him, and would not forgive him for marrying aunt Isabella. And you won't—*you* are the one to be blamed—he is willing to let *us* be friends, at least, Linton and I—and you are not."

My master, perceiving that she would not take his word for her uncle-in-law's evil disposition, gave a hasty sketch of his conduct to Isabella, and the manner in which Wuthering Heights became his property. He could not bear to discourse long upon the topic, for though he spoke little of it, he still felt the same horror and detestation of his ancient enemy that had occupied his heart ever since Mrs. Linton's death. "She might have been living yet, if it had not been for him!" was his constant bitter reflection; and, in his eyes, Heathcliff seemed a murderer.

Miss Cathy, conversant with no bad deeds except her own slight acts of disobedience, injustice, and passion rising from hot temper and thoughtlessness, and repented of on the day they were committed, was amazed at the blackness of spirit that could brood on and cover[22] revenge for years; and deliberately prosecute its plans, without a visitation of remorse. She appeared so deeply impressed and shocked at this new view of human nature—excluded from all her studies and all her ideas till now—that Mr. Edgar deemed it unnecessary to pursue the subject. He merely added,

"You will know hereafter, darling, why I wish you to avoid his house and family—now, return to your old employments and amusements, and think no more about them!"

Catherine kissed her father, and sat down quietly to her lessons for a couple of hours, according to custom: then she accompanied him into the grounds, and the whole day passed as usual: but in

22 Hide.

the evening, when she had retired to her room, and I went to help her to undress, I found her crying, on her knees by the bedside.

"Oh, fie, silly child!" I exclaimed. "If you had any real griefs, you'd be ashamed to waste a tear on this little contrariety. You never had one shadow of substantial sorrow, Miss Catherine. Suppose, for a minute, that master and I were dead, and you were by yourself in the world—how would you feel, then? Compare the present occasion with such an affliction as that, and be thankful for the friends you have, instead of coveting more."

"I'm not crying for myself, Ellen," she answered, "it's for him—He expected to see me again, to-morrow, and there, he'll be so disappointed—and he'll wait for me, and I shan't come!"

"Nonsense!" said I, "do you imagine he has thought as much of you, as you have of him? Hasn't he Hareton for a companion? Not one in a hundred would weep at losing a relation they had just seen twice, for two afternoons—Linton will conjecture how it is, and trouble himself no further about you."

"But may I not write a note to tell him why I cannot come?" she asked rising to her feet. "And just send those books I promised to lend him—his books are not as nice as mine, and he wanted to have them extremely, when I told him how interesting they were—May I not, Ellen?"

"No, indeed, no indeed!" replied I with decision. "Then he would write to you, and there'd never be an end of it—No, Miss Catherine, the acquaintance must be dropped entirely—so papa expects, and I shall see that it is done!"

"But how can one little note—" she recommenced, putting on an imploring countenance.

"Silence!" I interrupted. "We'll not begin with your little notes—Get into bed!"

She threw at me a very naughty look, so naughty that I would not kiss her good-night at first: I covered her up, and shut her door, in great displeasure—but, repenting half-way, I returned softly, and lo!—there was Miss, standing at the table with a bit of blank paper before her, and a pencil in her hand, which she guiltily slipped out of sight, on my re-entrance.

"You'll get nobody to take that, Catherine," I said, "if you write it; and at present I shall put out your candle."

I set the extinguisher on the flame, receiving as I did so, a slap on my hand, and a petulant "cross thing!" I then quitted her again, and she drew the bolt in one of her worst, most peevish humours.

The letter was finished and forwarded to its destination by a milk-fetcher who came from the village, but that I didn't learn till some time afterwards. Weeks passed on, and Cathy recovered her temper, though she grew wondrous fond of stealing off to corners by herself, and often, if I came near her suddenly while reading, she would start, and bend over the book, evidently desirous to hide it; and I detected edges of loose paper sticking out beyond the leaves.

She also got a trick of coming down early in the morning, and lingering about the kitchen, as if she were expecting the arrival of something; and she had a small drawer in a cabinet in the library which she would trifle over for hours, and whose key she took special care to remove when she left it.

One day, as she inspected this drawer, I observed that the playthings and trinkets, which recently formed its contents, were transmuted into bits of folded paper.

My curiosity and suspicions were roused; I determined to take a peep at her mysterious treasures; so, at night, as soon as she and my master were safe up-stairs, I searched and readily found among my house keys, one that would fit the lock. Having opened,[23] I emptied the whole contents into my apron, and took them with me to examine at leisure in my own chamber.

Though I could not but suspect, I was still surprised to discover, that they were a mass of correspondence, daily almost, it must have been, from Linton Heathcliff, answers to documents forwarded by her. The earlier dated were embarrassed and short;

23 The 1847 edition omits the direct object, "the drawer."

24 Nelly is separating the threads that are part of the ornamental borders of the window curtains.

gradually, however, they expanded into copious love letters, foolish as the age of the writer rendered natural, yet with touches, here and there, which I thought were borrowed from a more experienced source.

Some of them struck me as singularly odd compounds of ardour and flatness; commencing in strong feeling, and concluding in the affected, wordy way that a school-boy might use to a fancied, incorporeal sweetheart.

Whether they satisfied Cathy, I don't know, but they appeared very worthless trash to me.

After turning over as many as I thought proper, I tied them in a handkerchief, and set them aside, re-locking the vacant drawer.

Following her habit, my young lady descended early, and visited the kitchen: I watched her go to the door, on the arrival of a certain little boy; and, while the dairy maid filled his can, she tucked something into his jacket pocket, and plucked something out.

I went round by the garden, and laid wait for the messenger, who fought valorously to defend his trust, and we spilt the milk between us; but I succeeded in abstracting the epistle; and threatening serious consequences if he did not look sharp home, I remained under the wall, and perused Miss Cathy's affectionate composition. It was more simple and more eloquent than her cousin's, very pretty and very silly. I shook my head, and went meditating into the house.

The day being wet, she could not divert herself with rambling about the park; so, at the conclusion of her morning studies, she resorted to the solace of the drawer. Her father sat reading at the table; and I, on purpose, had sought a bit of work in some unripped fringes[24] of the window curtain, keeping my eye steadily fixed on her proceedings.

Never did any bird flying back to a plundered nest which it had left brim-full of chirping young ones, express more complete despair in its anguished cries and flutterings, than she by her single "Oh!" and the change that transfigured her late happy countenance. Mr. Linton looked up.

"What is the matter, love? Have you hurt yourself?" he said.

His tone and look, assured her *he* had not been the discoverer of the hoard.

"No papa—" she gasped. "Ellen! Ellen! come up-stairs—I'm sick!"

I obeyed her summons, and accompanied her out.

"Oh, Ellen! you have got them," she commenced immediately, dropping on her knees, when we were enclosed alone. "O, give them to me, and I'll never never do so again! Don't tell papa—You have not told papa, Ellen, say you have not! I've been exceedingly naughty, but I won't do it any more!"

With a grave severity in my manner, I bid her stand up.

"So," I exclaimed, "Miss Catherine, you are tolerably far on, it seems—you may well be ashamed of them! A fine bundle of trash you study in your leisure hours, to be sure—Why it's good enough to be printed! And what do you suppose the master will think, when I display it before him? I haven't shown it yet, but you needn't imagine I shall keep your ridiculous secrets—For shame! And you must have led the way in writing such absurdities; he would not have thought of beginning, I'm certain."

"I didn't! I didn't!" sobbed Cathy, fit to break her heart. "I didn't once think of loving him till—"

"Loving!" cried I, as scornfully as I could utter the word. "*Loving!* Did anybody ever hear the like! I might just as well talk of loving the miller who comes once a year to buy our corn. Pretty loving, indeed, and both times together you have seen Linton hardly four hours, in your life! Now here is the babyish trash. I'm going with it to the library; and we'll see what your father says to such *loving.*"

She sprang at her precious epistles, but I held them above my head; and then she poured out further frantic entreaties that I would burn them—do anything rather than show them. And being really fully as inclined to laugh as scold, for I esteemed it all girlish vanity, I at length relented in a measure, and asked, "If I consent to burn them, will you promise faithfully neither to send, nor receive, a letter again, nor a book, for I perceive you have sent him books, nor locks of hair, nor rings, nor playthings?"

"We don't send playthings!" cried Catherine, her pride overcoming her shame.

"Nor anything at all, then, my lady!" I said. "Unless you will, here I go."

"I promise, Ellen!" she cried catching my dress. "Oh put them in the fire, do, do!"

But when I proceeded to open a place with the poker, the sacrifice was too painful to be borne—She earnestly supplicated that I would spare her one or two.

"One or two, Ellen, to keep for Linton's sake!"

I unknotted the handkerchief, and commenced dropping them in from an angle, and the flame curled up the chimney.

"I will have one, you cruel wretch!" she screamed, darting her hand into the fire, and drawing forth some half consumed fragments, at the expense of her fingers.

"Very well—and I will have some to exhibit to papa!" I answered shaking back the rest into the bundle, and turning anew to the door.

She emptied her blackened pieces into the flames, and motioned me to finish the immolation. It was done; I stirred up the ashes, and interred them under a shovel full of coals; and she mutely, and with a sense of intense injury, retired to her private apartment. I descended to tell my master that the young lady's qualm of sickness was almost gone, but I judged it best for her to lie down a while.

She wouldn't dine; but she re-appeared at tea, pale and red about the eyes, and marvellously subdued in outward aspect.

Next morning I answered the letter by a slip of paper inscribed, "Master Heathcliff is requested to send no more notes to Miss Linton as she will not receive them." And, thenceforth, the little boy came with vacant pockets.

CHAPTER 8

Summer drew to an end, and early Autumn—it was past Michaelmas,[1] but the harvest was late that year, and a few of our fields were still uncleared.

Mr. Linton and his daughter would frequently walk out among the reapers: at the carrying of the last sheaves, they stayed till dusk, and the evening happening to be chill and damp, my master caught a bad cold that, settling obstinately on his lungs, confined him indoors throughout the whole of the winter, nearly without intermission.

Poor Cathy, frightened from her little romance, had been considerably sadder and duller since its abandonment: and her father insisted on her reading less, and taking more exercise. She had his companionship no longer; I esteemed it a duty to supply its lack, as much as possible, with mine; an inefficient substitute, for I could only spare two or three hours, from my numerous diurnal occupations, to follow her footsteps, and then, my society was obviously less desirable than his.

On an afternoon in October, or the beginning of November, a fresh watery afternoon, when the turf and paths were rustling with moist, withered leaves, and the cold, blue sky was half hidden by clouds, dark grey streamers, rapidly mounting from the west and boding abundant rain; I requested my young lady to forego her

1 September 29, 1800, a little more than a year before the date at the beginning of the novel.

2 Inclined to.

3 Continuance or grip.

4 On December 18, 1838, Brontë composed a poem about the bluebell, "the sweetest flower/ That waves in summer air." In the poem (published in 1850 under Charlotte's title, "The Bluebell") and in *Wuthering Heights,* Brontë has in mind the bluebell of Scotland and northern England, a species of Campanula that grows in summer and fall on open downs and hills. In her poem, its bell-shaped flowers, poised on "slight and stately" stems, "have the mightiest power/ To soothe my spirit's care."

ramble because I was certain of showers. She refused; and I unwillingly donned a cloak, and took my umbrella to accompany her on a stroll to the bottom of the park, a formal walk which she generally affected[2] if low-spirited; and that she invariably was when Mr. Edgar had been worse than ordinary, a thing never known from his confession, but guessed both by her and me, from his increased silence and the melancholy of his countenance.

She went sadly on; there was no running or bounding now, though the chill wind might well have tempted her to a race. And often, from the side of my eye, I could detect her raising a hand, and brushing something off her cheek.

I gazed round for a means of diverting her thoughts. On one side of the road rose a high, rough bank, where hazels and stunted oaks, with their roots half exposed, held uncertain tenour[3]: the soil was too loose for the latter; and strong winds had blown some nearly horizontal. In summer, Miss Catherine delighted to climb along these trunks, and sit in the branches, swinging twenty feet above the ground; and I, pleased with her agility and her light, childish heart, still considered it proper to scold every time I caught her at such an elevation; but so that she knew there was no necessity for descending. From dinner to tea she would lie in her breeze-rocked cradle, doing nothing except singing old songs—my nursery lore—to herself, or watching the birds, joint tenants, feed and entice their young ones to fly, or nestling with closed lids, half thinking, half dreaming, happier than words can express.

"Look, Miss!" I exclaimed, pointing to a nook under the roots of one twisted tree. "Winter is not here yet. There's a little flower, up yonder, the last bud from the multitude of blue-bells[4] that clouded those turf steps in July with a lilac mist. Will you clamber up, and pluck it to show to papa?"

Cathy stared a long time at the lonely blossom trembling in its earthy shelter, and replied, at length—

"No, I'll not touch it—but it looks melancholy, does it not, Ellen?"

"Yes," I observed, "about as starved[5] and sackless[6] as you—your cheeks are bloodless; let us take hold of hands and run. You're so low, I dare say I shall keep up with you."

"No," she repeated, and continued sauntering on, pausing, at intervals, to muse over a bit of moss, or a tuft of blanched grass, or a fungus spreading its bright orange among the heaps of brown foliage; and, ever and anon, her hand was lifted to her averted face.

"Catherine, why are you crying, love?" I asked, approaching and putting my arm over her shoulder. "You mustn't cry because papa has a cold; be thankful it is nothing worse."

She now put no further restraint on her tears; her breath was stifled by sobs.

"Oh, it *will* be something worse," she said. "And what shall I do when papa and you leave me, and I am by myself? I can't forget your words, Ellen, they are always in my ear. How life will be changed, how dreary the world will be, when papa and you are dead."

"None can tell whether you won't die before us," I replied. "It's wrong to anticipate evil—we'll hope there are years and years to come before any of us go—master is young, and I am strong, and hardly forty-five. My mother lived till eighty, a canty[7] dame to the last. And suppose Mr. Linton were spared till he saw sixty, that would be more years than you have counted, Miss. And would it not be foolish to mourn a calamity above twenty years beforehand?"

"But Aunt Isabella was younger than papa," she remarked, gazing up with timid hope to seek further consolation.

"Aunt Isabella had not you and me to nurse her," I replied. "She wasn't as happy as master; she hadn't as much to live for. All you need do is to wait well on your father, and cheer him by letting him see you cheerful; and avoid giving him anxiety on any subject—mind that, Cathy! I'll not disguise, but you might kill him if you were wild and reckless, and cherished a foolish, fanciful affection for the son of a person who would be glad to have him in his

The true bluebell or Campanula, a colored engraving by Victor from *Choix des Plus Belles Fleurs* after Pierre Joseph Redouté (1759–1840).

5 Frozen.

6 Dispirited.

7 Cheerful.

8 The hips are the fruit of the wild rose trees.

grave—and allowed him to discover that you fretted over the separation he has judged it expedient to make."

"I fret about nothing on earth except papa's illness," answered my companion. "I care for nothing in comparison with papa. And I'll never—never—oh, never, while I have my senses—do an act or say a word to vex him. I love him better than myself, Ellen; and I know it by this—I pray every night that I may live after him; because I would rather be miserable than that he should be—that proves I love him better than myself."

"Good words," I replied. "But deeds must prove it also; and after he is well, remember you don't forget resolutions formed in the hour of fear."

As we talked, we neared a door that opened on the road: and my young lady, lightening into sunshine again, climbed up, and seated herself on the top of the wall, reaching over to gather some hips[8] that bloomed scarlet on the summit branches of the wild rose trees, shadowing the highway side; the lower fruit had disappeared, but only birds could touch the upper, except from Cathy's present station.

In stretching to pull them, her hat fell off; and as the door was locked, she proposed scrambling down to recover it. I bid her be cautious lest she got a fall, and she nimbly disappeared.

But the return was no such easy matter; the stones were smooth and neatly cemented, and the rosebushes and blackberry stragglers could yield no assistance in re-ascending. I, like a fool, didn't recollect that till I heard her laughing, and exclaiming—

"Ellen! you'll have to fetch the key, or else I must run round to the porter's lodge. I can't scale the ramparts on this side!"

"Stay where you are," I answered, "I have my bundle of keys in my pocket; perhaps I may manage to open it; if not, I'll go."

Catherine amused herself with dancing to and fro before the door, while I tried all the large keys in succession. I had applied the last, and found that none would do; so, repeating my desire that she would remain there, I was about to hurry home as fast as I could, when an approaching sound arrested me. It was the trot of a horse; Cathy's dance stopped; and in a minute the horse stopped also.

"Who is that?" I whispered.

"Ellen, I wish you could open the door," whispered back my companion, anxiously.

"Ho, Miss Linton!" cried a deep voice (the rider's). "I'm glad to meet you. Don't be in haste to enter, for I have an explanation to ask and obtain."

"I shan't speak to you, Mr. Heathcliff!" answered Catherine. "Papa says you are a wicked man, and you hate both him and me; and Ellen says the same."

"That is nothing to the purpose," said Heathcliff. (He it was.) "I don't hate my son, I suppose, and it is concerning him that I demand your attention. Yes! you have cause to blush. Two or three months since, were you not in the habit of writing to Linton? Making love in play, eh? You deserved, both of you, flogging for that! You especially, the elder, and less sensitive, as it turns out. I've got your letters, and if you give me any pertness, I'll send them to your father. I presume you grew weary of the amusement, and dropped it, didn't you? Well, you dropped Linton with it, into a Slough of Despond.[9] He was in earnest—in love—really. As true as I live, he's dying for you—breaking his heart at your fickleness, not figuratively, but actually. Though Hareton has made him a standing jest for six weeks, and I have used more serious measures, and attempted to frighten him out of his idiocy, he gets worse daily, and he'll be under the sod[10] before summer, unless you restore him!"

"How can you lie so glaringly to the poor child!" I called from the inside. "Pray ride on! How can you deliberately get up such paltry falsehoods? Miss Cathy, I'll knock the lock off with a stone; you won't believe that vile nonsense. You can feel in yourself, it is impossible that a person should die for love of a stranger."

"I was not aware there were eaves-droppers," muttered the detected villain. "Worthy Mrs. Dean, I like you, but I don't like your

9 A deep, miry bog in John Bunyan's *The Pilgrim's Progress* into which the hero, Christian, sinks when he becomes aware of the weight of his sins. *Pilgrim's Progress* was very widely read from the time of its first publication in 1678, and Charlotte's early writings and her novels allude to it. The Brontës owned an edition of 1743 (Christine Alexander and Margaret Smith, eds., *The Oxford Companion to the Brontës* [Oxford: Oxford Univ. Press, 2003], p. 111).

10 Dead and buried.

11 Stories of goblins in the shape of bears invented by nurses to frighten their charges.

12 Directed our course.

double dealing," he added aloud. "How could *you* lie so glaringly, as to affirm I hated the 'poor child'? And invent bugbear stories[11] to terrify her from my door-stones? Catherine Linton (the very name warms me), my bonny lass, I shall be from home all this week: go and see if I have not spoken truth; do, there's a darling! Just imagine your father in my place, and Linton in yours; then think how you would value your careless lover, if he refused to stir a step to comfort you, when your father himself entreated him; and don't, from pure stupidity, fall into the same error. I swear, on my salvation, he's going to his grave, and none but you can save him!"

The lock gave way, and I issued out.

"I swear Linton is dying," repeated Heathcliff, looking hard at me. "And grief and disappointment are hastening his death. Nelly, if you won't let her go, you can walk over yourself. But I shall not return till this time next week; and I think your master himself would scarcely object to her visiting her cousin!"

"Come in," said I, taking Cathy by the arm and half forcing her to re-enter, for she lingered, viewing, with troubled eyes, the features of the speaker, too stern to express his inward deceit.

He pushed his horse close, and, bending down, observed—

"Miss Catherine, I'll own to you that I have little patience with Linton—and Hareton and Joseph have less. I'll own that he's with a harsh set. He pines for kindness, as well as love; and a kind word from you would be his best medicine. Don't mind Mrs. Dean's cruel cautions, but be generous, and contrive to see him. He dreams of you day and night, and cannot be persuaded that you don't hate him, since you neither write nor call."

I closed the door, and rolled a stone to assist the loosened lock in holding it; and spreading my umbrella, I drew my charge underneath, for the rain began to drive through the moaning branches of the trees, and warned us to avoid delay.

Our hurry prevented any comment on the encounter with Heathcliff, as we stretched[12] towards home; but I divined instinctively that Catherine's heart was clouded now in double darkness.

Her features were so sad, they did not seem hers: she evidently regarded what she had heard as every syllable true.

The master had retired to rest before we came in. Cathy stole to his room to inquire how he was; he had fallen asleep. She returned, and asked me to sit with her in the library. We took our tea together; and afterwards she lay down on the rug, and told me not to talk for she was weary.

I got a book, and pretended to read. As soon as she supposed me absorbed in my occupation, she recommenced her silent weeping: it appeared, at present, her favourite diversion. I suffered her to enjoy it a while; then, I expostulated, deriding and ridiculing all Mr. Heathcliff's assertions about his son, as if I were certain she would coincide. Alas! I hadn't skill to counteract the effect his account had produced; it was just what he intended.

"You may be right, Ellen," she answered; "but I shall never feel at ease till I know—and I must tell Linton it is not my fault that I don't write; and convince him that I shall not change."

What use were anger and protestations against her silly credulity? We parted that night hostile—but next day beheld me on the road to Wuthering Heights, by the side of my wilful young mistress's pony. I couldn't bear to witness her sorrow, to see her pale, dejected countenance, and heavy eyes; and I yielded in the faint hope that Linton himself might prove by his reception of us, how little of the tale was founded on fact.

1 In Greek mythology, the abode of the blessed after death, originally reserved for mortals related to the gods and other heroes. Nelly's classical allusion reminds us that Joseph enjoys his creature comforts at the Heights, despite his carping about the torments of hell and the dangers of worldly pleasures.

2 "No ! . . . No! you should go back where you came from."

CHAPTER 9

The rainy night had ushered in a misty morning—half frost, half drizzle—and temporary brooks crossed our path, gurgling from the uplands. My feet were thoroughly wetted; I was cross and low, exactly the humour suited for making the most of these disagreeable things.

We entered the farm-house by the kitchen way to ascertain whether Mr. Heathcliff were really absent; because I put slight faith in his own affirmation.

Joseph seemed sitting in a sort of elysium,[1] alone beside a roaring fire; a quart of ale on the table near him, bristling with large pieces of toasted oat cake; and his black, short pipe in his mouth.

Catherine ran to the hearth to warm herself. I asked if the master were in?

My question remained so long unanswered, that I thought the old man had grown deaf, and repeated it louder.

"Na—ay!" he snarled, or rather screamed through his nose. "Na—ay! yah muh goa back whear yah coom frough."[2]

"Joseph," cried a peevish voice, simultaneously with me, from the inner room. "How often am I to call you? There are only a few red ashes now. Joseph! come this moment."

Vigorous puffs and a resolute stare into the grate declared he had no ear for this appeal. The housekeeper and Hareton were invisible; one gone on an errand, and the other at his work, probably. We knew Linton's tones and entered.

"Oh, I hope you'll die in a garret! starved to death," said the boy, mistaking our approach for that of his negligent attendant.

He stopped, on observing his error; his cousin flew to him.

"Is that you, Miss Linton?" he said, raising his head from the arm of the great chair, in which he reclined. "No—don't kiss me. It takes my breath—dear me! Papa said you would call," continued he, after recovering a little from Catherine's embrace; while she stood by looking very contrite. "Will you shut the door, if you please? You left it open—and those—those *detestable* creatures won't bring coals to the fire. It's so cold!"

I stirred up the cinders, and fetched a scuttle full myself. The invalid complained of being covered with ashes; but he had a tiresome cough, and looked feverish and ill, so I did not rebuke his temper.

"Well, Linton," murmured Catherine, when his corrugated brow relaxed. "Are you glad to see me? Can I do you any good?"

"Why didn't you come before?" he said. "You should have come, instead of writing. It tired me dreadfully, writing those long letters. I'd far rather have talked to you. Now, I can neither bear to talk, nor anything else. I wonder where Zillah is! Will you (looking at me) step into the kitchen and see?"

I had received no thanks for my other service;[3] and being unwilling to run to and fro at his behest, I replied—

"Nobody is out there but Joseph."

"I want to drink," he exclaimed, fretfully, turning away. "Zillah is constantly gadding off to Gimmerton since papa went. It's miserable! And I'm obliged to come down here—they resolved never to hear me up-stairs."[4]

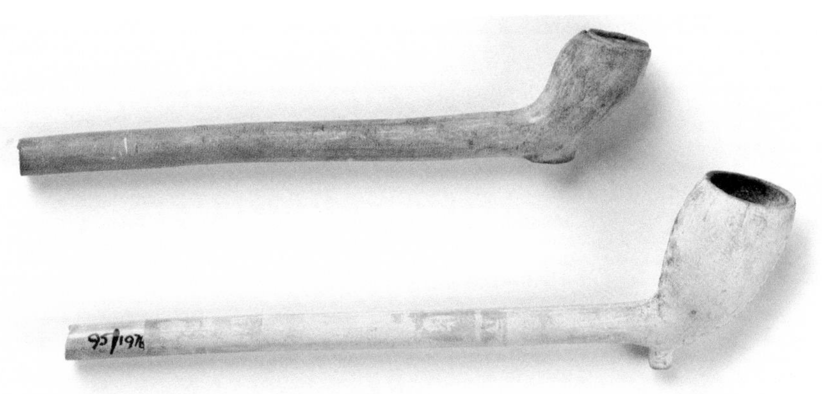

Two eighteenth-century clay pipes found in Birmingham. The novel describes Joseph's pipe as black and short.

3 Putting coals on the fire.

4 In the parlor.

5 There was no "shooting season" before the passage of the Game Act in 1831, and Brontë's implicit reference to the Act is anachronistic. It is now late October or early November (Chapter 8); after 1831, the shooting season would have begun on August 12.

"Is your father attentive to you, Master Heathcliff?" I asked, perceiving Catherine to be checked in her friendly advances.

"Attentive? He makes *them* a little more attentive, at least," he cried. "The wretches! Do you know, Miss Linton, that brute Hareton laughs at me—I hate him—indeed, I hate them all—they are odious beings."

Cathy began searching for some water; she lighted on a pitcher in the dresser, filled a tumbler, and brought it. He bid her add a spoonful of wine from a bottle on the table; and having swallowed a small portion, appeared more tranquil, and said she was very kind.

"And are you glad to see me?" asked she, reiterating her former question, and pleased to detect the faint dawn of a smile.

"Yes, I am—It's something new to hear a voice like yours!" he replied, "but I *have* been vexed, because you wouldn't come—And papa swore it was owing to me; he called me a pitiful, shuffling, worthless thing; and said you despised me; and if he had been in my place, he would be more the master of the Grange than your father, by this time. But you don't despise me, do you, Miss—"

"I wish you would say Catherine, or Cathy!" interrupted my young lady. "Despise you? No! Next to papa, and Ellen, I love you better than anybody living. I don't love Mr. Heathcliff, though; and I dare not come when he returns; will he stay away many days?"

"Not many," answered Linton, but he goes onto the moors frequently, since the shooting season commenced,[5] and you might spend an hour or two with me, in his absence—Do say you will! I think I should not be peevish with you; you'd not provoke me, and you'd always be ready to help me, wouldn't you?"

"Yes," said Catherine stroking his long soft hair, "if I could only get papa's consent, I'd spend half my time with you—Pretty Linton! I wish you were my brother!"

"And then you would like me as well as your father?" observed he more cheerfully. "But papa *says* you would love me better than him, and all the world, if you were my wife—so I'd rather you were that!"

"No! I should never love anybody better than papa," she returned gravely. "And people hate their wives, sometimes; but not their sisters and brothers, and if you were the latter, you would live with us, and papa would be as fond of you as he is of me."

Linton denied that people ever hated their wives; but Cathy affirmed they did, and in her wisdom, instanced his own father's aversion to her aunt.

I endeavoured to stop her thoughtless tongue—I couldn't succeed, till everything she knew was out. Master Heathcliff, much irritated, asserted her relation was false.

"Papa told me; and papa does not tell falsehoods!" she answered pertly.

"*My* papa scorns yours!" cried Linton. "He calls him a sneaking fool!"

"Yours is a wicked man," retorted Catherine, and you are very naughty to dare to repeat what he says—He must be wicked, to have made aunt Isabella leave him as she did!"

"She didn't leave him," said the boy. "You shan't contradict me!"

"She did!" cried my young lady.

"Well I'll tell *you* something!" said Linton "Your mother hated your father, now then."

"Oh!" exclaimed Catherine, too enraged to continue.

"And she loved mine!" added he.

"You little liar! I hate you now," she panted, and her face grew red with passion.

"She did, she did!" sang Linton sinking into the recess of his chair, and leaning back his head to enjoy the agitation of the other disputant, who stood behind.

"Hush, Master Heathcliff!" I said, "that's your father's tale too, I suppose."

"It isn't—you hold your tongue!" he answered, "she did, she did, Catherine, she did, she did!"

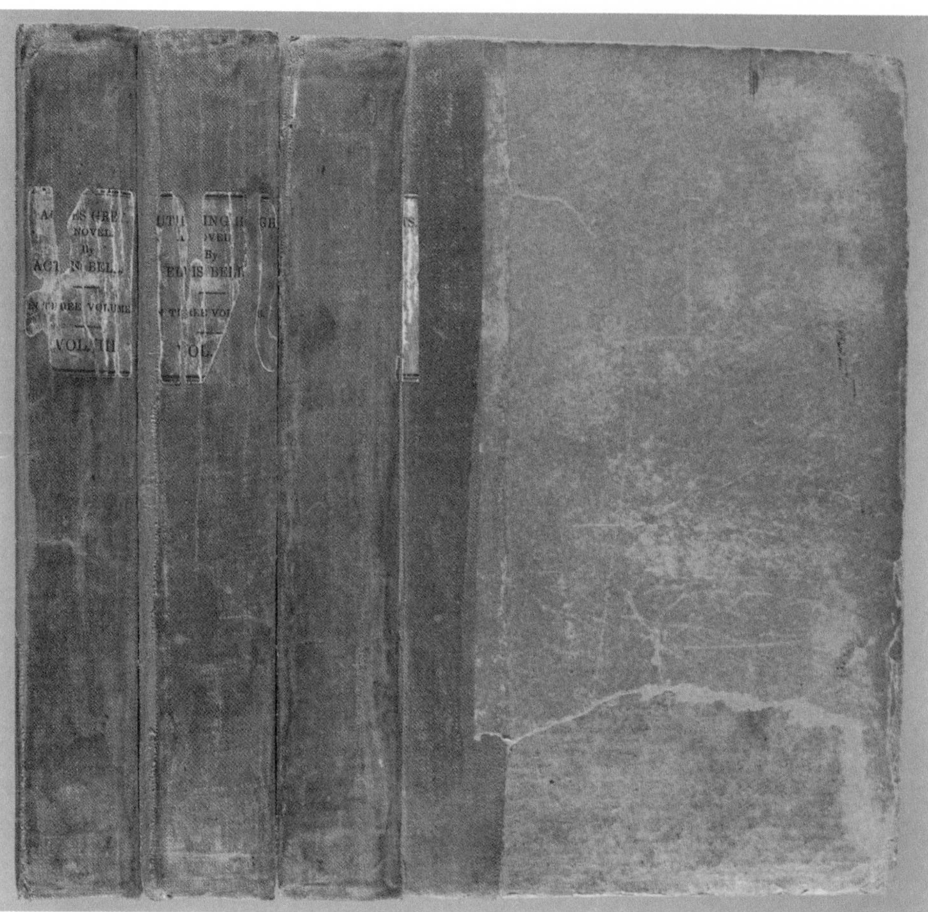

Wuthering Heights and *Agnes Grey,* bound together to comprise a three-volume novel, in 1847.

Cathy, beside herself, gave the chair a violent push, and caused him to fall against one arm. He was immediately seized by a suffocating cough that soon ended his triumph.

It lasted so long that it frightened even me. As to his cousin, she wept with all her might, aghast at the mischief she had done, though she said nothing.

I held him, till the fit exhausted itself. Then he thrust me away; and leant his head down, silently—Catherine quelled her lamentations also, took a seat opposite, and looked solemnly into the fire.

"How do you feel now, Master Heathcliff," I inquired after waiting ten minutes.

"I wish *she* felt as I do," he replied, "spiteful, cruel thing! Hareton never touches me, he never struck me in his life—And I was better to-day—and there"—his voice died in a whimper.

"*I* didn't strike you!" muttered Cathy chewing her lip to prevent another burst of emotion.

He sighed and moaned like one under great suffering; and kept it up for a quarter of an hour, on purpose to distress his cousin apparently, for whenever he caught a stifled sob from her, he put renewed pain and pathos into the inflexions of his voice.

"I'm sorry I hurt you, Linton!" she said at length, racked beyond endurance. "But *I* couldn't have been hurt by that little push; and I had no idea that you could, either—you're not much, are you, Linton? Don't let me go home thinking I've done you harm! Answer, speak to me!"

"I can't speak to you," he murmured, "you've hurt me so, that I shall lie awake all night, choking with this cough! If you had it you'd know what it was—but *you'll* be comfortably asleep, while I'm in agony—and nobody near me! I wonder how you would like to pass those fearful nights!" And he began to wail aloud for very pity of himself.

"Since you are in the habit of passing dreadful nights," I said, "it won't be Miss who spoils your ease; you'd be the same, had she never come—However, she shall not disturb you, again—and perhaps, you'll get quieter when we leave you."

"Must I go?" asked Catherine dolefully, bending over him. "Do you want me to go, Linton?"

"You can't alter what you've done," he replied pettishly, shrinking from her, "unless you alter it for the worse, by teasing me into a fever!"

"Well, then I must go?" she repeated.

"Let me alone, at least," said he "I can't bear your talking!"

6 This image of Linton and Cathy grotesquely parodies the images of Heathcliff and Catherine with which Volume II began.

She lingered, and resisted my persuasions to departure a tiresome while, but as he neither looked up, nor spoke, she finally made a movement to the door and I followed.

We were recalled by a scream—Linton had slid from his seat on to the hearthstone, and lay writhing in the mere perverseness of an indulged plague of a child, determined to be as grievous and harassing as it can.

I thoroughly guaged his disposition from his behaviour, and saw at once it would be folly to attempt humouring him. Not so my companion; she ran back in terror, knelt down, and cried, and soothed, and entreated, till he grew quiet from lack of breath, by no means from compunction at distressing her.

"I shall lift him on to the settle," I said, "and he may roll about as he pleases; we can't stop to watch him—I hope you are satisfied, Miss Cathy that *you* are not the person to benefit him, and that his condition of health is not occasioned by attachment to you. Now then, there he is! Come away; as soon as he knows there is nobody by to care for his nonsense, he'll be glad to lie still!"

She placed a cushion under his head, and offered him some water; he rejected the latter, and tossed uneasily on the former, as if it were a stone, or a block of wood.

She tried to put it more comfortably.

"I can't do with that," he said, "it's not high enough!"

Catherine brought another to lay above it.

"That's *too* high!" murmured the provoking thing.

"How must I arrange it, then?" she asked despairingly.

He twined himself up to her, as she half knelt by the settle, and converted her shoulder into a support.[6]

"No, that won't do!" I said. "You'll be content with the cushion, Master Heathcliff! Miss has wasted too much time on you already; we cannot remain five minutes longer."

"Yes, yes, we can!" replied Cathy. "He's good and patient, now—He's beginning to think I shall have far greater misery than he will, to-night, if I believe he is the worse for my visit; and then, I dare not come again—Tell the truth about it, Linton—for I mustn't come, if I have hurt you."

"You must come, to cure me," he answered. "You ought to come because you have hurt me—You know you have, extremely! I was not as ill when you entered as I am at present—was I?"

"But you've made yourself ill by crying, and being in a passion. I didn't do it all," said his cousin. "However, we'll be friends now. And you want me—you would wish to see me sometimes, really?"

"I told you, I did!" he replied impatiently.

"Sit on the settle and let me lean on your knee—That's as mama used to do, whole afternoons together—Sit quite still, and don't talk, but you may sing a song if you can sing, or you may say a nice, long interesting ballad—one of those you promised to teach me, or a story—I'd rather have a ballad though: begin."

Catherine repeated the longest she could remember. The employment pleased both mightily. Linton would have another, and after that another; notwithstanding my strenuous objections; and so, they went on, until the clock struck twelve, and we heard Hareton in the court, returning for his dinner.

"And to-morrow, Catherine, will you be here to-morrow?" asked young Heathcliff, holding her frock, as she rose reluctantly.

"No!" I answered, "nor next day neither." She, however, gave a different response, evidently, for his forehead cleared, as she stooped, and whispered in his ear.

"You won't go to-morrow, recollect, Miss!" I commenced when we were out of the house. "You are not dreaming of it, are you?"

She smiled.

"Oh, I'll take good care!" I continued, "I'll have that lock mended, and you can escape by no way else."

"I can get over the wall," she said laughing. "The Grange is not a prison, Ellen, and you are not my jailer. And besides I'm almost seventeen. I'm a woman—and I'm certain Linton would recover quickly if he had me to look after him—I'm older than he is, you know, and wiser, less childish, am I not? And he'll soon do as I direct him with some slight coaxing—He's a pretty little darling when he's good. I'd make such a pet of him, if he were mine—We should never quarrel, should we, after we were used to each other? Don't you like him, Ellen?"

"Like him?" I exclaimed. "The worst tempered bit of a sickly slip[7] that ever struggled into its teens! Happily,[8] as Mr. Heathcliff conjectured, he'll not win twenty! I doubt whether he'll see spring indeed—and small loss to his family, whenever he drops off; and lucky it is for us that his father took him—the kinder he was treated, the more tedious and selfish he'd be! I'm glad you have no chance of having him for a husband, Miss Catherine!"

My companion waxed serious at hearing this speech—To speak of his death so regardlessly wounded her feelings.

"He's younger than I," she answered, after a protracted pause of meditation," and he ought to live the longest; he will—he must live as long as I do. He's as strong now as when he first came into the North, I'm positive of that! It's only a cold that ails him, the same as papa has—You say papa will get better, and why shouldn't he?"

"Well, well," I cried, "after all, we needn't trouble ourselves; for listen, Miss, and mind, I'll keep my word—If you attempt going to Wuthering Heights again, with or without me, I shall inform Mr. Linton, and unless he allow it, the intimacy with your cousin must not be revived."

"It has been revived!" muttered Cathy sulkily.

"Must not be continued, then!" I said.

"We'll see!" was her reply, and she set off at a gallop, leaving me to toil in the rear.

We both reached home before our dinnertime: my master supposed we had been wandering through the park, and therefore he demanded no explanation of our absence. As soon as I entered, I hastened to change my soaked shoes and stockings; but sitting such a while at the Heights had done the mischief. On the succeeding morning, I was laid up; and during three weeks I remained in-

7 A small shoot taken from a plant for the purpose of propagation. The metaphor glances ironically at the function for which Heathcliff has purposed Linton. He will promote his father's claim to Thrushcross Grange, but not by propagating offspring.

8 "Happily" here means "perchance," not "fortunately."

capacitated for attending to my duties—a calamity never experienced prior to that period, and never, I am thankful to say, since.

My little mistress behaved like an angel in coming to wait on me, and cheer my solitude: the confinement brought me exceedingly low—It is wearisome, to a stirring active body—but few have slighter reasons for complaint than I had. The moment Catherine left Mr. Linton's room, she appeared at my bed-side. Her day was divided between us; no amusement usurped a minute: she neglected her meals, her studies, and her play; and she was the fondest nurse that ever watched: she must have had a warm heart, when she loved her father so, to give so much to me!

I said her days were divided between us; but the master retired early, and I generally needed nothing after six o'clock; thus the evening was her own.

Poor thing, I never considered what she did with herself after tea. And though frequently, when she looked in to bid me good night, I remarked a fresh colour in her cheeks, and a pinkness over her slender fingers, instead of fancying the hue borrowed from a cold ride across the moors, I laid it to the charge of a hot fire in the library.

1 Dislike, strong aversion. Both "disrelish" and "dis-relish" are accepted spellings of the word in the period.

2 Overcome.

CHAPTER 10

At the close of three weeks, I was able to quit my chamber, and move about the house. And on the first occasion of my sitting up in the evening, I asked Catherine to read to me, because my eyes were weak. We were in the library, the master having gone to bed: she consented, rather unwillingly, I fancied; and imagining my sort of books did not suit her, I bid her please herself in the choice of what she perused.

She selected one of her own favourites, and got forward steadily about an hour; then came frequent questions.

"Ellen, are not you tired? Hadn't you better lie down now? You'll be sick, keeping up so long, Ellen."

"No, no, dear, I'm not tired," I returned, continually.

Perceiving me immovable, she essayed another method of showing her dis-relish[1] for her occupation. It changed to yawning, and stretching, and—

"Ellen, I'm tired."

"Give over then and talk," I answered.

That was worse; she fretted and sighed, and looked at her watch till eight; and finally went to her room, completely overdone[2] with sleep, judging by her peevish, heavy look, and the constant rubbing she inflicted on her eyes.

The following night she seemed more impatient still; and on the third from recovering my company, she complained of a headache, and left me.

I thought her conduct odd; and having remained alone a long while, I resolved on going, and inquiring whether she were better, and asking her to come and lie on the sofa, instead of up-stairs, in the dark.

No Catherine could I discover up-stairs, and none below. The servants affirmed they had not seen her. I listened at Mr. Edgar's door—all was silence. I returned to her apartment, extinguished my candle, and seated myself in the window.

The moon shone bright; a sprinkling of snow covered the ground, and I reflected that she might, possibly, have taken it into her head to walk about the garden for refreshment. I did detect a figure creeping along the inner fence of the park; but it was not my young mistress; on its emerging into the light, I recognised one of the grooms.

He stood a considerable period, viewing the carriage road through the grounds; then started off at a brisk pace, as if he had detected something, and reappeared, presently, leading Miss's pony; and there she was, just dismounted, and walking by its side.

The man took his charge stealthily across the grass towards the stable. Cathy entered by the casement-window[3] of the drawing-room, and glided noiselessly up to where I awaited her.

She put the door gently to, slipped off her snowy shoes, untied her hat, and was proceeding, unconscious of my espionage, to lay aside her mantle, when I suddenly rose, and revealed myself. The surprise petrified her an instant: she uttered an inarticulate exclamation, and stood fixed.

"My dear Miss Catherine," I began, too vividly impressed by her recent kindness to break into a scold, "where have you been riding out at this hour? And why should you try to deceive me, by telling a tale. Where have you been? Speak!"

"To the bottom of the park," she stammered. "I didn't tell a tale."

"And no where else?" I demanded.

"No," was the muttered reply.

"Oh, Catherine," I cried, sorrowfully. "You know you have been doing wrong, or you wouldn't be driven to uttering an untruth to

3 A casement window has a hinged sash, so that it swings open like a door. In Vol. I, Chap. 6, Heathcliff and Catherine stood on a flowerpot under one of the drawing-room windows, spying on Edgar and Isabella.

A pair of linnets, small birds belonging to the finch family, in a color lithograph from W. Swaysland, *Familiar Wild Birds* (London: Cassell, 1883).

me. That does grieve me. I'd rather be three months ill, than hear you frame a deliberate lie."

She sprang forward, and bursting into tears, threw her arms round my neck.

"Well Ellen, I'm so afraid of you being angry," she said. "Promise not to be angry, and you shall know the very truth. I hate to hide it."

We sat down in the window-seat; I assured her I would not scold, whatever her secret might be, and I guessed it, of course, so she commenced—

"I've been to Wuthering Heights, Ellen, and I've never missed going a day since you fell ill; except thrice before, and twice after you left your room. I gave Michael books and pictures to prepare Minny every evening, and to put her back in the stable; you mustn't scold *him* either, mind. I was at the Heights by half-past six, and generally stayed till half-past eight, and then gallopped home. It was not to amuse myself that I went; I was often wretched all the time. Now and then, I was happy, once in a week perhaps. At first, I expected there would be sad work persuading you to let me keep my word to Linton, for I had engaged to call again next day, when we quitted him; but, as you stayed up-stairs on the morrow, I escaped that trouble; and while Michael was refastening the lock of the park door in the afternoon, I got possession of the key, and told him how my cousin wished me to visit him, because he was sick, and couldn't come to the Grange: and how papa would object to my going. And then I negotiated with him about the pony. He is fond of reading, and he thinks of leaving soon to get married, so he offered, if I would lend him books out of the library, to do what I wished; but I preferred giving him my own, and that satisfied him better.

"On my second visit, Linton seemed in lively spirits; and Zillah, that is their housekeeper, made us a clean room, and a good fire, and told us that as Joseph was out at a prayer-meeting, and Hareton Earnshaw was off with his dogs, robbing our woods of pheasants, as I heard afterwards; we might do what we liked.

"She brought me some warm wine and gingerbread, and appeared exceedingly good-natured; and Linton sat in the arm-chair, and I in the little rocking chair on the hearthstone, and we laughed and talked so merrily, and found so much to say; we planned where we would go, and what we would do in summer. I needn't repeat that, because you would call it silly.

"One time, however, we were near quarrelling. He said the pleasantest manner of spending a hot July day was lying from morning till evening on a bank of heath in the middle of the moors, with the bees humming dreamily about among the bloom, and the larks singing high up over head, and the blue sky and bright sun shining steadily and cloudlessly. That was his most perfect idea of heaven's happiness—mine was rocking in a rustling green tree, with a west wind blowing, and bright, white clouds flitting rapidly above; and not only larks, but throstles, and blackbirds, and linnets, and cuckoos pouring out music on every side,[4] and the moors seen at a distance, broken into cool dusky dells; but close by great swells of long grass undulating in waves to the breeze; and woods and sounding water, and the whole world awake and wild with joy. He wanted all to lie in an ecstacy of peace; I wanted all to sparkle, and dance in a glorious jubilee.[5]

"I said his heaven would be only half alive, and he said mine would be drunk; I said I should fall asleep in his, and he said he could not breathe in mine, and began to grow very snappish. At last, we agreed to try both as soon as the right weather came; and then we kissed each other and were friends. After sitting still an hour, I looked at the great room with its smooth, uncarpeted floor; and thought how nice it would be to play in, if we removed the table; and I asked Linton to call Zillah in to help us—and we'd have a game at blind-man's-buff[6]—she should try to catch us—you used to, you know, Ellen. He wouldn't; there was no pleasure in it, he said; but he consented to play at ball with me. We found two, in a cupboard, among a heap of old toys, tops, and hoops, and battledores,[7] and shuttlecocks. One was marked C., and the other H.; I wished to have the C., because that stood for Catherine, and the

4 Throstles are song thrushes. The linnets and larks of Cathy's imagined heaven also appear in one of Brontë's best-loved poems, "The linnet in the rocky dells," composed in 1844 and published in 1846. Brontë would have seen and heard all of these birds during her long walks across the moors. The setting Cathy imagines closely resembles the one Nelly described in Chapter 8, where Cathy spends summer afternoons in the Grange's extensive park, swinging in a "breeze-rocked" cradle of branches.

5 Brontë had already imagined Cathy's "whole world awake and wild with joy" in an early poem, "High waving heather 'neath stormy blasts bending." This is its first stanza:

> High waving heather 'neath stormy blasts bending
> Midnight and moonlight and bright shining stars
> Darkness and glory rejoicingly blending
> Earth rising to heaven and heaven descending
> Man's spirit away from its drear dungeon sending
> Bursting the fetters and breaking the bars

The poem's powerful swinging rhythms imitate and evoke a perpetually moving and mutable landscape and skyscape very like Catherine's "perfect idea of heaven's happiness."

6 An old game closely related to hide-and-seek and popular in the Victorian period. One player is blindfolded and has to find and tag the other players, who try to elude her. It is best played outdoors or in a large open space like the sitting room at the Heights.

7 A battledore is a small racket used to hit a shuttlecock. The first edition has "battledoor," probably a phonetic spelling of a word Brontë may never have seen in print.

Blind man's buff (later "bluff") in a watercolor by George Goodwin Kilburne (1839–1924). These Edwardian children are playing under the watchful supervision of their governess.

The Diverſion of Battledore and Shittlecock from an Original Deſign in Vauxhall Gardens.

"The diversion of Battledore and Shuttlecock from an original design in Vauxhall Gardens, London," English School engraving, eighteenth century.

H. might be for Heathcliff, his name;[8] but the bran[9] came out of H., and Linton didn't like it.

"I beat him constantly; and he got cross again, and coughed, and returned to his chair: that night, though, he easily recovered his good humour; he was charmed with two or three pretty songs—*your* songs, Ellen; and when I was obliged to go, he begged and entreated me to come the following evening, and I promised.

"Minny and I went flying home as light as air: and I dreamt of Wuthering Heights, and my sweet, darling cousin, till morning.

"On the morrow, I was sad; partly because you were poorly, and partly that I wished my father knew, and approved of my excursions: but it was beautiful moonlight after tea; and, as I rode on, the gloom cleared.

"I shall have another happy evening, I thought to myself, and what delights me more, my pretty Linton will.

"I trotted up their garden, and was turning round to the back, when that fellow Earnshaw met me, took my bridle, and bid me go in by the front entrance. He patted Minny's neck, and said she was a bonny beast, and appeared as if he wanted me to speak to him. I only told him to leave my horse alone, or else it would kick him.

"He answered in his vulgar accent. 'It wouldn't do mitch hurt if it did;' and surveyed its legs with a smile.

"I was half inclined to make it try; however, he moved off to open the door, and, as he raised the latch, he looked up to the inscription above, and said, with a stupid mixture of awkwardness and elation:

"'Miss Catherine! I can read yon, nah.'

"'Wonderful,' I exclaimed. 'Pray let us hear you—you *are* grown clever!'

"He spelt, and drawled over by syllables, the name—

"'Hareton Earnshaw.'

"'And the figures?' I cried, encouragingly, perceiving that he came to a dead halt.

"'I cannot tell them yet,' he answered.

8 The "H" probably stands for Hindley, not Heathcliff, but the two letters "C" and the "H" call attention to the motif of two children who are playmates and to the repetition of the initial letter "H" in the given names of all the Earnshaw males including Heathcliff.

9 Shuttlecocks are usually made of cork, but these are stuffed with bran.

10 Uncultured.

11 Learned or studied.

"'Oh, you dunce!' I said, laughing heartily at his failure.

"The fool stared, with a grin hovering about his lips, and a scowl gathering over his eyes, as if uncertain whether he might not join in my mirth; whether it were not pleasant familiarity, or what it really was, contempt.

"I settled his doubts by suddenly retrieving my gravity, and desiring him to walk away, for I came to see Linton not him.

"He reddened—I saw that by the moonlight—dropped his hand from the latch, and skulked off, a picture of mortified vanity. He imagined himself to be as accomplished as Linton, I suppose, because he could spell his own name; and was marvellously discomfited that I didn't think the same."

"Stop Miss Catherine, dear!" I interrupted. "I shall not scold, but I don't like your conduct there. If you had remembered that Hareton was your cousin, as much as Master Heathcliff, you would have felt how improper it was to behave in that way. At least, it was praiseworthy ambition, for him to desire to be as accomplished as Linton: and probably he did not learn merely to show off; you had made him ashamed of his ignorance before, I have no doubt; and he wished to remedy it and please you. To sneer at his imperfect attempt was very bad breeding—had *you* been brought up in his circumstances, would you be less rude?[10] He was as quick and as intelligent a child as ever you were, and I'm hurt that he should be despised now, because that base Heathcliff has treated him so unjustly."

"Well, Ellen, you won't cry about it, will you?" she exclaimed, surprised at my earnestness. "But wait, and you shall hear if he conned[11] his a b c, to please me; and if it were worth while being civil to the brute. I entered; Linton was lying on the settle and half got up to welcome me.

"'I'm ill to-night Catherine, love,' he said, 'and you must have all the talk, and let me listen. Come, and sit by me—I was sure you wouldn't break your word, and I'll make you promise again, before you go.'

"I knew now that I mustn't tease him, as he was ill; and I spoke softly and put no questions, and avoided irritating him in any way. I had brought some of my nicest books for him; he asked me to read a little of one, and I was about to comply, when Earnshaw burst the door open, having gathered venom with reflection. He advanced direct to us, seized Linton by the arm, and swung him off the seat.

"'Get to thy own room!' he said in a voice almost inarticulate with passion, and his face looked swelled and furious. 'Take her there if she comes to see thee—thou shalln't keep me out of this. Begone wi' ye both!'

"He swore at us, and left Linton no time to answer, nearly throwing him into the kitchen; and he clenched his fist, as I followed, seemingly longing to knock me down. I was afraid, for a moment, and I let one volume fall; he kicked it after me, and shut us out.

"I heard a malignant, crackly laugh by the fire, and turning beheld that odious Joseph, standing rubbing his bony hands, and quivering.

"'Aw wer sure he'd sarve ye aht! He's a grand lad! He's getten t'raight sperrit in him! *He* knaws—Aye, he knaws, as weel as Aw do, who sud be t'maister yonder—Ech, ech, ech! He mad ye skift properly! Ech, ech, ech!'[12]

"'Where must we go?' I said to my cousin, disregarding the old wretch's mockery.

"Linton was white and trembling. He was not pretty then—Ellen, Oh, no!—he looked frightful! for his thin face, and large eyes were wrought into an expression of frantic, powerless fury. He grasped the handle of the door, and shook it—it was fastened inside.

"'If you don't let me in I'll kill you; If you don't let me in I'll kill you!' he rather shrieked than said. 'Devil! devil! I'll kill you, I'll kill you!'

"Joseph uttered his croaking laugh again.

12 "I was sure he'd serve you right! He's a grand lad! He's getting the right spirit in him! *He* knows—Aye, he knows, as well as I do, who should be the master over there—Ech, ech, ech! He made you move properly! Ech, ech, ech!"

13 "There, that's the father! . . . That's his father [in him]! We've always got something of the other side in us. Don't pay any attention, Hareton, lad—don't be afraid—he cannot get at you." Linton, so far associated exclusively with his mother and the Lintons, can threaten as well as Heathcliff.

14 The violent cough and the blood gushing from his mouth indicate that Linton is in the late stages of consumption.

15 Going.

16 Stopped, taking hold of the reins.

"'Thear, that's t'father!' he cried. 'That's t'father! We've allas summut uh orther side in us—Niver heed, Hareton, lad—dunnut be 'feard—he cannot get at thee!'[13]

"I took hold of Linton's hands, and tried to pull him away; but he shrieked so shockingly that I dared not proceed. At last, his cries were choked by a dreadful fit of coughing; blood gushed from his mouth,[14] and he fell on the ground.

"I ran into the yard, sick with terror; and called for Zillah, as loud as I could. She soon heard me; she was milking the cows in a shed behind the barn; and hurrying from her work, she inquired what there was to do?

"I hadn't breath to explain; dragging her in, I looked about for Linton; Earnshaw had come out to examine the mischief he had caused, and he was then conveying the poor thing up-stairs. Zillah and I ascended after him; but he stopped me at the top of the steps, and said, I shouldn't go in, I must go home.

"I exclaimed that he had killed Linton and I *would* enter.

"Joseph locked the door, and declared I should do 'no sich stuff,' and asked me whether I were 'bahn[15] to be as mad as him.'

"I stood crying, till the housekeeper re-appeared; she affirmed he would be better in a bit; but he couldn't do with that shrieking and din, and she took me, and nearly carried me into the house.

"Ellen, I was ready to tear my hair off my head! I sobbed and wept so that my eyes were almost blind: and the ruffian you have such sympathy with, stood opposite; presuming, every now and then, to bid me "wisht," and denying that it was his fault; and finally, frightened by my assertions that I would tell papa, and that he should be put in prison, and hanged, he commenced blubbering himself, and hurried out to hide his cowardly agitation.

"Still, I was not rid of him: when at length they compelled me to depart, and I had got some hundred yards off the premises, he suddenly issued from the shadow of the road-side, and checked[16] Minny and took hold of me.

"'Miss Catherine, I'm ill grieved,' he began, 'but it's raything too bad—'

"I gave him a cut with my whip, thinking perhaps he would murder me—He let go, thundering one of his horrid curses, and I gallopped home more than half out of my senses.

"I didn't bid you good-night, that evening; and I didn't go to Wuthering Heights the next—I wished to, exceedingly; but I was strangely excited, and dreaded to hear that Linton was dead, sometimes; and sometimes shuddered at the thought of encountering Hareton.

"On the third day I took courage; at least, I couldn't bear longer suspense and stole off, once more. I went at five o'clock, and walked, fancying I might manage to creep into the house, and up to Linton's room, unobserved. However, the dogs gave notice of my approach: Zillah received me, and saying 'the lad was mending nicely,' showed me into a small, tidy, carpeted apartment, where, to my inexpressible joy, I beheld Linton laid on a little sofa, reading one of my books. But he would neither speak to me, nor look at me, through a whole hour, Ellen—He has such an unhappy temper—and what quite confounded me, when he did open his mouth, it was to utter the falsehood that I had occasioned the uproar, and Hareton was not to blame!

"Unable to reply, except passionately, I got up, and walked from the room. He sent after me a faint 'Catherine!'—he did not reckon on being answered so—but I wouldn't turn back; and the morrow was the second day on which I stayed at home, nearly determined to visit him no more.

"But it was so miserable going to bed, and getting up, and never hearing anything about him, that my resolution melted into air, before it was properly formed. It *had* appeared wrong to take the journey once; now it seemed wrong to refrain. Michael came to ask if he must saddle Minny; I said 'Yes,' and considered myself doing a duty as she bore me over the hills.

17 Sitting room.

18 I fear I may be.

"I was forced to pass the front windows to get to the court; it was no use trying to conceal my presence.

"'Young master is in the house,'[17] said Zillah as she saw me making for the parlour.

"I went in; Earnshaw was there also, but he quitted the room directly. Linton sat in the great arm chair half asleep; walking up to the fire, I began in a serious tone, partly meaning it to be true.

"'As you don't like me, Linton, and as you think I come on purpose to hurt you, and pretend that I do so every time, this is our last meeting—let us say good bye; and tell Mr. Heathcliff that you have no wish to see me, and that he mustn't invent any more falsehoods on the subject.'

"'Sit down and take your hat off, Catherine,' he answered. 'You are so much happier than I am, you ought to be better. Papa talks enough of my defects, and shows enough scorn of me, to make it natural I should doubt myself—I doubt whether I am not[18] altogether as worthless as he calls me, frequently; and then I feel so cross and bitter, I hate everybody! I *am* worthless, and bad in temper, and bad in spirit, almost always—and if you choose, you *may* say good-bye—you'll get rid of an annoyance—Only, Catherine, do me this justice: believe that if I might be as sweet, and as kind, and as good as you are, I would be, as willingly, and more so, than as happy and as healthy. And believe that your kindness has made me love you deeper than if I deserved your love, and though I couldn't, and cannot help showing my nature to you, I regret it, and repent it, and shall regret and repent it, till I die!'

"I felt he spoke the truth; and I felt I must forgive him; and, though he should quarrel the next moment, I must forgive him again. We were reconciled, but we cried, both of us, the whole time I stayed. Not entirely for sorrow, yet I *was* sorry Linton had that distorted nature. He'll never let his friends be at ease, and he'll never be at ease himself!

"I have always gone to his little parlour, since that night; because his father returned the day after. About three times, I think, we have been merry, and hopeful, as we were the first evening; the rest of my visits were dreary and troubled—now, with his selfishness and spite; and now with his sufferings: but I've learnt to endure the former with nearly as little resentment as the latter.

"Mr. Heathcliff purposely avoids me. I have hardly seen him at all. Last Sunday, indeed, coming earlier than usual, I heard him abusing poor Linton, cruelly, for his conduct of the night before. I can't tell how he knew of it, unless he listened. Linton had certainly behaved provokingly; however, it was the business of nobody but me; and I interrupted Mr. Heathcliff's lecture, by entering, and telling him so. He burst into a laugh, and went away, saying he was glad I took that view of the matter. Since then, I've told Linton he must whisper his bitter things.

"Now, Ellen, you have heard all; and I can't be prevented from going to Wuthering Heights, except by inflicting misery on two people—whereas, if you'll only not tell papa, my going need disturb the tranquillity of none. You'll not tell, will you? It will be very heartless if you do."

"I'll make up my mind on that point by to-morrow, Miss Catherine," I replied. "It requires some study; and so I'll leave you to your rest, and go think it over."

I thought it over aloud, in my master's presence; walking straight from her room to his, and relating the whole story, with the exception of her conversations with her cousin, and any mention of Hareton.

Mr. Linton was alarmed and distressed more than he would acknowledge to me. In the morning, Catherine learnt my betrayal of her confidence, and she learnt also that her secret visits were to end.

In vain she wept and writhed against the interdict; and implored her father to have pity on Linton: all she got to comfort her was a promise that he would write, and give him leave to come to the Grange when he pleased; but explaining that he must no longer expect to see Catherine at Wuthering Heights. Perhaps, had he been aware of his nephew's disposition and state of health, he would have seen fit to withhold even that slight consolation.

CHAPTER 11

These things happened last winter, sir," said Mrs. Dean; "hardly more than a year ago. Last winter, I did not think, at another twelve months' end, I should be amusing a stranger to the family with relating them! Yet, who knows how long you'll be a stranger? You're too young to rest always contented, living by yourself; and I some way fancy, no one could see Catherine Linton, and not love her. You smile; but why do you look so lively and interested, when I talk about her—and why have you asked me to hang her picture over your fireplace? And why—"

"Stop, my good friend!" I cried. "It may be very possible that I should love her; but would she love me? I doubt it too much to venture my tranquillity by running into temptation; and then my home is not here. I'm of the busy world, and to its arms I must return. Go on. Was Catherine obedient to her father's commands?"

"She was," continued the housekeeper. "Her affection for him was still the chief sentiment in her heart; and he spoke without anger; he spoke in the deep tenderness of one about to leave his treasure amid perils and foes, where his remembered words would be the only aid that he could bequeath to guide her."

He said to me, a few days afterwards, "I wish my nephew would write, Ellen, or call. Tell me, sincerely, what you think of him—is he changed for the better, or is there a prospect of improvement, as he grows a man?"

"He's very delicate, sir," I replied; "and scarcely likely to reach manhood; but this I can say, he does not resemble his father; and if Miss Catherine had the misfortune to marry him, he would not be beyond her control, unless she were extremely and foolishly indulgent. However, master, you'll have plenty of time to get acquainted with him, and see whether he would suit her—it wants four years and more to his being of age."[1]

Edgar sighed; and, walking to the window, looked out towards Gimmerton Kirk. It was a misty afternoon, but the February sun shone dimly, and we could just distinguish the two fir trees in the yard, and the sparely[2] scattered gravestones.

"I've prayed often," he half soliloquized, "for the approach of what is coming; and now I begin to shrink, and fear it. I thought the memory of the hour I came down that glen a bridegroom, would be less sweet than the anticipation that I was soon, in a few months, or, possibly, weeks, to be carried up, and laid in its lonely hollow! Ellen, I've been very happy with my little Cathy. Through winter nights and summer days she was a living hope at my side—but I've been as happy musing by myself among those stones, under that old church—lying, through the long June evenings, on the green mound of her mother's grave, and wishing, yearning for the time when I might lie beneath it. What can I do for Cathy? How must I quit her? I'd not care one moment for Linton being Heathcliff's son; nor for his taking her from me, if he could console her for my loss. I'd not care that Heathcliff gained his ends, and triumphed in robbing me of my last blessing! But should Linton be unworthy—only a feeble tool to his father—I cannot abandon her to him! And, hard though it be to crush her buoyant spirit, I must persevere in making her sad while I live, and leaving her solitary when I die. Darling! I'd rather resign her to God, and lay her in the earth before me."

1 Linton was born in the fall of 1784. Nelly's conversation with Edgar takes place in February 1801, when Linton is sixteen and a half years old.

2 Sparingly, thinly.

"Resign her to God, as it is, sir," I answered, "and if we should lose you—which may He forbid—under His providence, I'll stand her friend and counsellor to the last. Miss Catherine is a good girl; I don't fear that she will go wilfully wrong; and people who do their duty are always finally rewarded."

Spring advanced; yet my master gathered no real strength, though he resumed his walks in the grounds with his daughter. To her inexperienced notions, this itself was a sign of convalescence; and then his cheek was often flushed, and his eyes were bright; she felt sure of his recovering.

On her seventeenth birthday, he did not visit the churchyard; it was raining, and I observed—

"You'll surely not go out to-night, sir?"

He answered—

"No, I'll defer it, this year, a little longer."

He wrote again to Linton, expressing his great desire to see him; and, had the invalid been presentable, I've no doubt his father would have permitted him to come. As it was, being instructed, he returned an answer, intimating that Mr. Heathcliff objected to his calling at the Grange; but his uncle's kind remembrance delighted him, and he hoped to meet him sometimes in his rambles, and personally to petition that his cousin and he might not remain long so utterly divided.

That part of his letter was simple, and probably his own. Heathcliff knew he could plead eloquently enough for Catherine's company, then—

"I do not ask," he said, "that she may visit here; but, am I never to see her, because my father forbids me to go to her home, and you forbid her to come to mine? Do, now and then, ride with her towards the Heights; and let us exchange a few words, in your presence! We have done nothing to deserve this separation; and you are not angry with me—you have no reason to dislike me—you allow, yourself. Dear uncle! send me a kind note to-morrow;

and leave to join you anywhere you please, except at Thrushcross Grange. I believe an interview would convince you that my father's character is not mine; he affirms I am more your nephew than his son; and though I have faults which render me unworthy of Catherine, she has excused them, and, for her sake, you should also. You inquire after my health—it is better; but while I remain cut off from all hope, and doomed to solitude, or the society of those who never did, and never will like me, how can I be cheerful and well?"

Edgar, though he felt for the boy, could not consent to grant his request; because he could not accompany Catherine.

He said, in summer, perhaps, they might meet: meantime, he wished him to continue writing at intervals, and engaged to give him what advice and comfort be was able by letter; being well aware of his hard position in his family.

Linton complied; and had he been unrestrained, would probably have spoiled all by filling his epistles with complaints and lamentations; but his father kept a sharp watch over him; and, of course, insisted on every line that my master sent being shown; so, instead of penning his peculiar personal sufferings and distresses, the themes constantly uppermost in his thoughts, he harped on the cruel obligation of being held asunder from his friend and love; and gently intimated that Mr. Linton must allow an interview soon, or he should fear he was purposely deceiving him with empty promises.

Cathy was a powerful ally at home: and, between them, they at length persuaded my master to acquiesce in their having a ride or a walk together, about once a week, under my guardianship, and on the moors nearest the Grange; for June found him still declining; and, though he had set aside, yearly, a portion of his income for my young lady's fortune, he had a natural desire that she might retain, or at least return in a short time to, the house of her ancestors; and he considered her only prospect of doing that was by a union with his heir: he had no idea that the latter was failing almost as fast as himself; nor had any one, I believe; no doctor visited the Heights, and no one saw Master Heathcliff to make report of his condition, among us.

I, for my part, began to fancy my forebodings were false, and that he must be actually rallying, when he mentioned riding and walking on the moors, and seemed so earnest in pursuing his object.

I could not picture a father treating a dying child as tyrannically and wickedly as I afterwards learnt Heathcliff had treated him, to compel this apparent eagerness; his efforts redoubling the more imminently his avaricious and unfeeling plans were threatened with defeat by death.

CHAPTER 12

Summer was already past its prime, when Edgar reluctantly yielded his assent to their entreaties, and Catherine and I set out on our first ride to join her cousin.

It was a close, sultry day; devoid of sunshine, but with a sky too dappled and hazy to threaten rain; and our place of meeting had been fixed at the guide-stone, by the crossroads. On arriving there, however, a little herd-boy, despatched as a messenger, told us that—

"Maister Linton wer just ut this side th' Heights: and he'd be mitch obleeged to us to gang on a bit further."

"Then Master Linton has forgot the first injunction of his uncle," I observed: "he bid us keep on the Grange land, and here we are, off at once."

"Well, we'll turn our horses' heads round, when we reach him," answered my companion; "our excursion shall lie towards home."

But when we reached him, and that was scarcely a quarter of a mile from his own door, we found he had no horse, and we were forced to dismount, and leave ours to graze.

He lay on the heath, awaiting our approach, and did not rise till we came within a few yards. Then, he walked so feebly, and looked so pale, that I immediately exclaimed—

"Why, Master Heathcliff, you are not fit for enjoying a ramble, this morning. How ill you do look!"

Catherine surveyed him with grief and astonishment; and changed the ejaculation of joy on her lips, to one of alarm; and the congratulation on their long postponed meeting, to an anxious inquiry, whether he were worse than usual.

"No—better—better!" he panted, trembling, and retaining her hand as if he needed its support, while his large blue eyes wandered timidly over her; the hollowness round them, transforming to haggard wildness the languid expression they once possessed.

"But you have been worse," persisted his cousin, "worse than when I saw you last—you are thinner, and—"

"I'm tired," he interrupted, hurriedly. "It is too hot for walking, let us rest here. And, in the morning, I often feel sick—papa says I grow so fast."

Badly satisfied, Cathy sat down, and he reclined beside her.

"This is something like your paradise," said she, making an effort at cheerfulness. "You recollect the two days we agreed to spend, in the place and way each thought pleasantest? This is nearly yours, only there are clouds; but then, they are so soft and mellow, it is nicer than sunshine. Next week, if you can, we'll ride down to the Grange Park, and try mine."

Linton did not appear to remember what she talked of; and he had evidently great difficulty in sustaining any kind of conversation. His lack of interest in the subjects she started, and his equal incapacity to contribute to her entertainment, were so obvious, that she could not conceal her disappointment. An indefinite alteration had come over his whole person and manner. The pettishness that might be caressed into fondness had yielded to a listless apathy; there was less of the peevish temper of a child which frets and teases on purpose to be soothed, and more of the self-absorbed moroseness of a confirmed invalid, repelling consolation, and ready to regard the good-humoured mirth of others as an insult.

Catherine perceived, as well as I did, that he held it rather a punishment than a gratification to endure our company; and she made no scruple of proposing, presently, to depart.

That proposal, unexpectedly, roused Linton from his lethargy, and threw him into a strange state of agitation. He glanced fearfully towards the Heights, begging she would remain another half-hour, at least.

"But, I think," said Cathy, "you'd be more comfortable at home than sitting here; and I cannot amuse you to-day, I see, by my tales, and songs, and chatter; you have grown wiser than I, in these six months; you have little taste for my diversions now; or else, if I could amuse you, I'd willingly stay."

"Stay to rest yourself," he replied. "And, Catherine, don't think, or say, that I'm *very* unwell—it is the heavy weather and heat that make me dull; and I walked about, before you came, a great deal, for me. Tell uncle, I'm in tolerable health, will you?"

"I'll tell him that *you* say so, Linton. I couldn't affirm that you are," observed my young lady, wondering at his pertinacious assertion of what was evidently an untruth.

"And be here again next Thursday," continued he, shunning her puzzled gaze. "And give him my thanks for permitting you to come—my best thanks, Catherine. And—and, if you *did* meet my father, and he asked you about me, don't lead him to suppose that I've been extremely silent and stupid—don't look sad and downcast, as you *are* doing—he'll be angry."

"I care nothing for his anger," exclaimed Cathy, imagining she would be its object.

"But I do," said her cousin, shuddering. "*Don't* provoke him against me, Catherine, for he is very hard."

"Is he severe to you, Master Heathcliff?" I inquired. "Has he grown weary of indulgence, and passed from passive to active hatred?"

Linton looked at me, but did not answer; and, after keeping her seat by his another ten minutes, during which his head fell drowsily on his breast, and he uttered nothing except suppressed moans of exhaustion or pain, Cathy began to seek solace in looking for bilberries, and sharing the produce of her researches with me: she did not offer them to him, for she saw further notice would only weary and annoy.

"Is it half an hour now, Ellen!" she whispered in my ear, at last. "I can't tell why we should stay. He's asleep, and papa will he wanting us back."

"Well, we must not leave him asleep," I answered; "wait till he wakes and be patient. You were mighty eager to set off, but your longing to see poor Linton has soon evaporated!"

"Why did *he* wish to see me?" returned Catherine. "In his crossest humours, formerly, I liked him better than I do in his present curious mood. It's just as if it were a task he was compelled to perform—this interview—for fear his father should scold him. But I'm hardly going to come to give Mr. Heathcliff pleasure, whatever reason he may have for ordering Linton to undergo this penance. And, though I'm glad he's better in health, I'm sorry he's so much less pleasant, and so much less affectionate to me."

"You think he *is* better in health, then?" I said.

"Yes," she answered, "because he always made such a great deal of his sufferings, you know. He is not tolerably well, as he told me to tell papa, but he's better, very likely."

"There you differ with me, Miss Cathy," I remarked; "I should conjecture him to be far worse."

Linton here started from his slumber in bewildered terror, and asked if any one had called his name.

"No," said Catherine; "unless in dreams. I cannot conceive how you manage to doze, out of doors, in the morning."

"I thought I heard my father," he gasped, glancing up to the frowning nab[1] above us. "You are sure nobody spoke?"

Bilberry, otherwise known as the bog whortleberry *(Vaccinium uliginosum)*.

1 The summit of the Heights.

"Quite sure," replied his cousin. "Only Ellen and I were disputing concerning your health. Are you truly stronger, Linton, than when we separated in winter? If you be, I'm certain one thing is not stronger—your regard for me—speak, are you?"

The tears gushed from Linton's eyes as he answered—

"Yes, yes, I am!"

And, still under the spell of the imaginary voice, his gaze wandered up and down to detect its owner.

Cathy rose.

"For to-day we must part," she said. "And I won't conceal that I have been sadly disappointed with our meeting, though I'll mention it to nobody but you—not that I stand in awe of Mr. Heathcliff!"

"Hush," murmured Linton; "for God's sake, hush! He's coming." And he clung to Catherine's arm, striving to detain her; but, at that announcement, she hastily disengaged herself; and whistled to Minny, who obeyed her like a dog.

"I'll be here next Thursday," she cried, springing to the saddle. "Good bye. Quick, Ellen!"

And so we left him, scarcely conscious of our departure, so absorbed was he in anticipating his father's approach.

"Before we reached home, Catherine's displeasure softened into a perplexed sensation of pity and regret, largely blended with vague, uneasy doubts about Linton's actual circumstances, physical and social, in which I partook, though I counselled her not to say much, for a second journey would make us better judges.

My master requested an account of our on-goings: his nephew's offering of thanks was duly delivered, Miss Cathy gently touching on the rest: I also threw little light on his inquiries, for I hardly knew what to hide, and what to reveal.

CHAPTER 13

Seven days glided away, every one marking its course by the henceforth rapid alteration of Edgar Linton's state. The havoc that months had previously wrought was now emulated by the inroads of hours.

Catherine we would fain have deluded yet, but her own quick spirit refused to delude her. It divined, in secret, and brooded on the dreadful probability, gradually ripening into certainty.

She had not the heart to mention her ride, when Thursday came round; I mentioned it for her; and obtained permission to order her out of doors; for the library where her father stopped a short time daily—the brief period he could bear to sit up—and his chamber had become her whole world. She grudged each moment that did not find her bending over his pillow, or seated by his side. Her countenance grew wan with watching and sorrow, and my master gladly dismissed her to what he flattered himself would be a happy change of scene and society, drawing comfort from the hope that she would not now be left entirely alone after his death.

He had a fixed idea, I guessed by several observations he let fall, that as his nephew resembled him in person, he would resemble him in mind; for Linton's letters bore few or no indications of his defective character. And I, through pardonable weakness, refrained from correcting the error; asking myself what good there would be in disturbing his last moments with information that he had neither power nor opportunity to turn to account.

We deferred our excursion till the afternoon; a golden afternoon of August—every breath from the hills so full of life that it seemed whoever respired it, though dying, might revive.

Catherine's face was just like the landscape—shadows and sunshine flitting over it, in rapid succession; but the shadows rested longer and the sunshine was more transient, and her poor little heart reproached itself for even that passing forgetfulness of its cares.

We discerned Linton watching at the same spot he had selected before. My young mistress alighted, and told me that, as she was resolved to stay a very little while, I had better hold the pony and remain on horseback; but I dissented; I wouldn't risk losing sight of the charge committed to me a minute; so we climbed the slope of heath together.

Master Heathcliff received us with greater animation on this occasion; not the animation of high spirits, though, nor yet of joy; it looked more like fear.

"It is late!" he said, speaking short, and with difficulty. "Is not your father very ill? I thought you wouldn't come."

"*Why* won't you be candid?" cried Catherine, swallowing her greeting. "Why cannot you say at once, you don't want me? It is strange, Linton, that for the second time, you have brought me here on purpose, apparently, to distress us both, and for no reason besides!"

Linton shivered, and glanced at her, half supplicating, half ashamed, but his cousin's patience was not sufficient to endure this enigmatical behaviour.

"My father *is* very ill," she said, "and why am I called from his bedside—why didn't you send to absolve me from my promise, when you wished I wouldn't keep it? Come! I desire an explanation

—playing and trifling are completely banished out of my mind: and I can't dance attendance on your affectations, now!"

"My affectations!" he murmured, "what are they? For Heaven's sake Catherine, don't look so angry! Despise me as much as you please; I am a worthless, cowardly wretch—I can't be scorned enough! but I'm too mean[1] for your anger—hate my father, and spare me for contempt!"

"Nonsense!" cried Catherine in a passion. "Foolish, silly boy! And there! he trembles, as if I were really going to touch him! You needn't bespeak[2] contempt, Linton; anybody will have it spontaneously, at your service. Get off! I shall return home—it is folly dragging you from the hearth-stone, and pretending—what do we pretend? Let go my frock—if I pitied you for crying, and looking so very frightened, you should spurn such pity! Ellen, tell him how disgraceful this conduct is. Rise, and don't degrade yourself into an abject reptile—*don't.*"

With streaming face and an expression of agony, Linton had thrown his nerveless[3] frame along the ground; he seemed convulsed with exquisite terror.

"Oh!" he sobbed, "I cannot bear it! Catherine, Catherine, I'm a traitor too, and I dare not tell you! But leave me and I shall be killed! *Dear* Catherine, my life is in your hands; and you have said you loved me—and if you did, it wouldn't harm you. You'll not go, then? Kind, sweet, good Catherine! And perhaps you *will* consent—and he'll let me die with you!"

My young lady, on witnessing his intense anguish, stooped to raise him. The old feeling of indulgent tenderness overcame her vexation, and she grew thoroughly moved and alarmed.

"Consent to what?" she asked. "To stay? Tell me the meaning of this strange talk, and I will. You contradict your own words, and distract me! Be calm and frank, and confess at once, all that weighs on your heart. You wouldn't injure me, Linton, would you? You wouldn't let any enemy hurt me, if you could prevent it? I'll believe

1 Insignificant, ignoble.

2 Ask for.

3 Limp.

4 Heather.

you are a coward, for yourself, but not a cowardly betrayer of your best friend."

"But my father threatened me," gasped the boy, clasping his attenuated fingers, "and I dread him—I dread him! I *dare* not tell!"

"Oh well!" said Catherine, with scornful compassion, "keep your secret, *I'm* no coward—save yourself, I'm not afraid!"

Her magnanimity provoked his tears; he wept wildly, kissing her supporting hands, and yet could not summon courage to speak out.

I was cogitating what the mystery might be, and determined Catherine should never suffer to benefit him or any one else, by my good will. When hearing a rustle among the ling,[4] I looked up, and saw Mr. Heathcliff almost close upon us, descending the Heights. He didn't cast a glance towards my companions, though they were sufficiently near for Linton's sobs to be audible; but hailing me in the almost hearty tone he assumed to none besides, and the sincerity of which I couldn't avoid doubting, he said, "It is something to see you so near to my house, Nelly! How are you at the Grange? Let us hear! The rumour goes," he added in a lower tone, "that Edgar Linton is on his death-bed—perhaps they exaggerate his illness?"

"No; my master is dying," I replied, "it is true enough. A sad thing it will be for us all, but a blessing for him!"

"How long will he last, do you think?" he asked.

"I don't know," I said.

"Because," he continued, looking at the two young people, who were fixed under his eye—Linton appeared as if he could not venture to stir, or raise his head, and Catherine could not move, on his account—"Because that lad yonder, seems determined to beat me—and I'd thank his uncle to be quick, and go before him—Hallo! Has the whelp been playing that game long? I *did* give him some lessons about snivelling. Is he pretty lively with Miss Linton generally?"

"Lively? No—he has shown the greatest distress," I answered. "To see him, I should say that instead of rambling with his sweetheart on the hills, he ought to be in bed, under the hands of a doctor."

"He shall be, in a day or two," muttered Heathcliff. "But first—get up, Linton! Get up!" he shouted. "Don't grovel on the ground, there—up this moment!"

Linton had sunk prostrate again in another paroxysm of helpless fear, caused by his father's glance towards him, I suppose, there was nothing else to produce such humiliation.

He made several efforts to obey, but his little strength was annihilated, for the time, and he fell back again with a moan.

Mr. Heathcliff advanced, and lifted him to lean against a ridge of turf.

"Now," said he with curbed ferocity, "I'm getting angry—and if you don't command that paltry spirit of yours—*Damn* you! Get up, directly!"

"I will, father!" he panted. "Only, let me alone, or I shall faint! I've done as you wished—I'm sure. Catherine will tell you that I—that I—have been cheerful. Ah!—keep by me, Catherine; give me your hand."

"Take mine," said his father, "stand on your feet! There now—she'll lend you her arm . . . that's right, look at *her.* You would imagine I was the devil himself, Miss Linton, to excite such horror. Be so kind as to walk home with him, will you? He shudders, if I touch him."

"Linton, dear!" whispered Catherine, "I can't go to Wuthering Heights . . . papa has forbidden me . . . He'll not harm you, why are you so afraid?"

"I can never re-enter that house," he answered. "I am *not* to re-enter it without you!"

"Stop . . ." cried his father. "We'll respect Catherine's filial scruples. Nelly, take him in, and I'll follow your advice concerning the doctor, without delay."

5 Resolute or obstinate.

6 Open pasture for grazing cattle or sheep.

"You'll do well," replied I, "but I must remain with my mistress. To mind your son is not my business."

"You are very stiff!"[5] said Heathcliff, "I know that—but you'll force me to pinch the baby, and make it scream, before it moves your charity. Come then, my hero. Are you willing to return, escorted by me?"

He approached once more, and made as if he would seize the fragile being; but shrinking back, Linton clung to his cousin, and implored her to accompany him with a frantic importunity that admitted no denial.

However I disapproved, I couldn't hinder her; indeed how could she have refused him herself? What was filling him with dread, we had no means of discerning, but there he was, powerless under its gripe, and any addition seemed capable of shocking him into idiocy.

We reached the threshold; Catherine walked in; and I stood waiting till she had conducted the invalid to a chair, expecting her out immediately; when Mr. Heathcliff, pushing me forward, exclaimed—

"My house is not stricken with the plague, Nelly; and I have a mind to be hospitable to-day; sit down, and allow me to shut the door."

He shut and locked it also; I started.

"You shall have tea, before you go home," he added. "I am by myself. Hareton is gone with some cattle to the Lees[6]—and Zillah and Joseph are off on a journey of pleasure. And, though I'm used to being alone, I'd rather have some interesting company, if I can get it. Miss Linton, take your seat by *him.* I give you what I have; the present is hardly worth accepting; but, I have nothing else to offer. It is Linton, I mean. How she does stare! It's odd what a savage feeling I have to anything that seems afraid of me! Had I been born where laws are less strict, and tastes less dainty, I should treat myself to a slow vivifisection of those two, as an evening's amusement."

He drew in his breath, struck the table, and swore to himself.

"By hell! I hate them."

"I'm not afraid of you!" exclaimed Catherine, who could not hear the latter part of his speech.

She stepped close up, her black eyes flashing with passion and resolution.

"Give me that key—I will have it!" she said. "I wouldn't eat or drink here, if I were starving."

Heathcliff had the key in his hand that remained on the table. He looked up, seized with a sort of surprise at her boldness, or, possibly, reminded by her voice and glance, of the person from whom she inherited it.

She snatched at the instrument, and half succeeded in getting it out of his loosened fingers; but her action recalled him to the present; he recovered it speedily.

"Now, Catherine Linton," he said, "stand off; or I shall knock you down; and that will make Mrs. Dean mad."[7]

Regardless of this warning, she captured his closed hand, and its contents again.

"We *will* go!" she repeated, exerting her utmost efforts to cause the iron muscles to relax; and finding that her nails made no impression, she applied her teeth pretty sharply.

Heathcliff glanced at me a glance that kept me from interfering a moment. Catherine was too intent on his fingers to notice his face. He opened them, suddenly, and resigned the object of dispute; but, ere she had well secured it, he seized her with the liberated hand, and, pulling her on his knee, administered, with the other, a shower of terrific slaps on both sides of the head, each sufficient to have fulfilled his threat, had she been able to fall.

At this diabolical violence, I rushed on him furiously.

"You villain!" I began to cry, "you villain!"

A touch on the chest silenced me; I am stout, and soon put out of breath; and, what with that and the rage, I staggered dizzily back, and felt ready to suffocate, or to burst a blood-vessel.

7 Brontë uses the word "mad" in its full range of meanings, including "deranged" or "infatuated"; here she uses it in its modern colloquial sense to mean "angry" or "cross."

8 Bad temper.

The scene was over in two minutes; Catherine, released, put her two hands to her temples, and looked just as if she were not sure whether her ears were off or on. She trembled like a reed, poor thing, and leant against the table perfectly bewildered.

"I know how to chastise children, you see," said the scoundrel, grimly, as he stooped to repossess himself of the key, which had dropped to the floor. "Go to Linton now, as I told you; and cry at your ease! I shall be your father to-morrow—all the father you'll have in a few days—and you shall have plenty of that—you can bear plenty—you're no weakling—you shall have a daily taste, if I catch such a devil of a temper in your eyes again!"

Cathy ran to me instead of Linton, and knelt down, and put her burning cheek on my lap, weeping aloud. Her cousin had shrunk into a corner of the settle, as quiet as a mouse, congratulating himself, I dare say, that the correction had lighted on another than him.

Mr. Heathcliff, perceiving us all confounded, rose and expeditiously made the tea himself.

The cups and saucers were laid ready. He poured it out, and handed me a cup.

"Wash away your spleen,"[8] he said. "And help your own naughty pet and mine. It is not poisoned, though I prepared it. I'm going out to seek your horses."

Our first thought, on his departure, was to force an exit somewhere. We tried the kitchen door, but that was fastened outside; we looked at the windows—they were too narrow for even Cathy's little figure.

"Master Linton," I cried, seeing we were regularly imprisoned. "You know what your diabolical father is after, and you shall tell us, or I'll box your ears, as he has done your cousin's."

"Yes, Linton; you must tell," said Catherine. "It was for your sake I came; and it will be wickedly ungrateful if you refuse."

"Give me some tea—I'm thirsty—and then I'll tell you," he answered. "Mrs. Dean, go away. I don't like you standing over me.

Pencil sketch of St. Simeon Stylites, copied from an engraving by S. Williams, signed by Emily at the base of the pillar and dated March 4, 1833. St. Simeon was best known for having lived for thirty-seven years at the top of a pillar. Tennyson wrote a famous dramatic monologue in which the saint describes his "life of death" in 1833, but the poem was not published until 1842.

9 Heathcliff has not only threatened Linton but also bribed him with the promise that he can accompany Cathy back to the Grange once he and Cathy are married.

Now, Catherine, you are letting your tears fall into my cup! I won't drink that. Give me another."

Catherine pushed another to him, and wiped her face. I felt disgusted at the little wretch's composure, since he was no longer in terror for himself. The anguish he had exhibited on the moor subsided as soon as ever he entered Wuthering Heights; so, I guessed he had been menaced with an awful visitation of wrath, if he failed in decoying us there; and, that accomplished, he had no further immediate fears.

"Papa wants us to be married," he continued, after sipping some of the liquid. "And he knows your papa wouldn't let us marry now; and he's afraid of my dying, if we wait; so we are to be married in the morning, and you are to stay here all night; and, if you do as he wishes, you shall return home next day, and take me with you."[9]

"Take you with her, pitiful changeling?" I exclaimed. "*You* marry? Why, the man is mad, or he thinks us fools, every one. And do you imagine that beautiful young lady, that healthy, hearty girl, will tie herself to a little perishing monkey like you? Are you cherishing the notion that *anybody,* let alone Miss Catherine Linton, would have you for a husband? You want whipping for bringing us in here at all, with your dastardly, puling tricks; and—don't look so silly now! I've a very good mind to shake you severely, for your contemptible treachery, and your imbecile conceit."

I did give him a slight shaking, but it brought on the cough, and he took to his ordinary resource of moaning and weeping, and Catherine rebuked me.

"Stay all night? No!" she said, looking slowly round. "Ellen, I'll burn that door down, but I'll get out."

And she would have commenced the execution of her threat directly, but Linton was up in alarm, for his dear self, again. He clasped her in his two feeble arms, sobbing—

"Won't you have me, and save me—not let me come to the Grange? Oh!—darling Catherine!—you mustn't go, and leave me, after all. You *must* obey my father, you *must!*"

"I must obey my own," she replied, "and relieve him from this cruel suspense. The whole night! What would he think? He'll be distressed already. I'll either break or burn a way out of the house. Be quiet! You're in no danger—but, if you hinder me—Linton, I love papa better than you!"

The mortal terror he felt of Mr. Heathcliff's anger, restored to the boy his coward's eloquence. Catherine was near distraught—still, she persisted that she must go home, and tried entreaty, in her turn, persuading him to subdue his selfish agony.

While they were thus occupied, our jailer re-entered.

"Your beasts have trotted off," he said, "and—now, Linton! snivelling again? What has she been doing to you? Come, come—have done, and get to bed. In a month or two, my lad, you'll be able to pay her back her present tyrannies, with a vigorous hand—you're pining for pure love, are you not? Nothing else in the world—and she shall have you! There, to bed! Zillah won't be here to-night; you must undress yourself. Hush! hold your noise! Once in your own room, I'll not come near you, you needn't fear. By chance, you've managed tolerably. I'll look to the rest."

He spoke these words, holding the door open for his son to pass; and the latter achieved his exit exactly as a spaniel might, which suspected the person who attended on it of designing a spiteful squeeze.

The lock was re-secured. Heathcliff approached the fire, where my mistress and I stood silent. Catherine looked up, and instinctively raised her hand to her cheek—his neighbourhood revived a painful sensation. Anybody else would have been incapable of regarding the childish act with sternness, but he scowled on her, and muttered—

"Oh, you are not afraid of me? Your courage is well disguised—you *seem* damnably afraid!"

"I *am* afraid now," she replied; "because if I stay, papa will be miserable; and how can I endure making him miserable—when he—when he—Mr. Heathcliff, *let* me go home! I promise to marry

10 Nelly's point is that Heathcliff's forcing Cathy to marry Linton would constitute a felony. Her indignation is comic, given how much she has already put up with from Heathcliff, as is her eagerness to display her understanding of the law. Until 1827, when Parliament abolished benefit of clergy, clergymen were not subject to the authority of secular law.

11 Heathcliff reminds Cathy that her birth coincided with her mother's death.

Linton—papa would like me to, and I love him—and why should you wish to force me to do what I'll willingly do of myself?"

"Let him dare to force you!" I cried. "There's law in the land, thank God, there is!—though we *be* in an out-of-the-way place. I'd inform, if he were my own son, and it's felony without benefit of clergy!"[10]

"Silence!" said the ruffian. "To the devil with your clamour! I don't want *you* to speak. Miss Linton, I shall enjoy myself remarkably in thinking your father will be miserable; I shall not sleep for satisfaction. You could have hit on no surer way of fixing your residence under my roof, for the next twenty-four hours, than informing me that such an event would follow. As to your promise to marry Linton, I'll take care you shall keep it, for you shall not quit the place till it is fulfilled."

"Send Ellen then, to let papa know I'm safe!" exclaimed Catherine, weeping bitterly. "Or marry me now. Poor papa! Ellen, he'll think we're lost. What shall we do?"

"Not he! He'll think you are tired of waiting on him, and run off, for a little amusement," answered Heathcliff. "You cannot deny that you entered my house of your own accord, in contempt of his injunctions to the contrary. And it is quite natural that you should desire amusement at your age; and that you should weary of nursing a sick man, and that man, *only* your father. Catherine, his happiest days were over when your days began. He cursed you, I dare say, for coming into the world (I did, at least).[11] And it would just do if he cursed you as *he* went out of it. I'd join him. I don't love you! How should I? Weep away. As far as I can see, it will be your chief diversion hereafter: unless Linton make amends for other losses; and your provident parent appears to fancy he may. His letters of advice and consolation entertained me vastly. In his last, he recommended my jewel to be careful of his; and kind to her when he got her. Careful and kind—that's paternal! But Linton requires his whole stock of care and kindness for himself. Linton can play the little tyrant well. He'll undertake to torture any number of cats if their teeth be drawn, and their claws pared. You'll be able to tell his uncle fine tales of his *kindness,* when you get home again, I assure you."

"You're right there!" I said, "explain your son's character. Show his resemblance to yourself; and then, I hope, Miss Cathy will think twice, before she takes the cockatrice!"[12]

"I don't much mind speaking of his amiable qualities now," he answered, "because she must either accept him, or remain a prisoner, and you along with her, till your master dies. I can detain you both, quite concealed, here. If you doubt, encourage her to retract her word, and you'll have an opportunity of judging!"

"I'll not retract my word," said Catherine. "I'll marry him, within this hour, if I may go to Thrushcross Grange afterwards.[13] Mr. Heathcliff, you're a cruel man, but you're not a fiend; and you won't, from *mere* malice, destroy, irrevocably, all my happiness. If papa thought I had left him on purpose, and if he died before I returned, could I bear to live? I've given over crying; but I'm going to kneel here, at your knee; and I'll not get up, and I'll not take my eyes from your face, till you look back at me! No, don't turn away! *do* look! You'll see nothing to provoke you. I don't hate you. I'm not angry that you struck me. Have you never loved *anybody,* in all your life, uncle? *Never?* Ah!—you must look once—I'm so wretched—you can't help being sorry and pitying me."

"Keep your eft's fingers[14] off; and move, or I'll kick you!" cried Heathcliff, brutally repulsing her. "I'd rather be hugged by a snake. How the devil can you dream of fawning on me? I *detest* you!"

He shrugged his shoulders—shook himself, indeed, as if his flesh crept with aversion; and thrust back his chair: while I got up, and opened my mouth, to commence a downright torrent of abuse; but I was rendered dumb in the middle of the first sentence, by a threat that I should be shown into a room by myself, the very next syllable I uttered.

It was growing dark—we heard a sound of voices at the garden gate. Our host hurried out, instantly; *he* had his wits about him; *we*

12 Literally, a serpent identified with the basilisk and able to kill with its glance (see Vol. II, Chap. 3, note 27); figuratively, a traitor or a conspirator.

13 Cathy is interestingly uninformed about the laws regulating marriage, in particular the marriage of minors, yet another sign of Edgar's paternal care. The Marriage Act of 1753 stipulated that marriages had to be performed in a church and authorized by the publication of banns or a license. Parental consent was required for persons under the age of twenty-one to obtain a license, and a parent could also forbid the banns. In Scotland, where the Marriage Act was not in force, it was legal for boys to marry at fourteen and for girls to marry at twelve. Neither a license nor a minister was required.

14 Animal images animate Heathcliff's expression of his physical loathing of Cathy and also tell us what she is doing here—not just kneeling and looking up at him, but reaching out and touching him, perhaps attempting to turn him back toward her. He feels her fingers as the appendages of a newt or salamander; her embrace is more repellant than a snake's touch; and her dog-like behavior increases his hatred for her.

15 A ladder or steps leading to the garret.

had not. There was a talk of two or three minutes, and he returned alone.

"I thought it had been your cousin Hareton," I observed to Catherine. "I wish he would arrive! Who knows but he might take our part?"

"It was three servants sent to seek you from the Grange," said Heathcliff, overhearing me. "You should have opened a lattice, and called out; but I could swear that chit is glad you didn't. She's glad to be obliged to stay, I'm certain."

At learning the chance we had missed, we both gave vent to our grief without control; and he allowed us to wail on till nine o'clock; then he bid us go up-stairs, through the kitchen, to Zillah's chamber; and I whispered my companion to obey; perhaps, we might contrive to get through the window there, or into a garret, and out by its skylight.

The window, however, was narrow like those below, and the garret trap[15] was safe from our attempts; for we were fastened in as before.

We neither of us lay down: Catherine took her station by the lattice, and watched anxiously for morning—a deep sigh being the only answer I could obtain to my frequent entreaties that she would try to rest.

I seated myself in a chair, and rocked, to and fro, passing harsh judgment on my many derelictions of duty; from which, it struck me then, all the misfortunes of all my employers sprang. It was not the case, in reality, I am aware; but it was, in my imagination, that dismal night, and I thought Heathcliff himself less guilty than I.

At seven o'clock he came, and inquired if Miss Linton had risen.

She ran to the door immediately, and answered—

"Yes."

"Here then," he said, opening it, and pulling her out.

I rose to follow, but he turned the lock again. I demanded my release.

"Be patient," he replied; "I'll send up your breakfast in a while."

I thumped on the panels, and rattled the latch angrily; and Catherine asked why I was still shut up? He answered, I must try to endure it another hour, and they went away.

I endured it two or three hours; at length, I heard a footstep, not Heathcliff's.

"I've brought you something to eat," said a voice—"oppen t' door!"

Complying eagerly, I beheld Hareton, laden with food enough to last me all day.

"Tak it!" he added, thrusting the tray into my hand.

"Stay one minute," I began.

"Nay!" cried he, and retired, regardless of any prayers I could pour forth to detain him.

"And there I remained enclosed the whole day, and the whole of the next night; and another, and another. Five nights and four days I remained, altogether, seeing nobody but Hareton, once every morning, and he was a model of a jailer—surly, and dumb, and deaf to every attempt at moving his sense of justice or compassion.

1 Zillah's basket hangs from her arm, moving back and forth freely.

2 Handsome.

3 Hale and hearty.

CHAPTER 14

On the fifth morning, or rather afternoon, a different step approached—lighter and shorter—and, this time, the person entered the room. It was Zillah; donned in her scarlet shawl, with a black silk bonnet on her head, and a willow basket swung to[1] her arm.

"Eh, dear! Mrs. Dean," she exclaimed. "Well! there is a talk about you at Gimmerton. I never thought, but you were sunk in the Blackhorse marsh, and Missy with you, till master told me you'd been found, and he'd lodged you here! What, and you must have got on an island, sure? And how long were you in the hole? Did master save you, Mrs. Dean? But you're not so thin—you've not been so poorly, have you?"

"Your master is a true scoundrel!" I replied. "But he shall answer for it. He needn't have raised that tale—it shall all be laid bare!"

"What do you mean?" asked Zillah. "It's not his tale—they tell that in the village—about your being lost in the marsh; and I calls to Earnshaw, when I come in—'Eh, they's queer things, Mr. Hareton, happened since I went off. It's a sad pity of that likely[2] young lass, and cant[3] Nelly Dean.'

"He stared. I thought he had not heard aught, so I told him the rumour.

"The master listened, and he just smiled to himself, and said—

"'If they have been in the marsh, they are out now, Zillah. Nelly Dean is lodged, at this minute, in your room. You can tell her to

Albumen print portrait of William Makepeace Thackeray (1811–1863) by J. C. Watkins.

Mary Wollstonecraft (1759–1797), English writer, philosopher, feminist, and mother of Mary Shelley. Oil portrait by John Keenan c. 1793.

flit,[4] when you go up; here is the key. The bog-water got into her head, and she would have run home, quite flighty, but I fixed her,[5] till she came round to her senses. You can bid her go to the Grange, at once, if she be able, and carry a message from me, that her young lady will follow in time to attend the Squire's funeral.'"

"Mr. Edgar is not dead?" I gasped. "Oh! Zillah, Zillah!"

4 Be gone.

5 Kept her securely here. Heathcliff's use of the verb "fix" with a human direct object is unusual.

"No, no—sit you down, my good mistress," she replied, "you're right sickly yet. He's not dead: Doctor Kenneth thinks he may last another day—I met him on the road and asked."

Instead of sitting down, I snatched my outdoor things, and hastened below, for the way was free.

On entering the house,[6] I looked about for some one to give information of Catherine.

The place was filled with sunshine, and the door stood wide open, but nobody seemed at hand.

As I hesitated whether to go off at once, or return and seek my mistress, a slight cough drew my attention to the hearth.

Linton lay on the settle, sole tenant, sucking a stick of sugar-candy,[7] and pursuing my movements with apathetic eyes.

"Where is Miss Catherine?" I demanded sternly, supposing I could frighten him into giving intelligence, by catching him thus, alone.

He sucked on like an innocent.

"Is she gone?" I said.

"No," he replied; "she's up-stairs—she's not to go; we won't let her."

"You won't let her, little idiot!" I exclaimed. "Direct me to her room immediately, or I'll make you sing out sharply."

"Papa would make you sing out, if you attempted to get there," he answered. "He says I'm not to be soft with Catherine—she's my wife,[8] and it's shameful that she should wish to leave me! He says, she hates me, and wants me to die, that she may have my money, but she shan't have it; and she shan't go home! she never shall! she may cry, and be sick as much as she pleases!"

He resumed his former occupation, closing his lids, as if he meant to drop asleep.

"Master Heathcliff," I resumed, "have you forgotten all Catherine's kindness to you, last winter, when you affirmed you loved her, and when she brought you books, and sung you songs, and came many a time through wind and snow to see you? She wept to

6 The sitting room.

7 Brontë could not have found a better way to signal that Linton has now fallen to a new low point of self-involvement and cruelty. Her image of him sucking a stick of sugar candy while Cathy suffers upstairs recalls Heathcliff's infantilizing description of Edgar Linton as a "sucking leveret" (Vol. I, Chap. 11), but the sugar candy signals how much more contemptible Linton is than his uncle.

The cost of sugar candy depended on the number of refining stages required to produce it, and it is tempting to imagine Linton's treat as very white rather than tan or brown. A nasty child named Tom Billings lies and steals sugar in William Makepeace Thackeray's *Catherine: A Story,* which appeared in serial installments in *Fraser's Magazine,* one of the journals that came by subscription to the Parsonage.

Slavery was an inextricable part of the economy of sugar plantations, and Liverpool was both an important slave-trading port and a center of sugar production. English goods left Liverpool to be traded for African slaves, the slaves were transported from Africa to the West Indies to work the plantations, and the sugar was brought back from the West Indies to Liverpool. Jane Eyre's inheritance comes from her uncle, John Eyre, who made his fortune in the West Indian sugar plantations. In *A Vindication of the Rights of Woman* (1792), Mary Wollestonecraft asks whether sugar is "always to be produced by vital blood" and then goes on to compare the lives of European women to the lives of Caribbean slaves: "Is one half of the human species, like the poor African slaves, to be subject to prejudices that brutalize them, when principles would be a surer guard, only to sweeten the cup of man?" (ed. Carol H. Poston [New York: W. W. Norton, 1975], pp. 144–145).

8 The five days of Nelly's confinement provide ample time for Heathcliff to take Linton and Cathy across the Scottish border to be married, perhaps to Gretna Green, the most famous site of runaway marriages. For the parallel with Heathcliff's and Isabella's runaway marriage, see Vol. I, Chap. 12, note 20.

miss one evening, because you would be disappointed; and you felt then that she was a hundred times too good to you; and now you believe the lies your father tells, though you know he detests you both! And you join him against her. That's fine gratitude, is it not?"

The corner of Linton's mouth fell, and he took the sugar-candy from his lips.

"Did she come to Wuthering Heights, because she hated you?" I continued. "Think for yourself! As to your money, she does not even know that you will have any. And you say she's sick; and yet, you leave her alone, up there in a strange house! *You,* who have felt what it is to be so neglected! You could pity your own sufferings, and she pitied them, too, but you won't pity hers! I shed tears, Master Heathcliff, you see—an elderly woman, and a servant merely—and you, after pretending such affection, and having reason to worship her, almost, store every tear you have for yourself, and lie there quite at ease. Ah!—you're a heartless, selfish boy!"

"I can't stay with her," he answered crossly. "I'll not stay, by myself. She cries so I can't bear it. And she won't give over, though I say I'll call my father—I did call him once; and he threatened to strangle her, if she was not quiet, but she began again, the instant he left the room; moaning and grieving, all night long, though I screamed for vexation that I couldn't sleep."

"Is Mr. Heathcliff out," I inquired, perceiving that the wretched creature had no power to sympathise with his cousin's mental tortures.

"He's in the court," he replied, "talking to Doctor Kenneth, who says uncle is dying, truly, at last—I'm glad, for I shall be master of the Grange after him—and Catherine always spoke of it as *her* house. It isn't hers! It's mine—papa says everything she has is mine. All her nice books are mine—she offered to give me them, and her pretty birds, and her pony Minny, if I would get the key of our room, and let her out: but I told her she had nothing to give, they were all, all mine.[9] And then she cried, and took a little picture from her neck, and said I should have that—two pictures in a gold

9 The information Linton has received from Heathcliff is accurate. He will inherit his uncle's estate, and his marriage to Cathy has given him ownership of all her moveable property.

case—on one side her mother, and on the other, uncle, when they were young. That was yesterday—I said *they* were mine, too; and tried to get them from her. The spiteful thing wouldn't let me; she pushed me off, and hurt me. I shrieked out—that frightens her—she heard papa coming, and she broke the hinges, and divided the case and gave me her mother's portrait; the other she attempted to hide; but papa asked what was the matter, and I explained it. He took the one I had away; and ordered her to resign hers to me; she refused, and he—he struck her down, and wrenched it off the chain, and crushed it with his foot."

"And were you pleased to see her struck?" I asked, having my designs in encouraging his talk.

"I winked," he answered. "I wink to see my father strike a dog, or a horse, he does it so hard—yet I was glad at first—she deserved punishing for pushing me: but when papa was gone, she made me come to the window and showed me her cheek cut on the inside, against her teeth, and her mouth filling with blood: and then she gathered up the bits of the picture, and went and sat down with her face to the wall, and she has never spoken to me since; and I sometimes think she can't speak for pain. I don't like to think so! but she's a naughty thing for crying continually; and she looks so pale and wild, I'm afraid of her!"

"And you can get the key if you choose?" I said.

"Yes, when I am up-stairs," he answered "but I can't walk up-stairs now."

"In what apartment is it?" I asked.

"Oh, he cried, I shan't tell *you* where it is! It is our secret. Nobody, neither Hareton, nor Zillah, are to know. There!—you've tired me—go away, go away!" And he turned his face onto his arm, and shut his eyes again.

I considered it best to depart without seeing Mr. Heathcliff; and bring a rescue for my young lady, from the Grange.

On reaching it the astonishment of my fellow servants to see me, and their joy also, was intense; and when they heard that their little mistress was safe, two or three were about to hurry up, and shout the news at Mr. Edgar's door: but I bespoke[10] the announcement of it, myself.

How changed I found him, even in those few days! He lay an image of sadness and resignation, waiting his death. Very young he looked: though his actual age was thirty-nine, one would have called him ten years younger, at least. He thought of Catherine, for he murmured her name. I touched his hand, and spoke.

"Catherine is coming, dear master!" I whispered, "she is alive, and well; and will be here I hope to-night."

I trembled at the first effects of this intelligence: he half rose up, looked eagerly round the apartment, and then sunk back in a swoon.[11]

As soon as he recovered, I related our compulsory visit, and detention at the Heights: I said Heathcliff forced me to go in, which was not quite true; I uttered as little as possible against Linton; nor did I describe all his father's brutal conduct—my intentions being to add no bitterness, if I could help it, to his already overflowing cup.

He divined that one of his enemy's purposes was to secure the personal property, as well as the estate to his son, or rather himself; yet why he did not wait till his decease, was a puzzle to my master, because ignorant how nearly he and his nephew would quit the world together.

However, he felt his will had better be altered—instead of leaving Catherine's fortune at her own disposal, he determined to put it in the hands of trustees, for her use during life; and for her children, if she had any, after her. By that means, it could not fall to Mr. Heathcliff should Linton die.[12]

Having received his orders, I despatched a man to fetch the attorney, and four more, provided with serviceable weapons, to demand my young lady of her jailer. Both parties were delayed very late. The single servant returned first.

10 Stipulated for.

11 Which Catherine is Edgar thinking about when he murmers the name? Nelly assumes he is thinking of his daughter, but Edgar's startled response to her news that "Catherine is coming" (and his consistent reference to his daughter as "Cathy" and her mother as "Catherine") suggests he is thinking about his dead wife. If this is the case, then Edgar has more in common with Heathcliff than either of them imagines.

12 Toward the end of Chapter 11, Nelly reported that Edgar had set aside "yearly, a portion of his income for my young lady's fortune." Edgar cannot bequeath his estate to Cathy, but he can devise a legal instrument for putting her fortune out of her husband's (or her father-in-law's) control. Edgar fears Heathcliff, though he fails entirely to imagine his nephew's selfish disregard for Cathy and his power over her when he becomes her husband.

13 Most Victorians imagined Heaven as a place where families would be reunited. Edgar's death, as Nelly describes it, has all the features of a good Christian death. Dying has no terrors for him, and his confidence in his own salvation provides evidence of it. See Patricia Jalland, *Death in the Victorian Family* (Oxford: Oxford Univ. Press, 1996).

He said Mr. Green, the lawyer, was out when he arrived at his house, and he had to wait two hours for his re-entrance: and then Mr. Green told him he had a little business in the village that must be done, but he would be at Thrushcross Grange before morning.

The four men came back unaccompanied also. They brought word that Catherine was ill, too ill to quit her room, and Heathcliff would not suffer them to see her.

I scolded the stupid fellows well, for listening to that tale, which I would not carry to my master; resolving to take a whole bevy up to the Heights, at daylight, and storm it, literally, unless the prisoner were quietly surrendered to us.

Her father *shall* see her, I vowed, and vowed again, if that devil be killed on his own door-stones in trying to prevent it!

Happily, I was spared the journey, and the trouble.

I had gone down stairs at three o'clock to fetch a jug of water; and was passing through the hall, with it in my hand, when a sharp knock, at the front door, made me jump.

"Oh! it is Green"—I said, recollecting myself—"only Green," and I went on, intending to send somebody else to open it; but the knock was repeated, not loud, and still importunately.

I put the jug on the bannister, and hastened to admit him, myself.

The harvest moon shone clear outside. It was not the attorney. My own sweet little mistress sprung on my neck sobbing,

"Ellen! Ellen! Is papa alive?"

"Yes!" I cried, "yes, my angel, he is! God be thanked, you are safe with us again!"

She wanted to run, breathless as she was, up-stairs to Mr. Linton's room; but I compelled her to sit down on a chair, and made her drink, and washed her pale face, chafing it into a faint colour with my apron. Then I said I must go first, and tell of her arrival; imploring her to say, she should be happy with young Heathcliff. She stared, but soon comprehending why I counselled her to utter the falsehood, she assured me she would not complain.

I couldn't abide to be present at their meeting. I stood outside the chamber-door a quarter of an hour, and hardly ventured near the bed then.

All was composed, however; Catherine's despair was as silent as her father's joy. She supported him calmly, in appearance; and he fixed on her features his raised eyes that seemed dilating with ecstasy.

He died blissfully, Mr. Lockwood, he died so; kissing her cheek, he murmured, "I am going to her, and you, darling child, shall come to us," and never stirred or spoke again, but continued that rapt, radiant gaze, till his pulse imperceptibly stopped, and his soul departed. None could have noticed the exact minute of his death, it was so entirely without a struggle.[13]

Whether Catherine had spent her tears, or whether the grief were too weighty to let them flow, she sat there dry-eyed till the sun rose—she sat till noon, and would still have remained, brooding over that death-bed, but I insisted on her coming away, and taking some repose.

It was well I succeeded in removing her, for at dinner-time appeared the lawyer, having called at Wuthering Heights to get his instructions how to behave. He had sold himself to Mr. Heathcliff, and that was the cause of his delay in obeying my master's summons. Fortunately, no thought of worldly affairs crossed the latter's mind to disturb him, after his daughter's arrival.

Cathy escaping from Wuthering Heights by climbing out of the window in her mother's bedroom. This gouache painting by Lucien Joseph Fontanarosa (1912–1975) was published in the French translation of *Wuthering Heights, Les Hauts de Hurlevent* (1949).

Mr. Green took upon himself to order everything and everybody about the place. He gave all the servants but me notice to quit. He would have carried his delegated authority to the point of insisting that Edgar Linton should not be buried beside his wife but in the chapel, with his family. There was the will, however, to hinder that, and my loud protestations against any infringement of its directions.

The funeral was hurried over; Catherine, Mrs. Linton Heathcliff now, was suffered to stay at the Grange, till her father's corpse had quitted it.

She told me that her anguish had at last spurred Linton to incur the risk of liberating her. She heard the men I sent disputing at the door, and she gathered the sense of Heathcliff's answer. It drove her desperate—Linton, who had been conveyed up to the little parlour soon after I left, was terrified into fetching the key before his father re-ascended.

He had the cunning to unlock and re-lock the door, without shutting it; and when he should have gone to bed, he begged to sleep with Hareton, and his petition was granted, for once.

Catherine stole out before break of day. She dare not try the doors, lest the dogs should raise an alarm; she visited the empty chambers, and examined their windows; and, luckily, lighting on her mother's, she got easily out of its lattice, and onto the ground, by means of the fir tree, close by.[14] Her accomplice suffered for his share in the escape, notwithstanding his timid contrivances.

14 Cathy's egress through the window enclosed by the box-bed where Catherine once slept alongside Heathcliff constitutes yet another instance of the novel's symmetries by recalling her ghost-mother's desperate effort to come back into the Heights through the same window in Lockwood's dream (Vol. I, Chap. 3).

CHAPTER 15

The evening after the funeral, my young lady and I were seated in the library; now musing mournfully, one of us despairingly, on our loss; now venturing conjectures as to the gloomy future.

We had just agreed the best destiny which could await Catherine would be a permission to continue resident at the Grange, at least during Linton's life: he being allowed to join her there, and I to remain as housekeeper. That seemed rather too favourable an arrangement to be hoped for, and yet I did hope, and began to cheer up under the prospect of retaining my home, and my employment, and, above all, my beloved young mistress, when a servant—one of the discarded ones, not yet departed—rushed hastily in, and said, "that devil Heathcliff" was coming through the court, should he fasten the door in his face?

If we had been mad enough to order that proceeding, we had not time. He made no ceremony of knocking, or announcing his name; he was master, and availed himself of the master's privilege to walk straight in, without saying a word.

The sound of our informant's voice directed him to the library: he entered; and motioning him out, shut the door.

It was the same room into which he had been ushered, as a guest, eighteen years before: the same moon shone through the window; and the same autumn landscape lay outside. We had not yet lighted a candle, but all the apartment was visible, even to the

Oil portrait of Emily Brontë, painted by Patrick Branwell Brontë, c. 1833–1834. This portrait was originally part of the "Gun Group" painting of Charlotte, Emily, Anne, and Branwell, so called because Branwell represented himself holding a shotgun. Charlotte's widower, Arthur Bell Nicholls, inherited the painting in 1861 when Patrick Brontë died. We don't know when Nicholls cut Emily's portrait out of the "Gun Group" painting and destroyed the rest. Apparently, he believed that Branwell had failed to represent everyone but Emily accurately.

1 Heathcliff announces his intent to subject Cathy to the same debasing treatment he himself had, and has given to Hareton.

portraits on the wall—the splendid head of Mrs. Linton, and the graceful one of her husband.

Heathcliff advanced to the hearth. Time had little altered his person either. There was the same man; his dark face rather sallower, and more composed, his frame a stone or two heavier, perhaps, and no other difference.

Catherine had risen with an impulse to dash out, when she saw him.

"Stop!" he said, arresting her by the arm. "No more runnings away! Where would you go? I'm come to fetch you home; and I hope you'll be a dutiful daughter, and not encourage my son to further disobedience. I was embarrassed how to punish him, when I discovered his part in the business—he's such a cobweb, a pinch would annihilate him—but you'll see by his look that he has received his due! I brought him down one evening, the day before yesterday, and just set him in a chair, and never touched him afterwards. I sent Hareton out, and we had the room to ourselves. In two hours, I called Joseph to carry him up again; and, since then, my presence is as potent on his nerves as a ghost; and I fancy he sees me often, though I am not near; Hareton says he wakes and shrieks in the night by the hour together; and calls you to protect him from me; and, whether you like your precious mate or not, you must come—he's your concern now; I yield all my interest in him to you."

"Why not let Catherine continue here?" I pleaded, "and send Master Linton to her. As you hate them both, you'd not miss them—they *can* only be a daily plague to your unnatural heart."

"I'm seeking a tenant for the Grange," he answered; "and I want my children about me, to be sure—besides that lass owes me her services for her bread;[1] I'm not going to nurture her in luxury and idleness after Linton is gone. Make haste and get ready now. And don't oblige me to compel you."

"I shall," said Catherine. "Linton is all I have to love in the world, and, though you have done what you could to make him hateful to me, and me to him, you *cannot* make us hate each other! and I defy you to hurt him when I am by, and I defy you to frighten me."

"You are a boastful champion!" replied Heathcliff; "but I don't like you well enough to hurt him—you shall get the full benefit of the torment, as long as it lasts. It is not I who will make him hateful to you—it is his own sweet spirit. He's as bitter as gall at your desertion, and its consequences—don't expect thanks for this noble devotion. I heard him draw a pleasant picture to Zillah of what he would do, if he were as strong as I—the inclination is there, and his very weakness will sharpen his wits to find a substitute for strength."

"I know he has a bad nature," said Catherine; "he's your son. But I'm glad I've a better, to forgive it; and I know he loves me and for that reason I love him. Mr. Heathcliff, *you* have *nobody* to love you; and, however miserable you make us, we shall still have the revenge of thinking that your cruelty rises from your greater misery! You *are* miserable, are you not? Lonely, like the devil, and envious like him? *Nobody* loves you—*nobody* will cry for you, when you die! I wouldn't be you!"[2]

Catherine spoke with a kind of dreary triumph: she seemed to have made up her mind to enter into the spirit of her future family, and draw pleasure from the griefs of her enemies.

"You shall be sorry to be yourself presently," said her father-in-law, "if you stand there another minute. Begone, witch, and get your things."

She scornfully withdrew.

In her absence, I began to beg for Zillah's place at the Heights, offering to resign her mine; but he would suffer it on no account. He bid me be silent, and then, for the first time, allowed himself a glance round the room, and a look at the pictures. Having studied Mrs. Linton, he said—

"I shall have that at home. Not because I need it, but—"

He turned abruptly to the fire, and continued, with what, for lack of a better word, I must call a smile—

2 Cathy's words echo the words her mother spoke to Isabella when she tried to discourage her from pursuing a romantic relationship with Heathcliff: "I wouldn't be you for a kingdom, then!" (Vol. I, Chap. 10).

"I'll tell you what I did yesterday! I got the sexton, who was digging Linton's grave, to remove the earth off her coffin lid, and I opened it. I thought, once, I would have stayed there, when I saw her face again—it is hers yet[3]—he had hard work to stir me; but he said it would change, if the air blew on it, and so I struck one side of the coffin loose—and covered it up—not Linton's side, damn him! I wish he'd been soldered in lead[4]—and I bribed the sexton to pull it away, when I'm laid there, and slide mine out too, I'll have it made so, and then, by the time Linton gets to us, he'll not know which is which!"

"You were very wicked, Mr. Heathcliff!" I exclaimed; "were you not ashamed to disturb the dead?"

"I disturbed nobody, Nelly," he replied; "and I gave some ease to myself. I shall be a great deal more comfortable now; and you'll have a better chance of keeping me underground, when I get there.[5] Disturbed her? No! she has disturbed me, night and day, through eighteen years—incessantly—remorselessly—till yesternight—and yesternight, I was tranquil. I dreamt I was sleeping the last sleep, by that sleeper, with my heart stopped, and my cheek frozen against hers."

"And if she had been dissolved into earth, or worse, what would you have dreamt of then?" I said.

"Of dissolving with her, and being more happy still!" he answered. "Do you suppose I dread any change of that sort? I expected such a transformation on raising the lid, but I'm better pleased that it should not commence till I share it. Besides, unless I had received a distinct impression of her passionless features, that strange feeling would hardly have been removed. It began oddly. You know, I was wild after she died, and eternally, from dawn to dawn, praying her to return to me—her spirit—I have a strong faith in ghosts; I have a conviction that they can, and do exist, among us!

"The day she was buried there came a fall of snow. In the evening I went to the churchyard. It blew bleak as winter—all round

3 There is a natural explanation for the preservation of Catherine's corpse: she has been buried in a hollow in the corner of a churchyard where there are heavy deposits of peat. In Chapter 3 of Volume I, Lockwood recalled passing Gimmerton Chapel and described its setting "near a swamp, whose peaty moisture is said to answer all the purposes of embalming on the few corpses deposited there" (Vol. I, Chap. 3, note 20).

4 In Victorian England, those who could afford it might purchase double or triple coffins for burial. One of the layers in such coffins would be made of lead, which was thought to make the coffin more secure from bodysnatchers and also to slow down the process of decomposition. The coffins in *Wuthering Heights* are made of wood, but a lead coffin would suit Heathcliff's plans better than a wooden one since his aim is to keep Edgar's remains from mixing with Catherine's.

5 Heathcliff threatens Nelly (and the novel repeatedly tempts its readers) with the idea that he is not human. His warning that he won't stay buried connects him to the ghosts and vampires who terrorize and injure their former neighbors in Yorkshire ghost stories that go back at least to the Middle Ages. Although the usual remedies—prayers and promises of absolution—sometimes worked, the approved method of stopping revenants from tormenting their neighbors was to dig up their corpses and dismember or burn them.

was solitary: I didn't fear that her fool of a husband would wander up the den[6] so late—and no one else had business to bring them there.

"Being alone, and conscious two yards of loose earth was the sole barrier between us, I said to myself—

"'I'll have her in my arms again! If she be cold, I'll think it is this north wind that chills *me;* and if she be motionless, it is sleep.'

"I got a spade from the toolhouse, and began to delve with all my might—it scraped the coffin; I fell to work with my hands; the wood commenced cracking about the screws, I was on the point of attaining my object, when it seemed that I heard a sigh from some one above, close at the edge of the grave, and bending down.—'If I can only get this off,' I muttered, 'I wish they may shovel in the earth over us both!' and I wrenched at it more desperately still. There was another sigh, close at my ear. I appeared to feel the warm breath of it displacing the sleet-laden wind. I knew no living thing in flesh and blood was by—but as certainly as you perceive the approach to some substantial body in the dark, though it cannot be discerned, so certainly I felt that Cathy was there, not under me, but on the earth.

"A sudden sense of relief flowed, from my heart, through every limb. I relinquished my labour of agony, and turned consoled at once, unspeakably consoled. Her presence was with me; it remained while I re-filled the grave, and led me home. You may laugh, if you will, but I was sure I should see her there. I was sure she was with me, and I could not help talking to her.

"Having reached the Heights, I rushed eagerly to the door. It was fastened; and, I remember, that accursed Earnshaw and my wife opposed my entrance.[7] I remember stopping to kick the breath out of him, and then hurrying up-stairs to my room, and hers—I looked round impatiently—I felt her by me—I could *almost* see her, and yet I *could not!* I ought to have sweat blood then, from the anguish of my yearning, from the fervour of my supplications to have but one glimpse! I had not one. She showed herself,

6 Hollow.

7 Isabella narrated the extraordinarily violent events that followed Heathcliff's effort to embrace Catherine on the night of her funeral in Chapter 3.

8 The dried and twisted intestines of sheep, horses, and donkeys were used for the strings of musical instruments and for tools of various kinds.

as she often was in life, a devil to me! And, since then, sometimes more, and sometimes less, I've been the sport of that intolerable torture! Infernal—keeping my nerves at such a stretch, that, if they had not resembled catgut,[8] they would, long ago, have relaxed to the feebleness of Linton's.

"When I sat in the house with Hareton, it seemed that on going out, I should meet her; when I walked on the moors, I should meet her coming in. When I went from home, I hastened to return; she *must* be somewhere at the Heights, I was certain! And when I slept in her chamber—I was beaten out of that—I couldn't lie there; for the moment I closed my eyes, she was either outside the window, or sliding back the panels, or entering the room, or even resting her darling head on the same pillow as she did when a child. And I must open my lids to see. And so I opened and closed them a hundred times a-night—to be always disappointed! It racked me! I've often groaned aloud, till that old rascal Joseph no doubt believed that my conscience was playing the fiend inside of me.

"Now since I've seen her, I'm pacified—a little. It was a strange way of killing, not by inches, but by fractions of hair-breadths, to beguile me with the spectre of a hope, through eighteen years!"

Mr. Heathcliff paused and wiped his forehead—his hair clung to it, wet with perspiration; his eyes were fixed on the red embers of the fire; the brows not contracted, but raised next the temples, diminishing the grim aspect of his countenance, but imparting a peculiar look of trouble, and a painful appearance of mental tension towards one absorbing subject. He only half addressed me, and I maintained silence—I didn't like to hear him talk!

After a short period, he resumed his meditation on the picture, took it down, and leant it against the sofa to contemplate it at better advantage; and while so occupied, Catherine entered, announcing that she was ready, when her pony should be saddled.

"Send that over to-morrow," said Heathcliff to me, then turning to her he added, "You may do without your pony—it is a fine evening, and you'll need no ponies at Wuthering Heights; for what journies you take, your own feet will serve you—Come along."

"Good-bye, Ellen!" whispered my dear little mistress. As she kissed me, her lips felt like ice. "Come and see me Ellen, don't forget."

"Take care you do no such thing, Mrs. Dean!" said her new father. "When I wish to speak to you I'll come here. I want none of your prying at my house!"

He signed her to precede him; and casting back a look that cut my heart, she obeyed.

I watched them from the window, walk down the garden. Heathcliff fixed Catherine's arm under his, though she disputed the act at first, evidently; and with rapid strides, he hurried her into the alley, whose trees concealed them.

Kate Bush performing her debut single, "Wuthering Heights," in 1978. It topped the charts in the UK, Ireland, Australia, New Zealand, and Italy and remains her best-selling song. Bush, who shares a birthday (July 30) with Brontë, manages to sound like both a mercurial spirit and a feral creature.

CHAPTER 16

I have paid a visit to the Heights, but I have not seen her since she left; Joseph held the door in his hand, when I called to ask after her, and wouldn't let me pass. He said Mrs. Linton was "thrang,"[1] and the master was not in. Zillah has told me something of the way they go on, otherwise I should hardly know who was dead, and who living.

She thinks Catherine haughty, and does not like her, I can guess by her talk. My young lady asked some aid of her, when she first came, but Mr. Heathcliff told her to follow her own business, and let his daughter-in-law look after herself, and Zillah willingly acquiesced, being a narrow-minded selfish woman. Catherine evinced a child's annoyance at this neglect, repaid it with contempt, and thus enlisted my informant among her enemies, as securely as if she had done her some great wrong.

I had a long talk with Zillah, about six weeks ago, a little before you came, one day, when we foregathered[2] on the moor; and this is what she told me.

"The first thing Mrs. Linton did," she said, "on her arrival at the Heights, was to run upstairs without even wishing good-evening to me and Joseph; she shut herself into Linton's room, and remained till morning—then, while the master and Earnshaw were at breakfast, she entered the house and asked all in a quiver if the doctor might be sent for—her cousin was very ill.

1 Too busy (to visit with Nelly).

2 Met by chance.

"'We know that!' answered Heathcliff, 'but his life is not worth a farthing,[3] and I won't spend a farthing on him.'

"'But I cannot tell how to do,' she said, 'and if nobody will help me, he'll die!'

"'Walk out of the room!' cried the master, 'and let me never hear a word more about him! None here care what becomes of him; if you do, act the nurse; if you do not, lock him up and leave him.'

"Then she began to bother me, and I said I'd had enough plague with the tiresome thing; we each had our tasks, and hers was to wait on Linton; Mr. Heathcliff bid me leave that labour to her.

"How they managed together, I can't tell. I fancy he fretted a great deal, and moaned hisseln,[4] night and day; and she had precious little rest, one could guess by her white face, and heavy eyes —she sometimes came into the kitchen all wildered[5] like, and looked as if she would fain beg assistance: but I was not going to disobey the master—I never dare disobey him, Mrs. Dean, and though I thought it wrong that Kenneth should not be sent for, it was no concern of mine, either to advise or complain; and I always refused to meddle.

"Once or twice, after we had gone to bed, I've happened to open my door again, and seen her sitting crying, on the stairs' top; and then I've shut myself in, quick, for fear of being moved to interfere. I did pity her then, I'm sure; still I didn't wish to lose my place, you know!

"At last, one night she came boldly into my chamber, and frightened me out of my wits, by saying, 'Tell Mr. Heathcliff that his son is dying—I'm sure he is, this time.—Get up, instantly, and tell him!'

"Having uttered this speech, she vanished again. I lay a quarter of an hour listening and trembling—Nothing stirred—the house was quiet.

"'She's mistaken,' I said to myself. 'He's got over it. I needn't disturb them.' And I began to doze. But my sleep was marred a second time, by a sharp ringing of the bell—the only bell we have, put up on purpose for Linton, and the master called to me, to see what

3 A coin of little value; literally, a quarter of a penny.

4 Moaned to himself.

5 Bewildered.

6 Glad.

was the matter, and inform them that he wouldn't have that noise repeated.

"I delivered Catherine's message. He cursed to himself, and in a few minutes, came out with a lighted candle, and proceeded to their room. I followed—Mrs. Heathcliff was seated by the bedside, with her hands folded on her knees. Her father-in-law went up, held the light to Linton's face, looked at him, and touched him; afterwards he turned to her.

"'Now—Catherine,' he said, 'how do you feel?'

"She was dumb.

"'How do you feel, Catherine?' he repeated.

"'He's safe, and I'm free,' she answered, 'I should feel well—but,' she continued with a bitterness she couldn't conceal, 'you have left me so long to struggle against death, alone, that I feel and see only death! I feel like death!'

"And she looked like it, too! I gave her a little wine. Hareton and Joseph, who had been wakened by the ringing, and the sound of feet, and heard our talk from outside, now entered. Joseph was fain,[6] I believe, of the lad's removal: Hareton seemed a thought bothered, though he was more taken up with staring at Catherine than thinking of Linton. But the master bid him get off to bed again—we didn't want his help. He afterwards made Joseph remove the body to his chamber, and told me to return to mine, and Mrs. Heathcliff remained by herself.

"In the morning, he sent me to tell her she must come down to breakfast—she had undressed, and appeared going to sleep; and said she was ill; at which I hardly wondered. I informed Mr. Heathcliff, and he replied,

"'Well, let her be till after the funeral; and go up now and then to get her what is needful; and as soon as she seems better, tell me.'"

Cathy stayed up-stairs a fortnight, according to Zillah, who visited her twice a-day, and would have been rather more friendly, but her attempts at increasing kindness were proudly and promptly repelled.

A watercolor painting copied from an engraving of H. Corbould's drawing "The Disconsolate." Emily would have seen this engraving in the *Forget Me Not* annual for 1831, where it accompanied a poem by L. E. L. about a young woman deserted by her lover. L. E. L. was the penname of Letitia Elizabeth Landon (1802–1838), a popular poet and woman of letters. The title and signature appear to be in Emily's handwriting, although it has been suggested that Branwell may have made the painting to give to Emily.

Heathcliff went up once, to show her Linton's will. He had bequeathed the whole of his, and what had been her, moveable property to his father. The poor creature was threatened, or coaxed into that act, during her week's absence, when his uncle died. The lands, being a minor, he could not meddle with. However, Mr.

Heathcliff has claimed, and kept them in his wife's right, and his also—I suppose, legally at any rate, Catherine, destitute of cash and friends, cannot disturb his possession.[7]

"Nobody," said Zillah, "ever approached her door, except that once, but I . . . and nobody asked anything about her. The first occasion of her coming down into the house was on a Sunday afternoon.

"She had cried out, when I carried up her dinner, that she couldn't bear any longer being in the cold; and I told her the master was going to Thrushcross Grange; and Earnshaw and I needn't hinder her from descending; so, as soon as she heard Heathcliff's horse trot off, she made her appearance, donned in black, and her yellow curls combed back behind her ears, as plain as a quaker; she couldn't comb them out.[8]

"Joseph, and I generally go to chapel on Sundays." ("The Kirk, you know, has no minister now," explained Mrs. Dean, "and they call the Methodists' or Baptists' place, I can't say which it is, at Gimmerton, a chapel."[9]) "Joseph had gone," she continued, "but I thought proper to bide at home. Young folks are always the better for an elder's over-looking,[10] and Hareton with all his bashfulness, isn't a model of nice[11] behaviour. I let him know that his cousin would very likely sit with us, and she had been always used to see the Sabbath respected, so he had as good leave his guns and bits of in-door work alone, while she stayed.

"He coloured up at the news; and cast his eyes over his hands and clothes. The train-oil[12] and gunpowder were shoved out of sight in a minute. I saw he meant to give her his company; and I guessed, by his way, he wanted to be presentable; so, laughing, as I durst not laugh when the master is by, I offered to help him, if he would, and joked at his confusion. He grew sullen, and began to swear.

"Now, Mrs. Dean," she went on, seeing me not pleased by her manner, "you happen think your young lady too fine for Mr. Hareton, and happen you're right—but, I own, I should love well to

7 Because Linton is still a minor at the time of his death, he can make a will devising moveable property but not one devising real property. According to C. P. Sanger, Heathcliff has no right to Thrushcross Grange as Isabella's husband. His possession of Thrushcross Grange is therefore not legal, but Catherine lacks the friends and resources required to challenge it ("The Structure of Wuthering Heights," in Eleanor McNees, ed., *The Brontë Sisters: Critical Assessments* [Mountfield: Helm Information, 1996], 2, pp. 76–78).

8 Cathy is already dressed in black for her father, but a widow's mourning would be more severe and more drab still than a daughter's. Lacking the "cash and friends" to acquire a new mourning costume, she has tried to make herself look more severe by combing her natural curls behind her ears.

9 Nelly's inability to specify whether the chapel Zillah and Joseph attend belongs to the Methodists or the Baptists is not surprising. Like her employers, Nelly herself would worship at the established church. In her narration so far, she has used the terms "chapel" and "kirk" interchangeably, but Zilla's reference here to a "chapel" marks it as a place for Dissenters to worship.

In the period between 1801, when Lockwood arrives at the Heights, and 1847, when *Wuthering Heights* was published, membership in the Church of England declined, and attendance in Dissenting chapels increased. By the end of the eighteenth and the beginning of the nineteenth centuries, Protestant Dissent (Methodist, Baptist, Quaker, and so on) thrived alongside the established Church of England, which was itself divided by the Evangelical Revival.

10 Supervision.

11 Refined.

12 Oil extracted from whale blubber and used for various purposes, including cleaning gun barrels.

bring her pride a peg lower. And what will all her learning and her daintiness do for her, now? She's as poor as you, or I—poorer, I'll be bound—you're saving, and I'm doing my little all that road."[13]

Hareton allowed Zillah to give him her aid; and she flattered him into a good humour; so, when Catherine came, half forgetting her former insults, he tried to make himself agreeable, by the housekeeper's account.

"Missis walked in," she said, "as chill as an icicle, and as high as a princess. I got up and offered her my seat in the arm-chair. No, she turned up her nose at my civility. Earnshaw rose too, and bid her come to the settle, and sit close by the fire; he was sure she was starved.[14]

"'I've been starved a month and more,' she answered, resting on the word, as scornful as she could.

"And she got a chair for herself, and placed it at a distance from both of us.

"Having sat till she was warm, she began to look round, and discovered a number of books in the dresser; she was instantly upon her feet again, stretching to reach them, but they were too high up.

"Her cousin, after watching her endeavours a while, at last summoned courage to help her; she held her frock, and he filled it with the first that came to hand.

"That was a great advance for the lad—she didn't thank him; still, he felt gratified that she had accepted his assistance, and ventured to stand behind as she examined them, and even to stoop and point out what struck his fancy in certain old pictures which they contained—nor was he daunted by the saucy style in which she jerked the page from his finger; he contented himself with going a bit farther back, and looking at her, instead of the book.

"She continued reading, or seeking for something to read. His attention became, by degrees, quite centred in the study of her thick, silky curls—her face he couldn't see, and she couldn't see him. And, perhaps, not quite awake to what he did, but attracted like a child to a candle, at last he proceeded from staring to touch-

13 Charlotte removed a comma that follows "all" in 1847, and I have followed her emendation. Marsden and Jack position the comma after "little" to emphasize that "all that road" is "a common expression" (Hilda Marsden and Ian Jack, *Wuthering Heights* [Oxford: Clarendon Press, 1976], p. 432). Zillah's meaning is not obscure: she is doing everything she can, however little that is, to save her money. She is also fully aware that Cathy has not inherited her father's wealth and is entirely dependent on Heathcliff to maintain her. Her desire to humble Cathy repeats Nelly's desire to humble her mother.

14 Frozen.

15 Passion.

16 Tired.

17 Inconsiderable person.

18 Roused.

19 Take on Cathy's chores, perhaps specifically her care of Linton.

20 Zillah uses the title ironically to call attention to Cathy's airs.

ing; he put out his hand and stroked one curl, as gently as if it were a bird. He might have stuck a knife into her neck, she started round in such a taking.[15]

"'Get away, this moment! How dare you touch me? Why are you stopping there?' she cried, in a tone of disgust. 'I can't endure you! I'll go up-stairs again, if you come near me.'

"Mr. Hareton recoiled, looking as foolish as he could do; he sat down in the settle, very quiet, and she continued turning over her volumes, another half hour—finally, Earnshaw crossed over, and whispered to me.

"'Will you ask her to read to us, Zillah? I'm stalled[16] of doing naught—and I do like—I could like to hear her! Dunnot say I wanted it, but ask of yourseln.'

"'Mr. Hareton wishes you would read to us, ma'am,' I said, immediately. 'He'd take it very kind—he'd be much obliged.'

"She frowned; and, looking up, answered, 'Mr. Hareton, and the whole set of you will be good enough to understand that I reject any pretence at kindness you have the hypocrisy to offer! I despise you, and will have nothing to say to any of you! When I would have given my life for one kind word, even to see one of your faces, you all kept off. But I won't complain to you! I'm driven down here by the cold, not either to amuse you, or enjoy your society.'

"'What could I ha' done?' began Earnshaw. 'How was I to blame?'

"'Oh! you are an exception,' answered Mrs. Heathcliff. 'I never missed such a concern[17] as you.'

"'But I offered more than once, and asked,' he said, kindling up[18] at her pertness, 'I asked Mr. Heathcliff to let me wake[19] for you—'

"'Be silent! I'll go out of doors, or anywhere, rather than have your disagreeable voice in my ear!' said my lady.[20]

"Hareton muttered, she might go to hell, for him! and unslinging his gun, restrained himself from his Sunday occupations no longer.

"He talked now, freely enough; and she presently saw fit to retreat to her solitude: but the frost had set in, and, in spite of her pride, she was forced to condescend to our company, more and more.[21] However, I took care there should be no further scorning at my good nature—ever since, I've been as stiff as herself—and she has no lover, or liker, among us—and she does not deserve one—for, let them say the least word to her, and she'll curl back without respect of any one! She'll snap at the master himself; and as good as dares him to thrash her; and the more hurt she gets, the more venomous she grows."

At first, on hearing this account from Zillah, I determined to leave my situation, take a cottage, and get Catherine to come and live with me; but Mr. Heathcliff would as soon permit that, as he would set up Hareton in an independent house; and I can see no remedy, at present, unless she could marry again; and that scheme, it does not come within my province to arrange.

Thus ended Mrs. Dean's story. Notwithstanding the doctor's prophecy, I am rapidly recovering strength, and, though it be only the second week in January, I propose getting out on horseback, in a day or two, and riding over to Wuthering Heights, to inform my landlord that I shall spend the next six months in London; and, if he likes, he may look out for another tenant to take the place after October—I would not pass another winter here, for much.

21 Cathy is forced to spend more of her time in the company of the other members of the household because the only fire (apart from the cooking fire in the kitchen) is in the sitting room, which they occupy. When Linton was alive, a fire was also maintained in his room upstairs.

Emily's pencil sketch of another Brontë pet, "Grasper—from life," made in January 1834. Said to be an Irish terrier, Grasper has an uncharacteristically pointed nose. He preceded Keeper and was a favorite of Emily's. The label on his collar states his owner's name and address, as required by the dog tax law.

CHAPTER 17

Yesterday was bright, calm, and frosty. I went to the Heights as I proposed; my housekeeper entreated me to bear a little note from her to her young lady, and I did not refuse, for the worthy woman was not conscious of anything odd in her request.[1]

The front door stood open, but the jealous gate was fastened, as at my last visit; I knocked and invoked Earnshaw from among the garden beds; he unchained it, and I entered. The fellow is as handsome a rustic as need be seen. I took particular notice of him this time; but then, he does his best, apparently, to make the least of his advantages.

I asked if Mr. Heathcliff were at home? He answered, no; but he would be in at dinner-time. It was eleven o'clock, and I announced my intention of going in, and waiting for him, at which he immediately flung down his tools and accompanied me, in the office of watchdog, not as a substitute for the host.

We entered together; Catherine was there, making herself useful in preparing some vegetables for the approaching meal; she looked more sulky, and less spirited, than when I had seen her first. She hardly raised her eyes to notice me, and continued her employment with the same disregard to common forms of politeness, as before; never returning my bow and good morning, by the slightest acknowledgment.

1 See below, where Lockwood is "fearful" lest the note he carries to Cathy from Nelly will be thought to be a note he has written to her.

"She does not seem so amiable," I thought, "as Mrs. Dean would persuade me to believe. She's a beauty, it is true; but not an angel."

Earnshaw surlily bid her remove her things to the kitchen.

"Remove them yourself," she said, pushing them from her, as soon as she had done; and retiring to a stool by the window, where she began to carve figures of birds and beasts, out of the turnip parings in her lap.

I approached her, pretending to desire a view of the garden; and, as I fancied, adroitly dropped Mrs. Dean's note onto her knee, unnoticed by Hareton—but she asked aloud—"What is that?" And chucked it off.

"A letter from your old acquaintance, the housekeeper at the Grange," I answered, annoyed at her exposing my kind deed, and fearful lest it should be imagined a missive of my own.

She would gladly have gathered it up, at this information, but Hareton beat her; he seized, and put it in his waistcoat, saying Mr. Heathcliff should look at it first.

Thereat, Catherine silently turned her face from us, and, very stealthily, drew out her pocket-handkerchief and applied it to her eyes; and her cousin, after struggling a while to keep down his softer feelings, pulled out the letter and flung it on the floor beside her as ungraciously as he could.

Catherine caught and perused it eagerly; then she put a few questions to me concerning the inmates, rational and irrational,[2] of her former home; and gazing towards the hills, murmured in soliloquy.

"I should like to be riding Minny down there! I should like to be climbing up there—Oh! I'm tired—I'm *stalled*,[3] Hareton!"

And she leant her pretty head back against the sill, with half a yawn and half a sigh, and lapsed into an aspect of abstracted sadness, neither caring, nor knowing whether we remarked her.

"Mrs. Heathcliff," I said, after sitting some time mute, "you are not aware that I am an acquaintance of yours? So intimate, that

2 Cathy asks about the animal inhabitants of the Grange as well as its human inhabitants.

3 Tired. Italics emphasize Cathy's adoption of a dialect word to express her own feelings. It is not just any word in Hareton's dialect but a word he whispered to Zillah toward the end of the previous chapter, when he hoped she would ask Cathy to read to them. By using Hareton's word, Cathy shows she has been listening to him more intently than he knows.

4 Both Cathy and Lockwood are readers, and the novel repeatedly correlates reading with social mobility. Heathcliff certainly read while he was still being educated as Mr. Earnshaw's ward and Catherine's foster brother, and Nelly has improved herself by her good use of the library at Thrushcross Grange. When Cathy wanted to make her clandestine visits to the Heights, she bribed a groom at the Grange by giving him books. Hareton is not yet a reader but longs to become one.

5 "Chevy Chase" (or "The Ballad of Chevy Chase") tells the story of a hunt that provoked a bloody battle. The Cheviot Hills lie on both sides of the English-Scottish border, and the hunt is led by the hot-headed Englishman Henry Percy, the eldest son of the first Earl of Northumberland and the "Hotspur" of Shakespeare's *Henry IV, Part I.* Percy violates the law stipulating that no party may hunt in the border lands without notice and permission. The Scottish Earl Douglas, Percy's long-time rival, attempts to repel his trespass and is killed. The ballad and the episode that inspired it were an important part of the Brontë childrens' cultural heritage. An important character in Charlotte's and Branwell's Angrian saga, Alexander Augustus Percy, Duke of Northangerland, is based on Henry Percy. A fierce outlaw named Douglas figures in two of Emily's Gondal poems.

"The Ballad of Chevy Chase" was published in Thomas Percy's *Reliques of Ancient English Poetry* (1765), which may well be the book that Hareton has been trying to read. As Susan Stewart points out, it is humiliating that a Yorkshire yeoman and an avid hunter cannot pronounce the words of the ballad in their written form (Stewart, "The Ballad in *Wuthering Heights,*" *Representations,* 86:1 [Spring 2004], p. 191). Percy's *Reliques* aroused passionate, public enthusiasm for ancient ballads; contributed to the birth of Romanticism; and influenced two writers Brontë especially admired, Scott and Coleridge. As a child, Brontë chose Scott as her particular hero, and his influence on *Wuthering Heights* is pervasive. Several of her poems, in particular "A Day Dream" and "No coward soul is mine," show the influence of Coleridge's philosophy and poetry.

I think it strange you won't come and speak to me. My housekeeper never wearies of talking about and praising you; and she'll be greatly disappointed if I return with no news of or from you, except that you received her letter, and said nothing!"

She appeared to wonder at this speech and asked,

"Does Ellen like you?"

"Yes, very well," I replied unhesitatingly.

"You must tell her," she continued, "that I would answer her letter, but I have no materials for writing, not even a book from which I might tear a leaf."

"No books!" I exclaimed. "How do you contrive to live here without them, if I may take the liberty to inquire?—Though provided with a large library, I'm frequently very dull at the Grange—take my books away, and I should be desperate!"

"I was always reading, when I had them," said Catherine, "and Mr. Heathcliff never reads;[4] so he took it into his head to destroy my books. I have not had a glimpse of one, for weeks. Only once, I searched through Joseph's store of theology, to his great irritation: and once, Hareton, I came upon a secret stock in your room . . . some Latin and Greek, and some tales and poetry—all old friends. I brought the last here—and you gathered them, as a magpie gathers silver spoons, for the mere love of stealing! They are of no use to you—or else you concealed them in the bad spirit that as you cannot enjoy them, nobody else shall. Perhaps *your* envy counselled Mr. Heathcliff to rob me of my treasures? But I've most of them written on my brain and printed in my heart, and you cannot deprive me of those!"

Earnshaw blushed crimson, when his cousin made this revelation of his private literary accumulations, and stammered an indignant denial of her accusations.

"Mr. Hareton is desirous of increasing his amount of knowledge," I said, coming to his rescue. "He is not *envious* but *emulous* of your attainments—He'll be a clever scholar in a few years!"

"And he wants *me* to sink into a dunce, meantime," answered Catherine. "Yes, I hear him trying to spell and read to himself, and pretty blunders he makes! I wish you would repeat Chevy Chase,[5] as you did yesterday—It was extremely funny! I heard you . . . and I heard you turning over the dictionary,[6] to seek out the hard words, and then cursing, because you couldn't read their explanations!"

The young man evidently thought it too bad that he should be laughed at for his ignorance, and then laughed at for trying to remove it. I had a similar notion, and, remembering Mrs. Dean's anecdote of his first attempt at enlightening the darkness in which he had been reared, I observed, "But, Mrs. Heathcliff, we have each had a commencement, and each stumbled and tottered on the threshold, and had our teachers scorned instead of aiding us, we should stumble and totter yet."

"Oh!" she replied, "I don't wish to limit his acquirements . . . still, he has no right to appropriate what is mine, and make it ridiculous to me with his vile mistakes and mis-pronunciations! Those books, both prose and verse, were consecrated to me by other associations, and I hate to have them debased and profaned in his mouth! Besides, of all, he has selected my favourite pieces that I love the most to repeat, as if out of deliberate malice!"

Hareton's chest heaved in silence a minute; he laboured under a severe sense of mortification and wrath, which it was no easy task to suppress.

I rose, and from a gentlemanly idea of relieving his embarrassment, took up my station in the door-way surveying the external prospect as I stood.

He followed my example, and left the room, but presently reappeared, bearing half-a-dozen volumes in his hands, which he threw into Catherine's lap, exclaiming, "Take them! I never want to hear, or read, or think of them again!"

"I won't have them, now!" she answered. "I shall connect them with you, and hate them!"

6 This may or may not have been Johnson's *Dictionary*, first published in 1755 and reprinted several times in the eighteenth century. Hareton's dictionary study shows his determination to acquire a knowledge of English literature and much else. Johnson's "immediate predecessor and most important competitor for the market of dictionary buyers, Nathan Bailey," described his audience as the "Curious," the "Ignorant," "young Students, Artificers, Tradesmen and Foreigners." Johnson also designed his dictionary for "popular use" and especially for use by men seeking to improve themselves. He wanted his quotations to do more than provide examples pertinent to his definitions:

> When first I collected these authorities, I was desirous that every quotation should be useful to some other end than the illustration of a word; I therefore extracted from philosophers principles of science; from historians remarkable facts; from chymists complete processes; from divines striking exhortations; and from poets beautiful descriptions.

According to Robert DeMaria, Jr., Johnson accomplished "a remarkable portion of his scheme" (*Johnson's Dictionary and the Language of Learning* [Chapel Hill: Univ. of N. Carolina Press, 1986], pp. 7–13).

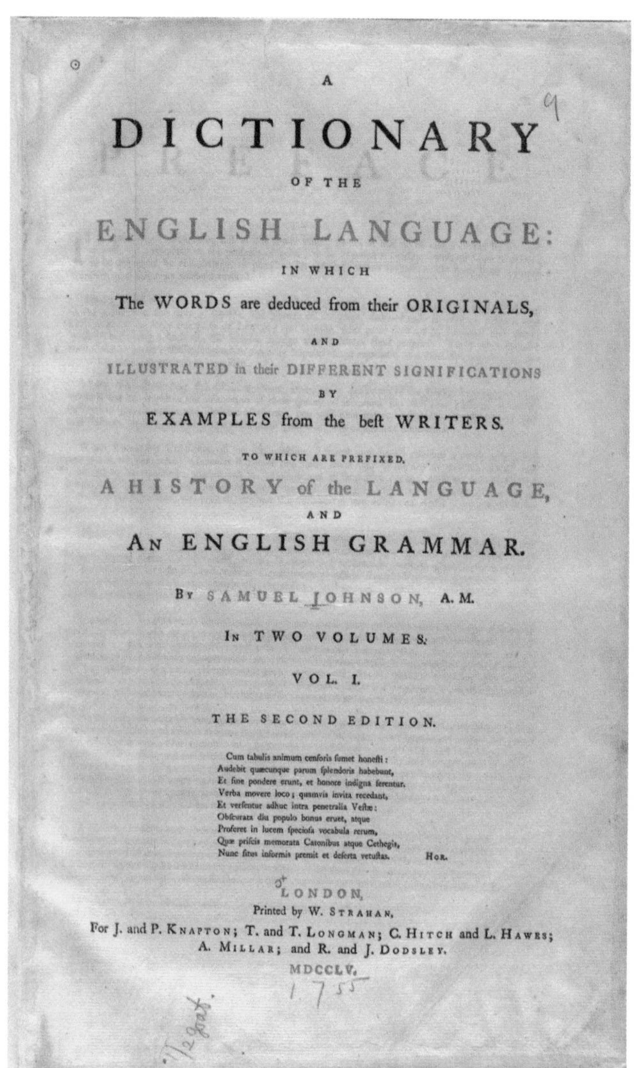

A

DICTIONARY

OF THE

ENGLISH LANGUAGE:

IN WHICH

The WORDS are deduced from their ORIGINALS,

AND

ILLUSTRATED in their DIFFERENT SIGNIFICATIONS

BY

EXAMPLES from the beſt WRITERS.

TO WHICH ARE PREFIXED,

A HISTORY of the LANGUAGE,

AND

AN ENGLISH GRAMMAR.

BY SAMUEL JOHNSON, A.M.

IN TWO VOLUMES.

VOL. I.

THE SECOND EDITION.

Cum tabulis animum cenſoris ſumet honeſti:
Audebit quæcunque parum ſplendoris habebunt,
Et ſine pondere erunt, et honore indigna ferentur.
Verba movere loco; quamvis invita recedant,
Et verſentur adhuc intra penetralia Veſtæ:
Obſcurata diu populo bonus eruet, atque
Proferet in lucem ſpecioſa vocabula rerum,
Quæ priſcis memorata Catonibus atque Cethegis,
Nunc ſitus informis premit et deſerta vetuſtas. HOR.

LONDON,
Printed by W. STRAHAN,
For J. and P. KNAPTON; T. and T. LONGMAN; C. HITCH and L. HAWES;
A. MILLAR; and R. and J. DODSLEY.
MDCCLV.

Title page of Samuel Johnson's *A Dictionary of the English Language* (1755–1756), not the first English dictionary but the most famous.

She opened one that had obviously been often turned over, and read a portion in the drawling tone of a beginner, then laughed, and threw it from her.

"And listen!" she continued provokingly, commencing a verse of an old ballad in the same fashion.

But his self-love would endure no further torment—I heard, and not altogether disapprovingly, a manual check[7] given to her saucy tongue—The little wretch had done her utmost to hurt her cousin's sensitive though uncultivated feelings, and a physical argument was the only mode he had of balancing the account and repaying its effects on the inflicter.

He afterwards gathered the books and hurled them on the fire. I read in his countenance what anguish it was to offer that sacrifice to spleen[8]—I fancied that as they consumed,[9] he recalled the pleasure they had already imparted, and the triumph, and ever increasing pleasure he had anticipated from them—and I fancied I guessed the incitement to his secret studies, also. He had been content with daily labour and rough animal enjoyments, till Catherine crossed his path—Shame at her scorn, and hope of her approval were his first prompters to higher pursuits; and instead of guarding him from one, and winning him the other, his endeavours to raise himself had produced just the contrary result.

"Yes, that's all the good that such a brute as you can get from them!" cried Catherine, sucking her damaged lip, and watching the conflagration with indignant eyes.

"You'd *better* hold your tongue, now!" he answered fiercely.

And his agitation precluding further speech, he advanced hastily to the entrance, where I made way for him to pass. But, ere he had crossed the door-stones, Mr. Heathcliff, coming up the causeway, encountered him and laying hold of his shoulder, asked,

"What's to do now, my lad?"

"Naught, naught!" he said, and broke away, to enjoy his grief and anger in solitude.

7 A slap across the mouth.

8 Pride.

9 Burned. The intransitive verb is rare. The *OED* cites Shakespeare's *Henry VI, Part 1*: "Breake thou in peeces, and consume to ashes."

Heathcliff gazed after him, and sighed.

"It will be odd, if I thwart myself!" he muttered, unconscious that I was behind him. "But when I look for his father in his face, I find *her* every day more! How the devil is he so like? I can hardly bear to see him."

He bent his eyes to the ground, and walked moodily in. There was a restless, anxious expression in his countenance, I had never remarked there before, and he looked sparer in person.

His daughter-in-law, on perceiving him through the window, immediately escaped to the kitchen, so that I remained alone.

"I'm glad to see you out of doors again, Mr. Lockwood," he said in reply to my greeting, "from selfish motives partly: I don't think I could readily supply your loss in this desolation. I've wondered, more than once, what brought you here."

"An idle whim, I fear sir," was my answer, "or else an idle whim is going to spirit me away—I shall set out for London next week, and I must give you warning that I feel no disposition to retain Thrushcross Grange, beyond the twelvemonths I agreed to rent it. I believe I shall not live there any more.

"Oh, indeed!—you're tired of being banished from the world, are you?" he said. "But if you be coming to plead off paying for a place you won't occupy, your journey is useless—I never relent in exacting my due, from any one."

"I'm coming to plead off nothing about it!" I exclaimed, considerably irritated. "Should you wish it, I'll settle with you now," and I drew my notebook from my pocket.

"No, no," he replied coolly, "you'll leave sufficient behind, to cover your debts, if you fail to return . . . I'm not in such a hurry—sit down and take your dinner with us—a guest that is safe from repeating his visit can generally be made welcome—Catherine! bring the things in—where are you?"

Catherine re-appeared, bearing a tray of knives and forks.

"You may get your dinner with Joseph," muttered Heathcliff aside, "and remain in the kitchen till he is gone."

She obeyed his directions very punctually—perhaps she had no temptation to transgress. Living among clowns and misanthropists, she probably cannot appreciate a better class of people, when she meets them.

With Mr. Heathcliff, grim and saturnine, on one hand, and Hareton, absolutely dumb, on the other, I made a somewhat cheerless meal, and bid adieu early—I would have departed by the back way to get a last glimpse of Catherine, and annoy old Joseph; but Hareton received orders to lead up my horse, and my host himself escorted me to the door, so I could not fulfil my wish.

How dreary life gets over in that house! I reflected, while riding down the road. What a realization of something more romantic than a fairy tale it would have been for Mrs. Linton Heathcliff, had she and I struck up an attachment, as her good nurse desired, and migrated together into the stirring atmosphere of the town!

CHAPTER 18

1802.—This September,[1] I was invited to devastate[2] the moors of a friend, in the North; and, on my journey to his abode, I unexpectedly came within fifteen miles of Gimmerton. The hostler,[3] at a roadside public-house, was holding a pail of water to refresh my horses, when a cart of very green oats, newly reaped, passed by, and he remarked—"Yon's frough Gimmerton, nah! They're allas three wick' after other folk wi' ther harvest."[4]

"Gimmerton?" I repeated; my residence in that locality had already grown dim and dreamy. "Ah! I know! How far is it from this?"

"Happen[5] fourteen mile' o'er th' hills, and a rough road," he answered.

A sudden impulse seized me to visit Thrushcross Grange. It was scarcely noon, and I conceived that I might as well pass the night under my own roof as in an inn. Besides, I could spare a day easily, to arrange matters with my landlord, and thus save myself the trouble of invading the neighbourhood again.

Having rested a while, I directed my servant to inquire the way to the village; and, with great fatigue to our beasts, we managed the distance in some three hours.

I left him there, and proceeded down the valley alone. The grey church looked greyer, and the lonely churchyard lonelier. I distinguished a moor sheep cropping the short turf on the graves. It was

1 Lockwood's last visit to the Heights in Chapter 17 occurred in the second week of January, 1802. In this chapter, he resumes his narrative after an interruption of about eight months.

2 Ravage. Lockwood has been invited to hunt, and his word choice is meant to be witty.

3 Someone who attends to horses at an inn.

4 "That's from Gimmerton! They're always three weeks later than everybody else with their harvest."

5 About.

sweet, warm weather—too warm for travelling; but the heat did not hinder me from enjoying the delightful scenery above and below; had I seen it nearer August, I'm sure it would have tempted me to waste a month among its solitudes. In winter, nothing more dreary, in summer, nothing more divine, than those glens shut in by hills, and those bluff,[6] bold swells of heath.

I reached the Grange before sunset, and knocked for admittance; but the family had retreated into the back premises, I judged by one thin, blue wreath curling from the kitchen chimney, and they did not hear.

I rode into the court. Under the porch, a girl of nine or ten sat knitting, and an old woman reclined on the horse-steps,[7] smoking a meditative pipe.

"Is Mrs. Dean within?" I demanded of the dame.

"Mistress Dean? Nay!" she answered, "shoo[8] doesn't bide here; shoo's up at th' Heights."

"Are you the housekeeper, then?" I continued.

"Eea, Aw keep th' hause,"[9] she replied.

"Well, I'm Mr. Lockwood, the master—Are there any rooms to lodge me in, I wonder? I wish to stay here all night."

"T' maister!" she cried in astonishment, "Whet, whoiver knew yah wur coming? Yah sud ha' send word! They's nowt norther dry nor mensful abaht t' place—nowt there isn't!"[10]

She threw down her pipe and bustled in, the girl followed, and I entered too; soon perceiving that her report was true, and, moreover, that I had almost upset her wits by my unwelcome apparition.

I bid her be composed—I would go out for a walk; and, meantime, she must try to prepare a corner of a sitting-room for me to sup in, and a bed-room to sleep in—No sweeping and dusting; only good fires and dry sheets were necessary.

She seemed willing to do her best; though she thrust the hearth-brush into the grates in mistake for the poker; and mal-

6 Elevated.

7 Steps provided for making it easier to mount a horse.

8 She.

9 "Yes, I keep the house." Except in the speech of this housekeeper, "Yes" is "Aye" in the novel's dialect. According to K. M. Petyt, "Eea" was a form less used, and used mainly by women. (See "The Dialect Speech in *Wuthering Heights*," in Hilda Marsden and Ian Jack, eds., *Wuthering Heights* [Oxford: Clarendon Press, 1976], p. 512.)

10 "The master! . . . What, who knew you were coming? You should have sent word. There's nothing either dry or proper about the place—there isn't!"

appropriated several other articles of her craft; but I retired, confiding in her energy for a resting-place against my return.

Wuthering Heights was the goal of my proposed excursion. An after-thought brought me back, when I had quitted the court.

"All well at the Heights?" I enquired of the woman.

"Eea, f'r owt Ee knaw!"[11] she answered, skurrying away with a pan of hot cinders.

I would have asked why Mrs. Dean had deserted the Grange; but it was impossible to delay her at such a crisis, so I turned away and made my exit, rambling leisurely along with the glow of a sinking sun behind, and the mild glory of a rising moon in front; one fading, and the other brightening, as I quitted the park, and climbed the stony by-road branching off to Mr. Heathcliff's dwelling.

Before I arrived in sight of it, all that remained of day was a beamless, amber light along the west; but I could see every pebble on the path, and every blade of grass by that splendid moon.

I had neither to climb the gate, nor to knock—it yielded to my hand.

That is an improvement! I thought. And I noticed another, by the aid of my nostrils; a fragrance of stocks and wall flowers, wafted on the air, from amongst the homely fruit trees.

Both doors and lattices were open; and yet, as is usually the case in a coal district, a fine, red fire illumined the chimney; the comfort which the eye derives from it renders the extra heat endurable. But the house of Wuthering Heights is so large that the inmates have plenty of space for withdrawing out of its influence; and, accordingly, what inmates there were had stationed themselves not far from one of the windows. I could both see them and hear them talk before I entered, and looked and listened in consequence, being moved thereto by a mingled sense of curiosity and envy that grew as I lingered.

11 "Yes, for all I know!"

"Con-*trary!*" said a voice as sweet as a silver bell—"That for the third time, you dunce! I'm not going to tell you, again—Recollect, or I pull your hair!"

"Contrary, then," answered another, in deep but softened tones. "And now, kiss me for minding so well."

"No, read it over first correctly, without a single mistake."

The male speaker began to read—he was a young man, respectably dressed, and seated at a table, having a book before him. His handsome features glowed with pleasure, and his eyes kept impatiently wandering from the page to a small white hand over his shoulder, which recalled him by a smart slap on the cheek, whenever its owner detected such signs of inattention.

Its owner stood behind, her light shining ringlets blending, at intervals, with his brown locks, as she bent to superintend his studies; and her face—it was lucky he could not see her face, or he would never have been so steady—I could, and I bit my lip, in spite, at having thrown away the chance I might have had, of doing something besides staring at its smiting beauty.

The task was done, not free from further blunders, but the pupil claimed a reward and received at least five kisses, which, however, he generously returned. Then, they came to the door, and from their conversation, I judged they were about to issue out and have a walk on the moors. I supposed I should be condemned in Hareton Earnshaw's heart, if not by his mouth, to the lowest pit in the infernal regions if I showed my unfortunate person in his neighbourhood then, and feeling very mean and malignant, I skulked round to seek refuge in the kitchen.

There was unobstructed admittance on that side also; and, at the door, sat my old friend, Nelly Dean, sewing and singing a song, which was often interrupted from within, by harsh words of scorn and intolerance, uttered in far from musical accents.

"Aw'd rayther, by th' haulf, hev 'em swearing i' my lugs frough morn tuh neeght, nur hearken yah, hahsiver!" said the tenant of the kitchen, in answer to an unheard speech of Nelly's. "It's a blaz-

WUTHERING HEIGHTS

A NOVEL,

BY

ELLIS BELL,

IN THREE VOLUMES.

VOL. I.

LONDON:
THOMAS CAUTLEY NEWBY, PUBLISHER,
72, MORTIMER St., CAVENDISH Sq.

1847.

WUTHERING HEIGHTS

A NOVEL,

BY

ELLIS BELL,

IN THREE VOLUMES.

VOL. II.

LONDON:
THOMAS CAUTLEY NEWBY, PUBLISHER,
72, MORTIMER St., CAVENDISH Sq.

1847.

The title pages of the first and second volumes of the first edition of *Wuthering Heights.* Although they identify *Wuthering Heights* as a three-volume novel, *Wuthering Heights* takes up Volume 1 and Volume 2, while Anne Brontë's *Agnes Grey* takes up Volume 3. The Brontë sisters chose pseudonyms—Currer, Ellis, and Acton Bell—that retained the initial letters of their given names but masked their gender as well as their identities. We don't know how they arrived at their pennames. "Bell" was the middle name of Patrick Brontë's curate, Arthur Bell Nicholls. He had recently arrived at the Parsonage and would marry Charlotte in 1854. Marianne Thormählen suggests that "Ellis" refers to Sarah Stickney Ellis (1799–1816), but she acknowledges that "some nerve" is required here, since this Ellis is best known as the author of popular conduct books for women ("The Brontë Pseudonyms," *English Studies* [1994], 3, p. 249). A more likely source for the name "Ellis" is George Ellis (1753–1815), poet, textual scholar, and popularizer of Middle English, Middle Scots, Anglo-Norman, and French poetry. Sir Walter Scott wrote two cantos of *Marmion* in Ellis's home and dedicated one of them to him:

> Dear Ellis! to the bard impart
> A lesson of thy magic art,
> To win at once the head and heart,—
> At once to charm, instruct, and mend,
> My guide, my pattern, and my friend.

ing shaime, ut Aw cannut oppen t' Blessed Book, bud yah set up them glories tuh Sattan, un' all t' flaysome wickednesses ut iver wer born intuh t' warld! Oh!—yah're a raight nowt; un' shoo's another; un' that poor lad 'ull be lost, atween ye. Poor lad!" he added, with a groan; "he's witched, Aw'm sartin on't! O, Lord, judge 'em, fur they's norther law nur justice amang wer rullers!"[12]

"No!—or we should be sitting in flaming fagots,[13] I suppose," retorted the singer. "But wisht, old man, and read your Bible, like a Christian, and never mind me. This is 'Fair Annie's Wedding'—a bonny tune—it goes to a dance."[14]

Mrs. Dean was about to recommence, when I advanced, and recognising me directly, she jumped to her feet, crying—

"Why, bless you, Mr. Lockwood! How could you think of returning in this way? All's shut up at Thrushcross Grange. You should have given us notice!"

"I've arranged to be accommodated there, for as long as I shall stay," I answered. "I depart again to-morrow. And how are you transplanted here, Mrs. Dean? tell me that."

"Zillah left, and Mr. Heathcliff wished me to come, soon after you went to London, and stay till you returned. But, step in, pray! Have you walked from Gimmerton this evening?"

"From the Grange," I replied; "and, while they make me lodging room there, I want to finish my business with your master, because I don't think of having another opportunity in a hurry."

"What business, sir?" said Nelly, conducting me into the house. "He's[15] gone out, at present, and won't return soon."

"About the rent," I answered.

"Oh! then it is with Mrs. Heathcliff you must settle," she observed, "or rather with me. She has not learnt to manage her affairs yet, and I act for her; there's nobody else."

I looked surprised.

"Ah! you have not heard of Heathcliff's death, I see!" she continued.

"Heathcliff dead?" I exclaimed, astonished. "How long ago?"

12 "I'd rather, by half, have them swearing in my ears from morning to night than listen to you, anyway! . . . It's a blazing shame that I cannot open the Blessed Book but you set up these songs praising Satan, and all the fearful wickednesses that ever were born into the world! Oh!—you're a right nothing; and she's another; and that poor lad will be lost between you. Poor lad! . . . He's bewitched, I'm certain of it! O, Lord, judge them, for there's neither law nor justice among our rulers!"

The phrase "neither law nor justice" turns up often in biblical commentaries but has no specific source in the Bible.

13 Hell.

14 The 1847 edition gives the title of the ballad Nelly is singing as "Fairy Annie's Wedding." That title is emended in accord with Colin Wilcockson's suggestion that the long puzzlement over which ballad Nelly sings here results from a simple printer's error: the addition of a "y" to "Fair" in the title as given in the manuscript. This is an example of the kind of error Brontë would have corrected on the proofsheets that Newby neglected, unless she intended to make Nelly guilty of a malapropism ("Fair[y] Annie's Wedding: A Note on *Wuthering Heights*," *Essays in Criticism*, 33:3 [1983], pp. 259–261).

In the ballad, a lord kidnaps fair Annie when she is a child and, after fathering seven illegitimate children with her, decides to marry a woman of wealth. On the eve of the wedding, the two women discover that they are sisters. The bride sails home, leaving part of her wealth as a dowry for her sister. Annie's subsequent wedding to the lord is implied. Wilcockson points to one "ironic" parallel between Brontë's story and the story the ballad tells. Heathcliff loves Catherine but marries her sister-in-law; his motive for marrying Isabella, like the lord's in "Fair Annie," is avarice. This situation is repeated with important variations in the story of the second generation of characters. Motivated by revenge and avarice, Heathcliff forces Linton to marry Cathy. Linton's death frees Cathy to marry her other cousin, Hareton, even though both of them are penniless. Nelly's account of how Cathy and Hareton are reconciled to each other follows her singing of "Fair Annie's Wedding."

"Fair Annie" is one of the 305 ballads published by Francis James Child in *English and Scottish Popular Ballads* in 1857, but many of the Child ballads would have been well known to the Brontës. As Child explains, there is "scarce an old historical song or ballad . . . wherein a Minstrel or Harper appears, but he is characterized by way of eminence to have been of 'the north countrye': and indeed the prevalence of the northern dialect in such compositions, shews that this representation is real" ("An Essay on the Ancient Minstrels in England," *Percy's Reliques of Ancient English Poetry*, available at https://archive.org/details/percysreliquesof01percuoft). This particular ballad was also printed in Scott's

"Three months since—but, sit down, and let me take your hat, and I'll tell you all about it. Stop, you have had nothing to eat, have you?"

"I want nothing. I have ordered supper at home. You sit down too. I never dreamt of his dying! Let me hear how it came to pass. You say you don't expect them back for some time—the young people?"

"No—I have to scold them every evening for their late rambles—but they don't care for me. At least, have a drink of our old ale—it will do you good—you seem weary."

She hastened to fetch it, before I could refuse, and I heard Joseph asking, whether "it warn't a crying scandal that she should have fellies[16] at her time of life? And then, to get them jocks[17] out uh t' Maister's cellar! He fair shaamed to 'bide still and see it."

She did not stay to retaliate, but re-entered, in a minute, bearing a reaming,[18] silver pint, whose contents I lauded with becoming earnestness. And afterwards she furnished me with the sequel of Heathcliff's history. He had a "queer"[19] end, as she expressed it.

"I was summoned to Wuthering Heights, within a fortnight of your leaving us," she said; "and I obeyed joyfully, for Catherine's sake."

My first interview with her grieved and shocked me!—she had altered so much since our separation. Mr. Heathcliff did not explain his reasons for taking a new mind about my coming here; he only told me he wanted me, and he was tired of seeing Catherine; I must make the little parlour my sitting room, and keep her with me. It was enough if he were obliged to see her once or twice a day.

She seemed pleased at this arrangement; and, by degrees, I smuggled over a great number of books, and other articles, that had formed her amusement at the Grange; and flattered myself we should get on in tolerable comfort.

The delusion did not last long. Catherine, contented at first, in a brief space grew irritable and restless. For one thing, she was for-

Minstrelsy of the Scottish Border (1802) under the title "Lord Thomas and Fair Annie."

15 Lockwood means Heathcliff. Nelly at first thinks he means Hareton, now the master of Wuthering Heights.

16 Fellows; admirers. Charlotte substitutes "followers" in 1850.

17 Provisions; in this instance, jugs of ale.

18 Foaming.

19 Used as an intensifier in Scottish and Irish English.

20 Doing the housework.

bidden to move out of the garden, and it fretted her sadly to be confined to its narrow bounds, as Spring drew on—for another, in following the house,[20] I was forced to quit her frequently, and she complained of loneliness; she preferred quarrelling with Joseph in the kitchen to sitting at peace in her solitude.

I did not mind their skirmishes; but Hareton was often obliged to seek the kitchen also, when the master wanted to have the house to himself; and, though, in the beginning, she either left it at his approach, or quietly joined in my occupations, and shunned remarking, or addressing him—and though he was always as sullen and silent, as possible—after a while, she changed her behaviour, and became incapable of letting him alone. Talking at him; commenting on his stupidity and idleness; expressing her wonder how he could endure the life he lived—how he could sit a whole evening staring into the fire, and dozing.

"He's just like a dog, is he not, Ellen?" she once observed, "or a cart-horse? He does his work, eats his food, and sleeps, eternally! What a blank, dreary mind he must have! Do you ever dream, Hareton? And, if you do, what is it about? But, you can't speak to me!"

Then she looked at him; but he would neither open his mouth, nor look again.

"He's perhaps, dreaming now," she continued. "He twitched his shoulder as Juno twitches hers. Ask him, Ellen."

"Mr. Hareton will ask the master to send you up-stairs, if you don't behave!" I said. He had not only twitched his shoulder, but clenched his fist, as if tempted to use it.

"I know why Hareton never speaks, when I am in the kitchen," she exclaimed, on another occasion. "He is afraid I shall laugh at him. Ellen, what do you think? He began to teach himself to read once; and, because I laughed, he burned his books, and dropped it—was he not a fool?"

"Were not you naughty?" I said; "answer me that."

Cathy (Juliette Binoche) making a peace offering to Hareton (Jason Riddington) toward the end of Peter Kosminsky's film adaptation of *Wuthering Heights* (1992). Kosminsky's is one of very few adaptations of Brontë's novel for film and television that represents the second generation of characters.

"Perhaps I was," she went on, "but I did not expect him to be so silly. Hareton, if I gave you a book, would you take it now? I'll try!"

She placed one she had been perusing on his hand; he flung it off, and muttered, if she did not give over, he would break her neck.

"Well I shall put it here," she said, "in the table drawer, and I'm going to bed."

Then she whispered me to watch whether he touched it, and departed. But he would not come near it, and so I informed her in the morning, to her great disappointment. I saw she was sorry for his persevering sulkiness and indolence—her conscience reproved her for frightening him off improving himself—she had done it effectually.

But her ingenuity was at work to remedy the injury; while I ironed, or pursued other stationary employments I could not well do in the parlour—she would bring some pleasant volume, and read it aloud to me. When Hareton was there, she generally paused in an interesting part, and left the book lying about—that she did repeatedly; but he was as obstinate as a mule, and, instead of

21 Joseph and Hareton are smoking pipes.

22 Making the linen ready for wearing; here Nelly is ironing it.

snatching at her bait, in wet weather he took to smoking[21] with Joseph, and they sat like automatons, one on each side of the fire, the elder happily too deaf to understand her wicked nonsense, as he would have called it, the younger doing his best to seem to disregard it. On fine evenings the latter followed his shooting expeditions, and Catherine yawned and sighed, and teased me to talk to her, and ran off into the court or garden, the moment I began; and, as a last resource, cried and said, she was tired of living, her life was useless.

Mr. Heathcliff, who grew more and more disinclined to society, had almost banished Earnshaw out of his apartment. Owing to an accident, at the commencement of March, he became for some days a fixture in the kitchen. His gun burst, while out on the hills by himself; a splinter cut his arm, and he lost a good deal of blood before he could reach home. The consequence was that, perforce, he was condemned to the fire-side and tranquillity, till he made it up again.

It suited Catherine to have him there: at any rate, it made her hate her room up-stairs, more than ever; and she would compel me to find out business below, that she might accompany me.

On Easter Monday, Joseph went to Gimmerton fair with some cattle; and, in the afternoon, I was busy getting up linen[22] in the kitchen—Earnshaw sat, morose as usual, at the chimney corner, and my little mistress was beguiling an idle hour with drawing pictures on the window panes, varying her amusement by smothered bursts of songs, and whispered ejaculations, and quick glances of annoyance and impatience in the direction of her cousin, who steadfastly smoked, and looked into the grate.

At a notice that I could do with her no longer, intercepting my light, she removed to the hearthstone. I bestowed little attention on her proceedings, but, presently, I heard her begin—

"I've found out, Hareton, that I want—that I'm glad—that I should like you to be my cousin, now, if you had not grown so cross to me, and so rough."

Hareton returned no answer.

"Hareton, Hareton, Hareton! do you hear?" she continued.

"Get off wi' ye!" he growled, with uncompromising gruffness.

"Let me take that pipe," she said, cautiously advancing her hand, and abstracting it from his mouth.

Before he could attempt to recover it, it was broken, and behind the fire. He swore at her and seized another.

"Stop," she cried, "you must listen to me, first; and I can't speak while those clouds are floating in my face."

"Will you go to the devil!" he exclaimed, ferociously, "and let me be!"

"No," she persisted, "I won't—I can't tell what to do to make you talk to me, and you are determined not to understand. When I call you stupid, I don't mean anything—I don't mean that I despise you. Come, you shall take notice of me, Hareton—you are my cousin, and you shall own[23] me."

"I shall have naught to do wi' you, and your mucky[24] pride, and your damned, mocking tricks!" he answered. "I'll go to hell, body and soul, before I look sideways after you again! Side out of t' gait,[25] now; this minute!"

Catherine frowned, and retreated to the window-seat, chewing her lip, and endeavouring, by humming an eccentric[26] tune, to conceal a growing tendency to sob.

"You should be friends with your cousin, Mr. Hareton," I interrupted, "since she repents of her sauciness! It would do you a great deal of good—it would make you another man, to have her for a companion."

"A companion?" he cried; "when she hates me, and does not think me fit to wipe her shoon![27] Nay, if it made me a king, I'd not be scorned for seeking her good will any more."

"It is not I who hate you, it is you who hate me!" wept Cathy, no longer disguising her trouble. "You hate me as much as Mr. Heathcliff does, and more."

23 Acknowledge (as kin).

24 Hateful.

25 "Get out of the way."

26 Odd or whimsical.

27 Shoes.

"You're a damned liar," began Earnshaw; "why have I made him angry, by taking your part then, a hundred times?—and that, when you sneered at, and despised me, and—go on plaguing me, and I'll step in yonder, and say you worried me out of the kitchen!"

"I didn't know you took my part," she answered, drying her eyes; "and I was miserable and bitter at every body; but, now I thank you, and beg you to forgive me, what can I do besides?"

She returned to the hearth, and frankly extended her hand.

He blackened, and scowled like a thunder cloud, and kept his fists resolutely clenched, and his gaze fixed on the ground.

Catherine, by instinct, must have divined it was obdurate perversity, and not dislike, that prompted this dogged conduct; for, after remaining an instant undecided, she stooped, and impressed on his cheek a gentle kiss.

The little rogue thought I had not seen her, and, drawing back, she took her former station by the window, quite demurely.

I shook my head reprovingly; and then she blushed, and whispered—

"Well! what should I have done, Ellen? He wouldn't shake hands, and he wouldn't look—I must show him some way that I like him, that I want to be friends."

Whether the kiss convinced Hareton, I cannot tell; he was very careful, for some minutes, that his face should not be seen; and when he did raise it, he was sadly puzzled where to turn his eyes.

Catherine employed herself in wrapping a handsome book neatly in white paper; and having tied it with a bit of ribband, and addressed it to "Mr. Hareton Earnshaw," she desired me to be her ambassadress, and convey the present to its destined recipient.

"And tell him, if he'll take it, I'll come and teach him to read it right," she said, "and, if he refuse it, I'll go up-stairs, and never tease him again."

I carried it, and repeated the message, anxiously watched by my employer. Hareton would not open his fingers, so I laid it on his knee. He did not strike it off either. I returned to my work: Catherine leaned her head and arms on the table, till she heard the slight rustle of the covering being removed; then she stole away, and quietly seated herself beside her cousin. He trembled, and his face glowed—all his rudeness, and all his surly harshness had deserted him—he could not summon courage, at first, to utter a syllable, in reply to her questioning look, and her murmured petition.

"Say you forgive me, Hareton, do! You can make me so happy, by speaking that little word."

He muttered something inaudible.

"And you'll be my friend?" added Catherine, interrogatively.

"Nay! you'll be ashamed of me every day of your life," he answered. "And the more, the more you know me, and I cannot bide it."

"So, you won't be my friend?" she said, smiling as sweet as honey, and creeping close up.

I overheard no further distinguishable talk; but on looking round again, I perceived two such radiant countenances bent over the page of the accepted book, that I did not doubt the treaty had been ratified, on both sides, and the enemies were, thenceforth, sworn allies.

The work they studied was full of costly pictures; and those, and their position, had charm enough to keep them unmoved, till Joseph came home. He, poor man, was perfectly aghast at the spectacle of Catherine seated on the same bench with Hareton Earnshaw, leaning her hand on his shoulder; and confounded at his favourite's endurance of her proximity. It affected him too deeply to allow an observation on the subject that night. His emotion was only revealed by the immense sighs he drew, as he solemnly spread his large Bible on the table, and overlaid it with dirty bank-notes from his pocket-book, the produce of the day's transactions. At length, he summoned Hareton from his seat.

"Tak' these in tuh t' maister, lad," he said, "un' bide theare; Aw's gang up tuh my awn rahm. This hoile's norther mensful, nor seemly fur us—we mun side aht, and seearch another!"[28]

28 "Take these in to the master, lad," he said, "and stay there; I'm going up to my own room. This room is neither proper, nor seemly for us—we must leave, and find another!"

“Come, Catherine,” I said, “we must ‘side out,’ too—I’ve done my ironing, are you ready to go?”

“It is not eight o’clock!” she answered, rising unwillingly. “Hareton, I’ll leave this book upon the chimney-piece, and I’ll bring some more to-morrow.”

“Ony books ut yah leave, Aw sall tak’ intuh th’ hahse,” said Joseph, “un’ it ’ull be mitch if yah find ’em agean; soa, yah muh plase yourseln!”[29]

Cathy threatened that his library should pay for hers; and, smiling as she passed Hareton, went singing up-stairs, lighter of heart, I venture to say, than ever she had been under that roof before; except, perhaps, during her earliest visits to Linton.

The intimacy, thus commenced, grew rapidly, though it encountered temporary interruptions. Earnshaw was not to be civilized with a wish; and my young lady was no philosopher, and no paragon of patience; but both their minds tending to the same point—one loving and desiring to esteem; and the other loving and desiring to be esteemed—they contrived, in the end, to reach it.

“You see,” Mr. Lockwood, “it was easy enough to win Mrs. Heathcliff’s heart; but now, I’m glad you did not try—the crown of all my wishes will be the union of those two; I shall envy no one on their wedding-day—there won’t be a happier woman than myself in England!”

29 “Any books that you leave, I’ll take into the sitting room, and you’ll be lucky to find them again; so, you may please yourself.”

CHAPTER 19

On the morrow of that Monday, Earnshaw being still unable to follow his ordinary employments, and, therefore, remaining about the house, I speedily found it would be impracticable to retain my charge beside me, as heretofore.

She got down stairs before me, and out into the garden, where she had seen her cousin performing some easy work; and when I went to bid them come to breakfast, I saw she had persuaded him to clear a large space of ground from currant and gooseberry bushes, and they were busy planning together an importation of plants from the Grange.

I was terrified at the devastation which had been accomplished in a brief half hour; the black currant trees were the apple of Joseph's eye, and she had just fixed her choice of a flower bed in the midst of them!

"There! That will be all shewn to the master," I exclaimed, "the minute it is discovered. And what excuse have you to offer for taking such liberties with the garden? We shall have a fine explosion on the head[1] of it: see if we don't! Mr. Hareton, I wonder you should have no more wit, than to go and make that mess at her bidding!"

"I'd forgotten they were Joseph's," answered Earnshaw, rather puzzled, "but I'll tell him I did it."

1 Topic.

2 Cathy has her mother's dark eyes, as does Hareton, whose resemblance to Catherine is striking.

We always ate our meals with Mr. Heathcliff. I held the mistress's post in making tea and carving, so I was indispensable at table. Catherine usually sat by me; but to-day, she stole nearer to Hareton, and I presently saw she would have no more discretion in her friendship than she had in her hostility.

"'Now, mind you don't talk with and notice your cousin too much," were my whispered instructions as we entered the room; "It will certainly annoy Mr. Heathcliff, and he'll be mad at you both."

"'I'm not going to," she answered.

The minute after, she had sidled to him, and was sticking primroses in his plate of porridge.

He dared not speak to her, there; he dared hardly look; and yet she went on teasing, till he was twice on the point of being provoked to laugh; and I frowned, and then, she glanced towards the master, whose mind was occupied on other subjects than his company, as his countenance evinced, and she grew serious for an instant, scrutinizing him with deep gravity. Afterwards she turned, and re-commenced her nonsense; at last, Hareton uttered a smothered laugh.

Mr. Heathcliff started; his eye rapidly surveyed our faces. Catherine met it with her accustomed look of nervousness, and yet defiance, which he abhorred.

"It is well you are out of my reach," he exclaimed. "What fiend possesses you to stare back at me, continually, with those infernal eyes?[2] Down with them! and don't remind me of your existence again. I thought I had cured you of laughing!"

"It was me," muttered Hareton.

"What do you say?" demanded the master.

Hareton looked at his plate, and did not repeat the confession.

Mr. Heathcliff looked at him a bit, and then silently resumed his breakfast, and his interrupted musing.

"Stone-Breakers on the Road," a drawing by George Walker for *The Costume of Yorkshire* (1814). Yorkshire roads were made of stone, which was brought in large pieces from nearby quarries. Machines had not yet been invented for breaking stones, and the tattered clothing of the men doing this hard labor suggest their poverty.

We had nearly finished, and the two young people prudently shifted wider asunder, so I anticipated no further disturbance during that sitting; when Joseph appeared at the door, revealing by his quivering lip, and furious eyes, that the outrage committed on his precious shrubs was detected.

He must have seen Cathy and her cousin about the spot, before he examined it, for while his jaws worked like those of a cow chewing its cud, and rendered his speech difficult to understand, he began:

"Aw mun hev my wage, and Aw mun goa! Aw *hed* aimed tuh dee, wheare Aw'd sarved fur sixty year; un' Aw thowt Aw'd lug my books up intuh t' garret, un' all my bits uh stuff, un' they sud hev t' kitchen tuh theirseln, fur t' sake uh quietness. It wur hard tuh gie up my awn hearthstun, bud Aw thowt Aw *could* do that! Bud, nah, shoo's taan my garden frough me, un' by th' heart! Maister,

Aw cannot stand it! Yah muh bend tuh th' yoak, an ye will—*Aw'm* noan used to't and an ow'd man doesn't sooin get used tuh new barthens—Aw'd rayther arn my bite, an' my sup, wi' a hammer in th' road!"[3]

"Now, now, idiot!" interrupted Heathcliff, "cut it short! What's your grievance? I'll interfere in no quarrels between you and Nelly—She may thrust you into the coal-hole for anything I care."

"It's noan Nelly!" answered Joseph. "Aw sudn't shift fur Nelly—Nasty, ill nowt as shoo is, Thank God!—*shoo* cannot stale t'sowl uh nob'dy! Shoo wer niver soa handsome, bud whet a body mud look at her baht winking. It's yon flaysome, graceless quean ut's witched ahr lad, wi' her bold een, un' her forrard ways—till—Nay! It fair brusts my heart! He's forgetten all E done for him, un made on him, un' goan un' riven up a whole row ut t' grandest currant trees i' t' garden!"[4]—and here he lamented outright, unmanned by a sense of his bitter injuries, and Earnshaw's ingratitude and dangerous condition.

"Is the fool drunk?" asked Mr. Heathcliff. "Hareton, is it you he's finding fault with?"

"I've pulled up two or three bushes," replied the young man, "but I'm going to set[5] 'em again."

"And why have you pulled them up?" said the master.

Catherine wisely put in her tongue.

"We wanted to plant some flowers there," she cried. "I'm the only person to blame, for I wished him to do it."

"And who the devil gave *you* leave to touch a stick about the place?" demanded her father-in-law, much surprised. "And who ordered *you* to obey her?" he added, turning to Hareton.

The latter was speechless; his cousin replied—

"You shouldn't grudge a few yards of earth, for me to ornament, when you have taken all my land!"

"Your land, insolent slut? You never had any!" said Heathcliff.

"And my money," she continued, returning his angry glare, and meantime, biting a piece of crust, the remnant of her breakfast.

3 "I must have my wages, and I must go! I *had* aimed to die, where I've served for sixty years; and I thought I'd lug my books up into the garret, and all my things, and they should have the kitchen to themselves, for the sake of quiet. It was hard to give up my own hearthstone, but I thought I *could* do that! But, now, she's taken my garden from me, and by the heart! Master, I cannot stand it! You may bend to the yoke, if you will—*I'm* not used to it and an old man doesn't soon get used to new burdens—I'd rather earn my food, and my drink, [breaking stones] with a hammer in the road!"

Building roads was particularly low and opprobrious labor. Depictions of the lives of the poor flourished in the 1870s, when Victorian social realism was at its height. Courbet's famous painting, *The Stone Breakers,* which represents an old and a young man breaking stones on the road, was first exhibited in Paris in 1850.

4 "It's not Nelly! . . . I shouldn't bother myself about Nelly—nasty, poor nothing that she is. Thank God!—*she* cannot steal anybody's soul! She was never so handsome, but that somebody might look at her without winking. It's that fearful, lost hussy that's bewitched our lad, with her bold eyes, and her forward ways—till—Nay! It almost bursts my heart! He's forgotten all I've done for him, and made of him, and gone and dug up a whole row of the grandest currant trees in the garden!"

Bringing plants from the Grange to the Heights and replacing bushes that produce edible berries with ornamental flowers mark Cathy's intent to civilize the Heights and make it more like the Grange.

5 Plant.

"Silence!" he exclaimed. "Get done, and begone!"

"And Hareton's land, and his money," pursued the reckless thing. "Hareton, and I are friends now; and I shall tell him all about you!"

The master seemed confounded a moment, he grew pale, and rose up, eyeing her all the while, with an expression of mortal hate.

"If you strike me, Hareton will strike you!" she said, "so you may as well sit down."

"If Hareton does not turn you out of the room, I'll strike him to Hell," thundered Heathcliff. "Damnable witch!—dare you pretend to rouse him against me? Off with her! Do you hear? Fling her into the kitchen! I'll kill her, Ellen Dean, if you let her come into my sight again!"

Hareton tried under his breath to persuade her to go.

"Drag her away!" he cried savagely. "Are you staying to talk?" And he approached to execute his own command.

"He'll not obey you, wicked man, any more!" said Catherine, "and he'll soon detest you, as much as I do!"

"Wisht! wisht!" muttered the young man reproachfully. "I will not hear you speak so to him—Have done!"

"But you won't let him strike me?" she cried.

"Come then!" he whispered earnestly.

It was too late—Heathcliff had caught hold of her.

"Now *you* go!" he said to Earnshaw. "Accursed witch! this time she has provoked me, when I could not bear it; and I'll make her repent it for ever!"

He had his hand in her hair; Hareton attempted to release the locks, entreating him not to hurt her that once. His black eyes flashed, he seemed ready to tear Catherine in pieces, and I was just worked up to risk coming to the rescue, when of a sudden, his fingers relaxed, he shifted his grasp from her head to her arm, and gazed intently in her face—Then, he drew his hand over his eyes, stood a moment to collect himself, apparently, and turning anew to Catherine, said with assumed calmness, "You must learn to avoid putting me in a passion, or I shall really murder you sometime! Go with Mrs. Dean, and keep with her, and confine your insolence to her ears. As to Hareton Earnshaw, if I see him listen to you, I'll send him seeking his bread where he can get it! Your love will make him an outcast, and a beggar—Nelly, take her, and leave me, all of you! Leave me!"

I led my young lady out; she was too glad of her escape to resist; the other followed, and Mr. Heathcliff had the room to himself till dinner.

I had counselled Catherine to get hers up-stairs; but, as soon as he perceived her vacant seat, he sent me to call her. He spoke to none of us, eat very little, and went out directly afterwards, intimating that he should not return before evening.

The two new friends established themselves in the house, during his absence, where I heard Hareton sternly check his cousin, on her offering a revelation of her father-in-law's conduct to his father.

He said he wouldn't suffer a word to be uttered to him, in his disparagement; if he were the devil, it didn't signify; he would stand by him; and he'd rather she would abuse himself, as she used to, than begin on Mr. Heathcliff.

Catherine was waxing cross at this; but he found means to make her hold her tongue, by asking how she would like *him* to speak ill of her father? And then she comprehended that Earnshaw took the master's reputation home to himself: and was attached by ties stronger than reason could break—chains, forged by habit, which it would be cruel to attempt to loosen.

She showed a good heart, thenceforth, in avoiding both complaints and expressions of antipathy concerning Heathcliff; and confessed to me her sorrow that she had endeavoured to raise a bad spirit between him and Hareton—indeed, I don't believe she has ever breathed a syllable, in the latter's hearing, against her oppressor since.

When this slight disagreement was over, they were thick again, and as busy as possible in their several occupations of pupil and teacher. I came in to sit with them, after I had done my work, and I felt so soothed, and comforted to watch them, that I did not notice how time got on. You know, they both appeared in a measure, my children: I had long been proud of one, and now, I was sure, the other would be a source of equal satisfaction. His honest, warm, and intelligent nature shook off rapidly the clouds of ignorance and degradation in which it had been bred; and Catherine's sincere commendations acted as a spur to his industry. His brightening mind brightened his features, and added spirit and nobility to their aspect—I could hardly fancy it the same individual I had beheld on the day I discovered my little lady at Wuthering Heights, after her expedition to the Crags.

While I admired, and they laboured, dusk drew on, and with it returned the master. He came upon us quite unexpectedly, entering by the front way, and had a full view of the whole three, ere we could raise our heads to glance at him.

Well, I reflected, there was never a pleasanter, or more harmless sight; and it will be a burning shame to scold them. The red firelight glowed on their two bonny heads, and revealed their faces, animated with the eager interest of children; for, though he was twenty-three and she eighteen, each had so much of novelty to feel, and learn, that neither experienced, nor evinced, the sentiments of sober disenchanted maturity.

They lifted their eyes together to encounter Mr. Heathcliff—perhaps, you have never remarked that their eyes are precisely similar, and they are those of Catherine Earnshaw. The present Catherine has no other likeness to her, except a breadth of forehead, and a certain arch of the nostril that makes her appear rather haughty, whether she will or not. With Hareton the resemblance is carried farther; it is singular, at all times—then it was particularly striking: because his senses were alert, and his mental faculties wakened to unwonted activity.

I suppose this resemblance disarmed Mr. Heathcliff: he walked to the hearth in evident agitation, but it quickly subsided, as he

6 Tools with a pointed or chisel edge, made of steel and used for breaking up hard ground.

looked at the young man; or, I should say, altered its character, for it was there yet.

He took the book from his hand, and glanced at the open page, then returned it without any observation; merely signing Catherine away—her companion lingered very little behind her, and I was about to depart also, but he bid me sit still.

"It is a poor conclusion, is it not," he observed, having brooded a while on the scene he had just witnessed. "An absurd termination to my violent exertions? I get levers and mattocks[6] to demolish the two houses, and train myself to be capable of working like Hercules, and when everything is ready, and in my power, I find the will to lift a slate off either roof has vanished! My old enemies have not beaten me—now would be the precise time to revenge myself on their representatives—I could do it; and none could hinder me—But where is the use? I don't care for striking. I can't take the trouble to raise my hand! That sounds as if I had been labouring the whole time, only to exhibit a fine trait of magnanimity. It is far from being the case—I have lost the faculty of enjoying their destruction, and I am too idle to destroy for nothing.

"Nelly, there is a strange change approaching—I'm in its shadow at present—I take so little interest in my daily life that I hardly remember to eat and drink—Those two, who have left the room, are the only objects which retain a distinct material appearance to me; and that appearance causes me pain amounting to agony. About *her* I won't speak, and I don't desire to think; but I earnestly wish she were invisible—her presence invokes only maddening sensations. *He* moves me differently; and yet if I could do it without seeming insane, I'd never see him again! You'll perhaps think me rather inclined to become so," he added, making an effort to smile, "if I try to describe the thousand forms of past associations and ideas he awakens, or embodies—But you'll not talk of what I tell you, and my mind is so eternally secluded in itself, it is tempting, at last, to turn it out to another.

"Five minutes ago, Hareton seemed a personification of my youth, not a human being—I felt to him in such a variety of ways, that it would have been impossible to have accosted him rationally.

"In the first place, his startling likeness to Catherine connected him fearfully with her—That, however, which you may suppose the most potent to arrest my imagination, is actually the least—for what is not connected with her to me?—and what does not recall her? I cannot look down to this floor, but her features are shaped on the flags![7] In every cloud, in every tree—filling the air at night, and caught by glimpses in every object by day, I am surrounded with her image! The most ordinary faces of men, and women—my own features—mock me with a resemblance. The entire world is a dreadful collection of memoranda that she did exist, and that I have lost her!

"Well, Hareton's aspect was the ghost of my immortal love, of my wild endeavours to hold my right, my degradation, my pride, my happiness, and my anguish—

"But it is frenzy to repeat these thoughts to you; only, it will let you know why, with a reluctance to be always alone, his society is no benefit, rather an aggravation of the constant torment I suffer—and it partly contributes to render me regardless how he and his cousin go on together. I can give them no attention, any more."

"But what do you mean by a *change,* Mr. Heathcliff?" I said, alarmed at his manner, though he was neither in danger of losing his senses, nor dying; according to my judgment he was quite strong and healthy; and, as to his reason, from childhood he had a delight in dwelling on dark things, and entertaining odd fancies—he might have had a monomania[8] on the subject of his departed idol; but on every other point his wits were as sound as mine.

"I shall not know that, till it comes," he said, "I'm only half conscious of it now."

"You have no feeling of illness, have you?" I asked.

"No, Nelly, I have not," he answered.

7 Flagstones.

8 Nelly's diagnosis of Heathcliff's mental condition is precise and ahead of the time in which she makes it. Monomania was a kind of partial insanity afflicting an otherwise rational mind and was often associated with obsession. According to James Cowle Prichard (1786–1848), an influential English physician, the monomaniac's "intellectual powers appear, when exercised on other subjects, to be in a great measure unimpaired." Sally Shuttleworth writes that monomania "constituted one of the most decisive innovations in nineteenth-century psychiatry," and that frequent references to it appeared in the periodical literature after 1830. (Pritchard is quoted in Shuttleworth, *Charlotte Brontë and Victorian Psychology* [Cambridge: Cambridge Univ. Press, 1996], p. 51.) Monomania made sense in the context of a new understanding of the mind as embattled and divided. In Charlotte Brontë's *Villette,* Lucy Snowe deplores Polly's "monomaniac tendency" and, later, her own.

"Then, you are not afraid of death?" I pursued.

"Afraid? No!" he replied. "I have neither a fear, nor a presentiment, nor a hope of death—Why should I? With my hard constitution, and temperate mode of living, and unperilous occupations, I ought to, and probably *shall*, remain above ground till there is scarcely a black hair on my head—And yet I cannot continue in this condition!—I have to remind myself to breathe—almost to remind my heart to beat! And it is like bending back a stiff spring . . . it is by compulsion, that I do the slightest act, not prompted by one thought, and by compulsion that I notice anything alive or dead which is not associated with one universal idea . . . I have a single wish, and my whole being and faculties are yearning to attain it. They have yearned towards it so long, and so unwaveringly, that I'm convinced it *will* be reached—and *soon*—because it has devoured my existence—I am swallowed in the anticipation of its fulfilment.

"My confessions have not relieved me—but they may account for some otherwise unaccountable phases of humour, which I show. O, God! It is a long fight, I wish it were over!"

He began to pace the room, muttering terrible things to himself; till I was inclined to believe, as he said Joseph did, that conscience had turned his heart to an earthly hell—I wondered greatly how it would end.

Though he seldom before had revealed this state of mind, even by looks, it was his habitual mood, I had no doubt: he asserted it himself—but not a soul, from his general bearing, would have conjectured the fact. You did not, when you saw him, Mr. Lockwood—and at the period of which I speak, he was just the same as then, only fonder of continued solitude, and perhaps still more laconic in company.

CHAPTER 20

For some days after that evening, Mr. Heathcliff shunned meeting us at meals; yet he would not consent, formally, to exclude Hareton and Cathy. He had an aversion to yielding so completely to his feelings, choosing rather to absent himself—And eating once in twenty-four hours seemed sufficient sustenance for him.

One night, after the family were in bed, I heard him go down stairs, and out at the front door: I did not hear him re-enter, and, in the morning, I found he was still away.

We were in April then—the weather was sweet and warm, the grass as green as shower and sun could make it, and the two dwarf apple trees, near the southern wall, in full bloom.

After breakfast, Catherine insisted on my bringing a chair and sitting, with my work, under the fir trees at the end of the house; and she beguiled Hareton, who had perfectly recovered from his accident, to dig and arrange her little garden, which was shifted to that corner by the influence of Joseph's complaints.

I was comfortably revelling in the spring fragrance around, and the beautiful soft blue overhead, when my young lady, who had run down near the gate to procure some primrose roots for a border, returned only half laden; and informed us that Mr. Heathcliff was coming in.

"And he spoke to me," she added, with a perplexed countenance.

"What did he say?" asked Hareton.

Study of a fir tree, c. 1842, in pencil. Brontë sketched this tree from life while she was in Brussels and gave it to one of her pupils. Blasted trees are an iconic element of Romantic paintings of the period and achieve their apotheosis in the work of Caspar David Friedrich (1774–1840). Emily's tree has two trunks, but only the topless one on the left still has sufficient life to produce leaves, and its angled branches reach out boldly. This drawing anticipates her poem "Death," composed three years later. The poem begins by exhorting Death to "Strike again, Time's withered branch dividing / From the fresh root of Eternity."

1 Cats breathe faster than humans, but very rapid breathing in cats is connected to illnesses of various kinds. Susan Stewart suggests that Nelly's reference to Heathcliff's breathing like a cat implies "both the 'cat-soul' who lies on the coffin or grave and the internalization of his dead Catherine" (Stewart, "The Ballad in *Wuthering Heights*," *Representations,* 86:1 [Spring 2004], p. 183).

"He told me to begone as fast as I could," she answered. "But he looked so different from his usual look that I stopped a moment to stare at him."

"How?" he enquired.

"Why, almost bright and cheerful—No, almost nothing—*very much* excited, and wild and glad!" she replied.

"Night-walking amuses him, then," I remarked, affecting a careless manner. In reality, as surprised as she was, and, anxious to ascertain the truth of her statement—for to see the master looking glad would not be an every day spectacle—I framed an excuse to go in.

Heathcliff stood at the open door; he was pale, and he trembled; yet, certainly, he had a strange joyful glitter in his eyes that altered the aspect of his whole face.

"Will you have some breakfast?" I said, "You must be hungry, rambling about all night!"

I wanted to discover where he had been; but I did not like to ask directly.

"No, I'm not hungry," he answered, averting his head, and speaking rather contemptuously, as if he guessed I was trying to divine the occasion of his good humour.

I felt perplexed—I didn't know whether it were not a proper opportunity to offer a bit of admonition.

"I don't think it right to wander out of doors," I observed, "instead of being in bed: it is not wise, at any rate, this moist season. I dare say you'll catch a bad cold, or a fever—you have something the matter with you now!"

"Nothing but what I can bear," he replied, "and with the greatest pleasure, provided you'll leave me alone—get in, and don't annoy me."

I obeyed; and, in passing, I noticed he breathed as fast as a cat.[1]

Yes! I reflected to myself, we shall have a fit of illness. I cannot conceive what he has been doing!

That noon, he sat down to dinner with us, and received a heaped-up plate from my hands, as if he intended to make amends for previous fasting.

"I've neither cold, nor fever, Nelly," he remarked, in allusion to my morning's speech. "And I'm ready to do justice to the food you give me."

He took his knife and fork, and was going to commence eating, when the inclination appeared to become suddenly extinct. He laid them on the table, looked eagerly towards the window, then rose and went out.

We saw him walking, to and fro, in the garden, while we concluded our meal; and Earnshaw said he'd go, and ask why he would not dine; he thought we had grieved him some way.

"Well, is he coming?" cried Catherine, when her cousin returned.

"Nay," he answered, "but he's not angry; he seemed rare[2] and pleased indeed; only, I made him impatient by speaking to him twice; and then he bid me be off to you; he wondered how I could want the company of any body else."

I set his plate, to keep warm, on the fender: and, after an hour or two, he re-entered, when the room was clear, in no degree calmer—the same unnatural—it was unnatural—appearance of joy under his black brows; the same bloodless hue: and his teeth visible, now and then, in a kind of smile; his frame shivering, not as one shivers with chill or weakness, but as a tight-stretched cord vibrates—a strong thrilling, rather than trembling.

I will ask what is the matter, I thought, or who should? And I exclaimed—

"Have you heard any good news, Mr. Heathcliff? You look uncommonly animated."

"Where should good news come from, to me," he said. "I'm animated with hunger; and, seemingly, I must not eat."

"Your dinner is here," I returned; "why won't you get it?"

2 In an unusual state.

"I don't want it now," he muttered, hastily. "I'll wait till supper. And, Nelly, once for all, let me beg you to warn Hareton and the other away from me. I wish to be troubled by nobody—I wish to have this place to myself."

"Is there some new reason for this banishment?" I inquired. "Tell me why you are so queer, Mr. Heathcliff? Where were you last night? I'm not putting the question through idle curiosity, but—"

"You are putting the question through very idle curiosity," he interrupted, with a laugh. "Yet, I'll answer it. Last night, I was on the threshold of hell. To-day, I am within sight of my heaven—I have my eyes on it—hardly three feet to sever me! And now you'd better go—You'll neither see nor hear anything to frighten you, if you refrain from prying."

Having swept the hearth, and wiped the table, I departed more perplexed than ever.

He did not quit the house again that afternoon, and no one intruded on his solitude, till, at eight o'clock, I deemed it proper, though unsummoned, to carry a candle and his supper to him.

He was leaning against the ledge of an open lattice, but not looking out; his face was turned to the interior gloom. The fire had smouldered to ashes; the room was filled with the damp, mild air of the cloudy evening, and so still, that not only the murmur of the beck down Gimmerton was distinguishable, but its ripples and its gurgling over the pebbles, or through the large stones which it could not cover.

I uttered an ejaculation of discontent at seeing the dismal grate, and commenced shutting the casements, one after another, till I came to his.

"Must I close this?" I asked, in order to rouse him, for he would not stir.

The light flashed on his features, as I spoke. Oh, Mr. Lockwood, I cannot express what a terrible start I got, by the momentary view!

Those deep black eyes! That smile, and ghastly paleness! It appeared to me, not Mr. Heathcliff but a goblin; and, in my terror, I let the candle bend towards the wall, and it left me in darkness.

"Yes, close it," he replied, in his familiar voice. "There, that is pure awkwardness! Why did you hold the candle horizontally? Be quick, and bring another."

I hurried out in a foolish state of dread, and said to Joseph—

"The master wishes you to take him a light, and rekindle the fire." For I dared not go in myself again just then.

Joseph rattled some fire into the shovel, and went; but he brought it back, immediately, with the supper tray in his other hand, explaining that Mr. Heathcliff was going to bed, and he wanted nothing to eat till morning.

We heard him mount the stairs directly; he did not proceed to his ordinary chamber, but turned into that with the panelled bed—its window, as I mentioned before, is wide enough for anybody to get through, and it struck me that he plotted another midnight excursion, which he had rather we had no suspicion of.

Is he a ghoul, or a vampire? I mused. I had read of such hideous, incarnate demons.[3] And then, I set myself to reflect how I had tended him in infancy; and watched him grow to youth; and followed him almost through his whole course; and what absurd nonsense it was to yield to that sense of horror.

"But where did he come from, the little dark thing, harboured by a good man to his bane?" muttered superstition,[4] as I dozed into unconsciousness. And I began, half dreaming, to weary myself with imaging some fit parentage for him; and repeating my waking meditations, I tracked his existence over again, with grim variations; at last, picturing his death and funeral, of which all I can remember is being exceedingly vexed at having the task of dictating an inscription for his monument, and consulting the sexton about it—and, as he had no surname, and we could not tell his age, we were obliged to content ourselves with the single word, 'Heath-

3 Ghouls were thought to rob graves and feed on corpses. Vampires suck the blood of the living. Goethe's *Braut von Korinth* (1797) helped to inspire the vampire vogue of the early nineteenth century and, more particularly, Jane Eyre's assertion that Bertha Rochester resembles "the foul German spectre—the Vampyre" (*Jane Eyre,* ed. Jane Jack and Margaret Smith [Oxford: Clarendon Press, 1969], vol. 2, ch. 10, p. 358). Byron's poem *The Giaour* (1813), subtitled "A Fragment of a Turkish Tale," is an even closer source for Emily's reference to vampires here. In Byron's poem, the giaour kills the man who has murdered the woman he loves, and the Muslim narrator predicts that the giaour will be turned into a vampire and condemned to suck the blood of everyone he loves.

John Polidori's *The Vampyre* (1817), widely attributed to Byron at the time of its publication, popularized the figure of the vampire in England and influenced representations of vampires for the rest of the century. Polidori had accompanied Byron to Geneva as his physician. He claimed that his vampire story was inspired by one Byron wrote there in response to the same challenge that resulted in Mary Shelley's *Frankenstein.*

4 The superstition muttering to Nelly goes back to a pagan world and is preserved in ballads and in literature, especially Scottish literature. Nelly is remembering stories of otherworldly visitors who enter human dwellings, in particular the Brownie or Brown Man of the Moors, a being who is "sullen, capricious, unpredictable." The Brownie "emerges from rural nature and disappears back into it," and he can be the "agent of a rough justice" as well as the bane of the humans who harbor him. Like Heathcliff's, his complexion is said to be dark and swarthy (Douglas Gifford, "Hogg, Scottish Literature and *Wuthering Heights* or Was Heathcliff a Brownie," *Studies in Hogg and His World* [The James Hogg Society, no. 23, 2013], pp. 5–22).

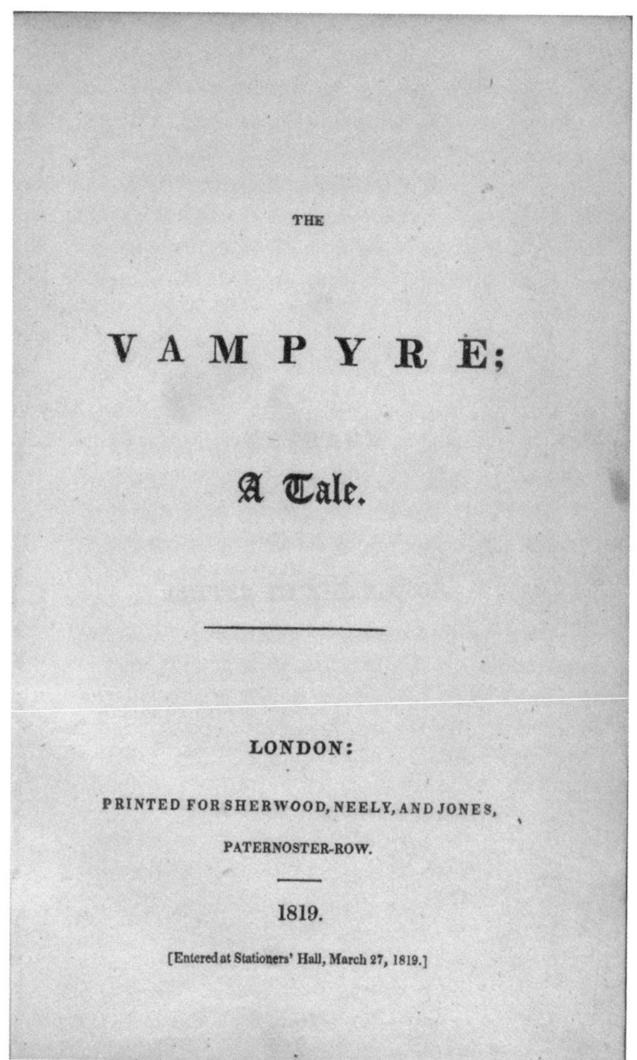
THE

VAMPYRE;

A Tale.

LONDON:

PRINTED FOR SHERWOOD, NEELY, AND JONES,

PATERNOSTER-ROW.

1819.

[Entered at Stationers' Hall, March 27, 1819.]

The title page of *The Vampyre: A Tale* (1819), the first modern vampire story, written by Dr. John William Polidori (1795–1821) but widely attributed to Byron. Polidori was Byron's personal physician and accompanied him on his European travels.

cliff.' That came true; we were. If you enter the kirkyard, you'll read on his headstone only that, and the date of his death.

Dawn restored me to common sense. I rose, and went into the garden, as soon as I could see, to ascertain if there were any footmarks under his window. There were none.

He has stayed at home, I thought, and he'll be all right to-day!

I prepared breakfast for the household, as was my usual custom, but told Hareton and Catherine to get theirs ere the master came down, for he lay late. They preferred taking it out of doors, under the trees, and I set a little table to accommodate them.

On my re-entrance, I found Mr. Heathcliff below. He and Joseph were conversing about some farming business; he gave clear, minute directions concerning the matter discussed, but he spoke rapidly, and turned his head continually aside, and had the same excited expression, even more exaggerated.

When Joseph quitted the room, he took his seat in the place he generally chose, and I put a basin of coffee before him. He drew it nearer, and then rested his arms on the table, and looked at the opposite wall, as I supposed, surveying one particular portion, up and down, with glittering, restless eyes, and with such eager interest that he stopped breathing, during half a minute together.

"Come now," I exclaimed, pushing some bread against his hand. "Eat and drink that, while it is hot. It has been waiting near an hour."

He didn't notice me, and yet he smiled. I'd rather have seen him gnash his teeth than smile so.

"Mr. Heathcliff! Master!" I cried. "Don't, for God's sake, stare as if you saw an unearthly vision."

"Don't, for God's sake, shout so loud," he replied. "Turn round, and tell me, are we by ourselves?"

"Of course," was my answer, "of course, we are!"

Still, I involuntarily obeyed him, as if I were not quite sure.

With a sweep of his hand, he cleared a vacant space in front among the breakfast things, and leant forward to gaze more at his ease.

Now I perceived he was not looking at the wall, for when I regarded him alone, it seemed, exactly, that he gazed at something within two yards distance. And, whatever it was, it communicated, apparently, both pleasure and pain, in exquisite extremes, at least the anguished, yet raptured, expression of his countenance suggested that idea.

The fancied object was not fixed either; his eyes pursued it with unwearied vigilance; and, even in speaking to me, were never weaned away.

I vainly reminded him of his protracted abstinence from food; if he stirred to touch anything in compliance with my entreaties, if he stretched his hand out to get a piece of bread, his fingers clenched before they reached it, and remained on the table, forgetful of their aim.

I sat a model of patience, trying to attract his absorbed attention from its engrossing speculation; till he grew irritable, and got up, asking why I would not allow him to have his own time in taking his meals?—and saying that, on the next occasion, I needn't wait; I might set the things down, and go.

Having uttered these words, he left the house; slowly sauntered down the garden path, and disappeared through the gate.

The hours crept anxiously by: another evening came. I did not retire to rest till late, and when I did, I could not sleep. He returned after midnight, and, instead of going to bed, shut himself into the room beneath. I listened, and tossed about; and, finally, dressed and descended. It was too irksome to lie up there, harassing my brain with a hundred idle misgivings.

I distinguished Mr. Heathcliff's step, restlessly measuring the floor; and he frequently broke the silence, by a deep inspiration, resembling a groan. He muttered detached words also; the only one I could catch, was the name of Catherine, coupled with some wild term of endearment, or suffering; and spoken as one would speak to a person present—low and earnest, and wrung from the depth of his soul.

I had not courage to walk straight into the apartment; but I desired to divert him from his reverie, and, therefore, fell foul of the kitchen fire; stirred it, and began to scrape the cinders. It drew him forth sooner than I expected. He opened the door immediately, and said—

"Nelly, come here—is it morning? Come in with your light."

"It is striking four," I answered; "you want a candle to take up-stairs—you might have lit one at this fire."

"No, I don't wish to go up-stairs," he said. "Come in, and kindle *me* a fire, and do anything there is to do about the room."

"I must blow the coals red first, before I can carry any," I replied, getting a chair and the bellows.

"He roamed to and fro, meantime, in a state approaching distraction: his heavy sighs succeeding each other so thick as to leave no space for common breathing between.

"When day breaks, I'll send for Green," he said; "I wish to make some legal inquiries of him, while I can bestow a thought on those matters, and while I can act calmly. I have not written my will yet, and how to leave my property, I cannot determine! I wish I could annihiliate it from the face of the earth."

"I would not talk so, Mr. Heathcliff," I interposed. "Let your will be a while—you'll be spared to repent of your many injustices yet! I never expected that your nerves would be disordered—they are, at present, marvellously so, however; and, almost entirely, through your own fault. The way you've passed these three last days might knock up a Titan. Do take some food, and some repose. You need only look at yourself, in a glass, to see how you require both. Your cheeks are hollow, and your eyes blood-shot, like a person starving with hunger, and going blind with loss of sleep."

"It is not my fault that I cannot eat or rest," he replied. "I assure you it is through no settled designs. I'll do both, as soon as I possibly can. But you might as well bid a man struggling in the water rest within arms-length of the shore![5] I must reach it first, and then I'll rest. Well, never mind Mr. Green;[6] as to repenting of my injustices, I've done no injustice, and I repent of nothing—I'm too happy, and yet I'm not happy enough. My soul's bliss kills my body, but does not satisfy itself."

"Happy, master?" I cried. "Strange happiness! If you would hear me without being angry, I might offer some advice that would make you happier."

"What is that?" he asked. "Give it."

"You are aware, Mr. Heathcliff," I said, "that from the time you were thirteen years old, you have lived a selfish, unchristian life; and probably hardly had a Bible in your hands, during all that period. You must have forgotten the contents of the book, and you may not have space to search it now. Could it be hurtful to send for some one—some minister of any denomination, it does not matter which—to explain it, and show you how very far you have erred from its precepts, and how unfit you will be for its heaven, unless a change takes place before you die?"

"I'm rather obliged than angry, Nelly," he said, "for you remind me of the manner that I desire to be buried in—It is to be carried to the churchyard in the evening. You and Hareton may, if you please, accompany me—and mind, particularly, to notice that the sexton obeys my directions concerning the two coffins! No minister need come; nor need anything be said over me—I tell you, I have nearly attained my heaven; and that of others is altogether unvalued and uncoveted by me!"

"And supposing you persevered in your obstinate fast, and died by that means, and they refused to bury you in the precincts of the Kirk?" I said, shocked at his godless indifference. "How would you like it?"

5 Brontë's poem "Death and Despondency" represents the afterlife as a "steadfast, changeless, shore" where the spirits of the dead survive, separated from the living by "Time's wide waters."

6 On his deathbed, Edgar Linton sent for Mr. Green in order to revise his will so as to protect Cathy's fortune from Heathcliff, but Heathcliff kept Mr. Green from getting to the Grange in time to do this. Here, Heathcliff has time to send for Green so that he can make a will, but he decides instead to die intestate. He thereby refuses the chance to do what he can to keep Hareton and Cathy from profiting by his death while at the same time refusing to repent for his "many injustices" toward them by willing anything to them.

7 A term of endearment; in northern dialect speech, a hen *(OED).*

8 Daybreak (chiefly poetical). Brontë may be remembering Coleridge's *Remorse:* "His tender smiles, love's day-dawn on his lips" (4, 2, 56).

"They won't do that," he replied, "if they did, you must have me removed secretly; and if you neglect it, you shall prove, practically, that the dead are not annihilated!"

As soon as he heard the other members of the family stirring, he retired to his den, and I breathed freer—But in the afternoon, while Joseph and Hareton were at their work, he came into the kitchen again, and, with a wild look, bid me come and sit in the house—he wanted somebody with him.

I declined, telling him plainly, that his strange talk and manner, frightened me, and I had neither the nerve nor the will to be his companion, alone.

"I believe you think me a fiend!" he said, with his dismal laugh, "something too horrible to live under a decent roof!"

Then, turning to Catherine, who was there, and who drew behind me at his approach, he added, half sneeringly.

"Will *you* come, chuck?[7] I'll not hurt you. No!—to you, I've made myself worse than the devil. Well, there is *one* who won't shrink from my company! By God!—she's relentless. Oh, damn it! It's unutterably too much for flesh and blood to bear, even mine."

He solicited the society of no one more. At dusk, he went into his chamber—through the whole night, and far into the morning, we heard him groaning and murmuring to himself. Hareton was anxious to enter, but I bid him fetch Mr. Kenneth, and he should go in, and see him.

When he came, and I requested admittance and tried to open the door, I found it locked; and Heathcliff bid us be damned. He was better, and would be left alone; so the doctor went away.

The following evening was very wet; indeed it poured down till day-dawn;[8] and, as I took my morning walk round the house, I observed the master's window swinging open, and the rain driving straight in.

He cannot be in bed, I thought; those showers would drench him through! He must either be up, or out. But I'll make no more ado—I'll go boldly, and look!

Having succeeded in obtaining entrance with another key, I ran to unclose the panels,[9] for the chamber was vacant—quickly pushing them aside, I peeped in. Mr. Heathcliff was there—laid on his back. His eyes met mine so keen and fierce, I started; and then, he seemed to smile.

I could not think him dead—but his face and throat were washed with rain; the bedclothes dripped, and he was perfectly still. The lattice, flapping to and fro, had grazed one hand that rested on the sill—no blood trickled from the broken skin, and, when I put my fingers to it, I could doubt no more—he was dead and stark![10]

I hasped the window; I combed his black long hair from his forehead; I tried to close his eyes—to extinguish, if possible, that frightful, life-like gaze of exultation, before any one else beheld it.[11] They would not shut—they seemed to sneer at my attempts, and his parted lips, and sharp, white teeth sneered too! Taken with another fit of cowardice, I cried out for Joseph. Joseph shuffled up and made a noise, but resolutely refused to meddle with him.

"Th' divil's harried off his soul," he cried, "and he muh hev his carcass intuh t' bargin, for ow't Aw care! Ech!—what a wicked un he looks girnning at death!"[12]—and the old sinner grinned in mockery.

I thought he intended to cut a caper[13] round the bed; but suddenly composing himself, he fell on his knees, and raised his hands, and returned thanks that the lawful master and the ancient stock were restored to their rights.

I felt stunned by the awful event; and my memory unavoidably recurred to former times with a sort of oppressive sadness. But poor Hareton, the most wronged, was the only one that really suffered much. He sat by the corpse all night, weeping in bitter earnest. He pressed its hand, and kissed the sarcastic, savage face that every one else shrank from contemplating, and bemoaned him with that strong grief which springs naturally from a generous heart, though it be tough as tempered steel.

9 Of the oak box-bed.

10 Stiff. The open window recalls Lockwood's desperate effort to shut the same window in Volume I, Chapter 3, and the wound on Heathcliff's hand recalls the bleeding wrist of the child-ghost. Brontë is also remembering the superstition that when someone dies, a window is opened to encourage the soul to leave the body.

11 The sharp contrast between Nelly's horror at Heathcliff's expression of "exultation" and her earlier approval of Edgar's "rapt, radiant gaze" on his deathbed calls attention to the difference between what each of Catherine's dying lovers sees at the time of his death, though both of them see Catherine. Edgar looks toward a reunion with her and, later, their daughter, Cathy, in heaven. Heathcliff imagines a triumphant leap across the distance that separates him from her. Compare these lines from "The Prisoner (A Fragment)":

> Then dawns the Invisible; the Unseen its truth reveals;
> My outward sense is gone, my inward essence feels:
> Its wings are almost free—its home, its harbour found,
> Measuring the gulf, it stoops, and dares the final bound.

12 "The devil's carried off his soul . . . and he may have his carcass into the bargain, for anything I care! . . . what a wicked one he looks snarling at death!"

13 Dance in a frolicsome way *(OED)*.

Kenneth was perplexed to pronounce of what disorder the master died. I concealed the fact of his having swallowed nothing for four days, fearing it might lead to trouble,[14] and then, I am persuaded he did not abstain on purpose; it was the consequence of his strange illness, not the cause.

We buried him, to the scandal of the whole neighbourhood, as he had wished. Earnshaw and I, the sexton and six men to carry the coffin, comprehended the whole attendance.

The six men departed when they had let it down into the grave: we stayed to see it covered. Hareton, with a streaming face, dug green sods, and laid them over the brown mould himself: at present it is as smooth and verdant as its companion mounds—and I hope its tenant sleeps as soundly. But the country folks, if you asked them, would swear on their Bible that he *walks.*[15] There are those who speak to having met him near the church, and on the moor, and even within this house—Idle tales, you'll say, and so say I. Yet that old man by the kitchen fire affirms he has seen two on 'em[16] looking out of his chamber window, on every rainy night, since his death—and an odd thing happened to me about a month ago.

I was going to the Grange one evening—a dark evening threatening thunder—and, just at the turn of the Heights, I encountered a little boy with a sheep, and two lambs before him; he was crying terribly, and I supposed the lambs were skittish, and would not be guided.

"What is the matter, my little man?" I asked.

"They's Heathcliff and a woman, yonder, under t' Nab," he blubbered, 'un' Aw darnut pass 'em."[17]

I saw nothing; but neither the sheep nor he would go on, so I bid him take the road lower down.

He probably raised the phantoms from thinking, as he traversed the moors alone, on the nonsense he had heard his parents and companions repeat—yet still, I don't like being out in the dark now

14 The suspicion that Heathcliff's death is a suicide. Nelly would then have to fulfill her promise to dig up his corpse and move it to the churchyard so that his dust can mingle with Catherine's.

15 Frank Kermode points to the kind of historical and sociological progress the story we have been listening to embodies. The ghosts of Heathcliff and Catherine "are of interest only to the superstitious, the indigenous now to be dispossessed by a more rational culture" ("*Wuthering Heights* as a Classic," in *Pieces of My Mind: Essays and Criticism 1958–2002* [London: Macmillan, 2003], electronic text). Lockwood belongs to this "more rational culture"; Hareton will more fully belong to it when he moves with Cathy from the Heights to the Grange. Nelly has seen herself as belonging to it from the beginning, but she still has enough of the country woman in her to feel frightened of Wuthering Heights.

16 Joseph sees Heathcliff and Catherine looking out of the window.

17 "There's Heathcliff and a woman, there, under the Hill . . . and I dare not pass them."

—and I don't like being left by myself in this grim house—I cannot help it, I shall be glad when they leave it, and shift to the Grange!

"They are going to the Grange then?" I said.[18]

"Yes," answered Mrs. Dean, "as soon as they are married; and that will be on New Year's day."[19]

"And who will live here then?"

"Why, Joseph will take care of the house, and, perhaps, a lad to keep him company. They will live in the kitchen, and the rest will be shut up."

"For the use of such ghosts as choose to inhabit it," I observed.

"No, Mr. Lockwood," said Nelly, shaking her head. "I believe the dead are at peace, but it is not right to speak of them with levity."

At that moment the garden gate swung to; the ramblers were returning.

"*They* are afraid of nothing," I grumbled, watching their approach through the window. "Together they would brave Satan and all his legions."

As they stepped onto the door-stones, and halted to take a last look at the moon, or, more correctly, at each other by her light, I felt irresistibly impelled to escape them again; and, pressing a remembrance[20] into the hand of Mrs. Dean, and disregarding her expostulations at my rudeness, I vanished through the kitchen, as they opened the house-door, and so, should have confirmed Joseph in his opinion of his fellow-servant's gay indiscretions, had he not, fortunately, recognised me for a respectable character by the sweet ring of a sovereign[21] at his feet.

My walk home was lengthened by a diversion in the direction of the kirk. When beneath its walls, I perceived decay had made progress, even in seven months—many a window showed black gaps deprived of glass; and slates jutted off, here and there, beyond the right line of the roof, to be gradually worked off in coming autumn storms.

18 "At one point," C. P. Sanger writes, he thought that Cathy and Hareton, "ill educated and incompetent, were to be left destitute. But that would be going too far." Cathy is "the sole living descendant of Mr. Linton. In some way or other, I need not go through the various alternatives, she must have become entitled to Thrushcross Grange, which is plainly by far the most valuable property. Heathcliff had been mortgagee in possession of Wuthering Heights for eighteen years, but this was not long enough to obtain an absolute title by adverse possession. Hareton, as Hindley's heir, would be entitled to the equity of redemption. Now if Heathcliff, who managed well, properly accounted for his profits during the eighteen years as he could be made to do, it may well be that they were sufficient, if he was charged a proper occupation rent, to pay off the mortgage. So that Hareton would get the house and land unencumbered or, at any rate, only slightly burdened. The personal property was comparatively unimportant, and we can only hope that the Crown did not insist on its rights, if it knew of them, or that if it did insist, the happy couple could buy out the Crown's claim out of the rent which Lockwood, as we know, paid" (Sanger, "The Structure of Wuthering Heights," in Eleanor McNees, ed., *The Brontë Sisters: Critical Assessments* [Mountfield: Helm Information, 1996], 2, p. 78).

19 January 1, 1803.

20 A tip.

21 A gold coin worth about a pound. This would have been a handsome tip.

I sought, and soon discovered, the three head-stones on the slope next the moor—the middle one grey, and half buried in heath—Edgar Linton's only harmonized by the turf, and moss creeping up its foot—Heathcliff's still bare.[22]

I lingered round them, under that benign sky; watched the moths fluttering among the heath and hare-bells;[23] listened to the soft wind breathing through the grass; and wondered how any one could ever imagine unquiet slumbers for the sleepers in that quiet earth.

THE END

22 Lockwood's description of Heathcliff's grave as "still bare" contradicts Nelly's earlier report that Heathcliff's grave is "as smooth and verdant as its companion mounds."

Christopher Heywood suggests that this scene has its source in Brontë's memory of "the graveyard at St. Oswald's Church, Thornton in Lonsdale, the last coaching stop before Cowan Bridge" ("Yorkshire Landscapes in 'Wuthering Heights,'" *Essays in Criticism*, 48:1 [Jan. 1998], p. 16). Brontë could have seen this graveyard when she traveled from Haworth to the Clergy Daughters' school in Cowan Bridge, a distance of about forty-five miles. She was six years old. Heywood suggests that she used maps and "regional, historical writing to supplement a sharp visual memory" ("Yorkshire Background," pp. 817, 825).

23 Lockwood is seeing bluebells (Campanula rotundifolia), which are sometimes called hare-bells, not wild hyacinths. Bluebells are much more common than hare-bells in the north of England and Scotland. Brontë wrote a poem about them, and Nelly urged Cathy to gather them to bring to her father when she hoped to raise her spirits.

BIOGRAPHICAL NOTICE OF ELLIS AND ACTON BELL [1850]

EDITOR'S PREFACE TO THE NEW EDITION OF "WUTHERING HEIGHTS" [1850]

FURTHER READING

ILLUSTRATION CREDITS

ACKNOWLEDGMENTS

BIOGRAPHICAL NOTICE OF ELLIS AND ACTON BELL

It has been thought that all the works published under the names of Currer, Ellis, and Acton Bell, were, in reality, the production of one person. This mistake I endeavoured to rectify by a few words of disclaimer prefixed to the third edition of *Jane Eyre.* These, too, it appears, failed to gain general credence, and now, on the occasion of a reprint of *Wuthering Heights* and *Agnes Grey,* I am advised distinctly to state how the case really stands.

Indeed, I feel myself that it is time the obscurity attending those two names—Ellis and Acton—was done away. The little mystery, which formerly yielded some harmless pleasure, has lost its interest; circumstances are changed. It becomes, then, my duty to explain briefly the origin and authorship of the books written by Currer, Ellis, and Acton Bell.

About five years ago, my two sisters and myself, after a somewhat prolonged period of separation, found ourselves reunited, and at home. Resident in a remote district where education had made little progress, and where, consequently, there was no inducement to seek social intercourse beyond our own domestic circle, we were wholly dependent on ourselves and each other, on books and study, for the enjoyments and occupations of life. The highest stimulus, as well as the liveliest pleasure we had known from childhood upwards, lay in attempts at literary composition; formerly we used to show each other what we wrote, but of late years this habit of communication and consultation had been discontinued; hence it ensued, that we were mutually ignorant of the progress we might respectively have made.

One day, in the autumn of 1845, I accidentally lighted on a MS. volume of verse in my sister Emily's handwriting. Of course, I was not surprised, knowing that she could and did write verse: I looked it over, and something more than surprise seized me,—a deep conviction that these were not common effusions, nor at all like the poetry women generally write. I thought them condensed and terse, vigorous and genuine. To my ear, they had also a peculiar music—wild, melancholy, and elevating.

My sister Emily was not a person of demonstrative character, nor one, on the recesses of whose mind and feelings, even those nearest and dearest to her could, with impunity, intrude unlicensed; it took hours to reconcile her to the discovery I had made, and days to persuade her that such poems merited publication. I knew, however, that a mind like hers could not be without some latent spark of honourable ambition, and refused to be discouraged in my attempts to fan that spark to flame.

Meantime, my younger sister quietly produced some of her own compositions, intimating that since Emily's had given me pleasure, I might like to look at hers. I could not but be a partial judge, yet I thought that these verses too had a sweet sincere pathos of their own.

We had very early cherished the dream of one day becoming authors. This dream, never relinquished even when distance divided and absorbing tasks occupied us, now suddenly acquired strength and consistency: it took the character of a resolve. We agreed to arrange a small selection of our poems, and, if possible, get them printed. Averse to personal publicity, we veiled our own names under those of Currer, Ellis, and Acton Bell; the ambiguous choice being dictated by a sort of conscientious scruple at assuming Christian names positively masculine, while we did not like to declare ourselves women, because—without at that time suspecting that our mode of writing and thinking was not what is called "feminine"—we had a vague impression that authoresses are liable to be looked on with prejudice; we had noticed how critics sometimes use for their chastisement the weapon of personality, and for their reward, a flattery, which is not true praise.

The bringing out of our little book was hard work. As was to be expected, neither we nor our poems were at all wanted; but for this we had been prepared at the outset; though inexperienced ourselves, we had read the experience of others. The great puzzle lay in the difficulty of getting answers of any kind from the publishers to whom we applied. Being greatly harassed by this obstacle, I ventured to apply to the Messrs Chambers, of Edinburgh, for a word of advice; *they* may have forgotten the circumstance, but *I* have not, for from them I received a brief and business-like but, civil and sensible reply, on which we acted, and at last made a way.

The book was printed: it is scarcely known, and all of it that merits to be known are the poems of Ellis Bell. The fixed conviction I held, and hold, of the worth of these poems has not indeed received the confirmation of much favourable criticism; but I must retain it notwithstanding.

Ill-success failed to crush us: the mere effort to succeed had given a wonderful zest to existence; it must be pursued. We each set to work on a prose tale: Ellis Bell produced *Wuthering Heights,* Acton Bell *Agnes Grey,* and Currer Bell also wrote a narrative in one volume. These MSS. were perseveringly obtruded upon various publishers for the space of a year and a half; usually, their fate was an ignominious and abrupt dismissal.

At last *Wuthering Heights* and *Agnes Grey* were accepted on terms somewhat impoverishing to the two authors; Currer Bell's book found acceptance nowhere, nor any acknowledgment of merit, so that something like the chill of despair began to invade his heart. As a forlorn hope, he tried one publishing house more—Messrs. Smith and Elder. Ere long, in a much shorter space than that on which experience had taught him to calculate—there came a letter, which he opened in the dreary expectation of finding two hard hopeless lines, intimating that Messrs. Smith and Elder "were not disposed to publish the MS.," and, instead, he took out of the envelope a letter of two pages. He read it trembling. It declined, indeed, to publish that tale, for business reasons, but it discussed its merits and demerits so courteously, so considerately, in a spirit so rational, with a discrimination so enlightened, that this very refusal cheered the author better than a vulgarly-expressed acceptance would have done. It was added, that a work in three volumes would meet with careful attention.

I was then just completing *Jane Eyre,* at which I had been working while the one volume tale was plodding its weary round in London: in three weeks I sent it off; friendly and skilful hands took it in. This was in the commencement of September 1847; it came out before the close of October following, while *Wuthering Heights* and *Agnes Grey,* my sisters' works, which had already been in the press for months, still lingered under a different management.

They appeared at last. Critics failed to do them justice. The immature but very real powers revealed in *Wuthering Heights* were scarcely recognised; its import and nature were misunderstood; the identity of its author was misrepresented; it was said that this was an earlier and ruder attempt of the same pen which had produced *Jane Eyre.* Unjust and grievous error! We laughed at it at first, but I deeply lament it now. Hence, I fear, arose a prejudice against the book. That writer who could attempt to palm off an inferior and immature production under cover of one successful effort, must indeed be unduly eager after the secondary and sordid result of authorship, and pitiably indifferent to its true and honourable meed. If reviewers and the public truly believed this, no wonder that they looked darkly on the cheat.

Yet I must not be understood to make these things subject for reproach or complaint; I dare not do so; respect for my sister's memory forbids me. By her any such querulous manifestation would have been regarded as an unworthy, and offensive weakness.

It is my duty, as well as my pleasure, to acknowledge one exception to the general rule of criticism. One writer, endowed with the keen vision and fine sympathies of genius, has discerned the real nature of *Wuthering Heights,* and has, with equal accuracy, noted its beauties and touched on its faults. Too often do reviewers remind us of the mob of Astrologers, Chaldeans, and Soothsayers gathered before the "writing on the wall," and unable to read the characters or make known the interpretation. We have a right to rejoice when a true seer comes at last, some man in whom is an excellent spirit, to whom have been given light, wisdom, and understanding; who can accurately read the "Mene, Mene, Tekel, Upharsin" of an original mind (however unripe, however inefficiently cultured and partially expanded that mind may be); and who can say with confidence, "This is the interpretation thereof."

Yet even the writer to whom I allude shares the mistake about the authorship, and does me the injustice to suppose that there was equivoque in my former rejection of this honour (as an honour, I regard it). May I assure him that I would scorn in this and in every other case to deal in equivoque; I believe language to have been given us to make our meaning clear, and not to wrap it in dishonest doubt.

The Tenant of Wildfell Hall by Acton Bell, had likewise an unfavourable reception. At this I cannot wonder. The choice of subject was an entire mistake. Nothing less congruous with the writer's nature could be conceived. The motives which dictated this choice were pure, but, I think, slightly morbid. She had, in the course of her life, been called on to contemplate, near at hand and for a long time, the terrible effects of talents misused and faculties abused; hers was naturally a sensitive, reserved, and dejected nature; what she saw sank very deeply into her mind; it did her harm. She brooded over it till she believed it to be a duty to reproduce every detail (of course with fictitious characters, incidents, and situations) as a warning to others. She hated her work, but would pursue it. When reasoned with on the subject, she regarded such reasonings as a temptation to self-indulgence. She must be honest; she must not varnish, soften, or conceal. This well-meant resolution brought on her misconstruction and some abuse, which she bore, as it was her custom to bear whatever was unpleasant, with mild, steady patience. She was a very sincere and practical Christian, but the tinge of religious melancholy communicated a sad shade to her brief, blameless life.

Neither Ellis nor Acton allowed herself for one moment to sink under want of encouragement; energy nerved the one, and endurance upheld the other. They were both prepared to try again; I would fain think that hope and the sense of power was yet strong within them. But a great change approached: affliction came in that shape which to anticipate is dread; to look back on, grief. In the very heat and burden of the day, the labourers failed over their work.

My sister Emily first declined. The details of her illness are deep-branded in my memory, but to dwell on them, either in thought or narrative, is not in my power. Never in all her life had she lingered over any task that lay before her, and she did not linger now. She sank rapidly. She made haste to leave us. Yet, while physically she perished, mentally, she grew stronger than we had yet known her. Day by day, when I saw with what a front she met suffering, I looked on her with an anguish of wonder and love. I have seen nothing like it; but, indeed, I have never seen her parallel in anything. Stronger than a man, simpler than a child, her nature stood alone. The awful point was, that, while full of ruth for others, on herself she had no pity; the spirit was inexorable to the flesh; from the trembling hand, the unnerved limbs, the faded eyes, the same service was exacted as they had rendered in health. To stand by and witness this, and not dare to remonstrate, was a pain no words can render.

Two cruel months of hope and fear passed painfully by, and the day came at last when the terrors and pains of death were to be undergone by this treasure, which had grown dearer and dearer to our hearts as it wasted before our eyes. Towards the decline of that day, we had nothing of Emily but her mortal remains as consumption left them. She died December 19, 1848.

We thought this enough; but we were utterly and presumptuously wrong. She was not buried ere Anne fell ill. She had not been committed to the grave a fortnight, before we received distinct intimation that it was necessary to prepare our minds to see the younger sister go after the elder. Accordingly, she followed in the same path with slower step, and with a patience that equalled the other's fortitude. I have said that she was religious, and it was by leaning on those Christian doctrines in which she firmly believed, that she found support through her most painful journey. I witnessed their efficacy in her latest hour and greatest trial, and must bear my testimony to the calm triumph with which they brought her through. She died May 28, 1849.

What more shall I say about them? I cannot and need not say much more. In externals, they were two unobtrusive women; a perfectly secluded life gave them retiring manners and habits. In Emily's nature the extremes of vigour and simplicity seemed to meet. Under an unsophisticated culture, inartificial tastes, and an unpretending outside, lay a secret power and fire that might have informed the brain and kindled the veins of a hero; but she had no worldly wisdom; her powers were unadapted to the practical business of life; she would fail to defend her most manifest rights, to consult her most legitimate advantage. An interpreter ought always to have stood between her and the world. Her will was not very flexible, and it generally opposed her interest. Her temper was magnanimous, but warm and sudden; her spirit altogether unbending.

Anne's character was milder and more subdued; she wanted the power, the fire, the originality of her sister, but was well-endowed with quiet virtues of her own. Long-suffering, self-denying, reflective, and intelligent, a constitutional reserve and taciturnity placed and kept her in the shade, and covered her mind, and especially her feelings, with a sort of nun-like veil, which was rarely lifted. Neither Emily nor Anne was learned; they had no thought of filling their pitchers at the well-spring of other minds; they always wrote from the impulse of nature, the dictates of intuition, and from such stores of observation as their limited experience had enabled them to amass. I may sum up all by saying, that for strangers they were nothing, for superficial observers less than nothing; but for those who had known them all their lives in the intimacy of close relationship, they were genuinely good and truly great.

This notice has been written, because I felt it a sacred duty to wipe the dust off their gravestones, and leave their dear names free from soil.

Currer Bell
September 19, 1850

EDITOR'S PREFACE TO THE NEW EDITION OF "WUTHERING HEIGHTS"

I have just read over "Wuthering Heights," and, for the first time, have obtained a clear glimpse of what are termed (and, perhaps, really are) its faults; have gained a definite notion of how it appears to other people—to strangers who knew nothing of the author; who are unacquainted with the locality where the scenes of the story are laid; to whom the inhabitants, the customs, the natural characteristics of the outlying hills and hamlets in the West-Riding of Yorkshire are things alien and unfamiliar.

To all such "Wuthering Heights" must appear a rude and strange production. The wild moors of the north of England can for them have no interest; the language, the manners, the very dwellings and household customs of the scattered inhabitants of those districts, must be to such readers in a great measure unintelligible, and—where intelligible—repulsive. Men and women who, perhaps, naturally very calm, and with feelings moderate in degree, and little marked in kind, have been trained from their cradle to observe the utmost evenness of manner and guardedness of language, will hardly know what to make of the rough, strong utterance, the harshly manifested passions, the unbridled aversions, and headlong partialities of unlettered moorland hinds and rugged moorland squires, who have grown up untaught and unchecked, except by mentors as harsh as themselves. A large class of readers, likewise, will suffer greatly from the introduction into the pages of this work of words printed with all their letters, which it has become the custom to represent by the initial and final letter only—a blank line filling the interval. I may as well say at once that, for this circumstance, it is out of my power to apologize; deeming it, myself, a rational plan to write words at full length. The practice of hinting by single letters those expletives with which profane and violent persons are wont to garnish their discourse, strikes me as a proceeding which, however well meant, is weak and futile. I cannot tell what good it does—what feeling it spares—what horror it conceals.

With regard to the rusticity of "Wuthering Heights," I admit the charge, for I feel the quality. It is rustic all through. It is moorish, and wild, and knotty as a root of heath. Nor was it natural that it should be otherwise; the author being herself a native and nursling of the moors. Doubtless, had her lot been cast in a town, her writings, if she had written at all, would have possessed another character. Even had chance or taste led her to choose a similar subject, she would have treated it otherwise. Had Ellis Bell been a lady or a gentleman accustomed to what is called "the world," her view of a remote and unreclaimed region, as well as of the dwellers therein, would have differed greatly from that actually taken by the homebred country girl. Doubtless it would have been wider—more comprehensive: whether it would have been more original or more truthful is not so certain. As far as the scenery and locality are concerned, it could scarcely have been so sympathetic: Ellis Bell did not describe as one whose eye and taste alone found pleasure in the prospect; her native hills were far more to her than a spectacle; they were what she lived in, and by, as much as the wild birds, their tenants, or as the heather, their produce. Her descriptions, then, of natural scenery, are what they should be, and all they should be.

Where delineation of human character is concerned, the case is different. I am bound to avow that she had scarcely more practical knowledge of the peasantry amongst whom she lived, than a nun has of the country people who sometimes pass her convent gates. My sister's disposition was not naturally gregarious; circumstances favoured and fostered her tendency to seclusion; except to go to church or take a walk on the hills, she rarely crossed the threshold of home. Though her feeling for the people round was benevolent, intercourse with them she never sought; nor, with very few exceptions, ever experienced. And yet she knew them: knew their ways, their language, their family histories; she could hear of them with interest, and talk of them with detail, minute, graphic, and accurate; but *with* them, she rarely exchanged a word. Hence it ensued that what her mind had gathered of the real concerning them, was too exclusively confined to those tragic and terrible traits of which, in listening to the secret annals of every rude vicinage, the memory is sometimes compelled to receive the impress. Her imagination, which was a spirit more sombre than sunny, more powerful than sportive, found in such traits material whence it wrought creations like Heathcliff, like Earnshaw, like Catherine. Having formed these beings, she did not know what she had done. If the auditor of her work when read in manuscript, shuddered under the grinding influence of natures so relentless and implacable, of spirits so lost and fallen; if it was complained that the mere hearing of certain vivid and fearful scenes banished sleep by night, and disturbed mental peace by day, Ellis Bell would wonder what was meant, and suspect the complainant of affectation. Had she but lived, her mind would of itself have grown like a strong tree, loftier, straighter, wider-spreading, and its matured fruits would have attained a mellower ripeness and sunnier bloom; but on that mind time and experience alone could work: to the influence of other intellects, it was not amenable.

Having avowed that over much of "Wuthering Heights" there broods "a horror of great darkness"; that, in its storm-heated and electrical atmosphere, we seem at times to breathe lightning, let me point to those spots where clouded daylight and the eclipsed sun still attest their existence. For a specimen of true benevolence and homely fidelity, look at the character of Nelly Dean; for an example of constancy and tenderness, remark that of Edgar Linton. (Some people will think these qualities do not shine so well incarnate in a man as they would do in a woman, but Ellis Bell could never be brought to comprehend this notion: nothing moved her more than any insinuation that the faithfulness and clemency, the long-suffering and loving-kindness which are esteemed virtues in the daughters of Eve, become foibles in the sons of Adam. She held that mercy and forgiveness are the divinest attributes of the Great Being who made both man and woman, and that what clothes the Godhead in glory, can disgrace no form of feeble humanity.) There is a dry saturnine humour in the delineation of old Joseph, and some glimpses of grace and gaiety animate the younger Catherine. Nor is even the first heroine of the name destitute of a certain strange beauty in her fierceness, or of honesty in the midst of perverted passion and passionate perversity.

Heathcliff, indeed, stands unredeemed; never once swerving in his arrow-straight course to perdition, from the time when "the little black-haired, swarthy thing, as dark as if it came from the Devil," was first unrolled out of the bundle and set on its feet in the farm-house kitchen, to the hour when Nelly Dean found the grim, stalwart corpse laid on its back in the panel-enclosed bed, with wide-gazing eyes that seemed "to sneer at her attempt to close them, and parted lips and sharp white teeth that sneered too."

Heathcliff betrays one solitary human feeling, and that is *not* his love for Catherine; which is a sentiment fierce and inhuman: a passion such as might boil and glow in the bad essence of some evil genius; a fire that might form the tormented centre—the ever-suffering soul of a magnate of the infernal world: and by its quenchless and ceaseless ravage effect the execution of the decree which dooms him to carry Hell with him wherever he wanders. No; the single link that connects Heathcliff with humanity is his rudely confessed regard for Hareton Earnshaw—the young man whom he has ruined; and then his half-implied esteem for Nelly Dean. These solitary traits omitted, we should say he was child neither of Lascar nor gipsy, but a man's shape animated by demon life—a Ghoul—an Afreet.

Whether it is right or advisable to create beings like Heathcliff, I do not know: I scarcely think it is. But this I know; the writer who possesses the creative gift owns something of which he is not always master—something that at times strangely wills and works for itself. He may lay down rules and devise principles, and to rules and principles it will perhaps for years lie in subjection; and then, haply without any warning of revolt, there comes a time when it will no longer consent "to harrow the vallies, or be bound with a band in the furrow"—when it "laughs at the multitude of the city, and regards not the crying of the driver"—when, refusing absolutely to make ropes out of sea-sand any longer, it sets to work on statue-hewing, and you have a Pluto or a Jove, a Tisiphone or a Psyche, a Mermaid or a Madonna, as Fate or Inspiration direct. Be the work grim or glorious, dread or divine, you have little choice left but quiescent adoption. As for you—the nominal artist—your share in it has been to work passively under dictates you neither delivered nor could question—that would not be uttered at your prayer, nor suppressed nor changed at your caprice. If the result be attractive, the World will praise you, who little deserve praise; if it be repulsive, the same World will blame you, who almost as little deserve blame.

"Wuthering Heights" was hewn in a wild workshop, with simple tools, out of homely materials. The statuary found a granite block on a solitary moor: gazing thereon, he saw how from the crag might be elicited a head, savage, swart, sinister; a form moulded with at least one element of grandeur—power. He wrought with a rude chisel, and from no model but the vision of his meditations. With time and labour, the crag took human shape; and there it stands colossal, dark, and frowning, half statue, half rock: in the former sense, terrible and goblin-like; in the latter, almost beautiful, for its colouring is of mellow grey, and moorland moss clothes it; and heath, with its blooming bells and balmy fragrance, grows faithfully close to the giant's foot.

Currer Bell

FURTHER READING

Primary Sources and Critical Editions of *Wuthering Heights*

Brontë, Emily. *Wuthering Heights,* a facsimile of the first edition of 1847. Washington, D.C.: Orchises Press, 2007.

Dunn, Richard J., ed. *Wuthering Heights.* New York: W. W. Norton, 2003.

Gezari, Janet, ed. *Emily Jane Brontë: The Complete Poems.* Harmondsworth: Penguin, 1992.

Heywood, Christopher, ed. *Wuthering Heights.* Peterborough, ON: Broadview Press, 2002.

Lonoff, Sue. *The Belgian Essays: A Critical Edition.* New Haven: Yale Univ. Press, 1996.

Marsden, Hilda, and Ian Jack, eds. *Wuthering Heights.* Oxford: Clarendon Press, 1976.

Peterson, Linda, ed. *Wuthering Heights: Case Studies in Contemporary Criticism.* New York: Bedford/St. Martin's, 2003.

Roper, Derek, with Edward Chitham, eds. *The Poems of Emily Brontë.* Oxford: Oxford Univ. Press, 1995.

Biographical and General

Alexander, Christine, and Jane Sellars. *The Art of the Brontës.* Cambridge: Cambridge Univ. Press, 1995.

Alexander, Christine, and Margaret Smith, eds. *The Oxford Companion to the Brontës.* Oxford: Oxford Univ. Press, 2003.

Allott, Miriam. *The Brontës: The Critical Heritage.* London: Routledge & Kegan Paul, 1974.

Barker, Juliet. *The Brontës.* London: Phoenix, 1994.

Dinsdale, Ann. *The Brontës at Haworth.* London: Frances Lincoln, 2006.

Gaskell, Elizabeth. *The Life of Charlotte Brontë.* Ed. Angus Easson. Oxford: Oxford Univ. Press, 1996.

Gérin, Winifred. *Emily Brontë: A Biography.* Oxford: Oxford Univ. Press, 1971.

McNees, Eleanor, ed. *The Brontë Sisters: Critical Assessments.* 4 vols. Mountfield: Helm Information, 1996.

Robinson, A. Mary. *Emily Brontë.* London: W. H. Allen, 1883.

Smith, Margaret, ed. *The Letters of Charlotte Brontë.* 3 vols. Oxford: Clarendon Press, 2000–2004.

Critical Studies: Books

Allott, Miriam, ed. *Wuthering Heights: A Casebook.* Basingstoke: Macmillan, 1970.

Bataille, Georges. *Literature and Evil.* Trans. Alistair Hamilton. London: Marion Boyars, 2001.

Bersani, Leo. *A Future for Astyanax: Character and Desire in Literature.* New York: Columbia Univ. Press, 1976, rpt. 1984.

Bloom, Harold, ed. *Emily Brontë's* Wuthering Heights. New York: Chelsea House, 1996.

Chitham, Edward. *The Birth of Wuthering Heights: Emily Brontë at Work.* Basingstoke: Macmillan, 1998.

Chitham, Edward, and Tom Winnifrith, eds. *Brontë Facts and Brontë Problems.* London: Macmillan, 1983.

Davies, Stevie. *Emily Brontë.* Plymouth: Northcote House, 1998.

———. *Emily Brontë: Heretic.* London: Women's Press, 1994.

DeLamotte, Eugenia C. *Perils of the Night: A Feminist Study of Nineteenth-Century Gothic.* Oxford: Oxford Univ. Press, 1990.

Eagleton, Terry. *Myths of Power: A Marxist Study of the Brontës.* London: Macmillan, 1975.

Gezari, Janet. *Last Things: Emily Brontë's Poems.* Oxford: Oxford Univ. Press, 2007.

Homans, Margaret. *Bearing the Word: Language and Female Experience in Nineteenth-Century Women's Writing.* Chicago: Univ. of Chicago Press, 1986.

Kermode, Frank. *The Classic: Literary Images of Permanence and Change.* Cambridge, MA: Harvard University Press, 1983.

Miller, J. Hillis. *Fiction and Repetition: Seven English Novels.* Cambridge, MA: Harvard Univ. Press, 1982.

Miller, Lucasta. *The Brontë Myth.* New York: Knopf, 2004.

Petit, Jean-Pierre. *L'Oeuvre d'Emily Brontë: la vision et les thèmes.* Lyon: Éditions L'Hermès, 1977.

Pykett, Lyn. *Emily Brontë.* Savage, MD: Barnes and Noble Books, 1989.

Stoneman, Patsy. *Brontë Transformations: The Cultural Dissemination of* Jane Eyre *and* Wuthering Heights. London: Prentice Hall/Harvester Wheatsheaf, 1996.

Thormählen, Marianne. *The Brontës and Education.* Cambridge: Cambridge Univ. Press, 2007.

———. *The Brontës and Religion.* Cambridge: Cambridge Univ. Press, 1999.

Critical Studies: Essays and Book Chapters

Armstrong, Nancy. "Emily's Ghost: The Cultural Politics of Victorian Fiction, Folklore, and Photography." *Novel: A Forum on Fiction,* 25:3 (Spring 1992), pp. 45–67.

Homans, Margaret. "Repression and Sublimation of Nature in *Wuthering Heights.*" *PMLA,* 93:1 (Jan. 1978), pp. 9–19.

Parker, Patricia. "The (Self-) Identity of the Literary Text: Property, Propriety, Proper Place, and Proper Name in *Wuthering Heights.*" In Mario J. Valdes and Owen Miller, eds., *Identity of the Literary Text.* Toronto: Univ. of Toronto Press, 1985, pp. 92–116.

Stevenson, W. H. "*Wuthering Heights:* The Facts." *Essays in Criticism,* 35:2 (1985), pp. 149–166.

Stewart, Susan. "The Ballad in *Wuthering Heights.*" *Representations,* 86:1 (Spring 2004), pp. 175–197.

VanGhent, Dorothy. "*Wuthering Heights.*" In Dorothy VanGhent, *The English Novel: Form and Function.* New York: Holt, Rinehart and Winston, 1953, pp. 153–170.

Von Sneidern, Maja-Lisa. "*Wuthering Heights* and the Liverpool Slave Trade." *ELH: English Literary History,* 62:1 (1995), pp. 171–196.

Williams, Anne. "Natural Supernaturalism in 'Wuthering Heights.'" *Studies in Philology,* 82:1 (Winter 1985), pp. 104–127.

ILLUSTRATION CREDITS

On the Moor, wood engraving by Clare Leighton for the series *Wuthering Heights,* 1930. Courtesy of the Allen Memorial Art Museum, Oberlin College, gift of Mrs. Malcolm L. McBride. *frontispiece.*

The world of *Wuthering Heights,* map by Isabelle Lewis. *vi*

Genealogical chart by Isabelle Lewis. *viii*

Emily Brontë's writing slope. Courtesy of the Brontë Parsonage Museum, Haworth, West Yorkshire. *3*

Emily Brontë's artist box and geometry set. Courtesy of the Brontë Parsonage Museum, Haworth, West Yorkshire. *6*

Portrait of the Brontë Sisters, oil on canvas by Patrick Branwell Brontë, c. 1834. National Portrait Gallery, London/ Bridgeman Art Library. *9*

Manuscript of Emily Brontë, "How long will you remain," 1839. Courtesy of the Brontë Parsonage Museum, Haworth, West Yorkshire. *11*

Emily Brontë's world, map by Isabelle Lewis. *14*

Title page, Currer, Ellis, and Acton Bell, *Poems* (London: Aylott and Jones, 1846). Courtesy of Houghton Library, Harvard University. *17*

Pub sign, Haworth, West Yorkshire. Photograph courtesy of Janet Gezari. *21*

Kristen Stewart as Bella Swan in *Twilight,* dir. Catherine Hardwicke (2008). *27*

Shibden Hall, Halifax, West Yorkshire. Mike Kipling Photography/Alamy. *42*

Top Withens, Pennine Way, in winter snow on Haworth Moor. Steven Gillis hd9 Imaging/Alamy. *45*

The Dog-Breaker, etching colored with aquatint by Robert and Daniel Havell, after design by George Walker, from George Walker, *The Costume of Yorkshire* (London: printed by T. Bensley, 1814), plate 4, opp. p. 9. Courtesy of Houghton Library, Harvard University. *47*

Stone plaque at Ponden Hall, West Yorkshire. Photograph courtesy of Charles O. Hartman. *48*

Keeper—from Life, watercolor on paper by Emily Brontë, April 24, 1838. Courtesy of the Brontë Parsonage Museum, Haworth, West Yorkshire. *50*

Sir Walter Scott, engraving by Charles Turner, 1810, after a painting by Sir Henry Raeburn. Yale Center for British Art, Paul Mellon Collection/Bridgeman Art Library. *53*

Oak box-bed, reconstruction used in *Emily Brontë's Wuthering Heights,* dir. Peter Kosminsky (1992). *65*

Nero, watercolor on card by Emily Brontë, October 27, 1841. Courtesy of the Brontë Parsonage Museum, Haworth, West Yorkshire. *67*

Whitefield Preaching in Moorfields, lithograph after Eyre Crowe, from H. D. M. Spence-Jones, *The Church of England: A History for the People,* c. 1910. Private collection/ Stapleton Collection/Bridgeman Art Library. *68*

Title page, William Gurnall, *The Christian in Compleat Armour,* part 3 (London: printed for Ralph Smith, 1662). Courtesy of Houghton Library, Harvard University. *70*

Jabez Burns. © Liszt Collection/Alamy. *72*

Jabez Bunting, calotype by David Octavius Hill and Robert Adamson, c. 1843–1848, Edinburgh University Library. With kind permission of the University of Edinburgh/Bridgeman Art Library. *72*

Mullioned Window, pencil on paper by Emily Brontë, January 19, 1929. Courtesy of the Brontë Parsonage Museum, Haworth, West Yorkshire. *73*

The Cuckoo, engraving on wood from Thomas Bewick, *A History of British Birds* (Newcastle: Beilby and Bewick, 1797–1804), 1:104. Courtesy of Houghton Library, Harvard University. *85*

Travelling on the Liverpool to Manchester Railway: A Train of the First Class of Carriages with the Mail; A Train of the Second Class, for Outside Passengers; A Train of Waggons with Goods, Etc.; A Train of Carriages with Cattle, from "Ackermann's Long Prints," plate 10, published by Rudolph Ackermann, 19th century. Private collection/ Bridgeman Art Library. *87*

Four-Masted Clipper Ship in Liverpool Harbour, oil on panel by Robert Salmon, c. 1810. Private collection/David Finlay Jr. Fine Art, NY/Bridgeman Art Library. *89*

Shannon Beer as Young Catherine Earnshaw and Solomon Glave as Young Heathcliff in *Wuthering Heights,* dir. Andrea Arnold (2011). *95*

Delftware "ship bowl," tin-glazed earthenware painted with enamels, possibly painted by William Jackson, Liverpool, c. 1765–1770. Transferred from the Museum of Practical Geology, Jermyn Street; Victoria and Albert Museum, London. *99*

"Parce que Cathy lui enseignait ce qu'elle apprenait," India ink drawing by Balthus, from *Wuthering Heights,* c. 1930s. Succession Alexina Duchamp; image courtesy of Houghton Library, Harvard University. *100*

The Crimson Drawing Room, Windsor Castle, chromolithograph after James Baker Pyne, 1838. Private collection/Stapleton Collection/Bridgeman Art Library. *102*

"Nous avons couru depuis le sommet des Hauts," India ink drawing by Balthus, from *Wuthering Heights,* c. 1930s. Succession Alexina Duchamp; image courtesy of Houghton Library, Harvard University. *105*

Poke bonnet, silk satin, beaver plush, velvet ribbon, ostrich feathers, ca. 1816. © Victoria and Albert Museum, London. *107*

Frames from "*Wuthering Heights* Part Two," *Hark! A Vagrant* webcomic by Kate Beaton. Courtesy of Kate Beaton. *109*

Christmas-Eve in Yorkshire, drawn by Dodgson, from *Illustrated London News, Christmas Supplement,* 1849. Courtesy of the Linda Lear Center for Special Collections and Archives, Connecticut College. *111*

Gitano, Head Study, oil on canvas by Henri Alexandre Georges Regnault, 19th century. Private collection/Archives Charmet/Bridgeman Art Library. *115*

"Alors, pourquoi as-tu cette robe de soie?" India ink drawing by Balthus, from *Wuthering Heights,* c. 1930s. Succession Alexina Duchamp; image courtesy of Houghton Library, Harvard University. *124*

Title page, Sir Walter Scott, *The Lady of the Lake: A Poem* (Edinburgh: John Ballantyne, 1810). Courtesy of Houghton Library, Harvard University. *135*

"No coward soul is mine," by Emily Brontë, from Thomas J. Wise and John A. Symingon, eds., *The Poems of Emily Jane Brontë and Anne Brontë* (Oxford: Shakespeare Head Press, 1934). *138*

George Gordon Byron, 6th Baron Byron, oil on canvas by Richard Westall, 1813. National Portrait Gallery, London/Bridgeman Art Library. *141*

Percy Bysshe Shelley, oil on canvas by Amelia Curran, 1819. National Portrait Gallery, London/Bridgeman Art Library. *143*

Leech jar, ceramic, English school, 19th century. © Royal Naval Museum, Portsmouth, Hampshire/Bridgeman Art Library. *151*

Portrait of George Sand, oil on canvas by Auguste Charpentier, 1832. Musée de la Ville de Paris, Musée Carnavalet, Paris/Giraudon/Bridgeman Art Library. *153*

Juliette Binoche as Catherine, Ralph Fiennes as Heathcliff, and Simon Shepherd as Edgar in *Emily Brontë's Wuthering Heights,* dir. Peter Kosminsky (1992). *157*

Wedgewood Slave Emancipation Society medallion, jasperware, designed by William Hackwood, c. 1787–1790. Private collection/Bridgeman Art Library. *158*

Mercenaries Embarking from Hesse to America, 1776, copperplate engraving, c. 1776. Photo © Tarker/ Bridgeman Art Library. *168*

Rotographs of the autograph ms. of *The Gondal Poems* by Emily Brontë, 1844–1848. British Library, Add. ms. 43483, f. 1. © British Library Board. *172*

Signpost, Haworth Village via Bronte Falls, Bronte Way at sunset, Haworth, Yorkshire, photo by Mark Sykes, 2003. © Travel and Landscape UK/Mark Sykes/Alamy. *175*

Movie poster, *Wuthering Heights,* dir. William Wyler (1939). © cineclassico/Alamy. *177*

Jorge Mistral as Alejandro and Lilia Prado as Isabel in *Abismos de pasión,* dir. Luis Buñuel (1954). *177*

Female and Male Lapwing, color engraving by Eduoard Travies, 19th century. Private collection/Archives Charmet/Bridgeman Art Library. *189*

Portrait of Matthew Arnold, engraving, English School, 19th century. Private collection/Bridgeman Art Library. *194*

Flossy, watercolor on paper by Emily Brontë, c. 1843. Courtesy of the Brontë Parsonage Museum, Haworth, West Yorkshire. *196*

Gretna-Green, from *The Illustrated London News,* September 9, 1848. Courtesy of the Linda Lear Center for Special Collections and Archives, Connecticut College. *198*

Portrait of Alfred Lord Tennyson, oil on canvas by Samuel Laurence, c. 1840. National Portrait Gallery, London/ Bridgeman Art Library. *219*

Heathcliff under the Tree, engraving by Fritz Eichenberg, from Emily Brontë's *Wuthering Heights,* 1943. San Diego Museum of Art/ Museum purchase/Bridgeman Art Library. Art © The Fritz Eichenberg Trust/Licensed by VAGA, NY. *239*

Heathcliff's Grief, wood engraving by Clare Leighton, for the series *Wuthering Heights,* 1930. Courtesy of the Allen Memorial Art Museum, Oberlin College, gift of Mrs. Malcolm L. McBride. *241*

Queen Victoria, 1843, oil on canvas by Franz Xaver Winterhalter, 1843. Royal Collection Trust © 2014 Her Majesty Queen Elizabeth II/Bridgeman Art Library. *243*

Pair of flintlock pistols with spring blades, steel, brass, and wood, Birmingham, UK, 1782/1783. Metropolitan Museum of Art, New York, gift of Charles M. Schott, Jr., 1917 (19.53.17, .18). *254*

Basilisk. Universal History Archive/UIG/Bridgeman Art Library. *256*

A Scotch Poney, Commonly Call'd a Galloway, hand-colored etching by James Gillray, published by Hannah Humphrey, 1803. © Courtesy of the Warden and Scholars of New College, Oxford/Bridgeman Art Library. *269*

Landscape scene from *Wuthering Heights,* dir. Andrea Arnold (2011). *270*

A Fashionable Lecturer Demonstrates the Art of Physiognomy through Reference to Busts, etching from *The Universal Museum and Complete Magazine,* vol. 1, September 1765. Courtesy of the Wellcome Library, London, record no. 34515i. *275*

Letter from Queen Victoria to Mrs. Charles Kean expressing sympathy on the death of her husband, 1868. Courtesy of the Victoria and Albert Museum, London. *278*

The Whinchat, engraving on wood from Thomas Bewick, *A History of British Birds* (Newcastle: Beilby and Bewick, 1797), 1:231. Courtesy of Houghton Library, Harvard University. *281*

Diary paper, Emily Brontë, June 26, 1837. Courtesy of the Brontë Parsonage Museum, Haworth, West Yorkshire. *294*

Diary paper, Emily Brontë, July 30, 1845, from Clement K. Shorter, *Charlotte Brontë and Her Circle* (New York: Dodd Mead, 1896), between pp. 152 and 153. Courtesy of Houghton Library, Harvard University. *297*

Campanula, colored engraving by Victor, after Pierre Joseph Redouté, from *Choix des Plus Belles Fleurs* (Paris: 1827–1833). Private collection/Bridgeman Art Library. *311*

Two clay pipes, Birmingham, UK, 18th century. Dorling Kindersley/UIG/Bridgeman Art Library. *317*

Spines and front cover, Emily Brontë, *Wuthering Heights* (London: Thomas Cautley Newby, 1847). Courtesy of Houghton Library, Harvard University. *320*

Linnets, color lithograph from W. Swaysland, *Familiar Wild Birds* (London: Cassell, 1883). Private collection/ © Look and Learn/Peter Jackson Collection/Bridgeman Art Library. *328*

Blind Man's Buff, watercolor on paper by George Goodwin Kilburne (1839–1924). Private collection/Bridgeman Art Library. *330*

The Diversion of Battledore and Shuttlecock from an Original Design in Vauxhall Gardens, London, engraving, English school, 18th century. Private collection/ © Look and Learn/Peter Jackson Collection/Bridgeman Art Library. *330*

Bog whortleberry (*Vaccinium uliginosum*), Siberia. Nature, berries/Russian Look/UIG/Bridgeman Art Library. *347*

St. Simeon Stylites, pencil on paper by Emily Brontë, March 4, 1833. Courtesy of the Brontë Parsonage Museum, Haworth, West Yorkshire. *357*

Portrait of William Makepeace Thackeray, albumen print by J. C. Watkins, 19th century. Private collection/Stapleton Collection/Bridgeman Art Library. *365*

Portrait of Mary Wollstonecraft, oil on canvas by John Keenan, c. 1793. Private collection/Bridgeman Art Library. *365*

Catherine, watercolor and gouache on paper by Lucien Joseph Fontanarosa, published in *Les Hauts de Hurlevent* (1949). Private collection/Association Lucien Fontanarosa/Bridgeman Arts Library. © 2014 Artists Rights Society, New York/ADAGP Paris. *371*

Emily Brontë, oil on canvas by Patrick Branwell Brontë, c. 1833. National Portrait Gallery, London/ © Stefano Baldini/Bridgeman Art Library. *373*

Kate Bush performing "Wuthering Heights," 1978. © Pictorial Press Ltd./Alamy. *380*

Forget Me Not, watercolor on paper, c. 1830. The Henry W. and Albert A. Berg Collection of English and American Literature, New York Public Library, Astor, Lenox and Tilden Foundations. *383*

Grasper—from Life, pencil on paper by Emily Brontë, January 1834. Courtesy of the Brontë Parsonage Museum, Haworth, West Yorkshire. *388*

Title page, Samuel Johnson, *A Dictionary of the English Language,* 2nd ed., vol. 1 (London: W. Strahan, 1755). Courtesy of Houghton Library, Harvard University. *392*

Title pages, Emily Brontë, *Wuthering Heights,* vols. 1 and 2 (London: Thomas Cautley Newby, 1847). Courtesy of Houghton Library, Harvard University. *399*

Juliette Binoche as Cathy in *Emily Brontë's Wuthering Heights,* dir. Peter Kosminsky (1992). *403*

Stone-Breakers on the Road, etching colored with aquatint by Robert and Daniel Havell, after design by George Walker, from George Walker, *The Costume of Yorkshire* (London: printed by T. Bensley, 1814), plate 7, opp. p. 19. Courtesy of Houghton Library, Harvard University. *411*

Study of a Fir Tree, pencil on paper from life by Emily Brontë, c. 1842. Courtesy of the Brontë Parsonage Museum, Haworth, West Yorkshire. *419*

Title page, John William Polidori, *The Vampyre: A Tale* (London: Sherwood, Neely, and Jones, 1819). Courtesy of Houghton Library, Harvard University. *424*

ACKNOWLEDGMENTS

This volume is indebted to the generations of Brontë scholars and critics whose imaginations have been touched by Emily Brontë and whose writing about her has informed mine. I am also grateful to the participants in two NEH summer seminars on the Brontës, and to students in my Brontë senior seminars and my Rise of the Novel course at Connecticut College, in particular one class in 2011, each of whose nineteen members read and commented on the notes for one chapter of the novel. They warned me against spoilers, flagged references that puzzled them, and reminded me not to burden the novel with explanations that would interfere with their own imaginative work. Special thanks to a few of the members of that class who did this assignment with unusual diligence: Sarah Seigle, Carissa Anderson, Matty Burns, and Bridget Byers.

John Kulka, my editor at Harvard University Press, was an incisive and supportive reader throughout the process; his stewardship was steady and gracious. I am also grateful to the anonymous readers for the Press, who saved me from some blunders and enriched my reading of the novel; to Christine Thorsteinsson, copyeditor par excellence, who shepherded the text through its last stages; and to Heather Hughes, who capably managed the illustrations. Everyone who studies the Brontës owes a large debt to the Brontë Society and the Brontë Parsonage Museum and Library staff. Special thanks to Ann Dinsdale, the Collections Manager, for valuable assistance during my last visit to Haworth; to Marianne Thormählen, a Brontë colleague whose company made that visit especially pleasant; to Donald J. La Rocca, the Curator of the Arms and Armor collection at the Metropolitan Museum of Art, who went beyond the call of duty to share his expertise; and to the Information Services staff at Connecticut

College, especially Fred Folmer and Michael Dreimiller, who provided assistance and support of various kinds. Charles Hartman generated an electronic version of the text at the start of this project, and I have profited from his thoughtful advice throughout the preparation of this edition. I am especially grateful to John Gordon and Julia Genster, who generously agreed to read and comment on the introduction and the notes at a late stage of the project.